Celebrating
Latino Folklore

Advisory Board

Celebrating Latino Folklore

An Encyclopedia of Cultural Traditions

Volume 1: A–D

MARÍA HERRERA-SOBEK
Editor

ABC-CLIO

Santa Barbara, California • Denver, Colorado • Oxford, England

Library of Congress Cataloging-in-Publication Data

Celebrating Latino folklore : an encyclopedia of cultural traditions / María Herrera-Sobek, editor.
    p. cm.
  Includes bibliographical references and index.
  ISBN 978-0-313-34339-1 (hard back : alk. paper) — ISBN 978-0-313-34340-7 (ebook)
1. Hispanic Americans—Folklore—Encyclopedias.   2. Hispanic Americans—Social life and customs—Encyclopedias.   3. United States—Civilization—Hispanic influences—Encyclopedias.
I. Herrera-Sobek, María.
  E184.S75C455 2012
   305.86'8073—dc23   2012013257

ISBN: 978-0-313-34339-1
EISBN: 978-0-313-34340-7

16 15 14 13 12   1 2 3 4 5

This book is also available on the World Wide Web as an eBook.
Visit www.abc-clio.com for details.

ABC-CLIO, LLC
130 Cremona Drive, P.O. Box 1911
Santa Barbara, California 93116-1911

This book is printed on acid-free paper ∞

Manufactured in the United States of America

Contents

VOLUME 2

Preface

Celebrating Latino Folklore: An Encyclopedia of Cultural Traditions is a groundbreaking piece of scholarship. This first encyclopedia to focus on the folklore of the Latino population in the United States will be useful for students, scholars, and the general public interested in Latino folklore cultural production for generations to come.

This project began in November 2006 when I was offered a contract by Greenwood Press after the publication of my book *Chicano Folklore: A Handbook* (2006). Many changes and transitions have occurred over the past six years, including the purchase of Greenwood by ABC-CLIO in 2008. The guidelines originally called for essays ranging in length from approximately 1,000 to 5,000 words, that is, the encyclopedia would have both short and long essays according to what the topic under discussion required. The short essays provide the reader with enough information to get an excellent idea of the meaning and importance of the topic discussed. Those topics requiring mostly short entries include most of the folk foods (e.g., tacos, tortillas, maize, sopas), and others such as alabados, baptism, and so forth. These entries usually range from 500 to 1,500 words. The longer essays cover topics that require a more sustained and detailed explanation, such as the folklore of Latin American counties (e.g., Argentina, Panama, Nicaragua, and Venezuela). These essays range from 3,500 to 8,000 words. Other longer essays cover important and extensive folklore topics (e.g., folk medicine, *Pastorelas* [shepherds' plays], folk tales, and distinguished scholars or people in folklore production). Editing the volumes and writing the entries has been a labor of love and a great commitment on the part of everyone involved, including over 100 contributors who wrote the 318 entries comprising this three-volume work.

Celebrating Latino Folklore covers a wide variety of folklore genres either as specific topics or under a general essay that provides an overview of various related topics. These folklore genres include the following:

- Folk Narrative
- Folk Speech
- Folk Theater
- Folk Saints
- Folk Religion
- Folk Celebrations
- Folk Songs
- Folk Singers and Musicians
- Folk Instruments
- Folk Dance

- Folk Food
- Folk Architecture
- Folk Trades
- Folk Artists
- Folk Heroes and Anti-Heroes
- Folk Characters
- Folk Belief
- Folk Ailments and Medicine
- Folk Rites
- Folk Sacred Spaces
- Folk Art
- Folk Garments
- Children's Songs and Games

Celebrating Latino Folklore includes a number of illustrations, which add to the interest and understanding of the entries. Each entry concludes with a section of "Further Reading" that provides additional print and electronic information resources on the entry topic. A detailed bibliography of Latino folklore scholarship will be very useful to students, scholars, and interested nonspecialist readers wishing to delve further into the various topics covered. An appendix on "Medicinal Plants" adds greatly to the topics of "Curaderismo" and folk medicine. I thank Antonio Noé Zavaleta for permission to use this excellent resource. Most entries also include a "See also" listing of cross-references to other related entries.

To recruit contributors to write entries, I undertook major drives or a "Call for Contributors." The drives disseminated a "Call for Contributors" message via e-mail to specific departments and programs throughout the United States and Canada. The departments and programs contacted were Spanish and Portuguese Departments, Latin American Studies Programs and Centers, English and Comparative Literature Departments, and Chicano Studies and Ethnic Studies Departments. I contacted the chairs/directors of these departments, programs, and centers, and asked them to distribute the "Call for Contributors" to their colleagues and graduate students. I am very grateful for the help these chairs and directors afforded me in publicizing the *Celebrating Latino Folklore* project. In addition to writing to departments and programs throughout the United States, I also contacted faculty members who are experts in the field of Chicano/Latino folklore or related fields, such as Chicano literature and culture. Some of these faculty members wrote entries, while others helped with this project by offering names of colleagues or recruiting their graduate students to write entries for the encyclopedia. Once contributors started to write entries, I asked them to contact their friends or colleagues. In this manner, I was able to recruit over 100 faculty and graduate students as well as independent researchers to write the entries included in these three volumes. The contributors for this project include many scholars from the United States, but also from Spain, Canada, Scotland, and Brazil. I thank all those individuals who participated in this important endeavor for their time, effort, and commitment.

In addition to the above extensive publicity carried out via various departments and programs, Norma E. Cantú graciously allowed me to advertise the

Celebrating Latino Folklore project through her *Society for the Study of Gloria Anzaldúa Newsletter*.

Celebrating Latino Folklore is not an exhaustive study or collection of Latino folklore. This would be impossible in a three-volume set given the enormous amount of folklore entries that exist for each Latin American country, indeed for each region and even for each city and village, and that much of this folklore has migrated with each Latino group that has come to the United States. What I have attempted to do in this three-volume encyclopedia is to provide the reader with a sampling of Latino folklore and to give a small glimpse of the rich cultural heritage that belongs to the Latino population and that has now become part of our American folklore treasure. The splendid folklore that all immigrant groups and other non-immigrant groups (such as Native Americans) living in the United States have is all part of our American national cultural heritage.

Given the limitations of size and time for this project, I have provided, via longer essays, only a sampling of the folklore of different Latin American countries, since these national folklores are the fount from which Latino folklore emanates. For South America, I feature Argentina, Bolivia, Chile, Peru, Venezuela, and Brazil; for Central America, El Salvador, Panama, Costa Rica, and Nicaragua; and for the United States I have longer essays for Cuban American, Puerto Rican, and Greater Mexico folklore (i.e., folklore of the U.S.-Mexico borderlands). Please also note that the folklore of Mexico and Mexican Americans (Chicanos/as) is represented throughout the encyclopedia by many entries on these two groups and their folklore.

In the same manner that I selected Latin American countries and their folklore, I also provide in the encyclopedia a sampling of entries on folklore scholars. Scholars have addressed the topic of Mexican American folklore specifically since the late nineteenth century and more recently have also focused on Latino folklore. I therefore have different essays representing the four generations of scholars I first delineated in my book *Chicano Folklore: A Handbook* (2006). Below are the scholars highlighted in the encyclopedia:

I. First Generation of Folklore Scholars: 1893–1930
  1. Captain John Gregory Bourke (1843–1896)
  2. Charles Fletcher Lummis (1859–1928)
  3. Aurelio Macedonio Espinosa (1880–1958)
  4. John A. Lomax (1867–1948)
  6. Elsie Clews Parsons (1875–1941)

II. Second Generation Folklorists: 1930–1950
  1. Jovita González de Mireles (1904–1983)
  2. Arthur León Campa (1905–1978)
  3. Juan Bautista Rael (1900–1993)
  4. Ralph Steele Boggs (1901–1994)
  5. Fabiola Cabeza de Vaca Gilbert (1898–1993)
  6. Cleofas Jaramillo (1878–1956)
  7. Aurora Lucero-White Lea (1894–1965)
  8. John Esten Keller (1917–2010)
  9. Nina Otero Warren (1881–1965)

10. Lomax, John Avery (1867–1948)
11. Alan Lomax (1915–2002)

III. Third Generation Folklorists: 1950–1970
    1. Américo Paredes (1915–1999)
    2. John Donald Robb (1892–1989)
    3. Luis Leal (1907–2009)
    4. Harriet Goldberg (1926–2001)
    5. Archie Green (1917–2010)
    6. John O. West (1925–2010)
    7. Shirley Lease Arora (1930–)
    8. Chris Strachwitz (1931–)

IV. Fourth Generation Folklorists: 1970–Present
    1. John H. McDowell (1946–)
    2. José E. Limón (1944–)
    3. Norma E. Cantú (1947–)
    4. Olga Nájera-Ramírez (1955–)
    5. Olivia Cadaval (1943–)
    6. Charles Briggs (1953–)
    7. Dan William Dickey (1953–)
    8. Enrique Lamadrid (1948–)
    9. James Nicolopulos (1945–2010)
    10. Tey Diana Rebolledo (1937–)
    11. Antonio N. Zavaleta (1947–)

Folklore is a scholarly discipline that is very enjoyable to study and learn. Readers will undoubtedly find this collection of entries on the folklore of Latinos in the United States written by outstanding scholars in the field a rewarding and gratifying experience.

Acknowledgments

I take this opportunity to thank the members of my advisory board—Carlos F. Ortega, Norma E. Cantú, Rafael Hernández, Tey Diana Rebolledo, and Antonio Noé Zavaleta—who graciously agreed to serve as board members despite their very busy schedules and research agendas. I am especially grateful to Professors Zavaleta, Hernández, and Ortega for working tirelessly this past year writing numerous entries. I also want to thank the other members of the advisory board, Professors Cantú and Rebolledo, for providing me with names of contributors and/or suggested topics for inclusion in this important project.

I extend my gratitude to my faculty advisors, who also graciously helped in various ways in the completion of this project either by suggesting topics to be included in the encyclopedia or by suggesting names of colleagues and/or graduate students who would be interested in writing entries.

Without the many contributors who participated in this massive project, *Celebrating Latino Folklore* would not have been possible. I offer my most sincere gratitude to the marvelous contributors who wrote the more than 300 entries. For all of us, it was a labor of love and expectation that these volumes containing information on Latino folklore will be a splendid resource for generations to come.

A project of this magnitude involves numerous people. I am exceedingly grateful for the graduate and undergraduate student assistants who helped me identify contributors throughout the United States. Graduate students Brianne Dávila, now an assistant professor at Willamette University in Salem, Oregon; Adrianna Santos; and especially undergraduate student, Stephanie Palmerín, who was able to locate numerous contributors this past year and helped me organize my spreadsheets, all deserve my everlasting thanks. I also thank Dr. Irene Checa García for her help in locating contributors.

Funding for my research assistants came from my Luis Leal Endowed Chair and a grant from the Chicano Studies Institute; I am most grateful to former Director of the CSI, Professor Carl Gutiérrez-Jones. I offer my sincere gratitude to the Chicana/o Studies Department and to the Chicano Studies Institute for this funding. My sincere thanks to Joann Erving and Theresa Peña for all the help they gave me in locating research assistants and in helping me process my grants.

I am very grateful to John Wagner, senior development editor at ABC-CLIO, for his patience and understanding in working these last three years with me on this project. I also want to acknowledge the wonderful staff at ABC-CLIO, especially Julie Dunbar who did the research and acquisition of the photographs included in the three volumes of the encyclopedia, and Carol Bifulco who worked on the copy-edited manuscript. To all, my most heartfelt "thank you."

As always, I thank my husband Joseph George Sobek for the many weekends I spent on this project instead of sailing with him in his boat in the beautiful harbor and ocean in Santa Barbara, California. I also thank my son, Erik Jason Sobek, and my daughter-in-law, Michelle López Sobek, for sharing their home and my twin granddaughters, Leah and Danielle Sobek, on my short visits to Orange County these last three years.

Introduction

Celebrating Latino Folklore is the first scholarly collection of Latino folklore published on such a large scale. Its primary focus is on the oral traditions, customs, material culture, architecture, and other aspects of the cultural production of the Latino population in the United States, which has significantly increased in number and importance since 1970. The U.S. Census Bureau provides relevant statistics regarding the growth of the Latino population in the last four decades and the projected numbers highlighting their continued growth (U.S. Census Bureau). The Hispanic/Latino population has grown from 9.6 million in 1970 to 48.4 million in 2009 (U.S. Census Bureau Statistical Abstract of the United States, 2011).

Definitions and History

The word "Latino" encompasses people whose ancestors are from the various Latin American countries, including Mexico, but who were born, raised, or now reside in the United States. The word "Chicano," which is also frequently used in the encyclopedia, encompasses people of Mexican descent who were born, raised, or now live in the United States and who generally self-identify as Chicanos; they may also have a heightened political consciousness regarding their history and status in the United States. The word "Mexican" refers to a citizen of Mexico and the term "Mexican American" identifies people born or raised in the United States who are of Mexican descent. The term "Hispano" generally designates a person of Hispanic or Mexican descent from New Mexico. Both "Hispanic" and "Latino" are umbrella terms encompassing people of Latin American or Mexican descent who were born, raised, or now reside in the United States. It should be pointed out that the media and government entities use the words "Hispanic" or "Latino" when speaking about this particular population. Hispanics or Latinos, on the other hand, prefer to be called by their country of origin, such as Puerto Ricans, Cuban Americans, and so forth. The term "Latin American" is also an umbrella term that refers to people who were born and raised in a Latin American country and still make their home there. Once they come to live in the United States, they are referred to as "Latinos." People from Spain are referred to as "Spaniards" or "Spanish"; however, once they migrate to the United States, they are generally considered either "Latinos" or "Hispanics." Some people who have migrated from Spain, either in past centuries or in the present, may choose the designation they desire, that is to be called Hispanic or Latino. Due to the fact that people from Spain have Spanish surnames, they tend to find it more difficult to assimilate completely into an Anglo-American identity unless they change their names to a more Anglo-sounding version. Some celebrities of Mexican American/Latino descent who found it easier to gain acceptance with a name change include Vickie Carr (Vickie Cardenas), Ritchie Valens (Richard Valenzuela), Raquel Welch (Raquel Tejada), and Rita Hayworth (Margarita Cansino).

Some Latinos, mostly Mexican Americans, trace their ancestry to the sixteenth and seventeenth centuries and the settlement of the Southwest, such as many Hispanos from New Mexico. Other Latinos, such as Puerto Ricans, became part of the United States after the Spanish American War in 1898 and are U.S. citizens.

At different points in time, particularly during the twentieth century, Latin Americans migrated to the United States for various reasons, e.g., to escape economic hardship or political turmoil, to join their families, or to take advantage of educational opportunities. Cuban Americans came in large immigrant waves during the 1960s and 1970s due to political unrest caused by the Cuban Revolution (1953–1959). Central and South Americans also entered the United States in large numbers in the 1970s and 1980s because of political instability in their countries during these decades. Mexicans came to what is now the United States as explorers, colonizers, and settlers during the Spanish Colonial Period (1527–1821); as Mexican citizens during the Mexican Period of the Southwest (1821–1848); and as immigrants after the United States–Mexico War of 1846–1848, which brought territory encompassing all or part of the present-day states of California, Texas, Arizona, New Mexico, Colorado, Nevada, and Utah into the United States. In the late nineteenth century, Mexican immigrants worked as cowboys on the cattle drives that brought Texas longhorn cattle from the Rio Grande to Chicago slaughterhouses. In the 1860–1910 period, Mexicans were heavily recruited to come to the United States to build railroads and to work in the expanding agricultural fields. The states of the American Southwest relied heavily on Mexican labor for their expansion. In the nineteenth and twentieth centuries, Mexican workers built the infrastructure needed for the opening and settlement of the Southwest, such as roads, highways, canals, and irrigation projects. Mexican agricultural workers helped the Southwest become a rich fruit- and vegetable-producing area. And of course the folklore of these Mexican immigrants migrated with them and established itself as part of the rich folklore heritage of the United States.

Because the Chinese Exclusion Act of 1882 and the Gentlemen's Agreement Act of 1907 limited Chinese and Japanese immigration, respectively, Mexican labor tended to fill the void left by excluded Asian workers. Mexican immigration to the United States also greatly increased at the beginning of the twentieth century as a result of the political unrest emanating from the Mexican Revolution of 1910–1917. This political strife, when coupled with the start of World War I in 1914 and the American entry into that European war in 1917, further stimulated the flow of Mexican migrants into the United States. World War I increased the need for workers in different areas of the U.S. economy, and Mexican labor filled that need. Between 1910 and the 1930s, Mexican American neighborhoods, known later as barrios or "Little Mexicos," were established in such metropolitan areas as San Antonio, Tucson, Phoenix, Los Angeles, Chicago, and San Francisco, as well as in some smaller towns and cities.

The Great Depression in the 1930s witnessed massive deportations and repatriations of Mexican nationals and American citizens of Mexican descent. However, World War II (1939–1945) initiated a new recruitment era for Mexican labor through what is popularly known as the Bracero Program (1942–1964), which was an accord between the U.S. and Mexican governments to import Mexican labor into the United States. This international agreement of the 1940s grew out of the deportations of the 1930s, when those deported were usually deposited at the Mexican border to fend for themselves. In the 1940s, Mexico was still recuperating from the tumultuous politics of the Mexican Revolution and the difficult economics of the Great Depression. When the United States began to request Mexican labor to work on the railroads and in agriculture and other industries, the Mexican government was leery of sending back its citizens, fearful that another economic downturn would see the resumption of deportations. The accord popularly known as the Bracero Program was signed in 1942. The word "*bracero*" comes from "*brazos*," meaning arms, that is, working arms. This accord stipulated certain rights for the imported braceros, such as the provisions of adequate housing, wages, and transportation. Thereafter, recruiting centers were established throughout Mexico to sign up men to work in the United States. The Bracero Program lasted until 1964 because it provided employers with a ready-made labor force that they could draw upon when needed. Millions of braceros migrated to the United States and stayed on either as legal or undocumented residents. The Bracero Program is one reason why the presence of Mexican immigrants (and folklore) increased in the twentieth century. The working braceros brought their folklore with them from all parts of Mexico; all the regions of Mexico have rich and varied cultural and folklore heritages, which are now all very much evident in the United States.

The ending of the Bracero Program did not stop Mexican immigration into the United States; instead, the years since 1964 have seen an increase in the number of both documented and undocumented workers streaming into the United States from Mexico. This migratory movement has continued up until the present, although the recession, high unemployment, and stricter immigration laws and enforcements have seen a slight decrease in Mexican and other Latin American immigration to the United States since about 2008.

Cuban Americans have settled to a high degree in the southern states, especially Florida. But this Latin American population also has significant communities in New Jersey, New York, Chicago, Los Angeles, and other parts of the United States. Central Americans, such as Nicaraguans and El Salvadorans have settled in California, especially in Los Angeles and San Francisco. Like other Latin American immigrants, Central Americans can also be found all over the United States. For example, a large Salvadoran community lives in Washington, D.C.

Latino folklore is characterized by its *mestizaje* or the mixing of the various cultural strands that characterize all Latin American populations. These cultural strands include folklore from the various Indigenous groups in Latin America as well as from native American peoples in the United States; Africans from various parts of Africa; Asians; and Europeans, particularly, but not exclusively, from Spain and Portugal.

Of course by virtue of living in the United States, Anglo-American folklore and customs have also been acquired and incorporated into Latino folklore. This can be seen in folk speech with language mixing or code-switching, in holidays and the manner these are celebrated, such as Christmas, Thanksgiving, the Fourth of July, Valentine's Day (*Día de la Amistad* or *Día de los Enamorados*), Halloween, Mother's Day, Father's Day, and so forth. Cultural and folklore *mestizaje* is a way of life for many people and Latinos are no different.

Definition of Folklore

The term "folklore" was first coined by William John Thoms in 1846 and basically encompassed the two words "folk," the German term for "people," and "lore," defined by the *American Heritage College Dictionary* (1993) as "accumulated facts, traditions, beliefs about a particular subject." Attempting to pinpoint an exact definition for the encompassing term "folklore" is a difficult endeavor. The Funk and Wagnall's *Standard Dictionary of Folklore Mythology and Legend* (1949–1950) cites no less than twenty-one definitions by highly respected scholars from the twentieth century, such as William R. Bascom, Aurelio M. Espinosa, George M. Foster, Stith Thompson, and Katharine Luomala. Furthermore, the definitions of "folklore" offered by these eminent folklore scholars are based mostly on enumerating the various genres encompassed by folklore. For example, Bascom states the following:

> In anthropological usage, the term folklore has come to mean myths, legends, folktales, proverbs, riddles, verse, and a variety of other forms of artistic expression whose medium is the spoken word. Thus folklore can be defined as verbal art. (398)

Other folklorists similarly enumerate categories of folklore genres in their definition. Most include the words "oral traditions" within their definitions.

The most useful and all-encompassing definition for the term "folklore" that I have found is one rendered by Alan Dundes in his article "What Is Folklore?" published in 1965:

> Folklore includes myths, legends, folktales, jokes, proverbs, riddles, chants, charms, blessings, curses, oaths, insults, retorts, taunts, teases, toasts, tongue-twisters, and greetings and leave-taking formulas (e.g., See you later, alligator). It also includes folk costume, folk dance, folk drama (and mime), folk art, folk belief (or superstition), folk medicine, folk instrumental music (e.g., fiddle tunes), folksongs (e.g., lullabies, ballads), folk speech (e.g., slang), folk similes (e.g., as blind as a bat), folk metaphors (e.g., to paint the town red), and names (e.g., nicknames and place names). Folk poetry ranges from oral epics to autograph-book verse, epitaphs, latrinalia (writing on the walls of public bathrooms), limericks, ball bouncing rhymes, jump-rope rhymes, finger and toe rhymes, dandling rhymes (to bounce children on the knee), counting-out rhymes (to determine who will be "it" in games), and nursery rhymes. The list of folklore forms also contains games; gestures; symbols; prayers (e.g., graces); practical jokes; folk etymologies; food recipes; quilt and embroidery designs; house, barn, and fence types; street vendor's cries; and even the traditional conventional sounds used to summon animals or to give them commands. There are such minor forms as mnemonic devices (e.g., the name Roy G. Biv to remember the

colors of the spectrum in order), envelope sealers (e.g., SWAK—Sealed With A Kiss), and the traditional comments made after body emissions (e.g., burps or sneezes). There are such major forms as festivals and special day (or holiday) customs (e.g., Christmas, Halloween, and birthday). (p. 3)

While folklore also has been defined succinctly as being an artistic communication between two people, the above definition by citing the various genres and items included in folklore provides the reader with concrete examples of what folklore is in everyday terms.

There is sometimes confusion between the terms "folklore" and "popular culture." Folklore is related to oral traditions whereas popular culture is that found in the mass media, in contemporary fashion, films, comic books, television, newspapers, magazines, and so forth. Of course, it should be pointed out that folklore genres and motifs can and do appear in the mass media. The confusion in Latin America between the terms "folklore" and "popular culture" is also derived from the fact that folklore is synonymous with *tradiciones populares* (popular traditions), although the word "folklore" itself exists in Spanish and may be found with a variety of spellings, mainly, *folklore, folclore,* and *folcor.*

Brief History of Chicano/Latino Folklore Scholarship

The history of Hispanic/Latino/Chicano folklore scholarship as a lived and practiced tradition in the United States is as old as the populations inhabiting what is now U.S. territory. These populations include Native Americans, Hispanics, Mexican Americans, Afro-Latinos, Asian Latinos, and so forth; these populations practiced their everyday customs, which of course include all the categories of folklore, before Anglo Europeans landed on the eastern shores of America. The Colonial Period (1527–1821) in the American South and Southwest witnessed the settlement of Hispanics together with their Indian and African servants and way of life. The Spanish language; European Mediterranean architecture; Spanish and Mesoamerican traditional foods; Catholic customs; and Native American and Spanish forms of art, food, dress, dance, and so forth became part of the Southwestern landscape. The Mexican Period (1821–1848) was fairly short-lived. Nevertheless, Mexican immigration actually increased with the heavy need for Mexican labor and recruitment of this labor. By 1848, when Anglo-American colonization and settlement of the Southwest began in full force, Hispanic/Mexican traditions were deeply entrenched and periodically renewed with each successive wave of Mexican and Latin American immigration.

Mexican American folklore scholarship dates back to 1893 with the publication of John G. Bourke's article, "The Miracle Play of the Rio Grande," in volume six of the newly founded *Journal of American Folklore (JAF)*. Bourke continued publishing on various aspects of Mexican American folklore. His essays, "Popular Medicine, Customs, and Superstitions of the Rio Grande" (*JAF,* vol. 6), "The Folk Foods of the Rio Grande Valley and of Northern Mexico" (*JAF,* vol. 8), and "Notes on the Language and Folk Usage of the Rio Grande Valley" (*JAF,* vol. 9) all focused on the oral traditions of the Mexican American population living on the southeastern tip of Texas by the United States–Mexican border.

As the Southwest opened up to Anglo-American settlement, writers from the east coast began to write about the customs and traditions of the Mexican American people they encountered. To easterners, Mexican Americans were an exotic people and, unfortunately, many early writings were steeped in negative stereotypes or focused on the more "exotic" or "quaint" mode of living practiced by the Mexican American population. Thus the works of Charles F. Lummis, who began writing in the late 1890s and early twentieth century, are not viewed kindly by contemporary Chicano/a scholars. Nevertheless, Lummis was one of the early Anglo-American authors interested in the folklore of Mexican Americans. He wrote numerous articles in the popular magazine *The Land of Sunshine* (1896). His book, *The Land of Poco Tiempo* (1952) focused on the New Mexican *penitentes*, a Catholic religious group. Lummis also collected numerous folk songs from California and published them under the title *Spanish Songs from California* (1923).

John G. Bourke and Charles F. Lummis belong to what I have designated as the First Generation of folklore scholars focusing on Mexican American folklore. The first folklore scholar of Hispanic descent belonging to this First Generation, Aurelio Macedonio Espinosa (1880-1958), was born in Colorado, but did much of his work on New Mexican folklore. Espinosa received his Ph.D. from the University of Chicago in 1909 and began teaching as a professor in the Spanish Department at Stanford University in 1910 and was there until 1947. Espinosa's work focused principally on New Mexican folk traditions, such as Spanish ballads, folk tales, and philology. His books include *Estudios sobre el español de Nuevo Méjico* (1934; 2 vols.), *Cuentos populares españoles* (1946–1947; 3 vols.), and *Romancero de Nuevo México* (1953).

Several folklorists belonging to the first generation of scholars published numerous works on different folklore genres. These scholars include Texas folklorist John A. Lomax, who collected Mexican American cowboy songs, and Eleanor Hague, who was also interested in the folk-song genre. In 1919, Mary Austin published an article on folk poetry entitled "New Mexican Folk Poetry," and later focused on folk drama.

The second generation folklorists writing on Mexican American folklore date from about 1930–1950. This group broke from first generation scholars with respect to the origins of the folklore of Spanish-speaking populations of the United States. With this second group, there is a shift from viewing folklore as being derived from Spain (Hispanists) to perceiving folklore as having definite Mexican roots (Mexicanists). The main figure positing this new theoretical paradigm of origins was Arthur León Campa (1905–1978), who, like Espinosa, did his major work on New Mexican folklore. His works covered various genres: folk theater; folk poetry, especially the *decima*; and folk songs. One of his major contributions is his book *Spanish Folk-Poetry in New Mexico* (1946). His other important works include *Treasure of the Sangre de Cristos: Tales and Traditions of the Spanish Southwest* (1963). Campa also contributed greatly to the study of folk theater with his publications and collections of this folk genre. His publications in this area include *Religious Spanish Folk-Drama in New Mexico* (1931) and *The Spanish Religious Folk-theater in the Southwest* (First Cycle) and (Second Cycle) (both 1934).

Other folklorists from the second generation period include Frank J. Dobie, Mody C. Boatright, Ralph Steele Boggs, George Carpenter Barker, and Mary R. Van Stone, among others. Hispanic folklorists from this era include three prominent women: Fabiola Cabeza de Baca Gilbert (1894–1991), Cleofas Jaramillo (1878–1956), and Aurora Lucero-White Lea (1894–1965). Cabeza de Baca Gilbert's most famous work is *We Fed Them Cactus* (1954), Jaramillo's is *Shadows of the Past* (1941), and Lucero-White Lea's is *Literary Folklore from the Hispanic Southwest* (1953). These three women folklorists were all from New Mexico, a region rich in folklore tradition. They all sought to record a Hispanic past that was fast disappearing under the onslaught of new Anglo-American settlers who were coming from the east coast and rapidly replacing the old Hispanos in New Mexico in terms of political and economic power.

The third generation of folklorists focusing on Mexican American folklore and whose major work falls within the decades of 1950–1970 encompasses the imposing scholarly figure of Américo Paredes (1915–1999). Paredes is rightly considered the "Father of Chicano Studies" and he certainly deserves the title given the ground-breaking work he did in Chicano folklore and cultural studies. His most well-known work is *"With His Pistol in His Hand": A Ballad and Its Hero* (1958), a book-length study that centers its lens on the *corrido* or ballad of Gregorio Cortez, a folk hero from Texas. Paredes was not only a brilliant scholar but a very productive one as well. He published books and a great number of seminal articles on different aspects of folklore, including the folk song, mainly the corrido, but also the *décima*, folk tales, folk speech, and jokes. Ramón Saldívar recently published a magnificent book-length study on Paredes titled *The Borderlands of Culture: Américo Paredes and the Transnational Imaginary* (2006).

Paredes's work departed from previous generations of scholars in that he not only collected folklore items but provided theoretical paradigms by which to analyze Mexican American folklore and the political underpinnings and meaning of this folklore. His theory of "culture conflict and culture clash" as the prime driving force in Chicano cultural production is still valid today. Furthermore, Paredes also introduced the concepts of class and race in the analysis and hermeneutics of Chicano folklore.

Other scholarly figures from this generation include Merle Simmons, Stanley Robe, and Vicente T. Mendoza. I date the Fourth Generation of folklorists as those publishing major works between 1970 and 2010. I include contemporary scholars in this group because most of them are still publishing today. Many of these folklore scholars from this generation, particularly Mexican American ones, have been influenced by the works of Américo Paredes. These folklorists include José Reyna, John H. McDowell, José E. Limón, Manuel Peña, Enrique Lamadrid, Norma E. Cantú, Richard Flores, Olga Nájera-Ramírez, Francis Aparicio, Yolanda Broyles González, Antonio Noé Zavaleta, and Peter García, among others. I include myself among this Fourth Generation of scholars who have been greatly influenced by the scholarship of Paredes.

Presently, a new generation of folklore scholars, the fifth generation, is centering their attention on Mexican American and Latino folklore. This new group of folklorists includes Rene Domino, Julián Carrillo, Eric César Morales, Nadia De León, Carleen Sánchez, Tamara Valdez, Diana Noreen Rivera, and many of the assistant professors and graduate students who wrote entries for *Celebrating Latino Folklore*. I am delighted to see a renewed interest in the study of folklore and a new crop of folklorists focusing their interest on Latino folklore. It is marvelous to see that the future study of Latino folklore is in excellent hands. I sincerely hope that future generations of folklorists find this three-volume encyclopedia a useful scholarly resource for their research.

Bibliography

Dundes, Alan. "What Is Folklore?" In Alan Dundes, ed. *The Study of Folklore*, 1–3. Englewood Cliffs, NJ: Prentice-Hall, 1965.

Herrera-Sobek, María. *The Bracero Experience: Elitelore Versus Folklore*. Los Angeles, CA: UCLA Latin American Studies Publications, 1979.

Leach, Maria, ed. Funk and Wagnall's *Standard Dictionary of Folklore Mythology and Legend* (1949–1950). New York: Funk and Wagnall's, 1972.

Saldívar, Ramón. *The Borderlands of Culture: Américo Paredes and the Transnational Imaginary*. Durham, NC: Duke University Press, 2006.

U.S. Census Bureau. "Hispanic Population of the United States." http://www.census.gov/population/www/socdemo/hispanic/hispanic_pop_presentation.html.

U.S. Census Bureau, Statistical Abstract of the United States: 2011. "Table 9: Resident Population by Race, Hispanic Origin, and Age: 2000 and 2009." http://www.census.gov/compendia/statab/2011/tables/11s0009.pdf.

Guide to Related Topics

AILMENTS AND FOLK MEDICINE

Botánicas
Brujería (Witchcraft)
Caída de Mollera (Baby's Fallen
    Fontanel)
Candles (Velas)
Charms
Conjuro/Hechizo (Magic Spell)
Embrujado/a
Empacho (Tripada or Pega)

Folk Medicine
Huesero (Bonesetter)
Limpias (Cleansings)
Magia (Magic)
Mal de Ojo (Evil Eye)
Partera (Midwife)
Spirit Possession and Exorcism
Susto
Yerbero/a

ARCHITECTURE

Adobe
Casitas

Graveyards
Mission Art and Architecture

ART

Altars
Calaveras (Skulls)
Cascarones
Castellánoz, Genoveva
Chicano/a Art and Folklore
Colonial Art
Descansos
Gravemarkers
Latino National Heritage Award
    Fellows (1982–2011)
Love and Rockets
Mission Art and Architecture

Molas
Nacimientos
Paper Arts (Papel Picado, Papier Mâché
    and Kites)
Piñata
Rascuache
Religious Folk Art
Retablos
Tattoos (Tatuajes)
Tin Work
Vejigantes
Yard Shrines

AZTEC FOLKLORE INFLUENCES

Aztec Empire
Aztlán
Cihuacóatl
Coatlicue
Greater Mexico and Its Folklore

Huitzilopochtli
Malinche
Quetzalcóatl
Tezcatlipoca
Tonantzin

Tonantzin in Chicana Literature and Art

Virgin of Guadalupe: History and Fiestas Guadalupanas

BELIEF
Cabañuelas (Weather Pronostication)
Candles (Velas)
Canícula (Dog Days of Summer)
Charms
Chirrionera
Conjuro/Hechizo (Magic Spell)
Con Safos (C/S)
Duendes
El Diablo (The Devil)

Espíritus Malignos (Evil Spirits)
Ghosts
Iconotheophany
La Santísima Muerte
Magia (Magic)
Mandas and Juramentos
Milagros
Myths
Spirit Possession and Exorcism

CELEBRATIONS AND FOLK EVENTS
Baptism
Bautizo (Baptism): Rites, Padrinos, and Celebrations
Charreada
Christmas (Navidad)
Cinco de Mayo (May 5th)
Cuaresma (Lent)
Día de la Raza
Día de los Muertos (Day of the Dead)
Día de los Muertos, Migration and Transformation to the U.S.
Fandango
Flor y Canto
George Washington's Birthday Celebration (Laredo, TX)
Holy Communion

Huelga (Workers' Strike)
Las Posadas
Los Reyes Magos (The Three Kings)
Matrimonio and Pedida de Mano (Marriage and Engagement)
Quinceañera
Relajo
Saint's Day (Día de Santo)
San Lorenzo, Feast Day of
Santiago, Feast Day of
September 16 (Mexican Independence Day)
Virgin of Guadalupe: History and Fiestas Guadalupanas
Wedding Customs

CHARACTERS IN LATINO FOLKLORE
Bato/a
Billy the Kid/El Bilito
Chili Queens
Cholos/Cholas
Coyote
El Tiradito (The Outcast)
Lowriders

Pachucos
Pachuquismo: 1940s Urban Youth
Peladito (Pelado)
Pocho/a
Tín Tán
Tío Taco

CHILDREN'S SONGS AND GAMES
Adivinanzas (Riddles)
Children's Songs and Games

La Vieja Inés y los Listones

CONVERSATIONAL GENRES, LANGUAGE

Adivinanzas (Riddles)
Agringado (Anglicized)
Alambristas (Undocumented Border
   Crosser)
Albures
Bato/a
Bomba
Califas (California)
Caló (Folk Speech)

Chicano Spanish
Con Safos (C/S)
Dichos (Proverbs)
Folk Speech and Folklore
Greaser
Los Rinches
Pochismos
Verbal Dueling

COUNTRIES AND REGIONS

Argentina and Its Folklore
Bailes Latinoamericanos
Bolivia and Its Folklore
Brazil and Its Folklore
Brazil, Myths and Legends from
Chile and Its Folklore
Costa Rica and Its Folklore
Cuban Americans and Their Folklore

El Salvador and Its Folklore
Greater Mexico and Its Folklore
Nicaragua and Its Folklore
Panama and Its Folklore
Peru and Its Folklore
Puerto Rico and Its Folklore
Spain and Its Folklore
Venezuela and Its Folklore

DANCE

Bachata
Bailes Latinoamericanos
Ballet Folklórico: Azteca
Ballet Folklórico: Jarabe Tapatío
Ballet Folklórico: Michoacán
Ballet Folklórico: San Luis Potosí
Ballet Folklórico: Tabasco
Ballet Folklórico: Tamaulipas
Ballet Folklórico: Veracruz

Casanova, Stephen (Steve)
Fandango
Flamenco
Limón, José
Mambo
Merengue
Rumba (Rhumba)
Tango

FOLK BUSINESS ORGANIZATIONS

Tandas and Cundinas

Nuyorican Poets Café

FOLK KINSHIPS

Comadre/Compadre

FOLKLORE ORGANIZATIONS

American Folklore Society (AFS)
Texas Folklore Society
Works Progress Administration (WPA)

FOLKLORE SCHOLARS, COLLECTORS

Arora, Shirley Lease
Boggs, Ralph Steele
Bourke, Captain John Gregory
Briggs, Charles Leslie
Cabeza de Baca, Fabiola
Cadaval, Olivia
Campa, Arthur León
Cantú, Norma E.
Dickey, Dan William
Espinosa, Aurelio Macedonio
Goldberg, Harriet
González de Mireles, Jovita
Green, Archie
Jaramillo, Cleofas M.
Keller, John Esten
Lamadrid, Enrique R.
Lea, Aurora Lucero-White
Leal, Luis
Limón, José Eduardo
Lomax, Alan
Lomax, John Avery
Lummis, Charles F.
McDowell, John Holmes
Nájera-Ramírez, Olga
Nicolopulos, James
Otero-Warren, Nina
Paredes, Américo
Parsons, Elsie
Rael, Juan Bautista
Rebolledo, Tey Diana
Robb, John Donald
Sahagún, Bernardino de
Strachwitz, Chris
West, John O.
Zavaleta, Antonio Noé

FOODS

Albóndigas (Meatballs)
Arroz con Leche (Rice Pudding)
Barbacoa
Birria
Buñuelos
Burritos
Cabrito
Capirotada
Carne Asada
Chalupas
Champurrado
Chicharrones
Chiles (Peppers)
Chili Queens
Elotes
Empanadas
Enchiladas
Fajitas
Feijoada
Frijoles
Gorditas
Guacamole
Lengua
Maíz
Menudo
Mole
Morcillas
Nachos
Paella
Pan Dulce (Mexican Pastry)
Pinole
Pozole
Pulque
Quesos
Rosca de Reyes
Salsa
Sopas (de Arroz, de Fideos)
Tacos
Tamales
Tequila
Torta de Camarón
Tortas
Tortilla

FUNERAL RITES AND PRACTICES

Descansos
Funerals
Funerary Practices

La Despedida (The Farewell)
Wakes

GAMES

Adivinanzas (Riddles)
Children's Songs and Games

Pelea de Gallos (Cockfighting)

GARMENTS

Rebozo
Sarape

Zoot Suit

HEROES AND ANTI-HEROES

"Ballad of Gregorio Cortez"
Billy the Kid/ El Bilito
Murieta, Joaquín
Niños Héroes de Chapultepec (Boy
    Heroes of Chapultepec)

Treviño, Jacinto
Vásquez, Tiburcio
Zorro, Legend of

INFLUENCES ON LATINO FOLKLORE

African Influence on Latino Folklore
Asian Contribution to Chicano/Latino
    Folklore

Aztec Empire

MUSIC

Afro-Colombian Music
Alabados
Alabanzas
Bachata
"Ballad of Gregorio Cortez"
Bomba
Boogie Woogie
Canción Ranchera
Canción Romántica
Conjunto
Corrido (Ballad)
Décima
Flamenco

Hip Hop
Indita Folksongs
"La Adelita"
"La Bamba"
Mambo
Merengue
Narcocorridos
Plena
Reggae
Reggaetón
Romance
Rumba (Rhumba)
Tango

MUSICIANS AND MUSICAL INSTRUMENTS

Baez, Joan Chandos
Conjunto
Folk Instruments

Guerrero, Eduardo "Lalo"
Jiménez, Santiago
Los Lobos

Los Pleneros de la 21
Mariachi

Mendoza, Lydia
Race Records

NARRATIVE FOLKLORE
Aztlán
Bailando con el Diablo (Dancing with
  the Devil Legends)
The Black Legend
Brazil, Myths and Legends from
Chupacabra
Cihuacóatl
Coatlicue
Coyolxauhqui
El Coquí
Fables
Folk Narratives: Folk Tales, Legends,
  and Jokes
Folk Tales
Ghosts
Huitzilopochtli
Iconotheophany
Jokes (Chistes)

Juan El Oso (John the Bear)
La Llorona (The Wailing Woman)
La Siguanaba
Malinche
Maximón (San Simón)
The Motif-Index of Folk Literature
Pedro de Urdemalas
Quetzalcóatl
Quinto Sol
Ridge, John Rollin
Tezcatlipoca
Tonantzin
Tonantzin in Chicano Literature and
  Art
Virgin of Guadalupe: History and Fies-
  tas Guadalupanas
Zorro, Legend of

RELATED DISCIPLINES AND FOLKLORE
Chicano/a Art and Folklore
Chicano/a Literature and Folklore
Hispano Culture

Latina Feminism and Folklore in the
  United States

SACRED SPACES
Altars
Chimayó
Descansos
Graveyards

Iconotheophany
Nacimientos
Pilgrimages (Peregrinaciones)
Yard Shrines

SAINTS AND FOLK RELIGION
Altars
Candles (Velas)
El Niño Fidencio (José Fidencio
  Síntora Constantino)
Iconotheophany
Jaramillo, Don Pedrito
La Santísima Muerte
Los Penitentes
Malverde, Jesús
Mandas and Juramentos

Milagros
Religious Folk Art
Retablos
Saints (Santos)
Santería
Santo Niño de Atocha (The Holy Child
  of Atocha)
Soldado, Juan
Urrea, Teresa

THEATER

Calaveras (Skulls)
"El Niño Perdido" ("The Lost Child")
Farmworkers' Theater
"Los Tejanos" (folk play)
Matachines (folk performance)
"Moros y Cristianos" (folk play)
Pastorelas (Shepherds' Plays)
Teatro de Carpas
Valdez, Luis

TRADES AND FOLK ARTISTS

Adobe
Charros (Horsemen)
Colchas (Quilts/Quilting)
Gravemarkers
Graveyards
Latino National Heritage Award Winners (1982–2011)
Lowriders
Molas
Paper Arts: Papel Picado, Papier Mâché, and Kites
Piñata
Rebozo
Religious Folk Art
Retablos
Sarape
Tandas and Cundinas
Tattoos (Tatuajes)
Tin Work
Vaquero
Yard Shrines

UNITED STATES AND LATINO FOLKLORE

Cuban Americans and Their Folklore
Greater Mexico and Its Folklore
Hispano Culture
Puerto Rico and Its Folklore

ADIVINANZAS (RIDDLES)

Adivinanzas, or riddles, form part of the oral tradition of people throughout Latin America, the United States, and other parts of the world. Various scholars have offered definitions for this folklore genre including Archer Taylor, who undertook extensive work on this area of expressive culture and perceived its basic structure to consist of comparisons to an object. He went on to state that "[t]he wit of such comparisons is found in the disclosure of an answer that fits the comparison quite as well as the object that has been suggested" (1952, 170). Other important definitions include one articulated by Elli Kongas-Maranda, who suggested that "the riddle is a structural unit, which necessarily consists of two parts: the riddle image and the riddle answer (quoted in McDowell 1979, 20). The riddle image may be posited by the person proposing it, often in terms of a question, but also in terms of a general definition. At least two persons are required to play the game of riddling, although since the object of riddling or of saying *adivinanzas* is to entertain, posing *adivinanzas* to a group is perhaps even more enjoyable. The person asking the *adivinanza* challenges an individual or a group to decipher the enigma being asked within the structure of the question or the statement enunciated. For example, one *adivinanza* states: "*Es, cuando no es; y no es, cuando es. ¿Qué es?*" The

Cover of *El Pequeño Adivinadorcito* no. 5, a chapbook of *adivinanzas* (riddles) published between 1890 and 1913 by Antonio Vanegas Arroyo, with engravings by José Guadalupe Posada. (Library of Congress)

answer is "*la nuez*." The answer actually is inscribed within the enigma posed (*no es=nuez*). Another popular *adivinanza* of this type that encodes the answer within its structure is:

> Agua pasa por mi casa
> Cate de mi corazón
> Si no me adivinas ésta
> Eres burro cabezón!

> Water passes by my house
> My dear Cate
> If you cannot answer this riddle
> You are a dumb donkey!

> (answer: *aguacate*, that is, the avocado)

In the above case, the *adivinanza* is structured as a four-line strophe with a rhyme scheme of abcb—the second line rhyming with the fourth one. Furthermore, the strophe is octosyllabic, that is, consisting of eight syllables. This structure is commonly seen in *adivinanzas*. The answer is inscribed within the four-line strophe with the first word of the riddle "*agua*" and the word "Cate" at the beginning of the second line.

Another example of an *adivinanza* structured in verse form is the following:

> Tito, Tito
> Capotito
> Sube al cielo
> Y tira un grito

> Tito, Tito (name of a person)
> With your little cape
> Climb to the sky
> And let out a yell.

> The *adivinanza* may end with the question: *¿Qué es?* (What is it?)

> (answer: *el cohete*, that is, the fire cracker)

The fun is in both playing with language since it is composed of rhyming syllables and in the challenge given to the audience to decipher the riddle. The enjoyment for the audience consists in either rising to the challenge and guessing the answer correctly, or in possibly being stumped and not figuring out the answer. Furthermore, feeling foolish at how easy it is to decipher the answer once it is given brings out laughter in the audience. The audience usually laughs at the ingenuity of the speaker posing the *adivinanza*; they enjoy the play with language and finally hearing the answer that was there for all to see, but was invisible to them at the time.

A second example of a four-line *adivinanza* with an abcb rhyme scheme is the following:

Vence al tigre y al león
Vence al toro embravecido
Vence a señores y reyes
Y a todos deja vencidos.

It vanquishes the tiger and the lion
It vanquishes the enraged bull
It vanquishes distinguished men and kings
And is victorious over everyone.

¿Qué es? (What is it?)

(answer: "sleep," since everyone succumbs to sleep)

Archer Taylor approved of classifying riddles according to what the objects were being compared with. Taylor proceeds to offer examples, stating that there are riddles that structure the comparison of "living creatures not identifiable as an animal or a man, to an animal; to a man; to a plant; to a thing" (1952, 170). Animals, as seen in the above riddle, are used to structure the comparison with sleep.

Another example that compares animals to an inanimate object is the following:

Chiquito chiquito como un ratón
Pero cuido más mi casa que un león.

Tiny, tiny as a mouse
But I guard my house better than a lion.

(answer: *el candado*, that is, the lock)

Non-scholars who collect *adivinanzas* tend to categorize them and organize them by subject matter, for example family, geography, food, vegetables, fruits, clothing, flora and fauna, astronomy, animals, nature, kitchen utensils, furniture, and so forth. Anything in the universe and in the world can be used to structure *adivinanzas*.

While *adivinanzas* are playful and delight children as well as adults with their ingenuity, wit, playfulness with words, language dexterity, and imagination, educators often see this rich repertoire of expressive folklore useful in the development of children's language skills and other forms of cognitive development. John McDowell, author of the superb study *Children's Riddling* (1979), certainly views *adivinanzas* as offering children more than light entertainment, while that is also important, of course. He states: "Riddles in the modern, industrial society serve as models of synthetic and analytic thinking. They encourage children to discover the archetypical set of commonalities binding diverse experiential realities into a single, coherent world view, and at the same time, they require children to confront the tentative status of conceptual systems, thereby fostering a flexibility of cognition evidently of some utility in a great many cultural settings" (1979, 20).

Adivinanzas are one of the most popular folklore genres of oral tradition in Latin American countries and with Latinos/as in the United States. They continue to be composed, and most people are able to tell you a few *adivinanzas*, which they have in their own personal repertoire. The *adivinanza* is a playful genre that brings a smile to people's faces whenever one discusses the topic. The Internet evidences numerous sites attesting to the popularity of this folklore genre. A few of these include "Welcome to adivinanzas.com," http://www.adivinanzas .com/, and "Abc de adivinanzas," http://www.dichos.galeon.com/adivinanza.htm.

María Herrera-Sobek

See also: Dichos (Proverbs)

Further Reading

Campa, Arthur L. *Sayings and Riddles in New Mexico*. University of New Mexico Bulletin, Language Series, vol. 6, no. 2. Albuquerque: University of New Mexico Press, 1937.

Jijena Sánchez, Rafael. *Adivina adivinador: Quinientas [500] de las mejores adivinanzas de la lengua española*. Buenos Aires: Albatros, 1943.

Lehmann-Nitsche, Roberto. *Adivinanzas rioplatenses*. Buenos Aires: Coni Hermanos, 1911.

McDowell, John. *Children's Riddling*. Bloomington: Indiana University Press, 1979.

Rueda, Manuel. *Adivinanzas dominicana*. Santo Domingo: Instituto de Investigaciones Folklóricas, Universidad Nacional "Pedro Henríquez Ureña," 1970.

Taylor, Archer. *The Riddle*. Indiana University Publications Folklore Series, no. 6. Bloomington: Indiana University Press, 1952.

West, John O. *Mexican-American Folklore: Legends, Songs, Festivals, Proverbs, Crafts, Tales of Saints, of Revolutionaries, and More*. Little Rock, AR: August House Publishers, 1988.

ADOBE

The word "adobe" is derived from the Arabic *al tob*, literally sun-dried brick, which became *adobar* in Spain, meaning to plaster or to daub, and finally, adobe in Spanish-colonial America with the current meaning. Adobe works best as a building material in arid climates because rain and moisture cause rapid deterioration of the soil compound.

Traditionally, adobe bricks are made from a mixture of clay, sand, and straw that is pressed into a wooden frame and allowed to dry and bake in the hot sun. A similar mixture of earth is used as a mortar when building walls, and the exterior and interior of a building are coated with adobe to create a smooth finish. Adobe buildings generally have flat roofs that are slanted only enough to allow water to run off. Though this type of building is not exclusive to the Southwestern United States and Mexico, it is most popular in these regions for the use of contemporary buildings and has been in use as a building material for over a thousand years.

Spanish colonizers who came to the United States saw Pueblo Indians build structures by placing one layer of adobe on a wall and allowing it to dry before adding another layer, so that walls were built with successive layers of adobe. This layering process is called "puddle" adobe. Bricks were also sometimes formed by hand and called "turtle-back" adobe because the bricks were rounded on one side. Colonizers had seen this type of building in Spain and introduced the use of wooden frames to shape uniform bricks, a process that the Indians quickly

St. Augustine Church, built in 1612, at the Isleta Pueblo in New Mexico. (iStockPhoto.com)

adopted. When properly maintained by periodic replastering of the walls, adobe buildings can last centuries. For example, the Taos Pueblo in New Mexico includes adobe buildings that have been continuously occupied for over 900 years. These buildings are multistory, and look somewhat like stacked blocks.

Spanish-colonial adobe buildings were of a different style. Mission churches and houses were frequently built with adobe because it was the most readily available building material. Because adobe walls are exceptionally thick (often two to four feet), recesses and alcoves could be built into the walls, and church bells could be set within a high wall instead of a bell tower. Spanish homes in America were generally one story and built as a hacienda for defensive purposes. The rooms of a hacienda were built around a central courtyard, or *placita*. All doors and windows opened to the interior courtyard and a single set of heavy doors provided the only external access to the courtyard. Haciendas were generally owned by wealthy settlers such as merchants and ranchers, who could afford to build large homes, but less affluent people also built their houses together in the shape of a hacienda. Even when built separate from a hacienda, builders of adobe homes attached rooms end to end to form a straight line, an L shape, or a U shape. Both Indian and Spanish buildings feature a dome-shaped fireplace that is located in the corner of a room. *Bancos*, or benches, are also often built from adobe along one or more walls and covered with blankets or cushions. Similar buildings that can be found in the Southwest are *jacals*, which are also made of a mud compound spread across wooden poles, but these structures are less permanent and not considered adobe because they do not use the sun-dried bricks.

The influx of Anglo-Americans in the nineteenth century brought an influx of new materials and styles for adobe buildings and caused the development of what is now termed "territorial-style" adobe buildings. The popularity of Greek Revival architecture in the Eastern United States and the greater availability of timber from the north brought by the railroads caused the introduction of porches that ran along the front of an adobe building and were supported by whitewashed wooden posts. The decrease in Indian raids and the increased availability of glass also made large external windows more practical. These windows were usually made of small panes of glass in a lattice-type frame. Anglos also introduced the floor plan of a single hall with rooms on each side, rather then the L- or U-shaped row of rooms.

Ironically, beginning in the early twentieth century, Anglos in the Southwest began to be concerned with preservation of adobe buildings and conservation of pre-territorial style structures. This period started the "Pueblo-revival" style. Individuals took an interest in preserving old churches and homes, and institutions such as the University of New Mexico began building structures in the Spanish and Pueblo styles. John Gaw Meem, who designed numerous buildings for the New Mexico government in the 1920s and 1930s, is one of the most famous architects who popularized the Pueblo-revival style. However, "[r]estoring old buildings and accommodating the regional style to modern technology (electricity, water pipes, etc.) was . . . an expensive matter which few Spanish Americans could afford. So-called Spanish residences were typically restored, built, and owned by affluent Anglos" (López 1974, 91). Hispanos did continue to build traditional adobe homes in New Mexico throughout the twentieth century, particularly in rural areas, and while the commercial construction of adobe buildings is a thriving industry in New Mexico today, some families and individuals still build adobe structures by hand using the traditional wood-frame method. The fact that adobe homes are environmentally friendly and conserve energy because of their thick, insulated walls, has recently increased their popularity, and commercially produced adobe usually contains an added compound that stabilizes the bricks and makes them more resistant to water.

Adobe homes and buildings are important settings in many folk stories and traditions. The thick, earthen walls provide a quiet internal space that is said to be incomparable, and the regular maintenance required provides a sense of continuity and connection with the natural environment and the community that works as a group to maintain the structures. Historically, women have played a vital role in constructing and maintaining adobe structures in both Indian and Hispano traditions where it was the women's role to replaster the adobe walls at regular intervals. Many domestic folk tales of the Southwest, such as those involving *duendes*, or house gnomes, feature adobe homes, and adobe buildings are a vital part of much contemporary Chicano and Latino literature.

ERIN MURRAH-MANDRIL

See also: Casitas; Duendes; Mission Art and Architecture

Further Reading

López, Thomas R. *Prospects for the Spanish American Culture of New Mexico*. San Francisco, CA: R & E Research Associates, 1974.

Lumpkins, William, E. Boyd, and Charlie Steen. *Adobe Past and Present*. Santa Fe: Museum of New Mexico, 1974.

Montaño, Mary. *Tradiciones Nuevomexicanas: Hispano Arts and Culture of New Mexico*. Albuquerque: University of New Mexico Press, 2001.

Smith, Edward W., and George S. Austin. *Adobe, Pressed-Earth, and Rammed-Earth Industries in New Mexico*. Rev ed. Socorro: New Mexico Bureau of Mines and Mineral Resources, 1996.

AFRICAN INFLUENCE ON LATINO FOLKLORE

Latino folklore in Latin and North America and the Caribbean has been influenced heavily by African elements since the sixteenth century; these elements have been passed down for generations and from one country to the other. The African legacy is considered one of the main roots for the development of the Latino community, and the evidence of its influence can be seen throughout Latin America's history, ethnicity, folklore, culture, and everyday life. The ways it is exposed vary from country to country, but the essence of African heritage still exists in the music, festivals and celebrations, folk beliefs, and food, to mention a few, that distinguish Latino folklore.

Origin

Starting in the sixteenth century and for more than 200 years, millions of African slaves were brought by Europeans to North and Latin America and the Caribbean to work on fields and to take the place of declining Indigenous communities. This represented a lucrative business for Europeans and the beginning of a new life for Africans who brought customs and traditions with them. Africans were forced to settle in the new lands and, due to the great number of slaves and their contact with European and Indigenous cultures, became one of the greatest influences on most aspects of future Latin American countries. Even though many of them were assimilated to European culture and customs, a great number of African traditions were preserved and are still considered an essential part of Latino identity and folklore.

Folk Music

With the arrival and settlement of African slaves, many of their musical traditions, rhythms, dances, and instruments were adapted to the European and Indigenous music already present in the new continent. African music spread throughout Latin American regions and became a significant part of the musical folklore of different societies. The greatest evidence of this influence can be seen mainly in countries of the Atlantic and Pacific coast of South America and also in the Caribbean, but other countries such as Peru, Bolivia, and Mexico, as well as the area of Central America, have also shown a great musical influence of the slaves' settlements that became established in their regions.

The Caribbean

The Caribbean was the first stop for most ships that transported slaves directly from Africa before taking them to their final destination in different parts of North and Latin America. A great number of slaves were forced to work on Caribbean plantations and made those islands their new home. Until today, the music that developed in Cuba, Haiti, the Dominican Republic, and Puerto Rico shows a very strong African influence, mainly through instrumental improvisation, sensual movements, and festive rhythms, which makes it unique and popular in Latin America and around the world.

There are many varieties of Afro-Caribbean folkloric music. For example, in Cuba two of the most popular folkloric rhythms are the *Lucumí* or *Regla de Ocha* and the famous Cuban rumba, which depending on the style is called *yambú*, *guaguancó*, or *columbia*, and what connects them together are the ritual drums and songs of various African ethnic groups. The starting point of much of the folkloric music in Cuba and other countries in the Caribbean is religious beliefs brought from different parts of Africa, especially from the Congo region and the Yoruba tradition (Nigeria). Other types, such as the *son cubano*, combine Spanish and African rhythms with percussion instruments to create an original mixture of sounds and beats. The mambo, even though more recent, is also considered part of the Afro-Cuban folkloric tradition because it mixes the sensual movements and rhythms of African and Cuban music with European country dance. Its popularity, along with the popularity of the rumba, spread to the United States and became part of important dance competitions in cities such as New York, Miami, and San Francisco.

In Puerto Rico, the two main examples of Afro-Caribbean folkloric music are the *bomba* and *plena*; both have almost exclusive African rhythms. The *bomba* was used to celebrate baptisms, marriages, or rebellions while the *plena* tells stories or current events of the town mixed with the sounds of drums and other musical instruments of African heritage.

The African folkloric music in Haiti is related to the Vodou religion and is considered a spiritual music. The music, dances, and rhythms are part of the religious rituals where participants make a combination of beliefs in African spirits with images of Roman Catholicism. The African influence is also present in the language used in the songs and combines West and Central African languages with the Creole spoken in the country.

The neighboring country, the Dominican Republic, also shows the African element in folkloric music such as the *baile de palos* (dance of sticks), also called *bambula* or *quiyombo*, *música de congos* (music of Congos), *cantos de hacha* (chaints of axe), and *música de Gagá* (music of Gagá), where African tones and rhythms are combined during festivities or religious ceremonies. The famous merengue dance, created and developed in this country, also shows some elements of African rhythms along with other countries' influences. It became very popular in the

United States during the 1970s due to immigration movements from Quisqueya to New York and until today is still one of the most popular dances in ballroom competitions.

Mexico and Central America

There is a strong African influence in the folkloric music of Mexico and Central America, mainly in the regions of the Caribbean coast. Although Central American countries keep the influence of Mayan culture as well as Spanish conquerors, it is because of the countries' proximity to the most important slave settlements such as Cuba, Haiti, and Jamaica that Afro-Caribbean music such as reggae, calypso, rumba, and other types of religious dances became an important part of the folkloric music of the region.

Mexico's folk music encompasses a great variety of influences, from the Indigenous and European communities, specifically the Spanish, to those of the African slaves and Afro-Caribbean groups that settled in different parts of the country. The Cuban rumba, for example, was popular among black Mexican slaves in Veracruz and Yucatán. Also, the Cuban *son* became very popular and was adapted to the Mexican style to create the *son jarocho* in Veracruz, where the famous folk song "La Bamba" was created and where the term "Bamba" is believed to be the name of an African tribe in Angola. Another kind of *son*, called *son huasteca*, was developed in the Sierra Huasteca, in the Mexican Gulf. Other Mexican folkloric dances called *negritos* are also part of the African tradition and are performed in the Sierra of Oaxaca, Costa Chica, Michoacán, and Puebla. Even though these dances also have Indigenous elements, the style and movements, specifically those of the Snake Dance, are related to the ones practiced by the slave community in Cuba and Haiti, all of which originated in the Congo regions of West Africa.

In Costa Rica, African influences appear in the constant use of special and difficult percussion rhythms. In El Salvador, it is more noticeable in festivals and celebrations, with the adaptation of their own style of Afro-Caribbean dances such as the merengue from the Dominican Republic, the *cumbia* from Colombia, and the Cuban rumba. In Guatemala, as well as in some other countries of Central America such as Honduras, Belize, and Nicaragua, the musical influence from West African immigrants is related to that of the Garifuna community of Afro-Caribbean descent. Their most popular dance, *punta*, is related to an ancient West African fertility dance.

Panama also shows a strong influence of African rhythms in its folkloric music because of the influence of the Afro-Caribbean diaspora that brought immigrants mainly from Jamaica, Trinidad, and Martinique. There, people adapted the music of the surrounding countries, such as the calypso, the merengue, the salsa, the reggae, and the *cumbia*, to develop their own genres of African heritage, such as the *congo*.

South America

Today, as a result of slavery, African-descendant communities are concentrated in the Atlantic coast and some of the Pacific coast, such as Ecuador and part of Colombia. Nevertheless, this does not mean that countries such as Bolivia, Argentina, or Uruguay did not have any contact with African communities and their culture.

A member of the Afro Brazilian dance group called Mandingueiros Dospalmares performs *capoeira*—a combination of dance and self-defense—during a rally in support of immigrant students in Boston. (AP/Wide World Photos)

In Argentina, even though the majority of the population shows an evident European heritage, the slave community that was brought to the country in the mid-1800s had a very strong influence. The word "tango," which is the name of the national dance of Argentina, is believed to be of African origin and was used to identify the place where slaves congregated to dance. In Uruguay and also some northern regions of Argentina, influences of African elements in folk music can be seen in the popular *candombe*. The *candombe* rhythm, instruments, and dances (also called tangos) are of Bantu heritage and are still performed in festivals and cultural events.

In Brazil, African influence is stronger than in many other nations of South America, mainly in music like *capoeira* and samba. In *capoeira*, Brazilians combine African rhythms, dances, beliefs, games, and martial arts to produce one of the most popular and unique practices of the country. *Capoeira* was created in an African slave community called Palmares, where it was initially used by slaves to make the Portuguese and Dutch believe that they were practicing harmless dances and rituals, instead of martial arts that would be used to get their freedom. Later it became the symbol of freedom for slaves and was spread through the main slaves' settlements throughout the country. In *capoeira*, the music is the main element; it controls the speed and rhythm of movements. Even though *capoeira* groups struggled for many years against the Brazilian government, today, the music is a symbol of Brazilian identity and folklore.

The Brazilian samba (*umbigada* or folk samba) was first developed in Rio de Janeiro. The dancing and singing combine styles similar to those from the Angola and Congo regions in Africa, but also have some influence of the Portuguese. Other types of Brazilian folk music with African influence are the *maracatu*, played in the regions of Recife and Olinda during carnivals using drums, bells, and shakers, and the *afoxé*, a religious music that is part of the Afro-Brazilian religion called *candomblé*.

The geographic position and the direct connection with the Atlantic and Pacific coasts give Colombia the advantage of being considered one of the South American countries with the most varied African influence. The *cumbia* is one of the most famous music styles of the Atlantic coast of Colombia and combines elements of Spanish and Amerindian melodies with African rhythms, musical instruments, and movements. The term "*cumbia*" originated from a dance named "*cumbè*" from the region of Guinea in Africa and was soon adapted to many other countries nearby, mainly in Central America and the Caribbean. The *bullerengue*, also developed in the Atlantic coast, is part of the Afro-Colombian folk heritage as well. The *bullerengue* is found in Panama and is a dance where women celebrate their initiation into puberty.

In the Colombian Pacific coast, the *currulao* is the most representative Afro-Colombian music. The origin of the name comes from the style of the dance that is called "*acorralado*" in Spanish ("cornered" in English). Usually the dance is accompanied by the rhythms of *tambora o bombo* (drums), the *guasa* (a hollow cylinder made of metal, wood or bamboo filled with light seeds or rice), and the *marimba* (a wooden xylophone-like musical instrument).

Ecuador also has a noticeable African influence in the country's folk music that includes the *bambuco*, also found in Colombia but with some variations. The *bambuco*, which is believed to be of Kikongo origin, is a combination of dance and rhythms where African musical instruments such as the *marimba, cununos,* and *bomos y guazá* are mixed with women's songs. It is a mythological dance that celebrates life. It also has different varieties such as *Jugá, Caderona, Berejú, Banbara Negra,* and *patacoré.*

The folk music with the strongest African influence in Bolivia is *la saya* (*saya* music), played mainly by Afro-Bolivians. The term *la saya* comes from *Nsaya*, of Kikongo origin, and means common work under the command of a main singer. In *la saya*, Andean instruments and clothes (from the Aymara community) are combined with African percussion and rhythms. The participants use music, dance, and poetry along with metaphors and satire to represent themes related to slavery and the country's present situation.

The slaves' settlements in Peru came from the west regions of the African continent and developed, as in many other places in South America, dances and songs that became part of the country's folklore. Those African influences can be found in styles like the popular landó, the zamba-landó, and the zamacueca. The landó was brought to Peru from the slaves of Brazil, Haiti, and the Antilles, who came from Angola. This kind of music mixes European elements with African rhythms, themes about slavery, and musical instruments that became a symbol of the Peruvian folklore, especially the cajón, a box-like drum.

The folk music in Venezuela shows the African influence by combining or adapting a different style of music from other countries like *calypso, merengue*, and Afro-Cuban rhythms. The strongest African element that survives today is the use of African-derived percussion. Also the popular *joropo*, of European origin and part of the Colombian folklore as well, has been modified on the central coast of Venezuela to give it the African touch with shorter verses, more improvisation, and the reduction of musical instruments to a harp and maracas, and one singer. Many songs are also evidently derived from West Africa, for example: the *fulia* (or work songs), the *velorio* (wake songs for children), the *golpe* (in the north region of the country, accompanied by drums), and the *tambor mina* (in the central and eastern regions).

Folk Musical Instruments

The musical instruments used to play folk music in Latin American countries show, in many ways, the strong influences of African heritage that are still alive in each country's culture. Even today, in some regions of Latin America, people still play musical instruments that are similar to those used by slaves to re-create the rhythms that distinguished the original songs and dances.

Drums and Similar Musical Instruments

Latin folk music would not be the same without the rhythm and beats of the percussion instruments that came from Africa, the most important being the drums. Even though the shapes, sizes, materials, and sounds of these percussion instruments differ from one to the other, they fulfill the musicians' goals of re-creating old dances and rhythms that are a fundamental part of Latin culture. In the Antilles, for example, drums, congas, and batás are the main instruments of Afro-Caribbean folk music. Each drum has a specific name and function, and most of the time is responsible for marking the beat. These instruments are also an essential component for religious rituals, as in the Dominican Republic, Cuba, and in the Vodou music of Haiti. In Cuba, the *batá* drums, of Yoruba origin, are used to play the Lucumíní, and congas are played to accompany the Cuban rumba. The name of the Cuban mambo comes from the name of a Bantu drum, used also for sacred and ritual purposes. While the *plena* in Puerto Rico also uses drums, congas, and *panderetas* (tambourines), the *bomba* music requires two main drums: the *buleador* and the *subidor*, both used to set the rhythm, but also to participate in a kind of competing dialog between dancers and drummers.

In South America, drums also play a main role in folk music. The folk music of Venezuela, for example, shows different classifications for percussive instruments by giving them names such as *corrío* (the largest drum), *cruzao* and *pujao* (used for improvisations), the *cumacao*, the *mina* (a large drum), the *quimbángano*, and the *chimbangle*, which are still played in festivals as a tribute to the ones played by the slaves in their dances and rebellions. Drums used to play Colombian *cumbia* are made of wood or animal skins and are played either with or without sticks. One of the peculiarities of *cumbia* drummers is the way they play the instruments by hitting them in almost every area of the wooden base and dry skin. Colombian drums also have various names: the *manguaré* and the *cununú* (with one membrane), and the *bombo* (with membranes in both sides).

In Peru and Cuba, the *cajón* (box) is a very peculiar percussion instrument that is played widely in Afro-Cuban and Afro-Peruvian folk music. It consists of a drum box made of plywood that is played by hitting the front side with the hands while the drummer is sitting upon it.

In Uruguay and parts of Argentina, the music *candombe* must be performed by a group of drummers called *cuerda*. In the *candombe*, as in many other kinds of

Latino folk music, the drums, in this case called *tamboriles* because of their barrel-like shape, have different names: *chico* (small), *repique* (medium), *piano* (large), and a larger drum called *bajo* or *bombo*. In the Bolivian *saya*, the bombos are an important part of the music and a specific process is required to make them so that they produce the sounds that are needed.

In Brazil, the drums called *atabaque* and *urucungo* are used to accompany *capoeira* music along with the *pandeiro* (a kind of tamberine). Drums in *samba* performances are also fundamental and every year Brazilian samba schools develop different styles for the drummers to go into a competition. There are different kinds of samba drums, all made with light materials so they can be easily carried. Some of them are the *surdu* (large bass drum), the *timbale* (of conical shape), the *caixa* (called Caixa de Guerra or war drum if it has metal snares and played with drumsticks), the *pandeiro*, the *tambourim*, and the *cuica*.

The Marimba

The marimba is one of the most important and representative instruments of the folk music of Central America and the southern region of Mexico. This popular instrument was brought to the region by African slaves during the sixteenth century and by Afro-Caribbean immigrants that came later from the Antilles. This percussion instrument is a sort of xylophone with bars made of rosewood that can be either supported on cords or placed over bamboo or metal tubes of varying lengths. It is played with two resonators made out of metal or locally grown gourds. Even though it is not played exclusively in Latino folk music of African heritage, it has become a symbol of the tradition and folklore of the countries of Central America as well as some regions of Mexico and the South American Pacific coast. In Ecuador and Colombia, for example, the marimba is used along with other percussion instruments and songs in the folk performances of the *curralao* dance. This instrument also plays an important role in the folk music of Cuba, where it is called marimba or *manimbula* and is made of a hollow box and strips of bands. The marimba is the national instrument of Guatemala and is especially popular in Costa Rica, Honduras, El Salvador, and Nicaragua during festivities and heritage celebrations.

Other Instruments of African Influence in Latino Folk Music

The drums and the marimba are symbols of the presence of the African element in Latino folk music, but are not the only instruments that are related to that influence. Traces of African musical traditions are still found in other instruments in Latin countries of the Caribbean as well as in Central and South America, such as the maracas or "shakers." These are also percussion instruments that are usually played in pairs and made of dried gourd shell or coconut shell filled with seeds or dried beans, although in some regions they are made of leather, plastic, or wood. In the Dominican Republic, the maracas used to perform folk music are still made with shapes and materials very similar to those brought by the slaves; examples of this are the *maraca Ocoeña*, played in the *música de Palos,* and the *yomo* or *maraca doble* (double maraca) played in the *música de Gagá.* The maracas are also popular in the folk music of Cuba, Puerto Rico, México, Colombia, Brazil, and Venezuela.

Other instruments brought to Latin America by the slaves were the *claves* or *palitos* (wooden sticks used to mark rhythm). In Brazil, instruments such as the *berimbau*, a string bow-like instrument with a gourd at the bottom and a tire wire for a string, and the *agogo bells* (that resembles two round cowbells together) played in capoeira music are part of the Afro-Latin folkloric tradition.

Folk Festivals and Celebrations

Festivals and celebrations are an integral part of Latino culture. They are celebrated in a great variety of ways throughout the year and are considered a distinctive feature of many Latin countries. Generally, the celebrations include all types of music, dances, food, parades, and costumes with the purpose of commemorating each country's history, culture, traditions, and heritage. Although some countries in Central and South America have a predominantly Indian or European population, the African influence on these types of events is noticeable and is fundamental to many of the countries' identity.

The Caribbean

Folk festivals and celebrations in Latin countries of the Caribbean are some of the most popular events. Each country has its own style and costumes at specific times of the year, but the African influence in all of them is easily recognizable. In Cuba, for example, the carnival of Santiago, the island's old capital and center of the sugar and rum industries in the country, is one of the most important folkloric events. It is celebrated during the summer, specifically in June and July, and its origin goes back to the times when slaves worked on sugar cane plantations. The main event in this celebration is called the *fiestas de mamarrachos*. Even though it is considered a celebration of Spanish origin, African slaves contributed to the tradition by adding the famous parades that proceed through the villages while playing instruments of African origin, in addition to the masks and costumes of vivid colors that have become a fundamental part of the carnivals. The *comparsas*, or group of dancers, of African influence as well, became very popular in Cuba and other Latin American festivals.

The African influence on the folk celebrations of the Dominican Republic and Puerto Rico are very similar to those in Cuba. In both countries, the masks, the lively sounds of drums, and other instruments of African origin, as well as the costumes of brilliant colors, are symbols of African heritage. The idea of using natural materials to make the masks and costumes was also brought by the slaves during the sixteenth century, and they used to believe in these objects as carriers of spiritual strength and good luck. Other elements of African heritage in the parades are the practice of scaring or making fun of people, the use of puppets, the singing styles, and the dance movements, typical in these folkloric celebrations.

Folk festivals in the Dominican Republic also have some influence of the African traditions of Haiti. An example of this is *Ga-Gá* dances, originally from the carnival known in Haiti as *Ra-Rá*. In both countries, those have a strong religious meaning and their purpose is to celebrate the earth's and people's fertility.

Many folk festivals in Puerto Rico are related to the recognition of the *bomba*, the *plena*, and the salsa as a fundamental part of the island's folklore. Different kinds of celebrations are organized every year to commemorate Puerto Rican folk music with dances, live shows, food, and crafts that honor the African heritage in the Puerto Rican culture.

Central and South America

Many countries in Central and South America show a very strong influence of the Indigenous and European communities. Nevertheless, the countries in the coastal regions keep showing and celebrating the importance of the heritage of the West African traditions brought by the slaves that settled there since the sixteenth century.

In Central America, the folk festival *Palo de Mayo* or *Mayo Ya* (Maypole), celebrated in Nicaragua, marks the combination of cultural elements that distinguish the Nicaraguan heritage. It is celebrated on the Caribbean coast, where most of the African influence of this country, as well as in Belize and Honduras, can be found. The celebration was initiated during the seventeenth century and it combines European and Afro-Caribbean traditions. The intense rhythms, sensual movements, colorful costumes, and musical instruments mark the influence of the African heritage of the festival. Another region in Central America where the African tradition can be found is in the coastal town Limón, in Costa Rica. The folk festival in this region is celebrated in October and includes a great variety of Afro-Caribbean music and dances. Other folk festivals, like the *Gara-Wala*, are celebrated in some regions of the coast by the *Garifuna* people, who still speak African tribal languages.

The African heritage in folk festivals is stronger in South American countries. Colombia, for example, is known for the big celebrations that include many elements of the country's African legacy. Proof of this is the carnival of Barranquilla, considered the second in size after the Brazilian carnival of Rio de Janeiro and celebrated for four days before Ash Wednesday, where the African *congos* and the *cumbia* are considered fundamental for its success. Other Colombian folk events are the *Festival de la Cumbia* (Festival of the Cumbia), celebrated in May, the *Carnaval de Negros y Blancos* (carnival of Blacks and Whites), celebrated in January and declared cultural patrimony of the country, and the *Festival de Luna Verde* (Festival of the Green Moon), an Afro-Caribbean celebration of the region of San Andrés Islas.

Venezuela also has important folk celebrations of African influence, mainly along the coastal villages. In the village of Barlovento, for example, the main African influence comes from the Bantu, Mandingo, and Yoruba people. There, one of the most important festivals is the *Fiesta de San Juan Bautista* (St. John the Baptist Festivities) celebrated in June. During the festivities, rituals of Catholicism, Vodou, and Santería are combined along with drums' rhythms and dances.

Also in the regions of Chota Valley and the Esmeraldas, in Ecuador, some West African traditions are still preserved in the folk festivals and celebrations. One of the most important events of this kind is celebrated the night of December 25th. This celebration combines dance and music with religion by having the main priestess initiating the dance and choosing a partner from the crowd. The rhythms are very similar to the ones in the Congo regions of Africa, with the drummers playing very slowly at first but drumming faster as more people join the dance.

The main folk carnival in Uruguay that honors the African heritage of the country is celebrated in January and February. These celebrations have the *candombe* as the main dance and take place in the south neighborhoods of old Montevideo. Besides playing and dancing the *candombe* during the carnival parade called Las Llamadas, the members of the *comparsas* also wear costumes that reflect the music's origin in the slave trade. This is the longest festival of all; it lasts forty days.

Some folk celebrations related to the African influence have taken place in Peru as well, like the *Son de los Diablos* (Son of the devils). The *comparsas* were part of it and they also wear masks and colorful costumes very similar to the Afro-Caribbean festivals. The main instrument is the *cajón*, also of African origin, that is played along with other instruments while the *comparsas* dance on the streets. The parades take place at different times of the year but most of the time their purpose is to celebrate important religious festivities.

Brazilian festivals are famous around the world and many of them have a very strong African influence that is fundamental to the country's folklore and identity. Many of those festivals are based on West African traditions that include dances, rhythms, and musical instruments brought by the slaves. Examples of two of the festivals that are part of the long list of the Afro-Brazilian folk-tradition are the carnival of Pernambuco in which the *maracatu* (an Afro-Brazilian genre strongly related to the *candomblé*) is performed and the world-famous carnival of Rio de Janeiro, celebrated in February, where great samba competitions take place.

Folk Beliefs

Santería

Santería, or cult of the lucumini, is an Afro-Caribbean religious tradition that was developed in Cuba, where the Yorubas were brought as slaves from some region of Nigeria. To assure their religious and cultural survival, the slaves had to adapt certain aspects of Christianity to their African beliefs. For that reason, there are many similarities between the functions and nature of the *orisha* (African divinities) and the Catholic saints. Every person initiated in *santería* has one's own *orisha* with an individual cult that sometimes requires sacrifices where herbs, drinks, and even animals are used. The *santería* is known to be spread into Haiti, the Dominican Republic, and Puerto Rico, but has also become popular in some areas of the United States where the rates of immigration from Caribbean and other Latin American regions have increased.

Vodou

Vodou or *Vodoun* (in creole) is the general name for the religious cults practiced by slaves that were brought to Haiti from Dahomey, a region of West Africa, during the sixteenth century. The *loa* (*loua*) or *mistè* are known to be family spirits; they are believed to be everywhere and could be good or evil. They are also related to the Catholic saints. The belief system of the Vodou also includes ceremonies with altars, food, dances, possessions, and music. The Haitian Vodou exists in the United States, specifically in New Orleans, but it has been given a negative reputation mainly because of the folk beliefs that associate it with zombies, witchcraft, and cannibalism.

Candomblé

The *candomblé* (not to be confused with the *candombe* of Uruguay and north of Argentina) is another West African cult tradition that can be found in Brazil, specifically in the state of *Bahía*. Although it is said to be similar to the Afro-religious traditions in Cuba and Haiti, the initiation rites in *candomblé* are more traditional. The religious ceremony consists of the evocation of various Yoruba protector deities called *orishas*, who are said to possess the participants during rituals. The rituals include animal sacrifices, sacrificial food, communal meals, songs (using the language of

A Candomblé priestess stands outside the temple door before a ceremony. Candomblé is one of the faiths brought to Brazil by African slaves and and still preserved by worshippers today. (AP/Wide World Photos)

the Yorubas mixed with Portuguese), drum music, and four forms of divinations or foretelling that are based on open and closed shells.

Macumba

Macumba is an Afro-Brazilian cult tradition that was originally based on Bantu traditions, but later assimilated elements from other cults and religions like the Yoruba traditions, Catholicism, and spiritism, to mention a few. The divinities are called orishas and are invoked by drumming, dancing, or drawing symbolic designs on the floor. The *Macumba* rites also include possessions that are wild and have more sexual character.

Umbanda

Umbanda is an Afro-Brazilian religion that combines elements of Spiritism and Catholicism. *Umbanda* rites and beliefs are very similar to the *Candomblé* and

Macumba, but have retained most of the authentic forms of West African music and dances, and have added elements of European magic and astrology as well.

Folk Aliments

African influence can also be found in the preparation of folkloric food in Latin America. Even though the slaves that settled in Latin America were originally from different regions of Africa and their traditional foods varied from one group to the next, they left a legacy that is an essential part of Latin American cuisine.

In the Caribbean, a great number of slaves were forced to work in fields, in construction, and in domestic labor. To feed slaves during their trip from Africa, Europeans brought African fruits and vegetables, which today are a fundamental part of the Latin countries' cuisine. A few examples are the *malanga* (cocoyam), the *ñame*, the *yautía*, the *batata* (sweet potato), and the *quimbombó* (okra), which are important components of the folkloric food in most of the Antilles. Many slaves also worked as cooks in the haciendas of plantation owners; this helped to expand specific ways of preparing food such as the famous "deep frying" (also popular in the south of the United States), the preparation of plantains (that became part of the folkloric food in the Caribbean, Central and South America as well), the use of certain mixes of spices, the preparation of certain kinds of food wrapped in banana leaves, and the preparation of aphrodisiacs. Because of their situation as slaves, Africans only had access to products that were provided by their masters: most of them leftovers, specific cuts of meat that they did not use (like intestines, tongues, or shoulders), and dry codfish. Nevertheless, slaves prepared delicious dishes like the well-known Mexican menudo, the Puerto Rican *morcillas*, and the Peruvian *tacu-tacu*, that today are considered a symbol of great traditional cooking.

African Influences on Latino Folklore in the United States

The Latino community is one of the largest ethnic groups in the United States and keeps growing and developing along with the North American culture. The Latino communities settled in the United States and brought with them the European, Indigenous, and African heritages that are a fundamental part of their folklore, culture, and identity. In states such as Florida, New York, Illinois, California, and Texas, many Latino organizations work to preserve their folklore and to share it with the community. The African influence is also there, mainly in the famous and contagious Latin dances and rhythms, musical instruments, and songs that go beyond the geographical limits of Latin America. Dancing schools, international competitions, festivals, carnivals, parades, and other social gatherings similar to the ones celebrated in their home countries are some of the ways the Latino community preserve their African heritage and share it with other cultures. Also, food of African heritage is well known in the United States for its flavor, variety, and unique combination of spices.

MARIANELA RIVERA-PÉREZ

See also: Afro-Colombian Music; Argentina and Its Folklore; Bomba; Brazil and Its Folklore; Costa Rica and Its Folklore; Cuban Americans and Their Folklore; El Salvador and Its Folklore; Folk Instruments; Greater Mexico and Its Folklore; "La Bamba"; Menudo; Merengue; Morcillas; Nicaragua and Its Folklore; Panama and Its Folklore; Plena; Puerto Rico and Its Folklore; Reggae; Reggaetón; Rumba (Rhumba); Santería; Tango; Venezuela and Its Folklore

Further Reading

Davis, Darién J., ed. *Beyond Slavery: The Multilayered Legacy of Africans in Latin America and the Caribbean.* Lanham, MD: Rowman & Littlefield, 2007.

De Carvalho, José Jorge. *Las culturas afroamericanas en Iberoamérica: Lo negociable y lo innegociable.* Bogotá: Universidad Nacional de Colombia, Facultad de Artes, 2005.

Joel, Miriam. *African Tradition in Latin America.* Cuernavaca: Centro Intercultural de Documentación, 1972.

Martínez Montiel, María. *Presencia africana en Centroamérica.* México, DF: Consejo Nacional para la Cultura y las Artes, 1993.

Moreno Fraginal, Manuel. *Africa in Latin America: Essays on History, Culture, and Socialization.* New York: Holms & Meier, 1984.

Palmié, Stephan, ed. *Africas of the Americas: Beyond the Search for Origins in the Study of the Afro-Atlantic Religions.* Boston: Brill, 2008.

Pradel, Lucie. *African Beliefs in the New World: Popular Literary Traditions of the Caribbean.* Translated by Catherine Bernard. Trenton, NJ: Africa World Press, 2000.

Santos, Beatriz. *La herencia cultural africana en las Américas.* Montevideo: Ediciones Populares para América Latina, 1998.

AFRO-COLOMBIAN MUSIC

Dating back to the beginning of the Spanish Conquest, the Colombian population's racial composition has been characterized by the complex process of *mestizaje*—cultural and racial mixing—in which the interactions among Africans, Indians, and Europeans played a major role. Within this social framework, Afro-Colombian communities, historically marginalized and exploited, have struggled to construct and maintain their cultural and musical traditions, which have now become an important part of Colombia's cultural heritage.

The Afro-Colombian population holds music and dance as core features of everyday life, granting them symbolic value as expressive components of class and ethnic identity. In this sense, the body becomes an important element of self-identification and distinctiveness, turning dancing and singing into political actions of cultural resistance. Because of the adaptive quality these musical practices bear, Afro-Colombian musical traditions have not only survived periods of socio-political oppression, but have actually transformed and developed during times of duress.

The first African slaves arrived in Colombian territory in the 1520s and their successors populated basically the same regions they inhabit today. This area includes the Pacific and Atlantic coastal regions, the extensive lower valleys of Magdalena and Cauca rivers, and the mining zones in the Cauca and Antioquia regions. Additionally, the archipelago of San Andrés in the Caribbean Sea, a former English colony mainly inhabited by African descendants, was acquired by Colombia in 1786. While the enslaved population was organized in social units called *cabildos*, the free and revolutionary blacks (*cimarrones*) sought refuge in the mountains and jungles and free black villages known as *palenques*.

During the colonial occupation of the seventeenth and eighteenth centuries, the Catholic-Spanish authorities struggled to restrict Afro-Colombian music and dance expressions because of the social cohesion and the possibility of organized resistance it provided. Though attempts were made to ban street drums, chants, and dance circles (*bundes* or *fandangos*), their popularity overwhelmed the mandates of local authorities. It was during this period of political resistance that the first continuous musical encounters between African descendants, Indigenous peoples, and the Spanish population took place.

In the process of historical construction of Afro-Colombian music, the traditional drums have played a fundamental role. Their loud, alluring, and communicative character was feared by Spanish authorities, who saw them as a tool of subversion. Traditional drums have retained their historical significance and symbolic value and continue to be a central component of many musical traditions such as *gaita*, *caña de millo*, *bullerengue*, *son de sexteto*, *vallenato*, and *son de negro* in the Atlantic region; *tambora* and *chandé* in the river valleys; and *marimba de chonta*, *chirimía*, *violín caucano*, and *arrullo* in the Pacific region.

On the other side, processes of acculturation and evangelization of Indian and black populations were accompanied by musical training in the churches, where the popular Spanish *villancico* song-style was imposed during colonial times. Its versification structure—octo-syllabic quatrains intertwined with a non-changing refrain—became immensely popular in Latin American territories. However, local processes of reinterpretation and resistance transposed this structure to many Afro-Colombian musical traditions such as *tambora, cumbia, vallenato, porro,* and *arrullo,* among others. Other styles, however, underscore the prominence of a "call and response" structure (*bullerengue, currulao*), which is thought to be a remainder of West African musical structures. Simultaneously, other genres present an intertwining of the two (*arrullo, son de sexteto,* and some *chalupas*).

Another result of Christian evangelization was the emergence of a syncretic musical phenomenon in which Catholic beliefs were appropriated through the lens of local popular religiosity. Specific examples are the chanting traditions dedicated to praising Catholic saints and the recent dead. Currently, some of these expressions are the *lumbalú* ritual in San Basilio de Palenque (Atlantic region), the *alabao* (*alabado*), and *arrullo* chants (Pacific coast), and songs and games for *velorio de angelito* (wake of child). These practices are public and many times involve processions through the streets of towns, villages, and cities. In parallel, the Baptist population in the archipelago of San Andrés practices chanting of hymns and other sacred music in choirs during their devotional activities.

During the eighteenth and nineteenth centuries, some Afro-Colombian communities adopted the recently arrived European salon dance genres. These expressions are still visible in the Caribbean archipelago of San Andrés and the northern Pacific coast, where local ensembles such as *conjunto típico* and *chirimí a chocoana*, respectively, still interpret them along with their own regional genres, for example, *mento* and *tamborito chocoano*, but continue to reflect local musical esthetics. Some salon genres performed even today are *polka*, *mazurka*, *waltz*, *country-dance*, *dance*, and the Colombian salon piece *par excellence*, the *pasillo*.

The nineteenth century brought the arrival of two European musical elements and propelled Afro-Colombian music into modernity: the diatonic accordion and the brass band ensemble. Popular layers of black society absorbed these resources immediately, a fact that gave birth to some significant musical traditions: *chirimía chocoana* (Pacific region), and *bandas pelayeras* and *vallenato* (Atlantic region). These ensembles have always been associated with numerous kinds of local festivities. Among these, however, patron saint celebrations constitute one of the most important spaces of sociability for Afro-Colombian communities. In these festive contexts, whole and small formatted bands interacted strongly with local traditional ensembles, interchanging repertoires, instruments, dances, and social manners. This approximation to western musical languages, which was partially forced by the temperament of European wind instruments, created a whole new melting pot of regional musical expressions.

Afro-Colombian musical processes in the twentieth century were strongly permeated with homogenizing tendencies that originated from different nationalistic movements and the emergence of the music industry. While a first nationalistic wave, which started in the late nineteenth century, completely ignored Afro-Colombian music in its symbolic representation of nation-state, a new wave of nationalism developed since the 1920s, when processes mediated by the emerging music industry started positioning some Afro-Colombian rhythms. Particularly, *porro* and *cumbia* became highly successful in national and international markets. The adaptation and arrangement of this traditional music to the *orquesta tropical* ensemble, commercial standard by that time, resulted in a process of "whitening" that favored its popularity in different regions. In this manner, from the 1940s to 1960s, the so-called *música tropical* transcended regional boundaries and became the most recognized Colombian music internationally and is still one of its most powerful popular expressions.

In the late 1960s, an emerging *salsa* movement led by Afro-Colombian populations in the cities of Cartagena, Cali, and Buenaventura turned into a boom of local orchestras in the subsequent decades. The new *Colombian salsa* sound oftentimes drew musical resources from Afro-Colombian traditions and it became very influential in local spheres, where people still listen and dance to it. Gradually, at the same time, musical consumption habits were changing drastically toward *vallenato*, a local tradition from the savannas of the Magdalena Grande region, which was a sum-up of different Afro-Colombian-influenced regional musics. Its construction and unification were politically mediated by regional elites, who to consolidate regionally consistent identities, tried to hide black musical heritage from this music.

In the 1950s and 1960s, a new generation of folklorists and researchers arose, whose fear of cultural loss due to the modernization processes resulted in the canonization and reification of regional music and dance practices. Many compilation-like publications and folkloric dance companies emerged, most of which lacked any rigorous processes of academic research. Nonetheless, some of these companies, like the one directed by the Zapata Olivella brothers, pioneered the international touring of traditional music and its ensembles. On the other side, its reified esthetics, based in the scholarly work of the time (such as the work of Abadía Morales), ultimately transcended in the forms of a myriad of regional "folkloric festivals," which were created by the government during the 1980s to support and preserve the local traditions.

Although *vallenato*, *salsa*, and *música tropical* remain the most massively consumed types of Afro-Colombian music, the late 1980s and 1990s witnessed the construction of two important popular musics, too: (i) *terapia* (or *champeta*), which is a local adaptation of African *soukus* and *highlife*; and (ii) *rap colombiano*, which is the local version of North American rap. Nowadays, both have become an important seal of identity in many urban Afro-Colombian communities.

The last years of the millennium witnessed a shift in governmental policies when the new 1991 political constitution recognized Colombia as a "pluriethnic" and "multicultural" nation. The new policies of recognition and representation for ethnic minorities as well as the emergence of neo-liberal cultural industries began to take place and ultimately developed in an important revival movement that was initiated in the cities of Bogotá, Cali, and Medellín. Basically, its ideology restates the value of Afro-Colombian musical traditions through two mechanisms, which should be understood as opposites of a continuum: (i) the re-enactment of traditional musics in urban frames, especially *gaita*, *bullerengue*, *marimba de chonta* (*currulao*), and *chirimía chocoana* traditions; and (ii) the development of musical fusion projects that merge sonorities from Afro-Colombian traditions with anything else, ranging from salsa and reggae to rock, funk, jazz, and avant-garde.

Afro-Colombian music traditions have had a tremendous impact on world music especially in other Latin American countries and the United States. *Cumbia* and salsa music, for example, are danced throughout the United States and are popular not only among Latinos/as but other racial and ethnic groups as well.

JUAN SEBASTIÁN ROJAS

See also: African Influence on Latino Folklore; Cuban Americans and Their Folklore; Folk Instruments; Reggae

Further Reading

Aja Eslava, Lorena. "Del *fair and dance* al reggaeton: Tensiones y dinámicas de la interculturalidad en la isla de San Andrés a través de su música y su danza." In M. Pardo, et al. *Música y sociedad en Colombia. Translaciones, legitimaciones e identificaciones*, 308–332. Bogotá: Universidad del Rosario, 2009.

Bermúdez, Egberto. "Las músicas afrocolombianas en la construcción de la nación." In Ministerio de Cultura. *50 años de la abolición de la esclavitud en Colombia. Desde la marginalidad a la construcción de la nación*, 706–725. Memoires from the VI Annual "Ernesto Restrepo Tirado" History Lecture. Bogotá: Aguilar, 2003.

Bermúdez, Egberto. "La tradición musical religiosa de las comunidades afroamericanas de habla inglesa. . . ." In *Las iglesias de madera de San Andrés y Providencia*, 82. Bogotá: Fundación de Música, 1998.

Bermúdez, Egberto. "Syncretism, Identity, and Creativity in Afro-Colombian Musical Traditions." In Gerard Béhague, ed. *Music and Black Ethnicity: The Caribbean and South America*, 225–238. Miami, FL: University of Miami North South Center Press, 1994.

Birenbaum, Michael. "Música afropacífica y autenticidad identitaria en la época de la etnodiversidad." In Mauricio Pardo, et al. *Música y sociedad en Colombia. Translaciones, legitimaciones e identificaciones*, 192–216. Bogotá: Universidad del Rosario, 2009.

Cifuentes, Alejandro. "Identidades, comunidades y prácticas de la chirimía chocoana en Bogotá." In M. Pardo, et al. *Música y sociedad en Colombia. Translaciones, legitimaciones e identificaciones*, 252–268. Bogotá: Universidad del Rosario, 2009.

Eastman, Juan Carlos. "El Archipiélago de San Andrés y Providencia. Formación histórica hasta 1822." In *Revista Credencial Historia*, vol. III, Jan.–Feb., no. 25–36. Bogotá: Banco de Occidente, 1992.

Escobar, Luis Antonio. *La música en Cartagena de Indias*. 1985. Biblioteca Luis Ángel Arango. http://www.banrepcultural.org/blaavirtual/musica/muscar/prohibe.htm#PROHIBICIÓN%20DE%20BAILES%20POPULARES.

Miñana Blasco, Carlos. "Entre el folklore y la etnomusicología—60 años de estudio sobre la música popular tradicional en Colombia." In *A Contratiempo. Revista de música en la cultura*, Second Stage: 36–49. Bogotá: Ministerio de Cultura, 2000.

Montoya V., César Alejandro. "Del palenque al municipio: Relatos y ritmos del tambor en Uré." In M. Pardo, et al. *Música y sociedad en Colombia. Translaciones, legitimaciones e identficaciones*, 289–307. Bogotá: Universidad del Rosario, 2009.

Pardo R., Mauricio. "Localidad y cosmopolitanismo en "la tambora" de Santa Marta, Colombia." In M. Pardo, et al. *Música y sociedad en Colombia. Translaciones, legitimaciones e identificaciones*, 333–367. Bogotá: Universidad del Rosario, 2009.

Rojas, Juan Sebastián. "El Bullerengue Grande de Urabá". Liner Notes from CD *Island Groove—Caribbean Roots Vol. 1*. Bogotá: Reef Records, 2009.

Rojas, Juan Sebastián. "Los gaiteros de Bogotá. Una perspectiva sobre el transplante musical de la gaita a la capital." In M. Pardo, et al. *Música y sociedad en Colombia. Translaciones, legitimaciones e identificaciones*, 269–288. Bogotá: Universidad del Rosario, 2009.

Sánchez M., Hugues. "De *bundes, cumbiambas* y *merengues vallenatos*: fusiones, cambios y permanencias en la música y danzas en el Magdalena Grande, 1750–1970." In M. Pardo, et al. *Música y sociedad en Colombia. Translaciones, legitimaciones e identificaciones*, 80–99. Bogotá: Universidad del Rosario, 2009.

Wade, Peter. *Música, Raza y Nación. Música tropical en Colombia*. Bogotá: Vicepresidencia de la República y Departamento Nacional de Planeación—Plan Caribe, 2002.

Waxer, Lise. "Hay una discusión en el barrio: El fenómeno de las viejotecas en Cali." In Ana María Ochoa and Alejandra Cragnolini, eds. *Cuadernos de Nación. Músicas en Transición*. Bogotá: Ministerio de Cultura, 2002.

AGRINGADO (ANGLICIZED)

Agringado is a term popularly used to refer to a Latino, more commonly a Chicano, who has abandoned one's traditional culture and become anglicized or American, that is, assimilated. *Agringado* is derived from the word "gringo" and literally means to become a gringo. The term is often used in a negative sense, to criticize someone who is trying to be an Anglo-American and, in turn, forsaking their heritage. *Agringado* is also used to jokingly call attention to someone's obvious and comical attempts to appear or be like an Anglo-American. This use of *agringado* is particularly popular in film and theater.

There are different ways in which one is identified by others as an *agringado*. Eating American foods, wearing American clothes, trying to speak like an American, or closely associating with Americans are some examples. Marriage to an American is another reason why one may be called an *agringado*, as is changing a Spanish name to one which is more American, such as Juan to John. It is important to note that regardless of what conscious decisions one makes to appear more American, it is usually others who identify that individual as an *agringado*. The negative sense of the term usually deters someone from identifying oneself as anglicized.

Pointing out when someone has or is attempting to become an *agringado* has become a popular form of joking among many Latino and Chicano families and communities. Folklorist José Limón has described this type of entertainment as *agringado* joking. Among family and friends, this type of comedic criticizing calls attention to a member of the group who may appear ridiculous in obvious attempts at being American. In this sense, *agringado* joking can help to reaffirm a Latino or Chicano identity among members of a family or social group.

At times, possibly as a result of *agringado* joking or harsher criticism, Latinos/as or Chicanos/as will make a conscious effort to appear less American to avoid being called an *agringado*. Rediscovering and emphasizing certain characteristics of Latino culture are examples of this affirmation of traditional heritage. These efforts are often characteristic of those who experience a struggle between two groups (for example, friends and family) which represent different cultures.

This struggle is often comically and/or dramatically displayed in popular films. For example, in the 1995 film *My Family, Mi Familia*, written and directed by Gregory Nava, one of the main characters, Memo, returns from college to introduce his American fiancée and her parents to his Chicano family. The differences between the *agringado* Memo and his family are emphasized in this scene and are characteristic of other films as well.

STEPHANIE REICHELDERFER

See also: Limón, José Eduardo; Tío Taco

Further Reading

Limón, José E. "Agringado Joking in Texas Mexican Society." In Ricardo Romo and Raymund Paredes, eds. *New Directions in Chicano Scholarship*, 33–50. La Jolla, CA: USCD Press, 1978.

Paredes, Américo. "On Gringo, Greaser, and Other Neighborly Names." In Mody C. Boatright, et al., eds. *Singers and Storytellers*. Publications of the Texas Folklore Society, no. 30. Dallas, TX: Southern Methodist University Press, 1961.

ALABADOS

Alabados are known as hymns of praise and sung by the brotherhood of Los Penitentes as they perform their rites during Lenten rituals, Holy Week processions, and other religious ceremonies. The Penitentes traditionally praise the Virgin Mary, Jesus Christ, or a patron saint by observing the Passion of Christ, which includes fasting, flagellation, the enactment of the Last Supper, and the singing of *alabados*. *Alabar* means to praise or to glorify, so most *alabados* begin with the words *alabado sea . . .* (praise be), although not exclusively. *Alabados* were introduced to the Americas by Franciscan priests. Seeking to convert Indigenous youth, the Franciscans integrated the singing of *abalados* with the teaching of the Bible.

Yet there seems to be little connection between the *alabados* of Spain and those in New Mexico. As far as the origins of the *alabados* in New Mexico, it appears cloudy, but by the mid-nineteenth century, the term was evident. While some make the distinction between *alabanzas* and *alabados* (see *Alabanzas*), the term *alabado* is used to refer to both since they are sung in a capella form; a leader will sing the verses and worshipers will sing the chorus.

Alabados are part of Hispano oral and musical culture in New Mexico and thus part of Latino folklore. They comprise a cultural worldview and long-standing tradition in Spain, Mexico, and the Southwest. During the Great Depression, writers of the WPA collected many *alabados* and concluded that this style of hymn was an outgrowth of the Gregorian chant. As hymns they are viewed as folk expressions with strong accented rhythms, melodies in sequential patterns, and with tonic-dominant harmony. They are performed very slowly with a mournful tempo, with religious fervor, and sometimes seem modal in their melody lines, giving the hymn a Moorish or Sephardic influence. The Sephardic influence has merit; when Jews were expelled from Spain in 1492, many came to the New World masquerading as Christians and thus avoided the Spanish Inquisition, which was also in practice in the Americas. Many of these Sephardic Jews ultimately made their way to New Mexico.

Alabados are generally associated with the Penitente Brotherhood, a lay order organized for penance as well as mutual aid. The Brotherhood's origins have always been in dispute, but it is recognized that by 1800, they were an active part of New Mexico Hispano society. Secretive in nature and controversial because of their rites of penance, the Penitentes are an important part of religion and folklore. During their evolution, Penitente ritual activities incorporated *alabados* into their practice, and they have become an important element of their activities. However, *alabados* are not unique to the Penitentes. In various communities in New Mexico, especially in the northern part of the state, there are selected individuals who as singers help to preserve *alabados* and oral traditions in general.

The melody is simple and repetitive, with many stanzas. For the most part there is no instrumental accompaniment; however, a *pito*, symbolic of the wail of the Virgin Mary and the souls of Purgatory, is at times played between the stanzas of individual *alabados*. The *pito* is a "fipple" instrument resembling a soprano recorder and is handcrafted of wood. Because there is no formula to the instrument's construction, no two have the same tuning.

As with much of New Mexico folklore, *alabados* have now been recorded in text and preserved on records or CDs. Many singers of *alabados* utilize notebooks containing individual hymns, which is viewed as a helpful practice because, as many Hispano elders believe, the older traditions are being forgotten by young generations. *Alabados* are also sung in context with the performance of the ritual. Thematically, the hymns are mystic in nature; many narrate the story of Christ's life, his anguish, betrayal, crucifixion, and resurrection, while others praise the virtues of suffering and penance. *Alabados* have also been sung as ritual prayers in homes, at dawn, noon, and at nightfall, as well as at funerals. Melodies are fused with Indigenous music and medieval chants. Stories from Mexican California tell of families singing *alabados* first thing in the morning, each member in his or her own room but at the same time. *Alabados* were used in wakes and funerals conducted by the Brothers of Our Father Jesus the Nazerene. These would be all-night affairs, unlike today where wakes are only two hours and held in a local mortuary.

Jesús de mi Vida is an example of a penitente *alabado* from New Mexico. Although performed by one individual, sometimes this *alabado* is performed by a group. In the latter case, each new stanza is sung by a different group member, who is then answered by the rest of the group who repeat the first stanza as a chorus. There are twenty-three stanzas to this *alabado,* which is sung with great emotion and expression. The first stanza will serve as an example.

Jesús de mi Vida

Jesús de mi vida,
De mi corazón,
Ya vas de partida,
Divino Señor.

Jesus of my life,
of my heart,
you are already departing,
Divine Lord.

CARLOS F. ORTEGA

See also: Alabanzas; Cuaresma (Lent); Los Penitentes; Works Progress Administration (WPA)

Further Reading

Briggs, Charles L. *Competence in Performance: The Creativity of Tradition in Mexicano Verbal Art.* Philadelphia: University of Pennsylvania Press, 1988.

Castro, Rafaela G. *Chicano Folklore.* New York: Oxford University Press, 2001.

García, Mario T. *Católicos: Resistance and Affirmation in Chicano Catholic History.* Austin: University of Texas Press, 2008.

Library of Congress. American memory. http://memory.loc.gov/ammem/rghtml/r.g.home .html.

Loeffler, Jack. *La Música de los Viejitos: Hispano Folk Music of the Rio Grande del Norte.* Albuquerque: University of New Mexico Press,1999.

ALABANZAS

Alabanzas are religious songs of praise. Religious folk practices in the Southwest are found in communities with a substantial Mexican-origin population. These practices are reflected in customs, rituals, and traditions centering on the role of the Catholic Church. After four centuries of activity in the Southwest, the Catholic

Church and local community have become integrated. The result is a myriad of practices, some old and traditional; others are much newer. One such practice can be found in traditional hymns and songs.

Alabanzas are folk expressions of a religious nature and date back to the sixteenth century. Located within the folk tradition, *alabanzas* are central to religious practice and known throughout the Americas. In the United States, *alabanzas* are most associated with New Mexico. In large measure, the significance of *alabanzas* is found in their history and preservation as well as in religious practice. In contrast, *alabados* are also religious in nature, but focus on events associated with Holy Week. They are mostly associated with the Penitentes, a secret society in New Mexico. The origins of the group have been linked to the order of St. Francis, and members of the sect practice rituals of penance. The rituals are extreme: flagellation and, at one time, crucifixion, now banned by the church. On the other hand, *alabanzas* are songs that praise the Virgin Mary, saints, or holy figures as well as commemorations of certain events in the lives of Christ and the Virgin Mary. They are usually sung a capella with one or more singers handling the verses and everyone else the chorus. They are also found in various musical styles and forms. The lack of a common style makes them hard to categorize. Some *alabanzas* appear to be hymns. Some are like *regativos*, which focus on prayers as opposed to praise. Each village has its own melody and lyrics.

J. B. Ralliere published one of the earliest collections of *alabanzas* in 1877. Titled *Cánticos Espirituales*, reprints followed in 1892 and 1933. Some editions contain only text and others, music and text. Another collection is *Once Misas,* which represents the Hispanic folk mass tradition, but contains some *alabanzas* from Tome, New Mexico. Although sometimes performed outside of the liturgy, these hymns have traditionally served as a vehicle for verbally and musically expressing religious sentiments. More important, these hymns became a way of cementing the community.

Themes are varied within *alabanzas*. Jesus, Joseph, and Mary; St. Joseph, St. Anthony; St Ignatius de Loyola; St. Isidore; San Ramón de Nonato; the Holy Sacrament; and the shrine at Chimayó, New Mexico, for example, represent some of the topics found in *alabanzas*. There are some songs that praise the Lord in his different forms: Lord of Esquipula and the Santo Niño de Atocha. Interestingly, each has its own counterpart in hand-carved and painted statues (*bultos*) and traditional paintings done on wood (*retablos*) of Jesus, Mary, and the saints; some go as far back as the nineteenth century.

The more popular saints of the Southwest are praised because of their relationship to frontier life. San Ramón de Nonato is the patron saint of captives, so individuals who were held prisoner by Indians or bandits would naturally pray to him. San Juan Nepomuceno was martyred for not revealing secrets of the confessional, thus a favorite of the Penitentes, whose rites were always kept secret. Settlers praised San Ysidro, the patron saint of agriculture. El Santo Niño de Atocha rescues people from all types of danger.

Alabanzas are performed during festivals marking the days of Catholic personages. There are many local communities in Latin America where one or more days are devoted to feasts, dancing, folk dramas, and other activities dedicated to a patron saint. During the feast of St. Isidore, for example, patron saint of the farmer, *alabanzas* alternated with prayers during the night, interrupted only for a communal meal at midnight. Later the saint's image would be carried through the fields.

Traditional *alabanzas* are still performed in the villages of New Mexico. One that praises the Virgin Mary is ¡*Dios te Salve, Luna Hermosa!* (God Save Thee, Beautiful Moon!). One verse reflects the sense of praise:

> *Los Angeles en el cielo*
> los hombres en alabanzas
> la boca llena digamos
> virgen, llena eres de gracia.
>
> The angels in the sky
> Mankind with songs of praise
> Declare with a full voice
> "Virgin, thou art full of grace."

J. D. Robb found four variants of this *alabanza* in different parts of New Mexico.

Tañita de Galisteo and *Milagros de San Antonio* are other well-known *alabanzas*. In Mexico, traditional *albanzas* include *Alabanza a la Virgen*. Its exact origin is unknown, but it contains typical lyrics: *Buenos dias paloma blanca, hoy te vengo a saludar, saludando a tu belleza, en tu reino celestial* (good morning white dove, today I come to greet you, greeting your beauty, in your celestial reign). There are *alabanzas* associated with Indigenous groups such as the Yaqui Indians of Sonora, Mexico, reflecting the power of religious conversion.

Alabanzas provide insight to religious practice, faith, and praise. Unlike contemporary religious songs heard today, *alabanzas* provide a link to the past and an understanding of religion in folklore.

CARLOS F. ORTEGA

See also: Alabados; Chimayó; Cuaresma (Lent); Los Penitentes; Robb, John Donald; Santo Niño de Atocha (The Holy Child of Atocha)

Further Reading

Briggs, Charles L. *Competence in Performance: The Creativity of Tradition in Mexicano Verbal Art*. Philadelphia: University of Pennsylvania Press, 1988.

Loeffler, Jack. *Hispano Folk Music of the Rio Grande del Norte*. Albuquerque: University of New Mexico Press, 1999.

Robb, John Donald. *Hispanic Folk Music of New Mexico and the Southwest: A Portrait of a People*. Norman: University of Oklahoma Press, 1980.

ALAMBRISTA (UNDOCUMENTED BORDER CROSSER)

Literally meaning "wire crosser," *alambrista* is a term used in popular and Latino culture for someone who has crossed or attempted to cross the United States–Mexico border by jumping or cutting the wire fence, especially along the California-Mexico border. *Alambrista!* is also the title of a 1977 film written and directed

An alleged undocumented immigrant sits in a Border Patrol vehicle after being captured in the Otay Mountain Range in 2006 in Otay Mesa, California. (Getty Images)

by Robert Young, which follows the fictional journey of an undocumented immigrant from Mexico who crosses into America via California. This term has gained importance in Latino culture as the number of undocumented immigrants to America increased dramatically during the late twentieth century.

Alambrista is similar to the term *mojado* or wetback, the latter a pejorative word used for an undocumented immigrant who attempts to enter into Texas by crossing the Rio Grande and thus getting "wet." This term *mojado* has come to mean any undocumented worker. *Alambrista*, on the other hand, is used specifically for those who travel across the land border. During the 1960s through the mid-to-late 1980s, many of these *alambristas* made the risky journey to the United States to find agricultural employment, mainly in California. The high number of both legal and undocumented Mexican immigrants who performed agricultural work for low wages inspired labor leader César Chávez to attempt to organize these laborers in 1965. These largely *alambrista* workers and their farm workers' movement formed close connections with local churches and other community institutions. The movement attempted to connect the undocumented worker with American Latino culture.

The agricultural work of the *alambristas* in the United States inspired Young to create his film of the same name. *Alambrista!* follows Roberto, a Mexican immigrant who leaves Michoacán to look for extra income to help support his new daughter. Roberto crosses into the United States illegally in search of employment and finds himself moving from one agricultural or manual job to another, constantly threatened by immigration raids and exploitative employers. Young's film displays the harsh reality of the life of an *alambrista* and helped in making the term culturally important.

As the occurrence of undocumented border crossings has increased, *alambrista* has become a common term in the folklore of Latino and American culture as a whole. *Alambrista* is commonly used by the media when discussing the tragic results of failed border crossings that end in death or injury. Also, the *alambrista* has become an important figure in legends and contemporary folk tales. In the 2006 film *Babel* (directed by Alejandro Gonzales Iñarritu), another portrayal of the *alambrista* is presented in the character of Amelia, a Mexican immigrant who finds employment as a nanny for the children of a San Diego, California, couple. After a babysitting mix-up, Amelia decides to take the two children with her to Mexico to celebrate the wedding of her son. Amelia's other son, who is driving while intoxicated, creates a scene at a border patrol station, frightening Amelia who flees into the desert with the two children. Eventually, the border patrol finds Amelia, and the audience learns that after being employed in the United States for sixteen years as a nanny, Amelia is deported to Mexico because she is an *alambrista*.

The *alambrista* Amelia's story is one which has become common and popular in Latino culture. The undocumented border crosser is an increasingly visible character in folk tales. The hazardous act of actually crossing the border has come to define the journey of the *alambrista*, with stories of undocumented border crossers often portraying those who successfully cross in a heroic fashion. Also, many stories and tales explain that those *alambristas* who manage to cross safely into the United States are aided by a divine force, normally the Virgin of Guadalupe. Such stories mix traditional characteristics of Latino folk tales (heroic struggles with supernatural forces) with the contemporary problems faced by *alambristas* and debates concerning undocumented immigration in the United States.

STEPHANIE REICHELDERFER

See also: Virgin of Guadalupe: History and Fiestas Guadalupanas

Further Reading

Carrasco, David, and Nicholas J. Cull. *Alambrista and the U.S.-Mexico Border: Film, Music, and Stories of Undocumented Immigrants.* Albuquerque: University of New Mexico Press, 2004.

Maciel, David, and María Herrera-Sobek. *Culture Across Borders: Mexican Immigration and Popular Culture.* Tucson: University of Arizona Press, 1998.

ALBÓNDIGAS (MEATBALLS)

Albóndigas is the Spanish word for meatballs. Traditional *albóndigas* are made with ground meat mixed with spices and sometimes rice, eggs, or grated bread. Even though beef is the common ingredient in traditional *albóndigas*, any other meat, such as game, poultry, or fish may also be used. *Albóndigas* are very popular in Spain, Mexico, and other Latin American countries, where they can be made in different sizes and served as a main course in soups, or as tapas. There are as many recipes for *albóndigas* as people who make them, but the variations depend on the country or region of origin; the cooking methods are also different—they could be steamed, boiled, or fried. Some food historians trace their origins back to Medieval Europe or even earlier to Roman times. In Spain, *albóndigas* are traced back to at least the time of the Islamic influence, which started with the Arab invasion of the Iberian Peninsula in AD 711 and ended with the expulsion of the Moors in 1492 by the Catholic rulers, Isabella and Ferdinand. In fact, the word *albóndiga* is of Arabic origin and derives from the Greek word for hazelnut.

As we mentioned, the most traditional *albóndigas* are made with beef or pork, but fish is also a common ingredient, particularly in Spain. They are often fried or served in a light sauce. In Mexico, they are commonly served in a soup (*sopa de albónigas*) or in a tomato and chipotle chili-pepper sauce (*albóndigas en chipotle*). In both cases, *albóndigas* are cooked separately by boiling. When they are done, the sauce is added. It is one of the most traditional comfort foods known. Some would even call *albóndigas* the food of the urban poor because of the tradition of using inferior cuts of meat for the dish and decreasing the amount of meat used with the addition of bread or rice. Usually, butchers save the cuts that do not sell well and mix them to prepare the *carne molida* or *carne picada* (ground meat), the essential ingredient in *albóndigas*. Sometimes they have the meat already prepared and sell it as meat *para albóndigas* (for meatballs). Most Mexicans, Spaniards, and Latin Americans recall their family recipe for *albóndigas* with nostalgia. All are similar, but one of the distinctive ingredients of the Mexican *albóndigas* is the addition of chopped mint, while in Spain it is common to add ground pork for flavor; also, in Mexico they are often boiled, while in Spain they are most likely fried.

The traditional recipe for Spanish *albóndigas* in tomato sauce is the following. Mix ground veal, lamb, or beef, with a little ground pork. Add one beaten egg, breadcrumbs, minced garlic, chopped onion, chopped parsley, ground cumin, coriander, salt, and pepper. Mix well, form small balls (most Spanish meatballs are bite-sized), and roll them in flour. In a hot frying pan, heat olive oil and fry the meatballs until firm, turning constantly, but carefully, to brown each one uniformly. Once they are done, add them to the tomato sauce. To prepare the sauce, heat some olive oil in a heavy pan and fry chopped red peppers, onions, and garlic until soft. Add the tomatoes seeded, peeled, and crushed, as well as a half glass of dry white wine or sherry, and one cinnamon stick. Bring the sauce to a boil, then reduce the heat and season with salt, pepper, and a little sugar. Let it simmer at a low heat until it is thick and all the flavors have combined. Once you add the meatballs, cook together for another twenty minutes or so. Once done, the *albóndigas* may be served with rustic bread or on small plates with toothpicks, as tapas.

In Mexico, the traditional *albóndigas* in soup are prepared in the following manner. Heat oil in a heavy pot. Add chopped onion and minced garlic. Once the onion is translucent, add beef stock and pureed tomatoes. When the mixture bubbles up, reduce the heat and simmer. Add carrots, peeled and cubed, and string beans, cut into small pieces. Cook for a while. Add the meatballs and let them simmer until cooked. Toward the end of the cooking time, add fresh peas. Cook, in the broth,

Traditional Spanish *albóndigas* (spicy meatballs) in tomato sauce.
(Dreamstime.com)

until the meat and vegetables are done and then serve. To prepare the meatballs, mix ground beef with chopped onion, a beaten egg, chopped mint, parsley, and rice. Form balls with the mixture (traditionally Mexican meatballs are bigger than Spanish meatballs) and add them to the soup. Another traditional way of preparing *albóndigas* in Mexico is in a rich chipotle sauce.

Chipotle albóndigas are prepared the following way. Mix ground beef, chopped onion, salt, and pepper, and form balls. Either broil them in the oven or fry them in hot oil. Once they are done, add the *albóndigas* to the chipotle and tomato sauce. Bring to a boil and simmer, covered, for a few minutes. When done cooking, let them rest for a few minutes before serving. Traditionally, they are served alone with tortillas and beans on the side, but they can also be served over rice, or with rice and beans. The sauce can be prepared while the meatballs cook in the oven by pureeing tomatoes, peeled and seeded, with chipotle peppers, seeded and rehydrated in hot water for at least one hour, as well as onions and garlic in a blender or food processor. Add the tomato and chipotle-pepper puree to a heavy pan with hot oil, season with salt and pepper, then simmer until the sauce thickens. At this point, the *albóndigas* may be added. Other variations exist with different meats and additional ingredients, depending on the country or region, but the basic recipe is very similar to the Mexican and Spanish way of cooking *albóndigas*.

RAFAEL HERNÁNDEZ

See also: Chiles (Peppers); Frijoles (Beans); Tortilla

Further Reading

Apicius, M. G. *Gastronomía en la antigua Roma imperial. Textos gastronómicos.* San Sebastián: R & G Ediciones, 1995.

Baez Kijac, María. *The South American Table: The Flavour and Soul of Authentic Home Cooking from Patagonia to Rio de Janeiro, with 450 Recipes.* Boston: The Harvard Common Press, 2003.

Coronado, Rosa. *Cooking the Mexican Way.* Minneapolis, MN: Lerner Publications Co., 1982.

Luard, Elisabeth. *The Food of Spain and Portugal: A Regional Celebration.* London: Kyle Books, 2007.

Norigea de Kuri, Maruca. *¿Qué hacer de comer? Tu primer libro de cocina.* México: Editorial Limusa, 2000.

ALBURES

Albures are verbal duels in which virtuosic individuals exchange insults that they embed within seemingly innocuous speech acts. Unlike the overt insults exchanged in African American–sounding traditions, speakers often mask insults within fast-paced, poetic speech that the respondent then decodes and, if possible, responds to in kind. The covert nature of *albures* adds to their potency as insults. This exchange between interlocutors can go on for an extended period of time, linking performers by a dialogic chain, or may lose poetic momentum after a single statement. While the insults employed by speakers are inflammatory, they are not unexpected and carry different implications and potency depending on the age or marital status of the intended target. This form of verbal sparring is not divisive, although there may be moments when one speaker may overstep the boundaries of playful ritual insults; rather it functions as a necessary part of social bonding that links insult to intimacy. However, there is always an element of personal risk when one enters into the performance space of those performing *albures*. Speakers learn to conceal insulting jibes by using everyday words, phrases, or rhymes that are aggressive and insulting by way of form or symbolic reference. Through concealing an insult, one is also concealing personal involvement, for it is a gifted *alburero* who is able to incite so much frustration in his competitor that the other will break the playful performance frame and acknowledge the bawdy game at hand. Renowned in Mexico, but potentially found in other areas of Latin America and the Caribbean, *albures* capitalize on *doble sentido*, or double meaning, to mobilize their often highly sexualized, playful banter from one speaker to another. Often touted as a masculine performance genre, *albures* are incorporated into the verbal repertoires of female performers as well, although there is less accompanying ethnographic data.

Much like other forms of verbal dueling, *albures* require an audience. It is common for a trio of individuals to duel, rotating the role of active speaker and audience from one to the other. Despite the discontent of language purists, who react negatively to the practice of *albures* much as they would to other vernacular speech forms that do not follow the grammatical and lexical rules of standard Spanish, the performance of *albures* facilitates in-group dialogues that serve as windows into systems of honor and shame, as well as the articulation of other social and cultural realities of Spanish-speaking communities all over Latin America.

Origins

Samuel Ramos describes the *albur* as the unique invention of an underclass of proletarian Mexican males, who have created a linguistic style to express themselves and their liminal social status. Octavio Paz notes that the skillful linguistic repertoire of the *alburero* is designed to create verbal traps for adversaries, and much like other forms of verbal dueling, the loser is marked by silence, or the inability to verbally defend himself any longer. Often, *albures* appear as linguistically mediated sexual acts, where verbal jibes are "thrust" at opponents and the loser must "swallow" the attacks of others (Limón 1998, 77–81; Haney 2007, 4).

The *albur* is part of the discourse of honor and shame in Mexico. Carlos Monsiváis (1988) asserts that they (honor and shame) are a different source for the inception of *albur* performances. While Ramos, and later Limón, converge upon the idea that the *albur* was fashioned from the *pelado*, Monsiváis sees the *albur* emerging from a disgruntled class of lawyers, writers, doctors, and priests, who use the *albur* to "disguise their literary meanderings" (Haney 2007, 5). Armando Jiménez, popular for his collection of *albures* from the *colonias,* or impoverished urban neighborhoods of Mexico City, titled *Picardía Mexicana*, looks to Indigenous peoples as the originators of *albures* in Mexico. His work surmises the origin of the *albur* was during the time of the Spanish conquest of the New World. *Albures* are thus part of a discourse of colonial resistance, and posited to be one way in which subjugated Indigenous peoples could verbally undermine the invading Spanish without detection.

The *Alburero*

Historically, the image of the *Mexicano pelado*, or the undereducated, proletarian, gratuitously vulgar Mexican male, is presented in international popular media as a monolithic male archetype, an aggressive philandering alcoholic who objectifies women and revels in his masculine superiority. What critics often fail to acknowledge is the pressure of maintaining social honor, propriety, and the economic burden often internalized as a male head of a household. The macho's identity as a man is highly complex and one discovers that although it is ambiguous and opaque at times, there are cracks in this façade—brief moments where we may view the system behind the macho. One such critical crack is unearthed in the critical analysis of everyday discursive strategies, such as *albures*. The *alburero* enters the cantina, or gathers among other men on a street corner and lays himself open and vulnerable to his peers. *Albures* help construct an alternative narrative of gendered behavior that facilitates potentially new ways of understanding certain behaviors as articulations of a complex character heavily influenced by the historical development of Mexico as a nation as well as the imposition of national discourses of gender and class systems. In this context of resistance toward state-imposed identities, the *albur* becomes a metalinguistic tool for propagating national tolerance of countercultural movements against authorities who impose homogenous moral values on Mexican society.

Form and Content

As a form of wordplay, the *albur* exposes the creative facility that each speaker has with the Spanish language resources at his disposal. *Albureros* employ all manner of verbal indirection and circular speech to avoid detection by an interlocutor. While the *albur* is rooted in insult, Peter Haney notes that what *albureros* are doing is not only insult, but also a form of mutual education where individuals bring together their vast, collective repertoires and genially swap materials. Jorge M. Alarcón notes that the general form of *albures* is described as a linguistic derivative of the *calambour,* a form of French wordplay where syllables of words are rearranged to create new words with new meanings. Interestingly, the term *"albur"* is a rearrangement of the word Spanish word *burla*, which refers to a mocking joke, a description that captures the intent of most *albur* performances. As a heightened part of everyday conversation, the exchange of *albures* is very subtle, and often extremely fast-paced, often eluding the novice, or unassuming speaker of Spanish. This fact comes into stark reality when the *albur* migrates to the United States into Mexican enclaves, where Spanish is not the primary language of all participants. This transition refunctionalizes the *albur* from an exchange of witty, skillfully timed insults, into a marker of cultural heritage. Recognition of the *albur* is an admission of specialized knowledge and indexes a broader connection to Mexican cultural heritage, which in turn isolates the Chicano or Mexican American from the recent immigrant.

Albures utilize vulgar epithets, expletives, and allusions to sexual and scatological symbolism to feminize male opponents. Players restructure these linguistic resources to communicate productively and metadiscursively with one another. The presence of *albures* within a conversation expresses a certain class-based solidarity, where blue-collar men find solace in a common, unique language. Despite their controversial content, *albures* take many creative forms. The most recognized is formal verbal dueling that occurs within a conversational setting. In these situations, speakers cloak insults in creative double-talk and insert them into the conversation in a similar fashion to linguistic code-switching. Here, the obscure poetics of *albur* forms serve as an embedded language within the matrix language of Spanish. Speakers insert words or phrases into conversations in three basic ways. The first involves taking an everyday word or phrase that has another term existing within it that, according to cultural mores, an opponent would deem insulting. For instance, the use of the word *anciano*, which means elder, has the word *ano*, or anus, embedded in its original form. This small segment referencing this particular body part is part of a known vocabulary of *albureros,* a reference that implies anal erotic or homoerotic sexual acts against the hearer. This reference, in the context of a male social gathering, is enough for one listening to respond, covertly in kind, to this sexual jibe that was aimed at undermining his masculinity. The second form, which utilizes the culturally determined symbolic relations between words, is equally popular. Here the term *leche* (milk), being used between two men, is potentially an inflammatory insult if the hearer assumes it is meant to reference a vernacular meaning that equates milk with semen. They also accompany such words or phrases with physical gestures that draw attention to the speaker's body. This is why a sneeze or cough might incite a verbal duel, because mucus here is also a functional equivalent to semen. The third type of expression utilized by *albureros* is a combination of the first two strategies and is the most difficult to execute properly within conversation. It involves making subtle changes to innocuous words or phrases within a conversation, transforming them, in whole or in part, into obscenities. For instance, an *alburero* will use the Spanish word *confundido*, which means "confused," but replace the latter part of this same word with *fundillo*, a vernacular term for "anus," making the new term *confundillo*. This second word has no literal meaning; rather it will functionally replace "*confundido*" in the speaker's statement, and will be difficult to detect by an untrained ear. Haney notes that *albures* may also be stylistically delivered with a characteristic verbal feint, or pause, that sets up a delayed expectation for the obscene word or phrase to follow. If an interlocutor does not notice the barb or subtle pauses indicating a transition into competition, his opponent has successfully penetrated his defenses. These different types are then categorized more broadly based on a sliding scale of comprehensibility. Víctor Hernández, a skilled *alburero*, notices two broad categories of *albures*. An *albur* whose humor lacks opacity is considered an *albur corriente*, which is most likely the product of a novice performer. The second broader category is the *albur fino,* which is virtually incomprehensible without prior knowledge and acute skill to both unearth and decode the intended message (Hernández 2006, 302–303). Prolonged hesitation or silence implies that an interlocutor has been beaten; however, true success is also accompanied by the jeering laughter of an audience.

In cultural systems that value linguistic eloquence and formality, these antagonistic speech acts are extremely potent, especially in moments of conflict. Each of these types of insults may be ignored depending upon the interpretation of the hearer who may or may not retaliate, regardless of the intentions of the speaker. A virtuosic speaker will be able to embed insults so skillfully within conversation that the speaker will fail to notice, and therefore not think to defend himself, making the initial speaker the ultimate victor. However, a truly gifted *alburero* will so skillfully place an insult within a complex poetic smoke screen that his fellow interlocutor will actually come away feeling complimented rather than insulted. While a speaker may use any amount of symbolically or lexically charged vocabulary without the intention of challenging another individual, *albureros* must always be ready to defend themselves from potentially damaging verbal onslaughts. While exchanges often employ sexual symbolism, these function as metaphoric references to power and may serve to elucidate broader socioeconomic system influences on class and gender relations.

The *albur* also transitions from an oral- to a text-based medium, which takes shape in the intertextual form of folk poetry and graffiti found on bathroom stalls called *latrinalia*. One of the most popular *albures* is *El Gallito Inglés* (The little English cock):

> *Este es el gallito inglés*
> Míralo con disimulo

Quítale pico y pies
Y métetelo por el culo.

This is the little English cock
Watch him with pretense
Take away his beak and claws
And stick him up your ass.

This rhyme is a particularly good, metadiscursive example of *albur* play. The rhyme describes how, if one deconstructs the image of the *gallito inglés,* or the *albur* itself, what one finds is penis symbolism and anal erotic violation.

Albures also emerge in conversation as *piropos*, or pick-up lines used by men to attract female attention on the street. For example, a man may offer a chile pepper to a woman, where the subtext of the statement is the functional equivalence of a chile pepper with a penis, making his statement a veiled, yet not wholly opaque, sexual advance. Here one sees how the same vocabulary for making sexual advances on women mirrors verbal jibes among men. Now, while the *albur* is most popular among male audiences, women do engage with men in these verbal bouts and their repertories appear quite similar. While individual performances have differential degrees of improvised materials, performance repertoires are often built up over time, and learned from different popular outlets, such as books, Internet, and film resources. *Albures* were also a part of *carpas*, or Mexican vaudevillian stage performances. The contemporary *albur* is a genre that capitalizes on both the Internet and cinematic outlets. There are numerous websites that bring together the repertoires of *albureros* from across the globe. Similarly, from 1960 to 1990, there was a rash of films circulating in Mexico that chronicled life in Mexico City and featured the comedic power of the *albur*. These include film adaptations of the popular books *Picardia Mexicana*, *Albures Mexicanos*, *Los Mofles y los Mecánicos*, and *El Rey de los Albures*, to name a few. This film genre known as sexy-comedies uses the crass vernacular style of the *albur* to appeal to audiences whose lifestyles were marginalized in the gilt-edged productions of Mexico's Golden Age of cinema. These films exhibit certain similarities with the elaborate double talk of one of the most famous comedians of Mexico's Golden Age of cinema, "Cantinflas" played by Mario Moreno Reyes, whose character has been included in the dictionary of the *Real Academia Española* (*Diccionario de la Real Academia Española*). Much like the famous films of Cantinflas, sexy-comedies illustrate the experiences of Mexicano *pelados* in the impoverished neighborhoods in Mexico City, while also incorporating female performers, and showing a connection between linguistic virtuosity and the circumstances of poverty in urban Mexico. They emphasize the way in which individual, linguistic articulations of poverty are microsocial cultural productions that respond to the social and political turmoil of macrosocial environments.

Alternately, there are variants of *albur* play known as *albures blancos*, or the white *albures*. While the different linguistic recourses used in *albur* performance assist in concealing its obscene character under multiple layers of implication and innuendo, this secondary form endeavors to further sanitize the traditional *albur* for supposedly more genteel, upper-class audiences by attempting to divorce the *albur* from noticeable vulgar allusions. While little ethnographic inquiry has been devoted to this facet of *albur* play, it nonetheless contributes to furthering an understanding of the way in which socioeconomic systems come to inform *albur* performances directly or tangentially.

During an *alburing* session, gender and sexuality appear to be on display. Although the content is sexual in nature, often implying homoerotic behavior (indeed it is the graphically sexual nature that renders it unappealing to many), the exchanges themselves function beyond this facilitating sexual façade. *Albureros* often note that they are not homosexual nor do they desire homosexual sex; in fact they use their speech to make their opponents symbolically into female sexual partners, which reveals underlying ambiguities in both sexual and gendered normativity. Their use of a contested and marginal identity in Mexico, that of gay males, exhibits their skill in using insults effectively within the norms of their cultural system in a way that calls into question those previously established social norms. Rather, these men are using sex as a metaphor for a system of social power, which they internalize and code in their repertoire. These performances are extremely self-invested, as a man who wishes to display his verbal prowess must also be ready to be verbally ravaged by an opponent. All participants are simultaneously aggressors and victims, states that allude to the dualistic nature of masculinity in Mexico. As noted earlier, these virtuosic performances are about creating a space for self-expression—particularly creating a space for the development of new discourses of masculinity across Latin America. This manner of speech serves the communicative needs of a subset of Mexican males who find themselves trapped in a web of controversial masculine ideals that foreground the assertion of dominance through violence. These elaborate exchanges allow men to create autonomous space, where interaction frameworks allow each performer to highlight and negotiate gender norms through humor and insult, which in turn facilitates an intimacy between the two that would traditionally fall outside the assumptions of normative heterosexual behavior.

Female Performers

The development of national discourses of gender in Mexican culture is not a new subject. While the term "machismo" is only as old as the 1930s in Mexico, it has had far-reaching effects on the external and internal perceptions of idealized and naturalized gender constructions in Mexican society and among Mexican-descent communities all over the Americas. The *albur* is predominately categorized as a masculine genre of folklore, performed by and for men in locations traditionally deemed male social spaces, such as bars, cabarets, and street corners. However, women also perform *albures*, oftentimes alongside male performers. In 2002, the winner of the third annual *alburing* competition held at the Autonomous University of Mexico City was a woman, Lourdes Ruiz. Similarly, the above-mentioned films that feature *albur* performances, do include a small minority of female comedic performers who ably compete alongside male *albureros*. These female characters use *albur*es as men would to bond with their male compatriots and coworkers. While women have not been the subject of inquiry regarding *albur* performances, their role in this genre of folklore will shed light on the way in which these seemingly sexual verbal bouts go beyond notions of rampant nationalized homophobia in Mexico. The presence of female performers allows one to refocus the study of contemporary *albur* performances as reactionary cultural productions both in and across stratified socioeconomic class systems. As cultural products that allow one to question the naturalization of gender and morality in Mexico, they also allow one to begin to understand how gender and culture are performed and negotiated across Latin America.

RACHEL VALENTINA GONZÁLEZ

See also: Greater Mexico and Its Folklore; Jokes (Chistes); Limón, José Eduardo; Peladito (Pelado); Verbal Dueling

Further Reading

Haney, Peter C. "'*Se Me Para . . . Liza la Lengua.' Doble Sentido* and the Dialectic of Desire and Respect in Greater Mexico." Paper presented at the Oberman Center for Advanced Studies Symposium on Obscenity, Iowa City, IA, March, 2007.

Hernández, Víctor. *Antología del Albur*. Charleston: Book-Surge, 2006.

Ingham, John M. *Mary, Michael and Lucifer: Folk Catholicism in Central México*. Austin: University of Texas Press, 1986.

Jiménez, Armando. *Picardía Mexicana*. 48th ed. México, D.F.: Editores Mexicanos Unidos, 1972.

Limón, José E. *American Encounters: Greater Mexico, the United States, and the Erotics of Culture*. Boston: Beacon Press, 1998.

Monsiváis, Carlos. *Escenas de Pudor y Liviandad*. México, D.F.: Editorial Grijalbo, 1988.

Paz, Octavio. *The Labyrinth of Solitude*. Translated by Lysander Kemp. New York: Grove Press, 1985. Originally published 1951.

Ramos, Samuel. *Profile of Man and Culture in Mexico*. Translated by Adela Palacios Vda. de Ramos. Pan American Paperbacks Series. 3rd ed. Austin: University of Texas Press, 1975. Originally published 1934.

ALTARS

Traditional altars, also called *ofrendas* (literally offerings), are structures that are created to honor a saint, a holiday, or for permanent remembrance in the home. In Latino communities, altars can be classified as either seasonal or permanent and can be located in a number of places including the home, church, or public places. *Ofrendas* can also be classified as artistic creations. Seasonal altars include *pesebres* (also called *nacimientos*, or nativity scenes) of Christmas, Day of the Dead (*Ofrendas*) of November 1st to 2nd, or particular short-term altars set up for special saints or feast days such as La Virgen de Guadalupe's feast day on December 12th. *Descansos*, or altars set up along the highways where someone has been killed, could also be included in a discussion of altars. While altars set up seasonally may contain the same essential elements and typically are short-lived (they are set up annually), home altars are permanent and have a different function in the prayers

A modern-day altar in Los Angeles, California to celebrate El Día de los Muertos (the Day of the Dead). (Courtesy of Julie Dunbar)

of the community. In addition to home or seasonal altars, artists have begun to use the altar aesthetic to create performance pieces as well as sculptures.

Pesebres, *Belenes*, or *Nacimientos* are usually set up in homes for the Christmas season that typically begins on December 12th and runs until February 2nd, with the celebration of La Candelaria. The host family invites family and friends for a *posada* where they pray the rosary and sing the *posada*—the request for lodging in Bethlehem by the Holy Family on Christmas Eve. Typically, a piñata is part of the *posada*. On Christmas Eve, the *acostar al niño* (the laying down of baby Jesus on the crib) ritual includes all of these plus an *arrullamiento* (putting the baby Jesus to sleep) and sometimes special prayers as well. The typical foods are tamales, *champurrado*, and *buñuelos*. After the adoration of the Christ child by everyone—often with a kiss or simply a tap on the forehead of the small statue—often held by the youngest child there, a special type of hard candy for the feast day, *colaciones*, is distributed to all in attendance.

The image of the Christ child stays *acostado* (laying down on the crib), until February 2nd, when family and friends again meet for a *levantar al niño* (picking up of the baby Jesus) ritual, where the Christ child is set up—usually on a tiny chair or other stand. In some cases, as the *pesebre* or *nacimiento* (nativity scene) is dismantled for the following year, the images are stored. Objects on the *nacimiento* include the nativity scene with a star, one or more angels, shepherds, animals, the three kings (or magi, of course), Mary, Joseph, and the Christ child. Elaborate *nacimientos* can have up to 500 pieces, including scenes from the folk play *La Pastorela* (Shepherds' play), which include the battle between the devil Luzbel (Lucifer) and the Archangel Michael. Adorning the *nacimiento* may be fresh or paper flowers, typically poinsettias, lights, or candles, and in many homes in the United States traditional elements found in a secular Christmas village are fused with the more religious elements.

For the Day of the Dead altars, or *ofrendas*, one typically finds flowers as well, but these are usually *cempasúchil*, or marigolds, the flower associated with the trip to Mictla, the land of the dead. Also, sugar skulls with the names of living persons are placed on the altars in addition to seasonal foods, drinks, and other favorite items of the person or persons the *ofrenda* is set up to honor. Thus, one often finds dishes of *mole*, candy, *pan dulce*—especially *pan de muerto*, a special "bread of the dead" prepared for the occasion—or bottles of tequila. Sometimes, Day of the Dead altars are set up in homes, but most typically they are set up at the cemetery, tombs, or sites for those who have passed away. *Papel picado*, punched colorful tissue paper with appropriate designs related to the Day of the Dead, often decorates the altar's perimeter along with written *calaveras*, short-rhymed, satirical poems for the living, which may also form a part of the Day of the Dead celebration and *ofrenda*.

The traditional Day of the Dead altar consists of three levels upon which various items are placed and must include candles, fresh flowers, and pictures of the person being honored, or called back for the special day. Each level corresponds to the levels of the underworld, world, and heaven, and items placed on each level correspond to what could be found there. Thus the photograph of the person or saint is at the very top, foods are at the middle level, and water, soap, small towel (so that the spirit can wash after the long journey), and candles, are at the first level. The two-day ritual includes special prayers, including a rosary, for the departed—on November 1st for children and on the 2nd for adults.

Day of the Dead *ofrendas* have become popular artistic events in public spaces as well as in homes and at the cemetery. Museums and restaurants most typically commission an artist or several artists to create the *ofrendas*. For example, Mi Tierra Restaurant in San Antonio, Texas, sets up an *ofrenda* every year—one year it was for the slain Tejana singer Selena, another year it was for the restaurant founding family members who had died. Also, museums and other arts spaces such as cultural arts centers prepare a display of Day of the Dead altars, but of course do not conform to the traditional dates; the artists invited to create the altar typically leave them up from mid-October to mid-November. Children's crafts complement the activities and include creating a sugar skull or making paper flowers, usually marigolds, to decorate the altars.

In many Latino/a homes, a space is reserved for holy images and statues that serve as the prayer anchor in the home. While the San Pascual image may appear in the kitchen in New Mexico, or San Martin Caballero over the doorway in Texas, the home altar—usually in the living room or bedroom—may include special patron saints of the family and, often, the image of the Virgin Mary that the household venerates (Virgen de la Caridad del Cobre, Virgen de San Juan, or Virgen de Guadalupe) as well as any number of saints whose intercession is being sought:

St. Jude for lost causes, St. Roque for healing cancer, St. Gerard for insuring a good pregnancy, and so on. The home altar, like the *pesebre* or *ofrenda*, also includes candles, water, and flowers as essential elements representing the elements of fire, water, and earth. Usually, photographs of those for whom prayers are offered are placed on the altar. Unlike the Day of the Dead altar, a typical home altar is one level and is cumulative, that is, items are added and rarely discarded. The elaborate home altar of one of the key families in the annual *Pastorela* in San Antonio, Texas, for example, includes the yearly ribbon decorations used in that folk play. In addition, home altars may display major or significant accomplishments in the family—graduation pictures, diplomas, or even citizenship papers—that signify prayers granted. Because of the risk of fire associated with having lit candles, many contemporary home altars use electric lamps or battery-operated sources of light. It is customary that the statues of the saints be buried should they be broken for any reason; in some cases they are buried in the casket with the altar's owner.

In addition, those Latinos/as who practice the *Santería* religion may keep an altar for specific rituals associated with that tradition. The altar might also be constructed for a specific ritual and can be set up outdoors as well as indoors. The *Babalawo*, or high priest, worships at a *Santería* altar that mixes African and Christian traditions. In a similar manner to Christian worshippers who honor the saints, including folk saints such as Don Pedrito Jaramillo, *Santería* worshippers, through the construction of home altars and decorations, also pay homage to their *Orishas*—often likened to Christian saints. In like fashion, they place items on the typically three-tiered altars that signify or call to the *Orisha*; these offerings may include the traditional fruit and flowers along with statues, seeds, beads, feathers, and fans and mirrors. In both altars, one may find incense or a small *sauhmero*, or cauldron, for burning copal or other aromatic resins. Sometimes an altar honoring the *Orishas* is referred to as a *boveda espiritual*, or spiritual altar, literally a spiritual vault.

Artistic constructions inspired by traditional *ofrendas, altares,* or *nacimientos* began appearing in Chicano/a cultural centers and art spaces in the 1980s. Renowned Chicana artist and MacArthur fellow Amalia Mesa Bain has been credited with creating the first artistic altars (*Altar for Santa Teresa de Avila,* 1984) and is widely recognized as the master of such a tradition. Her *Altar for Dolores del Río,* for example, has been exhibited along with many other installations that draw from the tradition of altars. Frida Khalo, Selena, and other popular culture icons have been the subject of artistic altars usually set up for the Day of the Dead or for special museum exhibits. The traditional altar has also inspired artists to construct installations for special events, such as the one dedicated to Gloria Anzaldúa at the conferences on Anzaldúa created by artists such as Deborah Vásquez (2009) and by members of the organizing teams, Patricia Trujillo in 2007 and Glenda Shaeffer in 2010.

The altar tradition in the Latino community has inspired artists and continues to be a vibrant everyday practice in seasonal celebrations of Day of the Dead and Christmas, and in countless homes as devotees of particular Christian saints or practitioners of *Santería.*

Norma E. Cantú

See also: Christmas (Navidad); Cuaresma (Lent); Día de los Muertos (Day of the Dead); Día de los Muertos: Migration and Transformation to the U.S.; Jaramillo, Don Pedrito; Nacimientos; Paper Arts (Papel Picado, Papier Mâché, and Kites); Pastorelas (Shepherds' Plays); Saints (Santos); Santería; Virgin of Guadalupe: History and Fiestas Guadalupanas

Further Reading

Flores-Peña, Ysamur, and Roberta J. Evanchuk. *Santería Garments and Altars: Speaking Without a Voice.* Jackson: University Press of Mississippi, 2010.

Japser, Pat, and Kay Turner. *Art Among Us—Arte entre nosotros: Mexican American Folk Art of San Antonio.* San Antonio: San Antonio Museum Association, 1986.

Mesa-Baines, Amalia, et al. *Imágenes e Historias/Images and Histories: Chicana Altar-Inspired Art.* Medford, MA: Tufts University Gallery, 1999.

Pérez, Laura E. *Chicana Art: The Politics of Spiritual and Aesthetic Altarities (Objects/Histories).* Durham, NC: Duke University Press, 2007.

AMERICAN FOLKLORE SOCIETY (AFS)

Founded in 1888, the American Folklore Society (AFS) is both a learned and a professional society, and one of several organizations that serve to stimulate and encourage interest and research in the field of folklore. The more than 2,200 members and subscribers of the AFS, who study and communicate knowledge about folklore throughout the world, include scholars, teachers, fieldworkers, ethnographers, and libraries at colleges and universities, public sector professionals in arts and cultural organizations, and community members involved in all aspects of folklore work. While the majority of members live and work in the United States, their folkloristic interests span numerous forms, genres, and cultural groups worldwide; at present about one in every eight AFS members is from outside the United States (AFSnet.org).

The Society is currently headquartered at The Ohio State University in Columbus, Ohio, where it sponsors publications, meetings, and resources to support and promote members' work, and to help them build professional and social networks. The AFS publishes the quarterly *Journal of American Folklore* (*JAF*); holds an annual meeting each October that brings together more than 700 folklorists from around the world to exchange work and ideas, and to create and strengthen friendships and working relationships; maintains the AFS website as a means for communication among Society members and between folklorists and the world at large; serves as a hub of a diverse field, developing means of communication and offering professional development opportunities; prepares position statements on a variety of cultural, educational, and professional issues as part of an ongoing program of advocacy for traditional cultural expression, and for the work of folklorists; supports the work of committees and special interest–group sections; awards prizes, travel stipends, and other forms of recognition and support for outstanding work and best practices; maintains active partnerships with other societies in the American Council of Learned Societies and the National Humanities Alliance; takes a leading role in folklore projects both national (such as the Ethnographic Archives Initiative and the Folklore and Health Policy Project) and international (such as the H-Folk international folklore scholarship listserv and the development of an ethnographic thesaurus), and in international deliberations concerning folklore, intellectual property, and intangible cultural heritage (www.afsnet.org).

As a scholarly discipline, folklore studies began in the nineteenth century, a modernist successor to past-oriented antiquarianism. Prevailing Western trends of Romanticism and Nationalism colored early methods and concepts—a search for origins and salvage concerns—that were reflected in the dominant interests of the founders of folklore societies (Clements 1988, 1).

The America Folklore Society was founded on January 4th, 1888 in Cambridge, Massachusetts, having been set in motion the previous year. The first proposal came in the form of a circular letter dated May 5th, 1887. When the follow-up letter was issued in October, the original seventeen signatures had grown to 104, and included representatives from various parts of the United States and Canada. Encouraged and inspired by the establishment of The Folklore Society (FLS) in the United Kingdom in 1878, the AFS membership likewise drew upon humanities scholars, museum anthropologists, and private citizens (www.afsnet.org). The primary goal was to establish a "scientific" journal in which to publish "the collection of the fast-vanishing remains of Folk-Lore in America," which included Old World survivals and contemporaneous lore of marginal groups and regions, such as the "Negroes in the Southern States of the Union," "Native American Tribes of North America," and "French-Canada and Mexico, etc." (*JAF* 1, 3).

The first volume of *The Journal of American Folklore* was published in 1888, under the editorship of Franz Boas, T. Frederick Crane, and J. Owen Dorsey. Serving as general editor, William Wells Newell began what would become eighteen years of pioneering leadership and service to the Society. Today, the *Journal of American Folklore* is one of the oldest and most respected folklore journals in the world.

The Society's first meeting was held in Philadelphia in 1889. Apart from moratoria in 1942 and 1943, AFS conferences addressing a variety of path-breaking intellectual folkloristic themes have been held annually and in dozens of United States cities. In 1959, the AFS annual meeting was held in Mexico City, Mexico, and in 2007, a joint meeting with The Folklore Studies Association of Canada (ACEF-FSAC) was held in Québec City, Canada. In 1945, the AFS was admitted to the American Council of Learned Societies and continues as an actively participating member.

The AFS hosts more than thirty interest-group sections that speak to common interests and several geographical and generic specializations, and their members dialogue within and without the AFS infrastructure. For example, the Chicano and Chicana Folklore Section and the Folklore Latino, Latinoamericano, y Caribeño Section are dedicated to the study, advancement, and awareness of their respective memberships in both scholarly and public sector arenas, and convene at the meetings of the AFS and other learned societies such as the Latin American Studies Association, and the National Chicano and Chicana Studies Association.

In 2002, largely due to the advocacy of then AFS Board member Norma E. Cantú, the AFS approved the creation of the Américo Paredes Prize, in recognition of the relentless and significant scholarship of Américo Paredes

(1915–1999). Each year, both the Chicano and Chicana Folklore Section and the Folklore Latino, Latinoamericano, y Caribeño Section, along with the AFS Task Force on Cultural Diversity, join with the AFS Executive Board to award the Américo Paredes Prize for "excellence in integrating scholarship and engagement with the people and communities one studies, or in teaching and encouraging scholars and practitioners to work in their own cultures or communities" (www.afsnet.org).

Since its inception, the AFS has taken a leading role in fostering intellectual dialogue, both in the United States and internationally. The Society has benefited from a sizeable Latino presence and participation. Hispanophone AFS officers past and present include Olivia Cadaval (AFS Nominating Committee, 1989–1991), Norma E. Cantú (AFS Board, 2000–2002), Aurelio Macedonio Espinosa (AFS president, 1923–1924), Mario Montaño (AFS Nominating Committee, 2006–2008), Olga Nájera-Ramirez (AFS Board, 2007–2009), Solimar Otero (AFS Nominating Committee, 2007–2009), and Américo Paredes (*JAF* editor, 1969–1973). Furthermore, notable service in committee and special-interest section work is evidence of Latino commitment at both the individual and community level, and of the American Folklore Society's commitment to education, transformation, and diversity.

María Teresa Agozzino

See also: Cadaval, Olivia; Cantú, Norma E.; Espinosa, Aurelio Macedonio; Nájera-Ramirez, Olga; Paredes, Américo; Texas Folklore Society

Further Reading

The American Folklore Society. http://afsnet.org.

Boas, Franz, T. Frederick Crane, J. Owen Dorsey, and William Wells Newell, eds. *The Journal of American Folklore* 1:1 (1888).

Bronner, Simon J. *American Folklore Studies: An Intellectual History*. Lawrence: University Press of Kansas, 1986.

Clements, William M., ed. *100 Years of American Folklore Study: A Conceptual History*. Washington, DC: The American Folklore Society, 1988.

Jackson, Bruce, Michael Taft, and Harvey Axlerod, eds. *The Centennial Index: 100 Years of the Journal of American Folklore*. Washington, DC: American Folklore Society, 1988.

Limón, José E. "Américo Paredes: Ballad Scholar." *Journal of American Folklore* 120:475 (2007): 3–18.

López Morín, José R. *The Legacy of Américo Paredes*. College Station: Texas A&M University Press, 2006.

Zumwalt, Rosemary Lévy. *American Folklore Scholarship: A Dialogue of Dissent*. Bloomington: Indiana University Press, 1988.

ARGENTINA AND ITS FOLKLORE

Argentina is the largest Spanish-speaking country in South America; it is located between the Andes mountain range and the Atlantic Ocean. Before the Spanish conquest, the Argentine territory was occupied by a diversity of Indigenous peoples. This consisted mainly of those populations in the northwestern regions that had become part of the Inca empire before the Spanish conquest. Some of the largest Indigenous peoples include the Guaraní, Mapuche, Tehuelches, and Toba. During the sixteenth and seventeenth centuries, the territories that now make up Argentina belonged to the Viceroyalty of Peru until the creation of the Viceroyalty of the La Plata River in the late eighteenth century. The Argentine Republic emerged during the nineteenth century, also characterized by a large influx of European immigrants—mostly Spanish and Italians—who continued migrating into the twentieth century past World War II. Argentine folklore is comprised of a variety of traditions with Indigenous and European roots, as well as pockets of African influence. Argentine folkloric traditions are as varied as its geography, from the southern regions of Patagonia, to the plains of La Pampa, to the subtropical north, and the Andean highlands. Argentina is often divided into the following regions: Northwest (provinces of Jujuy, Salta, Tucumán, Catamarca, and La Rioja), Gran Chaco (Formosa, Chaco, and Santiago del Estero), Litoral (Misiones, Entre Ríos, and Corrientes), Cuyo (San Juan, Mendoza, and San Luis), Pampas (Córdoba, Santa Fe, La Pampa, and Buenos Aires), and Patagonia (Río Negro, Neuquén, Chubut, Santa Cruz, and Tierra del Fuego).

The official language in Argentina is Spanish, although spoken with a very distinct accent. The Spanish spoken in Buenos Aires evidences strong influences from Italian and other European languages. There is also a very particular slang called *lunfardo,* which is referred to as *Rioplatense.*

Gaucho Culture

Gauchos were men of the eighteenth and nineteenth centuries who lived in the Pampas, or plains, of Argentina and Uruguay. Their particular way of life has become an important romanticized aspect of Argentine identity. It was characterized by a horse-riding, wandering existence with very particular customs, clothing, food, beliefs, and poetry. They raised cattle, valued their independence, and were considered superb

Gaucho in traditional attire, Argentina, ca. 1868. (Library of Congress)

horsemen. The *gauchos* wore a headscarf and hat, wide underpants or *bombachas*, and often a sort of wide, wrap-around pant called *chiripás*, with a *faja* (belt-like cloth) that held them in place, and sometimes a thick leather belt with coins, as well as spurs, a sort of boots or *alpargatas* as shoes, and a thick poncho as protection against the cold. They utilized large knives (*facones*) and *boleadoras*, a throwing weapon designed to capture animals by entangling their feet.

Foodways

Argentine cuisine is heavily influenced by Spanish and Italian traditions. Pasta and pizza, often homemade, are common meal items. Empanadas, a sort of stuffed pastry, are emblematic of Argentine cuisine. Their stuffing and style vary from region to region, and the art of preparing and sealing them with intricate patterns, called *repulgue,* is passed from generation to generation. Other important items include *facturas* (sweet pastries), *dulce de leche* (a milk caramel spread), and *alfajores* (made of two round cookies with a stuffing such as jam or *dulce de leche* in the middle and often covered with sugar, glaze, or chocolate).

Argentineans also consume and produce large quantities of wine and beef. The most traditional way to prepare meat is an *asado* or *parrillada,* similar to a barbecue. *Asados* are often large family or community affairs centered around the fire. They include a variety of types of meats (mostly beef, but also chicken and goat) and sausages (such as *chorizos, morcilla,* and *chinchulines*). The meat is not marinated, only salted, and grilled slowly over wood or wood coal. The art of grilling is often taught from generation to generation, and tends to be the affair of men, or *asadores.* The *asado* is often accompanied by red wine and salad, prepared by women, and served with *chimichurri*, a traditional sauce made of parsley, garlic, olive oil, vinegar, oregano, paprika, salt, and pepper.

Argentine cuisine is also characterized by a number of unique foods with Indigenous influences, such as *locro* (a heavy stew made of corn, beef, and vegetables), humitas (a variety of corn-based dishes), and *yerba mate.*

Mate

Mate is the national beverage of Argentina. It is made by steeping dried leaves of *yerba mate* (*llex* paraguarensis) in hot water and drinking the infusion. *Mate* was originally drunk out of special hollowed gourds, also called *mates*, although they are commonly made out of metal today, as well as other materials, such as wood or ceramic. The straw, called *bombilla*, is commonly metallic nowadays, although often it is made out of a hollowed cane. *Mate* is prepared by placing some of the commercially available mixture of dried and chopped leaves known as *yerba mate* into the *mate* gourd, filling it up a little more than half way. Some people also add sugar or other additives (such as orange peel or other herbs). The *bombilla* straw is then placed into the *yerba*. Then, hot water is poured into the *mate* gourd over the *yerba*. Since the *bombilla* has a strainer piece at the end, one can suck the filtered water infusion from the tip of the *bombilla* without ingesting the dried leaves.

Yerba mate **served with a** *bombilla,* **a straw usually made of silver. (Studioflara/Dreamstime.com)**

The vast majority of Argentineans drink it once or twice a day, in the manner that tea or coffee is consumed in other countries. However, unlike tea and, particularly, coffee, *mate* is almost a sacred practice of the private and intimate realm, consumed in small groups at home and not in commercial shops. It is usually shared with family or friends, by taking turns and passing around the cup, so that everyone may drink from it, utilizing the same straw. It is also the indispensable offering when someone comes to visit.

There is a complex *mate* drinking etiquette at play when people prepare and share this special Argentinean drink. The person who prepares and serves the *mate* is called the *cebador*. The *cebador* must always drink the first *mate* himself or herself, to make sure it is not too hot and good enough to be shared, and because the first batch of this tea tends to be unpleasantly strong. After the *cebador* has drunk the first *mate*, he or she serves one to the person on his right. Once that person drinks all the water in the *mate*, he or she gives it back to the *cebador*, who refills the water and passes it on to the next person in the circle, and so on. After a number of servings the infusion is no longer as strong and the *mate* is said to be *lavado* (washed out). Depending on the preferences of the drinkers, some people change some or all of the *yerba mate* one or several times in the same sitting to keep a strong infusion.

Before the arrival of the Spanish in the Americas, the Indigenous peoples of the area regularly consumed *mate*. It was called *ka'aygua* in the Guaraní language, which literally means something like "herb water." The term *mate* is the Spanish adaptation of the Quechua term *mati*, which means gourd. Nowadays the Spanish word *mate* is used to refer to the drink as well as the cup it is drunk from. It was quickly adopted by the *criollos* (people of Spanish descent born in the Americas) and became a staple of the life of the *gauchos*. The Jesuits helped popularize the consumption of *mate* by commercializing the *yerba mate*. It is still a staple of the Argentinean economy and one of its most important exportation products. Nowadays it can be found in most supermarkets in the United States although often in its teabag version.

Music and Dance

Tango

Tango emerged in the lower class neighborhoods of the port cities of Montevideo in Uruguay, and in Buenos Aires in Argentina—both of these cities located on the Río de la Plata estuary. The music is a 2/4 or 4/4 played with violins, piano, double bass, and *bandoneón* (*bandoleón*). The late-nineteenth-century tango was the music of the urban poor, and Argentinean high society disapproved of it as a low class music and dance. It was only later welcomed and, in fact, even considered fashionable among the middle and upper classes, once it had become fashionable in Europe in the 1930s and 1940s. At that point, the tango moved from bars and brothels in the poor neighborhoods of the marginalized city outskirts, to became associated with formal wear and downtown nightclubs. By the mid-twentieth century, and in some places even earlier than that, tango had become the Argentinean national dance and had come to represent Argentine culture. There are many styles of tango, as well as *milonga,* a related faster rhythm. Tango has now become internationally popular. In the United States, it is danced widely as one of the ballroom dance genres and performed in two styles: American and International.

Traditional Music and Dance

Argentine folk music compromises a variety of genres with various Spanish and Indigenous influences, most of which are also danced. Argentina has a large canon of institutionalized folk dances. Most genres are joyous courtship dances with 6/8 rhythms danced by couples who perform different figures and steps, including the male *zapateo* (stepping). The couple moves closer and further away from each other, but never, or rarely ever, touching. That is, they are not performed in a close embrace. The traditional outfits for the dances vary according to region and style, but women invariably wear wide skirts. Dancers often perform *castañetas,* or rhythmic snapping of the fingers, as they dance. Folk music is very much alive in Argentina, constituting a strong market with famous past and present musicians, large festivals, and a significant recording industry.

Baguala and Carnavalito

The *baguala* is a northwestern music genre popular among the Indigenous groups. It is played with a *caja.* The rhythm and lyrics are markedly uniform. This *carnavalito* genre has a characteristic Indigenous influence in its dance style and instrumentation. It is performed by numerous cheerful couples, in the northern region of Argentina, particularly during carnival. It is played with *charango, bombo, caja,* and local wind instruments (such as *quena, erke, anata,* or *siku*). The most famous *carnavalito* song in Argentina is "*El Humaguaqueño.*"

Chacarera

One of the best-known Argentine folk dance and music genres, *chacareras* are danced by one or two couples. The genre originated in the north, but has spread throughout most of the country. It is often performed with a guitar, violin, and *bombo*. Some famous *chacarera* songs include "*Chacarera de las Piedras,*" "*Chacarera de los Lagos,*" and "*Déjame que me Vaya.*"

Chamamé

The *chamamé* is a northeastern Argentine music and dance with Indigenous *Guaraní* roots, as well as Spanish and German influences. It is played with guitars and accordions. There are many different variants, which vary from the festive to the melancholic. Some very famous *chamamé* songs include "*María va,*" "*Merceditas,*" and "*Pedro Canoero.*"

Cueca

The *cueca* is a north-Argentine dance performed by one or two couples, derived from the *zamacueca*. There are a variety of versions in the different provinces in which it is popular. Some very famous *cueca* songs include "*Las Dos Puntas*" and "*Los Sesenta Granaderos.*"

Escondido

This is a one-couple dance of the Argentine northeast that owes its name to the fact that at some points the dancers seem to be hiding from each other. It is also played with a guitar, violin or accordion, and *bombo*. The rhythm is similar to the *gato*. The most famous song of this genre is perhaps a song named after the rhythm itself, "*El Escondido.*"

Gato

The *gato* is one of the couple dances of rural origins that is still a living tradition. It can be danced by one or two couples. The version called *gato con relaciones* includes breaks for the man to recite a few lines. Some other variations include the *gato correntino, gato cordobés, gato encantado, gato polkeado, gato de dos giros,* and *gato con zapateo cantado.*

Vidala

The *vidala* is a style of folk song from the Argentine northwest. The songs are accompanied by guitar and *caja,* and often performed during carnival. The melody and lyrical structure vary from region to region.

Zamba

A well-known Argentine folklore genre, the *zamba* dance is characterized by the waving of handkerchiefs in one or both hands by the dancing couple. The dance movements display a courtship of the woman by the man, who is accepted by the woman by the end of the dance. It originated in the Argentine northwest. Like the faster *cueca*, it is also derived from the *zamacueca*. Some very famous *zamba* songs include: "*Alfonsina y el Mar*," "*Balderrama*," "*La Pomeña*," "*Luna Tucumana*," "*Paisaje de Catamarca*," "*Zamba de mi Esperanza*," "*Zamba para no Morir*," and "*Zamba para Olvidarte*."

Musical Instruments

Wind Instruments

The accordion, of European origin, is an important instrument in Argentinean folk music. Equally important for playing the tango is the *bandoneón*, which is similar to a concertina. Other important *criollo* wind instruments include the harmonica, the very long *corneta* or *erke* (played particularly during carnival and Corpus Christi celebrations in the northwest), and several flutes (such as the *anata* and the *flauta tucumana*). Some of the best-known Indigenous wind instruments from the northern regions of Argentina include a number of flutes, such as the *quena*, *anata*, and *pinquillo*; the *sikus*, similar to the panpipes, with one or two rows of bamboo flutes, that come in different styles and sizes; the *erkencho*, belonging to the Argentine northwest and made with a cow horn and a cane mouthpiece; and ceramic ocarinas. Wind instruments from the southern regions include the *pifilka* or Mapuche whistle; and the *trutruka*, made out of the base of a cow horn and a cane several meters long, which is reserved for ritual and special occasions.

String Instruments

The famous *charango* is a ten-stringed (or sometimes five-stringed) instrument of the Argentine northwest, similar to the guitar, with a body made out of wood or the shell of an armadillo. The *requinto* of the Cuyo region is a smaller guitar with six sets of two strings. The guitar and the violin also

A *charango* is a South American acoustic instrument with 10 strings. (Dreamstime.com)

play an important role in Argentine folk music, as well as a local version of the harp in the Northeastern region. The *arco musical* is an Indigenous string instrument, which consists of a wooden arch with a single animal hair string played with another wooden arched piece. The Indigenous peoples of Argentina also utilize several instruments similar to the guitar and the violin: the five-stringed *Mbyá* guitar, and the three-stringed *Mbyá* rabel, the one-stringed *Tobá* violin or *N' biké*, and the four-stringed *turumí*.

Percussion Instruments

There are many types of drums, including the deep, rhythm-keeping *bombos*, made out of wood and animal skin. The *bombo tubular*, with a deep cylinder, and played with a soft-headed mallet and a stick on a single membrane, of which the *bombo legüero* is the loudest and most famous, is played while hanging on the side of the drummer with an arm wrapped around it. The *bombo chato* or *bombo de banda*, with a diameter much wider than its depth, is hit with a single soft-headed mallet. Other popular percussion instruments include the triangle; the *redoblante*; the *cajas*, small, round, flat, two-headed drums; the *sistro* or *clavelito*, with small metal jingles; and the *platillos*, two large metal circles attached through a string.

The Indigenous groups of Argentina utilize a wide variety of gourd rattles. The Mapuche of the south also utilize a rattle belt made out of wooden jingle bells, often worn for ritual dances. The Indigenous groups of the north utilize rattles made out of animal hoofs, nails, or bones. There are also a variety of drums, such as the *timbale de agua*, the *tambor de dos parches,* and the *kultrun,* a semi-spherical wooden drum with a decorated animal skin, hit with one or two strings, depending on the size.

Folk Narratives

Legends

There are many legends in the oral tradition of Argentine folk narratives. Some are Catholic in content and origin, and speak of figures, miracles, and saints. There are also a number of historic figures often referred to in Argentine culture that have become legendary and an important part of Argentine *gaucho* identity, such as Pancho Sierra, Bailoretto, as well as literary figures, such as Martín Fierro. Other legends belong to the many Indigenous groups, and often tell of how particular rivers, rocks, or other natural elements were formed; or of how certain animals, trees, flowers, or foodstuffs (like corn and *mandioca*) came to be. The Indigenous groups of Argentina also possess complex mythologies with their own deities and explanations of how the world came to be and where humans come from. The two examples below belong to the Guaraní Indigenous groups and talk about two very important items for Argentine identity: the impressive Iguazú waterfalls visited by many tourists; and the *ceibo*, the national tree and flower of Argentina.

Panambí

In the jungle surrounding the Iguazú waterfalls lived a gorgeous young Guaraní woman. She had a beautiful voice and sang along as she went down the river on her canoe to gather fruits. One day she passed a handsome man in his canoe. He looked her in the eye as she went by and she felt hypnotized. She came home late and her mother noticed her absent behavior. Every afternoon from then on, she looked forward to the same encounter. One day, as she was resting in her hammock, she heard a canoe coming by through the rough, agitated waters. She immediately ran to the shore and saw the man in his canoe. A force pulled her toward him, and as she stepped into the river, the waters became calm. She drowned, and the man in the canoe, who was none other than Pyra-yara, the lord of the river and the fish, took her in her canoe down the river and past the precipice of the waterfalls. Her body became a woman-shaped stone, and a slight current of white water covers it like the veil of a bride.

Anahí

In the jungles surrounding the Paraná River lived a young woman named Anahí. She loved her land and her people fiercely, and often walked around the jungle, singing to the plants and animals, as she had a beautiful voice. One day her people were attacked, some say by another tribe, some say by the Spanish, and a brutal war ensued. Anahí fought bravely, despite her youth. One day she fell prisoner. However, in the middle of the night, she was able to escape, killing the guard. Sadly, she was recaptured and sentenced to death by fire. When the flames rose around her, she sang asking for divine protection for her people and their homeland. When the sun rose, her body had been transformed into the vigorous *ceibo* tree with its beautiful flowers, red like fire, a symbol of courage and strength.

Folk Tales

Many folk tales are told by the peoples of the Argentine cities and countryside. Some of them involve treacherous men, like Paí Luchí, the liar; Goyo Cardoso, from the province of Entre Ríos; and Pedro Urdemales, who deceives the powerful (see the following example). The protagonists of some other folk tales are animals, such as El Sapo (the toad), a small animal that often ends up defeating the big and powerful; El Quirquincho (the armadillo); El Tigre (the tiger); and the cunning Zorro (the fox). An example of these folk tales is given below in the story of *Pedro Urdemales and the Boiling Pot*:

> Pedro was once cooking by the side of a stream. He had started a fire with some branches, and was boiling some vegetables in his old little pot, when he saw a group of men approaching. Quickly, he dug a hole in the sand, hid the ambers in it, and placed the pot on top. He hid all the ashes, leaving no sign of a fire, and sat down. Then, he started talking to the pot: "Boil, little pot, boil." When the men heard him, they laughed at him and told him to stop talking to the pot and start a fire if he wanted to cook. He explained that he did not need to do such work, since his pot boiled water on its own. When the men looked inside the pot and saw the stew boiling they wanted to purchase the pot. "How convenient for when one is on a rush, or it's windy, or it's rainy!" they said. "I am not interested in selling and you won't have enough money to buy it," Pedro answered. The men dug in their pockets and bags and gave him all the silver coins they had. Pedro finally agreed. "Just for you,"

he said, "but you will have to wait until I'm done eating." He took his time to eat, washed out the pot, and gave it to them asking in which direction they were traveling. Then, he took off in the opposite direction, picturing how funny the men would look talking to his old little pot.

Crafts

Some of the best-known Argentine crafts include intricate wood and leather work. Ornate *mate* gourds and silverwork are also very popular. The Indigenous groups of the north are also well known for their ceramic. Furthermore, Argentine native peoples create valued handmade weavings and textiles, such as *arpilleras*; woven Mapuche *fajas*; *ponchos*, sometimes made of alpaca wool; carpets, scarves, and winter wear made with sheep or llama wool; as well as bags, hats, and other items made of *chaguar* fibers.

Beliefs

The Argentine population is largely Roman Catholic, although the majority does not attend church regularly. There are also significant Christian Protestant, agnostic, Muslim, and Jewish minorities.

A number of supernatural beings populate the Argentine collective imagination. For example, there are several man-eating monsters, such as the *Caá-Porá*, a gigantic hairy monster of the Guaraní regions that smokes a skull pipe; and the *Familiar* of the northwestern provinces, who takes the shape of a ferocious black dog or some other animal. There are also a number of supernatural beings that are partially human, such as the *Lobisón*, a sort of werewolf of the northeastern provinces, a family's seventh continuous male child. Finally, there is the *Pombero*, a thin, tall man with a hat that steals children; the *Supay*, an amalgamation of the Indigenous lord of the underworld and the Catholic devil; the *Coquena*, a sort of dwarf that takes care of the llamas and other local camelids; the *Pujllay*, the spirit of carnival; and the troublemaking *duendes*, similar to European gnomes.

Celebrations and Costumes

Carnival

Carnival is a time of enjoyment before the beginning of the forty days of Lent. It usually takes place during February or March, and lasts for four entire days. It is a much more important celebration in the northern regions of the country. Some of the highlights of carnival include parades, music, dancing, and fireworks. People often throw water, flour, powder, confetti, and other things at each other. Carnival is mostly celebrated in the province of Buenos Aires and the northern regions.

Carnival in the Litoral provinces is heavily influenced by Brazilian carnival. Many towns in the provinces of Corrientes and Entre Ríos have *comparsas* (competing music and dancing teams) and the carnival parades take place in specially built locations called *corsódromos*. The outfits of those participating in the parade are made for the occasion and feature rhinestones, glitter, feathers, and sequins.

Carnival in the northwestern provinces is quite different. It is a tradition with stronger Indigenous roots, celebrated in February, in provinces like Salta and Jujuy, most importantly in *Quebrada de Huamahuacá*. Their carnival begins with the unburying of a dummy, which represents the *Pujllay*, lord of the carnival, sometimes equated to the devil, which was buried the year before. The unburying of the *Pujllay* represents the freeing of repressed desires. During carnival, people are allowed to get drunk and engage in behaviors otherwise outside of the norm. People dressed in colorful clothes perform traditional dances to live music, celebrate, and play dress up by wearing masks. The festivities last eight days and conclude with the burying of the *Pujllay*.

Señaladas

The *señaladas* is an annual celebration to mark (*señalar*, or brand) the animals, such as cows and sheep. They are gathered, counted, marked with a hot iron or through an ear incision, and in addition, sterilizations are performed when necessary. It is a festive work occasion, sometimes accompanied by a blessing of the animals or a symbolic marriage ritual of a male and a female animal in hopes of a fertile season.

Games

There are many traditional games that remain alive in Argentina. Two of the best known in the countryside are *sortija* (in which two teams of horse riders try to put a sort of pointer through a hanging ring) and *taba* (played by flipping a cow talus bone). There are also many traditional card games, such as *escoba* and canasta, and perhaps the best known, *truco* (a trickery card game full of signals, bluffing, and traditional calls adorned by verses). The most important sport is soccer, with a very significant role in Argentine popular culture.

NADIA DE LEÓN

See also: Chile and Its Folklore; Folk Instruments; Tango; Vaquero

Further Reading

Aramburu, Julio. *Las hazañas de Pedro Urdemales*. Buenos Aires: El Ateneo, 1949.

Belloso, Waldo, and Beatriz Durante. *Danzas folklóricas Argentinas: Su coreografía y su música*. Buenos Aires: Editorial Julio Korn, 1964.

Chertudi, Susana. *Cuentos folkóricos de la Argentina*. Buenos Aires: Instituto Nacional de Filología y Folklore, 1960.

Coluccio, Félix. *Culto y canonizaciones populares de Argentina*. Buenos Aires: Editorial del Sol, 1994.

Coluccio, Félix. *Diccionario de creencias y supersticiones*. Buenos Aires: Corregidor, 1990.

del Campo, Luzán. *Canciónero del mate: Folklore de Argentina, Brasil, Chile, Uruguay y Paraguay*. Buenos Aires: Editorial Lavalle, 1950.

Fitch, Melissa, David William Foster, and Darrel B. Lockhart. *Culture and Customs of Argentina*. Westport, CT: Greenwood Press, 1998.

Metraux, Alfred. *Myths and Tales of the Toba and Pilagá Indians of the Gran Chaco.* Philadelphia: Kessinger Publishing, 2007. Originally published 1946.

Pérez Bugallo, Rubén. *Catálogo ilustrado de instrumentos musicales argentinos.* Buenos Aires:
Editorial del Sol, 1993.

Simoneau, Karin, and Johannes Wilbert. *Folk Literature of the Mocovi Indians.* Los Angeles:
University of California Press, 1988.

Simoneau, Karin, and Johannes Wilbert. *Folk Literature of the Toba Indians.* Los Angeles:
University of California Press, 1982.

Vidal de Battini, Berta. *Cuentos y leyendas populares de la Argentina.* Buenos Aires: Ediciones
Culturales Argentinas, 1980.

AROR A, SHIRLEY LEASE (1930–)

Shirley Lease Arora is an active and prolific American folklorist whose research on
Hispanic paremiology (the study of *dichos* or proverbs, and folk legends) and work
as a paremiographer (a person who collects proverbs) have made her an internationally respected scholar. Born in Youngstown, Ohio, Arora grew up in southern
California, and earned her bachelor's (1950) and master's degrees (1951) in Spanish at Stanford University—where she studied with Aurelio Espinosa, Jr.—and
her doctoral degree at the University of California, Los Angeles (UCLA). Although
UCLA professors Wayland D. Hand and Stanley L. Robe directed her dissertation
entitled "Proverbial Comparisons in Ricardo Palma's *Tradiciones peruanas*" (1962),
later published as a book in 1966, she had begun her research on Palma under Juan
B. Rael at Stanford. Her second book, *Proverbial Comparisons and Related Expressions in Spanish Recorded in Los Angeles* (1977), also follows the model established
in *Proverbial Comparisons and Similes from California* (1954) by Archer Taylor, who
would become her mentor.

Arora's distinguished academic career flourished at UCLA, where she taught
colonial and nineteenth-century Latin American literatures and Hispanic folklore,
and served as chair of the Department of Spanish and Portuguese (1981–1991),
acting director of the Latin American Center (1995–1996), and member of the
Advisory Committee of the Interdepartmental Program in Folklore and Mythology, among many responsibilities, for almost forty years. At the California Folklore
Society, she delivered the Archer Taylor Memorial Lecture in 1990 and became a
Fellow of the American Folklore Society two years later.

Arora's contributions to Latino folklore center on folk narrative and proverbial
lore. Working with texts collected from the greater Los Angeles area and Mexico,
she explores how the figure of La Llorona (The Weeping Woman) has been modified in the United States in "La Llorona: The Naturalization of a Legend" (1981).
In other studies, she examines the figure of La Llorona as a symbol of ethnic and
cultural identity in a Mexican American "memorate," or encounter story; the dissemination of the legend among children in bilingual environments; and infanticide as a common theme. Her research project on La Llorona was funded in part
by the National Endowment for the Humanities (1991–1992).

As evidenced by her numerous studies on both English and Spanish proverbial
speech, proverbs are Arora's true passion. As the foremost American scholar in

Spanish paremiology, she has collected and written about proverbial comparisons, exaggerations, and patterns, and "true proverbs." Cognizant of the few works on proverbial lore in Spanish from California, Arora made significant contributions to the field by collecting proverbial expressions among informants from all over the Hispanic world, including Filipinos; compiling annotated bibliographies; examining the Mexican American proverbial tradition and the new hybrid forms; and developing a theoretical framework from which to determine what makes a statement proverbial in "The Perception of Proverbiality" (1984).

By and large, Mexican American proverbs can be defined as those used by individuals of Mexican origin or descent who live in the United States. While a large percentage of Mexican American and Latino proverbs have roots in the oral tradition of Spain and Spanish America, the ubiquitous coexistence of English, as the dominant language, and Spanish, creates a linguistic contact zone that facilitates the coinage of hybrid forms that Arora terms "crossover proverbs." These new expressions emerge from direct translation or linguistic interference, generally from English into Spanish. Some examples are the following:

- "*Más fácil dicho que hecho*" ("Easier said than done")
- "*Lo que fácil viene fácil se va*" ("Easy come, easy go")
- "*La mujer casada, descalza, en casa y embarazada*" (A married woman [should be kept] barefoot, at home, and pregnant), which combines excerpts from both the Spanish "*La mujer casada, la pierna quebrada y en casa*" ("A married woman [should have] a broken leg and [remain] at home") and the English "A wife should be kept barefoot and pregnant."

Arora's most celebrated work is "The Perception of Proverbiality," praised by critic Wolfgang Mieder as an "enlightening article" that must be read by all students and scholars of proverbs. Whereas proverbial speech might be easily recognized by the listener, defining what makes it proverbial has been hard to pin down. On the basis of results from a survey that asked informants to identify twenty-five sayings, of which twenty-three were made up, Arora argues that the more proverbial markers a statement displays, the greater are its chances of being perceived as a proverb. She asserts that if the pseudo-proverb is perceived as a genuine saying, then it becomes a proverb to the hearer. Thus, the scholar of proverbs must know the criteria which folk groups use to determine proverbiality. Retired since 2000, Arora is currently finishing a long-term project on proverbs in Spanish recorded in the Los Angeles area.

ALEJANDRO LEE

See also: Dichos (Proverbs); Folk Narratives: Folk Tales, Legends, and Jokes; La Llorona (The Wailing Woman); Myths; Rael, Juan Bautista

Further Reading

Arora, Shirley L. "La Llorona: The Naturalization of a Legend." *Southwest Folklore* 5 (1981): 32–41.
Arora, Shirley L. "The Perception of Proverbiality." *Proverbium* 1 (1984): 1–38.

Arora, Shirley L. *Proverbial Comparisons and Related Expression in Spanish*. Berkeley: University of California Press, 1977.

Arora, Shirley L. "Proverbs in Mexican American Tradition." *Aztlán* 13 (1982): 43–69.

Mieder, Wolfgang "Shirley L. Arora: Hispanic Paremiologist Par Excellence." *Proverbium* 12 (1995): 1–12.

ARROZ CON LECHE (RICE PUDDING)

Arroz con leche is an extremely popular dessert in the Spanish-speaking world, especially with children. It translates literally as "rice with milk," but it is the Latino version of what is known as rice pudding in the United States, although generally with a thicker consistency. Its ingredients are rice, milk, cinnamon, sugar, and lemon or orange peel. Other possible ingredients are butter, cream, and caramel, with multiple variations depending on what may be available or preferred in each particular region or country.

In Puerto Rico, for example, this dessert is cooked with coconut milk and known as *arroz con dulce*. In a similar manner to Mexico, the dish may also include a variety of spices and flavorings such as cloves, ginger, vanilla, chocolate, nutmeg, and sometimes even cayenne pepper. It is often served with raisins in Central America, which may have been soaked in sherry, rum, or tequila prior to cooking. In South American countries such as Venezuela or Peru, some condensed milk or cream may be added to make a thicker consistency.

This well-known dessert dates back to the time of the Romans, who perceived it as a medicine instead of cuisine, and doctors prescribed it to settle upset stomachs. However, at that time, rice was an expensive commodity, which had to be imported and, therefore, only available for the higher social classes. The Arabic presence in the Spanish peninsula and other parts of the Mediterranean from the eighth century onward changed the availability and price of this main ingredient of *arroz con leche*, since rice started being produced in the continent.

The availability of rice in Spain during the Middle Ages, together with Arabic influence of eating rice-based dishes, meant that *arroz con leche* was easily accepted in the country. Later it was introduced by the Spanish conquistadors to Latin America. It used to be prepared with honey or coarse cane sugar, since those were the available sweeteners.

FRANCISCA SÁNCHEZ ORTIZ

Further Reading

Davidson, Alan. *The Oxford Companion to Food*. Oxford: Oxford University Press, 1999.

ASIAN CONTRIBUTION TO CHICANO/ LATINO FOLKLORE

Asians have made many contributions to Chicano/Latino folklore over the past 400 years that have been generally overlooked. Unknown to most people, millions of Asians have lived in Latin America since the late sixteenth century and they have left an indelible mark upon its culture. Asian contributions to Chicano/Latino culture have gone largely unnoticed because the history of Asians in Mexico and other parts of Latin America is not well known. Major Asian contributions to Mexican culture and folklore relate to religion, fashion, art, food, flora, jokes, music, poetry, and even cartoons. These contributions, moreover, correspond with two specific historical time periods of Asian migration: 1565–1815 and 1882–1940.

The Manila Galleon Trade, 1565–1815

The Manila Galleon Trade opened up migration and cultural exchange between Asia and Latin America between the years of 1565 and 1815. During this time period, Manila galleons or "China ships" transported thousands of Asian migrants and a wide variety of goods and luxury items to colonial Mexico. The Manila galleons were Spanish trading vessels which sailed annually across the Pacific Ocean between Manila in the Philippines and the port of Acapulco, Mexico. The Manila Galleon trade began in 1565 when Andrés de Urdaneta discovered the Pacific Ocean route connecting Southeast Asia and the Americas, and came to a halt in 1815 because of the impending Mexican War of Independence.

It is estimated that 40,000–100,000 Asian immigrants came to Mexico during the two and a half centuries of the Manila Galleon trade. These immigrants came from China, Cathay, Japan, the Philippines, and India. Despite their diverse national roots, they were referred to collectively as *chinos* (Chinese) or *indios chinos* (Chinese Indians). This lumping together of all Asian immigrants was due largely to the fact that the word *chino* became a term which was used synonymously with Asia. To this day in Latin America and in Latino communities of the United States, the word *chino* is still used as a label for all Asians. Unknown to most Latinos/as, this use of the term *chino* has a 400-year history.

After arriving in Acapulco, Asian immigrants scattered themselves throughout colonial Mexico. They were to be found as far north as Baja California, and as far south as the Yucatan Peninsula. Most Asians, however, congregated on the western coast of Mexico in the districts of Guerrero, Jalisco, and Michoacan, as well as in Mexico City, Puebla, and Veracruz. Asian presence in central Mexico was so strong, in fact, that the roads connecting Acapulco to Mexico City were called "*el camino de China*," or "The Chinese Road." Many Mexicans today display Asian physical characteristics and it is possible that this can be traced back to Asian lineage from the colonial period.

Chinos of colonial Mexico worked in a variety of jobs ranging from sailors and servants, to vendors, dancers, and craftsmen. The largest group served as sailors on the Manila Galleons which travelled regularly between the Philippines and Mexico. These seamen were Filipinos, Chinese-Filipinos known as "*mestizos de Sangley*," and ethnic Chinese from the Filipino port city of Cavite. Slaves and servants comprised the second largest population of Asians. Slaves were transported to Manila from Africa, India, the Malay Peninsula, Japan, and China, and then shipped to Mexico. Many Asians also worked as indentured servants of Spaniards following the dramatic decline of the native population of Mexico in the early seventeenth century because of disease. Asian craftsmen were also a notable presence, and they sold textiles, pottery, porcelain, and glassware to the larger Hispanic community. *Chino* merchants sold food products such as *aguardiente*, molasses, chickens, confectionaries, sugar, and cacao. These merchants were noted for selling their items in an outdoor marketplace of the Plaza Mayor of Mexico City called the *Parián*, which was named and modeled after the Chinese emporium of Manila. Colonial records also cite Asians as holding a variety of odd jobs such as harp players, dancers, scribes, tailors, cobblers, and coachmen.

La China Poblana

The most famous person of Asian descent was a woman, a *china* from colonial Mexico whose name was Catarina de San Juan, better known as *"La China Poblana"* (the Chinese woman from Puebla). Much folklore and controversy surround the historical figure of Catarina de San Juan, but what is clear from most accounts is that she was a famous Catholic mystic who was brought as a slave to New Spain from India circa 1619. She was the only Asian person from colonial Latin America about whom extensive contemporary accounts were written. Three written accounts were penned about her life: (i) a sermon which was delivered at her funeral on January 24th, 1688; (ii) a three-volume biography which was written by her father confessor and published in 1689, 1690, and 1692; and (iii) a single-volume biography written by a second father confessor.

These biographies were originally written to support a request for Catarina's beatification in the Roman Catholic Church, and they are striking examples of *"chino* folklore" from colonial Mexico. According to these accounts, Catarina was originally named Mirrha and she was born in India in a country governed by the *"Gran Mogors,"* or "the Great Mughals." She claimed a royal lineage and held that her maternal grandfather was the ruler of all of India and Arabia. She was abducted from her home on the Arabian Sea, together with her brother, in 1618 or 1619 at the age of twelve years old. Following her abduction she was taken to the Philippines, sold as a slave, and placed on a Manila Galleon headed for Mexico. It is further asserted that she was disguised as a boy on the trip to Mexico to increase her value as a slave.

Upon arrival in Acapulco, Catarina was sold as a slave to a Captain Miguel de Sosa who lived in Puebla, Mexico. Similar to the biblical account of Joseph who was sold into slavery in Egypt, it is alleged that she rose quickly in rank and became a high-level servant for the Sosa family. Despite gaining her freedom in 1624 upon the death of her master, she went on to become a servant for a Spanish priest named Padre Pedro Suárez. After becoming a servant, she was persuaded in 1627 to marry Domingo Suárez, one of Pedro Suárez's Chinese slaves. She refused to consummate the marital union, however, stating that her life was dedicated to Christ who was her true husband. This refusal launched her famous public religious life.

According to Catarina, she had received numerous religious visions of Christ, the Virgin Mary, and various saints. Her earliest vision occurred while she was a young slave in Manila. On that occasion, she claimed that she received consolation about the loss of her parents from an image of Jesus, which passed by her during a religious street procession. In the vision, she was told that Jesus would take care of her from that point on and be her father. Catarina also asserted that the Virgin Mary had helped her mother to miraculously conceive and that the Virgin had made special prophecies about the special plans for Catarina's life. As a final sign of her unique religious calling, she claimed that she had received a Christ-like piercing on her side while she was a slave on the Manila Galleon that had brought her to Mexico. Finally, Catarina was also famous for her apparent abilities to heal the sick.

Despite her religious celebrity, the petition for Catarina's beatification was denied by Catholic officials. These officials further ordered, moreover, that all portraits and biographies of "*La China Poblana*" were to be destroyed. Four hundred years later, Mirrha-Catarina remains a deeply revered religious figure in Mexico.

Beyond her religious acclaim, "*la China Poblana*" is perhaps most famous for her centuries-long impact upon Mexican fashion. According to legend, she was the originator of "*la China Poblana*," the national costume of Mexico. As the story goes, upon her death, the native women of Puebla felt it befitting to bury Catarina in an elegant skirt, blouse, and shawl from her native India. They chose this special attire, instead of her humble nun's outfit, because of the significance of the occasion—she was at last going to meet her true husband, Jesus Christ. By sporting this outfit at her burial, Catarina became the first "*China Poblana*" (Chinese woman from Puebla), and she allegedly inaugurated a fashion trend which has survived into the twenty-first century.

Today, "*la China Poblana*" is considered the national dress of Mexico. The outfit consists of several items of clothing: (i) a shiny embroidered white blouse with colorful silk and beads arranged in floral designs; (ii) a castor skirt with sequins and beads; (iii) a white slip with zig-zagged lacework; and (iv) a silk shawl. The *China Poblana*

Representation of a *china poblana* wearing traditional clothing. The *china poblana* has evolved into an archetype of Mexican womanhood. (Arturo Osorno/Dreams time.com)

dress is commonly worn at Mexican cultural events and also by those seeking to express a sense of Mexican cultural nationalism.

As evidenced by the story of the *China Poblana*, the Manila Galleon Trade led not only to the migration of tens of thousands of Asian immigrants to Mexico, but also to a wide range of unique Asian cultural contributions. These contributions include clothing, food, and other types of cultural products, and they have become such integral parts of Chicano/Latino culture that most people have forgotten about their Asian origins.

Clothing

The *guayabera* shirt represents another type of Chicano/Latino clothing, which, according to some accounts, has its origins in Asia. Also known as a "Mexican Wedding Shirt," the *guayabera* is a men's shirt, which is popular in Cuba, Puerto Rico, the Philippines, Samoa, and even Zimbabwe, Africa. The shirt is often made of linen and has a number of distinguishing characteristics. It features two or four patch pockets and two vertical rows of fine, tiny pleats on the front and back of the shirt. Some styles also have three-inch slits and two or three adjusting buttons on the bottom of the shirt. *Guayaberas* traditionally come in white or pastel colors, but are now available in many colors.

The geographic origins of the *guayabera* are disputed. One theory states that the precursor to the modern *guayabera* shirt was brought to Mexico from the Philippines as part of the Manila Galleon trade. According to this explanation, this prototype to the modern *guayabera* originated on the island of Luzon before the advent of the Spanish colonization of the Philippines. It was longer than the present-day *guayabera*, reaching just below the waist, and was also translucent in color. This theory asserts, moreover, that this style of shirt was called *Filipina* during the Mexican colonial period, and that it spread from Mexico to other parts of Latin America and eventually became what we now call the *guayabera*. Other theories trace the origins of the *guayabera* to immigrant Spaniards living in Cuba in the early eighteenth century. Despite the competing theories about the origin of the *guayabera*, it is likely that the *Filipina* served as an influential prototype for the modern-day *guayabera*.

Ceramic Art

Colonial Latin America was influenced by Asian culture not only in the area of fashion, but also with regards to ceramic art. Thousands of barrels of Chinese porcelain were exported to Mexico during the years of the Manila Galleon Trade. This blue and white porcelain was made in large quantities in the Kiangsi Province of China specifically for western consumption, and it was shipped to Europe, the British colonies, and Mexico. Chinese porcelain was highly coveted throughout the western world because European artisans did not understand how it was manufactured. Because of its uniqueness, Chinese porcelain became a status symbol for the rich and wealthy of Europe and the Americas.

Chinese porcelain was transported to Mexico via the Philippines as part of the Manila Galleon Trade. The first Chinese porcelain is recorded to have arrived in

Mexico in 1573. Chinese porcelain plates were ordered by high-ranking families and religious officials and often featured coats of arms and other monogram designs. Chinese porcelain became so popular in Mexico that it became "bootlegged" by Mexican artisans in Puebla.

In the mid-seventeenth century, Puebla was famous for exporting a style of ware known as *Talavera*. Although the roots of *Talavera* lie in the city of Talavera de la Reina in Spain, potters were brought to colonial Mexico to replicate the trade. In the late seventeenth century, Spanish artisans deliberately modified their *Talavera* designs to make them look more like the blue and white Chinese porcelain which was being imported to Mexico from China. In fact, guild regulations from Puebla in 1682 specifically admonished artisans to imitate Chinese style, color, and relief work when manufacturing their pottery. Since Puebla was home to a large population of Asian immigrants during this time, it is probable that Asians assisted in the manufacture of this bootlegged *Talavera* porcelain. *Talavera* pottery remains a popular export of Puebla to the present day. Few consumers of *Talavera*, however, are aware of the strong Asian influences which have shaped its design.

Food

The Manila Galleon Trade also introduced a wide variety of foods from Asia. Rice is one major example. It's hard to imagine that there ever was a time when Latino food dishes such as Spanish rice, *arroz con pollo* (rice with chicken), *arroz con leche* (rice with milk), and black beans and rice did not exist. All of these dishes, however, were made possible because rice was introduced to Latin America from Asia during the colonial period. Although considered a staple of Mexican and Latin American cuisine, rice was first introduced to Mexico from the Philippines. Rice was first brought to Veracruz, Mexico in the 1520s. Veracruz was chosen as an ideal place to raise this crop because its warm and wet climate resembled the rice-growing regions of Asia. *Chinos* of colonial Mexico were known to have farmed rice in Pacific Coast cities such as Acapulco, Coyuca, San Miguel, and Atoya. Around the same time that rice was introduced to Mexico, the Portuguese introduced Asian rice to the colony of Brazil.

Mango is another food product that is closely associated with Mexico and Latin America, but has its origins in Asia. Today, Mexico is the leading supplier of mangos to the world, and Mexican mangos are known as the gold standard for the industry. Unknown to most people, mangos were first brought to Mexico from the Philippines in the seventeenth century. Today, mango production is centered in places such as the Yucatan peninsula and the Pacific coast—two regions which were *chino* hubs during the colonial period.

Coconut is another food product that is commonly found in Mexican cuisine, but which has its roots in Asia. Coconuts are used in cakes, cookies, flan, and soups, and are even known to make their way into drinks such as rice-milk *horchata*. One important species of coconuts was introduced to the Pacific coast of Mexico from the Philippines. A second variety was introduced to the Atlantic coast from Cape Verde and Santo Domingo. In cities such as Acapulco, San Miguel, and Colima, *chinos* were known to grow coconut palm trees well into the eighteenth century.

Chino *Decline in Colonial Mexico*

A strange phenomenon occurred in Mexico in the mid 1700s—the term *chino* became "Africanized." The word stopped being a reference to persons of Asian descent and instead began to refer to a person who came from a mixture of African and Indigenous descent. In a strange turn of events, Asians came to disappear as a distinct social group in Mexican historical records during the late colonial period.

One explanation put forth by scholars is that *chinos* had largely intermarried with Africans and Indians by this time. As a result, they became blended into the large mixed-race population of colonial Mexico. This theory seems persuasive because it accounts for the declining numbers of Asians who migrated to New Spain after 1700. Small numbers of Asians came to Mexico after these years because *chino* slaves were emancipated in the late seventeenth century. With fewer numbers of new Asian immigrants in Mexico, it is likely that the existing Asian population intermarried in large numbers with other ethnic groups and therefore lost their unique cultural presence.

Today, the term *chino* is often used as a nickname for someone with curly hair. This terminology is consistent with the meaning of the term *chino*, which developed in the 1700s. Since the word at this time was used to refer to individuals of African ancestry (who likely had curly hair), it is possible that the term evolved over the centuries to refer to a person with curly hair.

The Chinese in Mexico, 1882–1940

Following the decline of the *chino* population of Mexico in the late eighteenth century, Asians ceased to make significant cultural contributions to Mexican society for about 100 years. Such Asian cultural contributions resumed in the late nineteenth century following the resurgence of Chinese migration to Mexico after the passage of the United States Chinese Exclusion Act of 1882. This law, and its later legislative extensions, barred the immigration of Chinese laborers to the United States until 1943. Following the passage of the Exclusion Laws, many Chinese turned to Mexico as a popular immigrant destination. They went to Mexico for two reasons: (i) to get smuggled into the United States in circumvention of the Chinese Exclusion Laws; and (ii) in search of jobs and other economic opportunities.

An estimated 60,000 Chinese immigrated to Mexico between the years of 1882 and 1940. By 1926, at a size of more than 24,000, the Chinese came to comprise the second largest immigrant group in all of Mexico, second only to Spaniards. By 1910, moreover, the Chinese were to be found in every state of Mexico except for the state of Tlaxcala. These Chinese immigrants made a profound impact upon Mexican folklore and society.

The First "Undocumented" Immigrants

Although undocumented immigration in the present day is often viewed as an issue primarily impacting the Latino community, it was the Chinese who "invented" undocumented immigration from Mexico. In resistance to the Chinese Exclusion

Laws of the United States, the Chinese created a vast, multinational smuggling network involving Mexico, Cuba, Canada, and various cities throughout the United States. They also invented many of the undocumented immigration methods and practices which continue to the present day. By creating the infrastructure for contemporary undocumented immigration from Mexico, the Chinese left an important mark upon Mexican culture and society.

The Chinese smuggling network was coordinated by a multinational Chinese fraternal organization headquartered in San Francisco known as the Chinese Six Companies. According to one common smuggling practice developed by the Six Companies, Chinese residents of the United States would make smuggling arrangements for family members in China by first contacting their local Six Companies representatives. The immigrant friend or relative would then be instructed to travel to a port city in China such as Hong Kong. After arriving in the port city, they would be prepared for life in the United States by being taught English and American cultural etiquette. After receiving this basic training, they would be transported by steamship to a Mexican port city such as Mazatlan, Manzanillo, or Guaymas. Chinese immigrants were met in Mexico by Six Company representatives who transported them to Mexican border cities like Nogales, Mexicali, or Tijuana. From these border towns Chinese immigrants were smuggled into the United States by a Mexican *coyote*, or guide, who led them across secretive terrain. This use of a *coyote* is still a common practice to this day.

Upon arrival in the United States, Chinese immigrants were given the false identities of other Chinese individuals who were legally entitled to be in the country. To verify their identities in court, some smuggled Chinese were given false immigration documentation. This method of using fake "papers" is still a common practice used by undocumented immigrants from Mexico today.

Employment in Mexico

In addition to going to Mexico to get smuggled into the United States, many Chinese immigrants went there in search of work. Chinese immigrants held a wide variety of jobs in Mexico, including agricultural laborers, day laborers, tailors, bakers, and merchants. These diverse immigrants left a deep impression upon native Mexicans and influenced Mexican folklore and culture in important ways.

The Legend of "El Chinero"

One dark Mexican legend tells the story of "*El Chinero*." In Baja California, about thirty miles north of San Felipe, is a hill called "*El Chinero*." This hill is named after 160 Chinese immigrant laborers who are said to have died there in the early twentieth century. Brought to Baja, California to work as laborers in Mexico, they were abandoned in the border town of San Felipe. Unfamiliar with the severe weather conditions of the area, they attempted to walk across the 125-mile desert to Mexicali. Tragically, all 160 individuals died in the desert. Today, the desert hill is named in their honor.

Merchants and the Anti-Chinese Campaigns

As with Chinese laborers and the legend of "*El Chinero*," the memory of Chinese immigrant merchants in Mexico is also marked with tragedy. In the case of Chinese merchants, however, such misfortune was deliberately inflicted upon them by native Mexicans.

By the 1920s, Chinese immigrant merchants were extremely successful and monopolized small-scale trade in northern Mexico. Much like 7–11 convenience stores today in the United States, Chinese grocery shops dotted the Mexican landscape and were to be found on virtually every street corner in places like Sonora and Chihuahua.

Racist Jokes, Music, and Cartoons

Chinese economic success unfortunately engendered strong resentment on the part of many Mexican merchants who could not compete. This economic jealousy led to much racism against the Chinese and the development of organized anti-Chinese campaigns. As an expression of anti-Chinese sentiment, racist jokes, music, and cartoons became common features of Mexican popular culture and folklore of the era.

Similar to U.S. "Polack" jokes of the twentieth century, which targeted Polish immigrants, Mexican jokes portrayed Chinese immigrants as bumbling idiots. The Chinese were also mocked because of their strong accents and poked fun of because they could not properly pronounce certain letters of the Spanish alphabet such as the letter "r." Another common stereotype was that Chinese men would try to seduce Mexican women by offering them gifts, money, and a carefree life.

Unfortunately, Chinese Mexican intermarriage was not always treated lightly or with a humorous attitude. Songs, poetry, and cartoons of the era ruthlessly portrayed such intermarriage as a shameful phenomenon which led to the production of degenerative offspring and the downfall of the Mexican race. Mexican women who married Chinese suitors were chastised as "dirty," "lazy," and "unpatriotic." Interracial marriages were shunned as marriages of convenience which allowed lazy Mexican women to avoid work because of financial support from their Asian husbands. Cartoons depicted Mexican women as imprisoned slaves who suffered abuse and neglect at the hands of their Chinese husbands. The offspring of Chinese Mexican unions, moreover, were disparagingly portrayed as freaks of nature who resembled aliens from another planet.

In addition to decrying Asian Latino intermarriage, cartoons of the era also criticized the Chinese for being public health threats. They showed Chinese businesses as unsanitary places where disease, dirt, animals, and grime contaminated the food and groceries, which were later sold to consumers. Other cartoons depicted the Chinese as violent criminals who shot people in the streets and sold drugs to native Mexicans.

Unfortunately, such racist attitudes gained official expression in Mexican law. Sonoran Chinese public health laws unfairly targeted Chinese business proprietors, and anti-miscegenation laws prohibited Chinese Mexican intermarriage under penalty of fine.

The Mexican anti-Chinese movement gained widespread popularity in part because anti-Chinese sentiment became intertwined with revolutionary national- ~ies of the Mexican Revolution was that foreign business the United States had overrun the Mexican economy. ~ese were also decried as culprits in the foreign eco-

of Mexico won its ultimate victory in 1931 when ~ulation of Sonora was expelled from the state. In ~ution of the 1920s and 1930s, most Chinese fled ~iority returned to China, some relocated to more Baja California, and a few went to the United ~ion of Mexico dwindled to a size of about 5,000.

The Chinese population of Mexico remains small to the present day. One estimate places their numbers at approximately 5,000–7,000. The largest Chinese immigrant community is found in Mexicali, Baja, California. A second, smaller Chinese population can be found in Mexico City.

Food

The Chinese of Mexico today have made their most visible cultural contributions through food. Mexicali is home to the largest "Chinatown" in Mexico and it boasts of having the most Chinese restaurants per capita in the country. Mexicali's 100

Dancers perform the dragon dance in celebration of Chinese New Year in Mexico City's Chinatown. (AP/Wide World Photos)

plus Chinese restaurants have achieved international celebrity for their fusion of Mexican flavors with traditional Cantonese cuisine. In an effort to cater to the mainstream Mexican population, these restaurants create spicier versions of classic Chinese dishes using ingredients such as chiltepín peppers. Unlike Chinese restaurants in other parts of the world, moreover, they offer bottles of Tabasco sauce and bowls of Mexican limes at every table. Fusion dishes include *camarón a la mariposa* (butterflied shrimp stuffed with bacon and spread with toasted almonds), *sopa agria picante pikinesa* (Beijing-style hot and sour soup), and, reminiscent of the colonial Manila Galleon Trade, *pato a la Filipina* (Filipino-style duck).

ROBERT CHAO ROMERO

See also: African Influence on Latino Folklore; Arroz con Leche (Rice Pudding)

Further Reading

Chu, Clara. "Asians in Latin America: A Selected Bibliography, 1990–2002." http://libres.uncg.edu/ir/uncg/listing.aspx?styp=ti&id=2116.

Kuwayama, George. *Chinese Ceramics in Colonial Mexico.* Honolulu: University of Hawaii Press, 1997.

Morse, Kitty. "Woks Across the Border." *Los Angeles Times*, October 19th, 1997. http://articles.latimes.com/1997/oct/19/travel/tr-44325.

Romero, Robert Chao. *The Chinese in Mexico, 1882–1940.* Tucson: University of Arizona Press, 2010.

Rustomji-Kerns, Roshni. "Mirrha-Catarina de San Juan: From India to New Spain." *Amerasia Journal* 28, no. 2 (2002): 29–36.

Schurz, William. *The Manila Galleon.* Boston: E. P. Dutton, 1959.

Slack, Edward. "The Chinos in New Spain: A Corrective Lens for a Distorted Image." *Journal of World History* 20, no. 1 (2009): 35–67.

AZTEC EMPIRE

The rapid rise, expansion, and collapse of the Aztec, or Mexica, Empire has perplexed generations of scholars who continue to grapple with a host of questions regarding those variables that fed this Mesoamerican imperial juggernaut. From their island capital of Mexico-Tenochtitlán, situated in the midst of a shallow lacustrine basin identified with Lake Texcoco in the Valley of Mexico, the Mexica launched scores of major wars that achieved the conquest and subjugation of all those ancient Mesoamerican kingdoms and towns that lay in the path of empire. The topographically challenging central Mexican highlands were as such the stage for the momentous exploits of a sizeable group of Chichimec nomads who swept into the basin from the north Mexican frontier in the period spanning the twelfth through fourteenth centuries. It was, however, the Mexica contingent of this tribal diaspora that ultimately sought and found the promised land in the prophesied appearance of an eagle perched atop a *nopal* or prickly pear cactus at the site that would become the legendary city of Tenochtitlán.

Founded on March 13th, 1325, the city of Tenochtitlán bore many of those characteristics defining the legendary Mexica or Aztec place of origin, otherwise

Templo Mayor ruins at Tenochtitlán. (Corel)

identified with the mystical island settlement of Aztlán, the Place of Whiteness or Place of Egrets (*Crónica Mexicáyotl*). Aztlán was purported to lie north of the Valley of Mexico, and by some accounts, some 150 leagues or 517.8 miles distant from the future *altepetl*, community kingdom or city-state, of Tenochtitlán. According to legend, and those accounts derived from the sixteenth-century *Codex Boturini*, the Mexica and other allied *Nahua*-speaking tribes departed *Chicomostoc*, or the Place of Seven Caves, in the twelfth century. *Chicomostoc* was the ancestral place of origin for the seven primary Chichimeca tribes from whom the Mexica derived prior to the epic migration that would see them through an initial settlement at Aztlán, and then south to the Basin of Mexico. The Mexica eventually settled at the site of Chapultepec, or Grasshopper Hill, in about 1248. Located atop a hill situated on the southern margins of Lake Texcoco, elevation 2,236 meters above sea level, the Mexica occupied Chapultepec until ousted from their newfound homeland by the Tepanec kingdom of Azcapotzalco after an occupation spanning some twenty years. Forced to settle on the margins of the lake near the barren plains of Tizapan in 1299, the Mexica established themselves in 1325, selected the Lord Acamapichtli as their first *huey Tlatoani*, or great speaker, in 1375; and subsequently capitulated to the powers that be by way of their assignment to a tributary status as a vassal of Azcapotzalco to the northwest. Shortly thereafter, the earliest monuments identified with the *Templo Mayor* were erected.

By 1427, the plight of the Mexica would all change with the formation of an alliance by the Mexican *huey Tlatoani* or great speaker Itzcoatl (1427–1440) and the Acolhua Lord Netzahualcoyotl of Texcoco, who sought to fend off the impending aggression of Maxtla, the Tepanec warlord of Azcapotzalco. The son of the bellicose tyrant Tezozomoc, Maxtla was responsible for the assassination of the Mexica *huey Tlatoani* Chimalpopoca in 1426, as well as a host of aggressions against the Acolhua Lord of Texcoco. The Mexica-Acolhua alliance and engagement with the Tepanec thereby resulted in the death of Maxtla at the hands of Netzahualcoyotl, the utter annihilation of the former *altepetl* of Azcapotzalco and the destruction of its grandiose civic-ceremonial precinct, and the slaughter of the entirety of the Tepanec royal house by the Mexica and Acolhua forces led by Itzcoatl and Netzahualcoyotl. This decisive battle set the stage for a rapid succession of Mexica victories against their former Tepanec and Culhua overlords.

Tenochtitlán subsequently entered into a "Triple Alliance" with Texcoco and Tlacopán during the *Xochiyayotl* or "Flowery War" against Tlaxcala and Huexotzingo. Such wars, though long touted as ritualized combat, had as their prime motivation the wholesale encirclement and subjugation of the Tlaxcaltecan insurgency, as well as the corollary extraction of labor tribute, slaves, and *Ixiptla* (or deity impersonators) destined for the sacrificial altars of Tenochtitlán and allied communities. Through the course of Tenochtitlán's long history of attempts to vanquish the intractable Tlaxcalteca, the Mexica escalated the consequences of resisting the empire; and this proved catastrophic to Aztec attempts at vanquishing the Tarascan, or *Michhuacan*, Empire to the west. In this latter instance, the Mexica and their allies are purported to have suffered some 20,000 to 40,000 war dead in a single campaign. Thereafter, the Mexica retrofitted and manned the ancient fortress of Oztuma or Oztoman with the intent of keeping the Tarascan Empire and its bronze weaponry at bay indefinitely.

Where tribute collection was concerned, Tenochtitlán, Texcoco, and Tlacopan maintained a tribute ratio of 2:2:1, with Tenochtitlán and Texcoco sharing equally in the bounty of empire, and Tlacopán drawing but half of that tribute collected by either of its other alliance partners. According to such sixteenth-century accounts as the *Codex Mendoza*, some 2,000,000 cotton cloaks, battle uniforms, feathered headdresses, shields, and quantities of amber for incense were collected from tributaries on an annual basis. In addition, Tenochtitlán was the annual recipient of some 7,000 tons of maize, and 4,000 tons each of chia seeds, beans, and amaranth. To this should be added jaguar pelts, quetzal feathers, and cacao. Both cacao and copper axes served as a Mesoamerican form of currency, with the bulk of cacao, jaguar pelts, and quetzal feathers originating in the Aztec imperial province of Soconochco or Soconusco, located some 800 kilometers (as the crow flies) southeast of Tenochtitlán.

In addition to those immediate benefits that accrued from their hegemonic control of trade and tribute within the empire, the Mexica proved the ultimate beneficiaries of that body of science, technology, and medicine that sustained Mesoamerica more generally. Aztec medicine was as such a prime beneficiary, particularly in so far as battlefield medicine was concerned. In this latter regard, contact-era Spanish and other Europeans were awed by the medical practices, procedures, and innovations of early-sixteenth-century Aztec surgeons, who it is said could bind fractured bones through the insertion of an intramedullary nail or tie rod, or treat open wounds by way of stitches crafted from human hair. An abundant reservoir of acquired knowledge and legend was therefore available to Mexica nobles, scribes, warriors, midwives, teachers, priests, and poets; and where the arts were concerned, Mexi-- artisans excelled at extolling the virtues of life, death, and war.

Each successive ruling
to grow the empire by
ameliorate perceive
catl (1469–1481)
Tlatoani, or g
emperor A
Mexica
ident'
thr

generally.

In the years anticipating 1487, Anuitzotl the huey Teocalli, or great or divine God House devoted to the worship of Tlaloc, the earth lord or rain deity, and Huitzilopochtli, the preeminent Mexica avatar identified with both the sun and cosmic war. The Templo Mayor as such was dedicated to commemorating the War of Heaven by which the sun was replenished and restored with the excised hearts and blood of fallen warriors and Ixiptla deity impersonators and war captives. Although scholars continue to debate the total number of sacrificial captives sent to their deaths over the course of a four-day ceremony devoted to blood tribute and human heart excision commemorating the expansion and retrofit of the Templo Mayor of Tenochtitlán by the emperor Ahuitzotl, Aztec accounts inscribed in the Codice Telleriano Remensis indicate that some 20,800 captives were dispatched during the blood fest in question. The political dimensions of such a ritual exercise conducted on such a massive scale is made apparent by the fact that nobles from tributary provinces were explicitly invited to witness the spectacle firsthand, and were clearly awed and intimidated by the specter of such carnage.

Coincident with the expansion of the Mexica Empire were the growing demands for blood tribute, and thereby, the deployment of a host of technologies of terror inspired by both religious and political protocols and necessities. Such devices included the 60-meter-long huey Tzompantli, or great or divine Skull Rack or Skull Wall, of Tenochtitlán, purported to have held some 80,000 decapitated human heads in varying states of decomposition at the time of the Spanish entrada. Accordingly, the sixteenth-century Franciscan friar Bernardino de Sahagún noted that the huey Tzompantli in question was the largest of seven such macabre lattice-like structures situated within the main civic ceremonial precinct of Tenochtitlán. In addition to its monumental size, the huey Tzompantli maintained a commanding presence in the immediate forecourt of the huey Teocalli or Templo Mayor of that great city; and did so adjacent to the huey Teotlachco or great or Holy Ballcourt, which was in turn identified with blood tribute and human sacrifice. The mass immolation of war captives in 1487, and related facts pertaining to monuments regarding so dramatic an episode of ritualized excess, have been interpreted by some to exemplify a defining characteristic of the Mexica polity; mainly, the escalating demand for conquest victories and war captives, ritual theater on a massive scale, and ultimately, the celebration of Tenochtitlán's growing imperial power and authority.

Rubén G. Mendoza and Cristina Verdugo

See also: Aztlán; Cihuacóatl; Coatlicue; Greater Mexico and Its Folklore; Huitzilopochtli; Malinche; Quetzalcóatl; Tezcatlipoca; Tonantzin; Tonantzin in Chicana Literature and Art; Virgin of Guadalupe: History and Fiestas Guadalupanas

Further Reading

Aguilar-Moreno, Manuel. *Handbook to Life in the Aztec World.* New York: Oxford University Press, 2006.

Berdan, Frances F., and Patricia Rieff Anawalt. *Codex Mendoza.* 4 vols. Los Angeles: University of California Press, 1992.

Conrad, Geoffrey W., and Arthur A. Demarest. *Religion and Empire: The Dynamics of Aztec and Inca Expansionism.* Cambridge: Cambridge University Press, 1984.

Díaz del Castillo, Bernal. *The Conquest of New Spain.* Trans. J. M. Cohen. London: Penguin Books, 1963.

Durán, Fray Diego. *The History of the Indies of New Spain.* Trans., annotated, and with an introduction by Doris Heyden. Norman: University of Oklahoma Press, 1994.

Mendoza, Rubén G. "Aztec Militarism and Blood Sacrifice: The Archaeology and Ideology of Ritual Violence." In Richard J. Chacón and Rubén G. Mendoza, eds. *Latin American Indigenous Warfare and Ritual Violence*, 34–54. Tucson: University of Arizona Press, 2007.

Mendoza, Rubén G. "The Divine Gourd Tree: Tzompantli Skull Racks, Decapitation Rituals, and Human Trophies in Ancient Mesoamerica." In Richard Chacón and David Dye, eds. *The Taking and Displaying of Human Trophies by Amerindians*, 400–443. New York: Springer Press, 2007.

Ortiz de Montellano, Bernard R. *Aztec Medicine, Health, and Nutrition.* New Brunswick, NJ: Rutgers University Press, 1990.

Sahagún, Fray Bernardino. *Florentine Codex: General History of the Things of New Spain.* 12 vols. Trans. Arthur J. O. Anderson and Charles E. Dibble. Santa Fe: School of American Research and the University of Utah, 1951–1969.

Townsend, Richard. *The Aztecs.* New York: Thames and Hudson, 2000.

AZTLÁN

Aztlán was the primordial home of the Nahua peoples, where the Indigenous group traditionally is believed to have resided more than a thousand years ago. The Nahuatl word *Azteca* means, in fact, "people from Aztlán." In the 1960s and 1970s, during the Chicano Movement, Aztlán was claimed as the Chicano homeland. Today, Aztlán remains a powerful symbol of nationalism, unity, creativity, and self-definition for the Mexican American community.

Comparable to the mythological Atlantis, the existence of Aztlán has been the object of numerous investigations, yet its specific geographic location remains in the realm of speculation to this day. Aztlán might have been north of the Gulf of California in what is today the Southwest of the United States, and includes a variety of states that reach as far north as Colorado. According to the myth, in 1168, the Nahua people left Aztlán to follow a divine call. The Aztec god of war, Huitzilopochtli, guided them south and, in 1325, they founded Tenochtitlán, today Mexico City. The myth of Aztlán leaves many questions unanswered as historical sources are unable to provide satisfactory evidence or contradict each other. In fact, if Aztlán was a paradisiacal place where the Nahua peoples lived peacefully, as stated in the *Códice Ramírez* written in 902, it is not clear why they decided to leave. However, whether or not Aztlán actually existed, scholars agree that the Aztecs migrated into central Mexico from the north.

During the 1969 National Chicano Youth Liberation Conference in Denver, Colorado, in concomitance with the rising Chicano Movement in the United States, a group of young Chicano intellectuals produced the groundbreaking document *El Plan Espiritual de Aztlán* (The Spiritual Plan of Aztlán). The declaration, which emphasized self-determination and nationalism, brought to light a broad spectrum of issues that plagued the Chicano community: discrimination, economic exploitation, the need for education, land dispossession, and the threat of assimilation. Most importantly, despite emanating from an educated male minority, the plan reflected an awareness within the Mexican American community at large and represented the starting point for the recovery of a common history and the definition of a Chicano identity. Myth, in this case, functioned as a powerful cohesive force.

As its title suggests, the Plan, along with its political implications, also promoted a spiritual renaissance: Chicanos/as had to learn about the past to understand and confront the struggles of the present. Chicano intellectuals involved in the creation of the document, such as novelist and activist Oscar Zeta Acosta and poet Alurista, felt the urge to "decolonize" Mexican American history shadowed by centuries of both Spanish and Anglo domination. Like other minorities in the United States, Chicanos/as recognized that they had to explore their past outside of American textbooks and colonial discourses because, until that moment, the important contributions that Chicanos/as had made to North American history and culture had been neglected. *El Plan Espiritual de Aztlán* attempted to create discourses and images that could endow Chicanos with self-esteem and pride. The significance of Aztlán, in fact, lies also in the recovery and valorization of a Chicano Indigenous identity. Chicanos/as found in the Aztecs and, to a smaller extent, in the Mayas, a highly civilized culture that flourished prior to the foundation of the United States and whose military, artistic, and architectural achievements surpassed those of other Mesoamerican civilizations.

The identification of Aztlán as the Chicano homeland during the Chicano Movement implied also a reconceptualization of the North American territory. In considering the Southwest of the United States as the occupied northern part of Aztlán and of Mexico, Chicanos/as redefined the U.S.-Mexican border as an unnatural boundary separating a land and a people who historically and culturally belong together. Hence, the postulation of the existence of a Chicano "nation" must be understood in the larger realm of a North American geography of displacement and in the context of American domination: colonization and imperialism have disrupted the natural connection between place and people, and have imposed upon Chicanos/as and Mexicans an illegitimate boundary.

While the search for the geographical Aztlán keeps engaging historians, for the Chicano community, its importance transcends a concrete geographical location. Aztlán is a *real place* in the Chicano collective imagination. More than in political achievements, the legacy of Aztlán found resonance in the burst of creativity that has led to a vast artistic production after the creation of *El Plan*. In light of the fact that writers were mainly responsible for its adoption, it comes as no surprise that the myth of Aztlán was particularly significant for the arts. In fact, a boom of publications referring to the mythological Chicano homeland and elaborating upon a Chicano Indigenous identity followed the creation of *El Plan*. The first issue of *Aztlán*, the journal of Chicano studies, published by the Chicano Studies Research Center at the University of California, Los Angeles, appeared as early as 1970 and today continues to be one of the most prestigious publications covering almost exclusively Chicano topics.

During the Chicano Movement, poets and writers assumed the symbolic role of older, wiser leaders and acted as guardians of culture. They also adapted specific pre-Columbian stories and myths to connect them to a contemporary reality, make them accessible to the Chicano masses, or use them to re-interpret the position of the Chicano community within the United States territory. For instance, the playwright Luis Valdez, founder of the Teatro Campesino, adopted Indigenous myths and symbols in various works, such as *Bernabé* and *Pensamiento Serpentino*. Several Chicano writers wrote about the myth of Aztlán as a story able to move the masses and lead to political mobilization. For instance, Rudolfo Anaya's novel *Heart of Aztlán*, published in 1976, brings together Chicano struggles for equality and the Chicano reliance on Indigenous myths for political inspiration.

A crucial revision of Aztlán and Chicano Indigenous identity has come from female writers who felt excluded by the "Aztlanian Dream." Chicanas lamented that the Chicano Movement neglected their concerns and constructed an oppositional Chicana voice in their literature. As a response to Chicano machismo, many Chicanas reinterpreted pre-Columbian myths in a feminist light and de-romaticized Indigenous history by exposing those aspects of the Aztec and Mayan cultures that oppressed women. Gloria Anzaldúa and Cherríe Moraga, particularly, revaluated the significance of Aztlán from a lesbian-feminist perspective. Cherríe Moraga condemned the ideology of Aztlán for having served only the empowerment of male heterosexuals. Gloria Anzaldúa in her masterpiece *Borderlands/La Frontera: The New Mestiza*, first published in 1987, rewrote specific pre-Columbian narratives to challenge the dichotomy mother/whore that Mexican and Chicano societies have imposed upon women.

Today Aztlán continues to live in Chicano and Chicana literary works, theatrical productions, barrio folklore, murals, student organizations, publications, paintings, performance art, and much more. The focus, thus, cannot be on the historicity of Aztlán, but must be placed on its undeniable influence as a cultural symbol and on its enormous relevance for Chicano/a self-definition and creativity. During the Chicano Movement, for Chicanos/as, a people without a nation, Aztlán became a means of empowerment, a way of resisting hegemonic cultural forms and North American assimilation policies. It represented the Chicano intellectuals' attempt to emerge from the American "melting-pot" of Greek, Latin, and Manifest Destiny mythologies, to conceptualize an individual cultural and historical legacy, and to find a distinct Chicano voice.

MARZIA MILAZZO

See also: Aztec Empire; Cihuacóatl; Coatlicue; Greater Mexico and Its Folklore; Huitzilopochtli; Malinche; Quetzalcóatl; Tezcatlipoca; Tonantzin; Tonantzin in Chicana Literature and Art; Virgin of Guadalupe: History and Fiestas Guadalupanas

Further Reading

Anaya, Rudolfo, and Francisco Lomelí, eds. *Aztlán. Essays on the Chicano Homeland.* Albuquerque: Academia; El Norte, 1989.

Anzaldúa, Gloria. *Borderlands/La Frontera: The New Mestiza.* 2nd ed. San Francisco: Aunt Lute, 1999.

Huerta, Jorge. "Mythos or *mitos*: The Roots of a Chicano Mythology." In *Chicano Drama: Performance, Society and Myth*, 15–55. Cambridge: Cambridge University Press, 2000.

Leal, Luis. *No Longer Voiceless.* San Diego: Marin, 1994.

Moraga, Cherríe. "Queer Aztlán: The Re-formation of the Chicano Tribe." In Yolanda Broyles-González, ed. *Re-emerging Native Women of the Americas: Native Chicana Latina Women's Studies*, 236–253. Dubuque, IA: Kendall, 2001.

Pérez-Torres, Rafael. "Refiguring Aztlán." *Aztlán* 22.2 (1997): 15–41.

Smith, Michael. *The Aztecs.* Oxford: Blackwell, 1996.

B

BACHATA

Bachata is a music that originated in the Dominican Republic around the 1960s and has now become a well-known genre among followers of Latin American music. It combines characteristics of guitar-based music found all over Latin America with Afro-Caribbean elements. Though currently popular and accepted across social classes in the Dominican Republic and elsewhere, in its infancy as a genre, the listening public of *bachata* was limited to the rural and urban poor, considered a rudimentary musical form practiced by unskilled musicians with the basic instruments available to them. *Bachata* emerged as primarily live music played at parties, but eventually spread to the informal market through street-based music vendors, eventually gaining in popularity such that record labels signed *bachata* acts, and albums appeared in mainstream record stores and entertainment venues in the Dominican Republic and other Spanish-speaking music markets, particularly in Latin America and the United States in the 1990s. Given patterns of Dominican migration, especially to the United States and Puerto Rico, as well as its popularity among youth who have experimented and fused it with other genres such as *reggaetón*, *bachata* continues to gain popularity.

In the 1960s, mass migrations from rural regions to cities in the Dominican Republic, particularly Santo Domingo, resulted in the increased presence of rural traditions, including music, in the Dominican Republic's capital and largest city. One such tradition found in shanty towns built on the fringes of the city by arriving rural migrants is a type of social gathering featuring music led by guitar trios or quartets singing songs of romantic despair sometimes termed *música de amargue* (music of bitterness) and later *bachata*. As the genre spread throughout the Dominican Republic in the 1970s and 1980s, the term *bachata* became associated with this music, since *bachata* was the term used to describe the social gatherings where the music was played. One theory of the origin of the word *bachata* is that it is derived from the African words *cumbancha* and *cumbanchata*, meaning party or spree, shortened in Spanish to *bachata* or *bacha*. Due to the stigma attached to these gatherings and their music by upper-class Dominicans, some early practitioners have rejected the term *bachata* in deference to *música de amargue*. It is important to note that the name *bachata* did not come from the genre's marginalized practitioners as a form of solidarity, but rather from the wealthy Dominican class that maligned the music and its musicians. With the passage of time and shifts in popular music, *bachata* became a more accepted term for the music, though still associated with poverty.

The lyrical and instrumental styles of *bachata* belie its roots in rural and urban poverty. As a genre it incorporates a wide range of musical styles from the rhythmically slower, acoustic guitar-based Cuban *bolero*, which came to be known as *música de amargue* (music of bitterness), to faster rhythms featuring electric guitars and other technological elements referred to as *tecno-bachata*. Since its beginnings, the themes of romantic despair of *música de amargue* have been delivered via a raw and highly emotional voice style often compared to the lyrical style of Mexican *rancheras* and *corridos* narrating primarily romantic woes, but sometimes social commentary against racism and corruption. The equally raw guitar-driven music evolved from a pan–Latin American genre referred to as *música de guitarra* (guitar music), especially the traditional Cuban *bolero*, a genre depicting similar themes of romance and pain. *Bachata* ensembles typically combine string instruments—most commonly guitar though others such as the requinto are also used—with percussion instruments such as bongo drums, *claves* (wooden sticks slapped together) or gourd güiro scrapers. In addition to the Cuban *bolero*, other genres which have influenced *bachata* include: Cuban *son*, *guaracha*, and *guajira*, Puerto Rican *plena* and *jíbaro*, Colombian-Ecuadorean *vals campesino* and *pasillo*, as well as Dominican merengue, which was originally guitar-based.

From these origins, bachata has developed and changed in significant ways. As successive generations play the music, they have sped up its rhythm. The lyrical and vocal style has become bawdier. In addition to the vocally tight and extremely emotional call and response vocals of *amargue*, humorous and double entendre themes are more and more common as *bachata* evolves. Now that the rhythm is faster, *bachata* has evolved from a sing-along form of music to a danceable genre more visible in clubs. Perhaps the single most important innovation to *bachata's* sound has been the addition of technological instrumentation such as electric guitars, resulting in a genre termed *tecno-bachata*. One critical event in the Dominican music industry facilitated, if not outright legitimized *bachata* as mainstream, as opposed to marginal music of the poor. In 1990, Juan Luis Guerra, an immensely popular Dominican merengue star, decided to explore the relatively marginalized genre on his album *Bachata Rosa*. His international fame and identity as a middle-class musician associated with merengue, considered to be the Dominican national music, trained in a Dominican music conservatory, lent an air of respectability to the genre thus allowing for successive *bachata* performers to enter the mainstream Dominican and international Spanish language music markets.

JENNIFER DOMINO RUDOLPH

See also: African Influence on Latino Folklore; Afro-Colombian Music; Cuban Americans and Their Folklore; Folk Instruments; Puerto Rico and Its Folklore

Further Reading

Hernández, Deborah Pacini. *Bachata: A Social History of a Dominican Popular Music.* Philadelphia: Temple University Press, 1995.

IASO World Soul. The History of Bachata. http://www.iasorecords.com/bachata.cfm.

National Geographic. Bachata Music. http://worldmusic.nationalgeographic.com/view/
    page.basic/genre/contentgenre/bachata_690.

BAEZ, JOAN CHANDOS (1941-)

Joan Chandos Baez is a popular folk singer and one of the first Latinas to be issued the American Civil Liberties Union's Earl Warren Award and the Gandhi Memorial International Foundation Award. Unafraid to alienate an audience, Baez has never stood on the sidelines of history. With an unrivaled soprano voice Baez has used her talent to not only warm the spirit of millions, but has created music that gave meaningful clarity and continuity to her tireless peace and civil rights efforts. In doing so, Baez became not only one of the leading folk singers of the 1960s, but a transnational inspirational figure. Folk music has a long history of conveying social concerns so Baez's personality and the era of protest created a perfect synergy.

The daughter of a physicist, Baez was born in Staten Island, New York, on January 9th, 1941, the middle daughter of Albert Vinicio and Joan Bridget. Both of Baez's parents were born abroad but raised in the United States. Baez's father was born in Mexico while her mother, a drama teacher, was from Scotland. Baez's parents met at a college dance at Drew University in New Jersey. From this chance encounter, affection manifested into love and the two were married a year later. This bicultural family with a strong adherence to Quaker views and values encouraged a nonviolent global outlook. Since both Baez's grandfathers were clergymen, the family's commitment to peace and prosperity only intensified. In turn, Baez embraced this belief as it served to guide and shape her life and music. As an adolescent, Baez was a bit disillusioned with school, and so struggled with academics. Several years later, Baez learned she was dyslexic and the condition naturally made reading and other school exercises challenging. Despite this difficulty, Baez had the courage to follow a dream, the willpower to overcome adversity, and the

Joan Baez, folk singer and political activist. (AP/Wide World Photos)

determination to never give up. While in high school, Baez began to fully appreciate her talent for art and music. In fact, many illustrations from a high school sketch pad reproduced in her autobiography *And a Voice to Sing With* reveal Baez's talent.

At first Baez shared ideas about music and her gifted voice with only an inner circle of friends. In short order, however, Baez became a member of both church and high school choirs, which helped create opportunities to perform at local establishments. When the Baez family moved to Boston to advance her father's university career, young Baez's singing skill set not only blossomed but gained greater exposure. Initially, Baez enrolled at Boston University's School of Drama, but left after only one semester to concentrate strictly on music. As folk singing underwent a revival throughout the country, Baez took full advantage of the Cambridge youth scene. By listening and learning from "folk musicians such as Bob Gibson, Baez, despite an untrained voice, began performing in coffeehouses.

Coffeehouses were just proliferating in the late 1950s and early 1960s, so Baez's timing could not have been better. Baez promptly became inseparable from her guitar, learning to play while mastering folk songs, ballads, and blues. By the age of 18, Baez was performing at large venues, including such events as the 1959 Newport Folk Festival in Rhode Island. A year later, Baez signed with Vanguard Records, a small folk-friendly label that turned out her first self-titled album. *Joan Baez*, a collection of thirteen traditional folk songs, was released in the winter of 1960. That same year, Baez held a solo concert in New York City's prestigious Carnegie Hall. By 1962, Baez released three albums, all of them becoming best sellers.

As a woman who was bestowed such monikers as the "Queen of Folk Music" and the "Godmother of Modern Folk," Baez infused folk music with timely human rights messages, thereby becoming an iconic voice for a generation. Baez lyrics seemed to soothe and sort people's growing disdain for American institutions. In important ways, folk music complemented the mood of young people during the unpredictable 1960s. It was a decade characterized by protests from all sorts of historically marginalized groups. Joan Baez reflected this political mood, surfacing as one of the best-known folk singers. Gracing the cover of *Time* magazine in 1962 only reinforced Baez's growing influence on both the folk music genre and larger societal issues. Baez became increasingly involved with the broader Civil Rights Movement, often showing solidarity by performing at historically African American universities in an effort to help racially desegregate southern college campuses. Troubled by the Vietnam War and the disproportionate casualty rate among Mexican Americans, Baez protested in a number of anti-war marches.

Baez not only sang at protests, but actually got involved with student and community agency efforts. Baez marched with Martin Luther King Jr. and joined California college students in occupying administration buildings. By supporting César Chávez, coupled with countless Latinos/as, she helped to compel leaders in the agricultural world to address issues of reasonable wages, humane work and living conditions, pesticide misuse, and overall responsible business practices. Although not directly associated with the Chicano Movement, Baez did embrace important aspects of the movement's spirit by supporting a loyalty and love for ethnic Mexican heritage. Baez asserts, "I've always thought brown is beautiful, and every chance I've had to get into the sun I've done so, because I like being brown" (Fariña 1969, 29).

By the late 1960s, Baez became a national embodiment of nonviolent means toward forging equality, and used platforms at music festivals like Woodstock, Newport, and Big Sur to share messages. These efforts galvanized Baez to create the Institute for the Study of Non-violence in 1965 and Humanities International in 1979. The Institute concentrated on teaching the philosophy of pacifism, whereas the organization promoted human rights, disarmament, and nonviolence. Baez also helped create Amnesty West, a branch of the human rights organization Amnesty International.

Baez fostered a deep passion for drawing attention to deplorable and disingenuous acts because of ostracizing experiences as a youth. Baez's Spanish surname and overall phenotype, which reflected her father's heritage, often were at odds with peers. Baez found it difficult to fit in with Anglos or ethnic Mexicans because possessing both Anglo and Mexican cultural characteristics was not appreciated. On one hand, Baez had olive skin, consistent with many Mexican Americans, but an inability to speak Spanish impeded efforts to build lasting friendships with other Latinos/as. Similarly, Anglo classmates rejected Baez often on the pretext that she was different. Like many, Baez felt trapped in a culture in which she belonged to two worlds. Baez belonged to a Mexican heritage as well as the Anglo world, but neither recognized the unique cultural capital. Experiencing this sense of exclusion, Baez was determined to help others avoid feelings of isolation and persecution. In the aforementioned autobiography, Baez also shares that she developed a heart and mind imbued with fervor for justice by living abroad. In Baghdad, for example, Baez saw up close the face of poverty and its unyielding impact on children. As a ten-year-old child, the nameless faces and places of poverty and despair profoundly resonated with Baez.

By 1965, folk music gave way to rock music led by such groups as the Beatles and Rolling Stones. Folk music was much quieter and much more contemplative than rock and roll. Even though Baez appreciated this, she began to alter the scope and significance of her folk music style. Baez recorded several albums with a country music flare and a handful of rock ballads. By expanding her repertoire from mostly folk music to more fast-paced contemporary rock songs, Baez understood how young people were evolving their music tastes to coincide with the changing times.

Through the 1970s, 1980s, and 1990s, Baez continued to sing at concerts and support numerous causes. At Baez's concerts, she ensured the crowd was racially diverse while insisting that ticket prices were reasonable. In 1985, Baez participated at the Live Aid concert in Philadelphia to raise money for relief victims of famine in Africa. Seven years later, Baez was nominated for a grammy award for best contemporary folk recording for the album *Play Me Backwards*. For fifty years, Baez has been active through words and works sharing a vision for a better world. By the mid 1980s, Baez collected a handful of honorary doctorate degrees from such universities as Antioch University and Rutgers University. Recording more than thirty albums, of which eight went gold, while trekking around the globe investigating human rights abuses, Baez has challenged conventional wisdom and redefined folk music forever. From protesting the Vietnam War—one of the longest and most unpopular wars in American history—to the ongoing "War on Terror," Baez as an activist, author, and entertainer has remained consistent with her commitment to nonviolence.

DARIUS V. ECHEVERRÍA

Further Reading

Baez, Joan. *And a Voice to Sing With: A Memoir*. New York: Summit Books, 1987.

Baez, Joan. *Daybreak*. New York: Avon Books, 1969.

Baez, Joan, and David Harris. *Coming Out*. New York: Pocket Books, 1987.

Fariña, Richard. *Long Time Coming and a Long Time Gone*. New York: Random House, 1969.

Hajdu, David. *Positively 4th Street: The Lives and Times of Joan Baez, Bob Dylan, Mini Baez Fariña and Richard Fariña*. New York: Farrar, Straus, and Giroux, 2001.

Lutzow, Nancy. The Joan Baez webpages, Joan C. Baez/Diamonds & Rust Productions. http://www.joanbaez.com/.

BAILANDO CON EL DIABLO (DANCING WITH THE DEVIL LEGENDS)

Bailando con el Diablo, or the legend of dancing with the devil, is a popular tale within the Mexican and Mexican American community told across south Texas, the Southwest, and Mexico. The basic kernel of the legend features a young woman disobeying her parents and attending a local dance in the community against their wishes. At the event, the most attractive, sharply dressed, and best dancer there asks the young woman to dance and they spend the entire night on the dance floor, until she realizes the man she is dancing with is the devil himself. Modified to fit contemporary times and specific locations, the legend is usually told by adults as a lesson to their children of the consequences of disobeying their parents.

An example of a more detailed version of the legend is the following: A young girl is anxious to attend a local dance in the community. Against her parents' wishes, she attends the dance on her own, without a chaperone, and notices a dapper, handsome man on the dance floor, who asks her to dance. They spend the entire night on the dance floor together, when suddenly the young girl looks down and notices there is something wrong with her partner's feet. In fact, the man she is dancing with doesn't have feet at all. Instead, the legend describes the man as having a donkey, rooster, or goat foot, as well as a tail. Upon realizing the man she is dancing with is not a man, but the devil himself, the young girl screams into the night. Some variations of the story have the devil rushing off and disappearing into thin air, the strong stench of sulfur, a scent associated with the devil, left behind. Other versions have the young girl severely burned, the imprint of a man's hand burned into her back, or in other cases, even dying upon uncovering her dance partner's true identity.

The legend of *Bailando con el Diablo* is usually told by parents or other adults to children, especially young girls, as a means of social control, a way to scare the young children into listening to and obeying their parents, as well as frightening them away from talking or dancing with strangers, specifically strange men. Some variations of the story put the dance around the same time as a religious holiday or event tied to the Catholic Church, such as Good Friday, and frame the appearance of the devil as a sign, cautioning young children on the dangers of straying from the practices of the church.

Other versions of the tale are framed as a warning toward young women, to not only teach that youth must obey authority, especially their parents, but to also enforce purity and chastity as a means of preserving the family name. In traditional Mexican culture, young girls were not allowed to attend dances or social functions without a chaperone, much less dance with a man who was not a family member. The legend of *Bailando con el Diablo* works to not only enforce parental authority and portray a tale of what happens when you disobey your parents, as well as the consequences of straying from the traditional practices of the Catholic Church, but also specifically warns young girls of the potential dangers of associating with strange men.

An interesting phenomenon with respect to the Dancing with the Devil legend is its appearance and resurgence at certain points in time. During the 1970s, with the beginning of the disco dancing fever, the legend surfaced along the U.S.-Mexico border with multiple variants appearing. It was particularly popular with young people who told the tale to each other. The reappearance of the legend seemed to coincide with the popularity of disco dancing and the hundreds of discotheques built along both sides of the U.S.-Mexico border. As the 1970s legends tell it, the devil began to appear at these new dancing places. These "disco" legends bore the same kernel as above. As the disco craze subsided by the late 1980s and early 1990s, so did the round of Dancing with the Devil legends. By the 1990s, the tales were no longer as popular as they had been in the 1970s (see Herrera-Sobek 1988).

SYLVIA MENDOZA

See also: El Diablo (The Devil); Folk Narratives: Folk Tales, Legends, and Jokes; Folk Tales

Further Reading

Castro, Rafaela G. *Chicano Folklore: A Guide to the Folktales, Traditions, Rituals and Religious Practices of Mexican Americans*. New York: Oxford University Press, 2001.

Herrera-Sobek, María. "The Devil in the Discotheque: A Semiotic Analysis of a Contemporary Legend." In Jillian Benner and Paul Smith, eds. *Monsters with Iron Teeth: Perspectives on Contemporary Legend*. Vol. 3. Sheffield, UK: Sheffield Academic Press, 1988.

Limón, José L. *Dancing with the Devil: Society and Cultural Poetics in Mexican-American South Texas*. Madison: University of Wisconsin Press, 1994.

Scholsser, S. E. "American Folklore." 1997. http://www.americanfolklore.net/folktales/tx3.html.

BAILES LATINOAMERICANOS

Baile folklórico, Spanish for "folk dance," is the term for the various traditional dances practiced by Latin American people in Mexico and Central and South America. The lives and dances of Latin American people are intertwined and expressed through a close relationship to folk music, and most often the dance and music share the same name. Latin American dancers use native and borrowed folk dance to express social and religious ritual, as well as political statements. The Indigenous dance forms were significantly influenced by European and Afro-European dance, primarily Hispanic forms, but also dances such as the waltz, the polka, and the mazurka. The relationship has extended in the other direction as fashionable dances, especially from Cuba and Brazil, have been integrated into mainstream popular dance in the twenty-first century. The dance forms such as samba, salsa, and cha-cha-chá are just a few examples of the popular dances performed by Latin Americans today that have their roots in folk traditions.

The *cumbia* of Colombia, the *bachata* and *merengue* of the Dominican Republic, and the romantic *marinera* dance of Peru are all instances of Latin American dances rooted in social ritual. The dancers often use props, such as a handkerchief, to link the male and female during a typical courtship ritual. Dances such as the *cumbia* exhibit African influences from slave populations brought to the area. Many of these rituals, including the popular conga in Cuba, were originally considered vulgar by the upper classes because they were danced by the slaves, rural populations, and/or lower classes.

European and African contact in Brazil and the Caribbean led to a distinct fusion of styles that combined local dance with immigrant forms. The country with the most visible and international influence of style, Cuba, exemplifies a dance expression manifest in a highly politicized atmosphere. Refugees from the Haitian revolution in the early nineteenth century popularized the *habanera*, which would later lead the way for dances such as the *rumba*, the *danzón*, and eventually the popular *son* in the twentieth century. These would all contribute to one of the most prominent Latin American dance styles today, the salsa. It is important to note the political origins of these dance forms, for often Latin American folk dance was born in response to the delicate political context caused by colonization of the various regions.

Much of the Mexican folkloric tradition has recently been preserved through groups such as Amalia Hernández's Ballet Folklórico de Mexico. Ensembles have appeared in many regions with an intent to perform a wide-range of differing folk dances. In addition, the establishment of schools alongside these ensembles has allowed young people to continue in the folk dance tradition. This, however, is not the most common form of passing along folk traditions. Most often dancers learn a local form of dance through community festivals and competitions that exhibit the favorite dance(s) of the region.

Many folk dances that are similar in nature originate and are performed in different neighboring countries with slight variations in name or style. The *chacarera* is popular in Argentina, Bolivia, Paraguay, and Brazil; the *huayño*, a popular Andean region dance, and the *cueca,* the national dance of Chile, have strong influences in Peru, Bolivia, and Argentina as well. These dances are adopted by dancers in different regions and used to express the variances in cultural preference.

Latin American dancers have often used dance forms to mirror the political unrest in the region. The *capoeira* of Brazil and the *calinda* practiced in the

Ballet Folklórico members dance in traditional costume. The troupe is Mexico's national dance company, performing dances that highlight Mexico's regions, history, and culture. (Corel)

Caribbean nations are two dance forms with roots in the martial arts. These more violent rituals were originally a form of resistance whose traditions have been preserved through the vessel of folk dance.

MICHELLE TIMMONS

See also: Bachata; Ballet Folklórico: Azteca; Ballet Folklórico: Jarabe Tapatío; Ballet Folklórico: Michoacán; Ballet Folklórico: San Luis Potosí; Ballet Folklórico: Tabasco; Ballet Folklórico: Tamaulipas; Ballet Folklórico: Veracruz; Merengue; Rumba (Rhumba); Tango

Further Reading

Tenenbaum, Barbara A., ed. *Encyclopedia of Latin American History and Culture*. New York: Charles Scribner's Sons, 1996.

"BALLAD OF GREGORIO CORTEZ"

The "Ballad of Gregorio Cortez" is more commonly known as *El Corrido de Gregorio Cortez*, a Mexican folk-ballad that chronicles the tumultuous and violent encounter that took place in 1901 between the Texas Rangers and a young Texas-Mexican, Gregorio Cortez. Accounts suggest Cortez was a rather ordinary Texas-Mexican, an agricultural laborer living with his family in Karnes County (located southeast of San Antonio), when on June 12th, 1901, he became a fugitive after killing the local sheriff (and former Texas Ranger), W. T. Morris, in self-defense. The incident occurred after Sheriff Morris, following a lead concerning horse thievery, arrived at Cortez's home to speak to both Gregorio and his brother, Romaldo, about their possible involvement in the affair. Morris was suspicious of Gregorio's recent trading of a mare with a neighboring Mexican, Andrés Villareal, though later investigation proved Cortez had legally acquired the mare. After the brothers denied allegations of thievery and a subsequent general misunderstanding, Morris shot and wounded Romaldo, fired upon Gregorio, and was himself then shot down and killed. Gregorio immediately fled, fearing Ranger retribution. It was these events that stirred the folk imagination of the Texas-Mexican community. Soon after, *corridistas*, *corrido* folksingers, turned to the traditional ballad form to speak of Cortez's story and artistically render his adventurous ride to freedom.

"Corrido, the Mexicans call their narrative folk songs, especially those of epic themes, taking the name from *correr*, which means 'to run' or 'to flow,' for the *corrido* tells us a story simply and swiftly, without embellishments," writes Américo Paredes, the late influential ballad scholar and folklorist (Paredes 1958, 3). Paredes' intellectual precursor, Vicente T. Mendoza, suggests the *corrido* has its origins in national Mexico, for ballads concerned with heroic proletarian struggles against the *Porfiriato* emerge roughly around 1875. However, Paredes contends the Texas-Mexico border region to be the birthplace of the *corrido*, writing that "conflict— cultural, economic, and physical—has been a way of life along the border between Mexico and the United States" (Paredes 1993, 19). His scholarship suggests that intercultural conflict has played a central role in shaping and engendering new meanings and expressive practices throughout "Greater Mexico." He argues the emergence of the heroic *corrido* of border conflict, as a popular cultural expression, is tied to the transformation of Texas-Mexican society in the mid–nineteenth century, a consequence of the Texas Revolution (1836), the Mexican-American War (1846–1848), and the signing of the Treaty of Guadalupe Hidalgo (1848). This social transformation explicitly involved the rise of both capitalist modernity and a new racial-class social order, as a largely Texas-Mexican ranching society was violently transformed by Anglo-controlled commercial farming interests by the early twentieth century.

Accordingly, the *corrido* emerges in the 1850s along the Texas-Mexico border region with a specific generation of folk singers and musicians. Before its time, Spanish *décimas* and *romances* were the order of the day in Mexico and along the border; thus anything collected before 1850 was not a *corrido*. The oldest border *corrido* known is *El Corrido de Kiansis*, which chronicles the first cattle drives from Texas to Kansas in the late 1860s. Thereafter, similar *corridos*, in addition to those concerned with border heroes, such as Juan Nepomuceno Cortina, Catarino Garza, and Gregorio Cortez, became commonplace. The *corrido* itself, as ballad form, exists as a series of quatrains, usually octosyllabic 4-line stanzas rhyming abcb. They are strung together to construct a narrative cast in everyday direct language detailing the events in question, usually marked by a formal opening and departure or *despedida*. From the 1930s on, the *corrido* has transcended its folk status and enjoyed a fair amount of commercial success. *El Corrido de Gregorio Cortez* remains one of the more popular *corridos* in the traditional corpus of nineteenth- and early-twentieth-century Greater Mexican border ballads, though it too has been recorded commercially.

> *En el condado del Carmen*
> *miren lo que ha sucedido:*
> *murió el Cherife Mayor,*
> *quedando Román herido.*

> In the county of El Carmen
> Look what has happened;
> The Major Sheriff died,
> Leaving Román badly wounded.

> *Otro día por la mañana*
> *cuando la gente llegó,*
> *unos a los otros dicen:*
> *"No saben quien lo mató."*

> The next day, in the morning,
> When people arrived,
> They said to one another:
> "It is not known who killed him."

> *Se anduvieron informando,*
> *como tres horas después*
> *supieron que el malhechor*
> *era Gregorio Cortez.*

> They went around asking questions
> About three hours afterward;
> They found that the wrongdoer
> Had been Gregorio Cortez.

> *Ya insortaron a Cortez*
> *por todito el estado,*
> *que vivo o muerto lo aprehendan*
> *porque a varios ha matado.*

> Now they have outlawed Cortez,
> Throughout the whole state;
> Let him be taken, dead or alive;
> He has killed several men.

Decía Gregorio Cortez
con su pistola en la mano:
—No siento haberlo matado,
al que siento es a mi hermano.

Then said Gregorio Cortez,
With his pistol in his hand,
"I don't regret that I killed him;
I regret my brother's death."

Decía Gregorio Cortez
con su alma muy encendida:
—No siento haberlo matado,
la defensa es permitida.

Then said Gregorio Cortez
And his soul was all aflame,
"I don't regret that I killed him;
A man must defend himself."
(*Corrido de Gregorio Cortez*, Variant A, Quatrains 1–6, in Paredes, 1958)

ALEX E. CHÁVEZ

See also: Corrido (Ballad); Décima; La Despedida (The Farewell); Paredes, Américo; Romance

Further Reading

Flores, Richard. "The *Corrido* and the Emergence of Texas-Mexican Social Identity." *Journal of American Folklore* 105 (1992): 166–182.

Herrera-Sobek, María. *The Mexican Corrido: A Feminist Analysis*. Bloomington: Indiana University Press, 1990.

Limón, José. *Mexican Ballads, Chicano Poems: History and Influence in Mexican-American Social Poetry*. Berkeley: University of California Press, 1992.

Limón, José. "Américo Paredes: Ballad Scholar (Phillips Barry Lecture, 2004)." *Journal of American Folklore* 120 (2007): 3–18.

Mendoza, Vicente T. *El Romance Español y el Corrido Mexicano: Estudio Comparativo*. Mexico City: Ediciones de la Universidad Nacional Autónoma de México, 1939.

Mendoza, Vicente T. *El Corrido Mexicano: Antología, Introducción y Notas*. Mexico City: Fondo de Cultura Económico, 1954.

Menéndez Pidal, Ramón. *Los Romances de América y Otros Estudios*. Buenos Aires: Espasa-Calpe, 1943.

Paredes, Américo. *With His Pistol in His Hand: A Border Ballad and Its Hero*. Austin: University of Texas Press, 1958.

Paredes, Américo. *A Texas-Mexican Cancionero: Folksongs of the Lower Border*. Urbana: University of Illinois Press, 1976.

Paredes, Américo. *Folklore and Culture on the Texas-Mexican Border*. Austin: Center for Mexican American Studies, University of Texas, 1993.

Reyes, Judith. *El Corrido: Presencia del Juglar en la Historia de México*. México: Universidad Autónoma de Chapingo, 1992.

Simmons, Merle E. *The Mexican Corrido as a Source for Interpretive Study of Modern Mexico, 1870–1950*. Bloomington: Indiana University Press, 1957.

BALLET FOLKLÓRICO: AZTECA

Mexico possesses a rich Indigenous culture and almost every state can boast having Indigenous peoples within its borders. Each Indigenous group has its own unique style of dance or dances and specific costumes for dancing. Present-day Mexico City, standing on the site of the Aztec capital, Tenochtitlán, is where Aztec dances are most frequently represented and performed today.

Although Tenochtitlán fell to the Spanish in 1521, many people in Mexico still speak Nahuatl, and these descendants of the Aztecs still perform Aztec dances for ceremonial occasions. The Aztecs took dancing seriously because it was a sacred ritual; they danced before warfare and they danced to honor their gods and goddesses. Although many Aztec rituals have been lost, many of their dances have survived and are still practiced by ballet *folklórico* dance groups in Mexico and in the American Southwest, especially California. The dance attire varies, but typically men wear a highly decorated loin cloth that covers the groin area and a cape, with a *sonaja* (rattle) in one hand and, at times, a feather in the other hand. Women wear a *huipil*, a long skirt slit open on the outer thighs, which falls down below their hips. They also carry the *sonaja* and feathers. The costumes are usually brightly colored and at times carry the image of the *Virgen de Guadalupe* (Holy Mother). This is because after the Spanish conquest, Catholicism was introduced to the Aztecs. However, some dancers (*concheros*) are trained from childhood to follow the old ways of the Aztec dancer. For example, the feathers worn on the headdress are traditional and represent each member of one's family. Before being placed in the headdress, the

Vicente Téllez, head dancer and drummer of the Tlacopán Aztec Fire Dancers, performs at Olvera Street in Los Angeles, California. (Marilyn Gould/Dreamstime.com)

feathers are blessed and a person gives thanks to God. The ankle bracelets worn on the feet are called *huesos de fraile*. All dancers wear a *penacho* (headdress), which is decorated with bright feathers and almost looks like a crown worn by royalty. Painting on the face is rarely done; when the face is painted it represents the warrior preparing for battle. On the rare occasions that men carry a bow, it indicates that the performers are not just dancers, but also the protectors of the deity being honored in the dance.

Aztec dances are usually performed for special occasions, such as Mexican Independence Day on September 16th or the birthday of the *Virgen de Guadalupe* on December 12th. Before each dance, a performer blows a conch while facing in turn each corner of the world (north, south, east, and west). This is done to call on the ancestors for permission to dance and for their protection. The dances are considered holy and are taken seriously, which is why there are no smiles on the faces of the performers. Incense is present at times to purify the area and welcome the gods. The *sonajas* used in the dance help call on the gods, as do the *huesos* (bones) on the ankles. Because the Aztecs had a deep respect for nature, steps are grounded and the gaze of the dancer shifts from the ground to the sky, acknowledging both the sky and the earth and giving thanks to all living things. The current dances not only honor the ancient deities, but also the Catholic God and saints. Dancing traditional Aztec dances takes great strength and agility, but is also a privilege. The dancers feel it is important to respect and carry on the traditions inherited from their ancestors.

ANA C. FLORES

See also: Aztec Empire; Bailes Latinoamericanos; Ballet Folklórico: Jarabe Tapatío; Ballet Folklórico: Michoacán; Ballet Folklórico: San Luis Potosí; Ballet Folklórico: Tabasco; Ballet Folklórico: Tamaulipas; Ballet Folklórico: Veracruz; September 16th (Mexican Independence Day); Virgin of Guadalupe: History and Fiestas Guadalupanas

Further Reading

Coe, Michael D., and Rex Koontz. *From the Olmecs to the Aztecs*. New York: Thames and Hudson, 2008.

Covarrubias, Luis. *Mexican Native Dances*. N.p.: Eugenio Fischgrund, 1979.

Grabsky, Phil. *Ancient Warriors: The Aztecs*. DVD. Discovery Channel. Phil Grabsky. 2008.

Huajuca, Gladis. Grupo *Folklórico* Nacional de Guadalajara, personal communication, September, 2006.

Johnston, Edith. *Regional Dances of Mexico*. Dallas, TX: Banks Upshaw and Co., 1935.

McFeaters, Bea. Mexico: The Other Melting Pot, Houston Institute for Culture. http://www .houstonculture.org/mexico/ballet.html.

Nájera-Rámírez, Olga, Norma E. Cantú, and Brenda Romero. *Dancing Across Borders: Danzas y Bailes Mexicanos*. Urbana and Chicago: University of Illinois Press, 2009.

Sedillo, Mela-B. *Mexican and New Mexican Folkdances*. 2nd ed. Albuquerque: University of New Mexico Press, 1937.

Segovia, Eloisa M., and Cindy Clayman Wesley. *Folklóricos Regionales de México: A Textbook of Mexican Folk Dances*. Colton, CA: C and E Prensa, 1975.

BALLET FOLKLÓRICO: JARABE TAPATÍO

The *Jarabe Tapatío*, or "Mexican Hat Dance" as it is most commonly referred to in English, is a traditional Mexican folk dance and musical piece that narrates the story of a courtship between a woman and a male suitor. It typically consists of a male and female couple (or multiple couples) performing a series of choreographed moves meant to imitate a flirtatious encounter that ends in a scene of love. Since its inception, the dance, and the musical composition that accompanies it, has become a significant symbol of Mexican culture and was proclaimed the country's "national dance" in 1924. In modern times, the *Jarabe Tapatío* is performed at various celebratory gatherings within Mexican culture, including *Cinco de Mayo* celebrations and family parties. The dance stands as a symbol of Mexican unity and independence. Because both the dance and the composition draw from various ethnic traditions, the *Jarabe Tapatío* is considered a unifying cultural element for Mexican culture.

While the origin of the dance's name is still disputed, certain linguists suggest that the name *Jarabe Tapatío* is a combination of a type of Spanish dance known as a *Jarabe* (a fluid or syrupy dance) and *Tapatío*, which denotes that an object or person is originally from Guadalajara, Jalisco. Yet another theory states that *Jarabe*, which stems from the Arabian word for a mixture of herbs (*Xarab*), is meant to represent the mixture of traditions present in both the dance and the accompanying music.

History

Jesús González Rubio, a professor of music, composed the musical piece during the 1800s. The composition is a mixture of various Mexican folk melodies performed in an up-tempo manner. The dance was choreographed by Felipa López at the end of the Mexican Revolution to celebrate the country's new-found independence. However, it was not until 1919, when famous Russian ballerina Anna Pavlova discovered and assimilated the dance into her repertoire, that the *Jarabe Tapatío* began to take on a new national reverence. Pavlova performed the dance during her global tour, which aided in it becoming a symbol of Mexican culture worldwide. Her stage performance of the dance was done *en pointe*, a classical ballet method that uses pointed shoes. The *Jarabe Tapatío*'s growing popularity led the secretary of education, José Vasconcelos, to declare it the "national dance" of Mexico. This proclamation led to the dance being spread nationwide as a symbol of national pride and cemented the *Jarabe Tapatío*'s place as a cornerstone of Mexican culture.

Choreography

While usually performed by two people, the *Jarabe Tapatío* can also be done with one person or in a large group. The dance recounts the story of a woman being pursued by a male suitor. The two partners dance around each other in a circular motion. At the beginning of the performance, the couple flirt with each other as the man attempts to impress the woman with his *machismo*. He stomps and taps his feet in rhythm to the music, otherwise known as *zapateado*, and makes other romantic gestures to his female partner. The woman meets these actions by twirling her dress and tapping her feet opposite from her partner's. When the man notices that his initial movements impress the woman, he erupts into a moment of celebration that displeases his partner. At this point, the female partner considers the man to be a *borracho*, or drunkard, and pushes him away. The man persists, however, and throws his hat to the ground. This step is where the English title "Mexican Hat Dance" is derived from. The woman bends over to retrieve the hat, which allows the man to kick his foot over her head, a symbolic gesture that the man has "conquered" her or won her affections. The newly enamored couple now begin to dance in unison in a military march referred to as a *diana*. The final step of the dance involves the man placing his hat in front of the two partners' faces as they engage in a passionate kiss (this kiss is either actually performed or merely acted out, depending on the dancers). While every performance of the *Jarabe Tapatío* involves this same basic storyline, there are various versions of the specific movements that each dancer executes.

Another more generalized and less elaborate version of the dance involves two partners who kick out their feet in rhythm to the *Jarabe Tapatío* melody while alternating each arm from being crossed across to the body to being placed upright in an almost "waving" position. On the fourth count, each partner claps their hands twice in rhythm to the music. When the music changes to the second part of the melody, the partners lock elbows and dance around in a circle. These steps continue as the speed of the music increases. The dance concludes with a celebratory shout of "olé."

Costumes

The costumes used within the *Jarabe Tapatío* are as culturally significant as the dance itself. The female partner wears a dress referred to as a *china poblana*, which was a garb typically worn by Mexican peasant women in the nineteenth century. The *china poblana* is commonly adorned with beads, silk, and colorful designs. The male dancer wears a *charro* suit, which is a three-piece suit most recognized as the traditional dress of musicians in *mariachi* bands. The *charro* is a black pants, jacket, and vest combo covered in silver buttons and embroidery; the suit also includes a *sombrero* that the man throws to the ground near the climax of the dance.

COLTON SAYLOR

See also: Bailes Latinoamericanos; Ballet Folklórico: Azteca; Ballet Folklórico: Michoacán; Ballet Folklórico: San Luis Potosí; Ballet Folklórico: Tabasco; Ballet Folklórico: Tamaulipas; Ballet Folklórico: Veracruz; Mariachi

Further Reading

Greathouse, Patricia. *Mariachi*. Layton, UT: Gibba Smith, 2009.

Hellier-Tinoco, Ruth. *Embodying Mexico: Tourism, Nationalism and Performance*. New York: Oxford University Press, 2011.

Nájera-Rámirez, Olga, Norma E. Cantú, and Brenda Romero. *Dancing across Borders: Danzas y Bailes Mexicanos*. Urbana and Chicago: University of Illinois Press, 2009.

Naylor, Frank. *Latin-Americana: A Selection of Famous Melodies and Rhythms*. Skokie, IL: Harry J. Bosworth Co., 1977.

BALLET FOLKLÓRICO: MICHOACÁN

The western Mexican state of Michoacán is bordered by the Pacific Ocean and crossed by the Sierra Madre del Sur Mountains, as well as the region known as Tierra Caliente. The diversity of the region is reflected in the beauty and variety of its dances. The dances and performances of the Lake Pátzcuaro area, for example, derive from the Indigenous culture of the region and exhibit strong religious influences.

The dances that are representative of the state of Michoacán are also performed elsewhere in Mexico and in the United States. Many characteristics typical of the dances can be traced to Spanish influences, though the dances are often a blending of European and Indigenous population culture, particularly that of the P'urhépecha, who originally inhabited the region. Many of the popular Michoacán dances also have some religious aspects.

General Costume Characteristics

The women's dance costume in Michoacán is mainly influenced by local Indigenous attire. A black or dark-colored skirt often goes underneath a colorful embroidered apron. A blouse of unbleached muslin with kimono-cut sleeves is also beautifully embroidered as well. A black or dark-colored *rebozo* (shawl) is usually draped over the head and shoulders. Sometimes a hat is worn over the *rebozo* to hold it; at other times, pins secure the fabric behind the ears. Women sport braided hair and wear huaraches or sandals.

Men wear a standard white muslin long-sleeved shirt and trousers. Like the women, their clothes are colorfully embroidered. Most men wear kerchiefs around their necks. Men also carry a sarape (a long blanket-like shawl) around their shoulders, holding it securely behind the back. Alternatively, a *gabán*/poncho can be used. Straw hats can also be worn. Typically, men wear hard-soled huaraches.

Women from Michoacán are depicted as shy, often avoiding eye contact with men. The skirt is often held out to the front with a slight bend forward. Men dance with their hands on their side, sporting a more relaxed posture in comparison to dancers in the neighboring state of Jalisco.

Music and Dances

The music is carried rhythmically by the *jarana* (a small guitar) and can be accompanied by a violin or small orchestra. The *zapateado*, a basic step in *folklórico* dance, uses the feet to emphasize the rhythm of the music. In Michoacán, most *zapateados* are danced using the whole bottom of the foot, rather than alternating between heels and toes.

Among the best-known Michoacán dances are the *Jarabe Michoacano*, the *Jarabe de la Botella*, the *Jarabillo de Tres*, and the *Las Canacuas*. The *La Costilla* is a good example of the couple's interaction that characterizes many Michoacán dances. The song for the dance represents the companionship between a man and a woman, hence the name "*costilla*" (rib). This is often a name that a man calls a woman, meaning that she is as close to him as his rib or in reference to the biblical story of Eve's creation from Adam's rib. Hats are placed six feet apart in a line and couples dance around the hats often using the *zapateado*.

La Danza de los Viejitos and *Los Moros* are two dances that diverge from the typical Michoacán style. The *Danza de los Viejitos* ("Dance of the Old Men" or "Dance of the Ancients") is one of the most well-known and widely performed dances in Michoacán. Arising from the area of Lake Pátzcuaro, this style is representative of pre-colonial performances. Also known as *Huehues* or *Huehuenches*, the song is supposed to represent the god Huehueteotl, who is often depicted as a smiling ancient man doubled-over under the weight of a large brazier.

The dance costumes are based on the outfit a typical male from Michoacán wears, with some added features. Colorful ribbons are attached to the top of the hat and allowed to fall off the sides. The mask carries the face of an old man, with white hair, and a wrinkled toothless grin. A cane is part of the costume with the added feature that the handle is often in the shape of a deer's head and can be adorned with flowers.

Mexican dancers in masks and ribboned hats wait to perform the *Danza de los Viejitos,* or Dance of the Old Men. (Dreamstime.com)

This dance requires great skill, agility, and endurance to control the exaggerated steps that imitate those of a frail elderly man. The dancers are usually bent forward and dance with their feet as well as their canes. The *Danza de los Viejitos* is often performed by four dancers, one of whom is the leader while the other three imitate him.

Another religious dance is the dance of the *Moros* (the Moors), but unlike the "Dance of the Old Men," the main influence behind *Los Moros* stems from the time of the Spanish conquest. Dancers wear a silk turban decorated with ribbons and beads. The silk extends over the face, leaving only the eyes visible. Dancers carry a cape (usually black) over the shoulders. The cape can be decorated to the dancers' wishes and often has silver fish, representative of the fish in Lake Pátzcuaro.

The dance is characterized by heel clicks, the use of a staff, and a particular step called the *Los Moros* step. The dancers often wear boots with spurs to help accentuate the rhythm of the music and define the heel clicks.

Tierra Caliente

The Tierra Caliente (hot country) is a sub-region of Michoacán that shares the Michoacán dance repertoire. The dance costumes from the Tierra Caliente area differ from the strongly influenced Indigenous ones in the rest of the state in that the women's outfit consists of a long skirt and blouse of the same color. In addition, dancers in the Tierra Caliente area use the Spanish dancing shoes typical in many *folklórico* dances instead of the huaraches or sandals that are typical of other parts of Michoacán.

With respect to music in the Tierra Caliente, a string orchestra often performs the music for the dancers. Especially important for musicians of the region is the use of the *arpa* or harp. "*El Relampago*" is an example of one of the dances from this region.

María Cristina Carrillo

See also: Bailes Latinoamericanos; Ballet Folklórico: Azteca; Ballet Folklórico: Jarabe Tapatío; Ballet Folklórico: San Luis Potosí; Ballet Folklórico: Tabasco; Ballet Folklórico: Tamaulipas; Ballet Folklórico: Veracruz

Further Reading

Covarrubias, Luis. *Mexican Native Dances.* Mexico: Eugenio Fischgrund, 1979.

Johnston, Edith. *Regional Dances of Mexico.* Dallas: Banks Upshaw and Co., 1935.

McFeaters, Bea. "Mexico: The Other Melting Pot," Houston Institute for Culture. http://www.houstonculture.org/mexico/ballet.html.

Nájera-Ramírez, Olga, Norma E. Cantú, and Brenda Romero. *Dancing Across Borders: Danzas y Bailes Mexicanos.* Urbana and Chicago: University of Illinois Press, 2009.

Sedillo, Mela-B. *Mexican and New Mexican Folkdances.* 2nd ed. Albuquerque: The University of New Mexico Press, 1937.

Segovia, Eloisa M., and Cindy Clayman Wesley. *Folklóricos Regionales de México: A Textbook of Mexican Folk Dances.* Colton, CA: C and E Prensa, 1975.

BALLET FOLKLÓRICO: SAN LUIS POTOSÍ

Known for its abundant mineral deposits and agricultural products, the state of San Luis Potosí is located in central Mexico. It is bordered on the north by Nuevo León and Coahuila; on the northeast by Tamaulipas; on the south by Hidalgo, Querétaro, and Guanajuato; on the southeast by Veracruz; on the southwest by Jalisco; and on the west by Zacatecas. The states surrounding San Luis Potosí exert an important influence on the style of its *folklórico* dancing. In particular, Veracruz and Guanajuato are important influences for San Luis Potosí's "grounded" (close to the ground) footwork style. The region where San Luis Potosí is located is called La Hauasteca and the dance style that it produces is called *huapango*. *Huapango* is a Náhuatl word meaning "over the platform," and is also used for the music that is played for this style of dancing.

Because *huapango* is popular all over the Hauasteca region, a specific type of scenery is used on the platform where the dancing takes place. The images displayed on the decorated dance platform are rustic and picturesque, and include pictures of houses surrounded by trees, hay, and structures made of tin. The *huapango* conveys a social gathering where hardworking men meet their potential wives by courting them throughout the dance. The *huapangos* should take place every eight days in an important town or village, or on a ranch. The musicians use instruments such as the *jarana*, violin, and guitars; singing is done in a falsetto style. The singers decide when the dancers switch positions, and set the beat and rhythm of the dance, while the dancers try to match their steps to the beat of the music. The social scene of a *huapango* is similar to a party or fiesta. A *huapango* fiesta is announced by the lighting of fireworks. The men proceed to the dance right after work, keeping their work clothes on. They have the look of men who have had a hard day's work and their attire shows it. The women display a more innocent air as well as a certain shyness. They wear their hair in a braided style with flowers placed on the braids, and they are accompanied by their mothers.

The dancing commences when the women step on the dance floor followed by any interested men, who indicate their interest by taking off their hats. If others are interested in the same girl, they simply place their hats on top of the other man's and continue the dance. Sometimes, both sexes dance with a glass or a bottle on top of their head or with their feet tied up with a handkerchief. The steps to the dance may be fast or slow, depending on the tempo of the music. As previously mentioned, the steps to these dances are grounded, which means that when dancing the knees must be bent, with the feet kept close together and close to the floor.

The costumes for the women dancers are handmade with beautiful brightly colored fabric bearing Indigenous designs and graphics. Women also wear a shawl (*rebozo*) and sometimes also a v-shaped poncho (*quesquémetl*). The beautiful costumes demonstrate the joyful pride of the Potosi women. The male dancers wear a thin shirt and pants and a hat made from palm leaves. Both men and women dancers wear sandals. One of the most popular songs featured at the *huapango* fiestas of the Hauasteca region is "*La Malagueña*." The song is danced using the "grounded" steps characteristic of the region.

PATRICIA VIRAMONTES

See also: Bailes Latinoamericanos; Ballet Folklórico: Azteca; Ballet Folklórico: Jarabe Tapatío; Ballet Folklórico: Michoacán; Ballet Folklórico: Tabasco; Ballet Folklórico: Tamaulipas; Ballet Folklórico: Veracruz

Further Reading

Covarrubias, Luis. *Mexican Native Dances.* Mexico: Eugenio Fischgrund, 1979.

McFeaters, Bea. "Mexico: The Other Melting Pot," Houston Institute for Culture. http://www.houstonculture.org/mexico/ballet.html.

Múzquiz, Rodolfo. *Bailes y danzas tradicionales.* México: Coordinación General de Presentaciones Sociales, Coordinación de Promoción Cultural, Secretaría General, Unidad de Publicaciones y Documentación, Instituto Mexicano del Seguro Social, 1988.

Nájera-Ramírez, Olga, Norma E. Cantú, and Brenda Romero. *Dancing Across Borders: Danzas y Bailes Mexicanos.* Urbana and Chicago: University of Illinois Press, 2009.

Schwendener, Norma, and Averil Tibbels. *Legends and Dances of Old Mexico.* New York: A. S. Barnes and Co., 1934.

Sedillo, Mela-B. *Mexican and New Mexican Folkdances.* 2nd ed. Albuquerque: The University of New Mexico Press, 1937.

Segovia, Eloisa M., and Cindy Clayman Wesley. *Folklóricos Regionales de México: A Textbook of Mexican Folk Dances.* Colton, CA: C and E Prensa, 1975.

BALLET FOLKLÓRICO: TABASCO

The state of Tabasco is located in southeastern Mexico on the Gulf of Mexico and the Bahía of Campeche. The southern dance style is very "ground"-oriented, meaning lots of footwork with the feet held close to the floor, and does not require large amounts of skirt twirling, such as occurs in the state of Jalisco. Among Tabasco's neighboring states, such as Chiapas, Guerrero, Yucatan, Oaxaca, and Guanajuato, the dance style calls for women to hold their *huipils* (blouse) or skirts low; they are never raised above the hip. With respect to footwork, it is very grounded (i.e., focused and closed to the floor) and movement is fast for both the men and women dancers. The state of Tabasco is located in what was once Mayan territory, which extended from Yucatan to present-day Honduras, Guatemala, and El Salvador. The land is tropical, hot, and humid and boasts a rich culture. The Mayan lands were close to the Aztec Empire, which extended its domination into Mayan territory. The name Tabasco is itself derived from a Mayan word, the origin and meaning of which are still being debated.

Folklórico dancers in Tabasco who wish to achieve the *campesina*, or country-woman look, wear ruffled, full-circle skirts that are usually printed with flowers native to the land. The skirt is longer in the back, which creates the illusion that the dress is being dragged as a train. Women also wear a white blouse that is trimmed at the collar with a band of colorful embroidery. Usually the shirt reaches all the way to the woman's ankle to create a *fondo* (equivalent to a slip), or the top and *fondo* can be separate. The *rebozo* (shawl) is a common accessory for women; it is usually black but can also be brightly colored. Another accessory worn by female dancers is a *paliacate* (bandanna or handkerchief) placed on the right side of the woman's hip and tucked into her skirt. This is symbolic of the hot climate of the region and demonstrates the necessity of carrying a *paliacate* for wiping off perspiration. *Paliacates* may be seen in Veracruz as well. Another accessory worn by female dancers is a golden necklace displayed around the neck. In a similar manner to other *folklórico* costumes, a headpiece (*tocado*) decorated with hibiscus flowers is worn; it is representative of the tropical climate of Tabasco. The dancing footwear usually consists of black Spanish shoes (*folklórico* dancing shoes). A more Indigenous version of the costume uses a wrap-around skirt and *huaraches* (sandals) instead of shoes. A third style of dancing costume worn by Tabasco women, the more elegant *gala* style, is rarely used. The more typical one worn by *folklórico* groups is the *campesina* costume.

For the men, the typical dance costume is also the *campesino* (country) look. It consists of white pants accompanied by a tucked-in white shirt with a belt. The use of white in dance costumes is once again indicative of the heat of this tropical region. Black would be too hot to wear in this torrid climate. One of the accessories the male dancer wears, similar to what women display in their outfits, is the *paliacate* (bandanna). This is worn around the neck and used for the same reason the women wear them, to wipe off perspiration. A second accessory is a hat that is usually waved around while dancing on certain assigned steps, either above the head or across the lower body. The last accessory worn by male dancers from Tabasco is usually a small purse wrapped across the shoulder similar to a messenger bag. This purse is purely symbolic and does not have a dance function. The pouches represent the hard work the men and women do in the agricultural fields. The purses traditionally have seeds in them. Like the women, the men wear black Spanish boots (*folklórico* boots), or if they are dancing in the Indigenous style, they wear *huaraches* (sandals).

The music in Tabasco is unique because of its African, Spanish, and Mayan influence. The main instruments are the *jarana* (guitar), the *marimba* (similar to a xylophone), reed flutes, and drums played by ensembles called *Tamborileros*. The music of Tabasco has Mayan roots, but also a strong Afro-Caribbean rhythm that arrived with African slaves brought into the region during the colonial era. Some typical tunes played in Tabasco are *El Torito* (the little bull), *Son Chontal*, and *Tabasco Poppurri*.

The Tabasco dancing style has deep Indigenous roots. The steps are vigorous and quick, following the drum beats and the flutes. The women hold their skirts out in front of them at roughly a 45 degree angle. The steps are done in a *plie* (small bend in the knees) for both men and women. With few exceptions, the steps are meant to be done close to the ground; the goal is to get to the next step without lifting your feet too far from it. This style is derived from Mayan dancing; it represents a closeness to nature. Men typically have their hands behind their backs, right below the tailbone, unless they are using their hats, in which case only one hand stays behind their backs. The character of the woman can be a bit flirtatious when around her partner, but not seductive; she is almost shy in her aspect. As for the man, he is very proud, a pride that comes from knowing he works hard (i.e., what the costume represents). This type of dance is rarely performed because it is not as popular as other dances, such as those from Jalisco, but it does represent part of the Indigenous culture belonging to Mexico and its influence in *folklórico* dancing.

ANA C. FLORES

See also: Bailes Latinoamericanos; Ballet Folklórico: Azteca; Ballet Folklórico: Jarabe Tapatío; Ballet Folklórico: Michoacán; Ballet Folklórico: San Luis Potosí; Ballet Folklórico: Tamaulipas; Ballet Folklórico: Veracruz

Further Reading

Covarrubias, Luis. *Mexican Native Dances.* Mexico: Eugenio Fischgrund, 1979.

Fuentes, Jonatan V. "El vestuario tabasqueño." 2009. "Raíces Tabasco." http://www.raices tabasco.com/2009/05/el-vestuario-tabasqueno.html.

Johnston, Edith. *Regional Dances of Mexico.* Dallas: Banks Upshaw and Co., 1935.

"Mexican Dance-Tabasco." The Mexican Folkloric Dance Company of Chicago. 25 May 2011. http://mexfoldanco.org/mexican/folkloric/dance/tabasco.html.

Nájera-Ramírez, Olga, Norma E. Cantú, and Brenda Romero. *Dancing Across Borders: Danzas y Bailes Mexicanos.* Urbana and Chicago: University of Illinois Press, 2009.

Sedillo, Mela-B. *Mexican and New Mexican Folkdances.* 2nd ed. Albuquerque: The University of New Mexico Press, 1937.

Segovia, Eloisa M., and Cindy Clayman Wesley. *Folklóricos Regionales de México: A Textbook of Mexican Folk Dances.* Colton, CA: C and E Prensa, 1975.

BALLET FOLKLÓRICO: TAMAULIPAS

The state of Tamaulipas is located in northeastern Mexico. To the north, it is bordered by the U.S. state of Texas, to the east by the Gulf of Mexico, to the southeast by Veracruz, to the southwest by San Luis Potosí, and to the west by Nuevo León. The state's geography exerts a definite influence over the style of *folklórico* dancing found in the region. The traditional or well-known Tamaulipas costume is *La Cuera* (cowhide), which is found in southern Tamaulipas. The three regions of the state are the Franja fronteriza (Border) in the north, the Sierra de San Carlos and Plains of San Fernando in the center, and the Huasteca region in the south. Each of these regions has its own style of music and costume.

Franja Fronteriza

Three styles of dancing are performed in the northern Franja fronteriza area—Polka, Redova, and Chotís (Schottische). These styles have German, Swedish, and Czechoslovakian origins, but have been adopted by the people of Tamaulipas, who assimilated them into Mexican culture by adding more movement and joyfulness. The Tamaulipas versions of these dances also differ from the originals in other ways. Dance in Tamaulipas exhibits the gracefulness and flirtatiousness seen in the dancing of Mexican women, as well as the pulsating personality and untamed, virile character of the agile and strong *zapateado*, which is one of the basic steps found in *folklórico*. The instruments used to play the polka, *chotís*, and *redova* are the accordion, saxophone, bajo sexton, and contrabass.

In the north, the women's dancing costume is made of a checkered cotton or floral patterned fabric. Women wear a blouse and a skirt decorated with lace, ruffles, and pasalistones (strips of fabric that are intertwined with the blouse to facilitate the integration of a ribbon). The headpiece consists of a braid that has ribbons intertwined or a scarf of the same color as the dress. Men wear dark cowboy-style trousers made out of denim or tergal. They wear a cowboy shirt, bandanna or scarf, cowboy boots, and a *tejana* (a northern sombrero made of dark colored felt). The costumes, reflecting the idea of the western cowboy, illustrate the influence contact with Texas has had on the state.

Sierra de San Carlos and Llanos de San Fernando

The typical dance and music found in this region is known as *picota*, which means "*palo alto*" (high pole) or "*columna*" (column). It is believed to have its origins in the ancient dances dedicated to the fertility of the earth. This is a reference to the time when the people were exposed for their transgressions to public shame accompanied by the martial beat of the drum and clarinet. It originated in the Villa de San Carlos, which served as a refuge for the Indigenous people who ran away from their Spanish colonizers. As time passed, the people adopted this music and adapted it to the joyous rhythms and rhythmic character of the state. The instruments used are the clarinet and the drum. To announce festivities in the region, musicians climb the hills early in the morning to play their music. The intensity of the music tells the town the celebration is about to start, making everyone feel welcomed.

The fabric used to make the costumes of this region is *tela de manta* (white cotton fabric). The woman wears a v-neck with short sleeves and a dress that extends to her ankles. She wears a sash around her waist which is tied making a bow in back. The dress is adorned with ribbons of different colors with greca patterns. The headpiece consists of one large braid and white Nacahua flowers. Men wear laces around the neck of the shirt and wear a sash around their waist along with white pants; the color of the sash is determined by the color of dress the woman is wearing. Both can use huaraches (sandals) or dance barefoot.

Huasteca

In the Huasteca Tamaulipeca region, as in the rest of the Huastecas—Puebla, Veracruz, Hidalgo, Querétaro, and San Luis Potosí—there is only one type of music that's representative of this region, the *huapango*. The *huapango* is not just music for dancing, but also for telling anecdotes, to ask for Christmas gifts, to make fun of others with humor, and to taunt one's enemies. The dancers dance to the rhythms of this music on a platform. The instruments used are the violin, *jarana* (a small guitar with five strings that is used to keep the rhythm), *guitarra quinta* (fifth guitar), and the accompaniment of a Trobriander's voice, which wakes up the sensibility of the person listening to it. The famous *huapango* from this region is "*El Querreque*." In this song, the two singers alternate humorous repartees.

Three variations of the regional costume exist within this region. The costume in *campero* (country people) style is made of cotton because it is used along the coastal zone. The costume in *ranchero* (rancher) style is made of a combination of cotton that is comfortable to work in, but also has a leather jacket due to the harsh weather changes. Lastly, the gala costume is made completely of leather and is used to attend social events.

JESÚS ADRIÁN GALLARDO

See also: Bailes Latinoamericanos; Ballet Folklórico: Azteca; Ballet Folklórico: Jarabe Tapatío; Ballet Folklórico: Michoacán; Ballet Folklórico: San Luis Potosí; Ballet Folklórico: Tabasco; Ballet Folklórico: Veracruz

Further Reading

Covarrubias, Luis. *Mexican Native Dances.* Mexico: Eugenio Fischgrund, 1979.

Gobierno del Estado de Tamaulipas, México. http://tamaulipas.gob.mx/tamaulipas/tradiciones-y-costumbres/musica-danza-baile-y-vestimenta/.

Gobierno del Estado de Tamaulipas, México. http://tamaulipas.gob.mx/tamaulipas/tradiciones-y-costumbres/traje-tipico/.

Johnston, Edith. *Regional Dances of Mexico.* Dallas: Banks Upshaw and Co., 1935.

McFeaters, Bea. "Mexico: The Other Melting Pot," Houston Institute for Culture. http://www.houstonculture.org/mexico/ballet.html.

The Mexican Folkloric Dance Company of Chicago. http://www.mexfoldanco.org/mexican/folkloric/dance/tamaulipas.html.

Nájera-Ramírez, Olga, Norma E. Cantú, and Brenda Romero. *Dancing Across Borders: Danzas y Bailes Mexicanos*. Urbana and Chicago: University of Illinois Press, 2009.

Sedillo, Mela-B. *Mexican and New Mexican Folkdances.* 2nd ed. Albuquerque: The University of New Mexico Press, 1937.

Segovia, Eloisa M., and Cindy Clayman Wesley. *Folklóricos Regionales de México: A Textbook of Mexican Folk Dances.* Colton, CA: C and E Prensa, 1975.

BALLET FOLKLÓRICO: VERACRUZ

Veracruz is a gulf state and shares its borders (from north to south) with Tamaulipas, San Luis Potosí, Hidalgo, Puebla, Oaxaca, Chiapas, and Tabasco. The state itself is more than 400 miles long and extends no more than 100 miles inland. Veracruz is mostly a mountainous region with a narrow border of hot, humid coastland below the Sierra Madre Oriental, a range that occupies the center and western areas of Veracruz. It is also home to the volcano, Pico de Orizaba; it is the highest peak in Mexico rising to 18,700 feet. There are numerous rivers running through the state, a major one being Coatzacoalcos running in the southeast. To the north is the Tamiahua Lagoon, extending sixty-five miles across and containing many large islands. Because of heavy rainfall, Veracruz experiences a dense growth of vegetation. The region was once the center of an Indian civilization (which preceded that of the Aztecs) that has greatly influenced the culture and dance. The Spanish colonizers also exerted a great influence on the culture of Veracruz. In 1519, Cortez landed in its seaport merely two years after Cordoba landed in Yucatan. The dance typical of the Mexican state of Veracruz, like Yucatan, is highly Spanish-influenced.

Dancers perform a traditional Mexican dance during the celebration of International Dance Day in 2004 in Mexico City. (AP/Wide World Photos)

Some of the dance steps from Spain that are similar in the Veracruz dances are the Spanish *zapateado* (a dance from Southern Spain) and the same (dancing) leaps from the Spanish *jota* of Northern Spain. The dances from Veracruz are called *son jarocho* or *son huasteca*; a *son* is a melody and a *jarocho/Huasteca* refers to anything from the state of Veracruz.

Dance

Veracruz has a distinct style to its dance. The style is often called *son jarocho* or on *son huasteca*. These dances originated from flamenco dances and later acquired their own characteristics. The dance is characterized by dancing on a wooden platform with vigorous and complicated footwork. The platform has holes on its sides to convert it into a sounding board. The dance is often performed throughout an area extending from the Huasteca region of Tamaulipas to southern Veracruz. As stated above, another style of dance in Veracruz is the *son jarocho*. This style of dance was greatly influenced by the Spanish colonizers and dates from the seventeenth and eighteenth centuries. This style of music is often found in the southern half of Veracruz and has a very upbeat and joyous feel to it. As stated before, the *zapateado* and the *jota* were imported from Spain. The dance's movements are very Spanish; however, they lack the Spanish temperament. A Veracruzano's temperament is different from the Spaniard's. The dancers must stand erect (as in Spanish dances) and maintain control of their body movement. Dancers are subtly flirtatious and promiscuous. This character goes hand in hand with the lyrics of the music of Veracruz.

Many of the verses have double meanings, separating the *veracruzano* dance from the Spanish dance. These verses are often coquettish and even humorous at times. As for the dancing itself, the steps are synchronized and require a mastering of technique and skill. The *zapateado* requires a strong, high energy heel technique. The male dances with his arms to the side, the female dancer moves in a flirtatious manner and uses her dress to embellish her movements. This dance is very stylized and well-known as coming from the region of Veracruz. One song often performed from this region is "La Bamba." "La Bamba" is a song that tells of how the sailors flirt with the girls. The girls, in turn, enjoy the attention of the young men. This dance is often performed with a large group and/or with a solo couple. The solo couple dance and tie a bow with their feet. Veracruz is well known for this song.

Costume

A male dancer's costume is very similar to that of Yucatán. Because Veracruz is in a subtropical area, the costumes are usually white to reflect the heat. Men wear white, loose-fitting pants with a white, long-sleeve, loose-fitting shirt (also known as a *guayabera*). They also tie a necktie or handkerchief around their neck and another around their waist. This custom can be traced to the Spanish *vaquero* (cowboy). They also wear white boots with a heel, also of Spanish influence. Lastly, they wear a small straw hat that is similar to the Spanish *cordobés* in shape and size. The women wear a white, elaborate and beautiful fiesta dress. These dresses are very similar to the women of Seville, Spain.

Both costumes are embellished with ruffles and lace, and they require the women to wear their hair on top of their head. Their hair is braided with ribbon; it is then embellished with flowers and a gold colored *peine* (traditional Spanish comb often worn on the back and sides of the head). They wear a satin sleeveless blouse and a long petticoat decorated with lace. The petticoat is not full, but more A-line-shaped, gathered at the waist. A full skirt with ruffles at the bottom is worn over the petticoat. A white lace *mantilla* (shawl, from Spain) is worn around the shoulders that crosses in front, secured with a brooch. A black apron adorned with flower appliqués and bordered with black lace is worn at the waist. White hard-sole heels are worn for resonance and facility in their footwork. They often wear gold jewelry, rosaries and/or a cross to complete their outfit. The rosary/cross entered Mexico with the Spaniards. Much of the Veracruz dance costume was influenced or brought over from Spain, especially the women's dance outfit.

ADAM BARRIENTOS

See also: Bailes Latinoamericanos; Ballet Folklórico: Azteca; Ballet Folklórico: Jarabe Tapatío; Ballet Folklórico: Michoacán; Ballet Folklórico: San Luis Potosí; Ballet Folklórico: Tabasco; Ballet Folklórico: Tamaulipas; "La Bomba"

Further Reading

Segovia, Eloisa M., and Cindy Clayman Wesley. *Folklórico Regionales de México: A Textbook of Mexican Folk Dances*. Colton, CA: C and E Prensa, 1975.

Solomon, Loes. *Some Mexican Folk Dances as Found in Los Angeles, California*. Los Angeles: University of California at Los Angeles, 1941.

Trujillo, Lawrence. *The Spanish Influence on the Mestizo Folk Dance of Yucatan, Veracruz, and Jalisco, Mexico*. Denver: University of Colorado, 1974.

BAPTISM

Baptism is the first of the Christian sacraments, the initiation of an individual into the Christian life. It is prescribed and followed by the near majority of all Christian denominations, including the Roman Catholic Church (of which 70 percent of all Latinos/as are members), Anglican/Episcopalian, and classic Protestant denominations (Lutheran, Presbyterian, Methodist). This universality of acceptance, as well as its profound importance within Christian doctrine, makes baptism one of the most important rituals amongst Latinos/as. The 2003 Hispanic Churches in American Public Life survey found that 93 percent of Latinos/as consider themselves Christian; of those, almost all would have been baptized, independently of denomination and/or specific Latino community. Baptism has thus retained its overwhelming popularity despite liturgical changes, denominational fluctuations or historical moments of greater indifference to, or even hostility towards, organized Christianity.

Almost universally, baptism involves the presence of the baptizand in a church, where a priest will have him or her come into contact with baptismal water through one of four methods: immersion, submersion, aspersion or affusion. Affusion, the most common, involves pouring water over the head of the baptizand. Specific liturgies depend on the denomination, though in almost all of them the baptizand is assigned a godfather and godmother who are supposed to guarantee his or her Christian life and instruction. The Roman Catholic Church consecrates the baptismal water through a prayer of *epiclesis* either at the Easter Vigil or at the time of baptism. The person performing the ceremony will have the baptizand brought forward, them, draw the sign of the cross, proclaim the word of God, and pour the water over the baptizand's head whilst reciting the following: "[Name], I baptise you in the name of the Father, the Son and the Holy Spirit. Amen." The baptizand will then be anointed with the sacred chrism (perfumed oil consecrated by the bishop) and will be brought to the altar for the praying of *Our Father* (*Padre Nuestro*). At the baptism of newborns, the blessing of the mother also occupies a special place. The Catholic Church states that the ordinary ministers of baptism are the bishop, the priest and the deacon; however, in case of necessity, any person familiar with the ritual (even if they themselves have not been baptized) can perform it. The Church prescribes Sundays and the Easter Vigil as the most appropriate days for baptism. It is stipulated that godparents must be practicing Catholics, be of at least 16 years of age, and have received the First Communion; those living in adultery or *concubinaje* are ineligible to be godparents.

Christian doctrine establishes that everyone has a right to be baptized. There are therefore two types of candidates for baptism: newborns and adults. Newborns are baptized on the basis of their parents' faith (it is required that at least one of them consent to the child being baptized) and the guarantees of the godparents that the child will lead a Christian life. Adults are required by the Catholic Church to undergo a process of training in the doctrines of the Christian faith (catechumen). The strong tradition of religiosity amongst Latinos/as, however, ensures that most of them are baptized soon after birth. It also means they follow the usual baptismal liturgy, despite concessions made in the II Vatican Council (1965) allowing for the inclusion of native cultural elements within the ritual.

The meaning and importance of baptism are universal within Christianity. The belief that men are born with a fallen nature requires the spiritual cleansing which baptism provides and which neutralizes original sin, allowing for the possibility of salvation in the afterlife. Amongst Latinos/as, this effect is sometimes playfully articulated by referring to baptism as *cortar la cola* (cutting off the tail) or *sacarle el diablo* (removing the devil). The most recent catechism of the Catholic Church explicitly states that "the whole organism of the Christian's supernatural life has its roots in Baptism" (1266). Through this ritual, the individual enters into communion with the Holy Trinity and partakes in Christ's sacrifice. Though it is not usual for the baptized to receive the Eucharist (as he or she is usually a newborn), the praying of *Our Father* indicates the sacrament's orientation towards the participation in salvation guaranteed by the Host.

Baptism not only establishes a bond between the individual and God, it also establishes one between the individual and the rest of the Christian community. Baptism therefore has a strong social significance, which becomes even more prevalent amongst Latinos/as. Indeed, most of the particularities of the Latino practice of baptism have to do with its social dimension. A primary exponent of this is the particular strength of the relationship established between the child, its parents and the godparents, a relationship known as *compadrazgo*. The *padrino* and *madrina* are not only supposed to guarantee the child's learning of the Christian faith, but are also considered a close part of the family with concomitant rights and obligations, such as providing financial or other types of assistance in times of need, both to the child and to his or her parents. It must be noted that *compadrazgo* is a consequence of custom, not theology; it is a social practice that reinforces links within families or communities, often with a profoundly stabilizing effect.

Other baptism-related practices amongst Latinos/as include *el bolo*, the throwing of coins into the air upon emerging from the church where the baptism has been performed; this is considered a sign of good fortune, and is practiced principally by the Mexican American community. Another Mexican American and Cuban American tradition is *el ropón*, the baptismal gown which is passed along through generations of an entire family. In general, Latinos/as observe the practice of dressing the baptizand in a white gown, and having the parents and godparents (as well as other guests) wear their Sunday best to the ceremony. After the ceremony, it is customary to have a party or celebration either at the parents' home or the godparents' home. Friends and relatives join in on the celebration of this particular rite of passage with food and drink.

An exception in the universality of baptismal procedures amongst Latinos/as has been caused in recent decades by the growth amongst them of the Pentecostal movement. Various branches of Pentecostalism do not accept the Trinitarian formula for baptism (the invocation of the Father, Son, and Holy Spirit) and insist that those baptized under it need to be re-baptized invoking Christ's name only.

The insistence on unitary baptism eventually led to the creation of a Mexican One-ness Pentecostal/Apostolic movement. The Catholic Church, however, holds that baptism never has to be repeated, as no sin can erase its effect. Recent decades have also seen greater laxity in the Pentecostal requirement for re-baptism.

DAVID JIMÉNEZ TORRES

See also: Bautizo (Baptism): Rites, Padrinos, and Celebrations; Comadre/Compadre; Funerals; Holy Communion; Matrimonio and Pedida de Mano (Marriage and Engagement); Quinceañera

Further Reading

Avalos, Hector, ed. *Introduction to the U.S. Latina and Latino Religious Experience.* Boston: Brill Academic Publishers, 2004.

Geoffrey Chapman–Libreria Editrice Vaticana. *Catechism of the Catholic Church.* London: Continuum International Publishing Group, 1999.

Hinojosa, Gilberto Miguel, and Jay P. Dolan. *Mexican Americans and the Catholic Church, 1900–1965.* Notre Dame, IN: University of Notre Dame Press, 1994.

BARBACOA

Barbacoa is a traditional Mexican dish of seasoned, slowly-cooked beef. The process of cooking this meat is sometimes also referred to as *barbacoa*. Traditionally, a pit is dug in the ground, about three feet by three feet, and lined with rocks. The rocks are then covered with mesquite wood, and a fire is started. After the fire turns the mesquite into wood coals, the remaining wood is removed (so as to prevent an overly smoky taste) and maguey leaves are used to line the pit. Authentic *barbacoa de cabeza* ("head *barbacoa*") is made using an entire cow's head. The head is first cleaned and seasoned, placed in a damp burlap sack, wrapped in more maguey leaves, and then put into the pit. The pit is covered by a piece of tin and dirt. A fire is lit above the hole and it is left to cook overnight. The result is that the entire head of beef can be consumed, including brain, tongue, cheeks, and eyes. The slow cooking process leaves the meat very tender.

The traditional underground cooking method is not as common anymore, especially in the Southwest United States. Restricted by U.S. health codes and sanitation laws (due to the soil-meat contact) many Mexican and Tex-Mex restaurants prepare *barbacoa* in a pressure cooker or in an oven. Several recipes for preparing *barbacoa* easily in a slow cooker at home exist online. Since it remains a slow process, many restaurants only offer the delicacy on the weekends. In addition, sometimes the head of beef is substituted by tongue, cheeks, beef brisket, or chuck roast. It is often served for breakfast in tacos, with chopped onions and cilantro, as well as salsa. It can also be served in *tortas* (Mexican-style sandwiches).

The word *barbacoa* first appeared in the Spanish conquistador, Gonzalo Fernández de Oviedo's, *Historia general y natural de las Indias* ("General and Natural History of the Indies"). In this account, he uses the term to describe a type of scaffolding or frame made of wood and cane, which the Panama natives used to cook food (such as birds or iguanas) or to store grains.

During this same time, both the Aztecs and the Maya were cooking meat in underground pits. Today, the Nahuatl word *tatema* is used to describe such pit cooking, while the Maya term is *pibil*. Many authentic Mexican restaurants serve the Mayan steamed pork dish called *cochinita pibil*. Instead of maguey leaves, however, the Maya used banana leaves. Another pit-cooked dish is *birria*, a Mexican stew typical of Guadalajara. *Birria* is a spicy stew, whose broth is made from the juices of the meat cooked underground. It is usually prepared with goat meat, but can also be made with lamb, mutton, or iguana. The term *barbacoa* was also applied to similar underground cooking methods used in the Caribbean. While contested, the word *barbacoa* is thought to be the possible etymological origin of the English word "barbeque" or "barbecue' (also written "BBQ").

LORENA GAUTHEREAU-BRYSON

See also: Birria; Carne Asada; Salsa (Sauce); Tacos

Further Reading

Bendele, Marvin C. "Barbacoa? The Curious Case of a Word." In Elizabeth S. D. Engelhardt, ed. *Republic of Barbecue: Stories Beyond the Brisket.* Austin: University of Texas Press, 2009.

Fernández de Oviedo y Valdés, Gonzalo. *Historia general y natural de las Indias.* Madrid: Imprenta de la Real Academia de la Historia, 1851, *The Internet Archive.* http://www .archive.org/details/generalnatural01fernrich.

Walsh, Robb, ed. *Legends of Texas Barbecue Cookbook: Recipes and Recollections from the Pit Bosses.* San Francisco: Chronicle Books, 2002.

BATO/A

Bato/a, or alternately spelled *vato/a*, is an in-group term among Chicanos/as that creates a sense of emotional attachment between individuals and functions as a marker of one's in-group status in the barrio. While the term often takes on an overly simplified and generally pejorative meaning, *bato* has become emblematic of the social struggles of modern Chicanos/as. Following the pachucos of the 1930s and 1940s, a *bato*, a contemporary symbol of Mexican American manhood in the United States, has been the subject of early anthropologists and psychoanalysts who discussed the dangerous and uncontainable nature of Mexican virility and the plight of imported macho culture in the United States.

From an Anglo perspective a *bato* is a dangerous individual, a gang-banger who wears khaki pants, and Pendleton shirts, tattoos, and headscarves. He drives a low rider and dons a zoot suit to liken himself to his pachuco past. He is a cultural deviant whose identity is fluid. He fits neither into American nor Mexican culture, and thus is a representation of the unsteady bicultural experience of Mexican Americans in the United States. James Smethurst notes that while the *bato* is an acquired persona, one that resists cultural assimilation, he also embodies a kind of rugged individualism, which one can paradoxically liken to stereotypes of mainstream American individualism. The *bato* actively maintains his marginal status, choosing to self-identify with terminology, dress and personal esthetics that are shunned by others of Mexican descent (Smethhurst 1995, 120). Trapped by stereotypes, he finds pride in self-expressive, creative acts such as speech play, car art, and personal esthetic standards that come to mark him as both an individual and part of a larger marginalized class of poor brown people.

Bato is also an item of folk speech, specifically a term of address that transitioned from insult to referent. Its use is part of the vocabulary of *Caló*, and indexes a linguistic esthetic that aspires to self-determination. Its colloquial definition aligns with generic male terms of address, such as "guy" or "dude." The term originally derived from the older Spanish word *chivato*, which refers to a young male goat. This association connotes an air of insult as it is part of a broader system of intimate insults uttered by Mexican males that use goat symbolism to reference cuckolded or emasculated males. Appearing with both masculine and feminine adaptation in most aggregate vocabularies, speakers use it to address or reference any young person; however, the term and its variants are specifically used by those who speak forms of Chicano Spanish, or *Caló*. A speaker may modify the term to create compound terms that reference specific identities for unique individuals or groups of individuals. For instance, according to the *Dictionary of Chicano Spanish*, a *vato* is not necessarily a gang member despite social stereotyping; instead a "[v]ato-tirilongo" is a variant that specifically means a gang-affiliated male. A pachuco, would not have merely been a *bato,* but often a "[v]ato-tirili." A *bato-loco* is a potent contemporary image of an individual who exhibits a kind of controlled craziness or wildness that displays fearlessness, and unpredictable forms of destructive behavior. While a *vato* proves himself through violent and erratic behaviors, these extreme behaviors are also the cause of extreme violence and unwanted troubles perpetrated upon him (Vigil 1988, 438–439). These variants show the wide use of the term, inside and outside of what many deem delinquent culture.

While lexically the word is not complex, it is what it has come to symbolize that evokes a specialized meaning among Mexican American communities in the United States. Much like the term *cholo*, which is used in some parts of Latin America to categorize those that appear to occupy an intermediate position between metropolitan and Indigenous culture groups, the imagined *vato* represents Chicanos, situated between their Mexican heritage and the reality of their American lifestyle (Vigil 1988, 422). This terminology exists in part as a way for individual Chicanos in *barrio* communities to self-label and in part carve out their own lived social identity, one that fits into the social and cultural, albeit marginal, niches in which they feel they belong. The use of the word *bato* evokes a particular image of *barrio* youth culture, one that hinges on maintaining honor in the eyes of one's peers in the face of violence and poverty. While older definitions liken the term to mean "simpleton," it is currently used as an in-group reference to a system of fictive kinship, where insiders identify one another by a familiar, standardized vocabulary. Other terms similar to the term *vato* are *amigotes* or *cuates*, all of which denote the existence of a particularly close male friendship.

The metaphoric *vato* represents the bind or the paradox of contemporary masculinity among Mexican American males. He is an invisible man, living outside of the system. He is virile, yet weak. He is man in constant search of himself. In a sea of others just like himself he only finds small islands of camaraderie, peace—because social and cultural mores dictate that he stand alone. José Limón explains that the *bato* is the Mexican American male who is living in the cultural margins of society, taking comfort in the company of others like himself, and finding collective equality in the playful verbal exchanges they share. These exchanges serve to create the world of the Chicano male as it exists outside of the standards of American and Mexican social institutions. Despite his unstable and contested figure, the *bato* has become a potent image in ethnic writing, and a tool for cultural and social education of *Chicanismo*.

RACHEL VALENTINA GONZÁLEZ

See also: Caló (Folk Speech); Chicano Spanish; Limón, José Eduardo; Pachucos; Pachuquismo: 1940s Urban Youth

Further Reading

Limón, José E. *Dancing with the Devil: Society and Cultural Politics in Mexican-American South Texas.* Madison: University of Wisconsin Press, 1994.

Smethhurst, James. "The Figure of the Vato Loco and the Representation of Ethnicity in the Narratives of Oscar Z. Acosta." *MELUS* 20 (1995): 119–132.

Urrea, Luis Alberto. *Vatos.* El Paso, TX: Cinco Punto, 2000.

Vigil, James Diego. "Group Processes and Street Identity: Adolescent Chicano Gang Members." *Ethos* 16.4 (1988): 421–445.

BAUTIZO (BAPTISM): RITES, PADRINOS, AND CELEBRATIONS

Many first-generation Latinos/as evidence strong links to Mexican traditions and customs. Since they are reared in a devoutly Catholic home and family they learn early to love and fear God, paying particular attention to culturally based rites of passage.

In the Latino community, these rites are key transformative events—baptism, *quinceañera*, marriage, and death, that encapsulate a person's life by commemorating specific stages of life on earth and preparation for the next life. The Latino rites of passage are events rich with color, family ties, emotion, and music. Baptism, the first of seven Catholic sacraments, provides the family with the opportunity to present their infant to the Catholic community and budding spirituality. Baptism to a Latino is a solemn obligation deeply ingrained in their minds and is traditionally addressed within the first year of the child's life.

Baptism provides parents with an added layer of security and protection known as the "guardian angel," and the faster this angel assumes this responsibility the better the child is thought to be. Ensuring this spiritual protection takes precedence for the baby's parents as soon as the baby comes home. To Latinos/as, baptism initiates this new soul's path to heaven. Baptism is an event that welcomes new family members and celebrates the bonds of family and friendship. This important Catholic rite begins with the careful selection of the godparents or *padrinos* followed by a celebration of life and the bonds of family.

Padrinos, or Godparents

Selecting *padrinos* is among the first and most important duties of parents in the Latino culture. It is taken seriously not simply because it is one of the highest honors bestowed on individuals, but because *padrinos* will help create an extended family bond. The couple chosen to be *padrinos* is expected to be in good standing with the church and be firm believers in the faith. The bonds between parents and their co-parents, or *compadres*, is important and merits special consideration, since a spiritual and social relationship will form between them. It is also important for the godchild, or *ahijado*, and godparents, or *padrinos*, to see each other often to materialize both the symbolic and the spiritual bond which will last a lifetime.

Padrinos' Role

The role of *padrinos*, or godparents, is to be both a social and a spiritual guardian or advisor. The godparents will foment and continue to nurture the love of culture and belief. Godparents are the child's ritual parents responsible for watching over their godchild and providing all kinds of guidance when needed. The *ahijado* knows that one can consult with and trust the *padrinos* with one's trials and tribulations.

Traditionally godparents have the social and even legal obligation for the care of their godchild if something removes parents from the life of the child. This is one of the major reasons that Latinos/as often select extended family members such as uncles, aunts, or cousins to be godparents.

Both the godparents and parents work together for the common goal of assisting the godchild to incorporate both culture and faith into life's decisions. The godparents also serve as the child's safety valve, a place of comfort and solace away from home where issues regarding life's challenges may be discussed. Godparents and parents jointly teach the child the consequences of good or bad behavior and encourage the development of a strong personal ethic as well as the value of education, commitment, and hard work. Therefore, the relationship between the two couples must be constantly nourished because this partnership will guide the child into functional cultural and social adulthood.

Gifts

There are a series of gifts presented to the godchild, or *ahijado*, at baptism that symbolize the ties that will form between the child and the child's parents and the godparents. These gifts also symbolize the godparents' acceptance of their responsibility as the child's second set of parents.

The first and most important gift is the christening gown, or *ropón*. The *ropón* is a matter of tradition or personal taste and is always white, symbolizing purity, joy, and new life. The baptismal gown is purchased by the godparents, who also purchase accompanying white shoes, white socks, white blanket and a white hat or bonnet. Optional gifts such as "My First Bible," a gold bracelet, a small gold cross or medallion may also be provided by the godparents. While these gifts need not be expensive, their symbolism is very important. Additional gifts reflect the godparents' commitment to the bonds that will exist between them and their godchild. These gifts will also serve to remind the child that one's baptism is connected to a faith.

Day of Christening

On the day of christening, the godparents visit the child's home to begin their role as spiritual parents. After the brief reception, which includes refreshments, the godparents traditionally dress the baby with the entire christening wardrobe they purchased while parents look on and assist if needed. The tradition of the godparents dressing the baby symbolizes their long-term commitment to their role and obligation of caring and providing for their godchild. The christening mass can be a stand-alone ceremony for just friends and family or it may be part of a larger dedicated mass set aside for multiple baptisms. Depending on the parish, parents and godparents are required to attend from one to three pre-baptism training sessions. The purpose of these sessions is for the Church to remind couples that in requesting the sacrament of baptism parents and godparents are committing themselves to train the child in the practice of the faith.

Christening Mass

Latino christening masses are events that explode with music and family members. Priests celebrate each and every one of the baptisms by having all those in attendance applaud and sing after the water touches the head of each and every one of the children being baptized.

Most parishes acknowledge the joyful nature of the Latino community and incorporate a live parish band that plays a catchy rhythmic tune, "Alle, Alle, Alle, Alleluia," after each baptism. After the christening mass, either at the party or immediately on the steps of the church, friends and family wait for the godparents and parents to emerge from the church. As soon as both couples and the child emerge, adults and children chant "bolo, bolo, bolo." The godparents then throw coins into the air, the "bolo," and kids and adults scurry to pick them up as a measure of good luck. This tradition symbolizes good will as well as prosperity for the child.

The Christening Party

As soon as the christening mass is over, it is time for both parents and godparents to welcome friends and family to a christening party. The christening party is a celebration in which both sets of parents proudly present the child to the extended family. The party also serves to show the community which two families have fused socially and spiritually. The party itself is a matter of personal choice and affordability.

Traditionally the party was organized by the godparents, but due to the changing economic trends the organization and cost of the party are now divided between the parents and godparents and sometimes even throughout the extended family. A lot of thought and attention to detail goes into this social gathering. Among the first items to be considered are the christening favors, which are purchased or made by the *padrinos*.

Christening favors are often personalized with the date and with Spanish phrases like "*Recuerdo de mi Bautizo*" or English phrases like "Remembering my Christening." Personalized baptismal books are a thoughtful and practical way of sharing this important religio-cultural event with the guests.

The lunch or dinner menu is also traditional including classic entrées like *pollo en mole*, chicken in a spicy semi-sweet red sauce. The standard *asado de puerco* or braised pork with red chiles, *pozole*, a pork and hominy stew, and the classic *menudo*, honeycomb tripe and hominy stew. These dishes are accompanied by authentic Mexican rice, not to be confused with Spanish rice, refried beans, warm hot sauce, tortillas, and other garnishings that accompany the respective entrée. These traditional supper foods will vary according to the Latino sub-group hosting the baptism. For example, Cuban and Puerto Rican Latinos/as will favor Caribbean dishes.

Many Latino baptismal parties also include *piñatas* for the kids to break followed by a delicious and beautiful cake. Guests are not expected to bring gifts because this is not a birthday party, but many do. Some guests may decide to take a greeting card, a Bible, or Bible story books or some other religious artifact. These gifts are a nice thoughtful touch, but are not necessary. The Latino baptismal party bonds families as it initiates a new child into the faith.

GABRIELA SOSA ZAVALETA

See also: Baptism; Comadre/Compadre; Funerals; Holy Communion; Matrimonio and Pedida de Mano (Marriage and Engagement); Quinceañera

Further Reading

Vigil, Angel. *Una Linda Raza: Cultural and Artistic Traditions of the Hispanic Southwest.* Golden, CO: Fulcrum, 1998.

West, John O. *Mexican American Folklore: Legends, Songs, Festivals, Proverbs, Crafts, Tales of Saints, of Revolutionaries, and More.* Little Rock, AR: August House, 1988.

Williams, Norma. *The Mexican American Family: Tradition and Change.* New York: General Hall, 1990.

BILLY THE KID/EL BILITO (1859–1881)

Born on November 23rd, 1859, William H. Bonney, who is best known in the United States as Billy the Kid, was an American frontier outlaw and gunman who instigated the Lincoln County War. However, for *Nuevo Mexicano* farmers, Billy the Kid was known as *El Bilito* or *El Chivato*. He was born in New York's East Side and moved to Coffeyville, Kansas, when he was three. His mother became a widow and joined a large party of immigrants that were headed to Pueblo, Colorado, where she married a man named Antrim and later moved to Santa Fe, New Mexico. Billy grew up in Santa Fe and later his family moved to Silver City, New Mexico. Billy's breakaway from his family took him into the border towns of Arizona. During Billy's frontier border excursions, he often rode into Sonora, Mexico, speaking Spanish, playing cards, and finally partnered up with young Mexican gambler Melquiades Segura. Together they rode into Chihuahua, Mexico, where they gambled and robbed for thrills. *El Bilito* departed from Segura but later joined up with him; then they traveled back to Arizona to pair up with Jesse Evans. They gained far-flung notoriety in western Texas, northern and eastern Mexico, and along the Rio Grande in New Mexico for their many daring crimes, robberies, and gambling. Ranchmen in Mexico, Texas, and New Mexico were always on the lookout for Segura, Evans, and *El Bilito*. While *El Bilito* made his extended stay in Fort Sumner and Mesilla, he worked for the Murphy Dolan Store Company and

William H. Bonney, aka "Billy the Kid," western outlaw (1859–1881). (Hayward Circer, ed., *Dictionary of American Portraits,* 1967)

spent his time on the cattle ranges of the Pecos Valley and was later employed by John Tuntsall and the McSween store.

Many *Nuevo Mexicanos* did not see *El Bilito* as a ruthless killer. In fact, they cheered him on as their hero. He was against the politicians and the outsiders who tried to steal the property and the rights of *Nuevo Mexicanos*. It has been noted by scholars that the *Nuevo Mexicanos* called him *El Chivato*, their little Billy, as he became the social bandit that symbolized the voice of the poor and oppressed. Billy represented the underclass that was overtaken by the movement to impose law and order on the New Mexico Territory. The *Nuevo Mexicanos* trusted him and invited him into their homes and treated him as one of the family; he often would say to them: "Oh timid Mexicans, don't be afraid. Listen to the sound of the bullets, the bullets of those gringos say: chee chee cha ree, if you don't kill me, I shall kill thee" (Wallis, 244). After he escaped from the Lincoln County jail, Billy made his way into the Capitan Mountains and stayed with one of his oldest *compadres,* Yginio Salazar.

Billy the Kid was known as a protector of the Native New Mexicans. *El Bilito* made an impressionable presence with *Nuevo Mexicanos* with his work as a *vaquero,* sheepherder, and his frequent visits with the *Nuevo Mexicana* women.

Chicano poet, novelist, and playwright Rudolfo Anaya wrote the play *Billy the Kid* (1994), which tells the story of two narrators who claim to have close relationships with Billy the Kid. One is an Anglo perspective of Billy the Kid and the other is the *Nuevo Mexicano* perspective of *El Bilito* and his close relationship with many *Nuevo Mexicanos*. In the play, Anaya juxtaposes *El Bilito's* love interest for *Nuevo Mexicanas* such as Josefina Maxwell (Paulita Maxwell) and Rosa Anaya, sister of Paco Anaya, the play's narrator. In his play *Billy the Kid*, Anaya documents two *corridos* and a *melodía*, which serve as important storytelling documents expanding on the legend of *El Bilito* in New Mexico and his affable relations with the native Hispanos. The first *corrido* written by Anaya is narrated by a Hispano representing the native *Nuevo Mexicano* population and describes the mourning of Billy the Kid's death. This *corrido*, *Billy the Kid*, informs the audience about the fateful night of 1881 when Billy was shot by Sheriff Pat Garrett in Pedro Maxwell's house in Fort Sumner, New Mexico. This *corrido* sings about Billy's lover, Rosita, and her witnessing his death as well as how she cried as he fell in her arms. This type of *corrido* can be classified within the category of *corridos* about *bandidos*. The second *corrido* that Anaya incorporates in his play is *El Corrido del Bilito*, which serves as a cautionary *corrido*, or *exemplum*-type *corrido*, since it warns mothers and fathers about protecting their children.

> *El era valiente y muy arriesgado*/He was very brave and intrepid
> *amante del juego y de las mujeres*/Lover of gambling and of women
> *Con ellas bailaba, con ellas cantaba*/He danced with them and sang with them
> *pero con pistola, muy lista y muy brava*/But with his gun very brave and ready.

The lyrics of the ballad serve as a warning to steer clear of how *El Bilito* lived and lost his life to gambling and violence. The third musical composition that Anaya writes is a song, *Billy y Rosita*, describing the love between the lovers. The song is delivered by the communal voice of the native folk who comment on the relationship between Bilito and Rosita.

Undoubtedly, Billy the Kid is most well known for becoming one of the most popular legends of the lawless Wild West frontier. However, the play and songs of Rudolfo Anaya are proof of the long-standing folklore related to *El Bilito*. Billy the Kid represented the people's political and cultural struggles against the Anglo regime that had taken their lands, and the social change that the territory of New Mexico was undergoing during the nineteenth century. *El Bilito* made an enormous impression on *Nuevo Mexicanos*, as they were involved in creating legendary stories, folk songs, and plays that still exist within the communities that he engaged with. As a folk expression, *Nuevo Mexicanos* hold *El Bilito* as folklore and legend that are part of the history and the making of New Mexico's statehood.

CECILIA JOSEPHINE ARAGÓN

See also: Comadre/Compadre; Corrido (Ballad)

Further Reading

Anaya, A. P. "Paco." *I Buried Billy*. College Station, TX: Creative Publishing Co., 1991.
Anaya, Rudolfo. *Billy the Kid*. Albuquerque: Rudolfo Anaya, 1994.

Herrera-Sobek, María. *Northward Bound: The Mexican Immigrant Experience in Ballad and Song*. Bloomington: Indiana University Press, 1993.

Otero, Miguel Antonio. *The Real Billy the Kid: With New Light on the Lincoln County War*. New York: Rufus Rockwell Wilson, Inc., 1936.

Rivera, John-Michael. *The Emergence of Mexican America*. New York: New York University Press, 2006.

Wallis, Michael. *Billy The Kid*. New York: W. W. Norton and Co., 2007.

BIRRIA

Birria is a Mexican dish originally from the state of Jalisco and traditionally made with goat meat or mutton, although other meats can also be used, including beef and even chicken. It is a favored dish for big celebrations such as weddings, baptisms, and other important holidays like Christmas and Easter. It is also a popular remedy for hangovers, most likely due to the spiciness. There are two basic methods of preparing the dish, but in both cases it is served with hot corn tortillas, chopped onions, cilantro, and wedges of lime, so people can make tacos with the meat and tortillas, and garnish them with the onions, cilantro and a squeeze of lime. In the most traditional one of these methods of preparation, the meat is marinated in an *adobo* of spices, and *ancho* and *guajillo* chili peppers, which gives *birria* its characteristic color and flavor, and cooked with very little liquid or in a double boiler. To prepare the *adobo*, the chili peppers have to be simmered in water for a little while until they are soft and rehydrated; then they are pureed in a blender or food processor with garlic, onions, cumin, ginger, oregano, cloves, cinnamon, thyme, bay leaves, salt, and pepper. The meat then is covered with the *adobo* and left to marinate for a while. Once it has absorbed the flavors of the marinade, the meat is placed in a large pot and cooked either in a bain-marie or simmered in a large pot with very little liquid.

The other way of making this dish is to cook the meat with lots of spices in a broth of *ancho* and *guajillo* chili peppers to make a hearty soup. This broth is made by pureeing the chili peppers and the spices mentioned previously, although some of the ingredients may change depending on the recipe, the region, or even the cook. One of the most common variations includes *cascabel* chili peppers in addition to the *guajillo* and *ancho* chili peppers. Similar to the previous recipe, the chili peppers have to be simmered and pureed. Once this is done, the meat is placed in a large pot or Dutch oven with onion, garlic, and herbs, and a little vinegar, water, and the chili pepper puree, and simmered, covered, for a long time until the meat is tender, adding water as needed. When the meat is almost done, it should be uncovered and simmered for another few minutes. Once it is done, it should rest before it is served. Some people prefer to shred the meat before serving it, while others prefer to chop it and serve big chunks of it. In either case, the meat is placed in a bowl, traditionally a terracotta bowl called *cajete*, and the broth added on top of the meat. Then it is topped with chopped onions, cilantro, and a wedge of lime, and accompanied with hot corn tortillas. Another option is to serve the meat on a plate and the broth in a *cajete* so people can make tacos with the meat and the tortillas, and eat the broth as a soup.

Another traditional version of the dish is called *birria tatemada* (or charred *birria*). This is commonly made with goat meat, but like all other *birrias* can be made with mutton or even beef. This kind of *birria* is prepared in a very similar way to the previous recipe—by simmering the meat in a broth, having previously marinated it for a long time in a puree made with the *ancho* and *guajillo* chili pepper and spices. However, once the meat is done, it is removed from the pot and rubbed with some of the remaining puree, and then placed in a pan (more traditional recipes call for a clay pan or *cazuela de barro* covered with agave leaves), then put in a hot oven where it is left until some parts of the meat are crispy or a little burnt. Traditionally in Mexico, *birria* used to be made in a pit in the ground over hot coals and covered with agave leaves; however, more recently clay pans have been used in the preparation of the dish, and today mostly large aluminum pots are favored to make the *birria*. Nonetheless, the use of agave leaves is not unusual. Also even though different kinds of meats can be used for *birria*, the dish remains associated with goat and mutton; so much so that some people even claim that the name of the dish, *birria*, derives from the onomatopoeic word *berrear*, which in Spanish means to bleat.

Also traditional in Mexico, particularly ubiquitous in Guadalajara and other cities and towns of the state of Jalisco, are the restaurants called *birrierías*, which often advertise their products with cooked goat heads either hanging from a pole or placed on top of a table next to the *birria* pot. These *birrierías* are very popular establishments and they can be simple family-run restaurants or even improvised stands on street corners or in parks, as well as more elaborate *fondas* specializing in *birria*. Particularly traditional though are the *birrierías* of popular markets such as the Mercado de San Juan de Dios, the Mercado La Libertad or the Mercado Corona in Guadalajara, or the typical Mercado Juárez in Tlaquepaque. These restaurants are an authentic institution in Jalisco and each place has its own recipe for *birria*. Some specialize in preparing the traditional goat or mutton *birria*, while others prefer the beef *birria* or master the perfect *birria tatemada*. It is part of the local folklore that the *birrierías* in the same market compete with each other for costumers by calling them and advertising their *birria* with loud cries.

The importance of *birria* for the cultural identity of the *jaliscienses* (the inhabitants of the state of Jalisco) or even more for the *tapatíos* (as the people from the city of Guadalajara are known) is evident in the attempts of the local governments to promote the dish through gastronomic and cultural events like the *Feria de la Birría*, a culinary fair in which people sample different kinds of *birrias* and other traditional dishes from diverse regions of the state of Jalisco, sold in stands arranged along the paths of the Jardín Hidalgo, a public park in Tlaquepaque, a suburb of Guadalajara. The state office of tourism and the local chamber of commerce have embraced this event, as well as other similar ones like the Food and Wine Festival of Guadalajara. Although the traditional *birria* is the *birria* from Guadalajara—and the festivals try to promote this image—there are other regional versions in the neighboring states, like the *birria estilo Zacatecas* (Zacatecas-style *birria*) or the *birria de Colima*, the state where, legend has it, the dish was invented by accident during the eruption of a volcano, when a shepherd was forced to abandon his goats in a cave only to return a few days later to find out that the heat of the lava and the steam from the humidity in the cave had cooked them so perfectly, leaving the meat tender and the skin crunchy. In face of this tragedy, he had the idea of collecting the meat and of adding some hot sauce to it, thus creating the dish.

In Zacatecas, the typical *birria* is called *birria revolcada* (or smeared or wiped *birria*), which is made with mutton, sautéed with onions, serrano chili peppers, and salsa. This *birria* is served dry, topped with chopped onions, cilantro, and a wedge of lime, and with a side of *consomé de borrego* or mutton broth. All these *birrias* are similar; however, the ingredients used in each version could vary slightly. Although *birrias* are far less common in the United States than in Mexican restaurants or even *taquerías*, in part because of the resistance from most Americans to eat goat meat, there is a small yet significant presence of this culinary tradition in some American cities, particularly in those with a high concentration of Mexicans from the state of Jalisco and the Bajío region in general, like Chicago, Los Angeles, San Francisco, or El Paso, where it is not rare to find *birrierías* in traditional Mexican neighborhoods.

RAFAEL HERNÁNDEZ

See also: Barbacoa; Carne Asada; Chiles (Peppers); Salsa (Sauce)

Further Reading

Burum, Linda. "A Taste of Jalisco" in *Los Angeles Times,* August 10th, 2007. http://articles .latimes.com/2005/aug/10/food/fo-counter10.

Quintana, Patricia, and Ignacio Urquiza. *The Taste of Mexico.* New York: Stewart, Tabori & Chang, 1986.

Zaslavsky, Nancy. *A Cook's Tour of Mexico. Authentic Recipes from the Country's Best Open Air Markets, City Fondas, and Home Kitchens.* New York: Saint Martin's Press, 1995.

THE BLACK LEGEND

The "Black Legend" as a term was coined in 1914 by Julián Juderías as a way of explaining the antipathy toward Spain that originated with colonial settlement in the sixteenth century. English and Dutch writers and thinkers classified the Spanish as morally inferior through their use of the Black Legend. By the early eighteenth century, the Black Legend was widely known and disseminated. Popular lore held that the Spanish colonists were crueler to natives than were their English and Dutch counterparts.

Origins of Modern Representations

Bartolomé de Las Casas, a Spanish priest, is well known for his denunciation of Spanish behavior in colonial Mexico and Guatemala. He fought for the New Laws of 1542, which by outlawing forced Indian labor dealt a blow to the *encomienda* system that existed in New Spain. Las Casas found that the conditions for Natives violated his beliefs in fairness, humanity, and religion. He penned *A Brief Account of the Devastation of the Indies* (1542), which, because of its distribution in Europe, led to greater development of the Black Legend. The book detailed death, illness, and slavery at the hands of Spaniards, including priests. Garcilaso de la Vega also wrote histories during the 1500s. He was the son of a conquistador and an Incan noble-woman. His history of Peru also contributed to the Black Legend. Their accounts of Spanish behavior gained credence to further the Black Legend because they were Spaniards speaking ill of their own behaviors. Las Casas was especially influential as a Catholic priest condemning other priests' actions.

The books, while persuasive, only added to an idea that was preconceived by the English and Dutch. The growth of the Black Legend had religious underpinnings as Protestant propaganda led to the solidification of the Black Legend. Anthony Padgen sees the Black Legend as originating with the Spanish atrocities in the Netherlands and specifically the sack of Antwerp in 1576. The Duke of Alba's cruelty in the Netherlands contributed to propaganda from the English and Dutch as they attempted to show the Spanish Catholics as proud, cruel, overbearing, and menacing. In this way the Black Legend had little to do with Spanish behavior in New Spain; rather, European powers fed the Black Legend for their own gain on the continent and abroad.

The Inquisition adds to the concept of the Black Legend as Spain was the center of the Counter-Reformation and therefore the recipient of animosity from English and European Protestants. The exaggerated accounts of unique cruelty fed a stereotype of the Spanish as licentious, Machiavellian, bloodthirsty, and greedy according to William Maltby. By casting the Spanish as uniquely cruel, the English and Dutch sought to establish their own empires as humane and just as opposed to the barbarian Spaniards. English travel narratives frequently included references to the Black Legend; for instance, Sir Walter Raleigh's entry in Richard Hakluyt's 1589 twelve-volume collection of English travel narratives describes the Spanish mistreatment of Guiana natives.

As the eighteenth century evolved, the Black Legend was firmly ensconced into European consciousness and occurs in literary iterations. Daniel Defoe in *A New Voyage Round the World* (1724) draws heavily on Las Casas's narrative to create his Spanish character and the critique of English colonialism. Modern representations of the Black Legend appear in the 1947 Hollywood film *Captain from Castile*. In the film the Spanish have no respect for religion, their own or the natives'. Violence characterizes interactions the Spanish have with themselves and with the Other, both in Spain and in the New World. Spanish noblemen follow a violent religion that murders young women, chase slaves with dogs, and steal from (or attempt to kill) their leaders. This stereotype served American interests in an era that began with the Red-baiting of the McCarthy hearings. By reviving the black legend, the United States reasserted its claim to benevolent care of the Western hemisphere.

In 1971, renewed scholarly interest in the Black Legend led to the publication of four books in English. Most of these books focused on the colonial aspect of the Black Legend. They include: Philip Powell's *Tree of Hate*, Charles Gibson's *The Black Legend: Anti-Spanish Attitudes in the Old World and the New*, William Maltby's *The Black Legend in England, 1558–1660*, and Juan Friede and Benjamin Keen, eds., *Bartolomé de Las Casas in History*.

LEIGH JOHNSON

See also: Aztec Empire

Further Reading

"La Leyenda Negra (The Black Legend): Myths and Truths about the Spanish Colonization of the Americas." http://www.kwabs.com/leyenda_negra_black_legend1.html.

Padgen, Anthony. *Spanish Imperialism and the Political Imagination.* New Haven, CT: Yale University Press, 1990.

Rummell, Kathryn. "Defoe and the Black Legend: The Spanish Stereotype in 'A New Voyage Round the World.'" *Rocky Mountain Review of Language and Literature* 52:2 (1998): 13–28.

BOGGS, RALPH STEELE (1901–1994)

Ralph Steele Boggs was a noted linguist and scholar of Spanish and Latin American folklore who, through bibliographies and surveys, guided generations of folklorists through the field. He worked to establish and develop programs in folklore at several North American universities, including the University of North Carolina at Chapel Hill and Indiana University, and throughout his career encouraged communication and collaboration among folklorists of the Americas.

Though a regular contributor to academic publications such as *Southern Folklore Quarterly* and *Publications of the Modern Language Association*, Boggs perhaps proved most influential as a bibliographer. A tireless researcher, Boggs amassed a collection of primary and secondary sources that became well known within the field. Often, Boggs shared these sources: He published a partial list in 1939's *Biografía del Folklore Mexicano*, and again in 1940 with *Bibliography of Latin American Folklore*. The latter text separately treated every country in Latin America, and included listings related to food, dance, and tales among many other topics. Boggs's bibliographies not only aided future researchers in the field, but also provided librarians a blueprint with which to expand their collections as interest in Latino folklore grew.

Boggs encouraged dialogue between folklorists across the Americas. In 1940, a year after receiving his Ph.D. in Spanish and folklore at the University of Chicago, he founded and became editor of *Folklore Américas*—a bilingual journal of folklore not restricted by national boundaries, covering North, South, and Central America. The journal's birthday cards to its subscribers from around the world, according to Boggs, helped to form personal relationships with scholars of the field.

In 1954, he was chosen to write *El Folklore en Los Estados Unidos de Norteamérica*, the first book in the Biblioteca Americana de Folklore series, which was sponsored by the Club Internacional de Folklore and sought to produce authoritative surveys of folklore across the Americas. This text offered a survey of North American folklore, a bibliography for further research, and Spanish translations of North American tales. Furthermore, Boggs included a directory of North American folklore societies, scholars, publications, archives, and museums, again facilitating correspondence and collaboration within the field.

Boggs spent his later professional career at the University of Miami, and was a charter member of the Florida Folklore Society in 1981. He died in 1994, survived by his wife, noted Dominican folklorist Edna Garrido de Boggs. His papers are held in the University of North Carolina at Chapel Hill's Southern Historical Collection.

NICK BRAVO

Further Reading

Boggs, Ralph Steele. *Bibliografía del Folklore Mexicano*. México, DF: Instituto Panamericano de Geografía e Historia, 1939.

Boggs, Ralph Steele. *Bibliography of Latin American Folklore: Tales, Festivals, Customs, Arts, Magic, Music*. New York: The H. W. Wilson Co., 1940.

Boggs, Ralph Steele. *El Folklore en Los Estados Unidos de Norteamérica*. Buenos Aires: Editorial Taigal, 1954.

BOLIVIA AND ITS FOLKLORE

The landlocked Republic of Bolivia, home to more than eight million people, is a country rich in traditions, cultural values and belief systems of South America. Bolivian folklore is the product of a complex amalgam of cultures and ethnicities that go back centuries. The blending of Indigenous, African, and European traditional customs is manifested in music, dance, narratives, and religious beliefs. Religious events (such as commemorating a Christian or Indigenous saint or deity) and political events (independence, battles or revolutions) are celebrated with folk music, parades, processions, dancing and rituals, as well as eating and drinking. While there are nationwide celebrations such as Carnival, Independence Day, All Saints' Day and Christmas, the entire calendar year is filled with festivals and cultural events, most of which are celebrated according to the cultural diversity of the country.

There are three distinct regions in Bolivia that are important to understanding Bolivian folklore and folk practices: the western *Altiplano*, or high plains; the lower mountain or semi-tropical regions; and the eastern lowlands. The *Altiplano* is a territory between the Andean mountain ranges, and despite its extreme altitude, most of Bolivia's population resides here. While most western Bolivians are either direct or partially descendants of the Aymara and the Quechua, the lowland regions are more ethnically diverse. These low altitude regions are home to other Indigenous groups like the Guaraní, Chiquitano and Mojeño, as well as people from other ethnicities such as the Afro-Bolivians and people of European descent. However, all over Bolivia, the urban lower and middle classes and rural farmers who wear European clothes and speak Spanish consider themselves *mestizos*, while the upper classes who relate themselves with Western European society are considered "whites" (Klein 2003, xii). Yet, it is precisely these ethnic and socio-cultural differences that make Bolivian folklore so rich and complex.

Bolivians who uphold their Aymara and Quechua cultures, most of whom live in the western highlands and the lower mountains, keep their cultures alive in their customs, religious beliefs and language. For example, they pay their respects to ancient Andean deities such as *Pachamama* (mother earth), *Supay* (an evil god), and the *Ekeko* (god of abundance), among others. They practice the *ch'alla*

Bolivian Aymaras form a line to thank a llama prior to sacrificing it during celebrations of the Aymara New Year on the highest mountain near the village of Curahuara de Carangas, 122 miles southeast of La Paz, Bolivia. Aymaras, the country's most politically influential ethnic group, follow a calendar based mainly on the agricultural cycle. (AP/Wide World Photos)

(libations, in which people sprinkle alcohol over material goods to invoke a blessing) and the *t'inku* (a ritual fight between two moieties), and they use *aymarismos* and *quechuismos* in their everyday speech.

Other ethnic groups from the semi-tropical regions such as the small Afro-Bolivian population also strive to maintain their various African customs and rituals. Some of the cultural Afro-Bolivian practices, such as music and dance, have contributed richly to Bolivian folklore. One example is the *saya*, a traditional dance that their ancestors used to perform as a way of giving vent to the abuses they suffered as slaves during the colonial period (Angola Maconde 2000, 100). The smaller Indigenous groups of the eastern lowlands, such as the Mojeño, Chiquitano, and Guaraní, are characterized by their folk beliefs in curing shamans and evil sorcerers, as well by their folk dances such as the *macheteros* and *tobas*. Non-Indigenous people from this lowland region often follow some of these folkloric manifestations whether they identify themselves with these Indigenous groups or not.

The eastern lowland inhabitants have also been partly influenced by some Brazilian folk feasts, like the pompous Carnival, which is celebrated in the department of Santa Cruz with plenty of music and dance. In addition, Bolivians from the lower mountains tend to identify themselves with their Andalusian and Galician ancestry, and with the gaucho folklore of Argentina in their customs and folk practices. Festivals such as *Fiesta de Compadres* or Godparents' Feast (a celebration which originated in northern Spain), and dances like *chaqueña* and *cueca chapaca* are celebrated with a mix of several native and foreign instruments such as the *erke* (a wind instrument) and the violin.

Interestingly, these cultural and ethnic differences are concealed, if not forgotten, among Bolivians who have migrated to the United States. Most Bolivians who have settled in this country seek to maintain and even strengthen their ties to their homeland by practicing and teaching their children pan-Bolivian customs such as music, dances, and folk beliefs. However, a number of Bolivian immigrants are also willing to become part of the U.S. Latino population to assimilate better to this country (Griffith 1990, E1). This might be due to the fact that Bolivians only represent a 0.1 percent of the total population of Hispanic origin dispersed in the United States.

According to the 2000 U.S. Census Bureau, there are 45,188 Bolivians in this country compared to 38,073 in 1990. The largest communities of Bolivians and Bolivian Americans are in Washington, D.C., Los Angeles, and Chicago. These communities are noteworthy for their participation in Hispanic festivals where they represent Bolivian folklore in music, dance, and food. Other events such as celebrating Bolivian Independence Day or just having lunch or dinner in a Bolivian restaurant are important to the social fabric of this small immigrant community as they attempt to preserve Bolivian folklore in the United States.

Bolivian Folk Narrative

A Myth from the Western Highlands

Bolivia and its neighboring Andean countries share similar folk narratives, particularly those of the origins of their ancient civilizations. In Bolivia, one of those legends is that of the Tihuanacu (or Tiwanaku) culture, which predates the Incas. Although little is known about this culture and its ceremonial center located near the southeastern shore of Lake Titicaca in the department of La Paz, archeologists agree that this was a civilization of the Middle Horizon (AD 600–1000). At its imperial apex (AD 400–800) the city-state had a population of 20,000 inhabitants; and by 1200 Tihuanacu's population completely disappeared. Tihuanacu possibly collapsed due to environmental reasons, or invasion by another culture. However, folk legends attribute the destruction of the Tihuanacu people to their disobedience to one of the most important Andean deities, Viracocha.

Bolivian folklorist Antonio Díaz Villamil narrates that according to the legend, Viracocha created Lake Titicaca on a day of sadness. The lake was formed by one of his tears. Realizing that there was enough water for people to survive, he created humans with his hands, and gave them life with his divine breath. This was the Tihuanacu nation. As soon as the Tihuanacu people came to life, they started to sing and to speak and to work the landscape. They changed the landscape with the help of the water from Lake Titicaca and began farming potatoes and corn.

These people were obedient to the laws of Viracocha. They lived peacefully and with all justice, and therefore, they did not have weapons. Viracocha was pleased with such people and protected them from pain and sickness. He filled them with goods and favors. But it had been foretold that one day Supay, an evil deity, would play a role in the attitude of the Tihuanacu people. Supay came to live among them; he disguised himself as one of them. They started to believe his words, which were far from the teachings of Viracocha. The Tihuanacu people became greedy and evil; they started wars against other men and they were proud of it.

Viracocha first warned them by sending droughts and natural disasters, but they did not change their ways. Viracocha became angry with these people, and full of wrath transformed them all into stones. Their land was covered with monoliths, petrified men and women, which can be seen even today.

A Myth from the Lowland Region

Most of the myths from the lowland regions come from religious themes such as the appearance of the Virgin in a location, which is then made into a shrine. Other myths, however, explain how a particular reality came to be. The myth of the *Bibosi* (ficus), a large palm tree that produces a buttery fruit called *motacú*, narrates the love story of an eastern couple. According to the legend, there was a hard-working young man, who was very strong and diligent. He was in love with a young woman who belonged to a wealthy family. She was also in love with him.

When her parents found out about their love, they offered her hand to a rich man. Knowing that she had to accept this new relationship, she decided to meet with her beloved for the last time. They arranged a meeting one night before her wedding. When they saw each other, they cried and hugged with such passion that they fell dead. Immediately after their death, the first *Bibosi* tree grew up in that place.

Bolivian Traditions, Customs, and Beliefs

Bolivian folkloric narrative is also present in and combined with other folkloric expressions such as dances, songs and rituals. Most of the dances and songs are the essential part of folkloric feasts such as *Carnaval* (Carnival), Independence Day celebrations and religious pilgrimages. Other customs and beliefs are manifested in *Alacitas* (a miniature market) and All Saints' Day.

Carnaval

Carnaval is the biggest annual festival in Bolivia and takes place the week before Lent. Oruro's *Carnaval* is the most renowned and largest folkloric celebration of Bolivia. In the city of Oruro, candlelight processions and dance group practices begin several weeks before *Carnaval* itself, with a solemn pledge of loyalty to the Virgin in the sanctuary. The main event is the spectacular *entrada* (entrance procession) on the Saturday before Ash Wednesday. During the *entrada* the Archangel Saint Michael, the chief devil Lucifer, and a host of male and female devils, condors, and bears march and dance the *diablada* (the devil dance) on the streets.

The *diablada* is an old tradition that goes back to the colonial period. Various mythical and religious accounts explain its origins. One describes a miner who fell asleep in a shaft after making an offering to the devil. He awoke to find the devil dancing in front of him. The devil left the mine, still continuing his dance, and the man followed along in the first devil dance (Blair 1990, 3). Another legend tells the story of how the Virgin of *Candelaria* took pity on a man who was seriously injured by a traveler who took him for a thief. The Virgin helped him reach his home near the mine at the base of the mountain *Pie de Gallo*, and comforted him until he died. When the miners found him, they also found an image of the Virgin hanging over his head. Today, that mine is known as the *Socavón de la Virgen* (The Underground Chamber of the Virgin), and a large church, the *Santuario de la Virgen del Socavón*, has been built over it to house the Virgin and patroness of that town. One last account is that the *diablada* is a reenactment of the ancient rituals of the Uru people in which the dance represented a battle between a feminine Andean goddess and a mountain male god called Supay (Costas 1967, 141). This ceremony has been concealed in the form of a Catholic ritual with the triumph of good over evil.

The *Carnaval* of Oruro also features a dozen other dances such as the *caporales, llameradas, morenadas*, and *t'inkus*, which will be described later (pp. 128–130). The rest of the feast days of *Carnaval* are marked by family reunions and *ch'alla* libations, in which people sprinkle alcohol over material goods to invoke a blessing. The *ch'alla* is also common in other cities like La Paz and Potosí during the *Carnaval* celebration. People adorn their possessions with streamers and confetti only to pour alcohol on top of them in the hope of increasing their wealth in the next year. Despite the cold weather of these regions, young and adults initiate water balloon fights in the streets until *Carnaval* is over or "buried" on Sunday afternoon.

Carnaval in the lowland plains of Tarija is celebrated differently with the *Fiesta de Compadres* (Godfathers' celebration), the largest pre-*Carnaval* festival. This tradition originated in northern Spain. It was brought by some Spanish women during the colonial period, and adopted by the locals afterward. During this celebration there are special basket tableaux made out of a type of Galician bread called *bollus preñau*. There are also flowers, small cakes, and other gifts, which are exchanged between friends and relatives. Dances like *rueda, cueca chapaca*, and *montoneros* are accompanied by the sounds of traditional instruments called *erkes* (a wind instrument made of oxen horns) and *cajitas* (small percussion boxes). The celebrations end on Sunday afternoon when locals "bury" all their evil thoughts and deeds in preparation for Lent.

In the eastern lowlands, people also celebrate dancing, drinking, and playing with water balloons, colored flour, and confetti. The biggest show takes place in Santa Cruz with the coronation of the *Carnaval* queen, which attracts over 10,000 people. The traditional dances of this festivity are the *carnavalito, takiraris*, and the *macheteros*.

All Saints' Day

Todos (los) Santos or All Saints' Day is a blending of Andean rituals with Catholic beliefs. Traditions tell that on midday of the first of November the gates of heaven are open so that the dead return to earth, where they will remain until midday of the second of November. In the Andean calendar, this day marks the beginning of the rainy season, which will prepare the earth for agriculture.

During this celebration, relatives of the deceased visit their graves to spend time with them. They bring framed pictures of their late relatives and decorate their tombs with stucco and pastel colors. Family and friends of the deceased make a special type of bread called *t'antawawas*, which they bring to the cemetery along with fruits, candies and drinks. While much of the food, drinks and coca are offered to the dead, the remaining of it is given to children who offer to pray and sing for those souls.

During this festivity, people of Indigenous and non-Indigenous descent also pay their respect to *Pachamama* (Mother Earth) by pouring some of the liquids onto the ground of the graveyard as they reenact reciprocity rituals with the ancient deities. The All Saints celebration ends with somewhat quiet dances with accompaniment on a *charango* (a small guitar usually made from an armadillo shell) and *zampoñas* (panpipes).

Independence Day

Also called *Día de la Patria* is a national holiday that brings Bolivians together as they celebrate the ending of Spanish rule in 1825. Preparations for the main event, which takes place on August 6th in every city and town, begin weeks earlier as school-age children, teachers, government employees, and a number of national organizations rehearse their civic processions. After a recapitulation of the main events in the history of Bolivia, children and adults sing the national anthem, the popular song "Viva mi patria Bolivia" (Long life to my country Bolivia), and dance the most traditional and representative folkloric dances of Bolivia.

Pilgrimages and Other Religious Festivities

Religious festivities such as the feasts of the Virgin of Urkupiña, Virgin of Candelaria (or Copacabana), other local Virgins, as well as different patron saints are dispersed in the Bolivian calendar. They are celebrated everywhere in villages and towns, and play a vital role in the relationship between urban and rural Bolivia.

The feast of the Virgin of Urkupiña is celebrated every year in Quillacollo, Cochabamba for three consecutive days beginning on August 15th. Thousands of people come to participate in this festival. The pilgrims come to the Virgin's shrine to offer candles, flowers, and money. Similarly, the weeklong festival of Copacabana, a small town located near Lake Titicaca in La Paz, honors the image of the Virgin of Candelaria. Pilgrimage to this shrine, however, goes back to pre-Columbian times as the Incas organized processions to the temple of the sun in this location. On Good Friday, thousands of pilgrims, many of whom have journeyed the hundred kilometers from La Paz on foot (and some on their knees), climb the village's Hill of Calvary. They stop at the stations of the cross or the Via Crucis to do penance and to say prayers.

The *festividad de Nuestro Señor del Gran Poder*, or the Feast of the Great Power of Jesus, is perhaps the most lively festival of La Paz. *Gran Poder* is a popular district in La Paz, known for its commercial activity. Many Aymara migrants of this district have successfully become traders, merchants, craftsmen, and drivers, and have reached positions of respect and status. In a similar fashion to *Carnaval*, and after a procession of a Christ with native features, this festivity presents a number of folkloric dances sponsored by these merchants and traders along the main streets of La Paz. Although the *festividad de Nuestro Señor del Gran Poder* is a folkloric event, it is also an event in which these people compete against each other for status and recognition.

Similar events also take place in other Bolivian towns during the festivals for patron saints. These celebrations offer the migrants, who have settled elsewhere, the chance to maintain or strengthen their links with their hometowns. During the traditional celebrations migrants can achieve a higher status by their financial contributions to their hometown festivities or by donating money for different projects within the village, such as the construction of schools or roads.

Alacitas

Alacitas used to be a regional tradition of La Paz; however, it became a national custom with movable dates. *Alacitas* is a giant market of miniatures that extends over a continuously increasing area of a city or town. According to José Costas, *Alacita* is an Aymara term that means "buy from me" (*cómprame*). The celebration is also interpreted as the Feast of Plenty, named for a small figurine of a man carrying abundant objects, called the *Ekeko*. According to traditional accounts, the *Ekeko* is an Aymara god of the family, a symbol of prosperity, wealth, love, and fertility. References to this Andean god date from a few chronicles written in the seventeenth century. Part of the ritual consists in hanging the *Ekeko* with various desired miniature objects, which represent objects or wishes believers hope to achieve through this god's power (van Lindert and Verkoren 1994, 63). Though no dances are part of this celebration, traditional food such as *mote con queso* (cooked corn and cheese) is sold in several posts in this market.

Navidad

Christmas in Bolivia, as in other countries, is becoming more and more commercial. Old Bolivian traditions like nativity plays or Indigenous children singing *villancicos* (songs from the village) are slowly disappearing. The *villancicos* are a Spanish tradition that was imported to Bolivia around the eighteenth century. In different Bolivian cities and towns, Indigenous children dress up as shepherds and play musical instruments in the main streets. The pedestrians who listen to their songs give them a tip, so these children can afford to buy themselves something.

Around the country, Bolivian children eagerly await for Christmas Eve to open their presents. At midnight, all the family gets together for a toast and to eat the traditional *Picana de Navidad*, a sweet and spicy beef and chicken stew with vegetables. Dinner ends with an exchange of good wishes by every member of the family. Shortly after midnight, people attend mass to remember the meaning of Christmas and to say prayers. Following mass, there is a procession in honor of baby Jesus, and children and adults sing *villancicos* until dawn.

Bolivian Traditional Music

Music and dance are the utmost expressions of Bolivian folklore. These two elements are present in all the festivals described above as well in other small and local celebrations. Depending on the region and the event, the beat of the music changes from melancholic to cheerful. In the *Altiplano*, there are different types of wind, percussion and chord instruments. The best-known instruments are the *zampoña*, *quena*, *charango*, and the *bombo*. The *zampoña* is a panpipe that varies in size and consists of rows of pieces of reed joined to each other. The ideal *zampoña* has two rows that give the flute-player a range of two octaves (Costas 1967, 320). Another wind instrument is the *quena*, a long bamboo flute that produces both high and low tones. It has a notched mouthpiece, a variable number of finger holes in the front, and one thumb hole in the back. Bolivia has a number of different types of *quenas*, which produce a variety of sounds.

The *charango* is a string instrument traditionally made with the shell of the back of an armadillo (*quirquincho*), although today *charangos* are commonly made of wood. It usually has ten strings in five courses of two strings each. The *charango* player can play sustained melodies at rapid speed with an alternating thumb/finger pattern (Costas 1967, 221). An additional emblematic instrument of the Bolivian music is the *bombo*, a leather drum made of a hollow log, with the inside scraped and chiseled. The drumheads are made of animal skin, which produces a deep, dark sound. The *bombo* is played while hanging at the side of the drummer, who drapes one arm over the drum, to play it from above with a soft-headed mallet, while also striking it from the front with a stick (Costas 1967, 89). The *bombo* serves as a combination of bass and percussion that maintains the meter.

Other folkloric instruments of Bolivia are the *erke*, *pututu*, and the *caña*. The *erke* and the *pututu* are wind instruments made of horn of oxen. The *erke* is traditionally played in Tarija and other lowland plains. It has a short reed that extends from the end of the horn to produce low and high notes. The *pututu* is mostly played in Andean towns to summon a meeting. Unlike the *erke*, the *pututu* does not have a reed attached; therefore it only produces low sounds. The *caña* is an instrument similar to a trumpet, except it is not made of brass. The tube of the *caña* is made of reeds covered with oxen skin, which connects to a bended horn of an ox. The player of a *caña* blows to make the instrument vibrate to produce short and long notes with different rhythms.

A few Bolivian folk songs such as "El Cóndor Pasa" and "Llorando se fue" are known internationally. In the 1960s, "El Cóndor Pasa" was translated into English and recorded in France by Simon and Garfunkel (van Lindert and Verkoren 1994, 65). "Llorando se fue," Bolivia's most popular song, composed by *Los Kjarkas*, gave origin to the famous Brazilian *Lambada*. Other songs also played and sung by *Los Kjarkas*, mostly those from the Afro-Bolivian *saya*, have been declared as patrimonies of Bolivian folklore. A number of well-known folk groups like *Rumillajta, Wara, Raíces*, and *El Trío Oriental* among others have performed in international venues demonstrating Bolivia's rich and diverse folklore.

Bolivian devil dancers perform a traditional "Diablada" dance during carnival celebrations in the city of Oruro, south of Bolivia's capital, La Paz. (AP/Wide World Photos)

The Folkloric Dances of Bolivia

Most of the Bolivian dances share similarities with those of other countries like Peru, Chile, and northern Argentina. Although Bolivia has hundreds of different dances, the following are the most representative folkloric dances that Bolivians dance in their country and abroad.

Diablada

As described above, the *diablada* dance is performed in all the artistic and folkloric expressions of Bolivia, particularly during Carnival. The dance starts with the encounter between two powerful angelic beings. One represents harmony (the archangel Michael), and the other represents discontent and bitterness (Lucifer). The meeting takes place right on the edge of hell, and then the devil's army bursts in warlike attitude. At the call of Archangel Michael, heavenly legions arrive and the first battle starts. The first battle is won by the devils, who invade the earth to exterminate Christianity. Then the second battle takes place, and the mortals awaiting the outcome are frightened. When the battle is over, the devils are defeated, and they must suffer the shame of confessing their sins, "the Seven Deadly Sins," to the Holy Light.

Morenada

The dance of the *morenos* (darker-skinned people) dates back to the seventeenth century. The dance was an attempt to mock the ceremonial dances of the courts of the Viceroyalty of Peru. The heavy costumes used in this dance, which usually weigh sixty to eighty pounds, are a hyperbolic imitation of the court costume of Philip III. They also resemble the elaborated colonial archangels' garments. An interesting element of the *morenada* costume is the traditional mask of a black person, which apparently serves to highlight the ethnic and cultural miscegenation of this region. The *morenos* move slowly as they play their *matraca*, a wooden instrument that makes sharp sounds.

Llamerada

The dance of *llameros* (llama herders) imitates the daily life of the highland llama herders. Its choreography depicts the traditional Andean roundup to sheer the animals' wool. The dancers form a human fence to push the llamas together in a circle until they can reach them with their hands. The dancers' attire consists of a hat, woolen clothes, and slingshots, the latter being the most important part of the choreography and the costume. Most of the *llamerada* steps include the movement of the slingshots mimicking the driving of the llamas or the throwing of the stones.

T'inku

T'inku is a Quechua word, which means "encounter." In the form of a dance, it represents an ancient ritual conflict practiced by local people in the department of Potosí. In a local kinship system, people are divided into two moieties (two halves) of unequal status. These groups fight hand-to-hand in a symbolic and ceremonial dance. According to the ritual, the victors will have a prosperous year as well as more prestige. The dance is led by the male heads of each group, the women dance outside the male group holding flags that represent their moieties.

Cueca

The Bolivian *cueca* is a variation of the Chilean *cueca* and the Peruvian *marinera*. In Bolivia, the *cueca* is a popular dance that varies and is enriched by the dancers of each region. Therefore, there are several types of *cuecas*, such as the *cueca paceña* (from La Paz), *cueca cochabambina* (from Cochabamba), *cueca chuquisaqueña* (from Chuquisaca) and *cueca chapaca* (from Tarija). This dance requires a man and a woman, each carrying a handkerchief in the right hand. Through body language, the woman flirts with the man and attracts him with the handkerchief. The man is enticed to court the woman as he extends his handkerchief to her. Since this dance requires several parallel movements, it is usually performed in ballrooms rather than at outdoor events.

Caporales and Afro-Bolivian Saya

The *caporales* is a popular dance present in almost all Bolivian festivities and is often combined with the Afro-Bolivian *saya*, a dance that represents the relief of the black men and women after their onerous work in the fields. The *caporales* dance imitates the excessive control of the overseer (*caporal*) upon the black workers, and the *saya* highlights the social and cultural values of the people of African descent. For the black people of the Yungas region in the lower mountains, singing and dancing were and are the expression of all life matters. Singing is also a means to maintain and transmit their oral history. Their songs are led by a group of soloists who play drums and *wiros* (bamboo straws), while the women dance by shaking their hips and making small steps.

A few verses of a traditional Afro-Bolivian *saya* by Juan Angola Maconde say:

> Siempre ando solito
> buscando la felicidad
> llorando mi mala suerte
> hasta el día de mi muerte.
>
> I always walk by myself
> looking for happiness
> lamenting my bad luck
> until the day I die.
>
> . . . .
> Esta caja que yo toco
> tiene boca y sabe hablar
> solo los ojos le faltan
> pa' ayudarme a llorar.
>
> The drum I play
> has a mouth and can talk
> it only lacks a pair of eyes
> to help me cry.

As the *saya* dancers sing these or other lyrics, the *caporal* (overseer) enters as a commanding figure. The *caporal* depicts an old Spanish foreman wearing long boots with large rattles, carrying a whip in one hand and a hat in the other. In the modern version of this dance, all the men wear the *caporal* costume while the women wear short skirts, wide-sleeve shirts, and a bowler hat, which differs from the traditional attire of the Afro-Bolivian *saya* in which the women wear long skirts and embroidered shirts. Men and women dance in separated rows in a progressive march style. This dance has become very popular mostly among young men and women because it is invigorating.

Of all the folkloric dances of Bolivia, the ones represented most in Hispanic festivals in the United States are the *diablada*, *morenada*, and the *caporales/saya*. According to Tim Eigo, starting in the late twentieth century, Bolivian dances began to appeal to a broader audience in the United States. In 1996, for example, Bolivian folkloric dancers in Arlington, Virginia, participated in about 90 cultural events, nine major parades, and twenty-two smaller festivals (Eigo 2008, 7). Every year, Bolivian folkloric dancers of New York, San Francisco, Los Angeles, and Washington, D.C., perform their dances in schools, theaters, and other venues.

Bolivian Folk Food

A traditional Bolivian diet depends on the crops that grow in each region. The western highlands produce hundreds of different types of potatoes as well as quinoa and lima beans. The lower mountains supply more vegetables and fruits, and the eastern lowlands provide the country with rice, sugar cane, yucca, plantain, and a variety of tropical fruits. Fish from the rivers and lakes are also an important part of the Bolivian diet. The most traditional Bolivian dishes include different types of meat, potatoes, and rice as well as the essential *chuño* and *t'unta* (dry potatoes). The spicy sauce *llajwa* is optional for most people.

A few examples of folk dishes from the western region are: *thimpu*, a stew made of lamb, rice, *chuño*, potatoes and yellow peppers; *k'arachi*, a small fried fish with potatoes and rice; *chairo*, a broth made of diced *chuño*, cured meat, maize and wheat grains; and *salteñas*, oval baked pastries, stuffed with various fillings and eaten as a mid-morning snack. Dishes from the lower mountain region are the *sillp'anchu* (Quechua for "thin meat"), which are breaded beef cutlets served with an egg on top; *fritanga*, pork ribs cooked with red pepper, green onions and white potatoes; and *morcilla*, pork sausage with spices. Finally, traditional dishes from the eastern lowlands include the *pacú*, a fried river fish garnished with vegetables; *masaco de plátano*, ground green plantains crushed with jerked beef; and *caldo de peta*, turtle soup.

Bolivian Folk Speech

Bolivian Spanish has been influenced by the Aymara and Quechua languages, and a rich compendium of words are used in daily speech. A few examples provided by Gómez and Fernández Naranjo in their *Diccionario de Bolivianismos* are: *achachi* (an old person); *achuntar* (to be accurate); *ch'acha* (missing school without a valid reason); *ch'iti* (a disobedient child); *hach'a* (a large, robust man); *imilla* (an Indigenous girl); *k'ullu* (a stick); *laphincho* (a person who appears to have money, but in reality doesn't); *lloqalla* (an Indigenous boy); *manq'a-gasto* (a person who doesn't work or earn a living); *muru* (a person who shaves his/her hair), *q'elili* (a temperamental person); *t'inka* (a premonition); *tutuma* (the shell of a medium size fruit cut into two pieces, and used as a bowl).

Some common Bolivian phrases are: "ir a queso" (walking); "llegar a las quinientas" (arrive very late); "estar de ch'aki" (a person with a severe headache or other aftereffects caused by drinking an excess of alcohol); "gana y gusto" (a remark to refer to a rude person); "hasta por ahí nomás" (a phrase that indicates some kind of limitation; for example, "Yo hablo inglés hasta por ahí nomás," "I speak very little English"); "irse a Sucre" (to go mad; this phrase refers to the mental hospital of Sucre); "por si las moscas" (to have precaution, to be cautious); and "pucha caray" (an expression of frustration).

Bolivian folklore is rich and diverse. The examples provided in this entry are only a fragment of the numerous folkloric expressions of Bolivia. Bolivian folklorists like Antonio Paredes Candia, Antonio Villamil de Rada, Alberto Guerra Gutiérrez, and José Costas Arguedas have been pivotal to the scholarship of Bolivian folklore. However, most of their works have not been translated into English, which makes their access difficult to a broader audience. Understanding that Bolivian folklore is a mix of various traditional customs serves to recognize the overall identity of Bolivian immigrants in the United States.

Sara Vicuña Guengerich

See also: Peru and Its Folklore

Further Reading

Angola Maconde, Juan. *Raíces de un pueblo. Cultura Afroboliviana*. La Paz: Producciones Cima, 2000.

Blair, David N. *The Land and People of Bolivia*. New York: J. B. Lippincott, 1990.

Costas, José. *Diccionario del Folklore Boliviano*. Sucre: Universidad Mayor de San Francisco Xavier de Chuquisaca, 1967.

Díaz Villamil, Antonio. *Leyendas de mi tierra*. La Paz: Editorial Juventud, 2001.

Eigo, Tim. "Bolivian Americans." Every Culture. www.everyculture.com/multi/A-Br/Bolivian-Americans.html.

Griffith, Stephanie. "Bolivians Reach for the American Dream: Well-Educated Immigrants with High Aspirations Work Hard, Prosper in D.C. Area." *The Washington Post*. May 8, 1990, p. E1.

Guerra, Alberto. *Folklore Boliviano*. La Paz: Los Amigos del Libro, 1990.

Klein, Herbert S. *A Concise History of Bolivia*. New York: Cambridge University Press, 2003.

Paredes Candia, Antonio. *La danza folklórica en Bolivia*. La Paz: Editorial Popular, 1991.

van Lindert, Paul, and Otto Verkoren. *Bolivia. A Guide to the People, Politics and Culture*. London: Latin American Bureau, 1994.

BOMBA

The term *bomba* refers to a number of well-known folkloric Afro–Puerto Rican percussion-driven rhythms and associated dance styles. It emerged as early as the seventeenth century from the music and dance of the African slaves brought to Puerto Rico during the Spanish colonization. Its roots can be traced to the coastal regions and plantations of areas such as Loíza, Ponce, and Mayagüez.

Bomba is easily recognized by the Afro-rhythms played on two or three differently pitched barrel-shaped drums, known as *barriles* and played by hand, as well as the call-and-response structure of the lyrics, sung by a lead singer and a chorus. Other common instruments used to keep rhythms include a maraca (of Indigenous origin) and the palitos or *cuás*, two sticks hit against the wood of the *barriles* or any other piece of wood. The highest-pitched drum is known as the *subidor* or *primo*, while lower pitch drums are known as *buleador* and *segundo*. There are over a dozen different *bomba* rhythms, some examples are: *sica, yuba, cuembé, holandés, babú, belén, cunyá, yubá*, and *leró*. Some of the rhythms are duple meter while others are triple meter, often 2/4 or 6/8.

Bomba also features a unique dance style. The dancers engage in a challenge with the highest-pitched drum, in which the drummer follows the dancers' body movements. The dancers' movements focus largely, though not exclusively, on the hips, embellished with staccato movements in conversation with the drums, for example with the hands, feet, shoulder, head, or sometimes jumps. The dance is performed both by men and women. Women dancers often wear large skirts which they hold with their hands and move throughout the dance, challenging the drummer to catch the accented movements. The loose structure of the dance often includes an initial stroll around or *paseo*, a greeting to the drum, and a sudden jerk or *ponche* that initiates the improvisational dance consisting of a number of free-style moves or *piquetes*. Sometimes a couple dances together, challenging each other, although not touching, while other times there is a solo dancer.

Rather than simply a music genre, *bomba* is a social event and participatory performance in which musicians, singers, and dancers converse through rhythmic improvisation. A crowd often gathers around and people take turns participating in different ways. *Bomba* is a popular genre in Puerto Rico and the Puerto Rican diaspora in the continental United States, especially New York City. It is present at most Puerto Rican social gatherings and has come to be closely tied to Puerto Rican identity. Some important performers of *bomba* include: Rafael Cortijo, Ismael Rivera, the Cepeda family, Marciel Reyes, and Los Pleneros de la 21. *Bomba* is closely related to a more lyrical but similar Puerto Rican folkloric music genre known as plena. In fact, they are often referred to as *bomba y plena*. *Bomba* also had a strong influence in the emergence of the genre we have come to know as salsa.

NADIA DE LEÓN

See also: Los Pleneros de la 21; Plena

Further Reading

Aparicio, Frances. *Listening to Salsa: Gender, Latin Popular Music, and Puerto Rican Cultures.* Hanover, NH: Wesleyan University Press, 1998.

Flores, Juan. *From Bomba to Hip-Hop: Puerto Rican Culture and Latino Identity.* New York: Columbia University Press, 2000.

Manuel, Peter, Kenneth Bilby, and Michael Largey. "Puerto Rico." In *Caribbean Currents: Caribbean Music from Rumba to Reggae.* Philadelphia: Temple University Press, 2006.

Smithsonian Folkways. Soundscapes, *Puerto Rican Bomba and Plena: Shared Traditions—Distinct Rhythms.* http://www.folkways.si.edu/explore_folkways/bomba_plena.aspx.

BOOGIE WOOGIE

Boogie woogie is a piano-based style of the blues dating to the 1930s and 1940s. Though falling within the blues genre, boogie woogie is more about dancing rather than the visceral elements associated with blues music. Although the origins of this style are thought to be unknown, the same cannot be said for the approach to piano playing used by the early proponents of boogie woogie. Moreover, future styles of popular music would be influenced by the piano styles of boogie woogie music.

While some historians feel the origins of boogie woogie are not known, others claim that the boogie's piano bass patterns may have been created in logging camps and oil boomtowns in Louisiana, Mississippi, and Texas. Still others associate the style's history with honky tonk bars in the South (as captured by Alice Walker in her novel *The Color Purple*).

The boogie woogie rhythm was felt in the early part of the twentieth century, just as ragtime (an early form of jazz) was also becoming popular. Ragtime also used the "stride" form of piano playing, which would also be associated with boogie woogie. Jelly Roll Morton, one of the masters of ragtime, claimed that anyone who could get their hands on a piano would invent their version of the blues. These players were known to play barrelhouse or boogie woogie music. It did not stop here: Blues guitarist Huddie Ledbetter (Leadbelly) never showed interest in jazz. He favored the blues, which he learned in Texas in 1910. He especially worked at transposing the left-hand styles of boogie woogie piano players. This implies that while ragtime musicians were trained, could read music, understood theory and in some cases were composers, boogie woogie pianists were not.

Jimmy Yancey and Pine Top Smith were some of the better-known pianists. According to Marshall Stearns, early boogie-woogie pianists worked out their styles without any knowledge of how the European concert tradition emphasized how a piano should be played. Musicologists emphasize those piano players who were not trained, could not read music, and played piano in a manner allowing them to interpret what they wanted to play. And this was the key characteristic of boogie woogie.

But why would a seemingly American musical tradition find its way to a work on Latino folklore? To answer this question we turn our attention to New Orleans and the influence of Latin music. In the early part of the twentieth century, Afro Cuban rhythms began to influence music in the United States. New Orleans was the entry point as evidenced by the presence of Cuban musicians who brought with them various styles of music. At the same time, Mexican musicians, who, since the latter years of the nineteenth century, had been performing in the city, also brought popular styles to the growing musical traditions found there. In time, black musicians began incorporating Afro Cuban rhythms into the developing style of ragtime and the blues. This was especially noticeable in piano players, who incorporated syncopated rhythms, especially those from a popular Cuban dance, the *habanera*. This dance was the first Latin dance to influence U.S. music. Early proponents of this Afro Cuban influence were Jelly Roll Morton (ragtime) and W. C. Handy (jazz and blues). Both utilized a variation of the "stride," a

Composer, pianist, and bandleader Ferdinand "Jelly Roll" Morton, self-proclaimed "originator of jazz," is shown in 1938 in Washington, D.C., recording the priceless Library of Congress documentaries—playing, singing, and talking of the origins of jazz—for the Library's archivist Alan Lomax. (AP/Wide World Photos)

style of piano playing that borrowed from the habanera rhythms. It is from this style that boogie woogie, or barrelhouse, emerged.

Boogie woogie piano playing is basically a mirror of the "stride" piano playing of New Orleans, which involves cross rhythms and bass patterns that parallel Afro Cuban *tumbaos* (a way of playing musical phrases which are bass rhythms with the left hand on the piano paralleled by the upright bass, while the right hand improvises). New Orleans became the center of this trend, and the approach to piano playing went on to influence ragtime, blues, and boogie woogie, eventually influencing New York, Midwest, West coast musicians

So, Cuban music influenced piano playing in each of the three styles. In particular the habanera rhythm struck a chord on left-hand styles of piano playing. Though boogie woogie was popular in the early part of the twentieth century, this mixing of styles was going on as early as 1880. In 1896, for example, William H. Tyers published *La Trocha* with a strong *habanera* line. That is, pianists took the *habanera's ritmo de tango* (a basic element found in the Argentinean tango) and the *clave*, a rhythm counted as 2–3 or 3–2 and still a key element in Latin music. From these rhythmic elements, boogie woogie finds its use of syncopation. Found in ragtime, jazz, sometimes rock, syncopation is of African origin. A rhythm with an off-beat and played with the pianist's right hand, it made its way to the Americas via slavery from West Africa. Jimmy Yancey's left-hand bass-patterns and right-hand syncopation showed strong habanera and tango influences in his boogie-woogie playing. One only need hear songs such as "Memphis Blues" and "Panama" to grasp this rhythm.

And while boogie woogie does not sound "Latin" the key to understanding its importance is in the influence of Afro Cuban rhythms on its later development. Boogie went on to influence swing, country swing, and jump blues in the 1940s. Lalo Guerrero's recording of *Muy Sabroso Blues* and Don Tosti's *Pachuco Boogie* both reflect boogie woogie influence. This went on into the 1950s, where rock and roll and rockabilly also borrowed from boogie woogie and habanera rhythms.

CARLOS F. ORTEGA

See also: African Influence on Latino Folklore; Afro-Colombian Music; Cuban Americans and Their Folklore

Further Reading

Boogiewoogie.com. www.boogiewoogie.com.

Morales, Ed. *The Latin Beat: The Rhythms and Roots of Latin Music: From Bossa Nova to Salsa and Beyond.* New York: St. Martin's Griffin, 2003.

Roberts, John Storm. *The Latin Tinge: The Impact of Latin American Music on the United States.* 2nd ed. New York: Oxford University Press, 1999.

Stearns, Marshall. *The Story of Jazz.* New York: The New American Library, 1958.

BOTÁNICAS

A fixture in larger Latino communities in the United States, *botánicas* are storefronts that in addition to selling spiritual supplies also provide numerous social and therapeutic functions to their communities and are an integral part of the American religious fabric.

Patrons shop at the Botánica San Lazarito in the Jackson Heights section of Queens, New York. Long a staple in Hispanic culture, *botánicas* are flourishing in New York City neighborhoods and other urban locations with large immigrant populations. (AP/Wide World Photos)

The literal meaning of *botánica* is "plant or botany store" and some *botánicas* adhere to a secular function as natural pharmacies where customers purchase traditional plant and herb-based remedies. Other *botánicas* function solely in the spiritual realm where information is channeled from beyond and remedies are obtained from acts of magic and petitions to spirits. Most *botánicas* exist pragmatically between the two poles, mixing holistic remedies and metaphysical practices, depending on what is needed for each client. Altars and cash registers peacefully co-exist in the *botánica*, and there is no clear line between customer, client and practitioner.

With bright signs on the exterior and an interior filled from floor to ceiling and wall to wall with product and décor, the main purpose of a typical *botánica* is the sale of spiritual products including: candles, oils, incense, *limpias* or healing baths, talismans, *polvos* or magical powders, amulets, herbs, aromatic sprays, statues and esoteric books. While some will grow their own herbs, import or make their own products, increasingly *botánicas* obtain their stock from large international manufacturers such as Indio Products and Original Products Corporation.

Almost every *botánica* is owned by a resident reader or "worker" who, for a fee, will consult with clients on a wide range of issues: finding a job, legal difficulties, keeping a lover true, protection from enemies, or general luck and success. The size, stock and quality of a *botánica* is seen to reflect on the ability and success of its owner. Most give psychic readings in a separate and private space within the *botánica,* using cards, other divination tools such as a crystal ball, channeled spirits, or a direct intuitive reading. Some will also perform magico-spiritual work for clients: burning candles on their behalf, performing rituals or petitioning the saints. The reader counsels clients in the same manner a therapist would do while offering practical advice and remedies. Academic studies of *botánicas* and their treatment of physical ailments have found them often performing similar functions to other public health care institutions.

While some perceive *botánicas* as a solely Puerto Rican phenomenon tied to the practice of *Santería,* they are operated and patronized by practitioners of a myriad of faiths and beliefs from across the Americas including: *brujería,* Roman Catholicism, folk Catholicism, *curanderismo, spiritismo, Palo, Umbanda, Macumba, Candomblé,* Haitian Vodoun, African American Hoodoo, and in recent years those who follow Wicca, Pagan, or New Age beliefs. The *botánica* is often a space of cultural contact, where beliefs and practices of different cultures are introduced to one another, spread and synthesized. It is not unheard of to see Catholic saints placed alongside Yoruban orishas and Hindu goddesses, or to have a *santera* recommend a Lucky Buddha candle or a traditionally African-American High John the Conqueror root bath after a reading.

Most *botánicas* are dedicated by their owners to a patron saint or orisha and named accordingly as in "Botánica Oshun" and "Botánica San Miguel." Often they function as visible public spaces where immigrant communities can continue to practice their faith once removed from their home countries and a larger supportive culture of belief. Los Angeles, for example, is home to a *botánica* that functions as a rare public temple to the Mexican deity of death *Santa Muerte,* and another that doubles as a temple to the Guatemalan folk saint San Simón and holds a public parade and celebration on his feast day. As *botánicas* increasingly rely on large national manufacturers and Latinos/as continue to migrate into and within the United States, many localized saints, such as the Mexican Jesús Malverde and Juan Soldado, are gaining a popular, varied and widespread following.

The products sold in *botánicas* have been sold through the mail for at least a century, but neither mail order, telephone psychics or increasing internet sales can provide an alternative to what the *botánica* provides to its patrons, a cultural space where past traditions are linked to the present and believers can come together and find healing and relief.

PHILIP DESLIPPE

See also: Brujería (Witchcraft); La Santísima Muerte; Limpias (Cleansings); Malverde, Jesús; Maximón (San Simón); Saints (Santos); Soldado, Juan

Further Reading

Long, Carolyn Morrow. *Spiritual Merchants: Religion, Magic and Commerce.* Knoxville, TN: University of Tennessee Press, 2001.

Polk, Patrick Arthur. *Botánica Los Angeles: Latino Popular Religious Art in the City of Angels.* Los Angeles: UCLA Fowler Museum of Cultural History, 2004.

Zavaleta, Antonio, and Alberto Salinas, Jr. *Curandero Conversations: El Niño Fidencio, Shamanism and Healing Traditions of the Borderlands.* Bloomington, IN: Author House, 2009.

BOURKE, CAPTAIN JOHN GREGORY (1846–1896)

A prominent soldier and ethnologist of the late nineteenth century, John Bourke participated in numerous military campaigns against Indians in the U.S. West and eventually became an advocate for Indian rights. He is known for the meticulous diaries he kept throughout his life and the numerous books and essays he published detailing the folklore and cultural practices of Indians and Mexican Americans.

John Bourke was born in Philadelphia, Pennsylvania on June 23rd, 1846, to Edward Joseph and Anna Morton Bourke, who had emigrated from Ireland four years earlier. John Bourke attended St. Joseph's College from 1855 to 1859, when he quit after an argument with his professor. In August 1862, he lied about his age to enlist in the 15th Pennsylvania Volunteer Cavalry for the Union in the Civil War. He received an appointment to West Point Military Academy in 1865. Upon graduation, he became a 2nd lieutenant in the 3rd Cavalry, assigned to Fort Craig to fight Apaches. There he acted as aide-de-camp to Lieutenant Colonel George Crook, head of the military department of Arizona. Crook's extensive use of Apache scouts and his creation of mixed military units that incorporated enlisted men and Apache warriors allowed Bourke to observe Apache rituals and record them in his detailed diary. Bourke was also interested in Apache language, and, with the help of Indian friends, began compiling an Apache vocabulary that he would later expand into a comprehensive study of Apache languages. Though Bourke continued to view Indians as uncivilized throughout his life, his ethnological beliefs became troubled and contradictory at times. While he initially believed that all Indians should abandon their culture and fully assimilate into white society, he later felt that native cultural practices should be preserved not just in ethnological studies, but in the daily lives of Indians who should have the right to maintain their culture. Bourke's interest in ethnology began in the Southwest, when he became increasingly interested in Apache culture and befriended many of the Apache men he worked with while leading military campaigns against Indians in New Mexico and Arizona.

In 1875, Bourke became embroiled in the Sioux Wars when he was assigned to aid the U.S. Geological Expedition into the Black Hills. This was Lakota territory according to the 1868 treaty of Laramie, but discovery of gold in the Black Hills prompted the U.S. expedition that would recommend expulsion of Lakotas from the area. Bourke also participated in the resulting campaign against Lakotas and Cheyennes including the Battle of Rose Bud, in which Bourke commanded Crow and Shoshone warriors, the Powder River campaign, and the Big Horn and Yellowstone expeditions. Bourke continued his observation of Indian culture throughout the Sioux Wars, and afterward he worked closely with Indians at the Red Cloud and Spotted Tail agencies who shared their cultural knowledge with him.

Bourke's work in the military shifted after the Sioux Wars from combat to scholarship when, in 1881, he was assigned to ethnological duty by Lieutenant General Philip Sheridan. During this time, Bourke traveled throughout the Southwest and Great Plains areas gathering information about numerous tribes. While he acquired most of his information from Indians who openly shared their knowledge and invited him to religious rituals like the Oglala Sun Dance, Bourke was sometimes invasive and disrespectful, especially among the Pueblo Indians of the Rio Grande who were reluctant to reveal their beliefs and social organization. For example, in August 1881, Bourke observed the Hopi Snake Dance by entering *kivas* (rooms used by Puebloan peoples for religious rituals) where the ceremony was performed despite his knowledge that this violated the Pueblos' sacred rights.

Bourke interrupted his ethnological research in September of 1882 to aid Crook, who had returned to Apache territory to quell mounting hostilities. Bourke was disturbed by the corruption of Indian agents who had mismanaged the reservation and deprived Apaches of both government-issued food and a means to grow their own crops. He became involved in political disputes siding with Crook against Brigadier General Nelson A. Miles. Bourke was also outraged by the U.S. government's treatment of Geronimo and the other Apache leaders, and in 1886 he began leaking important information to the Indian Rights Association and he wrote *An Apache Campaign*, which defended Crook's actions.

From 1886 to 1891, Bourke worked in Washington, D.C., compiling his notes and fostering relationships with other intellectuals. His book *Snake Dance of the Moquis* impressed historian Francis Parkman whose friendship with Secretary of War William C. Endicott was instrumental in allowing Bourke the freedom to spend significant time on his scholarly pursuits. Bourke became an active member of the Anthropological Society of Washington (ASW) and the American Folk-Lore Society. He published numerous papers and three books during this period including *The Scatalogic Rights of All Nations*, a work about the use of human waste in cultural practices throughout the world, which Sigmund Freud would later call a "courageous" and "valuable undertaking" in his foreword to the book.

Bourke's time in Washington ended with his reluctant reassignment to Fort Ringold Texas in 1891. He considered the transfer punishment for his earlier dispute with Miles who was gaining political influence. Bourke began to focus his ethnological studies on the people of the lower Rio Grande, but his observation of the Mexican American population was strikingly less sympathetic than his work on Indian cultures. His notes from this period led to several publications in the *Journal of American Folk-Lore* including "The Miracle Play of the Rio Grande" (1893), "Popular Medicine, Customs, and Superstitions of the Rio Grande" (1894), "The Folk-Foods of the Rio Grande Valley and of Northern Mexico" (1895), and "Notes on the Language and Folk Usage of the Rio Grange Valley (With Especial Regard to Survivals of Arabic Customs)" (1896). While in Texas, Bourke also worked to capture Catarino Garza and his followers, the Garzistas, who were attempting to lead an uprising of *Tejanos* (Texas Mexicans) and northern Mexicans against Mexican president Porfirio Díaz. Bourke again became entangled in political disputes because of his aggressive tactics against the Garzistas, and consequently left Texas in February of 1893 to work for the Latin American Department of the World's Columbian Exhibition in Chicago. Bourke continued to write about the culture of the Rio Grande valley which he pejoratively termed "The American Congo" in an 1894 article for *Scribner's Magazine*.

Bourke died at the age of 49 from ongoing health problems, and even when he could no longer write he maintained his diaries by dictating to his wife, Mary

Horbach Bourke. Bourke is considered a foundational scholar in Native American and *Tejano* folklore and culture, and his detailed notes and diaries remain a source of important information for scholars.

ERIN MURRAH-MANDRIL

Further Reading

Bourke, John Gregory. "The American Congo." *Scribner's Magazine* 15.5 (May 1894): 590–610. Cornell University Library, Making of America. http://cdl.library.cornell.edu/moa/.

Bourke, John Gregory. *The Diaries of John Gregory Bourke*. Vols. 1–3. Edited by Charles M. Robinson III. Denton, TX: University of North Texas Press, 2003.

Bourke, John Gregory. *The Medicine Men of the Apache*. Glorieta, NM: Rio Grande Press, 1983.

Bourke, John Gregory. "Notes on the Language and Folk Usage of the Rio Grange Valley (With Especial Regard to Survivals of Arabic Customs)." *The Journal of American Folklore* 9 (1896): 81–116.

Bourke, John Gregory. *On the Border with Crook*. Chicago: Rio Grande Press, 1962. Originally published in 1891 by Charles Scribner's Sons.

Bourke, John Gregory. *The Scatalogic Rights of All Nations: A Dissertation upon the Employment of Excrementious Remedial Agents in Religion, Therapeutics, Divination, Witchcraft, Love Philters, etc., in All Parts of the Globe*. New York: American Anthropological Society, 1934.

Bourke, John Gregory. *The Snake Dance of the Moquis*. Chicago: Rio Grande Press, 1962. Originally published in 1884 by Charles Scribner's Sons.

Limón, José Eduardo. *Dancing with the Devil: Society and Cultural Poetics in Mexican-American South Texas*. Madison: University of Wisconsin Press, 1994.

Porter, John C. *Paper Medicine Man: John Gregory Bourke and His American West*. Norman: University of Oklahoma Press, 1986.

Turchenske, John A., Jr. "John G. Bourke—Troubled Scientist." *The Journal of Arizona History* 20 (1979): 323–344.

BRAZIL AND ITS FOLKLORE

The Roots of Brazilian Folklore

Home to nearly 200 million people, Brazil is the largest country in Latin America and the fifth-largest in the world in terms of population and land mass. Brazilian territory borders every country in South America except Ecuador and Chile, comprising 8.5 million square kilometers that are divided politically into 26 states (plus the Federal District of Brasília), and geographically into five major regions: north, northeast, south, southeast, and central-west. From the arid *sertão* of the northeast to the lush vineyards of the *serra gaúcha*, and from the *favelas* of the coastal megalopolises to the *pantanal* lowlands and the *floresta amazónica*, Brazilians inhabit a wide variety of climates and landscapes that have served—alongside a long, uneven history of colonialism and colonial legacies—to shape their popular traditions, stories, and cultural practices in radically diverging ways. Uniting the majority of Brazilians across this vast country—and abroad—is their shared mother tongue: while some 200 languages are used in Brazil (most of these by Indigenous peoples), over 99 percent of Brazilians speak Portuguese.

Considering the diversity of its territory and the profound heterogeneity of its people, Brazil's most enduring "lore," perhaps, resides in its old and always controversial categorization as a "racial democracy" in which descendants of Portuguese colonizers, African slaves, and Amerindians melded biologically, socially, and culturally (and with relative nonviolence) into the so-called *raça brasileira*, or "Brazilian race." This wishful rendering of national society, which was posited for decades in opposition to racism abroad (and especially in the United States), was compounded by the mythification or misreading of foundational accounts of the shared past, and in particular, of the work of Gilberto Freyre, whose 1938 *Casa Grande e Senzala* (*The Masters and the Slaves*) is one of the most-cited (if not most read) Brazilian texts of all time. In it, Freyre wrote not of "racial democracy" per se, but of the racialized "social democratization" of Brazilian society (Freyre 1938, xiii).

In light of Freyre's interest in and enthusiasm for "folk cultures" (and regardless of the terminology he used to describe them), it is perhaps not surprising that this inadvertent "father" of Brazilian sociology believed the field of Folklore Studies belonged squarely in the camp of the social sciences. At a roundtable discussion during the country's first official "Week of Folklore," which was sponsored by the National Folklore Commission in 1948 to overlap with National Folklore Day on August 22nd, Freyre suggested that the analysis of popular cultural forms would provide essential "supra-historical material" for understanding the complex relationships between people, time, and social space (Almeida 1964, 11).

Whether drawing on or departing from Freyre, subsequent scholars of folk culture in Brazil have done their share to foment the notion of a cohesive and homogenous "Brazilianness"—but not without a good deal of contradiction. Ethnographer, politician, and educator Darcy Ribeiro, for example, echoed Freyre's embrace of *mestiçagem* (racial mixing) while critiquing the latent desire for whitening on which it was premised (Ribeiro 1995, 219–227). This critique did not keep Ribeiro, however, from advancing a comparably evolutionist celebration of Brazil's "ethno-national" make-up, which he characterized (often using himself as an example) as a superior batch of mixed-race humanity—a "new Romanness" awash in its black and Indian blood (Ribeiro 1995, 453; Ribeiro 1996, 104–107). This penchant for appropriating and "improving" Otherness is paralleled in dominant society, as many advocates and practitioners of folk cultures (particularly traditional forms of music and dance) embrace them from a position of relative social power, with little recognition of, or fondness for their "subaltern" roots.

Considering the approximately five million Indigenous people living in Brazil at the time of its colonization and the more than eight million Africans and Afro-descendants who toiled on Brazilian soil before the enactment of the Law of the Free Womb in 1871 and the abolition of slavery in 1888, the contention that Brazilianness was forged out of the blood and sacrifice of black and Indigenous lives and labor is indisputable (Gomes 2000, 2; Ribeiro 1995, 220). Much of national folk culture derives from the knowledge, belief systems, and social practices of these two umbrella groups, which are already, unto themselves, both pluri-ethnic and pluri-lingual. And yet, to reduce national folklore to the dissemination and transformation of Iberian and pre-colonial African and Indigenous cultures in and through dominant *mestiça* society renders the situation both incomplete and overly simple; this version of the story would ignore the crucial fact that Brazil has also been a nation of migrants and (voluntary) immigrants.

Between 1884 and 1959, Brazil received more than 4.6 million new residents. While most arrived from Western Europe (primarily Portugal, Italy, Spain, and Germany), many also came from Bulgaria, Japan, Lebanon, Poland, Romania, Russia, Syria, Turkey, and Ukraine. The multiple flows of people, practices, and ideas to, from, and within Brazil have therefore long contributed to the complexity of its national folk culture. By the same token, the millions of Brazilians living outside Brazil—overwhelmingly in the United States, but also with significant numbers in Paraguay, Portugal, Spain, and Japan—serve as unofficial interpreters of, and ambassadors for their local, regional, and national traditions back home.

The vision of Brazil as a utopia of racial harmony was debunked more than a half-century ago by a well-known UNESCO study (Maio, 2001, 118) and has since been challenged by decades of scholarship examining Brazilian race relations—not to mention the personal experiences of those who suffer racism. The ideal of felicitous miscegenation lives on, however, in the realm of folklore, which is understood here as an ever-changing collection of ideas, beliefs, traditions, and practices that resonate in a romantic nationalism shared among individuals and groups. Though Brazil's highly classist society is far from embodying the egalitarian paradise that has been willed or imagined by generations of "racial democrats," the *practice* and *performance* of "Brazilianness" in and through folk culture still evokes the illusive "Freyrean dream." The adoption of marginalized cultural forms and social practices in and by dominant society thus sustains, to some degree, the old claim to racial progressiveness. As well-known composer and musician Sérgio Ricardo (b. João Lufti) once summarized this logic: "Every Brazilian is a *mestiço*—at least in his [or her] way of thinking."

Considering the countless micro-manifestations of folklore that travel, take root, and evolve throughout Brazil and the Brazilian Diaspora, it would be arbitrary and superficial to pretend to account for more than a fraction of them here. What follows, then, is a glimpse at some of the most popular national, regional, and local traditions and practices that make up the tale that Brazil likes to tell about itself. At the same time true and invented, this story—or assemblage of stories—is an important piece of cultural and affective "baggage" for the large and growing community of Brazilians abroad—including those who have made their home in the United States.

While the 2000 U.S. Census identified 212,636 Brazilian-born people living in the United States, unofficial estimates made by Brazil's Foreign Ministry six years later were much higher; these numbers approximate two million people—most of them undocumented (Miranda). Members of the documented group immigrate from all over Brazil, especially the states of Minas Gerais, Espírito Santo, Goiás, and Paraná. They have settled throughout the United States while concentrating in Florida (22 percent), Massachusetts (17 percent), California (11 percent), New York (10 percent), and New Jersey (10 percent). Smaller but still significant populations reside in Connecticut (5 percent), Texas (3 percent), Georgia, Maryland, Illinois, and Pennsylvania (all 2 percent each). These numbers do not include children born to Brazilian parents in the United States, and since U.S. population reports count Brazilians as Latin Americans but not as Hispanics or Latinos/as, the total number of "Brazilian-Americans" is difficult to calculate. In 2006, the U.S. Census Bureau accounted for 345,535 Brazilian-born people in the entire country (American Community Survey); even considering the large margin of error (+/- 16,181), this number is by several other accounts far below the mark. Nevertheless, documented and undocumented, officially and unofficially, Brazilians have been using and sharing their language and traditions on U.S. soil for many decades, contributing not only to the growth and development of Latino folklore, but also to the ever-changing pattern of North America's complex socio-cultural patchwork.

(Inter)National Manifestations of Brazilian Folklore

Carnaval: Between the Local and the Global

As the largest Catholic country in the world, Brazil is home to many popular celebrations with religious origins and significance, among them the widely-recognized *carnaval*. The country's most famous popular celebration is held annually during the two days preceding Ash Wednesday—in February or March, depending on the lunar calendar. Rooted in Greek and Roman spring festivals honoring Dionysus and Bacchus (gods of wine), the ancient festivities that eventually became *carnaval* existed for centuries in Europe before they were absorbed by the medieval Catholic Church as a precursor to Lent (a forty-day period of fasting and prayer before Easter). While the origin of the word is still disputed, many etymologists trace it to the Latin *carne vale* ("farewell to meat/flesh"), or *carne levamen* ("removal of meat/flesh"). These meanings can be read literally, as an allusion to the Church's mandate to refrain from eating meat during the Lenten period, or metaphorically, as a reference to Christian

Samba dancer dances in the Carnaval parade at the Sambodromo in Rio de Janeiro, Brazil. (David Davis/Dreamstime.com)

belief in the ascendance of spirit over body. The precursors to *carnaval* spread throughout Europe to the Spanish and Portuguese, who took their celebrations to the Americas in their military, cultural, and spiritual Conquest of the "New World."

By the 1840s, Brazilian *carnaval* had come to reflect a tropical amalgamation and reformulation of two traditions: first, the plebeian *entrudo* (a pre-Lenten "game" once played by tossing *limões de cheiro* (liquid-filled wax "lemons"), and *polvilho* (colored powders), at unsuspecting passersby in the streets; and second, high-society masquerade balls held by elites who imported their dress and music (typically waltz and polka) from Paris. In Brazil's urban centers—and especially Rio de Janeiro—this parallel *carnaval* structure was mediated by male-dominated parade societies that began to eclipse the *entrudo* component of the celebration by the end of the nineteenth century (Chasteen 1996, 38).

The *samba* music and dance now associated with *carnaval* developed out of the *lundu* and *maxixe* styles practiced primarily by Africans and Afro-descended Brazilians who migrated southeast after the end of the coffee boom in the early 1870s. Many came from Brazil's first capital city (Salvador, Bahia)—a major hub of the Atlantic slave-trade and vital center of Afro-Brazilian culture and cultural production. These *libertos* (freed slaves) and their kin helped make *carnaval* the popular public celebration it is today. With limited resources, and little or no access to the merrymaking of the (lighter-skinned) upper classes, they took to the streets in popular singing and dancing processions called *cucumbis* (in Bahia) or *congos* (elsewhere), which would later become known as *cordões*, *ranchos carnavalescos*, and *blocos* (block parties or informal processions). These ambulatory celebrations in which mixed-race and lighter-skinned Brazilians of all social classes also came to participate were antecedents of the *escolas de samba* ("samba schools") that now dominate the major *carnaval* celebrations (Tinhorão). The first of these, *Deixa Falar* (meaning "Let them say whatever they want; I / we don't care"), was formed in Rio de Janeiro in 1928.

Today, given that the massive celebrations in major cities like Rio, Salvador, and Recife are observed by millions around the world, and that thousands of foreigners flock to Brazil each year to partake of the festivities, *carnaval* has become a global event (as well as a capitalist spectacle). Rio dominates the national and international media, while other *carnavales* big and small reflect distinct local traditions in their themes, costumes, and music (e.g. *axé* in Bahia, *maracatu* or *frevo* in Recife). In the smaller, less publicized, and more rural manifestations of these festivities, many participants still celebrate with relative autonomy from the market and little or no outside influence (or interest). Some small-town commemorations are thus still aptly portrayed with the imagery used by folklorist A. M. Araújo over fifty years ago. There, as he explained, *carnaval*-goers assemble in the evenings with traditional instruments, including *pandeiros* (tambourines), *chocalhos* (rattles), *reco-recos* (gourds), *violas* (small guitars), *cavaquinhos* (ukuleles), and even pots and pans to form a *roda* (music circle) and *batucar* (play their rhythms) till the wee hours of the morning (Araújo 1964, vol. 1, 185).

Between the glamour and conspicuous consumerism of the *carioca* festivities (i.e., those in Rio de Janeiro) and the homemade simplicity of more intimate celebrations, the Brazilian diaspora in the U.S. celebrates *carnaval* throughout the country in cities as diverse as Boston, Chicago, Deerfield Beach (FL), Durham (NC), Houston, Los Angeles, Miami, New York, Newark (NJ), Portland (OR), and San Francisco. Like Mardi Gras in Louisiana (which was brought to the U.S. by the French in the seventeenth century) and pre-Lenten celebrations elsewhere, the "Brazilian-style" festivities involve music, dance, food, drink, and costume, and have few if any overt ties to religious beliefs or practices. Of course, since "Shrove Monday" and "Fat Tuesday" are not national holidays in the United States (except in New Orleans), Brazilian-American *carnaval* celebrations are often held on weekends rather than during the days leading up to Ash Wednesday. Uniting thousands of people across the country in celebration, they represent the largest and most frequent manifestation of Brazilian folk tradition outside Brazil.

Festas Juninas

Like *carnaval*, the "June festivals" represent the absorption of pagan rituals by the Catholic Church. Brought to Brazil by the Portuguese in the 1500s, they evolved over centuries of interaction with African, Indigenous, and other ethnic and cultural traditions, and are now practiced in a wide variety of ways throughout the country. In the northeast, the *festas juninas* can be just as important as *carnaval* or Christmas, and oftentimes still have strong religious and spiritual ties; in other regions, they have only a loose connection to Christianity. Originating with ancient European observances of the summer solstice or "midsummer" on June 21st, the festival was Christianized in the sixth century and moved to June 24th—the feast day of Saint John the Baptist (*a Festa de São João*). Over time, what were originally called *festas joaninas* (for São João) became *festas juninas*, because they continued to be held in June (*junho*). In the thirteenth century, the *festas* were expanded to incorporate the feast day celebrations of Santo Antônio (Saint Anthony) on June 13th, and São Pedro (Saint Peter) on June 29th ("Salve, Salve").

While the enactment of the *festas juninas* varies widely, particularly from north to south, much of their festive symbology is shared across the country, especially regarding the themes of purification and fertility inherited from the European tradition of a pre-harvest festival (and despite the fact that the European summer is wintertime in Brazil). The medieval Church reined in the popular association between free-flowing sexual energy (often manifested as orgies) and the fecundity of the land, and displaced it by focusing on the sacrament of marriage. This focus became tied to Santo Antônio, to whom female believers would pray to find a suitable husband. Their *pedidos* (petitions) often involve the physical manipulation of a statue or figurine of the Saint—placing him behind a door or in a well, or burying him up to his neck in the ground, for example (Araújo 1964, 104). Small figurines carried around in an *algibeira* (a small pocket sewn into an apron or dress) inspired folk prayers such as this one:

> *Meu querido Santo Antônio*
> *feito de nó de pinho,*
> *me arranje um casamento*
> *com um moço bonzinho.*

My dear Saint Anthony
made from hard pinewood,
arrange for me a marriage
to a man who is good.
(Araújo 1964, 105)

Along with pleas for love and marriage, *simpatías* (rituals meant to gain a wish or favor) are offered with faith—and sometimes in fun—to all the saints celebrated in the *festas juninas*. One of the *simpatías* used to gain protection and happiness from São João, for example, involves placing cloves, rosemary, and basil in a bowl of water, letting it sit, and pouring it over oneself while invoking the Saint's protection ("Salve, Salve").

Though some real weddings do take place during the *festas juninas*, it is more common in popular celebrations to see the performance of a *caipira* (country-style or peasant) "shotgun wedding." This practice reflects another important purpose of the event as currently celebrated: to pay tribute (albeit sometimes through parody) to rural Brazilian culture—a leitmotiv that is invoked through clothing, music, dance, and food. It is common, for example, to dress in "hillbilly-style" clothes: women and girls use gingham-print and flowered dresses and braid their hair; boys and men sport plaid shirts, patched-up overalls, and penciled-in mustaches and beards. Everyone wears bandanas, straw hats, painted freckles, and shows up ready to dance—in the north, *forró* (a rhythm played with an accordion, triangle, and bass drum or "*zabumba*"); and almost everywhere else, *quadrilhas* (from the nineteenth-century French *quadrille*, similar to square dancing). The celebrations are normally held outdoors in an *arraial* (campground) adorned with a tall mast pole bearing images of the saints (*o mastro de São João*) and hundreds or thousands of small colorful flags. In years past, these "*bandeirinhas*" were made of cloth and either painted or embroidered with symbols of the Catholic liturgy. Although they are now fabricated en masse out of paper or plastic, they remain the single most important and recognized symbol of the *festas juninas*.

Fireworks commonly used in the celebrations were once believed to awaken sleeping saints and scare off evil spirits, but have long served mostly an aesthetic purpose (Araújo 1964, 101). The release of hot-air balloons (invented in the early 1700s by Brazilian-born Portuguese priest Bartholomeu Lourenço de Gusmão) as an offering to the heavens for requests made or prayers answered was an important part of the celebrations until 1998, when the practice was outlawed for the risks it posed to public welfare (i.e., for starting fires and jeopardizing air travel). The massive *fogueiras* (bonfires) that still gather festival participants originally served to commemorate medieval European harvests and in Church lore came to symbolize the fire that São João's mother (Isabel) lit to advise her cousin Mary (mother of Jesus) that her son had been born. Fire is also meant to represent the renovation and liberation of baptism, and lore has it that São João visits homes (and other places) that are illuminated in celebration of his feast day.

Food and drink are an important component of the *festas juninas*, and traditional festival fare includes a variety of items that during the early colonial period were prepared by slaves, free servants, and others of limited economic means. Popular *quitutes* (a word of Angolan origin meaning "finger foods") are made from corn, peanuts, and *mandioca* (manioc), and include items like *pipoca* (popcorn), *bolo de milho* (corn bread), *milho cozido* (corn-on-the-cob), *paçoca* (peanut candy), *pé de moleque* (peanut brittle), *amedoim torrado* (roasted peanuts), *tapioca* (manioc pudding), and *beiju* (a manioc pancake). *Vinho quente* (hot wine) and *quentão* (hot cane liquor or *cachaça* with ginger and cinnamon) are popular drinks of choice.

Complete with music, dance, costumes, and many of these traditional treats, the *festas juninas* are widely celebrated by Brazilian and Brazilian American communities in the United States. Festivals take place from Miami, Deerfield Beach, and Newark on the east coast to Los Angeles, San Francisco, and Portland on the west coast, as well as in several less-than-likely locales in between: Colorado, Ohio, Michigan, and Minnesota. Massachusetts, however, is home to the greatest number of *festas juninas*, with celebrations held annually in Allston, Boston, Cambridge, Everett, Framingham, Lowell, and Somerville, as well as in several towns across Cape Cod.

Local and Regional Festivities and Celebrations

In addition to *carnaval* and *festas juninas*, dozens of other *folguedos* (popular festivals), each with hundreds of variations, are held throughout Brazil with celebrations that have specific local and regional ties and meaning—religious and otherwise. Among the most widely celebrated of these are the *Círio de Nazaré* in the north (Belém, Pará); the *folias de reis* in the southeast (and elsewhere); *cavalhadas* in the central-west (and elsewhere); *Oktoberfest* and the *Festa da Uva* in the south; and *Bumba-Meu-Boi* in the north and northeast (with variations elsewhere). Due to the country's intense history of migration, these celebrations and others like them have long extended beyond the geographical boundaries (including national borders) to which they were once confined.

Círio de Nazaré (north)

The *Círio de Nazaré* is a centuries-old holiday commemorating Our Lady of Nazareth, the patron saint of navigators and the Amazonian city of Belém (meaning Bethlehem). The celebration revolves around a figurine of the Virgin that was found on the banks of the Murucutú River in the early 1700s by a young man named Plácido de Souza, who was by some accounts the son of a Portuguese settler and an Indigenous woman, and by others an African slave. Lore has it that the statue, taken by Souza (and later, by others) to different locations for safekeeping, returned repeatedly and mysteriously to the very same spot, where a chapel was built in her honor and the *Basílica de Nazaré* now stands. The first *Círio* (from the Latin *cereus* for "of wax"—referring to a large devotional candle) was authorized by the Vatican in 1792 and organized the following year by the colonial governor (*capitão-mor*) of Pará, Francisco de Souza Coutinho. Since then, the festival has grown into an annual celebration of more than two million people who temporarily double the population of Belém.

Catholics gather during a procession of the Our Lady of Nazareth in Belem, Brazil. Thousands of people participate in the procession every year. (AP/Wide World Photos)

The main event of the *Círio* occurs on the second Sunday of October, when after fifteen days of preparation, hundreds of thousands of barefoot *romeiros* (pilgrims) accompany the statue from the *Cathedral de Belém* to the *Praça Santuário de Nazaré*. The Virgin sits inside a special sanctuary (*berlinda*) that rides atop a wheeled cart pulled by a 1,300-foot-long and 1500-pound rope made especially for the event. In a symbolic act of penance and gratitude, the faithful pack together for up to nine hours to touch or help pull the rope, which is believed by many to hold miraculous and healing powers. (If they are unable to secure the rope themselves, the *romeiros* aim to touch the clothing of those who can, thereby receiving the Virgin's positive energy vicariously.) In addition to heavy items like wooden crosses, caskets, and huge rocks, they carry hundreds of thousands of *votos* (religious symbols or offerings), usually in the form of wax and wooden replicas of body parts healed or material objects granted by the Virgin. Upon completing their sacrificial march, the *romeiros* retreat for a meal of *tacacá com tucupi* (duck with manioc sauce)—a traditional dish associated with the festival.

While this demonstration represents the culminating moment of the *Círio de Nazaré*, the two weeks that precede it are also of note, and include many smaller processions, liturgical celebrations, candlelight vigils, concerts, plays, fireworks, special food and drink, and a variety of artistic and cultural gatherings. As a testament to the "Golden Rule" (and to the chagrin of many Church officials), one of these is the *Festa da Chiquita*—a massive street party held in recognition of Brazil's gay and lesbian community, and more broadly, in support of an ethic of social tolerance. Highlights of the *Festa da Chiquita* include musical performances, a drag show, and the coronation of the *Veado de Ouro* ("Golden Fag") and *Rainha do Círio* ("Queen of the *Círio*")—titles of honor bestowed on prominent supporters of gay and lesbian rights. What began as a small meeting of artists, journalists, musicians, and intellectuals in the mid-seventies now includes tens of thousands of people— gay and straight, old and young, locals and visitors, and of varied class and ethnic backgrounds—all of whom share an interest in promoting social diversity, inclusiveness, and the "breaking of taboos" (*As filhas da Chiquita*).

Reisados, Pastoris, and Folias de Reis (rural southeast and throughout)

As in many predominantly Catholic countries, Christmas celebrations in Brazil extend from December 25th through the Epiphany or "Three Kings Day" (*Dia de Reis*) on January 6th, when the faithful celebrate the visit of Caspar, Melchior, and Balthazar to the child Jesus in Bethlehem. While the term *reisados* thus refers generally to celebrations invoking the three kings, the *pastoris* (pastoral celebrations) are reenactments of the manger scene in particular, and the *folias de reis* (kings' follies) refer specifically to the symbolic fusion of the three kings into one saint, the "Santo Reis." Commemorated in many parts of the country and most traditionally in the rural southeast, the *folias* are ambulatory music and theater ensembles that visit *lapinhas* or *presépios* (nativity scenes) on display. Often accompanied by members of the community who join in the procession, the *foliões* (*folia* participants) request permission to enter homes, churches, and other institutions to greet the baby Jesus. While the singing and oftentimes masked or costumed participants pay their visit, the homeowner holds a *bandeira* (flag) that represents *Santo Reis* and is said to improve the lives of those it touches. In return, the host offers the visitors a small meal or coins (*moedas dos reis*) believed to bring good fortune. The most famous *folias* take place in the states of Minas Gerais, São Paulo, and Rio de Janeiro, where many celebrations have now been institutionalized through the professional staging of formal presentations.

Festa do Divino (central-west and throughout)

The *Festa do Divino Espírito Santo* (Feast of the Divine Holy Spirit), known commonly as the *Festa do Divino*, corresponds to the celebration of Pentecost in the Catholic Church and dates to fifteenth-century Portugal. The feast day commemorates the descent of the Holy Spirit on the mother and apostles of Jesus Christ fifty days after his resurrection on Easter Sunday, and is celebrated in a variety of ways throughout the Lusophone world. In Brazil, where the commemoration dates to the 1600s, the best-known celebrations take place in small or medium-sized communities such as Pirenópolis (Goiás), Parati (Rio de Janeiro), São Luis do Paraitinga and Tietê (São Paulo), and Alcântara (Maranhão).

The *Festa do Divino* manifests the fusion of religious and non-religious beliefs and practices and the syncretism of Portuguese Christian, African, and Amerindian traditions that vary throughout the country (and over time). There are several customs common to most *Divino* celebrations, however, including the "coronation" of a child-emperor, the distribution of food to the poor, and a variety of popular music, dance, and processions. Participants in the *folias do Divino* sing and march their way through town, stopping to visit homes and other buildings along the way. They carry the flag of the *Espírito Santo*—a red banner that represents the fire through which, according to the Bible, God appeared to man. (The flag is adorned with a white dove symbolizing purity and the descent of the Holy Spirit.)

The *Festa do Divino* includes many other kinds of performance, ranging from "circle dances" or *danças de roda*, like *jongo* and *cururu*, to theatrical performances or processions like the *congadas* and *moçambiques*, which were practiced by slaves during the early colonial period to reenact the coronation of African kings and later came to represent offerings to *Nossa Senhora do Rosário*—the patron saint of people of color. Other popular reenactments depict struggles between warring African kingdoms and medieval battles between *cristãos e mouros* (Christians and Moors) known as the "*cavalhadas*." The largest such presentation takes place in the small city of Pirenópolis (Goiás), where for three days every year, lance-carrying horsemen dressed in elaborate medieval attire reenact the re-Conquest of the Iberian Peninsula. Held annually since 1819, the *cavalhada* in Pirenópolis ends (predictably) with the defeat of the "Moorish king" (*Mafona* or *Maomé*) and his subsequent conversion to Christianity.

While the celebrations of the *Círio de Nazaré*, *reisados*, and varied *Festa do Divino* traditions manifest the complex syncretism that characterizes so many religious practices in Brazil, they also reflect a deep spirituality and melding of religiosity and festivity that Brazilians take with them when settling abroad, including to the United States. The resurgence of the Catholic Church in the United States over the last half century is largely due to the growing Latino population overall, and in states like Massachusetts, New Jersey, California, Florida, and Georgia, a significant portion of this population is Brazilian. Hundreds of religious services are held across the United States in Portuguese on a regular basis, and the Feast of *Nossa Senhora da Aparecida* (patron saint of Brazil) is celebrated annually by thousands on October 12th (which is also commemorated by Brazilians in south Florida as the *Dia das Crianças* or "Children's Day"). The number of Evangelical, Protestant, and Spiritist Brazilian churches is also growing—not only in the typical immigrant enclaves (like Florida, for example, where alone there are at least 75), but also in Texas, Louisiana, Tennessee, Illinois, Maryland, and North Carolina (Comunidade Brasileira de Atlanta).

In addition to various forms of Christianity, the Fon, Bantu, and Yoruba-derived belief systems that arrived in Brazil with West African slaves, absorbed various elements of Catholicism and Amerindian tradition, and evolved into expressly Brazilian religions like *Candomblé* and *Umbanda*, are also on the rise in the United States. The Guaracy Temples in Berkeley, New York, and Washington D.C., for example, serve as spiritual homes for hundreds of Brazilians and non-Brazilians alike. As part of their regular schedule of *giras* (invocations of *orixás* or spirits), classes, and outreach work with local immigrant communities, members of the Washington Temple pay homage to *Iemanjá* (sacred Mother and spirit of the sea) at Delaware Seashore State Park (Templo Guaracy). While *capoeira* (a popular *jogo* or "game" created by African and Afro-descended slaves) is not an explicitly religious phenomenon, it also has strong ties to Yoruba-derived traditions, particularly *candomblé*. Scholars assert that serious "players" conceive of their practice as spiritual, especially regarding the trance-inducing potential of the music and chants around which it typically revolves. Over the last three decades, dozens of Brazilian *mestres* (masters) have brought their *capoeira* practices to the United States and set up specialized courses and academies all over the country, including in states as improbable as Maine, Iowa, Kentucky, and Utah. While some traditional practitioners equate the proliferation of *capoeira* as sport and spectacle with its transformation into a superficial "folkloric event," most *capoeira* schools in the United States conceive of their task as a historically-rooted philosophical and spiritual tradition (*Capoerista*).

Festa da Uva and Oktoberfest (south)

Although the Brazilian south is home to a diverse population that partakes of many of the African, Indigenous, and Portuguese-derived traditions mentioned here, the waves of Asian and European immigrants who poured into Paraná, Santa Catarina, and Rio Grande do Sul during the late-nineteenth and early-twentieth centuries also left their mark on local and regional folk celebrations and popular culture in general. Italian, Spanish, German, Japanese, Polish, Turkish, Romanian, Yugoslavian, Lithuanian, Syrian, Austrian, and Ukrainian settlers all brought their languages, customs, stories, cuisine, work habits, and agricultural expertise to their new homeland. They and their descendents would meet and mix not only with each other and the local population, but also with hundreds of thousands of migrants who left their homes in the northeast, Minas Gerais, and São Paulo, and headed south to pursue new economic opportunities, especially in the coffee industry. From 1940 to 1960 alone, the regional population surged from some 5.7 to over 11.8 million residents (Felipe 2000, 143).

Due to their relatively large numbers and long presence in the country, German and Italian-descended Brazilians have had a particularly enduring impact on popular cultural traditions in the south. Of the many events that celebrate this influence, *Oktoberfest* and the *Festa da Uva* are among the most important, together drawing over one million visitors to the south of Brazil each year. While the festivals themselves do not constitute folklore, the traditions and practices that they celebrate certainly do.

Oktoberfest, which takes its name from the famous Bavarian festival of Munich, originated in Itapiranga (Santa Catarina) in 1978 and has evolved into one of the largest celebrations of Teuto-Brazilian culture in Latin America. Although the city of Blumenau has long held the biggest and most popular *Oktoberfest* (with over 690,000 participants in 2007), smaller festivals are held all over Santa Catarina, Paraná, and Rio Grande do Sul to celebrate *chope* (beer) and the cultural lore of the approximately twelve million Brazilians who lay claim to Germanic ancestry (IBGE). The festival incorporates nearly two dozen "folkloric organizations" that work to cultivate their cultural traditions through dance, dress, song, theater, and the practice of Germanic languages. (Linguists have labeled the dialect spoken by a small population in the south "*Riograndenser Hunsrückisch*," or in Portuguese, *hunsriqueano riograndense,* which came from the Hunsrück region of Germany and has been heavily influenced by contact with Portuguese and other immigrant languages over the past two centuries.) In addition to various local beers (Eisenbahn, Bierland, Wunder Bier, Das Bier, Zehn Bier, and Schornstein), *Oktoberfest* features popular German-Brazilian meat dishes, like *Kassler, Eisbein,* and *marreco assado* (roast duckling); traditional music and dance forms, like *Schnupftabakpolka, Kaffee-kannenwalzer,* and *Zillertaler Hochzeitsmarsch;* re-creations of nineteenth-century "*dirndl*" (typical dress), like *Berchtesgaden, Miesbach, Boarisches);* and live demonstrations by hunting and rifle clubs (*Schützenvereinen*).

With the motto "*Uma vez imigrante, para sempre brasileiro*" (Once an immigrant, forever Brazilian), the *Festa da Uva* is held biannually in Caxias do Sul (Rio Grande do Sul) to recognize the culture and heritage of the Italian-Brazilians whose ancestors settled the city in the late nineteenth century. Begun in 1931 as a humble commemoration of the grape harvest, the *Festa* is now a major annual event that hosts dances, nightly parades, floats, a beauty contest, hundreds of food, wine, agricultural, and commercial exhibitors, and nearly a million visitors from home and abroad (Festa da Uva 2008). While the focus of the grape festival has been to showcase colonial customs and history, recent events have also featured icons of southern rural or *gaúcho* culture. Highlighted customs range from the culinary to the artistic, including traditional food and drink, like *churrasco* (grilled meat) and *chimarrão* (a strong tea drunk from dried gourd called a *cuia* or *porongo*), and a variety of music and dance forms, including *anú, chimarrita balão, balaio, chula, tirana do lenço, pezinho,* and the *dança dos fações.* Of primarily Spanish, Portuguese, and French origin, the *danças gaúchas* are practiced in a variety of forms in other regions of Brazil, as well as in neighboring Argentina and Uruguay.

Over the past two decades, the CTGs (*Centros de Tradições Gaúchas* or Center of Gaúcho Traditions) that proliferated in Brazil over the twentieth century and spawned a revival of "traditional southern culture" have also spread to North America. *Gaúchos* and their U.S.-born descendants have established the CTG Bento Gonçalves in Los Angeles, the CTG Nova Querência in Miami, the CTG Além Fronteira in Massachusetts, the CTG Saudade da Minha Terra in New Jersey, and several smaller cultural organizations in San Francisco, Atlanta, Maryland, Virginia, Pennsylvania, Connecticut, and New York (Garcia). Since 2005, these groups have been holding an annual *Encontro Tradicionalista Gaúcho* (Traditional Gaucho Convention) featuring typical food, dance, poetry, and garb, as well as a *missa crioula* (Portuguese-language mass) and "*Chimarrão* Ball." Other U.S. *gaúcho* organizations commemorate Brazilian independence and the *Data Farroupilha* (Farrapo Rebellion) with celebrations that incorporate traditional ball games (*jogo de bocha,* similar to bocce balls) and revere traditional *gaúcho* labor with presentations of *lides campeiras* (farming chores). In 2008, the "Fourth International Meeting of Gaucho Nativism" was held in New York City and featured cultural organizations from all over the United States, as well as representatives from Brazil and Canada. Participants ate, drank, danced, discussed cultural politics, and along with their non-*gaúcho* compatriots, carried the Brazilian flag down Sixth Avenue in the city's "International Parade of Immigrants."

Folguedos do boi (north, northeast, and throughout)

Another important celebration of rural-life Brazil is the *folguedo do boi* (roughly, "ox revelry"), which are known most famously as *Bumba-Meu-Boi* (Dance-My-Ox) in the states of Maranhão and Pernambuco. Related events are called *Boi-Bumbá* in Amazonas, *Boi-de-Mamão* in Santa Catarina, *Boi-a-Serra* in the central-west, *Boi-Pintadinho* in Rio de Janeiro, *Boi Calemba* in Rio Grande do Norte, *Reis-de-Boi* or *Bumba-de-Reis* in Espírito Santo, and *Cavalo Marinho* in Paraíba. In some regions the *folguedos do boi* take place around Christmas, while in others they accompany the *festas juninas*; almost all of them, however, involve a convoluted pastoral drama portraying the death and resurrection of an ox.

In the dominant version of the *boi* plot, a poor servant, slave, or cowboy (in older documents named Mateus and in more recent ones Francisco or Chico) kills his patron's prized ox for his pregnant wife, Catirina (*sic*), who suffers an unbearable craving for ox-tongue (or some other organ). Learning of the ox's "murder," the outraged patron calls on a local Indigenous group to capture the errant servant, whom he vows to spare only if the animal can be resuscitated. Unable to perform this miracle, Mateus/Francisco calls on a doctor and priest who are also unable to help him. Finally, an Indigenous healer or *pajé* is summoned to do the job and succeeds by dint of magic rituals. Mateus/Francisco is pardoned, and rejoicing ensues (Cavalcanti 2001).

This storyline or *ciclo do boi* includes dozens, and in some cases, hundreds of characters who invoke the realms of the human, the animal, and the supernatural; bridging these last two is the ox himself (typically one or several men sporting an elaborate costume of cloth, metal, leather, or papier mâché), who "chases" and "dances" for and sometimes among the spectators. One of the most famous versions of this celebration takes place every June (thus overlapping with *festas juninas*) on Tupinambarana Island in the Amazonian city of Parintins, where a "*bumbódramo*" ("*bumba* stadium"—like the famous "*sambódromo*" in Rio de Janeiro) holding 35,000 people is the site of the annual *bumba* competition between two competing "schools": *Caprichoso* ("Capricious") and *Garantido* ("Sure Thing"). The festival began in 1955 and is now one of the largest popular celebrations in the country; in 2008, the city of just over 100,000 residents received approximately 80,000 tourists in June alone (Parintins).

While the *bumba* tradition is not widely known in the United States, it gained recognition in the nineties when the Brazilian pop band (and one-hit wonder) Carrapicho released a song about the *boi* festival called "Tic, Tic, Tic, Tac" (from the album *Festa de Boi Bumba*). The single, which was produced by a French label, topped the charts in Europe and reached number eight on the U.S. charts in 1997 (Billboard 2008). The *bumba* lore has since adopted a more traditional format among Brazilian cultural groups in the northeastern United States, including the Massachusetts-based AfroBrazil. This organization teaches and performs a variety of music-related traditions, including a "Bahian-style" *bumba* show that has been featured in the Lowell Folk Festival—the largest of its kind in the country.

Despite (or perhaps because of) the growing popularity of these festivities, much debate still surrounds the origin of these stories and the ongoing practices of reinvention through which they are commemorated—both in and outside of Brazil. While some scholars tie them to ancient Egypt and Greece, or to the medieval Iberian theater, others believe they evolved out of African or Amerindian traditions. Most agree, however, that once planted on Brazilian soil, the *boi* phenomena flourished among Afro-descended populations in cattle-raising areas of the north and northeast.

The enduring search for the roots of this and so many other popular cultural practices and beliefs peaked during mid-twentieth century, when intellectuals like Mário de Andrade, Artur Ramos, Cecília Meireles, and Gilberto Freyre himself sought to link Brazil's official culture and national identity to the "authenticity" of folk practices and beliefs (Almeida 1964, 5–36). Caught up in the racist populism and nationalist fervor of the Vargas era, the intellectual elite dug deep and worked hard to find, standardize, and regulate popular culture, thus conferring upon themselves the duty of belying *"fakelore"* and teaching "proper" folklore to the folk (Almeida 1964, 35–36). To their great disappointment, however, there was and is no one, good, true thing to be unearthed. There are, instead, as many "genuine" versions of the story as there are tellers—from the Hudson to the Oiapoque to the Chuí, and lots of places in between.

Tracy Devine Guzmán

See also: African Influence on Latino Folklore; Brazil, Myths and Legends from; Cuaresma (Lent)

Further Reading

AfroBrazil. www.afrobrazil.org.

Almeida, Renato. *O Instituto Brasileiro de Educação, Ciência e Cultura e os Estudos de Folclore no Brasil.* Rio de Janeiro: Departamento de Imprensa Nacional, 1964.

American Community Survey. www.census.gov/acs/www.

Araújo, Alcéu Maynard. *Folclore Nacional.* Vols. 1–3. Rio de Janeiro: Edições Melhoramentos, 1964.

As filhas da Chiquita. Directed by Pricilla Brasil. Belém: Greenvision, 2006.

Billboard. "Chart Listing for the Week of July 12, 1997." December 2008. www.billboard .com.

Capoeiristas. www.capoeirista.com.

Cavalcanti, Maria-Laura. "The Amazonian Ox Dance Festival: An Anthropological Account." *Cultural Analysis* 2 (2001): 69–105.

Chasteen, John. "The Prehistory of Samba: Carnival Dancing in Rio de Janeiro, 1840–1917." *Journal of Latin American Studies* 28 (1996): 29–47.

Comunidade Brasileira de Atlanta. www.comunidadebrasileiradeatlanta.com.

Felipe, Carlos, and Maurizio Manzo. *O Grande Livro do Folclore.* Belo Horizonte: Editora Leitura, 2000.

Festa da Uva. www.festanacionaldauva.com.br.

Freyre, Gilberto. *Casa-Grande e Senzala.* Rio de Janeiro: Schmidt-Editor, 1938.

García, Paulo Roberto. "Desfile dos CTG em Nova York 2008." www.inema.com.br/mat/ idmat100906.htm.

Gomes, Mercio P. *The Indians and Brazil.* Translated by John Moon. Gainesville: University of Florida Press, 2000.

Gorham, Rex. *The Folkways of Brazil (A Bibliography)*. New York: The New York Public Library, 1944.

Instituto Brasileiro de Geografía e Estatística (IBGE). www.ibge.gov.br.

Lewis, J. Lowell. *Ring of Deception*. Chicago: University of Chicago Press, 1992.

Lima, Álvaro, and Eduardo Siqueira. "Brazilians in the U.S. and Massachusetts: A Demographic and Economic Profile." Boston: Mauricio Gastón Institute, 2008. www.gaston.umb.edu.

Maio, Marcos Chor. "UNESCO and the Study of Race Relations in Brazil: Regional or National Issue?" *Latin American Research Review* 36.2 (2001): 118–136.

Miranda, José Wilson. "Brazilians in U.S. Grow to Two Million." *Brazzil Magazine*. September 2nd, 2006. www.brazzilmag.com/content/view/7199/53/.

Parintins. www.parintins.com.

Portal Basília Santuário de Nazaré. www.ciriodenazare.com.br.

Ribeiro, Darcy. *O povo brasileiro: a formação e o sentido do Brasil*. São Paulo: Companhia das Letras, 1995.

Ribeiro, Darcy. *Mestiço é que é bom!* Rio de Janeiro: Editora Revan Ltd., 1996.

Templo Guaracy de Washington. www.tgwashington.org.

Tinhorao, José Ramos. *Pequenha história da música popular*. São Paulo: Círculo do Livro, 1974.

Weigl, F. D. Wilson. "Salve, Salve os santos padroeiros." *Bons Fluidos*. June 2004. www.abril.com.br.

BRAZIL, MYTHS AND LEGENDS FROM

Brazil was called Pindorama by the aborigines, meaning "land of palms" and, for a long time, it was believed that the origin of the name Brazil was the tree called "pau-brasil," the wood of which was exported to Europe during early colonization. From the ninth century on, this kind of wood was used by the Europeans and Arabs for the preparation of a red dye of great commercial value called "brasil" or "verzino" (Hollanda, 1977). Nevertheless, from the thirteenth to the sixteenth centuries, a fabulous island called *Hy-Brazil* could already be spotted on European maps (Hollanda 1977).

One of these maps had been made on the basis of a Portuguese original by order of Charles V, and can be found in the National Library of Paris (Silva 2007). The British Museum shelters a world map by Ranulf Nyggeder, dated from 1360, displaying an "Island of Brazil" on the same place as that of Charles V's (Silva 2007).

The Turkish admiral Piri Reis reported that he had used very ancient nautical charts for the drawing of his map dated from 1513, where not only the Brazilian coast, but also Antarctica were included. As a matter of fact, the navigations known in the Antarctic area only occurred after Ferdinand Magellan's expedition that departed from Spain in 1519.

Other popular Iberian legends influenced the first navigators sailing westwards such as Alexander the Great's who, in the company of a servant, came across a fountain that rejuvenated them as they traveled the *Terrae Obscurae*. Explorer Juan Ponce de León crossed a territory, corresponding to nowaday´s Florida, searching for this fountain of youth that he judged to exist in the new lands discovered in America. In his travel diaries, Christopher Columbus (Colombo 1999) reports his quest for the fantastic empire of the Great Khan described by Marco Polo, whose treasures would be worthy of the Thousand and One Nights stories. When his ships reached Cuba, Columbus asked the natives if they knew where to find the Great Khan for he was bringing him a letter written by the King of Spain.

Myths of Creation

Brazil's myths and legends are composed of the interaction of Indian, African and European cultures. This process, instead of creating a gap, generated a cultural and religious syncretism; it is difficult to find a myth or a legend in Brazil which would present a unique cultural branch of its own. Traces of these intertwined cultures can always be found. The Brazilian home was also a meeting spot for Europeans, Indians and slaves of African origin, which determined the folklore, the way of speaking, the cuisine, the architecture and the dressing style of the Brazilian people.

Tamandaré

The myths of deluge and formation of a new race after catastrophes can also be found in the culture and popular religiosity of Brazil. There is the myth of Tamandaré (Salles 1998) that inspired the end of the book *O Guarani* by José de Alencar (1857), when Indian Peri and his beloved Ceci manage to save themselves from a flood by climbing a palm tree, when Peri tells the story of Tamandaré, who repopulated the world after a deluge.

According to the original myth, after a battle fought against an enemy tribe, his brother, Aricute, meaning to insult him, tossed a dead enemy's arm against his shack. Fighting back, Tamandaré, thumping the ground with his feet, caused the flushing of a torrent that flooded the entire Earth, covering the trees and even the hills. To escape from death, Tamandaré climbed a palm tree with his wife. They fed from its fruits until the waters lowered. Aricute and his wife imitated them, climbing a genipap tree. After the flood, they repopulated the earth; Tamandaré and his wife gave birth to the Tupinambás Indians, and Aricute and his wife originated the Tomimis.

The Acaiaca Legend

Another legend says that, in the beginning of the world, there was a great flood, the rivers covered the lands. Only one couple of Indians survived because they managed to climb a tree that the Indians called Acaiaca, a *peroba* (a tree of the *Apocynaceae* family) that was on the top of the hill Ibitira, today called "Cruz das Almas" in the county of Diamantina. As the waters lowered, this primeval couple repopulated the Earth.

The Portuguese, to revenge the attacks of the Puris tribes of the area, cut the Acaiaca down because, according to the legend, the Indians would be invincible while it existed. A huge tempest of thunder and lightning struck the hill, and no trunk nor branch of the holy tree was ever found. It is said that, in the place of the Acaiaca's charcoal, the prospectors began to find little diamond stones (Moura 2000, n. 21, 18–37), which originated the city's name, Diamantina.

Sumé, the Civilizing Hero

In his *Cartas do Brasil*, dated from 1549, Father Manoel da Nóbrega described some legends of the Brazilian Indians on Sumé, or Zomé, or Zumé, which the Europeans associated with Saint Thomas (Nóbrega 1988, 91–102). This hero provided the Indians with moral rules and food, besides teaching them how to work the land, grow and prepare manioc (Cascudo 1972, 836). He allegedly left footprints on the rocks which, according to the Indians, would have been left behind during his escape from hostile natives (Nóbrega 1988, 91–102). The arrows aimed at him were shot back, killing the archers. Whenever Sumé fled from his persecutors, the wild growth would give way to him, as well as the waters of the river to let him pass without getting wet. According to the legend, he would have left for India, promising to come back because he had the power to cross the Earth and heavens as well, from where he could see all Indians, and look after them (Nóbrega 1988, 91–102; Cascudo 1972, 836).

Legends of Cobra-Grande

The Amazons

There is a popular story of Minas Gerais recorded in the research of Núbia Gomes and Edimilson Pereira (Gomes 1993) according to which, in the beginning of the world, women amused themselves, had children, and did everything without the presence of men, not caring for them. Men, therefore, complained to God that women were not interested in them. Then God came down to Earth to see what was happening, and found out that, at night, all women gathered in a cave where Cobra-Grande lived. There they danced, celebrated and had a great time with the serpent. God judged that was not right and cut Cobra-Grande in several pieces, fixing these between men´s legs. From then on, women started to become interested in men.

The Snake's Poison

Another legend says that, in the beginning of the world, a woman wanted to own the poison of the snake, and observed that, whenever the snake swam in the lake, it left its poison bag hidden on the edge. Once, as "God was not paying attention," she waited for the snake to enter the lake and quickly took possession of the poison bag (Gomes 1993). But God sees all and approached the woman, asking: "Woman, what are you hiding in your hands?" She replied: "Nothing," trying to get rid of the poison by rubbing her hands between the legs. And God asked again: "Woman, what are you hiding in your hands?" She replied: "Nothing," trying to get rid of the poison, rubbing her hands on her breasts. But there was still a little poison on her hands, and God asked again: "Woman, what are you hiding in your hands?" She replied: "Nothing," rubbing her hands on the nape of the neck to remove the rest of the poison. These are the parts where women have snake´s poison.

The Feathered Serpent of Lapa

In the county of Bom Jesus da Lapa, located on the right bank of the São Francisco River, there are limestone formations shaping many caves, which are considered sanctuaries. Legends and traditions on these caves turned the city into a pilgrims' and religious festivities center. In one of these caves there is a stone that, whenever struck, sounds like a cathedral bell. Another one was named "Serpent's Hole" for it was believed that it hid a winged serpent. In case it escaped, it would be the end of the world. In the eighteenth century, Friar Clemente, a religious member of the sanctuary, asked the locals to pray Our Lady's Office so that the serpent's wings were definitely deprived of feathers, disabling its flight. The cave remained closed until 1936. When it was opened, no traces of the serpent were found. According to popular belief, it had been defeated by the power of prayer.

Boiúna or Cobra-Grande

It is told that the most beautiful Indian girl of a tribe fell in love with Rio Branco, a river. For punishment, she was turned into a serpent, Cobra-Grande, or Boiúna, that would be responsible for the protection of her beloved, Rio Branco, living in its depths. Sometimes, Cobra-Grande emerges to the surface and wanders through the night with shining eyes illuminating the river like fire torches, confusing, scaring, and chasing fishermen and travelers by water. Many of them figure that it is a boat coming up, but only when they come closer they realize that it is Cobra-Grande.

Cobra Honorato and Maria Caninana

An Indian girl became pregnant by Cobra-Grande as she was bathing in the river, giving birth to twins in the shape of serpents, named Cobra Honorato and Maria Caninana. Since nobody knew she had given birth to two serpent-children, she tried to kill the newborns by throwing them into the river. Both survived because they were serpent-like and swam away. Honorato was good-natured, but his sister, Caninana, was bad-natured; she did evil to all; she hurt river fishes and sank boats by making leaks in their hulls allowing water in, drowning the crews. Once she heard that an enchanted serpent slept under the altar of the Óbidos Church in Pará, and that it sustained the altar with its body. But its tail was always at the bottom of the river. Out of evil, Caninana bit the serpent's tail to wake it up, and a great earthquake shook the entire area and everything began to fall apart. Cobra Honorato, her brother, was always trying to save the victims from the shipwrecks his sister caused and, during one of these struggles to avoid Caninana's atrocities, she hurt one of his eyes and he killed her. From then on, all that Honorato did was to drift along the river, and the riverside dwellers were free from Caninana's evildoings.

Cobra Honorato, for his good natural disposition, was cherished by all. At night, he left his serpent's skin on the banks of the river and participated in festivities in his human shape to dance, seduce women and be with everyone, young and old. To break the spell, someone would go to the riverside on a full moon's night, and, while he was asleep, put three drops of woman's milk into his mouth and hit his head with an iron bar. In the name of their friendship, many tried to disenchant him, but soon came back for fear of his primitive shape. But one day, one of his friends decided to give it a try, and Honorato appeared in his definite human shape holding a diamond to offer his savior. It is said that he still lives somewhere in the Amazon.

Water Beings

Boto

A myth similar to Cobra Honorato's is that of the Little Dolphin called Boto living in the Amazonian region. At night, Boto turns into a handsome youngster always wearing white. He never takes off his straw hat so as not to show a little breathing hole that dolphins have on the top of their heads. He usually goes to parties, dances all night, and seduces the village girls. Whenever one of them, single, appears pregnant, it is usually said that "it was Boto's fault." After parties and dates, he returns to the river and takes on his Boto original shape just to appear again whenever there is a party.

Anthropomorphic features are usually attributed to dolphins, whitch are also known for their closeness to human beings. Since ancient times, there are numberless cases of castaways saved by dolphins. Herodotus tells that a boat crew taking poet Arion back to his land decided to throw him into the sea to steal his possessions. But, before being cast into the sea, he asked to sing as he was used to. A dolphin, enchanted by his music, saved him and took him to the beach. By land, Arion managed to arrive before the mutinous boat, and King Periander punished the rebels (Herodotus 1998, Book I, 23–24). On Fernando de Noronha, a northeastern Brazilian island, a diver says that once he was surrounded by many dolphins, which kept swimming in circles, not letting him out. Only then he saw a shark trying to approach him. As the shark moved away, the dolphins did the same. The dolphins have an accurate perception of menstruating women as well, following the boats they are on. They are said to "cry as a child" when they get caught in fish nets. Moreover, they are considered taboos—it is said that the one who kills a dolphin will forever have bad luck.

Caboclo d'Água

A fisherman told about a man who was alone on his boat on a night of waning moon. Suddenly, the boat rocked violently from one side to the other and he saw a man's arm trying to tip it over. He struck it many times with the oar, cutting it into pieces. He noticed a piece of a black arm at the bottom of the boat, it was Caboclo d'Água's. This being, like other mythical characters, is called "enchanted," and is common in the Brazilian rivers mythology. He is also known as the Father of Fish. He is said to live at the bottom of rivers and chases those who fish for more than is necessary as well as those who do not give little fish back to the waters. Many tried to shoot Caboclo d'Água, but, since he is "enchanted," the bullets simply cross his body. To protect themselves from his anger, fishermen usually make him offers, throwing smoke and flour into the river waters.

Iara

Riverside peoples believe that during moonlit nights rivers sleep. Everything becomes silent. The waters stop their movement and fish stop to jump. The drowned emerge from the bottom of the river and go to the stars. Fishermen do not dare "wake" the river in this moment. This is when Iara appears beside a boat or on a stone bank of the river. While she combs her long golden hair, she chants songs that are echoed throughout the riverbanks. All those who hear them fall in love with her soft chants, and are taken by Iara to her enchanted palaces at the bottom of the rivers and never seen again. The native painters depict her as a woman of exuberant sensuality, nude breasts, surrounded by waterfalls. She is also known as Mãe d'Água, and in some other versions she is depicted as a water serpent.

Iemanjá

Iemanjá means "Queen of Fish," and in some regions, this goddess is also called "Dona Janaína." According to the Afro-Brazilian myths, the god Olodumaré created the Earth, Oxum the rivers and lakes, and Iemanjá the sea, becoming its protector. She also created fish and starfish. After having been raped by her own son, Iemanjá gave birth to the main divinities of the Afro-Brazilian pantheon called Orixás. Her colors are blue and silver which compose her followers' outfits in their Candomblé worship. She is associated with life cycles and rhythms, and with fertility as well.

She used to come to earth looking for lovers. The unwary, seduced by her rare beauty, are taken to her domain: the bottom of the sea. The following day, their bodies are found on the sands, returned by the tides. She symbolizes the twofold nature of love, and brings life and death to lovers.

Followers of African-Brazilian religious sects dance and pray next to offerings to Iemanjá, an African water goddess, in Rio de Janeiro, Brazil. On Iemanjá's Day, which corresponds with the Catholic feast of Our Lady of Navigators, thousands of followers go to the beach with offerings of flowers, perfume, and jewels. (AP/Wide World Photos)

The cult of Iemanjá takes place on the beaches of several Brazilian states on the first of January, and in Bahia on the second of February. During the ceremonies, women take to the beach flowers and little boats containing offerings like mirrors, pearls and perfumes which they believe will please the goddess. They ask Iemanjá to allow their husbands and lovers to come home safely after their journey at sea, bringing lots of fish. The human beings began to throw garbage and debris into Iemanjá´s house, the sea, which angered her. She then created the tides and waves to send back to land all the filth men had thrown into the sea.

Fruit and Food

The Legend of Guaraná

In a tribe of the Maué Indians a very beautiful boy was born, son of an Indian woman and a serpent. He was very strong, happy, joyful, and loved by all villagers. The god Jurupari got jealous because all the attention formerly given to him was now turned towards the child. So, he tried to find a way to get rid of him. He made the boy eat a forbidden nut, which was lethal. All mourned the child´s death, but from the boy´s eyes a plant was born; its fruit—the guaraná—comforted everyone, and is eaten and drunk as beverage all over Brazil.

Manioc

A tribal chief's daughter became pregnant. Although she protested, declaring never having been with a man, her father decided to punish her for the dishonor and was ready to kill her. Nevertheless, he dreamt of a very fair-skinned man who told him not to kill his daughter because she was innocent. Nine months later, a girl was born, and her name was Mani; her skin was as white as milk. She took after nobody in the tribe nor in the neighboring tribes. As she grew older, she became even more beautiful. She began to talk as soon as she was born, but when she was one year old, she got very sick. No witch doctor could heal her, and she died. On the very place she was buried, an unknown plant was grown. Its root was as white as Mani's skin, and the Indians called it *mandioca* (manioc), a word originated from Mani, which, juxtaposed to *oca,* means house, body, that is, Mani´s "house" or "body." The manioc, Indian in origin, is prepared in several ways in the Brazilian cuisine.

Fantastic Beings of the Earth and of the Forest

Many are the monsters that frighten children at night, such as the Boi da Cara Preta, or the monster that dwells under the bed and tries to catch their feet. Besides, there are the Cuca and the Bicho Papão, which carry children on their back in a sack, and who eat up those who refuse to sleep at the right time. Some Brazilian lullaby songs refer to these monsters, such as in the following lines:

> *Dorme neném, que a Cuca vem pegar*
> (Sleep baby, or Cuca will come and catch you)

Boi, Boi, Boi da Cara Preta
Pega este menino que não gosta de dormir
(Steer, Steer, Black-faced Steer,
Come and take this child who does not like to sleep).

Mula-Sem-Cabeça

This myth was spread over all the regions of Brazil, turning it into one of the most famous fantastic beings, also widespread in Portugal and Spain, where it was probably originated. The Mula-Sem-Cabeça gallops unbridledly on every full moon from Thursday to Friday night. It has the shape of a mule that, though headless, releases fire from its nostrils and sparks from its iron or silver paws, haunting the one who sees her. Its neigh is heard from far away and its gallop lasts till dawn, when the rooster sings for the third time. Then it returns to its human shape, that of the woman who has violated a taboo by becoming the lover of a priest. Its spell can only be broken if someone manages to remove the bits from its head or hurt it until it bleeds, or if the priest curses the woman seven times before celebrating the mass. In these cases, after the breaking of the spell, she can appear in the shape of some local girl, completely naked.

In some Brazilian regions, the Mula-Sem-Cabeça is called Burrinha do Padre (the priest's mule), with the same punishment peculiarity given to the priest's lovers. Nothing of the kind happens to the priest because the blame of seduction is always assigned to women in the Christian tradition. But if the priest celebrates the mass in the presence of the lover, the host will fall from his hand, accusing them.

Curupira and Caapora

In the legends of the Brazilian aborigines, there are representations of guardian beings of the forest and of the wild life, which are Curupira and Caapora. Curupira is represented in a child's body having its feet turned backwards, big and sharp ears, and is recognized by the way it strikes the tree trunks with its strong beats that can be heard far away. The word Curupira, according to Câmara Cascudo, is originated from *curu*, short for *curumi* which means "boy," and from *pira*, meaning "skin," and by extension, "body" (Cascudo 1972, 332–334). The translation of this word would then be "the one who has the body of a child."

Caapora has red-hot eyes, always mounting a *caititu* (a kind of wild pig) and smoking a terracotta pipe. Both are watchful of the hunt and of the wild animals. Caapora and Curupira severely punish all those who violate the taboos that forbid the useless killing of animals or the shooting of pregnant females or females with newborns.

João do Mato

An Afro-Brazilian community known as "the Arturos," named after their founder Arthur, celebrates a traditional festivity during weeding season: a community member covers himself with grass, dry leaves and boughs, and hides in the prairies—that would be the João do Mato. Then, all the other members begin to weed the fields of the plantation, singing and dancing to the rhythm of the hoes, bush hooks, and other tools. Many jests are made and, in some of the songs, João do Mato regrets the cutting of his grass. The workers, amid dancings and singings, try to justify the cutting of the grass to plant, which is obviously disputed by João do Mato. A fight between the opponents takes place represented by dancings and singings. At last, João do Mato is defeated and finally concurs with his opponents provided that the last bunch of grass, where he is hiding, remains untouched. At the end of the day, as the field is cleared, he comes out dancing. Next, he is enticed to pass under a row of hoes ordered in the shape of a cross. João do Mato is then taken to the main house where all come together to eat sweets and typical food, and drink cachaça (Brazilian firewater) and coffee. At the end of the party, João do Mato leaves the place singing his power of always going back to his wild growth, year after year (Salles 1998).

In some other cities of Minas Gerais, celebrations and festivities dedicated to João do Mato also take place but, besides the celebration dedicated to the plants that have to be cut out, auspices for a good crop are also made. In Ponte Nova's region, Minas Gerais, according to the research of Núbia Gomes and Edimilson Pereira, there is a variant of this theme: the João do Mato, who opposes the group of farmers, is known as "João Bunda" (Buttock Jack), and the workers, "João da Cara" ("Face Jack") (Gomes 1993). João Bunda, who dances freely in the wild, represents the wild nature still untamed by the "Cara." These festivities are very appreciated by the children of those communities, and the field workers comment that they are celebrated mainly because of the happiness that all express.

Famaliá

In the popular culture of Minas Gerais, there is a belief according to which, to obtain prosperity, a man must create a puppy-demon, named Famaliá. This creature will help its master except on Good Friday when it can harass him in any way it pleases, playing tricks, causing little accidents, whipping him, etc. As a token of their acknowledgement of the pact with Famaliá, the master or the lady of the house should leave all things imperfect, or else with a little sign that they have not been completed. For instance, in a hidden place of the house wall a brick should be missing, "Famaliá's brick." In new clothing, a small piece should be left unseamed, which would be "Famaliá's piece," and so on (Salles 1998). It is noteworthy that, as the master and/or lady have a relationship with it, they "bring it up," and it turns out to be more than a demon; it turns into an assistant to its master. Moreover, it makes its master aware of the incompleteness of all his tasks, which leads him to new personal conquests for we know that the consciousness of our incompleteness is the foundation of wisdom and every new discovery (Salles 1998). The word "Famaliá" is probably originated from Latin *famulus*, a term used to denote the domestic servants, or else the servants to some divinity (Salles, 1998). As a matter of fact, in the Christian culture, all gods or the ones devoted to pagan gods were relegated to the condition of demons.

The Trickster in Brazilian Culture

The word "trickster" denotes someone who is a humbug, a blunderer, one who makes use of artful tricks to accomplish a licit or unlawful goal. It is old French in origin—*trique, trikier*—and is used to denote undistinguished heroes who, by means of tricks, manage to accomplish deeds judged impossible by others. The sense of humor breaks the barriers of austerity and inflexibility of social rules. In the Brazilian culture, the trickster is mainly represented by the figures of Macunaíma, Pedro Malazarte, Saci Pererê, Exu, etc. Some folk tales also portray animals as tricksters in comic situations, especially the toad, the parrot, the monkey, the rabbit, and the fox. The jaguar is the main victim of the other animals.

The Party in Heaven

Some of the favorite themes on trickster animals are those referring to parties in heaven. In one of these stories, all birds were preparing to join the celebrations, and the nosy toad quickly tried to find out what it was all about, and asked his pal urubu, a Brazilian vulture:

> Is there going to be a party in heaven?
> Yes, but big-mouthed ones won't be allowed.
> And the toad, making a small mouth, answered:
> Poor pal alligator . . .

The turtle, very upset, after having unsuccessfully tried to be carried by the birds, hid itself inside the vulture's guitar so that it would be taken along to the party. In heaven, everyone was very surprised to see the turtle walking around, trying to understand how it had managed to get there. For the trip back to land, the turtle asked the vulture to take it along and entered the guitar again. But the vulture, on its descent, made some acrobatic movements so as to take a shortcut, and in one of the speedy curves, the turtle fell all the way down, squashing on the ground. Our Lady had mercy on it and sewed its broken cask. That is the reason why the turtle has a seamed cask.

Exu and Saci Pererê

The Catholic catechists transformed Exu into the Christian devil. Nevertheless, in Africa, he was both a trickster and a mediator between men and gods, like the Greek Hermes. In the Afro-Brazilian traditions, the myths of Exu mix with those of the Indian character Saci-Pererê. Among his ventures, once he persuaded the Sun and the Moon to exchange their houses, causing great commotion: day turned into night, and night into day. Some other time, Exu decided to terminate the friendship between two neighbors. He walked the dividing line of the houses wearing a hat black on one side and white on the other. He always carried a terracotta pipe in his mouth, and fixed another one to the nape of his neck. The two neighbors began an argument about the direction the stranger had taken, which ended in a fight because each could swear that he was right, accusing the other of being a liar.

The fight became so serious that the king interfered. Exu showed up to say that none was a liar, but that both were perfect idiots. As he confessed his trick, all tried to catch him, but Exu was faster. On his flight, he set fire to several houses. The dwellers tried to save their belongings and Exu offered to guard them. But instead of giving the belongings back to their owners, he spread them around, exchanging their places (Willis 1996, 274–275).

Saci Pererê´s outstanding adventures are inconsequential: he spoils popcorn, hides people´s belongings not to be found again. He is portrayed as a one-legged little negro, always wearing a red hood and carrying a terracotta pipe, like the original images of the African Exu. It is believed that he comes from the eye of a turmoil, which symbolizes the confusion he usually causes.

Pedro Malazarte

Pedro Malazarte or Malasartes is another hero of the kind. His stories originated in Iberia, although many are similar to those of other European peoples. His name comes from Old Portuguese "malas," bad, and "artes," pranks. In the opera version by Camargo Guarnieri, and Mário de Andrade´s libretto, Pedro Malazarte appears carrying all his belongings: a cat and his house door. He is searching for his lover from Bahia, whose husband is away. She then nicely prepares a dinner, but the husband returns. To conceal her lover's meal, she hides the plates and serves an improvised snack to her husband. The guest tells the husband that the cat can talk, and is a fortuneteller as well. Next, he begins to "translate" the cat´s meows and purrs, telling where "mysterious" dishes could be found—the ones hidden which were found one by one. The dazzled husband proposes to buy the prodigious talking cat. Malazarte, after having escaped from his adventure with good financial profit, leaves carrying his house door for new adventures. In other versions, he sells a vulture, "translating" its speech likewise.

Pedro Malazarte makes up a countercultural aspect because, in other tales, his pranks are against a despotic master who had assaulted and exploited his brother at work. Pedro Malazarte´s revenge against this boss is performed through pranks, and not by means of a direct confrontation in which he would be frankly handicapped.

Macunaíma

The buffoon's adventures are not always without consequence. In one of Macunaíma's legends, a trickster hero of the Brazilian Indians is eaten up by a vagina hanging from a tree. His brothers, worried about his disappearance, start to search for him everywhere, but soon are suspicious of that vagina because previously it was skinny and dry, and now it is fat and chubby. As it was beaten with a stick, it dropped Macunaíma, who came out laughing a lot. Mário de Andrade described Macunaíma as "a hero with no character at all" (Andrade 1978). Why is that? Because it is all about a personality in formation, about something that has not established itself so far, which has not achieved a social position yet. The same occurs with aspects which have not yet been completely developed in a given personality.

The Trickster as a Humbug in the Brazilian Culture

As an archetypal image, the trickster has a dual polarity and, in the identification with one of its poles, or in case of the non-transcendency of that phase, the result is what is called identification with the shadow: this with that which is not accepted, or has not been wholly integrated yet. Then, the identification with the impostor, swindler or humbug may occur. In the contemporary Brazilian culture, there are some allegories about these situations.

One of these Brazilian popular characters is the Pirate's Parrot. According to this allegory, after the pirate´s successful fight in a battle, when he could have lost a leg, an eye, or undergone any other hardship, the Pirate´s Parrot, which has been hiding, rests upon the pirate's shoulder to appear on the victory portrait. Like those who profit from efforts or merits of others.

Another controversial character in Brazil is João-Sem-Braço, who lends his name to a variety of strokes and trickeries. In one of his stories, a debtor proposed to pay the creditor half of the debts. The latter, judging everything was lost, agreed. And the debtor, João-Sem-Braço, answered: "All right, from now on you will only charge me half the debt. . . ." Greed, rampant sexuality and financial opportunism are ascribed to priests and nuns. Thus originated the term "conto do vigário" (vicar's tale) used as a synonym for swindle.

The Saints

The Brazilian religion can hardly be called monotheist because there are countless prayers and rites dedicated to each one of the Catholic saints or those of other beliefs. São Pedro (Saint Peter) is one of the favorite characters of the popular tales in which he is seen as the guardian of heaven´s gate and Christ's fellow wandering the world. One of these stories says that his mother was condemned to hell for her covetousness. As Saint Peter enjoyed great "prestige" in heaven, he managed her admission in spite of her background attitude. A rope was cast to lift her, and Saint Peter's mother began to mount. But other souls in hell witnessed the scene and tried to grab the rope. As she was very greedy and wanted the rope only for herself, she began to fight the other souls to push them away. She struggled so that the rope burst when she was on her way, and she got stuck between heaven and hell. This is the origin of the expression "like Saint Peter´s mother," meaning to be in between two places, that is, neither in one place nor in another.

São Cristóvão (Saint Christopher) is the patron saint of travelers for having carried a child to the other side of a river, who grew heavier and heavier. Only later he found out that the child was Our Lord, Jesus Christ. Buses and taxicabs in Brazil usually have an image of Saint Christopher on their panels or rearview mirrors.

Santo Antonio (Saint Anthony), for the fact that he saved his father from the gallows in Lisbon, receives prayers and devotion from the distressed, from those who are in desperate situations, and from spinsters who vehemently ask him for a husband. They hang the saint´s statuettes upside down or inside a well, saying: "I will only take you out of here, Saint Anthony, if you bring me a husband soon."

São Longuinho (Saint Longinus) is responsible for finding lost things. The one who gets something back should jump thrice saying: "I found it, Saint Longinus, I found it, Saint Longinus." He was the Roman blind soldier who crossed Christ's chest with his spear. His blood fell in his eye and he could see again. After this miracle, he converted to Christianity and his cult is celebrated on the same day as Hother's, the blind god of the Nordic mythology, who unintentionally killed Bader. The god's blood poured over his eye and he could see again, like Saint Longinus.

Santa Luzia (Saint Lucy), whose name derives from Latin *lux*, "light," is responsible for the cure of eye infirmities; Santa Isabel, for the lepers' assistance; Santa Efigênia protects against fires; Santa Cecília is the patron saint of musicians. In short, Brazilians have a saint for every situation in life. So as to have the protection of all the saints and to avoid any offense, the bay on which the city of Salvador, in the state of Bahia, is located was diplomatically called Baía de Todos os Santos, meaning, All Saints' Bay.

Matriarchy and Patriarchy

There is neither a clear hegemony of patriarchal power in the Brazilian culture nor in the Latin culture as in Protestant countries. Julius Caesar, in *De Bello Gallico,* highlighted the contrast between the patriarchal culture of the German barbarians and the "femininity" of the Civilized Provence (Meira Penna 1974). Nevertheless, the main peoples forming the Brazilian culture had particular characteristics.

Brazilian Natives and Patriarchal Culture

In "Cartas do Brasil," dated from 1549, Father Manoel da Nóbrega reports that the man-eating natives maintained captured enemies in the villages. They lived together with the others and could take wives. In a given time, they were eaten up together with the children of these unions for the natives believed that children descended only from their fathers, and not from their mothers (Nóbrega 1988, 90). These captives and their children served as fattening animals, could not have proper names, and were called "food."

Matriarchy in Afro-Brazilian Culture

In the Brazilian black religions and communities, the Grande Mãe (Big Mother) is given an outstanding role. The so-called "Mother's" house occupies the central position of the village. In the state of Bahia, Mãe Menininha do Gantois, the founder's great-granddaughter and Ialorixá of the Gantois Candomblé, stood as the spiritual leader of the entire state. At home, she kept a firewood stove lit to serve coffee with local specialties to visitors. Her hearty smile was endearing and she was responsible, among others, for the spreading of the cults of African origin. Mãe Menininha passed away in 1986 at the age of 92. At a rural community in the outskirts of Belo Horizonte, named the Arturos', workers used to quickly get the blessings of the "Mãe" first thing in the morning before work.

Worshippers light candles at the Basilica of Our Lady of Aparecida, in the town of Aparecida do Norte, Brazil. Thousands of pilgrims flock to this town to celebrate the day of Our Lady of Aparecida, patron saint of all Catholic Brazilians. (AP/Wide WOrld Photos)

Cult of the Virgin Mary

In Latin countries, the cult of Virgin Mary predominates over the cult of the Christian God, and even over that of Christ. In troubled times, Brazilians pray to the Virgin for help. The Patron of Brazil is Nossa Senhora Aparecida, or Our Lady Aparecida, celebrated on October 12th in the presence of thousands of faithful. Her name, Aparecida, comes from the fact that she "appeared" or was found by fishermen at the Paraíba River in the eighteenth century. According to the legend, they cast, in vain, the fish nets several times into the river, for they always returned empty. But suddenly, they noticed something in one of the nets; it was the body part of the statuette of a black Madonna. Next, the head of the statuette appeared. What follows is that their nets returned with plenty of fish. Many faithful came to know the saint, and a chapel was built to shelter her image. Soon, a village encircled the shrine. Nowadays, there are a city and a cathedral dedicated to her cult. Our Lady Aparecida is one of the few black Madonnas existent, counting about twenty around the world.

There are many images of Our Lady, with attributes and cults of their own. Prayers are addressed to Nossa Senhora do Parto (Our Lady of Labor), Nossa Senhora do Perpétuo Socorro (of Perpetual Assistance), Nossa Senhora das Dores (of Pains), Nossa Senhora do Bom Conselho (of Good Advice), Nossa Senhora dos Navegantes (of Sailors), etc. There is also Nossa Senhora da Boa Morte (Our Lady of the Good Death), which is to be placed at the foot of the bed of the dying ones to help them leave this life.

Cult of the Ancestrals

As infants under five years old die, they are called "little angels." It is believed they go to heaven for being free of sins, but those who die unbaptized go to limbo, the intermediate place between hell and heaven. When adults die, it is customary that friends keep vigil at the dead's house. The mourning family keeps serving typical food, coffee, cakes, cookies, etc. Those who stay for the vigil have a repertory of jokes and funny stories to distract them overnight. In colonial times, rich people usually donated their goods to the "souls" to shorten their stay in purgatory and hasten their way to heaven (d'Aves 2000). Once souls no longer manage earthly goods, the Church takes charge of this "difficult" task. It is also believed that the dead's souls are watchful over the troubled living.

The Enchanted

The *caboclos* (descendants of the miscegenation of Indians and whites) call the ancestral spirits and fantastic beings endowed with supernatural powers "encanta-dos" (enchanted). These beings allegedly dwell in the river waters or in the fields, and would also manifest themselves in the Caboclos' Candomblés, which are the outcome of a syncretism of African and Indian cultures besides the European Spiritism.

Kuarup

Kuarup, or Quarup, is a ritual of the Indians living in the National Park of Xingu to pay homage to the dead. It happens on full moon nights and during drought, when fish are easier to catch to feed all the guests coming from neighboring Indian tribes. Every guest brings his own hammock to sleep in the huts of the village that organizes the Kuarup, but if room is lacking, the hammocks can be fixed to the nearby trees. The *pajé*, or witch doctor, checks the surrounding trees to find out which of them "cries"—that would be the one sheltering an honored spirit. The "crying" trunks are cut, adorned with bunches of feathers, necklaces, cotton threads, feather armbands, and props evoking the dead, and then taken to the center of the village. All the Indians adorn their bodies with paintings, feather ornaments, and dance playfully; they say that the dead do not like to see their descendants ugly or sad. Only the members of the family are allowed to mourn the deceased, but for three days only. At night, the village men, holding their bows and arrows, sing and dance to pay homage to the ancestral spirits, opening the ceremony. This performance is repeated for several days until the trunk adornments "stop moving." According to the belief, this means that the dead have already left.

Candomblé

In Candomblé, a religious cult African in origin, death is seen as a change of state from one world to another, and there are many rites honoring the ancestrals. These cults aim at the communication with the spirits, and at the reception of positive influences emanating from their powers. I was given the opportunity to participate in one of these ceremonies on Itaparica Island, in Bahia, which was held all night long with dancing, typical food, and spiritual incorporation manifestations by the

Ialorixás (saints' daughters) and Babalorixás (saints' sons). These spirits of dead people are called Eguns or Egunguns and, when they manifest themselves in ritual dances, nobody is allowed to touch those who incorporated them. During the ceremony, it is forbidden to leave the Candomblé surroundings because, according to their belief, those who exit would become vulnerable and could be possessed by the spirits. These would be manifesting themselves to investigate if their descendants were doing right in the world that they had left.

CARLOS ALBERTO CORRÊA SALLES

See also: Brazil and Its Folklore; Folk Narratives: Folk Tales, Legends, and Jokes; Folk Tales; Myths; Saints (Santos)

Further Reading

Alencar, José de. *O guarani.* São Paulo: Ed. Ática, n.d. Originally published 1857.

Andrade, Mário. *Macunaíma. O Herói sem Nenhum Caráter.* São Paulo: Livraria Martins, 1978.

Cascudo, Luis da Câmara. *Dicionário do Folclore Brasileiro.* Rio de Janeiro: Tecnoprint, 1972.

Colombo, Cristóvão. *Diários da Descoberta da América.* Porto Alegre: L&PM Editores, 1999.

d'Aves, Alexandre. *As Representações da Morte em Minas Gerais.* Belo Horizonte: Seminário do Instituto C. G. Jung de Minas Gerais, 2000.

Gomes, Núbia. *Mitos serpentários no imaginário de Minas Gerais.* Belo Horizonte: Seminário do Instituto C. G. Jung de Minas Gerais, 1993.

Herodotus. *The Histories.* Oxford: Oxford University Press, 1998.

Hollanda, Sérgio Buarque de. *Visão do Paraíso.* São Paulo: Companhia Editora Nacional, 1977.

Meira Penna, José O. *Em Berço Esplêndido.* Rio de Janeiro: J. Olympio, 1974.

Moura, Antônio de Paiva. *A Dinâmica Cultural e Social Através das Lendas e Mitos de Minas Gerais.* Belo Horizonte: Revista da Comissão Mineira de Folclore, 2000.

Nóbrega, Manoel da. *Cartas do Brasil.* Belo Horizonte: Itatiaia, 1988.

Salles, Carlos Alberto Corrêa. *Somos Feitos da Matéria dos Sonhos.* Rio de Janeiro: Record, 1998.

Silva, Carlos Mário Alexandrino da. *Ecmésia Histórica Colonial.* http://www.portugal-linha.pt/opiniao/CAlexandrino/cronicas.html.

Willis, Roy, ed. *World Mythology.* New York: Henry Holt, 1996.

BRIGGS, CHARLES LESLIE (1953–)

Charles Leslie Briggs is a noteworthy American anthropologist and folklorist who has done admirable work with cultures in Cuba, Mexico, Venezuela, as well as with Latino cultures in the southwestern United States. His area of scholarship is expansive, covering citizenship and the state, linguistic and medical anthropology, modernity, race, social theory, and violence. His primary academic interest, however, is in extending Américo Paredes' theorization of the borderlands into how folklore defines borders by looking at the borders between groups: Chicano versus Anglo American, Indigenous versus non-Indigenous, academic versus non-academic. Currently, Briggs is a tenured professor at the University of California Berkeley, where he serves as the Alan Dundes Distinguished Professor of Folklore and Anthropology. He is also the co-editor of the journal *Pragmatics*, put out by the International Pragmatics Association.

Briggs began his advanced education at Colorado College in Colorado Springs, where he received a B.A. in 1974 through an independent major that combined anthropology, psychology, and philosophy. He graduated *cum laude* and was a member of the Phi Beta Kappa Society. Briggs then attended graduate school at the University of Chicago in Illinois, where he received an M.A. in Anthropology in 1978, followed by a Ph.D. in Anthropology in 1981. His dissertation was entitled "Our Strength Is the Land," and on his committee were Michael Silverstein, Marshall Sahlins, David Schneider, and Norman McQuown.

Over the course of his academic career to date, he has authored or co-authored eight books: *Hispano Folklife of New Mexico: The Lorin W. Brown Federal Writers' Project Manuscripts* (1978, co-authored with Lorin W. Brown and Marta Weigle); *Wood Carvers of Córdova, New Mexico: Social Dimensions of an Artistic "Revival"* (1980); *Learning How to Ask: A Sociolinguistic Appraisal of the Role of the Interview in Social Science Research* (1986); *Competence in Performance: The Creativity of Tradition in Mexicano Verbal Art* (1988); *The Lost Gold Mine of Juan Mondragón: A Legend from New Mexico Performed by Melaquías Romero* (1990, co-authored and co-edited with Melaquías Romero and Julián Josué Vigil); *Voices of Modernity: Language Ideologies and the Politics of Inequality* (2003, co-authored with Richard Bauman); *Stories in the Time of Cholera: Racial Profiling during a Medical Nightmare* (2004, co-authored with Clara Mantini-Briggs); and *Poéticas de vida en espacios de muerte: Género, poder y el estado en la cotidianeidad Warao* ("The Poetics of Life in Space of Death: Gender, Power, and the State in Warao Everyday Life") (2008). In addition to this, he has co-edited *Land, Water, and Culture: New Perspectives on Hispanic Land Grants* (1987) and *Disorderly Discourse: Narrative, Conflict, and Social Inequality* (1996).

Briggs grew up in Los Candelarias, then a working-class neighborhood in Albuquerque, New Mexico, predominantly composed of people of Mexican descent, and he attended high school at Valley High, which also included a sizable Native American population. The established cultural borderlines that existed in the area during this time, paired with the aftereffects of a concerted attempt on the part of school officials to quicken the process of assimilation by having discouraged the previous generation from speaking Spanish, created an interesting environment for Briggs to be raised in. Since childhood, his innate curiosity led him to explore the diverse cultures and social dynamics in his surroundings, nurturing within him an interest in aspects of Latinidad and indigeneity that would gain greater depth as he continued pursuing his academic interests, later forming the basis of much of his work.

Although Briggs was of European ancestry, many of his friends were Chicanos, and trips to the homes of their grandparents provided an opportunity for him to learn everything he could about the lives and cultures of the people in his area. He would spend time with people of different professions, helping a local beekeeper maintain his hives, assisting farmers with their day-to-day operations, and watching woodcarvers perform their art, all the while internalizing the lessons and life viewpoints that they shared with him. Briggs also had the good fortune to make trips to Córdova, New Mexico, and other nearby communities to collect Mexican and Mexican American folk songs with his grandfather, John Donald Robb, a composer and conductor who did extensive folk recordings in Mexico. This fascination and concerted effort to learn from older generations gave him greater exposure to the Spanish language, allowing him to begin learning Spanish as a young child, even when previous school policies had hindered the Spanish language development of many Chicanos and their children. By the age of 19, Briggs had developed a comfortable fluency, navigating both languages with ease.

At the end of his freshman year in college, Briggs transferred his natural inclination to learn about cultures into an academic context by taking a course in anthropology. This course provided him a window through which he could reexamine his childhood experiences, seeing the issues faced by the people of his community in New Mexico as occupying a problematic interracial and cultural borderline. It also allowed him to understand the elders he had interacted with as vernacular philologists/philosophers, profound thinkers who contributed greatly to the intellectual productivity of the area. With the understanding of these poetics, the discursive devices for the circulation of these forms of vernacular knowledge production helped lead him to study folkloristics.

As a graduate student, Briggs explored this dynamic in further depth on return trips to Córdova, using a community-based research paradigm that looks at how people want to be represented and what sorts of research projects they deem to be of value. These trips would later inform his book *Wood Carvers of Córdova, New Mexico: Social Dimensions of an Artistic "Revival,"* a publication that examined how the woodcarving industry of the area used racism to their own benefit by selling outsider "Anglos" models of their own stereotypes. The manuscript from this book was finished in 1978 and won the James Mooney Award that year from the Southern Anthropological Society for distinguished scholarship. On the award committee were Henry Glassie and Roger Abrahams, who advocated that Briggs receive this honor that normally went to individuals further along in their careers.

Briggs has since continued to produce exceptional work with a very meaningful impact on the communities he researches. In Venezuela, during and after a cholera epidemic, Briggs collaborated with a Venezuelan public health physician, Clara Mantini, to trace the narratives that showed a clear link between social inequalities and susceptibility to the cholera epidemic. The study showed the government's failure to properly educate the public about the health threat and its failure to deliver the necessary health care to the Indigenous of the area. Instead, the government equated cholera with the Indigenous populations to deflect responsibility from the institution to the victims. This work raised consciousness about the real issues still being faced when governments establish racial borderlines with inequities in social services and would later become the book *Stories in the Time of Cholera: Racial Profiling during a Medical Nightmare.* The book won the most important and respected awards in the fields of Latin American Studies and anthropology: The Bryce Wood Book Award from the Latin American Studies Association and the J. I. Staley Prize from the School of Advanced Research for outstanding scholarship in anthropology.

The amazing work Briggs has accomplished and continues to accomplish in his career falls in line with his desire to reposition folkloristics in theoretical terms so it is no longer seen as a marginal discipline, but rather as an important venue from which to understand communities. His contributions to the field have been recognized by numerous organizations, including the National Endowment for the Humanities, the Guggenheim Foundation, the National Science Foundation, and the American Folklore Society, which named him a Fellow in 1990.

Eric César Morales

See also: American Folklore Society (AFS); Paredes, Américo; Robb, John Donald; Venezuela and Its Folklore

Further Reading

Briggs, Charles L. *The Wood Carvers of Córdova, New Mexico: Social Dimensions of an Artistic "Revival."* Knoxville: University of Tennessee Press, 1980.
University of California Berkeley, Anthropology Department. http://anthropology.berkeley.edu/people/person_detail.php?person=8.

BRUJERÍA (WITCHCRAFT)

All human cultures, including the most modern and technological, have developed over time from tribal pre-Christian origins. As such, all human cultures have either active pagan nativistic beliefs or vestiges of those beliefs still extant in their cultures today. In the Americas, there is a tradition and practice of witchcraft called *brujería* in Spanish which has ancient origins. Those communities, which are the most geographically approximate to Indigenous ones, maintain the strongest traditions such as in the Mexican states of Veracruz and Oaxaca. In the Americas, Pre-Columbian belief systems and active native traditions continue to thrive side by side and are intertwined with five hundred years of influence by Roman Catholicism. Both the people we call Latinos/as and their belief systems have resulted from a racial and cultural mixing called m*estizaje.*

Latin American and Caribbean magico-Christian religious belief systems are largely the result of centuries of the mixing of symbols and beliefs, producing syncretic religions. In the Latino world, there are many active systems of belief that operate simultaneously with the Catholic Church. *Brujería, curanderismo,* and *espiritismo* are just a few of the traditions that develop in and around Catholicism using Catholic symbols.

Throughout Latin America and the Caribbean, native belief systems thrive in the shadow of the church. In the Caribbean, there are basically no surviving native populations remaining. However, beginning in the sixteenth century, the descendants of African slaves who were brought to the islands have maintained vigorous traditions derived from their points of origin. Yoruba slaves brought with them the belief system that is called *Santería* today while Congolese slaves imported *Palo Mayombe*. There are many other variants ascribed to specific African origin populations. While these legitimate religions are not of themselves *brujería,* many of their beliefs and practices have been adopted into the belief system others call *brujería* or witchcraft. This is the term chosen by the people themselves to describe their native beliefs and practices that attempt to alter the natural world by invoking the supernatural.

Many actively functioning native groups living in Mexico and Central and South America have maintained their pre-Christian traditions and adapted and modified their beliefs with Catholicism. Today they thrive and each one has a functioning system usually referred to as *brujería*. These contemporary belief systems migrate to the cities and across the border to the United States with the believer-participant. Native traditions and belief systems of the Aztec and Mayan descendant groups along with numerous other native cultures in Mexico such as the Otomí, Zapotec and Huastec, Huichol, and many others, today practice their traditional systems of belief simultaneously with Catholicism.

The term *brujería* is ubiquitous throughout Latin America and the Caribbean and in the United States as well. It must be understood that the term *brujería* is a generic word that refers to the syncretic practices and native rituals that are defined by a particular sub-culture, by language of the people, and by the geo-cultural region. Therefore, *brujería* is practiced on the island of Puerto Rico, in the lowland Amazonia of Peru, on the Sonoran desert of Mexico and in Chicago and throughout the United States as well, all in different forms.

There is, however, a common thread that runs through each variant of *brujería* defined by the interpretation of Catholicism practiced in a particular place mixed with the native practices of the place. This is the reality of what constitutes the world of *brujería* in the modern world. The non-Christian practice of *brujería* lives and even thrives side by side in the bustling modern communities of Latin America and in the United States. The person who is shopping the "esoteric marketplace" for the material culture supportive of their variant of *brujería* will find the effigies of the deities, spirits, and other artifacts of the local culture for sale alongside the statues and candles dedicated to both Catholic and popular saints. The materials available at the local level define the overarching *brujería*-Catholicism belief system and practice continuum at every specific location.

Throughout Latin American and the Caribbean Indigenous and rural agricultural communities are affiliated with larger central places. Central places are organized based on need around state capitals, and all are connected to the national capital. In Mexico, the national *brujería* center is *El Mercado Sonora,* known as the witch's market. This world-famous market provides the cultural material for the practice of *brujería* throughout Mexico. Items purchased in Mexico City on Monday are in shops on the U.S.-Mexico border the following day. *Brujería*-witchcraft cannot exist without the practitioner operating at the local level. With the exception of the most localized native "*brujos*" if male and "*brujas*" if female, the persons who consider themselves *brujos/as* and who actively practice *brujería* must rely upon the market place to supply the client with those items needed to complete a work or *trabajo*, or to reverse a spell or to heal the sick or lovelorn.

Every Latin American town of any significance has a *hierbería* or a *botánica,* that is, a shop that specializes in magical and witchcraft objects including medicinal plants. When a town or village is too small to have an actual store, these objects will be sold in the traditional native market. Interestingly, everyone from the common person on the street, to the major witches or *brujos mayores*, *curanderos* and *espiritistas* all utilize the same store. The objects for sale are the same while the purpose is different depending on the user and tradition.

Every village, town and city will have *brujos/as* and "*curanderos*" if male and "*curanderas*" if female. In some cases, they are the same person, but generally they do not overlap traditions. *Brujos/as* as witches are spell casters. They are commissioned by a person to either cast a spell on someone or to reverse a spell on someone. *Brujos/as* attribute their power to cast or reverse spells to either a regional deity or spirit or in the case of Catemaco, Veracruz to the devil himself. *Brujos* and *brujería* are universally thought of as negative or evil. This is because Christianity in all its forms has taught us so. However, the *brujos/as* and the common people usually do not associate evil with *brujería*.

In Latin America and the Caribbean, *brujería*, or witchcraft, has gradients or different forms which range from white magic or *magia blanca,* thought to be harmless, to black magic or *magia negra,* which is most definitely evil at work. There are many other colors in between, including green, yellow, red, and blue

White magic is performed or commissioned to influence relationships, the work place as well as other things in daily life that pertain to one's self or loved ones. Other forms of *brujería* are directed toward other people including the completely innocent and unaware. *Brujería* is commissioned to influence the outcome of a political race, or a sports contest, and more seriously to establish or break up marriages and relationships. In some cases the person commissioning the *brujo/a* seeks the death of the target. It is also not uncommon for a neighbor to commission a *brujo/a* to cast a spell on a neighbor or a co-worker. Because the incantations, spells, and rituals of *brujería* are so commonly known in Latin America and the Caribbean, often a professional *brujo/a* is not needed. Today's esoteric market contains a very complete section of books and pamphlets explaining *brujería* and how to perform it. This has resulted in many thousands of people dabbling in the practice of *brujería*.

Latin American *brujería* requires a petitioner and a practitioner who uses some system of divination such as the Spanish tarot cards, the *caracoles*, or cowry shells, and lesser known systems. It consists of the casting of spells called *trabajos*, which fall between benign white magic and malignant black magic. It also consists of the reversing or breaking of spells which may utilize a range from very simple incantation and recitation to more complex rituals including animal sacrifice.

Brujería may also be performed over distance. It is not necessary for the petitioner and the *brujo/a* to be in the same place to effect a spell against a third party who is located in some other location. *Brujería* spells may be cast across continents and countries. For example a *brujo* in Guatemala may cast a witchcraft spell against someone living in Dallas, Texas. It is generally believed that when a person's problem is identified as witchcraft or *brujería*, it must be resolved professionally by a spell-reversing *brujo/a*. Something as serious as a witchcraft spell cannot be left to chance or to the amateur to remove.

In the Indigenous communities of Latin America, the terms *nahual* or *chaman* are used to identify the native practitioners of witchcraft in these communities.

These persons are almost always born into a family of *brujos*. However, in cities *brujería* has become a quasi-profession and practitioners have either apprenticed with a *brujo/a* or simply picked up the practice, incantations and rituals along the way. As business people, those who are viewed as powerful survive and those who are not quickly go out of business. People desiring the accoutrements of *brujería* may purchase the printed incantations, the fetishes, the candles, necklaces, prepackaged plants, scapulars, prayer cards, statues, amulets, talismans and any other item needed for the practice of *brujería*.

Antonio Noé Zavaleta

See also: African Influence on Latino Folklore; Espíritus Malignos (Evil Spirits); Santería; Spirit Possession and Exorcism

Further Reading

Blea, Irene I. "*Brujería*: A Sociological Analysis of Mexican American Witches." In *Sex Roles, Language: Selected Papers*. Berkeley, CA: Tonatiuh-Quinto Sol, 1989.

"Brujería: Naturaleza e historia." http://www.corazones.org/apologetica/practicas/brujeria .htm.

Delgado, Edmundo R. *Witch Stories of New Mexico, Folklore of New Spain/ Cuentos de Brujas de Nuevo Mexico, Folklore de la Nueva España*. Collected by the Works Progress Administration, Santa Fe, NM, 1994.

Donnet, Beatriz. *Brujas, Ogros, Hechiceros y Otros Asustadores*. Mexico City: Quarzo, 2000.

Guiley, Rosemary Ellen. *The Encyclopedia of Witchcraft*. New York: Facts-on-File, 1989.

Zavaleta, Antonio, and Alberto Salinas, Jr. *Curandero Conversations: El Niño Fidencio, Shamanism and Healing Traditions of the Borderlands*. Brownsville: The University of Texas and Texas Southwest College, 2009.

BUÑUELOS

Buñuelos are a traditional pastry made with flour, butter, and eggs, well mixed and deep-fried in hot oil, until they puff up and are golden brown. After they are cooked, they can be either rolled on sugar or covered in syrup and served hot. They are traditional for Christmas and other festivities; and in Mexico they are also a popular street food often sold during religious celebrations outside of churches or in popular street fairs. The association between *buñuelos* and Christmas is evident in a popular Mexican *villancico* (Christmas carol) that literally says: *Esta sí que es noche buena, Nochebuena,/noche de comer buñuelos* (This Christmas Eve is truly a good night, a good night / a night to eat *buñuelos*). As is the case with most traditional Latino and Hispanic foods, there are many variations of the same dish, pastry, or drink, depending on the country or region as well as the ingredients available and the cultural and culinary traditions—and *buñuelos* are no exception.

The traditional Mexican *buñuelos*, for example, are made with flour, eggs, butter, milk, vanilla, and cinnamon, and they are similar to a thin fritter. The basic recipe calls for flour, a little bit of baking powder, salt, and cinnamon mixed in a bowl until incorporated. Separately, the milk is heated and the butter melted and mixed with the vanilla, and brought to a boil. In another bowl the eggs are mixed and added to the milk mixture; everything needs to be incorporated well by whisking quickly. All the ingredients must be mixed well and incorporated before working the dough on a floured surface. Once the mix is ready it should be rubbed well until it is smooth. When the dough is ready, it is divided it into several small balls, and each one should be rolled on a floured surface into very thin pies, until they resemble a tortilla (make them as big or as small as desired). Place these pies on a tablecloth and let them dry, then fry them in enough hot oil until they are golden brown and crispy, turning them only once so they can cook evenly on both sides. Be careful not to overcook them.

Unlike most *buñuelos*, Mexican *buñuelos* are very thin, almost like a flour tortilla, and can be relatively small or as large as a small pizza. In fact, the dough for the traditional Mexican *buñuelos* is worked like a pizza pie until is very thin and then it is fried in a huge pot of hot oil. Once they are done, they are usually placed in large piles or served immediately sprinkled generously with powdered cinnamon and sugar or with syrup of *piloncillo* (Mexican raw brown sugar) or sugar and fruit. Another version of the Mexican *buñuelos* makes the dough into small rosette fritters, usually crispy and rolled in sugar, and cinnamon. These cookies are also a favorite treat for Christmas and holidays and can be made easily at home if a mold is available. The mold has to be dipped in the hot oil and then in the batter of flour, sugar, eggs, butter, milk, and vanilla to collect enough batter for the cookie; then it is again dipped in the oil with the batter it carries and that is what makes the *buñuelos*. This version is also popular and can be found in bakeries all over Mexico, but also processed and packed by the Bimbo Company, which calls them Bimbuñuelos.

In Spain and other countries, *buñuelos* are simply little rolls fried in oil, similar to doughnuts or beignets made with flour, milk, butter, eggs, vanilla, cinnamon, and baking powder, mixed well, rolled in little balls that when fried in a neutral oil like canola, vegetable, or sunflower, expand, becoming spongy, and take different shapes and sizes. These pastries are then rolled in cinnamon sugar or powdered sugar. A variation of this pastry, typical of Spain, is *buñuelos de viento*, which are the same pastries just made fluffier and lighter and filled with pastry cream or marmalade. As is the case in Mexico, in Spain and other Latin countries *buñuelos* are traditional for big holidays such as Christmas, but in some regions, particularly Catalonia, they are also traditional during Lent and they are called *buñuelos de cuaresma*. In most of these traditions, *buñuelos* are a sweet treat covered in syrup, honey, sugar, liquor, or sweet wine, but some regions have also a tradition of savory *buñuelos*. These are less traditional and little known.

Among the savory type of *buñuelos* are the Colombian cheese *buñuelos*, which are prepared with similar dough to the other more traditional sweet *buñuelos*, but adding small chunks of cheese in the center of the pastry so it can melt inside when the *buñuelo* is fried. Other savory *buñuelos* are the *buñuelos de acelgas* (Swiss chard *buñuelos*) or *buñuelos de espinacas* (spinach *buñuelos*), *buñuelos de yucca* (yucca *buñuelos*) or even *buñuelos de bacalao* (codfish *buñuelos*), which are fish fritters; less traditional, and an example of the nouveau cuisine of Mexico, is a dish recently offered at the Tijuana restaurant Villa Saverios called *buñuelos de belly* (pork belly *buñuelos*, a combination of sweet and savory served as dessert). *Buñuelos* are as delicious as versatile and can be made sweet or savory and remain one of the foods most associated with holidays, particularly family holidays such as Christmas, Easter, and even Passover in the case of many Jewish families from Latin America. There is a dish similar to *buñuelos, sopapillas*, but usually the *sopapillas* are thicker corn cakes fried and drenched in syrup or other sweet liquid, or even ice cream.

Rafael Hernández

See also: Christmas (Navidad); Pan Dulce (Mexican Pastry)

Further Reading

Baez Kijac, Maria. *The South American Table: The Flavor and Soul of Authentic Home Cooking from Patagonia to Rio de Janeiro, with 450 Recipes.* Boston: The Harvard Common Press, 2003.

Luard, Elisabeth. *The Food of Spain and Portugal: A Regional Celebration.* London: Kyle Books, 2007.

Martínez, Zarela, with Anne Mendelson. *Zarela's Veracruz.* Boston and New York: Houghton, Mifflin, Co., 2001.

Quintana, Patricia, and Ignacio Urquiza. *The Taste of Mexico.* New York: Stewart, Tabori & Chang, 1986.

BURRITOS

A burrito, meaning "little donkey" in Spanish, is a type of food composed of a large, wheat flour tortilla wrapped around a number of ingredients. Burritos have become a staple of Mexican foodways, due to their ability to conveniently pack a considerable amount of food in an edible, portable, and flexible wrapper. There are endless varieties of the burrito. While typically beans function as the basic ingredient, common additions include cheese, tomatoes, sautéed strips of chiles and onions, beef, chicken, salsa, sour cream, etc.

The main component of the burrito, the tortilla, has roots that date back to Mesoamerica, with the Mayas (1500 B.C. to 1500 A.D.) and the Aztecs (1100 A.D.). The tortilla was originally made from dry maize kernels that were soaked in an alkaline solution, usually lime, a process called *nixtamal,* which makes the proteins and vitamins easier to absorb by the human body. The resultant kernels were then hulled and ground to make the *masa* that would later be flattened and cooked to make tortillas or used for other food products like tamales. Although maize was the most common grain used to make tortillas, the Aztecs were also known to make tortillas out of squash and amaranth. The finished tortilla would then be wrapped around a number of foods, including tomatoes, avocados, beans, mushrooms, and chile sauce. This food custom is widely considered to be the ancestor of the taco, the flauta, the enchilada, and, of course, the burrito.

The arrival of the Spanish in the sixteenth century brought about many changes to the Amerindian cuisine with the introduction of foreign ingredients, such as lentils, chickpeas, rice, sugar, and wheat. During colonization, the Spanish started a campaign to change the diet of the Amerindian population from being maize-based to the more European diet that was wheat-based. This dietary change took a significant hold in northern Mexico where climatic factors were favorable to the cultivation of this cereal plant and significantly fewer Amerindians inhabited the area than in the south. In the rural populations of the northern state of Chihuahua, for instance, there is evidence of the existence of adobe bread ovens that are hundreds of years old dating date back to the establishment of the first Catholic missions of the seventeenth century in the area the Spanish called Nueva Vizcaya, which encompassed all of Chihuahua as well as parts of other Mexican states. This preference for wheat by the Spaniards, paired with the existence of the Indigenous corn tortilla, gave rise to the wheat flour tortilla which has the benefit of being more pli-

Burritos stuffed with fresh ingredients. (Dreamstime.com)

able than its corn counterpart and can be used to wrap around a larger number of ingredients. The creation of the burrito can then be seen as a logical step in the fusion of two distinct cultures.

There are numerous stories that offer ideas as to when the innovation first occurred. One of the earlier and more popular theories is that in the nineteenth century *vaqueros* (cowboys) of northern Mexico created the burrito because of its high mobility value, allowing them to carry around this new food concoction in their saddlebags for convenience. An added benefit to the vaqueros was that the flour tortilla does not dry and harden as quickly as corn tortillas. People from the state of Sonora, an area known for its top-notch wheat flour tortillas, would fill their burritos with the region's famous *machaca* (dried, shredded beef) to create a food product that did well on long journeys through a characteristically arid land. The name burrito was given to this food as a term of endearment because it functioned as the sidekick to their horse, much like a donkey. This food trend was eventually picked up by miners and ranchers of the area.

Other stories place the creation of the burrito in the border city of Ciudad Juárez, Chihuahua. The earliest of the stories states that during the Mexican Revolution

(1910–1920), a street food vendor by the name of Juan Méndez had the idea to put his food inside a large, wheat flour tortilla and wrap it tightly so that it would not get cold. He would then put it under a little tablecloth to keep it warm. He would get so many delivery orders that he decided to buy a donkey to transport his food across the Rio Grande. His food was such a success that Mexicans and Americans began to arrive from everywhere in search of the food of the little donkey or "burrito."

A later story places it in Ciudad Juárez in the 1940s, when a street food vendor set up his stand outside a state-run middle school to sell his plates of food to the schoolchildren for lunch. The vendor would notice that the kids sometimes did not have enough money to buy a full plate of food or enough time to eat it all, so he decided to put a small portion of food in a wheat flour tortilla, wrap it, and sell it in this form for less money. When preparing these, he would often tell his kitchen helpers, "Hurry, my burritos are almost here!" In Spanish, *burro* can be used as a derogatory term, meaning dimwitted. In this context, the diminutive of the word was applied to the students. Eventually, the term was transferred to refer to the food product the students ate.

In today's society, the portability of the burrito is still highly valued, making it a popular food option across Mexico and the United States for people on the go. It is related to similar mobile foods from around the world, such as the American hoagie, the Italian panini, the Turkish döner kebab, etc. In addition, the versatility of its ingredients makes it palatable to a large swath of people with different tastes and permits it to be eaten at various times of the day. For example, a popular type of burrito found in the United States includes the breakfast burrito, which may consist of scrambled eggs, ham, potatoes, bacon, cheese, etc. Other variants of the burrito include the *chimichanga* (a deep-fried burrito popular in the Southwest) and the wrap, which has enjoyed increased popularity since the 1990s and experienced new undertakings as ingredients from fresh pear to scallions are incorporated and wrapped up tightly in the wheat flour tortillas.

ERIC CÉSAR MORALES AND JULIÁN ANTONIO CARRILLO

See also: Tortilla; Vaquero

Further Reading

Fox, Peter. End of the Burrito Trail. Audio recording from the archives of National Public Radio. http://www.npr.org/templates/story/story.php?storyId=1033459.

Janer, Zilkia. *Latino Food Culture*. Food Cultures in America Series. Westport, CT: Greenwood Press, 2008.

Pilcher, Jeffrey M. "Mexican American Food." In Andrew F. Smith, ed. *The Oxford Encyclopedia of Food and Drink in America*. New York: Oxford University Press, 2005.

CABAÑUELAS (WEATHER PROGNOSTICATION)

The *cabañuelas* is the Spanish term for a folk system of predicting the weather. This system of weather prediction is tied to natural climatological occurrences or to natural phenomena and persists as a folk tradition throughout the Spanish-speaking areas of the world as well as in the United States wherever Latinas/os live. The *cabañuelas* weather-predicting system is based on measurements and observations made during the month of January, although in some areas the period for tracking the shifts in weather to predict the year's climate conditions is the month of August.

No doubt, it is the need to have a sense of what the weather will bring during the year that led to these folk beliefs. In rural agricultural-oriented cultures it is imperative to have some type of guiding system for planting and harvesting crops. To insure a good yield, knowledge of weather patterns and climate changes must be acquired by the farmers and ranchers; thus we have a tradition that resembles the construction of a *Farmer's Almanac*. In a similar manner to the *Farmer's Almanac*, the *cabañuelas* began as a system based on observations of the moon's cycles.

Origins

Some people believe the origin of this method of weather forecasting, that is the *cabañuelas*, lies in the Mayan calendrical practices with their emphasis on the precise movements of astronomical bodies across the sky, while others believe it to be based on European traditions; more specifically, it is believed the system originated in Spain during the Muslim occupation of the Iberian peninsula. The *cabañuelas* appear to be a traditional form of weather prognostication dating from many centuries in Spain before traveling with the Spanish in the fifteenth and sixteenth centuries to the Americas, especially South America but also including the Caribbean, and even parts of Africa. As the Spanish moved north into what is now the United States, they brought with them the tradition. Thus while its origins may not be clear, we can surmise that it would have been a natural progression or combination of ancient Mayan and Spanish "science" coming together that gives us current-day practice of the *cabañuelas*.

In Mexico and the rest of South America and the American Southwest, the practice continues albeit not as essential to the groups' survival in an increasingly contemporary urban life style. In today's Spain, expert *cabañuelistas* have organized the Asociación Cultural Española de Cabañuelas y Astrometereología (ACECA) and claim that it is an empirical scientific method of weather prediction. Every year the members of the ACECA report the weather for the coming twelve months.

The association has been meeting since 1996 to insure that this ancient prehistoric method of predicting the weather survives threatened disappearance in these modern times.

The members of the Spanish ACECA also hold that the origin of the tradition lies thousands of years ago and that it is rooted in a system that used the moon and its cycles as a reference. They cite how the Egyptians would calibrate their measurement according to the levels of the Nile waters, the location of the Sirius star, and they also note that "the old base of cabañuelas was measured beginning in August and not the current January" (http://www.laopiniondemalaga.es/andalucia/2010/09/04/cabanuelas-anuncian-2011-olas-calor/365015.html, accessed June 23rd, 2011).

The Method

The intricate measurement that is taught from one generation to the next and has existed in oral tradition for centuries involves observing the changing weather for each of the thirty-one days of January. Each of the first twelve days represents a month of the year. January 1st represents January, January 2nd represents February; the 3rd is March, and so on. On the 13th day of January, the observation is reversed; that is, the 13th corresponds to December, the 14th is November, the 15th is October, and so on until the 25th when the measurement follows for six days, each half day representing a month: on January 25th midnight to noon stands for January, the afternoon from noon to midnight of the same day represents February; then the next twelve hours, of January 26th, will predict what March weather will be like and the afternoon will correspond to April's weather. On the 30th, the system shifts so that on the 31st, every hour corresponds to a month. So from midnight to 1:00 a.m. it is January; 1:00 to 2:00 corresponds to February and so on until noon when the months are reversed and from noon to 1:00 p.m. it is December; 1:00 to 2:00 November, and so on ending from 11:00 p.m. to midnight in January. The complete cycle must be meticulously observed and recorded to yield accurate predictions; the average of the corresponding measurement for the month—taking note of the average temperature during January 3rd, the 14th, and the 31st at 3:00 a.m. and 9:00 p.m. would show what to expect in March. Further, if on the corresponding dates and times it is chilly or rainy, the *cabañuela* would then indicate a chilly, rainy March.

The prediction is only accurate for the location where the observations are made. Thus, if in San Antonio, Texas the *cabañuelas* indicate a chilly rainy March, the same prediction would not hold for Albuquerque, New Mexico, and the observation for that location would be the one to consult for the expected weather in March. A report distributed by Europa Press titled "Las Cabañuelas anuncian un 2011 con 'muchas' olas de calor" (The Cabañuelas predict many heat waves for 2011) offer the predictions based on this method for Andalucía in southern Spain, more specifically for Malaga for 2011 (http://www.laopiniondemalaga.es/andalucia/2010/09/04/cabanuelas-anuncian-2011-olas-calor/365015.html, accessed July 1st, 2011).

Conclusion

While the meteorologist in the evening news presents an accurate and sophisticated rendering of the weather conditions for a region (indeed assisted by satellite images, they can predict with uncanny accuracy what time the rain will fall the next day), there are still some who retain the old traditional method rooted in folk tradition for predicting the weather. The folk knowledge that has been passed down via oral tradition survives as an odd curiosity and is no longer serving the same purposes it did during earlier times. However, in the United States, some of the elders in New Mexico and other parts of the Southwest still remember how to figure out the intricate measurements.

Norma E. Cantú

See also: Canícula (Dog Days of Summer)

Further Reading

Adame Martínez, Homero. "Las Cabañuelas, conocimiento empírico del clima." Laopin iondemalaga.es. http://www.laopiniondemalaga.es/andalucia/2010/09/04/cabanuelas-anuncian-2011-olas-calor/365015.html.

Alcón, Manuel B. *Lo de Mora*. Victoria, BC: Trafford Publishing, 2005. http://www.laopin iondemalaga.es/andalucia/2010/09/04/cabanuelas-anuncian-2011-olas-calor/365015 .html.

Madridejos. http://www.madridejos.net/cabanuel.htm.

Mexicodesconocido. http://www.mexicodesconocido.com.mx/las-cabanuelas-conocimiento-empirico-del-clima.html.

Yucatan Today. http://yucatantoday.com/en/topics/cabanuelas.

CABEZA DE BACA, FABIOLA (C. 1894–1991)

A New Mexican writer, Fabiola Cabeza de Baca described the folklore of northern New Mexico through cookbooks, memoirs, and teaching. She was born in La Liendre, part of her family's ranch in northern New Mexico. The exact date of her birth is uncertain, as 1898 is most common, but her younger sister was born in 1897. Her school records seem to indicate that 1894 is most likely. The ranch upbringing sparked an interest in preserving the way of life she had known growing up. She had a long career as a teacher, writer, extension agent, and cultural advocate.

Cabeza de Baca was raised by her grandmother, a woman whose own folk ways were included in the autobiographical and fictional *We Fed Them Cactus* (1954, republished 1995) as a strong woman and to some degree a *curandera*. Cabeza de Baca attended the Loretto Academy in Las Vegas, New Mexico, and later New Mexico Normal, graduating in 1921 with a teaching degree. She then taught school in one-room schoolhouses in northern New Mexico. As a rural schoolteacher, she lamented that her students had little exposure to the history of the Southwest. She taught in both English and Spanish, even though the schools in the Southwest were largely expected to Americanize the Hispano students.

She was an agricultural extension agent for more than thirty years after receiving a B.S. from New Mexico State University in 1927. During this time, she wrote *Historic Cookery* (1942) about the native New Mexican diet, replete with folklore and chile recipes, and *The Good Life* (1949), which emphasized the nutritional benefits of regional cuisine and the herbal remedies known in the northern regions of the state. She traveled to Mexico as a representative of the United Nations and worked with Indigenous communities there.

In *We Fed Them Cactus*, Cabeza de Baca shows how her father's heart broke when the homesteaders destroyed the productivity of the land in New Mexico. The years of drought and encroachment by homesteaders meant that the family had to move all their cattle by train to another part of the state. They fed the herd cactus in hard times—the Depression—leading to the title of the book. She also discusses the disappearance of the Comanche and the buffalo on the Llano while simultaneously preserving the Nuevomexicana presence.

Cabeza de Baca draws relationships between her family and their place in New Mexico history. As part of the Folklore Society in New Mexico, she shows how Anglos renamed places that already had names, such as the Los Barrancos Amarillos being changed to Amarillo. The family names also carry significance, which is explained as if it is implicitly understood when El Cuate notes in *We Fed Them Cactus*, "The Paezes had less money, but better blood than the Salcedos" (34). The pioneer families of northern New Mexico are all interconnected and their relationships form the basis of the historic events of the state.

In *The Good Life*, almost all of the characters are women and the alternative voices are the recipes included in the text. The book also focuses on the *curandera* (healer) figure as an important woman in the community. Her folklore collections made women central through food, domestic activities, and medicinal herbs.

As Tey Diana Rebolledo points out, Cabeza de Baca's writing uses multiple narrative strategies of resistance. Some of these include the use of cultural signs, Spanish names, and social banditry to show knowledge of colonization and folklore works to combat that colonization. In the books she represents a nostalgic unified Hispano community that contrasts to the fragmented community emerging in the 1950s. Certainly, Cabeza de Baca mixes genres, using recipes, community voices for storytelling, memoir, folk tales, and fiction.

LEIGH JOHNSON

See also: Rebolledo, Tey Diana

Further Reading

Cabeza de Baca, Fabiola. *We Fed Them Cactus*. 2nd ed. Albuquerque: University of New Mexico Press, 1998.

McMahon, Marci. "Transnational Domesticity: Fabiola Cabeza de Baca's Agricultural Extension Work in New Mexico and Mexico (1929–1957)." Paper presented at the annual meeting of the American Studies Association Annual Meeting, Hyatt Regency, Albuquerque, New Mexico, October 16th, 2008.

Rebolledo, Tey Diana. *Women Singing in the Snow: A Cultural Analysis of Chicana Literature*. Tucson: University of Arizona Press, 1995.

CABRITO

Cabrito, or little goat, refers to the meat of a young goat, usually between four and eight weeks of age, as well as the variety of dishes prepared with this meat. Due to the young age of the kid and the fact that it is still being fed by the mother's milk, the meat tends to be very tender and the flavor not as gamey as that of older goats. In cooking goat, tender cuts can be roasted, broiled, or fried, although by far the most common way of cooking goat is by grilling it. Less tender cuts are best in stews or even braised. In some parts of Mexico, *cabrito* is slowly cooked in a hole in the ground filled with hot rocks and lit coals and covered with maguey or banana leaves. This method of cooking *cabrito* is very effective since the meat could very easily lose moisture and the meat can become very tough quickly if exposed to high cooking temperatures. The Spanish and Portuguese who arrived in the Americas brought with them some of their culinary traditions and agricultural practices, among them farming and raising domestic animals, and mixed them with Indigenous practices like cooking in the ground with maguey, a native cactus.

In the arid northern states of modern Mexico and some other mountainous regions and areas of rough terrain in the continent, the conditions seemed particularly favorable to raise goats, and especially appreciated was *cabrito asado*. The Spanish and Portuguese settlers also raised sheep and cattle, and favored the production of *carne seca* (dry meat or goat or cow jerky). Usually all parts of the animal are used, including the innards or organ meats. Today's *cabrito* is prepared in many ways following a variety of recipes with added ingredients and spices. However, the most common ways of preparing it are grilled or in a stew with traditional spices and sometimes chili peppers. The tender cuts of goat meat are the legs, ribs, portions of the shoulder cut, the line roast and the breast; and these cuts are better prepared grilled. Less tender cuts of goat, like ribs and shanks, are usually stewed. But in general, the best way of preparing *cabrito* is to cook it slowly so it will not dry, remaining tender and more flavorful.

Cabrito asado remained very popular in northern Mexico, particularly in the city of Monterrey, where it is considered the regional dish. Traditionally in preparing

Roasting goat at a traditional Argentinean restaurant in Buenos Aires. (iStockPhoto.com)

cabrito, all parts of the animal are used, including the internal organs, and the meat is cut according to the method of preparation, with the carcass of the animal often split open in the middle, ready to be grilled whole. But there are really many different ways of preparing the meat, and depending on the region, each community or even each family may have a recipe for *cabrito*. Although cooking in general is customarily an activity dominated by women, men often are in charge of grilling the *cabrito* or making the *barbacoa* (cooking it in a pit).

Cabrito al pastor, or *cabrito* shepherd-style, is the traditional way of preparing *cabrito* in Monterrey and many other cities in Mexico. It is usually prepared by inserting the carcass of the kid on a long stick or rod and placing it over a fire. A more traditional way of preparing it is putting first the kid in a large stockpot with water, salt, and vinegar, letting it rest for at least two to three hours. Once it has marinated for that time, a pile of mesquite wood is built on the ground, and burnt down to white coals. The *cabrito* is then placed over the hot coals, and roasted for two to three hours, or until it is done, basting occasionally with a little salted water. It is important to turn the *cabrito* often so that the meat cooks evenly. When cooked and placed on plates, it is usually garnished with onions, tomatoes, and cilantro, and served with *frijoles charros* or *frijoles de olla* and salsa. *Cabrito* in stew or braised can be eaten in tacos; cooked this way, the meat is tender and the flavor more concentrated. These tacos are usually topped with pico de gallo or a red salsa.

Another traditional way of eating the *cabrito* is by shredding the cooked meat and stuffing fried tacos, or *flautas*, with it. The *flautas* then are placed on a plate and topped with lettuce, sour cream, and fresh cheese.

There are other traditional ways of cooking *cabrito*, particularly in Mexico, Spain, and some South American countries. One recipe calls for sautéing some onions and garlic in olive oil and then sealing the *cabrito* cut into big pieces. Once all the pieces are browned, some saffron, pepper, salt, a bay leaf, and white wine are added, and left to simmer for a little while. After the meat is half done it is moved to a hot oven to finish cooking, basting it with the sauce from time to time and adding hot water as needed. In Mexico, in particular, the *cabrito* can also be marinated by soaking it in a mixture of anchos chili peppers, tomatoes, vinegar, onions, garlic, and olive oil before putting it in the oven. This dish is sometimes called *cabrito enchilado*.

A *cabrito* dish popular in Mexico is the traditional *cabrito en su sangre* (literally kid in its own blood). Like the previous stews, it begins with the pieces of *cabrito* sautéed with onions. Once they are browned, they are moved to a pot with pureed tomatoes, and when it starts to boil, the heat is lowered and the ingredients are left to simmer for a while. Then garlic is added as well as cumin, coriander, oregano, and pureed ancho chili peppers. Add some water and simmer until it is almost done, add the blood blended to make it smooth and, if desired, finely chopped vegetables, and cook until done.

Also traditional in many places is the *cabrito* in tomato sauce, in which the *cabrito* is fried in oil and then simmered in a sauce of onions, garlic, and tomatoes. In Peru and Ecuador, *cabrito* is prepared in a sauce with chili peppers, garlic, cilantro, and beans; usually it is accompanied with yucca. In Venezuela, in addition to the *cabrito* and beans, the *cabrito* can be cooked in a sauce of onions, garlic, tomatoes, and fresh coconut milk. This dish is called *cabrito al talkari*, a dish made for big, popular celebrations that is believed to have originated in Trinidad and Tobago.

RAFAEL HERNÁNDEZ

See also: Barbacoa

Further Reading

Baez Kijac, Maria. *The South American Table: The Flavor and Soul of Authentic Home Cooking from Patagonia to Rio de Janeiro, with 450 Recipes.* Boston: The Harvard Common Press, 2003.

Quintana, Patricia, and Ignacio Urquiza. *The Taste of Mexico.* New York: Stewart, Tabori & Chang, 1986.

CADAVAL, OLIVIA (1943–)

Olivia Cadaval is a well-known researcher of the Latin American migrants' cultural manifestations in Washington, D.C.; she was born in Mexico City, but lives now in Washington. Since 1988, she has been chair of cultural research and education and also a folklife specialist at the Center for Folklife and Cultural Heritage of the Smithsonian Institution. Cadaval has also worked as a co-curator in the following programs: the "Colombia Folklife Festival" (displayed in 2011); the "Mexico Folklife Festival" (displayed in 2010); "Nuestra Música: Music in Latino Culture" (between 2004 and 2009); "Música del Pueblo: Latino Music Virtual Exhibition" (since 2007); "Las Américas: Un mundo musical—The Americas: A Musical World" (displayed in 2009). As a project director, she has been engaged in the "Latino Cultural Resources Network" since 1996. From 1991 to the present, she has been a board member of "Sol & Soul. Arts for Social Change."

With one exception, Cadaval's education is strongly linked to two emblematic institutions based in Washington, D.C.: the George Washington University and the Smithsonian Institution. Her professional development began in 1972 when she earned a B.A. in Philosophy at the George Washington University. Between 1981 and 1982, she was a fellow at the Smithsonian Institution. The next year, in 1983, she left her position as a teaching assistant at the George Washington University and attended the International Summer Institute for Semiotics & Structural Studies in Bloomington, Indiana. Immediately after, she did field research for the Italian American History Project. Three years later in 1987 (and until 1988) she came back to the Smithsonian Institution, as a pre-doctoral Fellow of the Office of Folklife Programs (now called Center for Folklife and Cultural Heritage). One year after, in 1989, she received her Ph.D. in American Studies/Folklife at the same university where she had obtained her B.A.

Her dissertation was entitled "The Hispanic American Festival and the Latino Community: Creating an Identity in the Nation's Capital." This thesis of 363 pages, directed by John Michael Vlach, focuses on the new cultural groupings created by the continuous flow of new immigrants coming because of the sociopolitical and economic crisis in the Third World countries and the persisting illusion of an economic paradise in the United States. Using perspectives from cultural history, ethnic studies, cultural anthropology and ethnography of experience, Cadaval's thesis analyzed the cultural dynamics of a very recently emergent multiethnic community in Washington, D.C., as manifested by an annual community ritual: the "Hispano-American Festival" or "Latino Festival." The climax of the festival is the parade, which according to Olivia Cadaval represents the most ceremonial symbolic act of identity in the event. Through three parade case studies she highlights the tensions between the major themes in the negotiation of identity.

Cadaval shows how the Latino community of the nation's capital records its growing multiethnic composition, enacts its emergent group dynamics, stakes its claim in the city and the U.S. federal government, and last but not least culturally marks and defines its living space. Cadaval examines the Latino Festival also in the context of other festivals and Ibero American traditions. She explores the relationships between the ritual and ethnicity (as characterized in the 1960s and 1970s), contemporary Latin American immigration, neighborhood decline and urban renewal, and emerging "Third World ideology." It is interesting to notice the importance of kiosk food sales found in this study. Along with the parade it is considered a dominant cultural expression within the festival. The organization of kiosks marks and qualifies the use of space, reinforcing relationships within the community and with the national society.

Almost simultaneous with her dissertation, Cadaval published a book whose revised edition is expected soon: *Adams Morgan: The Core of the Latino Community* (1988). Strongly linked with her thesis, this book is an ethnographic study of the Latino community in Washington, D.C. Also centering on its annual ritual, the book looks at the social and cultural contexts of the beginning and the history of the community and its festival, its participants and the kiosks.

Cadaval has researched on these topics from the late 1970s until the present. A brief recounting of her main publications can give a good idea of their relevance in her academic work: "The Art of Festival" (1977); "Festivals and the Politics of Culture" (1979); "Apuntes sobre el festival Latino" (1986); "Latinos in Washington D.C." (1990); "Tirarlo a la Calle/Taking to the Streets: The Latino Festival and the Making of Community" (1993); "The Latino Community: Creating an Identity in the Nation's Capital" (1996); "Creating a Latino Identity in the Nation's Capital: The Latino Festival" (1998); "Our Voices in the Nation's Capital: Creating the Latino Community Heritage Center of Washington, D.C." (2002) and "Many Americas in the Shadow of the Capitol: Latinos in Washington, D.C." (2006). Articles like these published in journals and newspapers illustrate the importance of Latin American migrants' cultural expressions, particularly those that transcend national borders. This has also been the usual topic of her participation in the panels of the American Folklore Society between 1981 and 2006 (like "Spectacle and Enactment: Political Expression in an Ethnic Parade" in 1984; "Tradition Invented: The Construction of Reality in Performance" in 1985; "D.C. Latinos: A Journey from Invisibility to Civil Society" in 1995; "Borders and Identity: A Workshop" in 1996; and "Mestizaje, Cultural Hybridity, and Cross Cultural Mimesis" in 2001).

There are other two works of Cadaval on which it would be interesting to focus: "Culture and Environment in the Río Grande/Río Bravo Basin: a Preview" (1998) and "El Río: Culture and Environment in the Río Grande/Río Bravo Basin" (2000). In both of them, she examines identity politics and transnational projects, highlighting relationships among traditional knowledge, cultural identity, and sustainable development. There is also media and educational material associated with this topic co-directed by Cadaval: "El Río: Do-Your-Own-Exhibition Kit" and "Borders and Identity Educational Kit."

These are part of an exhibition that opened at the Smithsonian Institution's Center for Folklife and Cultural Heritage in Washington, D.C., in 2003. Since then, the exhibition traveled to different places (the University of Texas–Pan American in Texas; the "Museo del Desierto" in Coahuila, Semilla; the "Museo-Centro de Ciencia y Tecnologia" in Chihuahua City; the Centennial Museum at the University of Texas–El Paso; and the Maxwell Museum at the University of New Mexico). This exhibition offered a panoramic view of the river that anchors the Rio Grande/Rio Bravo Basin on the border of the United States and Mexico (around two thousand miles across varied terrain extending from the mountains of Colorado through the rugged landscapes of New Mexico and Texas into northern Mexico). It focuses on the complex social relations that link the people of the basin with (i) both the United States and Mexico, (ii) with the environment and culture, and (iii) with modern technologies and traditional practices.

These are some of the questions explored by Cadaval here: How are cultural identity, traditional knowledge, and sustainable development related in a particular space at a particular time? How are identities created and maintained? How does place affect culture? What is the relationship of the communities of the United States and Mexico to the Río Grande/Río Bravo basin? And finally, How do the natives perceive themselves as carriers of traditional knowledge about the environment?

Questions like these have widely influenced the studies in other regions until the present (which is the case of the Andes). Concerning other regions, there is a particular work of Cadaval that stands out because of its comparative effort. In 1994, she published *Festival of American Folklife,* edited by Carla Borden and P. Seitel. Here Cadaval studies cases from Brazil, Chile, Guatemala, Ecuador, Mexico and Bolivia. The perspectives of Cadaval have been even more broadening with the case of the U.S. Virgin Islands' folklore (studied between 1990 and 1993).

As important in Cadaval's career as her written work is her role as project director. Among some of the projects directed by her are the Conference in the National Center for Urban Ethnic Affairs (in 1978 and 1979); the Exhibit Ethnic Ensemble Senior Project "Animo: Poetry in Motion" (1981 and 1982); the Institute for Contemporary Culture (between 1981 and 1984); and the "Talleres de la Frontera: A Workshop and Performance Series on Border Culture" (between 1995 and 1997). Between 1982 and 1991, she was the coordinator and fieldwork researcher at the following institutions: the Renwick Gallery, the George Washington Folklife Association, the Inter American Foundation for the Cultural Programs Evaluation Seminar at the Gatazo Hospital of Ecuador, the American Folklife Center of the Library of Congress, the Office of Folklife Programs of the Smithsonian Institution, and the Michigan Traditional Arts Program of the Michigan State University Museum.

Cadaval has been a curator of the following exhibitions of the Smithsonian Folklife Festival Program: "Cultural Encounters in the Caribbean" in 1989; "U.S. Virgin Islands" in 1990; "Knowledge and Power: Land in Native American Cultures" in 1991; "Mexico–United States Borderlands" in 1993; and "Culture and Development in Latin America and the Caribbean" in 1994. Along with her role in exhibitions, she has also been active in teaching. She has been visiting lecturer in the Spanish Department of George Mason University in 1984; the Community Arts Administration Seminar of the Sangamon Institute, between 1981 and 1984; George Washington University between 1986 and 1993; the University of Maryland in 1988; the Frostburg State University in 1990; and the Network of Educators on Central America in 1991.

JUAN JAVIER RIVERA ANDÍA

See also: Religious Folk Art

Further Reading

Cadaval, Olivia. *Creating a Latino Identity in the Nation's Capital: The Latino Festival.* New York: Garland Press, 1998.

Cadaval, Olivia. "The Latino Community: Creating an Identity in the Nation's Capital." In F. Cary and J. Jordan, eds. *Urban Odyssey*, 231–249. Washington, D.C.: Smithsonian Institution Press, 1996.

CAÍDA DE MOLLERA (BABY'S FALLEN FONTANEL)

In Spanish, the folk ailment resulting from a sunken or fallen anterior or frontal fontanel (fontanelle) on the top front of a baby's head is known as a *caída de mollera* or *mollera caída*. *Caída de mollera* is the more commonly cited description although both are correct.

Modern medicine began to encounter Mexican folk illnesses in the early twentieth century. Before the Mexican Revolution of 1910 Mexican immigration was for the most part limited to the U.S.–Mexico border area and the Southwestern United States; hence little was known about Mexican folk illnesses.

Mexican immigration to the United States increased during the revolution and there was a rapid rise in immigration associated with the industrialization of the United States from 1910 through the decade of the 1920s. Mexican workers along with their folk beliefs regarding health and illness were drawn into the American Southwest and Midwestern cities of the country.

The Mexican Bracero Program, that is the agreement between Mexico and the United States drawn when the United States entered World War II and designed for Mexican workers to emigrate to the United States to help in the war effort (1942–1964), drew a new and extended wave of Mexican immigration into the United States. Therefore, during the period 1910 to the present day we have steadily learned about and studied the etiology and proper treatment of Mexican/Latino folk illnesses.

There are generally five or six illnesses and conditions that are considered the most commonly presented to doctors and clinics and *caída de mollera* is one of those folk illnesses. It is considered very serious because if untreated the condition usually results in death. Therefore, any discussion of Mexican folk illness must include *caída de mollera*.

At birth the soft bones of the baby's skull are not articulated allowing the skull to pass through the birth canal. The soft and unarticulated bones of the head also allow for rapid brain growth. By two years of age the anterior fontanel of most children has closed. This means that the bones of the front part of the skull have fused closing the fontanel.

The folk illness known as *caída de mollera* commonly afflicts infants during the first year of life. The most common folk explanation for the condition is improper treatment of the infant including the infant being dropped or roughed up and/or the infant being quickly removed from the mother's breast during feeding, in other words, overall maternal neglect. Today we know that is not true. *Caída de mollera* is a common condition which has always been treated by experienced female relatives and/or local folk healers known as *curanderas* and is directly related to dehydration of the infant, which may bear no relation to maternal neglect.

Historically physicians and other allied health personnel have been insensitive to the understanding of folk illnesses when presented in clinic. Medicine's failure to take into consideration culturally defined illnesses and conditions may be combined with the hesitancy of Mexican mothers to describe the condition to doctors. This double failure has resulted in the improper diagnosis and failure to treat *caída de mollera* resulting in the loss of many lives.

The most common folk remedies for the condition are equally ineffective and rarely result in a raised fontanel except by accident. Common remedies include attempts to raise the fallen fontanel by sucking on it or drying liquids or eggs on the child's head in an attempt to raise the fontanel. Another common remedy is to gently press the palate at the roof of the mouth, thinking that the resulting pressure will raise the fontanel. A final, and sometimes effective folk remedy requires that the baby be held upside down and held by the ankles while gently tapping the bottoms of the feet. The resulting pressure on the baby's head sometimes returns the fontanel to its correct position if only temporarily. These folk remedies may work with varying degrees of success depending on the severity of the sunken fontanel and luck. Enlisting a *curandera* to "properly" perform the remedy adds a supernatural aspect to the cure and enlists the support of saints and ultimately God.

Medical anthropology has shown, and it is known conclusively, that the fallen fontanel or *caída de mollera* is due to severe dehydration of the baby due to multiple conditions including diarrhea, loss of appetite and failure to nurse or drink. Excessive diarrhea and or vomiting is often due to the mixing of contaminated water with infant formula resulting in intestinal dysentery and similar bacterial diseases. If an infant is experiencing a bacterial or viral disease causing diarrhea and vomiting, it is just a matter of time before the frontal fontanel will sink. If the dehydration is not treated, the infant will most likely die from severe dehydration and heart failure.

ANTONIO NOÉ ZAVALETA

See also: Folk Medicine

Further Reading

"Common Latino/Hispanic Folk Illnesses." http://itdc.lbcc.edu/chispa/DYKT/chispa_folkill.htm.

Guarnaschelli, John, John Lee, and Frederick W. Pitts. "Fallen Fontanelle (Caída de Mollera)." *JAMA (Journal of the American Medical Association.* http://jama.ama-assn.org/content/222/12/1545.abstract.

Trotter, Robert T. "Caida de Mollera: A Newborn and Early Infancy Health Risk." *Migrant Health Newsline: Clinical Supplement* 4, no. 5 (1987). National Migrant Referral Project, Inc. Austin, Texas.

CALAVERAS (SKULLS)

Found in traditional Mexican folk religions that originate with the Olmecs, Toltecs, Aztecs, and Mayans, the celebration of the dead that includes the use of skulls and skeletons to represent both the living and the dead has found its way into the homes and hearts of Americans in the Southwest or wherever Mexican immigrants and Mexican Americans live. The festival began as a celebration of death dedicated to a female deity known as the "Lady of the Dead" and was celebrated from the beginning of August when the corn crop was gathered lasting the entire month. With the coming of the Spaniards, survival of such folk traditions required they be combined with established Catholic practices. The date was moved to the first of November to coincide with All Saints' Day, called "Day of the Innocents" or "Day of the Little Angels" because on this day the souls of dead children are believed to return to be with their loved ones. The celebration was carried over to November 2nd, All Souls' Day, called "Day of the Dead" because adult souls are said to return. Eventually, the female deity was replaced with the modern day "Catrina."

Calaveras, or *calacas*, considered symbols of resurrection, are incorporated into the modern celebration in three important ways: (i) as hard-sugar skulls given as gifts with the name of the living recipient or the dead individual being honored inscribed on the forehead, (ii) as complete stylized skeletons dressed or partially dressed to represent well-known figures, professions, or stereotypical characters, and (iii) as short rhymes about a person that speaks of the person as dead even if one is not. These rhymes are known for their irony and sharp satiric humor.

The hard-sugar skulls are made in varying sizes from those that can fit into the palm of your hand to life-sized skulls. They are usually the color of bleached bones, hollow and decorated with piped sugar flowers, swirls, and flourishes in many different colors. The forehead is left undecorated and the purchaser may choose to have a name monogrammed with colored sugar piping. These are gifts given only to special friends and loved ones. The skulls, considered symbols of the continuity between life and death, also form an important part of the altars or

Calaveras (sugar skulls) in a store window in Mexico City, part of its Days of the Dead celebrations beginning annually on October 31. (AFP/Getty Images)

ofrendas set up in homes and on graves in cemeteries to welcome the souls of the dead upon their return.

The creation of stylized skeletons took hold in the eighteenth century when José Guadalupe Posada, a graphic artist, decided to use skeletons in drawings to depict famous persons and scenes. He is known to have depicted Emiliano Zapata as a skeleton with his famous handlebar moustaches, a large charro hat and crossed bandoliers, a rifle in one hand and a drawn sword in the other. Posada is the artist who popularized the skeletal *Catrina*, the upper-class female "dandy" dressed in the rich finery of the day with a large hat covered in flowers and feathers. Posada also produced his art forms with the *calaveras* that were the satiric rhymes accompanying them. From these drawings, the practice of dressing up as "Catrinas," "His Majesty Death," or well-known people in skeletal costumes has become popular in Mexico. Such costumes may also be seen in U.S. celebrations, while the production of skeletal *Catrinas* (female dandies) and *Catrinos* (male dandies) as well as other *calavera* and *calaca* figurines has been popularized. These figurines are most often fashioned from *papier mâché*, but they can be made from other materials as well. Such figurines can be found in most Mexican markets and craft shops throughout the Southwest of the United States.

The creation of short poems also called *calaveras* became popular in the late eighteenth or early nineteenth centuries. These epitaphs filled with sarcasm mockingly describe the habits and interests of those to whom they are dedicated often offering comic anecdotes. This practice began as a series of tombstone epitaphs published in a tongue-in-cheek article narrating a dream about a futuristic grave-yard. The practice was soon adopted appearing every November and the graphic images of artists like Posada were added. Below is an example of one such *calavera* (translation my own) written by a famous chronicler, Chantecler, who wrote during and after the Mexican Revolution. The Pablo Carreras to whom it was dedicated was actually Pablo González who was nicknamed "Pablo Carreras." *Carreras* means "races" and he was known to run as fast as he could when a battle broke out to report the event to Venustiano Carranza who at that time was Emiliano Zapata's rival for control of the Mexican government. Zapata saw Carranza as a dictator and Pablo "Carreras" as his lacky.

> PABLO CARRERAS
> Se le apodaba "Carreras",
> porque en cuanto presentía
> el menor peligro, huía
> dejando las chaparreras.
> Se quiso presidenciar,
> causando coraje y risa,
> mas le dieron tal paliza
> que al osario vino a dar.
>
> His nickname was "Races"
> 'cause as soon as he felt
> the slightest danger, he ran
> leaving behind his chaps.
> A leader he wanted to be,
> causing anger and laughter,
> but he took such a drubbing
> that in the ossuary he landed.

Similar rhymes appear in Spanish-language newspapers throughout the United States every November.

Anywhere that communities of Mexicans and Mexican Americans can be found, elements of the Day of the Dead celebrations have taken hold. Just as occurred when the Spaniards arrived in Mexico, these celebrations have taken hybridized forms combining elements of both cultures. In all these festivities from Hollywood to Missoula, Montana, to Texas and Boston the *calavera* plays a central role in the altars and processions organized to honor the dead.

Norma A. Mouton

See also: Día de los Muertos; Día de los Muertos: Migration and Transformation to the U.S.; La Santísima Muerte

Further Reading

Chantecler. "Tiros al Blanco: Calaveras Trasnochadas." *El Heraldo de México* [Los Angeles, CA], 4 Nov. 1919: 5.

Hollywood Forever. "Día de los Muertos." LA Day of the Dead. Hollywood Forever Cemetery, 2010. http://www.ladayofthedead.com.

Walkup, Nancy. "Teaching Sensitive Cultural Traditions." *School Arts* (November 2001): 23+.

CALIFAS (CALIFORNIA)

Califas is a Chicano in-group term for California. The word has been in continuous use since the 1940s, although it's likely the term was known before this time. The etymology of California is uncertain. It has been attributed to an Indian tribe of Baja California known as Kalifornos, meaning "high hills." Most likely the term is derived from the Arab word for Caliph (supreme ruler), or calophant (sovernignty), or *khalijah* (successor). In general, the term is associated with Pachucos of the 1940s.

Califas, like most of the terminology used by pachucos, has been referred to as jargon while others refer to their speech as criminal argot. The reliance on the words "argot" and "jargon" has helped focus the image of Pachucos as gang members, criminals, or a person active in any type of underground activity. Argot is a vocabulary peculiar to a group or class of people. This meaning has been tied to criminal groups by linguists, anthropologists, and in dictionaries. Argot also conveys a private source of communication or identification. Jargon simply means a vocabulary associated with a trade, profession, or group, but also something unintelligible, uncommon, or vague in meaning. The word Califas as jargon or argot is associated with a sub-dialect known as caló and was used by second-generation Mexican Americans who did not identify with their parents' Mexican traditions but at the same time did not fit into Anglo society for social or racial factors.

Caló as pachuco speech was varied and fluid. One tendency was to shorten words and improvise with rhyme or sound. Thus Arizona becomes *Arisa* and California becomes *Califas*. Califa was also a barrio on the east side of Los Angeles in the 1940s. When in the 1940s El Paso pachucos settled in Los Angeles, they often formed gangs and went to "war" with local gangs called "Califas," in reference to local gangs. While it is still in use today, fourth and fifth generation Mexican Americans are slowly moving away from using this term. Califas, like caló, has long been used in Chicano literature, film and music. But the folkloric sense of the term did not begin with pachucos.

The name California may have first come into literary use as a result of an eleventh-century epic poem: "The Song of Roland." The poem itself is a narrative surrounding the defeat on August 15th, 778, of King Charlemagne's army, commandeered by his nephew, Roland, who at the time was in retreat from the Saracens, a Muslim group who were taking control of the Iberian Peninsula. The battle itself is known as the Battle of Roncevauk Pass in the Pyrenees Mountains. In verse number CCIX (209), line 2924, the word *Califerne* is one of the mentioned lands, with no geographic location though named after a reference to Africa (*Affrike*). Could the poet have derived *Califerne* from *caliph*?

The first clear example of the word Califas was when author García Ordóñez de Montalvo used the word Califas to refer to an island of the Amazons in the novel *La Sergas de Esplandian* (the Adventures of Esplandian) in 1510. The novel describes the island of California as being "on the right hand of the Indies . . . very near the Earthly Paradise." The island was ruled by Queen Califa. It is possible Montalvo may have also been influenced by the names such as *Californo* and *Californinci* in Sicily or *Calahorra* in Spain. A work of the imagination, the story became reality as the ideas expressed in the novel were taken literally by the Spanish as evidenced by their explorations of the northwest regions. After the conquest of the Mexica Empire in 1521, the Spanish looked north for new lands to conquer. In so doing, they projected their own myths onto the regions that came to be known as the American Southwest. Tying together these mythic possibilities was the view of Eden, a paradise that became the goal of Spanish exploration and subsequent colonization of southwestern lands.

In his fourth letter (*Carta de Relación*), Hernán Cortés (October 15th, 1524) writes of an island of women without men abundant in pearls and gold. Not surprisingly, he left for this area shortly after and claimed land that he called (Baja) California. The information came to Cortés from a captain who had heard of this island. Ironically, Columbus also wrote of the island in his diary following his first voyage. The word was later used by Diego de Becerra and Fortun Ximénez who landed in what is Baja California in 1533, thinking they had landed on the island of California from Montalvo's novel. From here on, explorers referred to the region as California.

With respect to the Mexican American community, however, the term Califas is associated with an urban code developed by synthesizing varieties of language spoken by Mexican Americans in the southwest. These include standard Spanish, popular Spanish, loanwords from English and code-switching (Spanglish). Though viewed by some as an urban phenomenon, a type of slang, caló was actually spoken by urban gypsies in Spain as far back as the sixteenth century, eventually making its way to New Spain and then to the American Southwest. This makes the use of the word *Califas* a fascinating possibility. Was the word an invention of young Pachucos during the first half of the twentieth century, or did the word find its way from sixteenth-century Spain to the New World where it remains today in use among members of the Mexican American community? The possibility questions the urban code of Pachucos: Was it criminal argot, a linguistic invention forced by two languages, or a historical code that merged with contemporary language use?

CARLOS F. ORTEGA

See also: Caló (Folk Speech); Pachucos; Pachuquismo: 1940s Urban Youth

Further Reading

Barker, George Carpenter. *Pachuco: An American-Spanish Argot and Its Social Functions in Tucson, Arizona.* Tucson: University of Arizona Press, 1950.

Castro, Rafaela. *Chicano Folklore.* New York: Oxford University Press, 2001.

Chávez, John. *The Lost Land.* Albuquerque: University of New Mexico Press, 1985.

Hiller, Peter. "Califa: The Story Behind the Legend." *California Tour and Travel Magazine* (2001): 59, 63.

Scott, C. K., trans. *The Song of Roland.* Ann Arbor: University of Michigan Press, 1959.

CALÓ (FOLK SPEECH)

Caló is a type of modified Spanish with specialized vocabulary that is used alongside traditional Spanish grammar to produce a hybrid speech register that was popularized among Mexican American urban youth, or *pachucos,* in the southwestern United States in the 1930s and 1940s. As a language with no singular origin and which draws on both Spanish and English, it has come to be emblematic of the bicultural status of Mexican descent communities in the United States.

Academic investigations of *Caló* situate it as a class- and gender-based argot, which was first the language of the Spanish-speaking underworld in Spain as well as bullfighters, and today is a living form of Spanish prevalent in contemporary Chicano communities all over the United States. Susan Berk-Seligson highlights how *Caló* functions to communicate more than direct information; rather, its usage serves to index an intimate relationship of an individual speaker to the politically charged and socioeconomically stratified Chicano working-class culture and history. However, there are numerous studies that conflate the term *Caló* with any number of terms that reference nuanced forms of vernacular Spanish in the United States including the following: *Pachuco, Chicano Spanish, Spanglish, Pochismos, Hispanicized English, Anglicized Spanish, Tirili,* and generalized *jergas.* Despite the variety of external labels imposed upon it, this argot and its many variants serve as a private, intracultural form of communication that situates itself within the liminal space between Spanish and English, thus situating its speakers on a similar border between Mexican and American, insider and outsider, marginal and mainstream.

As a language of the pachuco, *Caló* is often associated with delinquent social behavior, gang culture, and poverty. Few, however, focus on the truly creative nature of the *Caló* speaker, who actively mobilizes his personal agency through the continual assimilation of new, innovative terminology to add to the ever-changing vocabulary of *Caló.* Ortega notes that *Caló* originates from the speech of gypsies who arrived in Spain from North Africa in the latter half of the fifteenth century. They called their dialect Zincaló, which eventually was shortened to Caló (Ortega, 1977, 3). It emerged in the Golden Age of the Spanish Empire, and became a salient feature in its cultural and political discourses of social control. In the early 1970s, *Caló* was thought to be merely a set of vocabulary words to be assimilated into the mainstream vocabulary of standard Spanish. However, this transition never occurred, and *Caló* remains today the independent jargon of contemporary Chicanos. Some scholars attempt to frame *Caló* as an impoverished speech genre for impoverished lives that reflects a fractured Mexican American worldview. However, it is also a complementary part of the varied language identity of Latin America like *Lunfardo* in Argentina, Peru, Uruguay, and Paraguay; or *Coa* of Chile; and *Hampa and Jiria* of Mexico.

Caló originally found a new cultural and geographic space to occupy among pachucos in the Southwest, especially El Paso, Texas and was viewed in direct contrast to Peninsular Spanish from Spain and the posh Spanish of Mexico City. Because it appears to distance its speakers from fluency in both standard Spanish and standard English, pachuco speak or *Caló* was considered highly detrimental to the productive educational development of Mexican American youth. At the same time, George Barker notes that *Caló* was also an attempt to meet the challenges of biculturalism that speakers formed as a way of circumventing linguistic and cultural rigidity in both Mexican and American culture beginning in the 1930s. *Caló* and its variants are a part of the language heritage of Spanish speakers in the American Southwest, and figure prominently in the burgeoning Chicano Studies discourses of the 1960s as emblematic of a unique Chicano or Mexican American worldview. While most studies of *Caló* focus on male speakers, recent studies acknowledge the linguistic repertoires of Chicanas. Letticia D. Galindo shows how female Chicana prisoners adopt *Caló* as a sign of camaraderie, and to convey the intimacy and commonality of their social experiences (Galindo 1993, 34). *Caló* as a hybrid cultural product and linguistic esthetic is valorized by Chicanos as a marker of cultural nationalism that is rooted in embracing barrio culture, recognizing the strength and virtues of language within a quest for self-determined cultural roles. Curtis Márez notes that this marker of an active "brown style" helps refigure the image of the Chicano, not as culturally fractured, but as an ingenious cultural *bricoleur* who carves out his own cultural destiny. In its remarkable versatility and inevitable instability *Caló* is not constitutive of Chicano or pachuco culture, but rather provides insight into an active process of ongoing cultural self-determination among Mexican descent communities in the United States.

RACHEL VALENTINA GONZÁLEZ

See also: Califas (California); Chicano Spanish; Pachucos; Pachuquismo: 1940s Urban Youth

Further Reading

Barker, George Carpenter. *Pachuco: An American-Spanish Argot and Its Social Functions in Tucson, Arizona.* Tucson: University of Arizona Press, 1950.

Fuentes, Daboberto, and Armando López. *Barrio Language Dictionary: First Dictionary of Caló.* Los Angeles: Southland Press, 1974.

Galindo, Letticia D. "The Language of Gangs, Drugs and Prison Life among Chicanas." *Latino Studies Journal* (September 1993): 23–43.

Márez, Curtis. "Brown: The Politics of Working-Class Chicano Style." *Social Text*, No.48 (1996): 109–132.

Ortega, Adolfo. *Caló Tapestry.* Berkeley, CA: Editorial Justa Publication, Inc., 1977.

Polkinhorn, Harry, Alfredo Velasco, and Malcom Lambert. *El Libro De Caló: The Dictionary of Chicano Slang.* Mountain View, CA: Floricanto Press, 1988.

CAMPA, ARTHUR LEÓN (1905–1978)

Arthur León Campa was an author, anthropologist, and folklorist whose scholarly work on Hispanic culture and folklore in the Southwestern region of the United States has become a widely respected resource in the Mexican American studies field. Campa wrote numerous academic books during his career, ranging from anthropologic histories of the Spanish language in the Southwest to accounts of

Hispanic folk theatre. Campa's work focused on the influences of Hispanic culture within the United States, and on the role that Hispanic folklore played within the Southwestern states. His major contribution with respect to New Mexican folklore was his theoretical position that New Mexican folklore derived its major influence from Mexican folklore and not from the folklore of Spain as Aurelio Macedonio Espinosa had previously posited. Aurelio Macedonio Espinosa had previously written in his scholarly publications that the folklore of New Mexico came directly from Spain. Campa took the position that and detailed in his work how New Mexican folklore came from Mexican sources and not directly from Spain.

Biography

Campa was born on February 20th, 1905, to Daniel Campa and Delfia López de la O. in Guaymas, Sonora, Mexico. Daniel Campa was a lieutenant in the Federal Army who was killed by Pancho Villa's revolutionaries in 1914. After her husband's death, Delfia moved her family (consisting of Campa and his four siblings) to a ranch outside of El Paso, Texas. Later, the family relocated to Albuquerque, New Mexico, where Delfia became a local business owner.

Campa received his bachelor's and master's degrees from the University of New Mexico in 1928 and 1930, respectively. In 1940, he earned a doctorate from Columbia University in New York. Campa taught at the University of New Mexico from 1932 to 1942 and again from 1945 to 1946. His first published work was *A Bibliography of Spanish Folk-lore in New Mexico* (1930). Later academic publications included *Spanish Religious Folktheatre in the Southwest* (1934), *Sayings and Riddles in New Mexico* (1937), *Los Comanches: A New Mexico Folk Drama* (1942), *Spanish Folk-Poetry in New Mexico* (1946), and *Hispanic Culture in the Southwest* (1979). From 1946 to his retirement in 1974, Campa was the head of the Department of Modern Languages and Literature at the University of Denver.

Campa married Lucille Cushing, a well-known dancer, in 1943. The couple had four children. Campa died on May 13th, 1978, of a heart attack; at the time of his death, he was in the process of publishing his final book, *Hispanic Culture in the Southwest*, which was published a year after his passing.

Hispanic Culture in the Southwest

Considered by many in the academic world to be his most important contribution to academia, Campa's *Hispanic Culture in the Southwest* describes the history of the Hispanic population in the southwestern region and discusses issues of nomenclature, history, and influence from American and Spanish culture. The text has been cited by numerous scholars discussing Southwestern history.

Although *Hispanic Culture in the Southwest* has been highly praised, Campa's work on folk theater is also very important. For New Mexican folk theater, Campa collected and published many folk plays, including the following (* indicates plays that can be found in the Museum of International Folk Art in Santa Fe, New Mexico):

- Old Testament Drama
- *Adán y Eva**
- *Caín y Abel**
- New Testament Drama
- *Los pastores**
- *Los reyes magos**
- La pastorela
- El auto de los pastores
- El nacimiento
- El coloquio de los pastores
- El Niño Dios
- Los pastores chiquitos
- Camino de la pastorela
- *El niño perdido**
- *El coloquio de San José**
- La pasión
- Event or Struggle Dramas
- *Los Comanches**
- *Los Tejanos**
- *Los Moros y Cristianos**
- *Las cuatro apariciones de Nuestra Señora de Guadalupe**
- *Los Matachines** (Montaño 2001, 169).

Campa's interest in folklore spanned the gamut from folk theater and folk tales to folk poetry, particularly the decimal, a ten-line stanza folk song and folk poem. Campa's work is indispensable for understanding and appreciating the rich cultural heritage of New Mexican folklore.

COLTON SAYLOR

Further Reading

Campa, Arthur León. *A Bibliography of Spanish Folk-lore in New Mexico*. Albuquerque: The University of New Mexico, 1930.

Campa, Arthur León. *Hispanic Culture in the Southwest*. Norman: University of Oklahoma Press, 1979.

Campa, Arthur León. *Hispanic Folklore Studies of Arthur L. Campa*. New York: Arno Press, 1976.

Campa, Arthur León. *Los Comanches : A New Mexican Folk Drama*. Albuquerque: University of New Mexico Bulletin 7, 1942.

Campa, Arthur León. "The New Mexican Spanish Folktheater." *Southern Folklore Quarterly* 5 (1941): 127–131.

Campa, Arthur León. "Religious Folk Drama in New Mexico." *New Mexico Quarterly* 2 (1932): 3–13.

Campa, Arthur León. *Sayings and Riddles in New Mexico*. Albuquerque: The University of New Mexico, 1937.

Campa, Arthur Leon. *Spanish Folk-Poetry in New Mexico*. Albuquerque: The University of New Mexico Press, 1946.

Campa, Arthur León. *The Spanish Folksong in the Southwest*. Albuquerque: University of New Mexico Press, 1933.

Campa, Arthur León. *Spanish Religious Folk-theatre in the Southwest*. Albuquerque: University of New Mexico Press, 1934.

Campa, Arthur León. "Spanish Religious Folk Theater in the Southwest (First Cycle)." *University of New Mexico Bulletin*, Language Series 5, no.1 (1934).

Campa, Arthur León. "Spanish Religious Folk Theater in the Southwest (Second Cycle)." *University of New Mexico Bulletin*, Language Series 5, no. 2 (1934).

Campa, Arthur León. "Spanish Traditional Tales in the Southwest." *Western Folklore* 6 (1947): 322–334.

Campa, Arthur León. *Treasure of the Sangre de Cristos: Tales and Traditions of the Spanish Southwest*. Norman: University of Oklahoma Press, 1963.

Castro, Rafaela. *Chicano Folklore: A Guide to the Folktales, Traditions, Rituals and Religious Practices of Mexican Americans*. New York: Oxford University Press, 2001.

Montaño, Mary. *Tradiciones Nuevomexicanas: Hispano Arts and Cultures of New Mexico*. Albuquerque: University of New Mexico Press, 2001.

CANCIÓN RANCHERA

The *ranchera* folk song genre is a particular musical style, which grew into commercial popularity shortly after the Mexican Revolution (1910–1917). Singers traditionally used straightforward lyrics expressing nationalistic, regional pride and sentiment. Musically, *ranchera*s are performed by different ensembles: from mariachi duets, accordion-based groups such as in *conjunto Tejano* or *norteño* (Northern Mexico and Texas-Mexican style), to guitar-based groups, such as *trios* (group of three singers generally playing guitars). The term is used for a song style sung in a *ranchero* style, here referring to sartorial mariachi dress, vocal and performance style, especially if accompanied by a mariachi group. In performance, a polka 2/4 time can be used, but also a slower waltz 3/4 time is appropriate. Thus one will hear of a polka *ranchera* or *bolero ranchero*, a *ranchera* played with polka or *bolero* rhythms.

For example, the *bolero-ranchero* is associated with singer Javier Solis, who in the 1960s interpreted the *bolero* song style, a romantic song-style, by singing open-voiced, as a soloist and with mariachis as backup. *Ranchera*s are also associated with the Mexican state of Jalisco, where the style is thought to have evolved.

A *ranchera* is not a narrative, such as with the *corrido*, but an introspection focusing on love, loneliness, sadness, or mourning. *Ranchera*s tend to be male-centered, and singers such as Pedro Infante, Vicente Fernández, Chavela Vargas, Lola Beltrán, Lucha Villa, Amalia Mendoza, and others have captured the sentiment of what it means to sing *ranchera*s. Performances in this genre tend to be emotional and dramatic, allowing the singer to draw audience empathy.

The *canción ranchera* has also been defined as a "ranch song," a song sung on a ranch or hacienda, or a song style situated among poor unsophisticated persons; but more appropriately, a song conveying nationalistic pride. However, definitions classifying *ranchera*s as "ranch songs" misrepresent the commercial and international popularity of this style. Further, the historical evolution of *ranchera*s is lost in simple definitions. In fact, the development of this style is reflected in musical fusion and urban appropriation of rural styles, of commercialization, while at the same time associated with music of the people. As a folk style it must be remembered that the *canción ranchera* has leaped borders throughout the Americas and its commercial popularity reflects the strength of this style among its legions of followers.

Origins

Its beginnings in Mexico go back one hundred and fifty years and its evolution begins with a genre simply referred to as *canción*. These types of songs had a lyrical and sentimental text and melody. *Canciónes* are also more varied making it difficult to classify them. Some are classified as religious, civic, or secular. The last two concern this article. Civic songs are patriotic or official in nature. The Mexican national anthem, for example, is civic in nature. Secular *canciónes* of the nineteenth century were of two additional types: one was rooted in the mestizo tradition and originated from a rural population. The other consisted of *canciónes* in *bel canto* style—an open, full-voiced quality associated with operatic tenors—and sung in musical salons of the upper and middle classes.

The *canciónes* emanating from the rural tradition were simple in structure, with thematic verses dealing with love. They came to be known as *canción mexicana* or *típica*. These might have been sung in Spanish *tonadillas* (a form of musical comedy) in Mexico City in the early nineteenth century. The other *canción*, of *bel canto* style, was introduced in the 1830s to Mexico City's upper and middle classes and was a popular urban style. The *canción* was likely influenced by Italian opera, popular at the time. This gave rise to *canciónes románticas* in music salons. In time this style was introduced to rural areas through the efforts of local composers and troubadours.

After Mexican independence, nationalistic ideas (civic) mixed with Italian operatic traditions, the 3/4 waltz time and *bel canto*, a vocal style where an open, full-voiced quality was the standard. Singers were trained and had superb command of breathing techniques. The formal elements of opera, then, were assimilated not only from the aristocracy but by the Mexican populace: idiom, versification, orchestra, singers, and style—in short, all the techniques.

The development of the *canción mexicana* was not simply the result of urban popularity. The early part of the nineteenth century was a watershed for Mexico. From 1810 to 1821, Mexico fought its war of independence against Spain; the newly independent republic also endured fifty military regimes through the years 1824–1836. It lost territory as a result of the Texas Revolt (1836) and later, half of its territory resulting from the war with the United States (1846–1848). By 1850, Mexico was poor and destitute. Those who lived in rural areas found themselves needing to escape their conditions. Their target was Mexico City and other urban areas. Along with their possessions, they brought their music where operatic styles of the day fused with the rural folk music of the migrants. By 1850, the *canción mexicana* was popular throughout Mexico.

During the Juárez era of the 1860s, the *canción mexicana* was introduced and performed during theatre interludes. This was also the period of French intervention in Mexico. The political antagonisms felt by the populace led to outcries of nationalistic fervor and cultural expression. In theatres, professional entertainers promoted music of the common people. The *canción mexicana* they performed took on a nationalistic focus. As the trend grew in popularity, the *canción mexicana* came to be regarded by urban folk as "authentic country-style" music. In time, the traditional rural lyrics were being discarded and new ones (by urban composers) were adapted to the melodies. In fact, the *ranchera's* popularity led to commercially successful imitations such as "El Chinaco" (the beggar) composed in the 1860s, and performed in the theater by actors dressed as charros (in what was then called the chinaco style although this sartorial dress was different from the contemporary charro outfit). Chinaco was also the nickname given to Juárez's soldiers. "El Chinaco" has also been classified as a corrido, although its text does not reflect the corrido structure.

During the rule of Porfirio Díaz, the music played at theaters and music salons took on a different focus. Orchestras, opera, and dances, such as the *habanera*, *paso doble*, *mazurkas*, polkas (European), and waltzes were the norm. The Porfiato was characterized as a period where European culture was promoted. Songs of the common people, such as *corridos*, were rejected. It became one of the harsh realities of the time. This is not to say that the *canción mexicana*, the *corrido*, and other genres were not heard.

Among the working Mexican population, these genres were heard in neighborhoods and gatherings. Styles such as *huapangos*, *jarabes*, *corridos*, *canciónes*, *rancheras*, and mariachi music were popular. But in theaters and salons, European-based music was considered more "respectable." Not until the start of the Mexican Revolution does this perspective change. When Díaz left the presidency (1910), residents of Mexico City, especially songwriters, performers, and audience members, again promoted nationalistic ideas through music. This saw the revival of the *canción mexicana*. This next stage of development would see the birth of the *ranchera* as known today.

The Mexican musicologist Sordo Sorti wrote that the "country" songs played on haciendas were popularly called *rancheras* although in Mexico City the word *ranchera* was not used before 1910 as the name of a song style. Interludes at the theater consisted of a couple dancing a *jarabe* or a singer performing songs. These songs would be described in the program as *rancheras*, as opposed to *canción mexicana*, perhaps then to the contemporary *ranchera* as known today. The singer would not necessarily learn the song from a published text but rather from talking to members of the working class. This urban *ranchera* would be accompanied by typical orchestras (*orquestas típica*) with instruments such as the *psaltery*, marimba, and flute. Musicians would be dressed in national costumes. Songs such as "Alborotada" by Lauro de Uranza were examples of *rancheras* performed in Mexico City during the revolution.

However, before 1920 there was no popular music common to all social classes. There were only two types: European-based music popular with the upper and middle classes and another emerging from Indigenous, mestizo, and poor populations. The post-revolutionary period saw an outburst of nationalistic ideology. In practice, all things Mexican were to be promoted and all western ideas and values were to be rejected. This was a key reason why the upper classes promoted *rancheras*. The traditional *ranchera* remained popular until the 1930s when it gave way to a commercial *ranchera*. Although the *ranchera* was still viewed as a "country style" by urban folk, most *ranchera* singers came from Mexico City.

Revolutionary leadership also helped promote the ideology of *lo ranchero*. Whether viewed as an ideology or myth, this concept is considered to be a component of romantic nationalism. This idea was manifested during the Mexican Revolution of 1910 and with the post-revolutionary generation. This form of nationalism exerts a perceived unifying influence when appealing to the nation's unique heritage. Thus *lo ranchero* as a concept and its symbols—*música ranchera*—contribute to the ideology by enabling the existence of hacienda and rural life in general as idyllic. This ideology was further promoted through film and musical recordings, but usually in combination. *Lo ranchero* shapes an ideal quality of Mexicans: manliness, self-sufficiency, candor, simplicity, sincerity, and patriotism (*mexicanismo*). This ideology was also evident on both sides of the border. In Texas, *lo ranchero* has been a prominent ideology in *Tejano* music. By capturing a range of moods, attitudes and values in a musical moment, *lo ranchero* crossed the border and situated itself among Mexican American and Mexican immigrant communities.

Ranchera as Commercial Product

The *ranchera* flourished with the rise of popular media and the popularity of folk-derived ensembles such as the mariachi—a string ensemble not resembling the contemporary mariachi. The establishment of XEW radio in 1930 and the national broadcasting system took the *ranchera* to new heights. The popularity of the songs also led to the making of films—the equivalent of U.S. cowboy films, which ironically were also becoming popular at the time—that also became popular in Mexican American communities. Films such as *Allá en el Rancho Grande* (1936) were so popular that a string of such films were made (*Rayando el Sol* and *Pajarillo*, for example). These films also made stars of singers such as Pedro Vargas, Pedro Infante, Jorge Negrete, Lupe Vélez, and Lucha Reyes—on both sides of the border! Both Negrete and Vargas began their careers in opera and quickly moved to more popular formats because better income was involved! They also portrayed the idealized ranchero, charros, and other stereotypes singing *ranchera* with messages of love, betrayal, and exploits. Pedro Infante and Jorge Negrete in particular made *ranchera* films popular in Latin America and the United States with its ever-growing Mexican and Mexican American population. What is remarkable is that although these artists have long passed, their music and films remain popular. Accessible by Internet, new CD collections of artists past and present, as well as films (VHS and DVD), continue to sell.

Even in 1930s Los Angeles, the mariachi popularized the *ranchera* due to the number of *ranchera* singers living in the city. So when "Canción Mexicana" was composed in 1936 and recorded by Lucha Reyes in 1940 for RCA-Victor, the song was an immediate hit. *Rancheras* thus flourished in the United States during the 1930s and 40s in spite of the trauma created by the repatriation movements against Mexicans and Mexican Americans in the era of the depression and the racial conflicts spurred by the Sleepy Lagoon Murder Case and the Zoot Suit Riots of the 1940s.

In Texas in the first half of the twentieth century, *la canción romántica* and *canción ranchera* became popular. As a result of the historical conditions of the time, the *canción rancheras* were clearly adopted by working-class *Tejanos*. For these individuals the *ranchera* was charged with class and gender implications. Given the social and economic changes awash in Texas and other Southwestern states enduring themes related to wealth and poverty, power and marginalization, shaped the *ranchera*. Moreover, these themes were often reflected within the subject of betrayed love. Thus gender is displayed by the traitorous woman, seldom the man, although Lydia Mendoza, in her classic *border canción* "Mal Hombre" (1934), saw things differently.

Rancheras hit their stride in the early 1950s thanks to the compositions of José Alfredo Jiménez (1926–1973). In the course of his career, he composed some 500 songs, many classics to this day and a requirement for all young *ranchera* singers to know and perform as part of their repertoire. The poetics found in these songs are heard in "Ella," "Camino a Guanajuato," and "La Vida no Vale Nada." While Jiménez never learned to read or write music, nor play an instrument, he was always writing. He would take his verses to Rubén Fuentes, arranger for Mariachi Vargas de Tecalitlán, who would then organize and notate his written fragments. It was no surprise Jiménez came to be known as *el hijo del pueblo* (the people's son). He was especially popular in Los Angeles where he often performed at the Million Dollar Theater, a center of Mexican cultural life.

In this period of commercial popularity and growth the *ranchera* vocal style became established. The songs were sung in a straightforward manner with straightforward lyrics and singers drawing out the final notes to a verse. These drawn-out notes are actually written out on the song charts. In addition, the singer will add a glissando, a gliding over a series of notes that has become typical of *ranchera* style, creating a more passionate delivery reminiscent of the *bel canto* style that was popular in the nineteenth century. *Bel canto* influenced traditional mariachi singing, which is one reason why *ranchera*s fit so perfectly with this ensemble (witness the richness of Vicente Fernández and Lola Beltrán's voices).

Some even came to view this song style as music of the working class. Amalia Mendoza once said the *canción ranchera* expressed the sensibility of people and thus could explain these songs' popularity. *Ranchera*s in her view came to reflect the "personality" of the people, the humanness or commonality of the masses. Accepting this point of view, and many do, is what makes the link between folklore and *canción ranchera*. And while this seems to have some truth to it, musical compositions have shown remarkable popularity among most Mexicans, regardless of social class. Javier Solis's recording of the *bolero-ranchero* "Sombras" in the mid-sixties sold two hundred thousand copies as a single! This does not include album sales.

Whether an ensemble trio, *conjunto*, mariachi, or a soloist, the songs captured not only emotion and sentimentality, but *ranchera*s also captured the memory of family cultural expression as found in gatherings where someone would pull out a guitar and sing the latest *ranchera*.

Crossover

John Storm Roberts made the case for Mexican influences in country, rock, and folk. Increasingly, producers in Nashville utilized a mariachi sound, which revolved around horn instruments and guitar solos. The use of 3/4 time gave many songs a *ranchera* feel. Artists such as Crystal Gayle, Kris Kristofferson, Willie Nelson, Hoyt Axton and others helped shape music in the 1970s with the use of these sounds. Rock artists such as Doug Sahm, Captain Hook, and Maria Muldar utilized these sounds to give a mariachi feel to their music.

What is fascinating about *canción ranchera* is its trajectory from traditional performances to popular musical expressions among Chicano musicians. In *Tejano* repertoire, the works of Little Joe y la Familia, the late Freddy Fender (Baldemar Huerta), and Johnny Rodríguez serve as examples.

In *Tejano* music, *ranchera* has always been a staple of the many musicians who perform this regional music. Little Joe y la Familia have always made these type of songs a key component of the act. But their release of "Para la Gente" (1970) took *canción ranchera* to another level. The first track contains the traditional *ranchera*, "Las Nubes." Utilizing an ensemble dominated by horns, the song explodes into a traditional *Tejano* arrangement, but by including violins during the instrumental middle, Little Joe helped create a bimusicality that had not before been heard.

Freddy Fender's *ranchera* influence was manifested in various ways. In some of his country-inspired recordings his vocals brought elements of *ranchera* sentimentality. Prime examples are "Wasted Days and Wasted Nights" and "Before the Last Teardrop Falls." And while he had no trouble singing traditional *rancheras*, at times he could have fun with them as well. Fender pulls this off with a lighter version of "(I Love) My Rancho Grande," which he did in both English and Spanish. His music always left the impression that *ranchera* and country were made for each other in emotion and the use of 3/4 or 2/4 time.

A little-known CD by Johnny Rodríguez, "Coming Home" (1990), also took *Tejano* music and *rancheras* to new heights. His recording of José Alfredo Jiménez's "Cuando Vivas Conmigo" turns this song into a *Tejano* ballad complete with violins and electric guitar solos. He also uses traditional *Tejano* arrangements to record *rancheras* such as "El Venadito" and "El Senderito" as well.

Even rock and pop singers have emerged with very special recordings indeed. Linda Ronstadt has made a name for herself as a rock singer and a chanteuse by forging into styles such as standards, country, and pop. In 1985, she released *Canciones de Mi Padre*, a collection of Spanish language songs she grew up listening to as a little girl in Tucson, Arizona. Her parents of German and Mexican background regularly played *ranchera* music at home parties. Ronstadt remembers listening to Lola Beltrén and being awed by the power of her voice. While these *ranchera* rhythms were not evident in her early music, the passion that is evident in *ranchera* singing was. One only need listen to her rendition of "Blue Bayou." Not until the

Freddy Fender performs on stage at the Country Music Festival held at Wembley Arena, London, in April 1988. (Getty Images)

release of *Canciones de Mi Padre* was Ronstadt able to capture the impact *ranchera* music had on her vocal style.

Los Lobos, the roots music band from East Los Angeles, has also made *canción ranchera* a staple of their repertoire. On their album of traditional Mexican music, *Just Another Band from East L.A.* (1978), they recorded "El Pescado Nadador," "Feria de las Flores," and the *bolero-ranchero* "Imploración." What is evident in these examples is that in the United States the *ranchera* flourishes with the performances of traditional Mexican singers but also among Chicano singers and ensembles.

In 2009, George Strait released his CD *Twang*. On it was his rendition of "El Rey," the José Alfredo Jiménez–penned classic *ranchera*, in Spanish no less! Arranged in traditional mariachi format, the feel is Nashville's long embrace of mariachi sounds and guitar runs. Now how does a country traditionalist, who also has a large Mexican American following, arrive at making such a recording? It may have been growing up on his father's ranch in Poteet, Texas, where he heard the song. One can imagine him listening to Mexican workers singing the song after the day was done or sitting with them listening to the song on radio. Certainly, in his own press release he mentions he had heard the song for years but never knew what it meant. After reading a translation, he decided to record the song in Spanish because in his own words, "it's a cool song."

While *rancheras* are firmly established in Mexico, music teachers in the American Southwest are teaching mariachi and guitar classes where they introduce to young musicians and vocalists the art of performing *rancheras*. This promises to keep this musical style alive for years to come.

CARLOS F. ORTEGA

See also: Canción Romántica

Further Reading

Broyles-González, Yolanda. *Lydia Mendoza's Life in Music*. New York: Oxford University Press, 2001.

Geijerstam, Claes. *Popular Music in Mexico*. Albuquerque: University of New Mexico Press, 1976.

Mendoza, Vicente T. *La canción mexicana: Ensayo de clasificasión y antología*. Mexico City: Universidad Nacional Autónoma de México, 1969.

Mendoza, Vicente T. "Some Forms of the Mexican Canción." In Mody C. Boatright, ed. *Singers and Storytellers*. Dallas: Southern Methodist University Press, 1961.

Peña, Manuel. *Música Tejana*. College Station: Texas A & M University Press, 1999.

Roberts, John Storm. *The Latin Tinge: The Impact of Latin American Music on the United States*. 2nd ed. New York: Oxford University Press, 1999.

Stevenson, Robert. *Music in Mexico: The Only Complete History of Mexican Music from Aztec to Modern Times*. New York: Apollo Editions/Thomas Y. Crowell, 1952.

CANCIÓN ROMÁNTICA

The *canción romántica* is a specific genre with a thematic structure and focus on romantic and sentimental verses. Musicologists have agreed, though not completely, that this genre is of Italian influence, certainly of European influence. In its most classical forms, the *canción romántica* was formed by verses of eleven-syllable lines and was sung in the *bel canto* style, which was of operatic influence. Its modern usage is also associated with the *bolero*, now the standard genre for romantic and sentimental song.

What is the *canción* as a genre and its types? In general the *canción* can literally refer to any song or in this case, specific types of songs. While *corridos* maintain a narrative structure of text, *canciones* maintain a lyrical and sentimental quality of text and melody. *Canciones* are written in *copla* form, that is, a verse of four lines (sometimes eight) with eight syllables per line, and the second and fourth line rhyming. The origins of the *canción* are uncertain though some reflect the Spanish *canción* romance.

The function of the *canción* falls into three categories: religious, civic, and secular. Examples of the religious *canción* include *alabados* and *alabanzas*. Many of these songs were viewed as popular music until the Reform Movement of the 1850s. Civic songs consisted of patriotic or official songs, such as the national anthem. The *canción romántica* falls under the third category: secular *canciones*. During the nineteenth century, secular songs were based on economic and social divisions within Mexican society. One group was tied to *mestizo* society and had originated in rural areas. The musical influence was largely Spanish. The second group was those *canciones* sung in *bel canto* style.

Classifications of secular group songs include *canciones epitalámicas*, wedding songs with a traditional Spanish flavor; and *versos de aliento entrecortado*, verse forms that begin, and then stop for a pause, and then the full line is sung, as for example in the following example:

> Estando . . . estando amarrado un gallo
> Se me re . . . se me reventó el cordón
> Si será . . . si será mi muerte un rayo
>
> While a rooster was tied
> The cord was ri . . . ripped
> I shall die, I shall die by a thunder bolt

Other sub-genres of the *canción* style were: *canción folklórica*, a rural style of song largely dominated by Spanish influences, and *canción ranchera*. Joining these classifications is *la canción romántica*.

Historical Overview

Sometimes called *la canción romántica mexicana*, its introduction to Mexican society occurred around 1820 or 1830, directly into Mexico's middle class and aristocracy. The people who followed *la canción romántica* were part of the post-Independence generation who had rebelled against Spanish colonialism and through their efforts founded the republic of Mexico. Most of this class was *criollo*, the sons and daughters of Spanish parents born in Mexico. Raised with Spanish traditions their forefathers had initiated the entry of European music into New Spain. Sufficient evidence exists to show that European opera had made its way to the Spanish colonies as early as 1711. Up to the time of independence, opera and other theatrical forms such as *tonadillas* (musical comedies) were regularly performed in Mexico City. Italian opera was introduced to Mexico in 1820. It should not be assumed that there existed a sound tradition of opera and musical theatre. Some musicologists maintain these traditions were weak and in no way exhibited the strong traditions found in Europe. Nevertheless, between 1821 and 1911, curricula and student programs found in musical conservatories were grounded on Italian opera. Mexican independence was to signal a change in musical traditions. A refinement in composition, performance and musicality set the stage for *la canción romántica*, a stage linked to three influences. These are the influences of Italian opera, the *bel canto* style of singing, and Mexican literary romanticism.

Singing of opera in Italian did not begin until after independence. Before this period opera was sung in Spanish. It was not until the Spaniard Manuel García came to Mexico following major success in Europe and New York that singing in Italian began. At age fifty-two, *García* was contracted to sing Rossini's *Il barbieri* and later his own work, a *tonadilla*, *El Abufar*; both in Italian. Although he had his detractors claiming Italian opera should be sung in Spanish, no doubt for nationalistic reasons, his concerts were major successes. So much so that by the 1830s, Italian became the only language in which opera was sung.

Opera's popularity among the middle class and aristocracy saw the development of Mexican composers whose work focused on opera. Luis Baca (1826–1855): *Leonor y Giovanna*; Ceniobio Paniagua (1821–1882): *Catalina de Guisa*; and Melisio Morales (1838–1908): *Ildegonda*. These and the operas of Bellini—*La Sonnambula*; Donizetti—*Lucia di Lammermoor*; Rossini—*Il barbieri* and others had one thing in common that went on to influence *la canción romántica*. It was the standard among all Italian operas: the vocal style known as *bel canto*.

Bel canto is a style of singing that flourished in Italy from the mid-1700s through the early decades of the nineteenth century. Associated with the works of Rossini, Bellini, and Donizetti, Italian opera became popular among enthusiasts in Mexico of the nineteenth century. Originally, *bel canto* referred to a beautiful voice or the singing of a beautiful melody. This was achieved by singing legato—that is, smooth and connected without breaks between the successive tones of a melody. There was no moving up or down vocal ranges and it required excellent breath control. In cases where embellishments were included, their execution was to have been effortless.

As the Romantic period captured the hearts and minds of nineteenth-century Europe, the demand for operatic drama grew. Newly composed works called for more intense and powerful singing. The other aspect of *bel canto* was the operas themselves. More and more operas were composed so as to showcase this vocal tradition. Specific melodies became the heart of arias but also the scenes containing them. Composers would construct full melody and conversational recitation. That the works of Donizetti, Rossini, Bellini, and Verdi became standards of Mexico's opera tradition should be of no surprise. European singers but also the local talent graduating from musical conservatories became masters of the *bel canto* tradition.

The aristocracy enjoyed opera which descended to salon music of the middle class, then descended to the popular or folk strata. At each level, *bel canto* changed by losing its operatic dimension, but the sense of beautiful singing did not. Music salons and their middle-class audience applauded singers of the day who could capture the nuances of *bel canto* as they performed selected arias. Amongst salon audiences, singers and composers later transmitted—through the help of local troubadours who learned *bel canto* by listening to professional opera singers—this vocal style to rural areas. *Bel canto* eventually made its way to the masses throughout Mexico which went on to influence the vocal styles of *la canción*.

The third influence which impacted the development of *la canción romántica* was European Romanticism. A complex artistic, literary, and intellectual movement, Romanticism evolved during the second half of the eighteenth century. Situated in Western Europe at the start, Romanticism spread and strengthened during the Industrial Revolution of the nineteenth century. Viewed as a revolt against social and political values of the aristocracy during the Age of Enlightenment, this movement was most evident in art, music and literature. At the center of this movement were instinct against reason, and emotion against science. It was opposed to realism and to classicism. The assumption to create, write, or fashion whatever moved the artist was at the center of Romanticism.

Romantic music, for example, was not necessarily about romance. Rather it was a musical concept referring to a period of theory, compositional practice, and canon from about 1800 to 1910. Romanticism refers to the development of musical structures within a composition, making pieces more passionate and expressive. Add to that, *bel canto* in Italian opera and one begins to see how the movement and the vocal were merged. Romantic love did make its way into romantic opera. Considering the poets of the day, it was only a matter of time. It was this movement that also gained popularity and strength in Mexico.

After Mexican Independence, international literary trends such as Romanticism, Realism, and Modernism also took hold in the new republic and came to influence Mexican writers such as Ignacio Manuel Altamirano (1834–1893), José López Portillo y Rojas (1850–1923), Amado Nervo (1870–1919), all of whom came to reflect Romanticism through their poetry. But it was perhaps Fernando Calderón (1809–1845) and Ignacio Rodríguez Galván (1816–1842) who came to be known as the best of the Romantic writers. Calderón was a dramatist and poet. Galván worked as a narrator, poet, playwright, journalist, and politician. He was considered to be the first of the Mexican Romantics. Galván's poems such as "*A la muerte de mi amigo*" and "*Adios, oh patria mía*" influenced compositions of *la canción romántica*. For one, poems such as *Adios, oh patria mía*, were written in copla format (eight syllables per line) and eight-lined verses. Thematically, his ideas of friendship, love and nationalism came to capture romance in popular music.

Age of *La Canción Romantica*

The *canción romántica* was in its prime from 1850 to 1900 at least according to Oscar Myer Serra. Musicologists point to the work of composer and troubadour A. Zúniga as an important link in the genre's development at this time. Borrowing from Italian musical structures rather than Spanish, Zúniga's work came to define the essence of the *canción romántica*: harmony, diverse melody lines, and time structures are different from the typical Spanish ones. However, not all musicologists are in agreement.

Musicologists Carmen Sordo Sodi and Juan S. Garrido both denied Italian influences in the nineteenth-century *canción* beyond the urban areas of Mexico and gave as an example the folkloric *canción* which was influenced by Spanish rhythms and melodies. They believed few Mexicans came into contact with Italian opera and therefore believed Italian influences were minimal, other than *bel canto*. But those who sang in this style were not necessarily using opera as their foundation.

But other difficulties arose in classifying *canción romántica*. The use of the word *mexicana* has never been clear. Sordo Sodi took the view that the word indicated the composer as Mexican, written in a Mexican style or that the theme of a song concerned a national interest. Juan Garrido defined the genre of *canción mexicana*, whether the word *romántica* was used or not, as a mix of Spanish influence with a "Mexican way of thinking." He added that when the term was coined by Manuel

Ponce in 1910, the thinking was that *mestizos* sang Spanish and Mexican songs in a way different from the Spanish way of singing them. That is, in a completely different style. This was evident in performance style and in a type of Mexican melodies common in *canciones románticas* at the beginning of the twentieth century.

However, the development of *la canción romántica* was also influenced by Cuban music which for some time had also been popular in Mexico; in particular, from 1860 to 1900. A dance that entered urban popularity was the *habanera*, a dance style which in the beginning was instrumental though in time was characterized by vocal lyrics. One of the first habanera songs to become popular in Mexico was "*La Paloma*" by Sebastián Yradier. So great was its popularity that it was eventually considered a *canción mexicana,* perhaps the first evidence of musical appropriation of Cuban music by Mexico. Regardless, the habanera and other Cuban musical pieces made Caribbean styles popular in Mexico. The habanera took the form of a *canción* in the *ritmo de hamaca* (hammock rhythm), a slow or moderately slow 2/4 time. It is also syncopated. Along with "*La Paloma*," Narciso Serardell's "*La Golondrina,*" became the prototypes for *la canción romántica* from 1870 to 1900.

In 1896 alone, the following romantic and *habanera* songs captured the sentiment of Mexico: "*Pregúntale a las estrellas*" (Ask the Stars), "*Ilusiones perdidas*" (Lost Hope), "*Bonaerges*" (a character from the novel *El Martir de Golgota*), "*Tristezas*" (Sadness), "*Horas de luto*" (Hours of Mourning), "*Corazones de marmol*" (Hearts of Marble), "*Guarda esa flor*" (Keep This Flower), and "*Resignación*" (Resignation). The titles clearly give a sense of the themes, and slowly Mexican audiences literally took them to heart. The spread of these lyrics was also helped by the introduction of the gramophone in 1897, which for those who could afford it could now bring home the lyrics of love.

Juan Garrido viewed the *canciones* of this early period as Spanish with no Mexican influence at all. In fact, he dated the style to 1896. In his view the song "*Perjura*" (1901) by Miguel Lerdo de Tejada was the first *canción romántica mexicana.* Although romantic lyrics had been heard before, Tejada's verses went to another level as in the following example:

> Cuando mis labios en tu albo cuello
> Con fiebre loca en mi bien posé,
> Y en los transportes de amor excelso
> No se hasta donde mi alma se fue.
> (When feverishly on your alabaster neck
> my lips I did lay
> and in transported love, I know not where
> My soul did make its way.)

With a melody line no different from other *canciones* of the nineteenth century, a *bel canto* arrangement focusing on love as a theme, with influence from the Cuban *bolero*, this musical style was developed by composers such as Lerdo de Tejada, Alfonso Esparza Oteo, and Tata Nacho.

Lerdo de Tejada (1869–1941) was always committed to popular music. Along with "*Perjura*" and "*México bello,*" he was the first Mexican composer to introduce his melodies with his own orchestra. Alfonso Esparza Oteo (1887–1950) grew up a classical pianist and had fought with Francisco (Pancho) Villa during the Mexican Revolution (1910–1917). While living in Mexico City he formed, with the aforementioned composers, Los Cuatro Ases de la Canción. He served as director of Columbia Records, Discos Brunswick and of radio stations in Mexico. He led La Orquesta Típica and is known for his classic song "*Un viejo amor.*" Tata Nacho, whose real name was Ignacio Fernández Esperón, was a composer, researcher of folkloric music who was active in film and radio, and later was director of Orquesta Típica de la Ciudad de Mexico. He composed *canciones* such as "*La Borrachita,*" "*Adios mi chapparita,*" and "*Nunca, nunca, nunca.*" Many of these songs were accompanied by a waltz or *habanera* rhythm.

Even through the violent times of the Mexican Revolution, *la canción romántica* flourished because of poetry. Among the middle class these songs harked back to a romantic period when Romantic poetry captured the sentiment of something pure and innocent. But there was to be one additional development: the *bolero*.

The *Bolero* in Mexico

La canción romántica would now come to epitomize the whole of Mexican popular music. Although in the nineteenth century this style drew from *bel canto*, now vocal styles would only be different in that they were not operatic. But the sense of feeling and sentiment were more powerful than ever. According to various sources, the *bolero* arrived in Mexico at the turn of the twentieth century from Havana where it had been evolving for some time. The earliest known *bolero* was "*Tristeza*" (1885) by José Pepe Sánchez. Besides being a popular composition, it was the song that made popular the term *bolero*. The Cuban *bolero* was also momentous for its structure, which facilitated the merging of its rhythms to the verses of romantic poets of the day. The verses of Adolfo Utrera and the music of composer Nilo Meléndez, for example, helped create "*Aquellos ojos verdes*" (Those Green Eyes) around the turn of the twentieth century. Today, it still remains a classic.

By 1919, the style was adopted by Mexico's own when Armando Villarreal composed "*Morena mía*" (My brown girl). The first of the classic *boleros*, and the one solidifying the style as Mexican, was "*Presentimiento*" (Premonition) in 1924. With words by Spanish poet Pedro Mata, and music by Emilio Pacheco, the *bolero* was about to take hold of Mexico and establish itself as the premier style not only in the country but in the rest of the Americas as well.

In the state of Veracruz, a young composer named Augusto "Guty" Cardenas Pinelo (1905–1932) was crafting songs such as "*Rayito de luna*" and María Grever (1884–1951), who lived much of her life in New York City, composed songs such as "*Júrame,*" "*Cuando vuelva a tu lado,*" and "*Muñequita linda.*" In the period of the 1930s and 1940s, the development of the *bolero* became the next stage of *la canción romántica mexicana*. In fact, it came to be known as *el bolero romántico*. The important proponents of this form were Roberto Cantoral, Armando Manzanero, Antonio Muñoz, and Consuelo Velásquez. In addition, the *bolero* merged with *la canción ranchera* to become *bolero-ranchero*. Also relying on *bel canto* influence one only need listen to Jorge Negrete, Pedro Infante, Miguel Aceves Mejía, Javier Solís, and Vicente Fernández to hear a style of singing that many struggled to achieve but only a few mastered.

But the 1930s saw the popularity of Agustín Lara as lyricist and musician reveling in the notion of *canción romántica*. But his was not traditional sentimentalism. A romantic poet who worshipped "marginalized women" as writer Carlos Monsivais put it, the use of language by Lara helped create a fiction of what falling in love was all about. Lara was in fact criticized by Mexican clergy for the romantic themes found in his songs. What made Lara so important to Mexico was that he presented to everyday people the desires of love and passion by taking the essence of *la canción romántica* to different heights: out of music salons and into the lives of the populace. What could not happen in the nineteenth century, Lara made possible for all. Still, his most popular song *Granada* (1935) remains a test for singers who wish to capture for their audiences a throwback to *bel canto*.

The *bolero romántico* became popular in the United States where it came to be known as International Latin. Lara's "*Sólamente un vez*" and María Grever's "*Cuando vuelva a tu lado*" became hits as "You Belong to My Heart" and "What a Difference a Day Makes," respectively.

The stature of the *bolero romántico* was further cemented by the many soloists or duos who included them in their repertoire. But the guitar trios of the 1940s, 1950s, and 1960s perhaps did more to bring the *bolero romántico* to national and international audiences. The Trío Los Panchos, for example, not only were successful in Mexico, but also in the United States. In record and in film the trios brought the *bolero* to such heights that the songs themselves have become the standards of Mexican popular music. Whether referred to as *bolero* or *canción romántica*, these styles are rooted in nineteenth-century musical traditions related to Italian opera, *bel canto*, and Romanticism. The development of themes and lyrics related to romance took these styles to new heights at the end of the nineteenth century and the beginning of the twentieth century. With the migration of the *bolero* to Mexico, *la canción romántica* entered a new dimension in music and with it a rare instance where the folkloric and popular merge and help shape a national music style that remains popular today in Mexico, Latin America, and with the Chicano/Latino population of the United States.

Carlos F. Ortega

See also: Canción Ranchera; Romance

Further Reading

Geijerstam, Claes. *Popular Music in Mexico*. Albuquerque: University of New Mexico Press, 1976.

González y González, Luis. "The Period of Formation." In Marjory Mattingly Urquidi, trans. *A Compact History of Mexico*, 67–111. Mexico City: El Colegio de México, 1974.

Monsiváis, Carlos. "Bolero: A History." In John Kraniauskas, trans. *Mexican Postcards*, 166–195. London: Verso Press, 1997.

Morales, Ed. *The Latin Beat: The Rhythms and Roots of Latin Music from Bossa Nova to Salsa and Beyond*. New York: De Capo Press, 2003.

Roberts, John Storm. *The Latin Tinge: The Impact of Latin American Music on the United States.* 2nd ed. New York: Oxford University Press, 1999.

Stevenson, Robert. *Music in Mexico: The Only Complete History of Mexican Music from Aztec to Modern Times.* New York: Thomas Y. Crowell Co., 1971.

CANDLES (VELAS)

Belief in the unseen and the supernatural is one of the most important tenets in the human belief system. For thousands of years, human beings have attempted to communicate with the supernatural and enlisted many different forms of communication. Early human populations saw evidence of the supernatural all around them in the natural environment and were in awe of it. Protection from harm was most likely one of the earliest reasons for communicating with the supernatural. Requesting favors and giving thanks for favors granted are some of the earliest foundations of human religion that continue to this day. Channels of communication between this world and the netherworld are critical and take many forms.

The concept of God as a superior entity is also one of humanity's earliest concepts since it was felt that the invisible was more powerful than the visible on earth. Additionally it was believed that the superior entity which looked over humans needed to be propitiated in some form or another to ensure continued protection. Prayer in the form of meditation or speaking silently and prayer spoken out loud in the form of a chant were two of the most common forms of contacting the gods. Additionally, the supernatural could be contacted both by individuals and by approved specialists called shamans or priests.

Before the advent of electricity, human beings in communities and in communion with nature gathered around the protective communal fire because it was believed that wild and dangerous animals would not approach it, and it also served as humanity's first altar. Those who gathered around the fire and were possibly led by their appointed communicator, watched as the flames danced and produced smoke which twisted and spiraled its way up to the heavens. The smoke carried prayers, wishes and dreams to the supernatural world for consideration.

Early humans believed that their words and chants were carried from the earthly fire to the gods on the smoke generated by the flames. If a sign was produced on earth as a result of their activity, then that counted as proof that their prayers or requests had been received and were being considered.

Candles have always had multiple purposes for man, one to produce light in a dark and dangerous environment and in this way lighting the way to safety, and secondly, to serve as a personal system of communication with the supernatural. Candles which are used for supernatural communication are called votive or prayer candles. The existence of candles used in religious ceremonies can be traced back several thousand years to the ancient Chinese and other ancient cultures. Candles were produced and used for religious purposes from the dawn of human existence.

The art of candle making has been kept alive and flourishes today in a combination of mainstream religious and pseudo religious movements including the New

Candles glow in a Mexican cathedral. (iStockPhoto.com)

Age movement and many forms of witchcraft including those forms utilized by Latinos/as.

Before the industrial age, candles were made from animal fat or tallow, certain plants that produced wax naturally, by beeswax and through the production of paraffin. Before electricity, the art of candle making was an essential component of every household and this is still true in many parts of the world. Today candle making is left to mass production in factories.

There is a major difference between the producer of the raw material used to make candles such as paraffin wax or the collection of beeswax and the preparation of candles. Today, many people who prepare candles for sale purchase the raw material and then further prepare the wax by adding color, aroma and magical objects before it is poured into the desired container and labeled. Contemporary prepared candles are hugely popular and thus the process of preparation of votive candles for prayer is also a growing industry.

If a candle is to be used for votive or prayer purposes every aspect of its manufacture, preparation and handling is important. Candles are widely used in many contemporary religions and most are purchased commercially by the case. Votive candles are very popular within Roman Catholicism and all of its folk variations. For example, the Latino population is comprised of Spanish-speaking populations from throughout the Americas. Each primary region of the Spanish-speaking Americas, including the Caribbean, Mexico, Central and South America has its favored variations of Christ, the Virgin Mary, Saints, and other Catholic hierarchy such as the Holy Spirit. Then there are the multitudes of folk saints each with his or her special candle.

Generally, votive candles are produced depending upon the demands of the regional market. For example, votive candles for a favored South American saint would probably not be found in the smaller markets of the United States, but may be found in the larger ones such as Los Angeles, Chicago, New York, and Miami. Even "prepared" candles are produced en masse but the true believers and those whose reputation depends on the effectiveness of the candle would most certainly prepare an important candle themselves.

In addition to their religious use, candles are utilized by practitioners of witchcraft or *brujería*. Candles are produced in explicit male and female forms including specific body parts and in different colors. Black candles are also produced specifically for the purpose of black magic or *magia negra*. Color magic is very important in the magical use of candles.

The colors associated with candles are the same as the colors associated with magic in general and are consistent in magical practices throughout the world and across cultures. The color white is associated with good and purity and thus most religious votive candles are white wax. If a candle carries a label it will portray the acknowledged symbol of the saint or entity on the front and sometimes it will have a prayer on the reverse side. Therefore, white candles are most common for religious purposes and black candles for black magic.

Many other colors may be used but the most common are red which is used in matters of passion, romance or bravery, yellow is used for protection, green is used for fertility, and gold is most commonly used for attracting financial gain.

Once a candle has been purchased or prepared, the actual use of the candle is also important. The importance includes where it is to be burned on a home altar, how and when it is lighted, the prayers that are said that accompany it and finally the interpretation of the action of the candle as it burns down.

A candle that burns cleanly is thought to be functioning properly. Conversely, a candle that is smoky is thought to have detected witchcraft or some other problem in the house and is signaling this fact. Some candles will not stay lit and this is also an indication of a problem. A candle that has a strong flame, is not smoky, and burns down properly as expected is considered to have properly performed its job and carried its message forward.

Votive candles have inadvertently started many house fires. Practioners are advised to place a votive candle in a nonflammable or Pyrex container with a little water at the bottom. Votive candles purchased in local neighborhood stores will very often crack and can be dangerous. When a candle has burned down completely and is out, it has no further spiritual use or significance and may be simply discarded.

ANTONIO NOÉ ZAVALETA

See also: Brujería (Witchcraft); Magia (Magic)

Further Reading

Newman, Jon. *Candles (History and Making Your Own Candles)*. Charlotte, NC: Baker and Taylor, Thunder Bay Press, 2000.
Oppenheimer, Betty. *The Candlemaker's Companion: A Complete Guide to Rolling, Pouring, Dipping, and Decorating Your Own Candle*. North Adams, MA: StoreyBooks, 2001.

CANÍCULA (DOG DAYS OF SUMMER)

The Spanish word *canícula* is a term used to designate the hottest time of the year (around July and August). It is similar to the English phrase "the dog days of summer," and both, the English phrase and the term *canícula*, allude to the same weather phenomena and originate in folk beliefs related to weather. This Spanish folk concept is still used by the older generation in Spanish-speaking countries.

Etymology and History

The term "*canícula*" is derived from the Latin word for "dog" (canis) and can be translated as "little dog." As is true for many other folk beliefs related to weather, the origin of the word and beliefs surrounding it are closely associated with the heavenly stars and constellations. In this case, the term is derived from a star, the dog star Sirius in the constellation Canis Major (also called the Alpha Canis Majoris), which rules the heavens during the summer period of long days and short nights; thus this period of intense heat came to be known as the "dog days."

For the Romans, the time when Sirius ruled the heavens was a good omen and Romans waited until Sirius appeared in the horizon to build their homes and temples as they situated their buildings in alignment with the star's position as it rose in the horizon. Thus, they waited for the "*canícula*" to build. Over time as the weather and climate were linked to the astral observations, the period came to signify the hottest time of the year, and the association with a building's orientation was forgotten.

For the Egyptians, Seth, as they called Sirius, held a special significance as well, and they began their year when the constellation Sirius rose; the year was called *annus canarius*. The climatological conditions aligned with Sirius and the Nile were such for Egyptians that they honored Sirius as a sun, a major influence in daily life.

In the state of Yucatan in Mexico, the phenomenon is observed in July and August as the sun's rays beat down on the Gulf and the temperatures rise. People will comment on the hot summer days as the time of the *canícula*, and this is done generally with apprehension and exasperation for it is viewed in negative terms both in terms of the physical discomfort due to the suffocating heat and also because it is deemed to be a "bad" time of the year. This negative view of the *canícula* season is due to the fact that people believe it is particularly dangerous for cuts and wounds becoming infected.

While in the United States the period is said to begin in July and end in August, in other places it begins with the summer solstice on June 21st, the longest day of the year when the sun shines the longest. The sun on this day is at the equator and thus it is said to mark the beginning of the dog days, *el tiempo de perros*/the time of the dogs.

Obviously, for the southern hemisphere, South America, the term has little meaning for this is not the hottest time of the year but the coldest. As the earth spins on its axis after the summer solstice, June 21st, the sun hits the northern hemisphere, but it is about a month later, in July, when it produces the hottest temperatures, just as it is approximately a month after December 21st, the winter solstice, that brings the coldest period for North America.

It was particularly in the nineteenth century and the early twentieth, when many Chicanos and Mexican immigrants in the United States were farmworkers, that the term had wide currency. Thus, for those who work the land, it becomes a period rich in lore. For Mexican American farmworkers this hottest time of the year, a time of drought and little harvesting, is known as "*la canícula*" (the dog days) or "*tiempos de canícula*" (the time of the dog days).

La Canícula, as it exists as a natural phenomenon in Chicano and Latino folk culture, has been relegated to those who recall the agricultural cycles along with recent immigrants for whom the traditional name for the "dog days" persists.

NORMA E. CANTÚ

See also: Cabañuelas (Weather Prognostication)

Further Reading

Bañuelos, Marta. "Las víctimas de la canícula: Ola de calor provoca alto costo de vidas en Europa." *Siempre* 50, Issue 2619 (2003): 56.

Cantú, Norma E. *Canícula: Snapshots of a Girlhood in la Frontera*. Albuquerque: University of New Mexico Press, 1997.

Juárez Núñez, Apolonio, and Pedro Ochoa Sánchez. "La canícula." http://www.cienciasap licadas.buap.mx/Divulgacion/ArticulosDivulgacion/Tierra/lacanicula.htm.

CANTÚ, NORMA E. (1947–)

Norma E. Cantú Ramón was born on January 3rd, 1947, in Nuevo Laredo, Tamaulipas, México, and raised in the border town of Laredo, Texas. She is an internationally known and recognized Chicana writer, activist, folklorist, and educator. Cantú is most notably known for her award-winning autobioethnography, *Canícula: Snapshots of a Girlhood en la Frontera* (1995) and is currently a professor of English at the University of Texas, San Antonio. Her areas of teaching and research interest include Chicana/o literature, border studies, folklore, women's studies, U.S. Latina/o studies, and creative writing. Since she was raised along the U.S.-México borderlands, the border and its cultures remain the focus of Cantú's academic and creative work, and the tales from, and of, the people on the Texas/México border to which she spent her earliest years listening serve as a creative influence on her work as a folklorist, teacher, and writer.

Cantú received her bachelor's and master's degrees from Texas A&M University, Laredo in 1973 and Kingsville in 1976, respectively, and her Ph.D. from the University of Nebraska, Lincoln in 1982. She received a Ford Foundation Graduate Fellowship (1977–1979), a Fulbright-Hays Research Fellowship to Spain (1979–1980), a Ford Foundation Chicano Dissertation Completion Grant (1982), and a Fulbright-Hays Post-Doctoral Research Fellowship to Spain (1985). In addition to the Ford Foundation and Fulbright Hays Fellowships, Cantú has received numerous awards including the Modern Language Association's Chicano Studies Section Scholar of the Year Award, the American Folklore Society's Américo Paredes

Award, the Elvira Cordero de Cisneros Award from the Macondo Foundation, the American Folklore Studies Women's Section Elli Köngäs-Maranda Prize, and she was honored as a Veteran Feminist of America.

Cantú held the positions of assistant professor (1980–1987), associate professor (1987–1993), and full professor (1993–2000) at Texas A&M International University (formerly named Laredo State University). Cantú also served as Senior Arts Specialist for the Folk and Traditional Arts Program of the National Endowment for the Arts (1993–1995) and Acting Director of the Center for Chicano Studies at the University of California, Santa Barbara (1998–1999). Cantú has served on the boards of the Federation of State Humanities Councils (1998–2002) and the American Folklore Society (2000–2002), and was appointed by the Librarian of the Library of Congress to the Board of Trustees of the American Folklife Center at the Library (1998–2006).

In addition to authoring *Canícula: Snapshots of Girlhood en la Frontera*, which is currently in its fifth printing and received the Premio Aztlán and Webb County Heritage Award in 1996, Cantú's in-progress creative works consist of the novels *Papeles de Mujer* and *Champú: or Hair Matters*, a collection of poetry, *Meditación Fronteriza: Poems of Life, Love and Work*, and an ethnographic study of a traditional religious dance tradition, *Soldiers of the Cross: Los Matachines de las Santa Cruz*, a longitudinal study of a group in Laredo, Texas. *Cabañuelas: A Love Story* is Cantu's latest forthcoming creative work. In addition to creative works, Cantú has edited and co-edited numerous other publications. She is editor of *Flor y ciencia: Chicanas in Mathematics, Science, and Engineering* (2006), *Moctezuma's Table: Rolando Briseño's Mexican and Chicano Tablescapes* (2010), and *The Art of Liliana Wilson* (in progress).

Cantú is co-editor of *Telling to Live: Latina Feminist Testimonies* (2001) with the Latina Feminist Group, *Chicana Traditions: Continuity and Change* (2002) with Olga Nájera-Ramírez, *Prietas y Güeras: Proceedings of the First Conference on the Life and Work of Gloria Anzaldúa* (2009) with Christina L. Gutiérrez, *Dancing Across Borders: Danzas y Bailes Mexicanos* (2009) with Olga Nájera-Ramírez and Brenda Romero, *Inside the Latina Experience: A Latino Studies Reader* (2010) with María Fránquiz, *The Plays of Silviana Wood* (in progress) with Rita Urquízo-Ruiz, and *Entre Malinche y Guadalupe: Tejanas in Literature and Art* (forthcoming) with Inés Hernández Avila.

In addition to her work as an author and editor, Cantú is responsible for founding, in 2005, the Society for the Study of Gloria Anzaldúa (SSGA), which focuses on the scholarship and writings of Chicana feminist theorist Gloria Anzaldúa. The SSGA is housed in the Women's Studies Institute of UTSA and is an affiliate organization of the Society for the Study of American Women Writers. SSGA hosts an international conference every eighteen months in San Antonio to provide a place for scholars, students, and community to come together with the intention of engaging in the continued study of Anzaldúa's intellectual and spiritual work. Cantú, along with Pablo Miguel Martínez, Celeste Guzmán Mendoza, Deborah Parédez, and Carmen Tafolla, is also a founder of CantoMundo, a national Latina poets organization.

Cantú's folklore studies began as a graduate student when she presented at meetings of the Texas Folklore Society in the mid 1970s. Her dissertation, "The

Offering and the Offers: The Illocation of a *Laredo Pastorela* in the Tradition of the Shepherd's Play" (1982), further deepened her work in folklore studies as her semiotic analysis of a traditional Christmas folk play, *La Pastorela,* integrated Chicano/a folkloristics within contemporary literary theory. Folklore studies also form part of Cantú's teaching specializations and, for the last six years, she has taught a class titled "The Spanish Roots of Chicana Folklore," a graduate seminar, in Toledo, Spain, at the Universidad de Castilla/La Mancha.

In her creative work, Cantú writes what she refers to as autobioethnography and thus creates a genre that fuses ethnographic information with literary production, mostly poetry and fiction. As a founding member of the Folklore and Creative Writing Section of the American Folklore Society, she has presented at the section's sponsored panel at the Associated Writing Programs and at the AFS annual meetings. In October 2008, Utah State University Press published *The Folklore Muse: Poetry, Fiction, and Other Reflections by Folklorists*, edited by Frank deCaro; the book collects the creative work of folklorists who belong to the AFS Creative Writing section. Cantú and María Herrera-Sobek were instrumental in the establishment of the Chicana/o Section at AFS, and as the first conveners for the section set forth an active presence at the annual meetings.

Cantú's own edited works, specifically *Chicana Traditions: Continuity and Change* and *Dancing Across Borders: Danzas y Bailes Mexicanos*, expand the field of folklore studies. *Chicana Traditions: Continuity and Change* provides an anthology of Chicana culture, exploring issues ranging from the role and art of *santeras* to contemporary reconfigurations of *La Llorona* (the Wailing Woman). The collection received the Susan Koppelman Award given by the joint Women's Caucus of the Popular Culture Association/American Culture Association, the Elli Köngäs Maranda Prize from the Women's Section of the AFS, and was chosen as an Outstanding Academic Book by *Choice Magazine*. Her other collaborative collection, *Dancing across Borders: Danzas y Bailes Mexicanos,* explores traditional Mexican dances along the U.S.-México border and addresses issues of authenticity and the role of cultural tourism.

Cantú has also prepared reports on traditional arts for a number of agencies. In 2008 as part of fieldwork research she prepared "Dressing San Antonio" for the Smithsonian Museum of American History and, in 2004, *Latinos/as in the South* for the Southern Arts Federation. She worked with Brazilian folklorist from the Idaho Arts Commission, María Gambliel, to conduct focus interviews in Southern Idaho and prepared *Latino Folklife in Idaho—2000–01: A Survey of Idaho Latino Traditional Arts* (2003) for the Idaho Commission on the Arts. She also wrote the *Report on Latino Culture and Traditional Arts in Tennessee* (2000) for the Tennessee Arts Commission Folk Arts Program.

MAGDA GARCÍA

See also: American Folklore Society (AFS); La Llorona (The Wailing Woman)

Further Reading

Cantú, Norma E. *Moctezuma's Table: Rolando Briseño's Mexican and Chicano Tablescapes.* College Station: Texas A&M University Press, 2010.

Cantú, Norma E. "The Semiotics of Land: Los Matachines de la Santa Cruz." In *Dancing across Borders: Danzas y bailes mexicanos*. Urbana: University of Illinois Press, 2009.

Cantú, Norma E. *Latinas and Latinos in the South*. Atlanta: Southern Arts Federation, 2004. http://www.southarts.org/atf/cf/%7B15E1E84E-C906-4F67-9851-A195A9BAAF79%7D/Latino_Report_English.pdf.

Cantú, Norma E. "Pastoras and Malinches: Women in Traditional Folk Drama." In *Recovering the U.S Literary Heritage Project*. Vol. 5. Houston: Arte Público Press, 2003.

Cantú, Norma E. "La Quinceañera: Towards an Ethnographic Analysis of a Life-Cycle Ritual." *Southern Folklore* 56, no. 1 (1999).

Cantú, Norma E. "La Virgen de Guadalupe: Symbol of Faith and Devotion." In *Familia, Fé y Fiestas/Family, Faith and Fiestas: Mexican American Celebrations of the Holiday Season*. Fresno, CA: Arte Américas and Fresno Arts Council, 1996.

Cantú, Norma E. *Canícula: Snapshots of a Girlhood en la Frontera*. Albuquerque: University of New Mexico Press, 1995.

Cantú, Norma E. "Los Matachines de la Santa Cruz de la Ladrillera: Notes Toward a Socio-Literary Analysis." In Ramón Gutiérrez, ed. *Feasts and Celebrations in U.S. Ethnic Communities*. Albuquerque: University of New Mexico Press, 1995.

Cantú, Norma E. "The Wound That Will Not Heal." Program Book for the *Festival of American Folklife*. Washington, DC: Smithsonian Institution, 1993.

Cantú, Norma E. "Los Matachines de la Santa Cruz: Un acto de resistencia cultural." *Mito y Leyenda*. Tijuana: Colegio de la Frontera Norte, 1992.

Cantú, Norma E. "Costume as Cultural Resistance and Affirmation: The Case of a South Texas Community." Texas Folklore Society, *Hecho en Texas*. Denton: University of North Texas Press, 1992.

Cantú, Norma E., and Olga Nájera-Ramírez. *Chicana Traditions: Continuity and Change*. Urbana: University of Illinois Press, 2002.

Cantú, Norma E., and Ofelia Zapata. "Mexican American Quilting Traditions in Laredo, San Ygnacio and Zapata." *Hecho en Texas*. Denton: University of North Texas Press, 1992.

De Caro, Frank, ed. *The Folklore Muse: Poetry, Fiction, and Other Reflections by Folklorists*. Logan: Utah State University Press, 2008.

Nájera-Ramírez, Olga, Norma E. Cantú, and Brenda M. Romero. *Dancing across Borders: Danzas y Bailes Mexicanos*. Urbana: University of Illinois Press, 2009.

CAPIROTADA

Cooking and cuisine embody history, language, and cultural identity. For many Mexican and Chicano/a cooks, making *capirotada* triggers memories of home, childhood, and the spicy, cinnamon aroma of their mothers' kitchens. "Each person knows at least one recipe that has been with him or her throughout life . . . [a]nd each recipe has its own story [that is] continually retold in a particular manner" (Hernández Fuentes 2005, 458). Chicano author Alberto Alvaro Ríos recalls the elaborate process of making *capirotada* when he was a child growing up in Nogales, Arizona. He remembers that "[t]he ingredients for *capirotada* had to be gathered from across the line, in Nogales, Sonora, or else certainly from Mexico—and this is one of the things that defined its making. It was not from here" (Ríos 1999, 85).

Capirotada is commonly known in Mexico and the United States as a sweet dish or dessert. In English it is often called Mexican bread pudding. Although there are many versions of the recipe, the basic ingredients are similar: layers of toasted and sliced white bread, spiced syrup made of cinnamon, clove, anise seeds, and *piloncillo*, or brown sugar, peanuts, raisins, prunes, and cheese. The name evokes a friar's hood. Similarly, the fried egg or the layer of brown and bubbling cheese covers the dish to give it a cloaked appearance.

Capirotada was traditionally prepared in a *cazuela*, a glazed Mexican earthenware dish, and served during Lent. Although the Lenten fast has long been abolished, many Mexican and Chicano families continue to observe the Catholic religious practice of not consuming meat on Fridays and throughout Lent. In commenting on the Lenten association, Ríos compares the dish to a food piñata: "[y]ou put everything into it the same way you just gave up everything for a week. It's a food that helps you make up in one sitting for everything you couldn't have before" (87). Because it has no meat, *capirotada* has become associated with this religious ritual.

"There are as many different recipes for *capirotada* as there are households in Mexico," asserts Arnaldo Richards (Grodinsky 2008). Instead of peanuts some cooks add pine nuts, almonds, or pecans as well as fresh fruit, such as bananas, apples, pears, pineapples, or mangos. "The cheese," according to Peggy Grodinsky, "may be Cheddar or Monterey Jack, manchego, queso fresco, cotija, añejo, or Chihuahua" (Grodinsky 2008). She adds that "[t]he bread may be supermarket white, bolillos (Mexican baguettes), or French bread; it's sometimes deep-fried, other times merely toasted. *Capirotada* is a good use for stale bread" (Grodinsky 2008). Some cooks like to add coconut, candied cactus, or brightly colored sprinkles like the kind used on ice cream. Another variation of the recipe requires soaking bread in eggs, heavy cream, and butter, adding *piloncillo,* cinnamon, and cheese, and drizzling the dessert with sherry-flavored *rompope*, a Mexican eggnog. The result is a combination of standard American bread pudding and traditional *capirotada*.

This is a María Herrera-Sobek family recipe for capirotada given to her by grandmother Susana Escamilla de Tarango:

Grease with vegetable oil a Pyrex (oven-proof) large bowl and have it ready.

Ingredients:
Four large buns of French-style bread cut into small cubes or pieces and toasted in pan with butter or oil
Eight small corn tortillas (toasted lightly in grill, not hard tortillas just warmed up)
1 cup of peanuts
2 cups of sliced banana
1 cup of raisins
1 1/2 cups of cheese cubes (Mozzarella, Monterey Jack or Longhorn cheese can be used
2 sticks of cinnamon
1 cup of small, hard colorful candy (Mexican colaciones if you can find them but hard candy can be substituted)
2 cups of brown sugar
1 cup of water

Boil water, cinnamon, and brown sugar to make a sweet liquid mixture. Line a large glass bowl with tortillas. Mix raisins, cheese, peanuts, bread, sliced bananas, and colorful hard candy and place mixture in bowl. Pour sweet brown sugar liquid mixture over ingredients to moisten them. Put in 350 degree oven for 1/2 hour or until cheese is slightly melted.

Serves 6

Some cooks prefer to create a different taste and texture altogether. They diverge from the sweetness by mixing tomatoes, onions, cilantro, bay leaves, and fig leaves with bread to create a layered casserole or stew. The original recipe for *capirotada* was a soup whose roots can be traced to seventeenth-century Spain and before that to ancient Rome. Culinary historian and cookbook author Maricel Presilla explains:

> You have recipes for *capirotada*, or things that are very similar, in very old books through the centuries. In one version, onions, tomatoes and garlic were fried in lard. A splash of water yielded tomato broth, which was poured over layers of bread sprinkled with cheese. The soup was ready to eat when the bread had absorbed the broth. Similar soups [still] exist in Spain. (Grodinsky 2008)

Moreover, Mario Montano claims that a recipe for *capirotada* calling for different kinds of meats and cheeses appeared in the 1667 cookbook of Felipe Martínez Montino, a chef for King Philip IV of Spain.

MARGARET B. CROSBY

Further Reading

Castro, Rafaela G. "Capirotada." *The American Mosaic: The Latino American Experience.* Santa Barbara, CA: ABC-CLIO, 2010. http://0-latinoamerican2.abc-clio.com.topcat .switchinc.org/.

Grodinsky, Peggy. "Capirotada Recipes. The Sweet Smell of Home." *Houston Chronicle,* 4 February 2008. http://www.chron.com/disp/story.mpl/life/food/5506982.html.

Hernández Fuentes, Lourdes. "Cuisine." In Suzanne Oboler and Deana J. González, eds. *The Oxford Encyclopedia of Latinos and Latinas in the United States,* 458–466. Translated by Felipe Ehrenberg. New York: Oxford University Press, 2005.

Montano, Mario. "The History of Mexican Folk Foodways of South Texas: Street Vendors, Offal Foods and Barbacoa de Cabeza." Dissertation, University of Pennsylvania, 1992. http://0-latinoamerican2.abc-clio.com.topcat.switchinc.org/.

Ortiz, Elisabeth Lambert. "Capirotada." In *The New Complete Book of Mexican Cooking,* 295–296. New York: Harper Collins, 1998.

Ríos, Alberto Alvaro. "Capirotada." In *Capirotada: A Nogales Memoir,* 84–86. Albuquerque: University of New Mexico Press, 1999.

CARNE ASADA

Carne asada can be defined as a thinly sliced, spicy beef often grilled over an open barbeque. However, such a denotation is limited in that it fails to recognize the utter significance that this preparation of beef has had and continues to have on many people who choose to identify or are labeled as Latino/a today. *Carne asada,*

Tacos de carne asada—tacos filled with thinly sliced, grilled beef.
(Dreamstime.com)

and even more specifically, the *taco de carne asada*, has a rich history that goes as far back as the arrival of the Spaniards in the New World in the early sixteenth century. The Spanish explorers and conquistadores, beginning with Christopher Columbus, Hernán Cortés, Francisco and Gonzalo Pizarro, as well as Hernando de Soto—just to name a limited few—were accustomed to an Agro-pastoral economy and way of life in the Extramaduran and Castilian territories from which they originated.

Knowing that these men relied on land and livestock in their home countries and regions helps us to understand the cultural customs and values that traveled with them to the New World—oftentimes at the expense of the Indigenous people, their land, and their way of life. Analyzing the history of beef in the New World, however, also helps us to contextualize the subsequent mixing of traditions that produced what is now referred to as Latin America—which includes Mexico, Central America, South America, and parts of the Caribbean. Today, for those who enjoy eating it, the *taco de carne asada* may be one example of the many wonderful fusions that took place as the cooking customs of Indigenous peoples of the Americas blended with the preferences of the Spaniards.

The New World did not have domesticated animals, such as pigs, goats, sheep, and chickens, among others. As the Spanish explorers and conquistadores were accustomed to eating these types of meats, they made sure to bring them along on their voyages. Furthermore, they were mandated by the Spanish Crown to do so to secure resources for settlements in the New World. So commonplace and necessary was meat to the Spanish that they had a hard time imagining any other way of life. They relied on it for nutrition and their livelihood, and therefore transferred that knowledge into the lands they conquered. The arrival of pigs predated the arrival of cows in the New World, and they played a vital role in the conquest and colonization of the Americas. Although the horses, dogs, and asses that the Spanish brought with them were crucial as instruments of war, pigs proved to be the primary source of sustenance for their soldiers during the first part of the Spanish invasion. Cattle arrived in the New World in 1521, but their slaughter was forbidden until their numbers grew. By 1526, Mexico City was being regularly supplied with beef. Cattle as well as other livestock were both destructive and beneficial to the Indigenous people and their lands.

Indigenous people were, for the most part, vegetarians until the arrival of the Spanish. *Maize* and *frijoles* were staple foods, and the few meat sources were provided by localized and seasonal fowl, such as ducks and turkeys. There was much variation due to the extensive geographic spaces spanning the New World. Although it has been stated that the natives gained a quicker appreciation for beef than for pork, the cattle served to displace them in many ways. For example, the natives' plots of land had to make way for the larger Spanish pastures that came to dominate. Due to grazing, the cattle eventually displaced the natives by destroying their croplands. It seems that cattle came to hold more prestige than swine since the natives were oftentimes forced (and sometimes permitted) to be swineherds; however, they were prevented from raising cattle or horses. Nevertheless, cows became the most important livestock, particularly in Mexico since they provided milk, cheese, and hides which were sold throughout the Americas and exploited for high profits. Many conflicts occurred between the *españoles* and the *indigenas*, the results of which are still apparent today. However, the fusion of foods that took place between these two cultures is an example of at least one harmonious blend. When the Spanish introduced beef to the New World, it eventually met with the *tortilla de maiz*, or corn tortilla. The legacy of that early encounter is still recognized, appreciated, and savored by many Latino families that incorporate the *taco de carne asada* into their leisurely and celebratory family activities.

For apart from its historical significance, the *taco de carne asada* reveals important connections that exist among race, ethnicity, and leisurely activities insofar that certain patterns become apparent regarding the practices, habits, and values of a people. Leisure activities can be defined as those done apart from working hours and doing things for personal enjoyment. Leisure activities are oftentimes associated with food. For many people of Mexican and Central American heritage, specifically, in California and other Southwest regions of the United States, the *taco de carne asada* has become synonymous with leisurely activities that often coincide with family gatherings. It is oftentimes prepared and served when families reunite for weekend gatherings or other festive occasions.

Although there are several regional variations regarding the preparation of *carne asada*, there are still many standards. *Carne asada* is typically seasoned with salt, pepper, garlic salt, and other spices. Additionally, it is marinated in citrus juices and/or beer. Some may even marinate it with *chorizo*. Once prepared, the meat is then grilled *al carbon*—in an outdoor barbeque grill. Typically, large-bulbed green onions are grilled alongside the meat. Once grilled, the seasoned/marinated meat is characteristically placed into a *tortilla de maiz* to create a *taco de carne asada*. Distinctive sides that are served along with the *taco* are *salsa de pico de gallo* (finely diced mixture of onions, green, hot peppers, and tomatoes) and *guacamole*. Also, *frijoles* (beans), *nopales* (tender cactus leaves), *arroz* (rice), or *fideos verdes* (vermicelli) may also accompany the *taco de carne asada*.

For many Latinos, *carne asada* itself is not just something to eat but it also names an experience that is connected with spending time with both immediate and extended family (as in we are going to a *carne asada*). In this way, *carne asada* becomes a symbol of culture and connotes family togetherness or unity. Childhood memories are often filled with occasions in which *carne asada* was prepared. The preparation might have been as simple as going to the local *carnicería* (butcher shop) and having it prepared by a *carnicero* (butcher), or it may have included more elaborate preparations involving multiple family members at home. The complexity of the preparation also has to do with geographic location. For instance, in many other countries outside of the United States, it is common for the family members to slaughter and *destazar* the cow on their own property. Regardless of the simplicity or complexity of the preparation, the end result is that the family members are unified by the preparing, cooking, and eating of the *carne asada*. More simple types of occasions, such as relaxing weekend gatherings in someone's backyard or at the park, result in more simple types of preparations. More festive celebrations, such as a *bautizo*, *cumpleaños*, *aniversario*, or other festive or religious occasion might result in more elaborate preparations; however, other selections of beef such as *barbacoa* might be more common.

When people are connected, exchanges take place, so that if people are connected by food, the specificities of the origins of that food for the people preparing it are significant. When elders prepare a food, they are also communicating information about their own regional origins and traditions. These traditions are often passed down orally and visually as the younger generations learn by what they hear, see, smell, touch, and taste. In this sense, the exchange of food is a layered experience that connects people to past places, people, eras, and memories. These experiences often make us feel connected to home—whether it is a tangible place or the remnant of a distant memory. As a person grows up eating a certain type of food, such as a *taco de carne asada*, it becomes associated with an experience that ultimately synthesizes into the person's sense of identity. *Tú eres lo que comes*—you are what you eat. Such a statement can have multiple meanings. Culturally speaking, it helps us to recall that maize was as pivotal for the Indigenous peoples of the Americas as was beef for the Spaniards. These staple foods continue to thrive in the encounter that occurs between them in the *taco de carne asada*. And it is obvious that nearly five hundred years of history still live in the mouths of the many who savor eating it.

SILVIA TOSCANO VILLANUEVA

See also: Barbacoa; Frijoles (Beans); Maíz; Tacos

Further Reading

Chávez, D. J. *Mexican-American Recreation: Home, Community and Natural Environment.* USDA Forest Service Pacific Southwest Research Station, 2003.

Sobek-Herrera, María. *Chicano Folklore: A Handbook.* Westport, CT: Greenwood Press, 2006.

Zadik, B. J. "The Iberian Pig in Spain and the Americas at the Time of Columbus." M.A. Thesis, Latin American Studies, University of California, Berkeley, 2000.

CASANOVA, STEPHEN (STEVE) (1949–2009)

Dr. Steve Casanova, a grandfather of tradition, *abuelo de tradición*, was a Chicano scholar, mentor, visionary, and Indigenous spiritual leader-elder. He died on January 22nd, 2009, and will be remembered for leaving his strong and remarkable footprints in the places he worked and in the hearts he touched with his generosity, wisdom and gentle compassion. He was born and raised in San Antonio, Texas, earning his B.A. degree in 1978 from Southwest Texas State University. He moved his family north to earn his M.A. degree in 1987 and his Ph.D. in 2001 from the University of Wisconsin-Madison. He was appointed Associate Professor in the Ethnic Studies Program at St. Cloud State University (SCSU), St. Cloud, Minnesota, and served as Director of the Chicano Studies Program from 1998 to 2009. He later also served as Associate Director of the Library's Multicultural Resources Center in 2007 and 2008, respectively. He developed the SCSU's International Study Abroad program with Chihuahua, Mexico.

At the national level, Dr. Casanova brought a framework to create a curriculum with Native American Studies. He developed collaboration opportunities for scholars whose academic interests were about the recognition of the negative effects of colonization. He was a member of the National Association of Chicana and Chicano Studies (NACCS) and a founder of the Indigenous Caucus within this group. He was a well-known spiritual leader and sundancer. He was a council member of the Tap Pilam Coahuiltecan, who are the original inhabitants of San Antonio, Texas. His family members were also descendents of the Canary Islands. Dr. Casanova was recently working on a book about mesquite trees and how they were used by the original inhabitants.

Dr. Casanova arrived to teach at St. Cloud State University during a time of campus change in the late 1990s. The St. Cloud Campus and other higher education institutions in Minnesota were experiencing the need to adapt to the increasingly diverse student body. Young Chicano students in particular were interested in learning more about their Indigenous roots and wanted to enroll in history and cultural courses pertaining to their heritage. Students were learning about Indigenous Mexican dance, their Indigenous spiritual heritage including sweat lodges, and about their *mestizo* mixed blood roots, and favored the Indigenous identity at national student conferences and regional meetings. The student passion for knowledge and change in the *status quo* led to a campus-wide hunger strike and sit-in demonstration by Chicano, white, African American and Asian students, and their supporters to bring attention to their unmet academic needs. They were advocating for more library acquisitions and materials about Chicano and Mexican American heritage, understanding about racial harmony and racism's alienation, and for the funding and recruitment of a faculty tenure track position to develop and teach such courses in the ethnic studies program.

The administration made an effort to accommodate students' concerns and "demands," creating a faculty position in the ethnic studies program. Dr. Steve Casanova was the first person to occupy this position and was very effective in his role of teacher and mentor. He made a decision to live in St. Cloud, a community that was known to not be very receptive to people of color. Most other faculty of color commuted an hour and a half south to live instead in the cities of Minneapolis or St. Paul. St. Cloud, home of St. Cloud State University, is located close to the meat processing poultry farms where Chicanos and those of Mexican heritage work and live with their families. Steve was known to mentor his students in his home which he shared with his sons who joined him in his move to Minnesota. He also brought his younger son often with him to Mexico when he developed the international study abroad in Chihuahua. He often spoke about being very proud of participating in NACCS conferences.

Steve Casanova and other faculty developed curriculum on race and spent over ten years building the library Multicultural Resources Center at SCSU. Not only did he serve as Associate Director, he served the community with great devotion and commitment to bridge communities together. In October 2006, the Multicultural Resources Center sponsored an evening called "Deporting of Columbus" to bring attention to the true history of immigration whereby faculty could present their research. Although it was challenging to colonial history, Steve Casanova was able to combine his passion for his own Indigenous roots and his knowledge of oral traditions and storytelling. He shared the scientific investigations based on evidence in South America that migrations were coastal and on-going for over 50,000 years. This contradicted the existing belief that the arrival occurred 12,000 years ago through the Bering Straits. He gave an academic framework to the concepts that the American Indian origin stories have solely American roots. He linked ancient history to recent history for students and his audiences, sharing that Mexico was once part of the Southwest.

During his tenure at St. Cloud State University, he fostered a student-centered environment, supported students, and student-led creativity. Students sponsored poetry nights, and Dr. Casanova and other faculty read poetry. Professor Casanova read his poem "Philosophy of Harmony," describing in his poem the Mexican cultural hang-over remedy of *menudo* made from tripe, chile, hominy, and salsa. He will be remembered as an active member of the Minnesota Network of Latinos in Higher Education (MNLHE), representing the central region in 2007 and 2008, and encouraging college graduation for students.

From behind the scenes, he was a tremendous support to Minnesota's dance groups, the Indigenous movement, and to individuals who were on their path. In 1998, when he first arrived in Minnesota, he drove from the St. Cloud Campus right after his last class to the Holy Rosary Church in Minneapolis to attend the Cuauhtemoc group dance for a 52-year-old's new fire ceremony. That night groups of people danced with their dance attire, held spoken word, and feasted on tamales. The circle of people was full because he also brought a number of his students to the ceremony. He advised about inter-tribal nation relations and respectful action. With the start of the Mexico women's moon dance with the obsidian pipe in 2007, he offered his Powwow drum without hesitation, if it was needed in Mexico. His community work created positive feelings for many. People who knew Casanova are aware that he left powerful footprints in his life journey. On February 7th, 2009, Cuauhtemoc of Minnesota danced in the Atwood Ballroom, St. Cloud Campus and led the memorial ceremony for Dr. Casanova in a tradition of *el abuelo*. This memorial ceremony was attended by hundreds who came to remember him. In testimony to his legacy, the Dr. Stephen Casanova Scholarship Fund website is under construction with the St. Cloud State University Foundation.

SYLVIA LEMUS SHARMA

Further Information

Dr. Stephen Casanova Scholarship Fund
SCSU Foundation
720 Fourth Avenue S.
St. Cloud, MN 56301

Further Reading

Cuauhtémoc Danzantes of Minnesota. www.cuauhtemoc.org.
National Association of Chicana and Chicano Studies. www.naccs.org.

CASCARONES

The Spanish word *cascarones* is literally translated in English as eggshells; however, the items are much more meaningful to Latino folklore when placed in a cultural and historic context. The standard definition of a *cascarón* is a chicken egg that has been properly cracked, emptied, and washed, and is subsequently filled with confetti. The hole is covered with colored tissue paper and the outside of the eggshell is painted in bright designs. Eggshells may be decorated with a wide range of supplies including food coloring and egg dyes, crayons, felt-tipped pens, or paint. Small seeds, pasta shapes, sequins, ribbons, lace, and scraps of felt are common choices for detailing. *Cascarones* may be decorated in solid colors, with designs or to resemble objects, animals, or icons. Caricatures of recognizable people are also extremely popular. They are made by individuals or families for private functions or sold in shops or street corners for public events.

Culturally, *cascarones* are party favors, specifically designed for unexpectedly cracking on people's heads concurrent with various activities of celebration. The recipient is then covered in a decorative shower of confetti. Because of the fragility of chicken eggs, the victim is rarely hurt, most often simply surprised. Many people believe that the confetti shower brings good luck to the recipient. Alternatively, they can be filled with candy or toys for children and used as small tokens or prizes. They are often used rambunctiously at many different kinds of celebrations such as festivals, holidays, weddings, anniversaries, fiestas, graduations, parades, religious ceremonies, birthday parties, and other special events. Similar to *piñatas*, *cascarones* are made to be destroyed. *Cascarones* are also made and sold for fundraisers by various church and school groups, especially around Easter, cultural

A basket of *cascarones*—eggshells filled with confetti that are used for celebrating Old Spanish Days in Santa Barbara, California. (Dreamstime.com)

celebrations such as Fiesta de San Antonio, or other city-wide parties, especially in the Southwest United States.

The decorated eggshells range in appearance from the very simple to elaborate or even *rasquache*. There is much variation regionally in differing communities of Latinos/as and other cultural and religious groups in the United States. *Cascarones* are not only painted solid colors or with swirling and striped designs, they can be decorated to look like various animals or flowers or with the logo of the local favorite sports team or many times like prominent historical figures. There are also *cascarones* with iconic religious or political symbols and those with faces resembling family members. The amount of creativity and detail is all up to the decorator's imagination. For example, in southern Arizona, the eggshell is decorated with paints, glue and glitter, or marking pens, often with elaborate and imaginative patterns. It is then placed on the end of a cone of newspaper covered with cut and fringed *papel de China*. It is made with meticulous attention to detail and then subsequently destroyed in an exuberant festival setting. Some, however, are kept as remembrances and displayed as art in individual homes or public galleries or shops.

The tradition of decorating eggs is not exclusively Latino, or even American. Many cultures include various traditions of colored eggs, especially centering on, but not exclusive to, the widely celebrated holiday of Easter. Even before Christianity came to Europe, however, eggs were viewed as a symbol of fertility and the rebirth of nature in springtime celebrations. Throughout the centuries, decorating eggs to give away as gifts became a very popular Easter tradition. Different styles of decorated eggs developed among the European nations. However, it was in Mexico that the confetti-filled eggs came to be known as the *cascarón*, or *cascarones*. Although the egg does not figure prominently in the solemn Mexican religious tradition of Easter or *Pascua*, *cascarones* are a staple in the *Carnaval* or Mardi Gras celebration that signals the beginning of Lent, another important marker of the Easter Season that has moved from a strictly religious event to a popular cultural activity.

It is generally thought that the tradition of decorated and stuffed eggshells began in the Manila Galleons in Asia. The eggs were filled with a perfumed powder and given as a gift. Marco Polo is credited with bringing the idea to Italy and the tradition eventually spread to other parts of Western Europe. While the origin of the modern-day *cascarón* is hard to accurately pinpoint due to the various likely historical influences, Carlotta, the wife of Emperor Maximilian, is most often credited for bringing decorated eggs filled with liquid perfume from Europe to Mexico during her husband's rule in Mexico in 1864. This particular tradition is believed to have begun in Italy, where men would douse women to whom they were attracted with the perfume-filled colored eggs as an indication of romantic interest. This behavior can still be witnessed amongst the young men and women engaging in innocent forms of flirtation with *cascarones* during fiestas, carnivals, wedding receptions, anniversaries, *quinceañeras* and other celebrations of merriment and union. While the interior make-up of the decorated eggshells may have morphed from this liquid model, the tradition of celebration, surprise and courting ritual remains in practice with the contemporary usage of *cascarones*.

Other early variations, connected to pre-Lenten celebrations, were filled with foul-smelling colored water and sealed with a plug of wax. These more unpleasant versions of *cascarones* were often used to replicate war games. There are historical accounts of the riotous Carnival celebrations in Mazatlán in the nineteenth century referencing gatherings known as *papaqui*, simulated battles that featured rival labor groups at war with *cascarones* as their ammunition. This specific tradition survives today in other Farewell to the Flesh or Fat Tuesday celebrations as party-goers, young and old, pelt each other with *cascarones* in an unrestrained display of assertion that can often involve friendly competition or rivalry for affection.

While it remains unknown exactly how or when the confetti-filled eggs specifically called *cascarones* were invented, it is widely believed that eventually the tradition of perfume and other manner of liquid was replaced with brightly colored strips of paper, hence creating the confetti egg. The Latino tradition of cracking *cascarones* on the heads of friends, rivals, family members, potential lovers, and even strangers has become a widely accepted form of amusement throughout the country, especially in the Southwest. They are especially popular in Mexican American or Latino celebrations. However, like so many other Latino traditions, it is beginning to merge with an overall sense of American tradition as well, having been used in so many different kinds of events and communities throughout history. *Cascarones* are no longer just a party favor, but have moved into the place of folk art, displayed in the homes of a diverse population of people from various cultural backgrounds.

ADRIANNA M. SANTOS

See also: Cuaresma (Lent); Paper Arts (Papel Picado, Papier Mâché, and Kites); Piñata; Quinceañera; Rascuache

Further Reading

Garza, Carmen Lomas. *Cascarones.* Copyright 2001 Hispanic Research Center, Arizona State University. All Rights Reserved. http://mati.eas.asu.edu:8421/ChicanArte/html_pages/garza17.html.

Southern Arizona Folk Arts. Mexican American Paperwork. *Cascarones.* August 11th, 2008. The University of Arizona. http://parentseyes.arizona.edu/folkarts/cascarones.html.

CASITAS

Casitas, literally meaning "little houses," refers to a type of housing structure found in the Caribbean that Puerto Ricans living in the diaspora have replicated in their new environment. These multi-use buildings have come to symbolize Puerto Rican cultural identity, particularly in New York City, where Puerto Ricans continue to struggle to retain their place in various neighborhoods. *Casitas* are typically named in honor of a hometown or famous person. The construction and history of *casitas* mirror the migration, settlement, and economic conditions of Puerto Ricans in major U.S. cities. Through the construction, naming, celebratory events housed within their walls, and in some cases demolition, *casitas* reveal processes of community formation, gentrification, and displacement.

Though primarily used as housing stock in the Caribbean, *casitas* in urban neighborhoods in the United States host neighborhood events such as holiday celebrations, family celebrations, and cultural events. The physical structure of *casitas* resembles houses found in the Caribbean as closely as possible. They are patterned after a form of architecture which dates back to the nineteenth and early twentieth centuries when increased trade and travel between the United States and the Caribbean resulted in the transformation and modernization of the region and its architecture. They are part of a family of balloon-frame wooden structures (shacks, bungalows, or cottages) which are built on stilts. The balloon-frame construction technique emerged as a result of the development of the sugar economy in the lowlands of Puerto Rico where this newer technique was part of the modernization of the island and a shift from an agricultural economy. *Casitas,* usually painted in bright colors, feature corrugated metal gable roofs, shuttered windows, and ample verandas. They are often surrounded by vegetable gardens. The architecture of *casitas* encompasses both the above transition to an industrial, capitalist economy through the vegetable garden, and the mixed cultural heritage of Puerto Rico, which is comprised of Tainos (a pre-Columbian Indigenous group), Africans, and Spaniards. While the roof and building designs resemble the Taino hut, the rituals associated with *casitas* reflect African heritage, and the presence of shutters and verandas recalls the arrival of Spanish culture on the island. Displaced agricultural laborers in the lowlands built *casitas* and vegetable gardens as a means of subsistence farming. With the passage of time and economic shifts in Puerto Rico and the United States, *casitas* have come to symbolize a folkloric past on the island, and a struggle against economic displacement for those living on the mainland.

From the 1950s to the mid-1970s, the Puerto Rican presence in New York City and Chicago increased due to U.S. economic intervention promoting migration from the island to the mainland for low-wage industrial jobs. This coincided with programs for urban renewal that displaced many working poor, a pattern which persists to the present. Forced to live under conditions of poverty and lack of municipal services such as adequate policing, Puerto Ricans constructed *casitas* as a means of place-making and beautification amid crumbling tenements and vacant lots. To this end, community members erected *casitas* in neighborhoods in the South Bronx, East Harlem (*el Barrio*), the Lower East Side (*Loisaida*), and Brooklyn. The case of *casitas* illustrates the tensions between the marginalized Puerto Rican community and the municipal government of New York City. While residents used the buildings as a place for social gathering and cultural events, city officials feared that they would become squatters' settlements and thus have demolished many built on municipal land; for example a group of eight units on 119th Street in *el Barrio* were demolished by the city in 1996.

Though *casitas* in the United States are primarily associated with the Puerto Rican community in New York, Chicago also houses one of the largest Puerto Rican populations living outside of the island, and thus Chicago Puerto Ricans have also adopted the *casita* tradition. On Chicago's Paseo Boricua, a cultural and business district in the heart of Humboldt Park, the most strongly established Puerto Rican neighborhood on Chicago's near northwest side, La Casita de Don Pedro serves as a cultural and physical anchor of Puerto Rican spatial identity. La Casita de Don Pedro differs from most of the *casitas* in New York City in that it is not built on abandoned property, but rather a private lot, which makes it less vulnerable to municipal efforts to remove ethnic identity markers as part of neighborhood redevelopment. In 1997, La Casita de Don Pedro, so named in honor of Puerto Rican independence leader Dr. Pedro Albizu Campos, was inaugurated on an empty lot on Paseo Boricua as the product of a joint venture between Pedro Albizu Campos High School and Architreasures Inc. Unlike some *casitas* that feature indoor plumbing as well as electricity, La Casita de Don Pedro features only electricity. It hosts many cultural events such as *bomba* and *plena* lessons which are free and open to the public. In Chicago, as in New York City, the *casita* not only marks Puerto Rican identity but also stands as a statement against gentrification which had already established a strong foothold in Humboldt Park by the late 1990s and continues in the present.

JENNIFER DOMINO RUDOLPH

See also: Adobe

Further Reading

Aponte-Parés, Luis. "Appropriating Place in Puerto Rican Barrios: Preserving Contemporary Urban Landscapes." In Arnold R. Alanen and Robert Z. Melnick, eds. *Preserving Cultural Landscapes in America*. Baltimore: Johns Hopkins University Press, 2000.

Sciorra, Joseph, and Martha Cooper. "'I Feel Like I'm in My Country': Puerto Rican Casitas in New York City." *The Drama Review* 34.4 (1990): 156–168.

Urban Agriculture. http://www.cityfarmer.org/casitas.html.

CASTELLÁNOZ, GENOVEVA (1932–)

Genoveva Castellánoz was born on November 18th, 1932, in Guanajuato, Mexico, and moved to the United States with her family to the Rio Grande Valley of Texas where she was trained in traditional arts including *colcha* quilting, crocheting, knitting, and embroidery, as well as making paper flowers. Her father soon began contract work and the family traveled as migrant workers to the Northwest. Shortly after her marriage, Castellánoz and her family settled out of the migrant stream in Nyssa, Oregon, where she soon became an important member of the community due to her knowledge of traditional practices, including many traditional arts.

Castellánoz served the area's Mexican American community in a variety of ways, most importantly as the person they would go to for paper and wax flowers for baptisms, weddings, and *quinceañeras*. For the latter, it is traditional that the young woman wear a *corona*, or tiara, a central item of the *quinceañera* event. Because of her skill and because there was simply no one else to make the *coronas*, Castellánoz became the go-to person, and people came from hundreds of miles to request a *corona* for a wedding or a *quinceañera*. But aside from her artistry, she is also a recognized folk healer and community scholar assisting local and regional folklorists in documenting the traditional arts of the Mexican American community in the Northwest.

Genoveva Castellánoz looks at an art exhibit called "People, Places and Perceptions: A Look at Contemporary Northwest Latino Art" in July 2005 at the Maryhill Museum in Goldendale, Washington. The exhibit celebrated Latino artists of the Pacific Northwest and showed how living there had permanently changed their work. (AP/Wide World Photos)

A traditional folk artist, Castellánoz is also known as a community scholar. In 1987, the National Endowment for the Arts recognized Castellánoz by awarding her the National Heritage Award. In 2011, folklorist Joanne Mulcahey published *Remedios: The Healing Life of Eva Castellánoz*, documenting Castellánoz's contributions to the traditional arts and chronicling a life of healing from Texas to Oregon and back. Castellánoz's work as a *curandera*, folk healer, relies on the knowledge passed down from her grandmother whose Indigenous knowledge weaves a holistic health perspective with other traditional herbal lore. Castellánoz is also known for working with youth and often demonstrates the making of the *corona* in festivals and school programs.

NORMA E. CANTÚ

See also: Matrimonio and Pedida de Mano (Marriage and Engagement); Quinceañera

Further Reading

Mulcahy, Joanne B. *Remedios: The Healing Art of Eva Castellánoz*. San Antonio, TX: Trinity University Press, 2010.

CHALUPAS

Chalupas are small corn cakes shaped like little boats and filled with meat, beans, or other foods; they are a popular snack all over Mexico. For most Mexicans, *chalupas* are associated with the central part of the country, Mexico City, and the state of Mexico, but more precisely with the states of Puebla, Tlaxcala, and Hidalgo. *Chalupas*, however, are a popular street food all over the country and can be found in many variations in most city streets and even restaurants in Mexico. The traditional *chalupa*, that of the city of Cholula in the state of Puebla, is a small, somewhat thick pie of corn dough, fried in hot oil, and dressed with many garnishes and sometimes meat. For the untrained eye and palate, the *chalupa* may seem like a *sope* or a huarache, or even a thick tortilla, but they are different enough with a distinctive flavor and preparation to justify giving them different names. One of the main differences is the size and shape of the *chalupas*, which are smaller and thicker than *sopes*, with an elongated shape with a shallow center that resembles a little boat or *chalupa*—thus the name.

Like little boats, the *chalupas* are then loaded with all kinds of garnishes, although traditional *chalupas* from Cholula are dressed only with salsa, shredded lettuces, and crumbled cheese. This cheese can be either fresh or *añejo*, and the salsa can be either a green tomatillo–based or red tomato–based salsa. Other variations of the *chalupas*, depending on the region or the restaurant, could have cheese and lettuce, shredded chicken, pork, or chorizo in addition to the salsa. However, the simplicity of the fresh, crispy masa, fresh salsa, and cheese, the classical combination, really complements the ingredients, creating a balance of flavors and making the *chalupa* a perfect snack to accompany drinks or a glass of cold beer. The *chalupas* are also favorite hors d'oeuvres and in many restaurants and bars they could be served as complimentary *botanas* (Mexican tapas or snacks).

Other variations of the *chalupas* are more elaborated and include a bean spread, salsa, chicken or chorizo, as well as cheese, lettuce, sour cream, or even guacamole on top. Some even include marinated pork and other vegetables, like the *chalupas* from Chiapas, which, according to some authors, are topped with pork, carrots, and cabbage. The basic *chalupas* are small and shallow and fried in hot oil until they are crispy on the outside, but not hard or undercooked inside. Then they are spread with a bean paste, salsa, or guacamole, and topped with shredded meat and grated cheese, and finished with shredded lettuce or *pico de gallo*. The combination of the crispiness of the pie with the creaminess of the bean paste, guacamole, or sour cream is a rich layer of flavors that work well without overpowering each other. Inexpensive, simple, and delicious, *chalupas* are a classic Mexican appetizer that has roots in pre-Hispanic cooking and is a testimony to the versatility of corn or maize, the grain widely cultivated in the Americas, which was originally domesticated in Mexico over eight thousand years ago.

The ancient native cultures of modern-day Mexico discovered and transformed a wild native grass called *teosinte* into the first maize, a cereal they called the grain of humanity. After the domestication of corn, the crop spread north and south of Mexico and from group to group because of exchange or commerce or because it moved along with the nomadic and semi-nomadic groups who migrated and first colonized the continent. These early exchanges made it possible for different varieties of corn to emerge and thrive due to the grain's adaptability. At the same time, the high levels of production of the plant favored an explosion of the population. The domestication of corn is believed to have had a fundamental influence in the shift of Mesoamerican cultures from nomadic clans of hunters and gatherers to more sedentary and complex societies able to cultivate their own food and therefore capable of living and prospering in any region they wanted.

By the time of the arrival of the Spaniards in Mexico in the sixteenth century, many different types of corn had already been developed; a series of techniques to prepare corn for human consumption had also been developed by the sixteenth century, and the Aztecs and other native cultures were already preparing tortillas in the same ways they can still be prepared today in some rural parts of Mexico and other communities in Central America—by cooking the corn with lime, grinding the grains into a dough on a stone, and patting this dough into round tortillas or thin patties, and cooking them on a comal (flat griddle). Numerous accounts of the conquistadores and early chroniclers relate the importance of tortillas for the Indigenous cultures and the early European settlers. Soon after their arrival in Mexico, the Spaniards introduced to the Americas a variety of foods previously unknown in the continent, including wheat, poultry, pork, beef, and milk, which were used along with native products and techniques.

Tortillas, the way we know them today, were mostly the food of the people, but Fray Bernardino de Sahagún has recorded several different variations of tortillas that the Aztec nobility ate, for example *veiltexcalli*, which were big, white, thin, and soft tortillas; *tlaxcalpacholli*, a white or brown, very tasty tortilla sometimes made with blue corn; *quauhtlacualli*, a white, thick, rough tortilla sometimes made with young corn and called *tlaxcales*; *tlaxcalmimilli*, small, rounded cakes, the size of a fist, similar to *chalupas*, sometimes filled with a bean, fava bean, or split pea paste; and *tlacepaollilaxcalli*, a puff pastry that was considered a delicacy. Tortilla means little torta, or cake, or patty in Spanish. Because of the Mexican influence in the United States, particularly of its cuisine and its language, what most people call tortilla in North America is the generic name given to the Mexican unleavened bread made with corn masa or wheat flour.

Also, because of this influence, many Mexican foods related to tortillas are popular in the United States, which due to the proliferation of Mexican and Mexican-inspired restaurants all over the country are well known and consumed nationwide. This is the case also of *chalupas*, which are typical appetizers in many Mexican restaurants and almost inevitable items in most books and websites on Mexican cooking. But the popularity of *chalupas*, and the reason they entered the mainstream American consciousness and vocabulary, is owed mostly to the introduction of an item of the same name by the fast-food chain Taco Bell. The Taco Bell *chalupa* is very different from the original Mexican snack and is similar to a taco, except that it uses a thick fried tortilla as a shell and is filled with seasoned ground beef, sour cream, salsa, shredded lettuces, cheese, and diced tomatoes, which is described by Taco Bell as crispy, flakey, chewy, and tasty, but remains a very distant relative of the Mexican *chalupa*.

RAFAEL HERNÁNDEZ

See also: Maíz; Sahagún, Bernardino de; Salsa (Sauce); Tacos; Tortilla

Further Reading

Benitez, Ana M. de. *Pre-Hispanic Cooking/Cocina Prehispánica*. Mexico: Ediciones Euroamericanas, 1974.

Galinat, Walton. "El Origen del Maíz: El Grano de la Humanidad. The Origen of Maize: Grain of Humanity." *Economic Botany* 49, no. 1 (January–March, 1995): 3–12.

Quintana, Patricia, and Ignacio Urquiza. *The Taste of Mexico*. New York: Stewart, Tabori & Chang, 1986.

Zaslavsky, Nancy. *A Cook's Tour of Mexico: Authentic Recipes from the Country's Best Open Air Markets, City Fondas, and Home Kitchens*. New York: St. Martin's Press, 1995.

CHAMPURRADO

Champurrado is a thick, creamy, sweet porridge made with corn, chocolate, and water, or milk. This drink is just another way in which Mexicans utilize corn, the grain that originated in Mexico thousands of years ago and has become a staple food in many parts of the world, from Africa where it has been one of the most important food crops since its introduction by the Portuguese in the sixteenth century, to Europe where it is consumed even in traditional cuisines like Italian, to Asia as well as, of course, North America, where it is traditionally served for breakfast as corn flakes, or grits, or as garnish in salads, and a side dish in many meals. Corn is the grain of a widely cultivated plant, which was originally domesticated over eight thousand years ago. The ancient native cultures of what is today

Mexico discovered and transformed a wild native grass called *teosinte* into the first maize. After the domestication of corn, the crop spread north and south of Mesoamerica and from group to group because of exchange, commerce, or because it moved along with the nomadic and seminomadic groups who migrated and first colonized the continent. These early exchanges made it possible for different varieties of corn to emerge and thrive due to the grain's adaptability. At the same time, the high levels of production of the plant favored an explosion of the native population.

The domestication of corn is believed to have had a fundamental influence in the shift of Mesoamerican cultures from nomadic clans of hunters and gatherers to more sedentary and complex societies able to produce their own food and therefore capable of living and prospering in any region they wanted. Corn remains the main staple food of Mexico where it is consumed in soups and stews, as a vegetable, or in traditional dishes, like tamales and *pozole*, as well as beverages such as *atole* and *champurrado*. *Atole*, or *atolli* in Nahuatl, is an aromatic drink made with corn dough and milk or water and sugar, honey, and other aromatic spices such as cinnamon or vanilla. The traditional *atolli* among pre-Columbian peoples was made only with water since they did not have cattle and it was often savory and flavored with herbs and chili pepper; occasionally it was sweetened with honey and fruits or berries. With the arrival of the Europeans the drink was adapted to the Spanish taste, and milk and sugar were added.

Similarly, chocolate used to be prepared by pre-Columbian societies with water and spiced with chili peppers, but like *atole*, chocolate also was adapted to a more European taste. What we call *champurrado* today is the combination of these two traditional drinks adapted to a more modern palate. We can say, then, that *champurrado* is a thicker, creamy *atole* with chocolate or a chocolate-flavored *atole*. The traditional *champurrado* is still prepared with corn dough dissolved in water instead of milk and sweetened with *piloncillo* (hard, unrefined brown sugar in the shape of a cone), and to make the drink thick enough, it is whipped while it simmers with a *molinillo*, a wooden whisk or spatula. The most common method of preparing *champurrado* is the following. Dissolve the dough in half the water or milk, preferably by hand; strain in the rest of the liquid and mix well. Bring to a boil and then add the *piloncillo*, chocolate, and a drop of vanilla; simmer for a while. While simmering, whip the liquid with the *molinillo* by placing it in between your palms and rubbing them rhythmically up and down until the chocolate and *piloncillo* have dissolved. Berries and other fruits can be added, if desired, at the end.

Champurrado is a traditional drink in most homes for Christmas and other holidays, particularly popular during *las posadas*, the festivities celebrated with carols, prayers, and food every night for nine days before Christmas to remember Mary and Joseph's journey to Bethlehem. This drink can also be served for special occasions and even for breakfast or for *merienda* (a snack meal in the late afternoon) with *churros*, *buñuelos*, or tamales, or any other type of pastries or sweet bread; not only is it smooth and delicious, but very fulfilling and packed with calories, making it an ideal breakfast. According to the first Spanish missionaries, the Aztecs used to drink a bowl of *atole* for breakfast, which was enough to keep them satisfied all morning. In Mexico today *champurrado* is also common for birthday parties where it is served with cake, tamales, and pastries. But *champurrado* is also sold in the morning in most street corners in Mexico City and other urban centers, typically together with tamales or *guajolotas* (a tamale in a roll) as a popular working-class breakfast as well as in popular fairs and kermises.

Although the traditional way of preparing the *champurrado* calls for a variety of ingredients and fresh corn dough mixed by hand and whipped with a *molinillo*, most people today can make *champurrado* with an *atole* instant mix sold pre-packed in most stores and supermarkets in Mexico and in special stores in the United States. The most popular brand of pre-packed mix is Maizena and it comes in different flavors from pineapple and strawberry to *cajeta* (caramel) and, of course, chocolate to make *champurrado*. This brand of cornstarch is so popular that sometimes *atole* and *champurrado* are referred to as *maizena*, as in "Could I offer you a strawberry *maizena*?"

RAFAEL HERNÁNDEZ

See also: Aztec Empire; Maíz

Further Reading

Galinat, Walton. "El Origen del Maíz: El Grano de la Humanidad. The Origen of Maize: Grain of Humanity." *Economic Botany* 49, no. 1 (January–March, 1995): 3–12.

Quintana, Patricia, and Ignacio Urquiza. *The Taste of Mexico*. New York: Stewart, Tabori & Chang, 1986.

Soustelle, Jacques. *Daily Life of the Aztecs on the Eve of the Spanish Conquest*. Stanford, CA: Stanford University Press, 1970.

Zaslavsky, Nancy. *A Cook's Tour of Mexico: Authentic Recipes from the Country's Best Open Air Markets, City Fondas, and Home Kitchens*. New York: St. Martin's Press, 1995.

CHARMS

Charms are objects, substances, or incantations that are ascribed a supernatural virtue believed to be capable of influencing the mind, body, or spirit. They function as an aspect of folk belief, can be found all over the world, and are as varied and unique as the cultures which use them. Charms can consist of a nearly endless assortment of things, including dirt, bones, herbs, essential oils, gems, crystals, coins, rings, pendants, necklaces, and so forth. They can be kept close to the person to create a stronger connection or secreted away so as not to be seen or touched by others so that energy is not inadvertently transferred. In many Latino cultures, charms are commonly associated with religious beliefs like folk Catholicism, Santería, Espiritismo, Palo Monte, and other belief systems.

The terms "charm," "amulet," and "talisman" are often used synonymously, but cultures may differentiate between them. Some state that charms are for luck, amulets are for protection, and talismans are used for power. Originally, the word "charm" derived from the French word *charme*, which previously referred to song and later applied to the way a blessing or incantation was sung. Spoken charms began to be used in conjunction with objects and the term started to define the objects as well. On the other hand, the term "amulet" has its roots in the Latin word *amuletum*, which referred to an object that was used as a protective device. The linguistic origins of "talisman" are in the Arabic word *tilasm*, and in Greek *telesma*, and it stood for initiation into a mystery or completion of an act. Gradually, amulets and talismans began to be used interchangeably, and later the term "charms" incorporated all definitions cited above.

Charms are believed to be governed by the principles of sympathetic magic, which stipulates that there exists a connection between a particular charm and a person or event due to inherent similarities. It therefore may be called an imitative charm if deemed to have inherent similarities; or if it is derived from an established contact, it is called a contagious charm. By understanding and exploiting this sympathetic connection, a person can be influenced or an event can be manipulated for a desired outcome. For instance, a person's private possession, such as an item of jewelry, can be used to assert some sort of control over her because an established connection between the two has already been forged. For example, a gold coin can be used as a charm to bring about financial prosperity because of the millennia-old association that gold has had with wealth.

Common forms of charms found across much of Latin America are *milagros*, meaning "miracles" in Spanish. These very popular protection charms in folk Catholicism are small metal talismans, ranging in size from half an inch to several inches, and are often found hammered to crosses kept in the home. They can depict a wide variety of images that hold a specific significance, from farm animals to books to body parts. *Milagros* of animals can be used in asking for help in

Milagros (charms) being sold at a street stall to the faithful outside the church of Our Lady of Guadalupe in Mexico City. (Francesca Braghetta/Dreamstime.com)

healing sick livestock or for livestock to be fertile. *Milagros* of a body part, such as a heart, might represent a prayer for the healing of a heart condition or for help with matters of love. The use of *milagros* is often connected with fulfilling a vow, known as *promesas* or *mandas*. This is where a person will ask a favor of a saint, and once it is granted the person will make a pilgrimage to the shrine of that saint, taking *milagros* to leave there as a sign of gratitude and devotion, often pinning them to the clothing of saint statues, such as the Virgin Mary. In cathedrals and churches of Latino neighborhoods, it is very common to see *milagros* hanging by little red ribbons or threads from the altars and to see small prayers of thanks written on a piece of paper and added to a shrine.

Charms are inherently tied to cultural contexts, and the power they possess becomes void if pulled out of that context, but there are certain charms, such as crystals and gems, that are found across diverse cultures. These crystals and gems are considered by many to be naturally endowed with metaphysical properties specific to each stone. It is common practice, however, to increase the efficacy of these charms through cultural specific incantations or rituals. A good example of this are *collares de Santería*, also known as *elekes*. They are necklaces commonly made out of glass beads or small crystals, and each necklace provides the wearer with the blessing and protection of a particular *orisha,* meaning "saint." The components of the necklaces are strung to correspond with an *orisha*, and a series of rituals must be followed in making the necklace and bestowing it to the wearer. Certain dictates must also be followed in where and how it is worn. Because of the mandates that such charms have to follow to be effective, many people choose to acquire their charms through spiritual merchants knowledgeable about the cultural attributions of each charm, how to charge them, and the best means by which to use them.

In Latino communities, when it comes to the acquisition and proper use of charms, people tend to consult with *curanderas*, "medicine women" (folk healers), or in more urban environments, with the clerks at local *botánicas* or *hierberías*, which are small, Latino-run, independent establishments that carry an assortment of folk and religious paraphernalia available for purchase. The clerks at these establishments have a breadth of knowledge concerning spiritual charm traditions. They sell a wide variety of charms, many of their own creation, made from essential oils, herbs, stones, and in some instances, with substances like dirt from graveyards. Many of these clerks are available for spiritual consultations or simply to offer guidance in choosing the right charm for the right purpose, be it wealth, luck, or love.

In recent years, there has been a growing trend of mass-producing charms and selling them prefabricated. These commercial products are not considered to be as powerful as handmade charms, since no rituals are performed to spiritually charge them and they tend to be made of lesser quality materials. But due to the fact that they are more economical, they have become increasingly common and can easily be found for purchase in *botánicas*, via mail orders, or at internet retailers.

Eric César Morales

See also: Botánicas; Folk Medicine; Mandas and Juramentos; Milagros; Saints (Santos); Santería

Further Reading

Long, Carolyn Morrow. *Spiritual Merchants: Religion, Magic, and Commerce*. Knoxville: University of Tennessee Press, 2001.

Polk, Patrick Arthur, and Donald Cosentino. *Botánica Los Angeles: Latino Popular Religious Art in the City of Angels*. Los Angeles: UCLA Fowler Museum of Cultural History, 2004.

Webster, Richard. "Llewellyn Worldwide—Articles: Amulets, Talismans, & Charms." http://www.llewellyn.com/journal/article/583.

CHARREADA

The *charreada* (derived from *charro*, or cowboy) is a transnational equestrian sporting event that originated in Mexico in the colonial period. Popular with the Mexican American community in the borderlands, it is frequently performed in the United States in large rodeo arenas. It is characterized by specialized maneuvers that feature the dexterity of the *charro* with respect to horsemanship and cattle management. The *charreada* is linked to the management of livestock, which required enormous physical strength, control, and discipline on the part of the early *vaqueros*, or cattle workers, who toiled among large herds in much the same way as contemporary cowboys do today.

The arrival in the Americas in the sixteenth century of horses and cattle from the Iberian Peninsula resulted in significant changes in the lives of the Indigenous communities that encountered these new, previously unknown animals. The *charreada*, with its carefully orchestrated public aspect, stemmed from the colonized people's initial contact with large animals. It was also linked to Spain's colonization endeavors, social control, and economic development through ranching, land appropriation, and agriculture. From these closely aligned activities, performance events emerged that displayed the talents of highly skilled equestrians, or *charros*, whose presence continues today even in geographic areas beyond Mexico, such as the southwestern part of the United States.

The *charreada* came to comprise highly organized performance events that sought to please large audiences that had high expectations of well-executed horsemanship maneuvers. A premium on style and elegance was expected rather than brute strength or stamina. The *charreada* became a dynamic event for the public display of ranching traditions associated with Mexico and its borderlands regions. Bravery, manual dexterity in the handling of livestock, ostentation in costuming, and the public demonstration of these and other virtues underscore these traditional equestrian events. The *charreada* comprises the following distinct but closely related events:

- *cala de caballos*—A maneuver intended to demonstrate the horses' aptitude in learning the most basic commands of the *charreada* and the *charros'* ability to bring horses to an abrupt stop from a full-speed gallop.
- *piales*—The competitor brings a horse to a complete stop by roping its rear legs only.
- *coleada*—The *charro* brings down a running bull by grabbing the animal's tail by the hand in full gallop.

- *jineteo de toros*—Riding a bull to a point where the bull simply stops bucking.
- *terna*—Three *charros* alternately demonstrate their abilities with the *reata* (lasso) to rope a bull.
- *jineteo de yeguas*—Wild mare riding.
- *manganas*—Wild mare lassoing, which is accomplished on foot or while riding horseback.
- *paso de la muerte*—The culminating spectacle of the *charreada,* the *paso de la muerte* is a dangerous maneuver requiring the *charro* to dismount from one horse and then remount another mare while in continuous motion around the arena. More than any of the other events, the *paso* demonstrates the rider's courage, athletic ability, and expert timing. A single competitor performs most of these events. In certain maneuvers, teams of three equestrians accomplish the feats. Competitors in the *charreada* win points by demonstrating dexterity in the least amount of time and with the most grace and efficiency.

Mexico's paintings and archival photographs record a stunning array of images that depict men on horseback executing ranching activities in the open range, the closed corral, or in military campaigns. Some artists, especially nineteenth-century painters such as Francisco Alfaro, Manuel Serrano, and Ernesto Icaza, were particularly adept at portraying Mexican equestrians involved in such activities as camaraderie, athleticism, and playfulness within the *charreada* events. Their portrayals of Mexican equestrians highlight the elegance and decorum of these activities by paying careful attention to the accoutrements of the competitors' costuming and the associated regalia of the equally caparisoned horse.

Although women's presence is largely absent in the visual record—that is in the paintings and photographs depicting nineteenth- and early-twentieth-century equestrian events—they constitute an important and significant aspect of the events of *charrerías* in the United States and Mexico. Women on horseback in the nineteenth century appear in elegant, if subdued, attire and, for the most part, sit on motionless horses in the lithographic images of Karl Nebel and in elite portraits.

Daniel Franco, 8, stops his horse in a horse-reining event during a *charreada* (Mexican rodeo) at the San Antonio Charro Ranch in San Antonio, Texas. The *charreada* began in the 16th century. (AP/Wide World Photos)

Similarly, the photographic record of the Mexican Revolutionary period (1910–1917) depicts women on horseback but not necessarily riding at full gallop or maneuvering such large animals in a performance, exhibition, or wartime settings. However, women have become key performers in the *charreada* through their participation in the events of the *escaramuza*. *Escaramuza*, which may be loosely translated as "skirmish," is a deliberately gendered word used to describe differences between the historically all-male activities of the sport and those of the women in the sport. Recognition of women in the sport came in 1989 with the official sanctioning by the Mexican Federation of Charros. Thereafter, a formalization of rules determined by *charras* (the female equivalents of *charros*) guided women's participation in the *charreada*. As the sport attracted more women, select events evolved into specialized maneuvers on horseback. These complex routines departed significantly from showy pageants and carousels (equestrian performances set to music), and led to an overt athleticism required for the stylish handling of horses. Women dressed in fine costumes are able to provide skillful horseback-riding performances today. The extraordinary competitiveness and skill of *escaramuza* teams constitute a popular part of the spectacle of the *charreada*.

Costuming is another significant component of the *charreada*. Rules provide precise descriptions of the required pieces of clothing worn by both men and women for the various activities of the performances. It is worth noting that clothing worn for events in the arena differs from that of more formal *charrería* affairs. The required costume for women participating in *charreadas* is dramatically different from the dusty, often muddy, environment of the *lienzo*, or alley, and the *rueda*, or ring, since the adjacent quarters house horses, competitors, and assistants.

The so-called "Adelita" costume, an ensemble consisting of a long dress, knee-high boots, sombrero, and full ruffled blouse, is designed to fully cover the *charra's* body to preserve modesty and impart propriety. It is presumably derived from the costuming choice of the *soldaderas* of the Mexican Revolution. From the very beginning, women's participation lent an air of decorum to the equestrian sport. Nevertheless, female equestrians always underscored and demonstrated their horse-handling skills and have included both young girls and seasoned veterans. *Escaramuzas* must perform in teams of at least eight *charras*, and their performances begin with the *desfile*, or parade, followed by ten events that are performed in patterns that demonstrate precision, expert timing, and the women's competent handling of their horses. Moreover, women are required to ride side-saddle, which is considered more difficult than riding astride as the male equestrians do. Most importantly, it should also be noted that the patterns of the *escaramuza* events must flow smoothly and continuously without interruptions or glaring transitions. The *escaramuza* riders perform their exercises while mounted on a single horse, and there is never any contact with bulls or any other horses. In addition, their routines must be accomplished in a very short period of time relative to that of the male performers. The audiences expect a great deal of expertise and skill from the women performing in the *escaramuzas*.

The key differences between the *charreada* events performed in Mexico and the United States lie in the expectations that audiences have of this very specialized cultural event. These expectations may differ because the more knowledge a person has regarding the various complex components of the *charreada*, the more he/she is likely to enjoy it. Prior experience on the part of the audience with respect to *charreada* events is therefore very important. The *charreada* requires specialized knowledge regarding the quality and the skill of both horse and rider for its complete enjoyment.

ROLAND RODRÍGUEZ

See also: Charros (Horsemen); Vaquero

Further Reading

Chávez, Octavio. *La Charrería: Tradición Mexicana.* 2nd ed. México, D.F.: Casa Pedro Domecq, 1993.

Islas Escárcega, Leovigildo, and Rodolfo García Bravo y Olivera. *Diccionario y Refranero Charro.* México, D.F.: Edamex, 1992.

Lepe, José I. *Diccionario Enciclopédico sobre Asuntos Ecuestres e Hípicos.* México, D.F.: Editorial Porrua, S.A. 1972.

Rincón Gallardo, Carlos. *El Libro del Charro Mexicano.* 3rd ed. México, D.F.: Editorial Porrúa, 1960.

Sands, Kathleen Mullen. *Charrería Mexicana.* Tucson: The University of Arizona Press, 1993.

Valero Silva, José. *El Libro de la Charrería.* México, D.F.: Banco BCH, S.N.C., 1985.

CHARROS (HORSEMEN)

Although the term *charro* originated in Salamanca, Spain, where it designated inhabitants of the rural areas of that region, it is now perhaps more widely known as referring to the traditional Mexican horseman. The creation and evolution of the Mexican *charro* would not have been possible if the Spanish conquistadores had not brought with them to New Spain (colonial Mexico which included today's American Southwest) their horses and other livestock. Nevertheless, the relative isolation of the farms and ranches with respect to New Spain's cultural centers allowed the Mexican *charro* to develop and progress into a unique figure considered to be entirely Mexican. Consequently, the *charro* has become a symbol of national identity and pride in that country.

In the case of Mexican Americans, this ethnic group has inherited the *charro* tradition from its cultural connections to Mexico and the Colonial Period of New Spain (1521–1821), which included the American Southwest. Today, Mexican American *charros* can be seen in southwestern parades such as the New Year's Rose Parade in Pasadena, California, and the Spanish Fiesta Parade in Santa Barbara, California, the first week of August. Other *charro* parades are also common in the states of Texas, New Mexico, and Arizona. There are also *charro* clubs throughout the Southwest, which meet regularly and are ready to display their horses, their *charro* finery, and skills during annual parades and festivals.

The typical *charro* is depicted as a self-reliant figure that embodies physical strength in addition to being capable and knowledgeable in all matters regarding

A Mexican cowboy rides a horse in a rural rodeo arena in Los Banos, California. (iStockPhoto.com)

ranching, farming and cattle raising. He is, of course, primarily known for being an exceptional horseman. Later, the *charro* would be called upon to participate in the war for Mexican independence and other important wars and battles in Mexico's history. It is during these periods of conflict that *la charra* becomes particularly important. The *charras* regularly followed their male counterparts into battle and served as female companions and nurses for many of the soldiers and wounded men.

The romanticized image of the *charro*, which probably solidified around the time of Mexico's independence or shortly thereafter, also includes the idea of the *charro* as principal defender of the homeland in addition to being a perfect gentleman. This romantic image is the one that has been reproduced and idealized in much of Mexican literature, music, and art. There are of course *charros* who do not live up to these ideals, and they are generally depicted as the villains in their respective representations in Mexican cultural production.

As wars and changes in political power left farms destroyed or proprietors dispossessed of their lands, many Mexicans gradually began to migrate towards the cities and, as a result, the traditional *charro* began to disappear. In his place, however, the practitioner of the national sport, *la charreada* or *la corrida*, developed as a tribute to the horsemen who had been so important throughout Mexican history. In this sport, typical activities associated with the *charro* are perfected and performed before a live audience. The first association of *charros* was formed in 1921, and there are now more than 300 such associations which seek to maintain the cultural practices of the Mexican *charro*. Every year a conference and national championship are held to remember, honor and practice the important Mexican tradition of *la charrería*.

Traditional Variations

The term *charro* refers in general to any Mexican horseman or rider that practices all the activities typically associated with raising livestock, cattle herding, or farming. There are, however, specific categories that designate more clearly the position and duties of the various *charros*. The *vaquero*, for example, is usually responsible for carrying out the instructions of his superiors with regard to moving and herding the livestock as well as general care taking and maintenance. The *caporal*, on the other hand, would be held accountable for the livestock as the *vaqueros* would typically report to him and be under his authority. The *caporal* may also have limited veterinary knowledge that would allow him to perceive and remedy the livestock's minor health issues. The *picador*, or *amansador*, was generally charged with taming and training the horses, as well as overseeing their care. The *administrador* had the task of overseeing the entire ranch or farm, including managing issues related to both the livestock and any crops being cultivated on the property. He would typically give the *caporal* his instructions on moving and herding the livestock. The prototypical charro is the *hacendado*. This kind of *charro* owns his farm or ranch and takes direct responsibility for overseeing its day-to-day management. He is intimately acquainted with and capable of performing all the tasks and chores necessary to successfully manage and maintain his farm. Another class of *hacendado*, on the other hand, would prefer to live in the city, only occasionally visiting his ranch in the country. Although he may own the property, he leaves its general management to others.

La Charrería

As previously noted, the traditional *charro* performed all the activities related to maintaining a ranch or farm. As this lifestyle developed into a national pastime, however, several skills were emphasized over the others: *lazar*, *colear*, *jinetear*, and *calar*. *Lazar* refers to the skill of roping or lassoing various kinds of animals by the foot, head or tail. *Colear* is similar to *lazar* in that this skill requires one to rope a moving bull by the tail and to consequently bring one's horse to an abrupt stop, causing the bull to lose its footing and fall to the ground. *Jinetear* refers to a rider mounting an untamed mare or bull and attempting to remain mounted for as long as possible. *Calar* indicates that a rider will control his mount using only the reins. In a typical *charreada* or *corrida* the riders, which may include women in a slightly more limited variety of tasks, are judged by the degree of skill and artistry with which they perform the above-mentioned tasks. The *charreada* is a sport still widely practiced in Mexico and is similar to the American rodeo.

LAURA M. QUIJANO

See also: Charreada; Vaquero

Further Reading

Bishko, Charles Julian. "The Peninsular Background of Latin American Cattle Ranching." *The Hispanic American Historical Review*. 32.4 (1952): 491–515.

Islas Carmona, Roberto. "The Charro's Apparel." *El arte de la charrería* 99 (1967): 26–38.

Islas Escárcega, Leovigildo. "Historical Synthesis of Charrería." *El arte de la charrería* 99 (1967): 19–21.

Nájera-Ramírez, Olga. "Engendering Nationalism: Identity, Discourse, and the Mexican Charro." *Anthropological Quarterly* 67.1 (1994): 1–14.

CHICANO/A ART AND FOLKLORE

At the height of the Civil Rights Movement during the late 1960s and 1970s in the United States of America, several minority groups of color asserted pride in the legacies of their historical heritages and cultures; they also demanded political liberation from the oppression of Anglo-dominant, materialistic power structures. Ethnic Mexicans (primarily Mexican American students) of this era made these assertions and demands via documents, such as *El Plan Espiritual de Aztlán* (1969) and *El Plan de Santa Bárbara* (1969). Those documents represented the beginning stages of the Chicano movement—*el movimiento*, which moved the people to consider the importance of a cultural nationalist ideology.

Cultural nationalism was supposed to function as the common denominator for a diversity that existed among ethnic Mexicans from varying social classes and backgrounds. *El Plan Espiritual de Aztlán* (1969) promoted cultural nationalism as key to organizing this diverse group of people, and it was supposed to "transcend all religious, political, class, and economic factions or boundaries." The document also specified that culture was at the center of this newly envisioned nationalism, for from it emerged the "values of our people" that would "strengthen our identity" and provide the "moral backbone of the movement" (*El Plan Espiritual de Aztlán* 1969). This manifesto proclaimed that all Chicano writers, poets, musicians, and artists should produce literature and art that was appealing to the people and that related to their revolutionary culture.

Chicano/a art has been and continues to be one of the most powerful manifestations of self-determination. The work of early Chicano/a artists served the very important purpose of presenting history from an insider's perspective, thus achieving a level of authenticity and truth that was otherwise unavailable from the mainstream sources of a dominant society—a society that had been and continues to be very anti–Hispano-Mexican. From these artists, people were made aware of both ancient and modern Mexican history as well as contemporary Chicano history as it evolved. The audiences, for the many prolific artists of the 1960s–1970s, consisted of *la gente del barrio*—or the people from the local communities. Because of this, the art work not only served the purpose of expressing the artists' thoughts but also of educating as well as empowering the people. The affirmation of Mexican cultural values became visible through the images, themes, and motifs that celebrated the folk traditions, beliefs, tales, and practices that had been and continue to be passed down orally (or by observation and everyday practice).

The word "folklore" was first coined by the British scholar William Thoms in 1846 to give a new name to the study of ancient customs and traditions. In the North American tradition, folklore can be divided into different categories: oral lore, material lore, and behavioral/cognitive lore. Oral lore includes songs, lullabies, games, poetry, jokes, tales, riddles, proverbs, myths, and sayings. Material lore consists of jewelry, puppets, quilts, clothes, musical instruments, home decorations, and even recipes or food preparations. Behavioral/cognitive lore refers to family and community celebrations as well as the ways in which a person's own thoughts take shape. These categories also correspond to Mexican and Chicano folklore respectively.

In fact, one cannot begin to understand Chicano/a art without examining the ways in which it is deeply rooted in Indigenous iconography as well as Mexican folklore. Over the past several decades, these roots have extensively multiplied, so that now people can study Chicano folklore in addition to Mexican folklore—as each cultural experience offers uniquely heterogeneous variations. The heterogeneity of Chicanos, for example, is influenced by both the Mexican and Anglo-American cultures in varying degrees. Indeed, as Felipe de Ortega y Gasca (1978) has indicated, Chicanos may manifest behaviors drawn from either Mexican or Anglo-American cultures. Behaviors associated with the latter arise, primarily, due to environmental contact and the oppressive conditions that accompany it. Ortega y Gasca also pointed out that Chicano folklore traditions, in addition to having mixed elements of primarily Mexican and Anglo customs, also have the potential to interactively mesh languages, such as Spanish and English, and one can even add the Indigenous tongues, such as Náhuatl or Mayan among several others.

The result, a Chicano culture, according to de Ortega y Gasca, is neither a synthesis of cultures nor a hybrid culture in itself but is rather "purposive in its tenacity to develop its own cultural identity" (25). Therefore, to understand a significant aspect of Chicano cultural identity is to also know the legends, heroes, and sayings that have emerged from the Mexican American imagination expressed in the forms of songs, dramas, dances, and tales. Ultimately, as Ricardo L. García (1976) has so perceptively articulated, Chicano folklore "represents the Mexican American's unconscious attempts at self-definition, and with this process, the Mexican American unfolds profound ethnicity, saddened by tragedy, enlightened by comedy, and balanced by self-criticism and parody" (87). García's statement has remained invariable throughout the decades, especially within the realm of Chicano/a art.

For the very act of creating an art piece is, in itself, an act of self-definition that has the potential to not only connect to others but also result in a collective experience. The fact that García also points to the role of the unconscious is vital to unlocking a key aspect of the Chicano experience in the United States that relates to the psychological impact of oppression on people—as well as how that impact is permanently imprinted within the realm of memory. The profound ethnicity that García defines in relation to the Mexican American, specifically, has evolved as a result of the tragedies linked to multiple forms of discrimination (and the memories associated with them). Nevertheless, it is these very same discriminatory practices and injustices that have strengthened the people's survival strategies and have resulted in an inspiring spirit of *sobrevivencia* (survival).

Comedy, self-criticism, and parody are a few survival tactics that García identifies. These and other strategies are visible throughout the various decades of artwork produced by Chicano/as. Ultimately, the creation of a Chicano folklore has occurred as a result of the appropriation, by Chicano/as, of Mexican customs, practices, and beliefs that have come to be negotiated within the context of living in a racialized and capitalist-driven United States of America.

Chicano/a art was certainly a catalyst for the unfolding of a profound ethnicity that focused on reclaiming and affirming Mexican customs, practices, and beliefs. This movement emerged during the 1970s in numerous barrios throughout what many refer to as the American Southwest. One such instance was the Barrio Logan struggle for Chicano Park in San Diego, California. The documentary *Chicano Park* (1988) contextualized this struggle within the myth of Aztlán. The documentary also provided a historical overview of the community and highlighted several examples of the ways in which Mexicans (throughout the United States) have had their choices as well as their access to resources limited due to their socially prescribed status as second-class citizens. Such (non)status has made ethnic Mexicans residing in the United States the recipients of both low- and high-intensity violence and warfare. They have also been on the receiving end of racially discriminatory public policies that have served *only* to guarantee the lack of equality of opportunity.

Although the Barrio Logan community is but one example out of many that could be mentioned, it does help to exemplify the commitment to self-determination that continues to provide inspiration for *La Causa* (the cause) of the Chicano people, which in large part is an intricate project aimed at preserving their dignity amidst oppressive and exploitative conditions in all facets of society affecting everyday life. In addition, a very important point conveyed in the documentary *Chicano Park* (1988) is the fact that many of the Chicano/a artists involved with the original Barrio Logan struggle for Chicano Park gained inspiration from the Mexican muralists who experienced the Mexican Revolution, which took place between the years 1910 and 1920 and whose effects continued for decades following the fratricide.

Sal Rojas wrote in a discussion of Chicano Park that "during the Chicano movement of the sixties and seventies, Chicano artists looked to the Mexican muralist[s] of the past for their direction of the future." Rojas also explained that from "the ashes of the Mexican Revolution, Mexico experience[d] a Cultural Revival behind the brush strokes of Diego Rivera (1886–1957), José Clemente Orozco (1883–1949), and David Alfaro Siqueiros (1898–1974)." At this point, it is vital to clarify that a primary force stimulating this cultural revival was the role of José Vasconcelos (1882–1959) who held office first as Rector of the National University of Mexico (1920–1921), and then as Minister of Education (1921–1924).

One would be remiss to overlook the connection between Vasconcelos's influential role and the visibility of the artwork produced by the aforementioned Mexican muralists. Vasconcelos secured his various roles under the presidency (during the years 1920–1924) of Álvaro Obregón Salido. During the years 1911–1920, the Mexican presidency changed at least three times due to assassinations in each case—Francisco Ignacio Madero González (1911–1913), José Victoriano Huerta Márquez (1913–1914), and Venustiano Carranza de la Garza (1917–1920). Between the years 1914 and 1917, Mexico was ruled for a time by a series of weak presidents. These men did not have any real power. Those with power consisted of the four renowned revolutionaries: Venustiano Carranza, José Doroteo Arango Arámbula (aka Pancho Villa), Álvaro Obregón, and Emiliano Zapata Salazar. Of the four, Carranza (a former politician) had the best case to be made president, and he did have much influence over the executive branch during that chaotic time (Minster 2010).

The chaos of the times undoubtedly affected Vasconcelos's philosophy which focused, in large part, on repairing so many years of damage done to the Mexican psyche and imagination. According to Encinas (1994), there was an eighty per cent illiteracy rate, an acute shortage of schools and schoolteachers in the state education system, as well as a very inadequate capacity for teacher training. Thus, Vasconcelos's philosophy maintained that education was a means of emancipation for the people.

The role of education in this context was to help the Mexican people to rediscover their own country, both in the classroom and on the street, since educational action was not just for children but for the entire community at multiple social sites. Vasconcelos took on a national education project that promoted literacy as well as a revival of the fine arts, and he was able to secure a very large budget. Vasconcelos decided to use the funds to heavily promote a sense of nationalism that would serve to unify a fragmented country since racial, cultural, social, economic, and geographical differences had been brought to light by the revolution (Encinas 1994).

A key component of Vasconcelos's educational philosophy was that it centered on an ethics of aesthetics which was understood as a means by which liberation of the mind could be attained. Hence, Vasconcelos promoted all types of popular artistic expressions that had been disregarded and forgotten by the dictatorial, pro-French Porfirio Díaz regime (also known as El Porfiriato, which lasted from 1876 to 1910). Vasconcelos's approach to education resulted in the rediscovery of pre-Hispanic archaeology (Encinas 1994). It also prompted the mural upsurge whereby Vasconcelos offered the walls of public buildings where the muralists could produce nationalist-inspired works.

Undoubtedly, the three major Mexican muralists—Diego Rivera, José Clemente Orozco, and David Alfaro Siqueiros—were impacted by this politically ideological and nationalist climate of their times. Other artists who were critical to this emerging iconography and cultural reclamation in post-revolutionary Mexico were Saturnino Herrán, Gerardo Murillo, known as Dr. Atl, María Izquierdo, Miguel and Rosa Covarrubias, and Frida Kahlo. According to Venegas (2007), by the 1930s these well-known Mexican artists and intellectuals helped inform a national aesthetic that began collecting native Mexican popular arts as a natural extension of the people's life interests, passions, and pursuits. Mexican painting, especially the public mural, became a dominant vehicle of transmitting not only a revolutionary consciousness, but a didactic tool in challenging the political color hierarchy in

Mexico (Venegas 2007). Indigenous cultures, history, and peoples dominated the emerging visual landscape appearing on the public walls of Mexico.

This artwork was commissioned by Vasconcelos insofar as it coincided with his ideological perspective—a perspective that argued for a unified nationalist spirit. This spirit could supposedly be attained by rediscovering the native values of a people (Encinas 1994). The native values were promoted in opposition to the decadence of Europe and the pragmatism of North America. Vasconcelos claimed that a Western mentality was restrictive and would limit future potentialities because it was impatient, greedy, and materialistic. On the other hand, the national spirit could only be attained through rediscovery of and respect for the native values of a people. For Vasconcelos, the native values carried a seed of original, creative energy (Encinas 1994). Although there are several critiques that can be made about Vasconcelos (primarily his use of colonialist, if not paternalistic rhetoric), it is important to highlight that his ideology in conjunction with his political role facilitated and funded the Mexican muralists that later came to inspire Chicano/a artists.

Interestingly, Vasconcelos's emphasis on the importance of native forms seems to have been preempted by another pivotal figure of inspiration for the Mexican muralists—José Guadalupe Posada (1852–1913). Diego Rivera and José Clemente Orozco received direct training from José Guadalupe Posada, who is best known for his black and white cartoons depicting *calaveras* (skeletons) and *La Muerte* (The Death) that asserted political and social commentary as well as satire. Posada captured an essential element in Mexican folklore by way of focusing on the image of the *calavera*—an image that acknowledges the duality of life in death/death in life; he also highlighted the need for balance in the day-to-day experiences of Mexicans living under the tyranny of El Porfiriato (1876–1910). Posada took the popular traditions, such as those played out during the *Día de los Muertos* celebrations, and gave them material form in his role as a cartoonist and printmaker. By doing so, he cultivated his own organic ideological stance.

His work and his collaborations with Antonio Vanegas Arroyo (1850–1917) questioned and criticized the inequality and social injustice of the Porfiriato regime of their day. Both men incorporated the *calavera* as a central image in their use of political satire. Their work highlighted the issues of a society in conflict prior to the revolution, and they utilized their art form as an outlet for protest and a way to move people forward by way of rediscovering their lost native forms. In this way, Posada and Vanegas remained in solidarity with the poor, bonded with the Mexican past, and fought for a more hopeful Mexican future. Fernando Gamboa (1944) specifically revered Posada for not having "the slightest shadow of European influence," and he acclaimed him as

> a popular artist in the deepest and highest sense of the word; popular because of his humble origin; popular, because of the definite class feeling he brings into each of his works; popular, because he was not an artist without antecedents, a phenomenon foreign to the world in which he lived, but rather the outburst of the feelings of a striving people; popular, because of the way he studied and lived in direct contact with life and the way in which he conscientiously listened to the demands of Mexico.

Illustration by Mexican artist José Guadalupe Posada entitled *Calaveras from the Heap*, 1910. The broadside shows the skeleton of a drunken peasant holding a bottle of Aguardiente de Parras—a reference to Francisco Madero's family's maguey plantation and distillery operation. (Library of Congress)

Gamboa's statement regarding Posada's commitment to a striving people is also applicable to the efforts of the early Chicano/a artists. Appropriating the pre-Columbian imagery and the revolutionary-inspired styles of the Mexican muralists was a resistive strategy employed by early Chicano/a artists to combat the effects of a heritage of internal colonialism in the United States. Barrera, Muñoz, and Ornelas (1972) noted that the barrio could be best perceived as an internal colony (466). The authors also explained that although the majority of the residents living in barrios occupied a status of formal equality within society, they, ironically, were quite powerless when it came to political and economic organization.

Furthermore, the dominant society had historically waged a constant attack on Chicano values and other (specifically Mexican) cultural traits through schools, media, and other institutions (Barrera, Muñoz, Ornelas, 469). Because of the prevalence of these oppressive conditions, Chicano/a artists used their works as a medium for decolonization—as a way to reclaim their culture and heritage and prevent it from dissipating within a melting pot ideology. Although many Chicano/a artists of the early phases of *el movimiento* drew affinities between their own cultural nationalist movement and the nationalist agenda of the Mexican muralists, it is very important to note that the former were also focused on reconstructing their identities in ways that were relevant to their own lived experiences.

Hence, the Chicano experience was an entirely exclusive cultural phenomenon specific to Mexican Americans living in the United States of America during the 1960s–1970s. Ultimately, the art grew from the particularities of this experience—from the various economic, political, social, national, geographical, and psychological struggles of the era. Mark Vallen, a renowned artist in his own right, has confirmed that Chicano art has had many influences and that most certainly "Mexican artists like José Guadalupe Posada, Frida Kahlo, and David Siqueiros have had their effect, but so have American comic books, Cuban political posters, and spray-painted barrio calligraphy" (Vallen 2010). The Chicano experience has thus been a diverse one, and this diversity has been reflected in the heterogeneity of the art itself.

Today, one can appreciate photographs, sculptures, engravings, weavings, embroideries, textiles, sketches, and a multiplicity of graphic arts. In addition, there are numerous types of multi-media projects that incorporate diverse modes of expression. Guerilla, graffiti, and tattoo artists infuse urban locales with their critical perspectives and creativity. Chicana/o art is also wearable through clothes and accessories. However, all of these aforementioned artistic expressions can trace their origins, in many ways, to the artwork of *el movimiento*, which included posters, prints, paintings, and murals. These were, and continue to be, the primary outlets of engaging people in and moving them toward political protest.

The early artists were, in many cases, the sons and daughters of Mexican workers who worked labor-intensive jobs without much recognition from the dominant society. They were part of a new era where voices emerged as well as the pride and dignity of a people who had long been demeaned and ignored. Chicano Park in San Diego, California represents a community that continues to put forth an exemplary effort to uphold the value of honoring, preserving, and representing their roots in Mexican culture and history. The struggle in the early 1970s of the Barrio Logan community to fight for Chicano Park reiterated the battle cry of the Mexican revolutionary Emiliano Zapata for *¡Tierra y Libertad!* (Land and Liberty!),

Mona Mills—known around San Diego's Chicano Park as Mona del Mundo—paints a mural, *Dual Creation,* in the park located in the Barrio Logan section of the city. Chicano Park is a four-acre parcel of land that is viewed as a monument to one of the key victories of the Chicano movement: one community's peaceful battle to save the soul of their neighborhood. (AP/Wide World Photos)

and the space encouraged communal unity among the *niños*, *viejitos*, and *familias* (children, elders, and families).

A key element of the park was the decision to erect a kiosk in the style of a pre-Columbian structure. This generated an affirmation of Indigenous history and identity that could simultaneously link the past to the present and offer guidance and hope for the future. Other Indigenous iconography visible among the murals at Chicano Park included: the Mexica warrior and his female counterpart that symbolize strength and the duality of the male/female dichotomy; various depictions of the god Quetzalcóatl (the plumed serpent or precious twin who also embodies intelligence, self-reflection, and creation); the eagle (or *águila*)—a symbol of Mexican nationalism that also points to the myth of migration of the Azteca/Mexica from Aztlán to Anahuac; the Mesoamerican Indigenous icon, referred to as the Mexica Sun Stone, which is described as a great monolithic sculpture that is probably the greatest "history book" of the Americas because it is the book of Tonatiuh, the sun, and the Mexica who gave the name to the land still called Mexico today; and the *calavera* (skeleton) or image of *La Muerte* (The Death) that points to the duality extant everyday between life and death.

The theme of carrying death into life is very well illustrated by a continued persistence of Mexican revolutionary heroes in the artwork of Mexicans and Chicano/as. The revolutionaries, such as Miguel Hidalgo y Costilla, José María Teclo Morelos y Pavón, Emiliano Zapata, Francisco "Pancho" Villa, and Ricardo Flores Magón, to name a few, are radical figures as well as folk heroes who have played a vital role in both Mexican and Chicano iconography. The Mexican mural movement of the 1920s provided critiques of the many manifestations of oppression, and it also provided a testament to the individual heroes as well as the communities who struggled to demand and defend their rights. In the spirit of this legacy, Chicano/a artists also recognized that empowerment could be gained through the visual arts. The need to promote a sense of empowerment is still quite apparent in the murals located in various geographical spaces throughout the United States, most specifically where *barrios* exist.

A famous Mexican American hero who has been memorialized by Chicano/a artists, and indeed in the process has been transformed into a folk hero, is César E. Chávez. At the core of Chávez's political persona was the principle of militant non-violence. This form of political action sought to retain a commitment to social change but at the same time disassociated that commitment from aggression against other individuals or groups (Mariscal 2005, 146). This led to a strong, Christian-based empathy for the oppressor. Chávez himself drew upon Mexican Catholic iconography and rituals and promoted the idea that it is the poor who carry out God's work. This resonated deeply with the foundational working-class membership and principles of the majority of Chicano movement organizations (Mariscal, 153).

Dolores Huerta, a folk heroine, is often represented alongside César E. Chávez because they co-founded the UFW (United Farm Workers) union together. Huerta directed the UFW's national grape boycott, taking the plight of the farm workers to the consumers. She has also continued to be visible as a highly politically active woman, lobbying in favor of (and against) numerous California and federal laws affecting Spanish-speaking peoples as well as those working in agricultural labor. Huerta has maintained a solid commitment to progressive causes through her involvement with organizations centering on social justice and equity. She is an exemplary model for Chicano/as since she became a leader among men and women because she was willing to take risks, work hard, study intensively, and make many personal sacrifices to achieve her goals (Mullikin and Jones 1997).

Also, Chávez and another family member created the UFW (United Farm Workers) logo—a black stylized eagle with wings shaped like an inverted Aztec pyramid. The logo had a very basic style and color scheme of red, black, and white. The UFW logo became a highly recognizable icon in the union's boycott efforts, legislative proposition campaigns, and a victorious symbol of its successful contract negotiations. It appeared prominently on all official UFW graphics, and it became a key symbol of the Chicano movement as well since its inclusion on unrelated posters made by Chicano artists signaled support for the union ("United" 2003).

Whereas Chávez, Huerta, and the UFW logo symbolized militant non-violence, Ernesto "Che" Guevara and Fidel Castro represented the opposite. For many, Chicano history was formed in the legacy of honoring heroes of the Mexican Revolution, such as Pancho Villa and Emiliano Zapata. Thus Che Guevara and Fidel Castro stood in as younger and contemporary exemplars of the Latin American revolutionary tradition. These figures were living signifiers for the utopian desire of many young, angry people around the world; furthermore, Cuba stood as the foremost Latin American example of decolonization and anti-U.S. imperialism (Mariscal 2005, 100).

By the 1970s many Chicano/a artists and activists had incorporated the image of Che into their discursive repertoire. Some had even converted the Argentina-born and honorary Cuban Guevara into a Chicano and so the image of the mestizo head with three faces that was widely distributed in Raza communities at times featured Che as its central figure (Mariscal 2005, 117). There were multiple cultural objects drawn from poetry, the visual arts, and especially muralism that concretized the meaning of Che and Cuba for Chicano/a activists (103).

Obviously, Che became appropriated by a Chicano consciousness that was also marginalized. However, the Che/Chávez dichotomy also represents the diversity and complexity of Chicano thought and behavior. The fact that Chicanos could embrace both nonviolent protest and militant aggression emphasizes that there were many intersecting facets affecting their lived experiences. Although *el movimiento* did begin with a culturally nationalist perspective, that perspective was never easily disassociated from other significant factors, such as class exploitation, racial discrimination, and gendered (or sexualized) expectations among others.

What can be appreciated today is that despite these challenges, the Mexican and Mexican American cultures in the United States have continued to persist and thrive. They have, in some cases, also forged successful alliances with other groups such as Indigenous nations in North America, Mexico, Central and South America as well with others falling into the "Hispanic" category used in the United States. *El movimiento* attempted to instill dignity from within the communities rather than to have the people endure shame from without. The artwork that has emerged as a result of this historical time period continues to celebrate the people that inhabit (or have inhabited) the barrios of this country: children, students, housewives, factory workers, lawyers, activists, mothers, grandmothers, professors, administrators, educators, domestic workers, daughters, and so much more.

Carmen Lomas Garza is an artist who was inspired by the Chicano movement of the late 1960s. She became dedicated to the depiction of everyday and special events in the lives of Mexican Americans based on her own childhood memories of living in South Texas. Garza saw the need to create images that would elicit recognition and appreciation among Mexican Americans while at the same time serve as a source of education for others not familiar with the culture. She stated, "It has been my objective since 1969 to make paintings, prints, installations for the Day of the Dead, paper and metal cutouts that instill pride in our history and culture in American society."

Garza and many other artists have sought to honor the folklore of Mexicans and Chicano/as by focusing on the community, the family, the day-to-day struggles as well as the many customs and traditions. Some of Garza's themes include the importance of multi-generational and communal unity found in events such as hosting *tamaladas* (tamale-making parties), attending *ferias* (fairs or carnivals), painting *cascarones* (confetti eggs), cutting *nopalitos* (prepared pads of the prickly pear cactus), and listening to *cuentos* (stories). Celebratory themes focusing on *quinceañeras* or *Día de los Muertos* are also common. The younger generations are depicted by way of showing their preferences for dancing and other forms of self-expression, such as low-riders and graffiti. She has also highlighted the central role of Mexican Catholicism by illustrating the presence of La Virgen María de Guadalupe, La Virgen de Zapopan, and crucifixes throughout various household rooms. *Curanderismo* is also represented by way of showing how *limpias* are performed during bouts of *susto* (fright) or other ailments.

Day laborers, *eloteros*, or other push-cart vendors as well as those selling flowers or fruit near freeway off-ramps have become central images in more contemporary works that show the struggles that exist with regard to city developers and city bureaucrats. Keller (2002) has also noted other significant themes to be found in contemporary Chicano/a art. Some of the themes include the barrio; the border and *indocumentados* (undocumented people); *bebida y comida* (beverages and food); *El Día de los Muertos*; farm worker iconography; fathers and sons; heroes, anti-heroes, and role models; *la lotería* (Mexican game); lowriders; mothers and daughters; *mujeres por mujeres* (women for women); pre-Hispanic elements; statues of liberty (United States and Mexico); *vatos*, *cholos*, and *pachucos*; *Vírgenes* (virgins); and *luchadores* (wrestlers) (Keller 2002).

Despite the diversity of themes, there is one constant theme that is visible throughout many Chicana/o works. The influence of folk tales—*los cuentos y las leyendas* (the stories and the legends)—is significant. For in honoring those tales, those who told them and the places from which they came are also, simultaneously, revered—if not resurrected. The artist Santa Barraza in describing her own early inspiration wrote: "[We wanted to] tell our real story; not to tell the dominant culture's story, but tell the story of what we knew through our own history and a lot of it was folklore—stories that have been told from grandmother to child, to son and daughter, parents to children" (Córdova 2003).

One legendary folk tale that has evolved as a popular motif in Chicana/o art, music, theatre, and literature is that of La Llorona. There are many variations to the story and to the descriptions of La Llorona herself; however, those familiar with the tale know her as the woman who drowned her children and who howls in the night while wandering eternally along the shores of rivers, lakes, or canals, searching for them (Pérez 2008). Within the greater Mexican culture, La Llorona serves a similar role to El Cucuy (a version of the bogeyman); both El Cucuy and La Llorona play a role in generating fear in children for them to behave.

Pérez (2008) suggested that one can trace this paternalistic role of La Llorona (as punisher of bad behavior) to the Spanish priests and missionaries who drew upon their knowledge of European figures such as the German *Die weisse Frau* (The White Lady), the tragic Greek figure Medea, and the Christian Eve (Pérez 2008). Identifying these European figures as precursors to La Llorona allowed the Spanish priests and missionaries to allegorize transgression and punishment for the Indigenous population.

However, for many Chicana/o artists, La Llorona has actually served as a catalyst to reconnect to Indigenous origins—to Mesoamerican cosmology in particular. Santa Barraza's incorporation of Cihuateteo into her artwork serves as an example of this decolonial imaginary. Cihuateteo (literally women goddesses), according to Key (2008), appear in the pantheon of Mesoamerican cosmology as mortal women who died in childbirth and were then deified. They also traversed the heavens, the underworld, and the earthly plane in regular cycles (Key 2008). Daily they dwelt with the stars in the western sky in the heavenly region called Cihuatlampa (place of women) and accompanied the sun from noon to sunset, then through the night as it lit the underworld.

Also, every fifty-two days in the ritual calendar, they descended to earth to reign for a day associated with the west (Key 2008). Their regularity placed them habitually in the lives of Mesoamericans. Although La Llorona is not said to have died in childbirth, but is instead responsible for the murder of her own children, the folklore tradition situates her as a woman who also traverses worlds. For Barraza, the Cihuateteo that she used in her works were also the "origin point or the original point of initiation for the folklore of the Llorona."

Pérez (2008) contended that La Llorona has precursors in pre-Christian Mayan and Mexica goddesses. Pérez identified two possible Mayan origins: *xtaj* (lust woman) and *xpunch* (wailing woman). Also, the Mexica deity Coatlicue represents a horrific mother with the power to create and destroy life. Rebolledo (1995) has suggested that La Llorona, like Coatlicue, "approximates in popular folklore all those ancient Nahuatl deities who had life-giving and destroying abilities" (76). Fernández (2008), in her description of pre-Hispanic gods in Mexico, has mentioned that Coatlicue is the most complicated and fascinating of Nahua deities, for she simultaneously represents life and death. She is at once noble and maternal, embodying the mother and grandmother of humanity, yet she is also recognized as a ferocious, rabid assassin.

Cihuacóatl is Coatlicue's most characteristic designation. In this manifestation, she is recognized by her skirt of serpents, which may represent her vast knowledge of the earth, of high celestial spaces, and of the lowly underworld. Cihuacóatl is also the protector of the Cihuateteo (mortal women who died in childbirth and were deified). She also possessed the ability to change herself into a serpent or a beautiful young woman. Hence, both Coatlicue's and Cihuacóatl's conflations of predator and nurturer lend insight into La Llorona's similarly dualistic aspects.

Chicana/o artists have rearticulated La Llorona's relevance in contemporary society. She has been summoned as the main character in new narratives that strive to decolonize the past, present, and future. For example, as Pérez (2008) has thoroughly summarized:

> Contemporary artists, such as Santa Barraza, Rosa María Calles, Isauro de la Rosa, Tony Ortega, and Victor Zubelchía, and performance artists and playwrights, such as Dorinda Moreno, Cherríe Moraga, Carmen Toscano, and Silvia Gonzalez, have created visual and dramatic renderings of La Llorona that are, in some instances, nightmares brought to life. These representations include images of La Llorona wielding a knife, sweeping in on the wind to carry children away in the dark, and being tried for eternity for her alleged crimes.

The cultural potency of La Llorona can be attributed to her intersectionality across historical time periods: pre-Hispanic, colonial, and contemporary. She is continually reimagined and thus resurrected as a symbol of empowerment and a catalyst for transformation.

Another significant figure in Mexican history that has also continued to be reclaimed by Chicana/o artists is Malinalli Tenepal, who was also known as Malintzin (and was later christened Doña Marina), but who gained infamous notoriety as La Malinche, which became synonymous with the word "traitor." Although Hernán Cortés was also referred to as Malinche, it was Malinalli who came to bear the absolute negative connotation of the name—until Chicana feminists reclaimed it in various literary and artistic forms nearly 500 years later.

In Mexico, La Malinche had been cast as a villain and was memorialized as such with support of the elite intelligentsia of the 1920s. In Octavio Paz's book *The Labyrinth of Solitude* (1980), he referred to Mexicans as Sons of Malinche or *hijos de la chingada* (literally translated as sons of the fucked one). Stella Pope Duarte (1997) has noted that Malinalli in 1519, at the time of Hernán Cortés's arrival, was living among the Mayans as a slave in what is now Mexico. She had been sold into slavery by family members in her own personal tale of betrayal. She was later presented to Cortés as a gift in Cozumel before he ever reached the shores. Cortés's "success" in that region could not have occurred without Malinalli as she was one of the few in the city who spoke Náhuatl. Her ability to translate messages in at least three languages—Spanish, Mayan, and Nahuatl—was indispensable in bringing to fruition the conquest of the Mexica.

Ramón A. Gutiérrez (1993) has noted in a detailed analysis of Chicana history that "for activist Chicanas, the historical representations of Malinche as a treacherous whore who betrayed her people were but profound reflections of the deep-seated misogynist beliefs in Mexican and Mexican American culture" (52). Malinche became vindicated in the literature of writers, such as Adelaida R. del Castillo (1977), Cordelia Candelaria (1980), and Sylvia González (1989). These women and other Chicana feminists launched important critiques of the Chicano movement, the women's movement, and the gay/lesbian movement, "challenging each to think about the ways racism, sexism, and homophobia are all embedded and interconnected, not only in contemporary society, but in our own movements as well" (Gallardo 2004).

Obviously, it was (or is not) necessary for a woman to identify as a Chicana feminist to assert a valid critique or challenge. In fact, Gallardo (2004) points out that "it's important to realize that many women of Mexican descent call themselves Mexicans, *Mexicanas*, Latinas, Mexican-American, or even Hispanic for a variety of significant, often personal, reasons." However, it is necessary to note that many who do choose to identify as Chicana feminists often do so within a critical framework that examines inequalities along the intersectionality of race, class, gender, and sexuality as they affect women of Mexican descent and others in the United States.

Malinche, as an icon, embodies the multiplicity of these inequalities, for her affinities to multiple Indigenous nations complicated her identity within a society that enslaved her despite her previously higher rank in society. She was seen as a valuable possession because of her beauty, yet this did not necessarily empower her—only to the extent that it motivated the males around her to empathize with her plight. Chicanas, however, have sought to reclaim Malinalli from different points of view altogether, views which are non-patriarchal. Chicanas have re-envisioned her and reclaimed her by emphasizing her positive, agential qualities, such as her intelligence, initiative, adaptability and leadership.

Santa Barraza has also depicted La Malinche as a symbol of strength and fertility amidst an impending background of destructive change and oppression. Her piece titled "La Malinche" (1991) depicts the Indigenous woman as young and beautiful with her gaze turned down so that she does not meet our eyes. Behind her appear references to the Spanish conquest, the introduction of Christianity, and the violence of both. While it does not deny the horrors of Christian conquest, it paints a world where beauty and violence co-exist. Another prominent Indigenous figure surrounded by beauty and violence that has appeared in many different versions is La Virgen María de Guadalupe. It can be stated that Our Lady, La Virgen Maria de Guadalupe, the mother of God who appeared in Mexico in 1531, is the common denominator of an immensely diverse land and people. She has given Mexicans a sense of both nationalism and patriotism, and their brotherhood can arguably be said to come from the strength of intense faith rooted in Indigenous attributes, images, symbols, magic and myth.

A brief history of the origins of La Virgen and her pivotal role in shaping Mexican history helps to explain why she has been and continues to be a prevalent figure in artistic representations, particularly for Chicana/os. According to Elizondo (1999), La Virgen, the Virgin Mary, appeared to Juan Diego in 1531 at Tepeyac, a small hill and former sanctuary to the Aztec goddess Tonantzin—located in what is now Mexico City. Mary asked Juan to request that the local bishop build a church on that site. Bishop Juan Zumárraga, in disbelief, asked for a heavenly sign. Our

Lady appeared to Juan Diego on the top of the hill, which was covered with beautiful flowers blooming out of season. Arranging the cut flowers on his cloak, known as a tilmátli, Mary sent him on his way. When Juan unfolded his tilmátli before the bishop, the image of Our Lady of Guadalupe appeared on it.

Elizondo (1999) also explained that Juan Diego's original name, Cuauhtlatoazin ("one who speaks like an eagle"), means one who speaks with great authority. It is a fitting description due to the fact that because of Juan Diego's evangelization, an estimated nine million Indigenous people converted to the Christianity of La Morenita (the beloved dark virgin). As she came to be known as the "Queen of Mexico," she also became the unifying symbol of the nation. Evidence of her connection to national pride can be seen in various examples.

For one, Miguel Hidalgo, in the Mexican War of Independence that lasted from 1810 to 1821, carried flags bearing the image of La Virgen María de Guadalupe. Next, José María Morelos, who assumed the leadership of the independence movement after the execution of its founder Miguel Hidalgo and who led insurgent troops in the Mexican south, adopted the Virgin as the seal of his Congress of Chilpancingo, inscribing her feast day into the Chilpancingo constitution and declaring that Guadalupe was the power behind his victories. Also, Emiliano Zapata and his troops carried Guadalupan banners when they entered Mexico City during the Mexican Revolution (1910–1920).

It is clear that La Virgen, as both a religious and national figure, played a pivotal role in unifying the very young nation of Mexico; however, Chicana/o artists have appropriated her image in a way that allows them to venerate the way in which she speaks to their own multifarious experiences, which have often centered on identity development and self-determination. By affirming the Indigenous aspects of La Morenita, Chicana/os simultaneously reclaim their own Indigenous identities. Doing so challenges the colonial effects of detribalization. Detribalization has resulted in a "mestiza/o consciousness," which, for many, results in a confused and marginalized sense of self. This confusion and sense of marginalization continue to manifest despite theoretical postulations that a mestiza/o consciousness is beneficial insofar that it allows for multiple subjectivities. Hence, the prevalence of La Virgen María de Guadalupe in Chicana/o art as a *specifically* Indigenous (and *exclusively* pre-Hispanic) icon confirms her role as an ancient expression of sacredness that is still relevant today.

However, she not only symbolizes the Chicana/os' rootedness in Mexican history and tradition; she also serves as a muse and symbol of empowerment for *mujeres*, specifically. The following artists (though not exclusively)—Ester Hernández, Yolanda López , and Alma López—have each, respectively, depicted La Virgen María de Guadalupe in their visual presentations. These artists chose to retain some of La Virgen's original manifestations, such as her cloak (with stars/gold trim) and even to some extent her ties to Indigenous culture and identity by way of preserving her brown skin as well as her relationship to the serpent as a symbol of the power of divine knowledge. The most obvious changes have been in regard to La Virgen's posture, for instead of downcast, averted eyes, she glares straight ahead, she runs, stands assertive, and even kicks.

Ester Hernández's "The Virgin of Guadalupe Fighting for the Rights of Xicanos" (1975), though not a self-portrait, has personalized La Virgin by positioning her in an aggressive, opposing stature wearing a karate uniform and kicking an invisible enemy. She becomes a symbol of power and strength—the defender of a people. Hernández believes it is important to produce and disseminate positive images of the varied lives of Chicanos; the work counteracts the stereotypes of *mujeres* as either passive victims or demonized creatures (Thomas 2011).

Yolanda López's "Self-Portrait as the Virgin of Guadalupe" (1978) focuses on women, Mexican culture, and on honoring the working class. It pays homage to working women by creating a new icon as a model Chicana. The work also attests to the critique of traditional Mexican women's roles and religious oppression with a sense of self-fashioning new identities (Thomas 2011). Alma López's "Our Lady" (1999), also a self-portrait, speaks to alternative identities as well and the lived realities of lesbian Chicanas. Mesa-Bains has asserted that this type of Chicana art provokes through satire while simultaneously retaining the transfigurative liberation of the icon (1993, 187). Such work subverts, recontextualizes and thus transforms culturally traditional images into feminist icons (Mesa-Bains 1993, 136).

Another example of the transformation that has taken place with regard to culturally traditional images is that of the exclusively Mexican male revolutionaries. These images have been expanded so that Miguel Hidalgo, Pancho Villa, and Emiliano Zapata have not remained the only options available for tracing an iconography of resistance associated with Mexican history. Chicana/os have also gained inspiration from Mexican women (from the past and present) who have been identified as revolutionary either by way of their ideological expressions or their presence on the frontlines of combat.

Early on, women's resistance to colonialism was inevitable. Elizabeth "Betita" Martínez (2008) provided several examples of lower-class women in colonial Mexico who chose not to conform to the oppressive conditions surrounding them. In 1680 in Santa Lucia, many villagers forced officials to leave, and they were purportedly led by Mariana de Oaxaca. Women were also imperative in the Great Rebellion of 1680 in New Mexico where many Pueblo people resisted Spanish colonization in their area. Also, in 1692 hundreds of women rose in Mexico City's Corn Riot; they burned down the Viceroy's palace and the mayor's office.

In 1722, in Nayarit, apostates rebelled in Nayarit, and a woman, Juana Burro, held out the longest. In 1785, Toypurina, the native daughter of a shaman and herself a medicine woman, watched with rage as her people at the San Gabriel Mission in southern California suffered. At the age of twenty-four, she was asked to support a revolt with her divine presence as a medicine woman. Although she was tried and exiled, her defiance set an unforgettable example. Artists such as Judith F. Baca and Raul Gutierrez have paid tribute to the strength of these Indigenous women.

Another important female figure (though a blend of Spanish and *criollo* lineage) connected to Mexican history is the seventeenth-century poet Sor Juana Inés de la Cruz, who lived approximately from 1648 to 1695. She was also at the center of Octavio Paz's (1982) in-depth study, *Sor Juana Inés de la Cruz, o, las trampas de la fe*. Kantaris (1992) has explained that the major theme of Sor Juana's work was the right of women to have access to learning. Kantaris also clarified that in the context of seventeenth-century New Spain, knowledge was a dangerous commodity that was carefully controlled by the religious hierarchy and rigorously policed by the Holy Inquisition. Scientific knowledge posed a threat to the basis of religious power.

Furthermore, in the hands of a woman, any claim to knowledge would have been triply suspect because access to knowledge of the "Divine Order" (whether scientific or theological) was strictly mediated through a patriarchal hierarchy of men. It is hardly surprising to find that Sor Juana's meditations on knowledge are peppered throughout her work with silence, hermeticism, and contradiction. Kantaris's (1992) analysis helps to elucidate why Chicano/a artists would view Sor Juana as a symbol of strength and resistance as well.

Despite the intensity of Sor Juana's critiques, the legacy of female suppression in Mexico continued long after her life had ended. Prior to the Mexican Revolution (1910–1920), the Mexican government passed the Mexican Civil Code in 1884, which functioned in a way that assisted in dramatically restricting women's rights at both home and at work. The Mexican Civil Code of 1884 sustained inequality between husbands and wives and restricted the rights of all women while also nullifying their personalities (Jandura). However, as the Mexican Revolution of the early twentieth century progressed, some women began to find a place in society where they could live their public lives as well as control their fate.

Mexican women were essential to the revolution insofar that they were involved politically, advocated for causes fervently, and fought on the battlefields valiantly. For example, Dolores Jimenez y Muro was successful as a political activist, and Hermila Galindo also succeeded in interrogating the male double standard as practiced in Mexican society for centuries. She also advocated for sex education for women, divorce, and anti-clericalism in 1916 (Pérez 1999). It should be noted that these women sought an audience of literate, middle-class women; nevertheless, there were other, more direct, involvements with the revolution as demonstrated by those women who showed a selfless support and commitment to the male troops. These *soldaderas* (also referred to as *adelitas* or *rieleras*) joined men on the frontlines and supported them in a way that allowed troops to succeed.

From their direct involvement on the frontlines emerged the iconic image of the Mexican female revolutionary: with a blouse, long skirt, sombrero, and ammunition across her chest. This image has been infused throughout Mexican (and Chicano) culture in songs, books, plays, films, and calendars to name a few examples. In these forms, she has often been popularized and romanticized by male storytellers who have placed them as sexual beings rather than heroines. Aside from being viewed as a sex symbol, Chicano/a artists have also represented the *soldadera* as a brave champion of a people or even as a proto-feminist. These artists offer a mix of diverse media—video, painting, photography, and printmaking. They each bring a layer of complexity as they offer powerful, personal, defiant, intimate, and lyrical portrayals of femininity (Hernández 2010).

Frida Kahlo, though not a *soldadera*, but definitely a defiant woman, is another iconic Mexican figure appropriated by Chicana/os. Although Kahlo lived during the Mexican Revolution, she came from an elite economic class and she benefited from the education that came as a result of her social status. Nevertheless, she suffered physical and emotional pain due to her bout with polio at the age of six and the devastating accident she lived through when she was eighteen. Her self-portraits depict her pain and suffering through images that show bleeding, injury, wounds, victimization, and symbols of death. She married Diego Rivera at the age of twenty-one and this allowed her to further socialize with progressive intellectuals and wealthy citizens. During this time, she joined the communist party. This non-conformity was preceded by Kahlo's bold, rebellious spirit that constantly challenged social norms specifically associated with her gender. By wearing trousers and smoking in public, she repeatedly broke social taboos.

Frida Kahlo's *Self-Portrait with Curly Hair* (1935). (AP/Wide World Photos)

Kahlo's appeal is not limited to her resilient exterior. She also captured in her art and in her life a very true sense of duality: a constant negotiation and balance between fearfulness and fearlessness. Frida Kahlo lived a marginalized existence and her artwork communicates the essence of that turmoil, which might explain why Chicana/os have an affinity toward her. For Kahlo reminds us that life is painful and unjust and that humanity has the capacity to endure and triumph over many aspects of pain, suffering, and tribulation (Hernández 2009). Her image confirms that illogical events and circumstances are part of this world, and perhaps the reasons for human sorrow may only be understood from a cosmic dimension (Hernández 2009).

Clearly, the appropriation by Chicano/a artists of Mexican figures goes beyond basic aesthetic appreciation—beyond an art historian's perspective that might only emphasize the importance of observing design elements of line, shape, color, value, and texture. Although Chicano/a art is visually stimulating, the intentionality of the style can be linked to the artistic attempt at constructing an identity of resistance. For this reason, this entry cannot end without discussing the profound impact that the images associated with the EZLN (Ejército Zapatista de Liberación Nacional or Zapatista Army of National Liberation) have had on Chicana/os.

On January 1st, 1994, a previously unknown force, the EZLN, emerged in Southern Chiapas, Mexico and seized control of four towns. Since that time, the Zapatistas have gained international recognition and support for their struggle, which also parallels the struggles of other peoples throughout the world seeking to decolonize and regain Indigenous control over their local resources, especially land. Brock Pitawanakwat (2002) has pointed out that the Zapatistas themselves have employed the use of consensus versus conflictive symbols.

According to Pitawanakwat (2002), the Zapatista symbols include "Emiliano Zapata, land, Indigenous identity, Indigenous languages, the role of women, leading by obeying, the ski mask, power of the word, weapons as well as armed resistance, and Subcomandante Marcos" (Pitawanakwat 2002). These symbols are interdependent, and because of this, they transcend categorical distinction. The power of these symbols and of the words that accompany them has enabled the Zapatistas and those who align with them to wage a parallel war of words and symbols, which is an effective decolonization of public language (Pitawanakwat 2002, 55).

Ideas of redemption and words of freedom are also extremely relevant today in the United States of America, where reactionaries have heightened their long-standing anti-immigrant campaigns and have continued to militarize the U.S.-Mexico border as they criminalize anyone who looks Mexican (read illegal). The Chicano/a affinity for the Zapatista struggle (as well as the symbols, words, and tactics it evokes) exists because it mirrors their own struggle. This struggle includes the need to respect the land, human dignity, and self-determination for our cultures and planet to survive.

This entry has sought to broadly present the influences of Indigenous iconography and Mexican folklore on Chicano/a art. Because of this, it has been necessary to adopt a socio-historical perspective applicable across two nations—Mexico and the United States. Furthermore, the task has not been easy given the immense amount of work that has been produced by Chicana/o artists since the 1960s. Several volumes have been and still need to be written about the specific inspirations of individual artists and their collaborators. Nevertheless, it is important for those truly vested in promoting an appreciation of Chicano/a art to do so while also uplifting the people it is intended to represent.

Undoubtedly, Chicana/o art is fundamentally rooted in Indigenous iconography and Mexican folklore. These roots, however, are also accompanied by rhizomes which are distinct from roots because they have very diverse forms that divide in all directions (Deleuze and Guattari 1987, 10–11). *Camotes* (yams) and *jicamas* (Mexican turnips), for example, were rhizomes that were essential to Indigenous cultures that did not produce or could not procure meat or fish. The versatility of these staples, however, allowed for new savory creations to be made that added color, flavor, pungency, texture/consistency, and intensity. Similarly, Chicano/a art—though rooted to some degree in *cultura Mexicana* (Mexican culture)—has continuously flourished beyond it, constantly shifting directions while adding color, intensity, and a *sabor* (flavor) all its own.

Silvia Toscano Villanueva

See also: Aztec Empire; Aztlán; Chicano/a Literature and Folklore; Cihuacóatl; Coatlicue; Greater Mexico and Its Folklore; La Llorona (The Wailing Woman); La Santísima Muerte; Malinche; Quetzalcóatl; Tonantzin; Tonantzin in Chicana Literature and Art; Virgin of Guadalupe: History and Fiestas Guadalupanas

Further Reading

Baca, Judy, and UCLA students (Artists). "Toyporina" (Digital Mural), 1996, US, SPARC. www.sparcmurals.org.

Barraza, S. (Artist). "La Malinche" (Painting), 1991, U.S., Private Collection.

Barrera, M., and M. Mulford (Producers). *Chicano Park.* (VHS). 1988. Available from Film Arts Foundation, San Francisco, CA.

Barrera, M., C. Muñoz, and C. Ornelas. "The Barrio as an Internal Colony." In Harlan Hahn, ed. *People and Politics in Urban Society.* Beverly Hills, CA: Sage, 1972.

Córdova, C. "Oral history interview with Santa Barraza in Kingsville, TX." November 21–22, 2003. *Archives of American Art.* http://www.aaa.si.edu/collections/interviews/oral-history-interview-santa-barraza-13254.

de Ortega y Gasca, F. "Chicanos and Concepts of Culture." Paper presented at a conference sponsored by the Intercultural Development and Research Association. Brownsville, TX, 1978.

Deleuze, G., and F. Guattari. *Thousand Plateaus: Capitalism and Schizophrenia.* Minneapolis: University of Minnesota Press, 1987.

Duarte, S. P. "In Search of La Malinche." *Waco Tribune Herald.* May 1997.

El Plan de Santa Bárbara. Chicano Coordinating Council on Higher Education. University of California, Santa Barbara, 1969.

El Plan Espiritual de Aztlán. First National Chicano Liberation Youth Conference, a March 1969 convention hosted by Rodolfo Gonzales's Crusade for Justice in Denver, CO, March 1969.

Elizondo, V. "Our Lady of Guadalupe. A Guide for the New Millennium." *AmericanCatholic.org, St. Anthony Messenger Magazine Online.* http://www.americancatholic.org/Messenger/Dec1999/feature2.asp.

Encinas, R. "José Vasconcelos (1882–1959)." *PROSPECTS: Quarterly Review of Comparative Education* XXIV, nos. 3–4 (1994): 719–29.

"Exploring Everyday Folklore." 2006. http://teacher.scholastic.com/writewit/mff/folklore_what.htm.

Gallardo, S. "What's Chicana feminism?" *Making face, making soul . . . a Chicana feminist homepage.* 2004. http://www.chicanas.com/whowhat.html#Wha.

Gamboa, F. *Posada: Printmaker to the Mexican People.* Chicago: Art Institute of Chicago, 1944.

García, M. T., ed. *A Dolores Huerta Reader.* Albuquerque: University of New Mexico Press, 2008.

García, R. L. "Overview of Chicano Folklore." NCTE's (National Council of Teachers of English) *English Journal* (February 1976): 83–87.

Garza, C. L. "Artist statement." 2001–2008. http://www.carmenlomasgarza.com/artiststatement.html.

Gaspar de Alba, A. *Chicana Art: The Politics of Spiritual and Aesthetic Alterities (Objects/Histories).* Durham, NC: Duke University Press Books, 2007.

Gaspar de Alba, A. *Chicano Art Inside/Outside the Master's House: Cultural Politics and the CARA Exhibition.* Austin: University of Texas Press, 1998.

Gutiérrez, R. A. "Community, Patriarchy, and Individualism: The Politics of Chicano History and the Dream of Equality." *American Quarterly* 45, no. 1 (March 1993).

Hernández, B. F. "Frida Kahlo: A Mexican Icon." *Lowrider Arte* (February 2009). http://www.lowriderarte.com/featuredartists/0309lra_mexican_artist_frida_kahlo/index.html.

Hernández, E. (Artist). "La Virgen de Guadalupe defendiendo los derechos de los Xicanos/The Virgin of Guadalupe fighting for the rights of Xicanos" (Etching), (1975), U.S., collection of the artist.

Hernández, J. "After Adelita: Myths, Heroes, and Revolutionaries." *Fine Art America.* (September 2010). http://fineartamerica.com/events/after-adelita-myths-heroes-and-revoluctionaries.html.

Hernández, S. F. "Santa Barraza, pionera de 'La Causa.'" *Flores de Nieve.* http://www.floresdenieve.cepe.unam.mx/quince/cepe-silvia205.htm.

Jandura, T. "Revolutionary Mexican women." http://www.ic.arizona.edu/ic/mcbride/ws200/mex.htm.

Kantaris, G. "Sor Juana Inés de la Cruz (Juana Ramírez de Asbaje)." Lecture for Part I SP2: Introduction to Hispanic Texts. 1992. http://www.latin-american.cam.ac.uk/culture/SorJuana/.

Keller, G. *Chicano Art for Our Millennium: Collected Works from the Arizona State University Community.* Tempe, AZ: Bilingual Review Press, 2004.

Keller, G. *Contemporary Chicana and Chicano Art: Artists, Work, Culture, and Education.* Tempe, AZ: Bilingual Review Press, 2002.

Key, A. "The Cihuateteo." *Matrifocus: Cross Quarterly for the Goddess Woman* 8.1 (2008). http://www.matrifocus.com/SAM08/key.htm.

López, A. (Artist). "Our Lady" (Iris print on canvas), 1999, U.S.

López, Y. "Portrait of the Artist as the Virgin of Guadalupe" (Oil pastel on paper), 1978, U.S.

Mariscal, George. *Brown-Eyed Children of the Sun: Lessons from the Chicano Movement, 1965–1975.* Albuquerque: University of New Mexico, 2005.

Martínez, E. B. *500 Years of Chicana Women's History/500 años de la mujer Chicana.* Bilingual ed. New Brunswick, NJ: Rutgers University Press, 2008.

Mesa-Bains, A. *Ceremony of Spirit: Nature and Memory in Contemporary Latino Art.* San Francisco: San Francisco Mexican Museum, 1993.

Minster, C. "The Mexican Revolution: Ten Years That Forged a Nation." *Latin American History* (2010). http://latinamericanhistory.about.com/od/thehistoryofmexico/a/mexicanrevo_3.htm.

Mullikin, C. M., and C. L. Jones. "Dolores Huerta: César Chávez' Partner in Founding the United Farm Workers Union in California." 1997. http://www.csupomona.edu/~jis/1997/Mullikin.pdf.

"Murals." 1997–2011. http://www.brownpride.com/murals/default.asp.

Paz, O. *The Labyrinth of Solitude: Life and Thought in Mexico.* New York: Random House, [1980] 1988.

Pérez , D. R. *There Was a Woman: La Llorona from Folklore to Popular Culture.* Austin: University of Texas, 2008.

Pérez, E. *The Decolonial Imaginary.* Bloomington: Indiana University Press, 1999.

Pitawanakwat, B. *The Mirror of Dignity: Zapatista Communication and Indigenous Resistance.* University of Victoria, 2002. http://dspace.library.uvic.ca:8080/bitstream/1828/383/1/joerger_2004.pdf.

Rebolledo, T. D. *Women Singing in the Snow: A Cultural Analysis of Chicana Literature.* Tucson: University of Arizona Press, 1995.

Rojas, S. "Chicano Park." http://www.brownpride.com/murals/default.asppride.com.

Sobek-Herrera, M. *Chicano Folklore: A Handbook.* Westport, CT: Greenwood Press, 2006.

Thomas, S. "Context Clues: The Appropriation of Malinche and the Virgin of Guadalupe." Yale–New Haven Teachers Institute. 2011. http://teachers.yale.edu/curriculum/search/viewer.php?id=initiative_07.04.03.

"United Farm Workers Logo." May 2003. *Social Design Notes.* http://backspace.com/notes/2003/05/united-farm-workers-logo.php.

Vallen, M. "Just another poster? Chicano graphic arts in California." http://www.art-for-a-change.com/Chicano/chicano.htm.

Venegas, S. "Golden Age of Mexico." *Chicanoart.org.* 2007. http://www.chicanoart.org/index2.html.

CHICANO/A LITERATURE AND FOLKLORE

Because folklore reflects the ingenuity, value system, humor, and reverence of a community, Chicano writers often use it as a source of inspiration and exploration. Mexican American literature from the early twentieth century to the late 1950s prominently featured folk stories, legends, and practices for a variety of reasons. Early writers initially incorporated folk motifs partly in response to the dominant culture's growing obsession with folk art and literature. During the modernist fascination with primitive cultures and the rise of the "Spanish Revival" art movement, women writers in particular emphasized folklore as a way to express their cultural heritage and to access the publishing industry. Although these writers depicted romanticized versions of the past, they wrote out of an acute fear that their cultural traditions were disappearing with the advent of a growing Anglo-American presence. Other writers produced fiction explicitly based on folk stories because they were academically trained as folklorists. For these scholars, Mexican American folklore constituted an important field of study that required specialists who could accurately document, preserve, and interpret their communities' cultural heritage. Their folk-based literature and their academic writing served as a corrective to denigrating stereotypes of Mexican Americans circulated in history books, newspapers, and popular fiction.

The Chicano Movement of the mid-1960s and 1970s inspired a renewed embrace of folklore in art, music, and literature. Writers turned to folklore to assert pride in their cultural heritage and to resist social pressures to assimilate to the dominant culture. Literary folklore also helped to mobilize individuals around important political and social issues by serving as the foundation for collective identity and solidarity. The literary output of this period introduced a generation of Chicanos to ancient Mesoamerican civilizations, Indigenous deities, and icons from the Mexican Revolution.

Post-Movement Chicano literature continued to focus on folklore as a way to explore its cultural influence on contemporary Chicano identity. Writers interested in examining collective norms and beliefs about race, gender, and sexuality returned to folkloric figures to make feminist or social demands for equality. Writers from the 1980s began reinterpreting the legacies of maligned historical figures such as La Malinche. They also use folklore in an ironic way to engage in a self-critique of repressive cultural values and traditions. Rather than discard or reject patriarchal folk beliefs completely, writers often use them to construct new models of empowerment and agency.

Chicano literature is also infused with strong Christian, specifically Catholic, beliefs that influence cultural notions of good and evil, life and death, sin and salvation. While the Catholic faith dominates Mexican American communities, it has always been imbued with resilient Indigenous spiritual traditions that have survived since Spanish colonization. This combination of Western and native traditions has produced a folklore that expresses unique views on death, spirits, religious intermediaries, and folk healers. The literature reflects the power and creativity of spiritual folk beliefs within Chicano communities. It also demonstrates how writers use folklore to engage in a constant process of reinvention and adaptation. In general, contemporary Chicano literature is less concerned with re-creating faithful renderings of an original folklore than with adapting folklore to express modern desires, beliefs, and anxieties.

Folklore in Early Mexican American Literature: 1913–1958

One of the earliest writers to incorporate folklore into her short fiction was María Cristina Mena (1893–1965). Between 1913 and 1916, Mena published short stories in leading literary magazines including *Century Magazine*. Born in Mexico City to an upper-class family, Mena moved to New York City in 1907 to live with friends. While New York became her permanent home, she wrote predominantly about Mexican life. She used her literary talents to bring Mexican cultural traditions and folk beliefs to an Anglo American readership eager to read about exotic locales. Through her writing, Mena hoped to satisfy the demand for stories about Mexican culture and to simultaneously challenge U.S. misperceptions of Mexicans.

A few of her stories focus on Anglo-American tourists in Mexico who encounter Mexican folk beliefs without initially understanding their significance. Through sophisticated plots and characterization, Mena's stories educate both her characters and readers about centuries-old religious beliefs that influence Mexican culture. For example, in "The Gold Vanity Set" (1913), Miss Young, an American tourist in a small Mexican village, loses her cosmetic vanity set. Eventually, she learns that Petra, a young Mexican woman, has found the set and considers it to be responsible for a series of positive changes in her marriage. As a result, Petra attributes sacred properties to the set and places it on a shrine to la Virgen de Guadalupe, Mexico's patron saint. Mena's story is one of the earliest depictions of religious devotion to la Virgen, one of the most prevalent figures found in Chicano literary folklore.

Writing a couple of decades after Mena, Jovita González (1904–1983) used her own graduate research on Texas folklore as the basis for her fiction. Born in the Texas-border town of Roma, González went on to earn degrees in Spanish and History. While earning her M.A. degree in History at the University of Texas at Austin, she met J. Frank Dobie, a leading scholar in the field of folklore studies. Her M.A. thesis examined the cultural norms and practices of the Texas-Mexican communities in three South Texas counties. González joined and eventually became president of the Texas Folklore Society, an organization of researchers that collected and studied folklore. During the 1930s, she wrote two novels: *Caballero: A Historical Novel* co-written with Eve Raleigh and *Dew on the Thorn*, which incorporated folk motifs drawn from her extensive research.

Dobie not only served as a professional mentor, but his views on literary folklore also influenced González's fiction writing. In contrast to some scholars who believed that folklore should be preserved in its original form, Dobie advocated the literary embellishment of folklore. He believed that folk tales could be transformed into longer, developed literary narratives that would appeal to a non-folk audience. Scholar José Limón argues that Dobie's views influenced González's *Dew on the Thorn*, a collection of interrelated folk tales, legends, and motifs. Limón further explains that González also challenged Dobie's views on Mexican folklore. Whereas Dobie's own writing on Mexican folklore avoided political analysis and emphasized a romanticized view of folk practices, González's novels incorporated folklore as a way to comment on colonization, gender inequality, and racial confrontation.

In the field of drama, Josephina Niggli (1910–1983) wrote and performed folk plays about pastoral Mexican life and key historical events. Born in Monterrey, Mexico, to Scandinavian American parents, Niggli spent her childhood in northern Mexico. During Niggli's teen years, her family moved back and forth between San Antonio, Texas, and Mexico to avoid the turmoil of the Mexican Revolution (1910–1920). Niggli would eventually graduate from college and go on to pursue a master's degree in playwriting at the University of North Carolina at Chapel Hill. While there, she joined Professor Frederick Koch's Carolina Playmakers, a university drama troupe that performed folk plays. Koch defined folk drama as plays that depicted primitive societies and their cultural traditions. Within the context of an increasingly industrialized, mechanized, and impersonal society, the peoples depicted in folk drama harkened back to a time when life was supposedly simpler.

As a student of Koch's, Niggli wrote the kind of folk plays that celebrated romanticized depictions of pre-modern Mexican communities. Most of Niggli's plays centered on Mexican history and culture. In 1938, she published *Mexican Folk Plays*, a collection of five one-act plays. The collection included three comedies that depicted the humor and charm of village life and two dramas about Mexican historical events. Soon afterward, the University of North Carolina Press approached Niggli to write a book about Mexican folklore. Unlike her contemporary Jovita González, Niggli had no academic training as a folklorist. Instead of submitting a manuscript on Mexican folklore, Niggli submitted several short stories based on folk practices. The Press accepted these replacements, which soon became the basis for her first novel *Mexican Village* (1945).

During the period of 1880 to 1930, a cultural and academic movement known as the "Spanish Revival" promoted a romanticized image of the U.S. Southwest as a land forgotten by time. Charles F. Lummis's *The Land of Poco Tiempo* (1893) is noted for beginning a trend among Anglo authors of moving to New Mexico and writing romanticized ethnographies of New Mexican landscapes and communities. Following his lead, Willa Cather among others began writing about New Mexican folk cultures. For many of these writers, New Mexico's relative geographical and cultural isolation from major urban centers enabled them to imagine a place untainted by the violence, greed, and stress of a modernizing world.

Revival literature often depicted the "Spanish" folk customs of ethnic Mexicans, portraying them as "pure" descendants of the original Spanish colonizers of the Southwest. Many Hispanos, particularly from the upper classes, supported the Spanish Revival movement because it reflected their own views on the value of Spanish heritage and whiteness. In response to the Revival, Cleofas Jaramillo (1878–1956) founded La Sociedad Folklórica de Santa Fe (the Folklore Society of Santa Fe) in 1930 to promote the preservation of Spanish folklore. The Sociedad felt that Revivalist depictions were not always accurate or sensitive to regional differences and beliefs. Furthermore, the Sociedad believed the region's Spanish heritage was threatened by the increasing incursion of Anglo American cultural and economic expansion.

Jaramillo's literary preservation of Spanish folklore began in 1939 with a cookbook, *The Genuine New Mexico Tasty Recipes*, and a collection of twenty-five folktales entitled *Cuentos del hogar/Spanish Fairy Stories*. She is best known for her autobiography *Romance of a Little Village Girl* (1955) that combined memoir and an ethnography of Arroyo Hondo, New Mexico. *Romance* describes the history of New Mexico beginning with the Spanish colonizers up to the time of her own family's settlement in New Mexico. Throughout her text, she describes the cultural practices, religious traditions, and local beliefs that shaped her childhood. Her account emphasizes life in a pastoral community that remained largely isolated from Anglo American influence for many decades.

Fabiola Cabeza de Baca (1894–1991), a distant cousin of Jaramillo's, also published books that preserved Spanish heritage. Cabeza de Baca traveled throughout the state as a home economist who worked with rural Hispano and American Indian women to promote nutrition and modern homemaking practices. Her interest in history and her work as home economist exposed her to Spanish folk customs and stories. Her book *The Good Life: New Mexico Traditions and Food* (1949) depicts an imaginary family, the Turrietas, to illustrate the preservation of local recipes and rituals associated with cooking and sharing meals. Her later memoir *We Fed Them Cactus* (1954) recounts her childhood in the ranching community of Llano Estacado. She describes the cultural practices maintained through centuries to cope with life in New Mexico's rugged terrain including feeding cactus to starving herds of cattle during periods of drought.

Later Chicano critics would criticize Jaramillo, Cabeza de Baca, and other Hispano writers for glorifying the Spanish racial identity and heritage over the region's equally significant mestizo and Indigenous roots. However, their emphasis on the past and on Spanish folklore, in particular, was motivated by their fear of cultural erasure. Their interest in folklore also enabled them to experiment with narrative forms as they combined oral traditions, recipes, folk tales, history, and poetry. These hybrid texts represented innovative narratives that sometimes challenged the inaccuracies and misinterpretations found in Spanish Revival texts written by nonnative writers.

Américo Paredes (1915–1999) is perhaps the most well known folklorist and author; his works have been described as forming the foundation for contemporary Chicano/a literature. Born in Brownsville, Texas, Paredes grew up in a ranching community in which members would often tell folk tales and sing ballads as a way of sharing information, news, and entertainment. Paredes's later interest in folklore would be informed by his childhood exposure to a community reliant on oral traditions. After serving in World War II, he returned to Texas and enrolled at the University of Texas at Austin where he eventually completed his Ph.D. in English and Spanish with an emphasis on the study of folklore. The University subsequently hired Paredes to teach folklore in 1957, a position that enabled him to expand research on folklore and Mexican Americans.

While Paredes wrote and published poetry, short stories, and novels, he is best known for his academic study of the *corrido,* or folk ballad, in *"With His Pistol in His Hand": A Border Ballad and Its Hero* (1958). Based on his dissertation, the text presents an exhaustive study of the *corrido* of Gregorio Cortez. In 1901, Cortez killed a Texas sheriff in self-defense and immediately began a period on the run from law enforcement. Paredes's study explains the history of the Lower Rio Grande Border region and describes how the *corrido* depicts Cortez as a man who defended himself against the social injustices that often plagued the *Tejano* community. Paredes then presents Cortez's life based on available documentary material. In a final section, Paredes compiles variants of the ballad to reconstruct what the original *corrido* sounded like. Scholar Ramón Saldívar argues that *Pistol* is one of the most influential and foundational texts of the Chicano literary tradition. For Saldívar, *Pistol's* oppositional stance to social repression and its emphasis on a heroic, masculinist cultural identity influenced later Chicano writers from the mid-1960s and beyond.

Paredes's approach to folklore focused on the contexts in which folklore was practiced and on the artists who performed it. For Paredes, folklore served a vital function within the community because it helped individuals relay important information about cultural events, legendary figures, regional histories, and cultural identity. Rather than being only a study of the past, folklore scholarship was an examination of the ways in which Mexican Americans lived in the present and how they expressed their fears, hopes, and beliefs.

Folklore and the Formation of Chicano Identity: 1960–1987

The mid-1960s and 1970s witnessed a cultural and literary renaissance of Chicano writing and artistic production. The renaissance coincided with a large-scale mobilization of Chicanos/as around diverse issues that included the struggle for farm workers' rights, economic justice, political representation, and an anti-war campaign. To mobilize a heterogeneous population of Chicanos, Movement leaders relied on writers and artists to inspire and educate Chicanos about their cultural history. The literary turn to folklore also helped Chicanos resist the pressures to assimilate into a dominant Anglo-American culture. Writers turned to their past to find culturally-affirming motifs and figures on which to write that were distinct from mainstream American culture and values.

One of the early movements to use folklore in the service of Chicano activism was the Teatro Campesino, or Farm Worker's Theater, in 1965. Founded by Luis Valdez, the son of migrant farmworkers, the Teatro began as the theatrical unit of the United Farm Workers' union. Valdez viewed theater as the ideal mode of mobilizing workers and community members to support the Union's efforts. The Teatro used *actos,* or improvisational skits, performed by actual workers to illustrate the migrant's struggle against economic and racial oppression. As the Teatro grew in popularity, Valdez began to write more structured scripts that expressed themes dealing with social injustice and cultural pride.

The Teatro's success partly stemmed from its use of folklore to galvanize diverse Chicano communities around California. The Teatro often used popular forms of verbal expression, dialects, and proverbs in their plays along with props based on folkloric objects. It also utilized the folk tradition of storytelling as it incorporated *cuentos* or tales into its performances. Because *cuentos* often focus on tales of good versus evil, they are useful dramatic vehicles to instruct audiences about acceptable cultural values and mores. In addition to *cuentos,* Valdez used *corridos* as the basis for his plays because of their dramatic quality, their embedded moral lessons, and their energy. In the early 1980s, the Teatro staged a production entitled *Corridos: Tales of Passion and Revolution* which later aired in 1987 as a televised performance on the Public Broadcasting System. The production was a compilation of *corridos* that mostly focused on patriarchal violence against women and the social control of women's sexuality.

Muralists, poets, and fiction writers turned to an Indigenous Mexican past to educate Chicano audiences about Mesoamerican history and myth. Alberto Baltazar Urista Heredia (1947–), more commonly known as Alurista, was one of the first Movement writers to introduce a new generation to Aztec mythology and legendry. Chief among his contributions to the Movement's artistic and political vision was the concept of Aztlán. Based on his study of Aztec civilization, Alurista wrote poetry that described Aztlán as the lost homeland of Aztec descendants who had originated in what is now the U.S. Southwest. Working with Rodolfo "Corky" Gonzales, a leader of the Chicano Movement, Alurista incorporated Aztlán into the Movement's key manifesto, "El Plan Espiritual de Aztlán" (1969). The concept of Aztlán enabled Chicanos to assert their sense of belonging and permanence on the land as it proved that their historical forebears were indigenous to the region long before the imposition of the U.S.–Mexican border. Due to his detailed historical study and his fluency in Nahuatl, the language of the Aztecs, Alurista's poetry is infused with references to Indigenous mythologies. He often combines Catholic figures with Aztec, Toltec, and Mayan symbols and icons.

Like Alurista, Chicana poet, essayist, and scholar Gloria Anzaldúa (1942–2004) used Aztec references to promote a feminist reinterpretation of women's role in Mexican and Chicano culture. She is best known for writing *Borderlands/La Frontera* (1987), a text that blends history, autobiography, ethnography, and poetry.

Anzaldúa weaves narratives about present injustices within the Chicano community and references to Indigenous female deities to articulate her concept of the "new mestiza consciousness." For example, she describes pre-Columbian figures such as Coatlicue, the fertility goddess who embodies both birth and death. For Anzaldúa, Coatlicue serves as a symbol of how contradictions can co-exist in individuals and communities without leading to violence and repression. By reclaiming the folklore of Amerindian cultures, Anzaldúa argues that Chicanos/as can begin to face both negative and positive aspects of their cultural heritage as they strive for a more holistic and empowering sense of identity.

Icons, Legends, and Mythic Figures in Contemporary Chicana/o Literature

Three of the most prevalent female archetypes found in Chicano literary folklore include La Virgen de Guadalupe, La Llorona, and La Malinche. These maternal figures embody cultural and religious conceptions of good and evil that have shaped Mexican and Chicana womanhood. As the Mexican version of the Virgin Mary, La Virgen represents the legacy of Spanish colonization in the Americas. In 1531, La Virgen appeared to the native Juan Diego and asked that a church be built in her name on the ruins of an Aztec temple at Tepeyac. It is believed that many natives associated La Virgen with the Aztec deity Coatlopeuh, thus transforming the Catholic figure into a fusion of Christianity and pre-conquest Indigenous spirituality.

References to La Virgen in Chicano literature often position her as a mediating and consoling figure that emanates a strong sense of love and encouragement to women who endure social, economic, and physical hardships. In *The Miraculous Day of Amalia Gómez* (1991), John Rechy follows the spiritual journey of his Chicana protagonist Amalia Gómez. Despite her devout faith in the Catholic religion, Amalia remains excommunicated from the Church for reasons beyond her control. For Amalia, only La Virgen understands her history of sexual violence and withholds judgment on her troubled past. Writers like Cherríe Moraga also use the symbolic power of La Virgen to depict contemporary social struggles. In her play *Watsonville* (2002), La Virgen appears to a Chicana worker who goes on strike with other women in a Watsonville cannery for improved conditions and higher wages. La Virgen's image miraculously appears on an oak tree as a symbol to strikers to continue their struggle.

While La Virgen represents maternal comfort and virginal purity, the figure of La Llorona (The Weeping Woman) represents infanticide and seduction. According to most versions of the legend, La Llorona was a woman who drowned her own children out of vengeance on a cheating husband. As a consequence for her sins, she was condemned to roam at night along bodies of water, weeping for her lost children. As one of the oldest and widespread legends in Mexican and Chicano folklore, La Llorona is found in all Chicano genres. In *The Legend of La Llorona* (1984), Rudolfo Anaya places his version of the haunting figure during the arrival of Spanish conquistador Hernán Cortés. In his account, La Llorona fears that her children will be forcibly taken to Spain as slaves, so she murders her children by drowning them in a lake. Helena María Viramontes's "The Cariboo Café" (1984)

Chicano author Rudolfo Anaya poses at Weems International Artfest in 2005 in Albuquerque, New Mexico. (Getty Images)

depicts a nameless Central American refugee as the representative Llorona. Rather than keeping with the typical narrative of a murderous mother, a Central American dictatorship orders the senseless killing of the protagonist's child. Anaya's and Viramontes's texts represent the diverse representations of the La Llorona myth in Chicano literature.

Like La Llorona, La Malinche exemplifies sexual promiscuity and treachery. Malintzin Tenepal, later renamed La Malinche, was an Indigenous woman who was sold to Hernán Cortés and eventually served as his guide, consort, and translator. Because of Cortés's conquest of the Aztecs, later generations of Mexicans regarded La Malinche as a traitor to her own people for assisting Cortés. Chicana writers, in particular, often take a more understanding approach in their depictions of La Malinche. In *Puppet: A Chicano Novella* (1985), Margarita Cota-Cárdenas incorporates La Malinche as a character who critiques the Chicano community's perpetuation of a misogynist history that continues to use her name to denigrate Chicanas who challenge contemporary forms of patriarchy. Sandra Cisneros's short story "Never Marry a Mexican" (1991) features a character named Clemencia who has an affair with a married man. Clemencia embodies the role of La Malinche because she has chosen a white lover over a Mexican man and because she uses her sexuality as a way of gaining power over men. Cisneros's version of Malinche presents a complex portrayal of an imperfect woman whose life is influenced by folklore about acceptable women's behavior.

One of the most prevalent male figures in Chicano literature is Francisco Doroteo Arango, better known as Pancho Villa. Villa was the leader of a rebel army from the northern state of Chihuahua that attempted to overthrow the Mexican government during the Mexican Revolution of 1910. Villa along with Emiliano Zapata is often depicted in Chicano art as an iconic revolutionary figure who epitomizes justice, courage, and strength. However, alternative interpretations of Villa's legacy can be found in Chicano literature and drama. Josephina Niggli's *This Is Villa!* (1938)

is one of the earliest depictions of Villa that portrays him as a temperamental and irrational figure. Writing almost 30 years later, Luis Valdez's *The Shrunken Head of Pancho Villa* (1964) uses Villa to inspire Chicano activism in the struggle for Chicano civil rights. The play also features another important folk hero, Joaquín Murrieta, the outlaw who eluded capture during the 1850s at the height of the California Gold Rush. Valdez uses Villa and Murrieta to symbolize the need for Chicanos to reclaim the radical spirit of past revolutionaries.

In 1981, Valdez brought one of the most popular twentieth-century Chicano folk heroes to life in the play and subsequent movie *Zoot Suit*. Set during the Zoot Suit riots of 1943, the play prominently features El Pachuco. A precursor to the contemporary Latino gang member, the Pachuco wore flamboyant suits, spoke in the vernacular of *caló,* and exhibited the stylized mannerisms of disaffected Mexican American urban youth. The Pachuco became a symbol of resistance to social repression, racial discrimination, and authority figures. The figure also represented how Mexican American youth actively formed their own folk traditions based on various cultural influences.

Folkloric Narratives of Death, Spirituality, and Healing

Recurrent references to death, spirits, cultural healers, and saints highlight the unique influence of Catholicism and Indigenous belief systems on Chicano culture. During holidays such as *Día de los Muertos* (Day of the Dead), many Chicanos commune with the deceased by constructing altars, decorating gravesites, and preparing symbolic foods. Such rituals help individuals accept the passing of loved ones and lessen the fear of death. These cultural beliefs about death are often found in Chicano literature. For example, Socorro Valdez, member of the Teatro Campesino, personified Death on stage by wearing black leotards painted with the white outline of a skeleton. Her character, La Muerte (Death), appeared in plays such as *Soldado Razo* (1971) and *La Gran Carpa de la Familia Rasquachi* (1974) as a figure that foreshadowed the fate of various characters.

In some novels, spirits of the deceased pose a menacing presence to the living. In Sandra Cisneros's *Caramelo* (2002), the young protagonist named Lala stands at her father's sickbed and argues with her deceased grandmother's spirit over his fate. The grandmother agrees to let go her grip on her son if Lala promises to tell her life story. Caught in a kind of purgatory, the grandmother cannot cross to the other side until her living relatives forgive her past behavior. *Caramelo* exemplifies how some Chicano writers use spirits to create opportunities for inter-generational dialogue among characters and to challenge the finality of death.

The topic of death, within a Catholic context, often produces narratives of heaven and hell. In these narratives, the Devil appears in different forms. Tomás Rivera's *. . . y no se lo tragó la tierra/ . . . And the Earth Did Not Devour Him* (1971) includes the story of a boy who is overcome with anger at seeing his family suffer from injustice, exploitation, and sickness while God and the Church fail to help his family. At one point, he summons the Devil and is surprised to find that no Devil appears. He then realizes that if there is no Devil, there must also be no heaven or God. In Aristeo

Author Sandra Cisneros sits for a portrait in San Antonio, Texas, in 2002. (AP/Wide World Photos)

Brito's *The Devil in Texas/ El Diablo en Tejas* (1976), the Devil appears in a variety of disguises and mingles with the townspeople. In one scene, he dresses up as a blond man, enters the church, and winks at a woman who later dies. Brito fashions his version of the Devil after common folk tales about a menacing figure who walks among the people taking advantage of human frailties and faults while instigating violence or death.

To counterbalance narratives of pain, trauma, and evil, Chicano literature often includes narratives of saints and spiritual healing. There are a vast number of officially and unofficially recognized saints who are revered for providing certain forms of assistance or protection to those who pray to them. Saints are particularly prevalent in Chicano literature as models of proper behavior. Yet, some writers like Arturo Islas, explore how Catholic expectations are often impossible to achieve. In *Migrant Souls* (1990), the family matriarch raises her daughters to emulate the Carmelite Saint Therese of Lisieux and to believe that women are meant to suffer in life while awaiting the glory of heaven. The daughters resist their mother's religious philosophy and create the "Order of Saint Wretched" to mock the inevitability of female misery. Ana Castillo's *So Far from God* (1993) names the protagonists Fe, Esperanza, and Caridad after the three daughters of Saint Sophia who were martyred in Rome under Hadrian's rule. While the three characters are martyred in her novel as well, Castillo emphasizes their struggles against social injustice and sexual repression as lessons for the contemporary reader.

In addition to religious figures, Chicano literature often features folk healers known as *curanderas*. *Curanderas* use Indigenous folk practices dating to pre-Columbian times to heal both physical and psychical maladies. They are often associated with supernatural powers because individuals seek their aid in curing illnesses such as *mal de ojo* (the evil eye) or *susto* (the loss of one's soul). Using herbs, chants, and rituals, the *curandera* embodies the healing knowledge of traditional communities and is seen as a non-Western resource of hope and guidance. Rudolfo Anaya's *Bless Me, Ultima* (1972) is perhaps the best-known novel featuring a *curandera* and her mystical practices. Ultima, the *curandera,* teaches a young boy named Antonio about the folk art of healing which he eventually practices as he assists her in saving his bewitched uncle's life. The novel focuses on Antonio's struggle with his faith in Catholicism and *curanderismo.* Yet, Ultima shows Antonio that both belief systems can help him understand philosophical questions about his destiny. Like Anaya, Alex Espinosa shows how *curanderas* are complementary spiritual advisors to the church. *Still Water Saints* (2007) features Perla Portillo, a *curandera* who owns a religious supply shop that sells charms, candles, and herbs. As troubled members of the town seek her advice, she gives them healing herbs and directions to pray to particular saints. Organized around the Feast Days of Saints, the novel presents a fictional example of how Chicano communities often blend church and folk practices in their search for spiritual guidance and emotional peace.

BELINDA LINN RINCÓN

See also: Aztec Empire; Aztlán; "Ballad of Gregorio Cortez"; Cabeza de Baca, Fabiola; Chicano/a Art and Folklore; Cihuacoatl; Coatlicue; Corrido (Ballad); Día de los Muertos (Day of the Dead); Día de los Muertos: Migration and Transformation to the U.S.; El Diablo; Farmworkers' Theater; Folk Narratives: Folk Tales, Legends, and Jokes; Folk Tales; Greater Mexico and Its Folklore; Jaramillo, Cleofas; La Llorona (The Wailing Woman); La Santísima Muerte; Lummis, Charles F.; Malinche; Murieta, Joaquín; Pachucos; Pachuquismo: 1940s Urban Youth; Paredes, Américo; Valdez, Luis; Virgin of Guadalupe: History and Fiestas Guadalupanas; Zoot Suit

Further Reading

Contreras, Sheila Marie. *Blood Lines: Myth, Indigenism and Chicana/o Literature.* Austin: University of Texas Press, 2008.

González, Jovita. *Dew on the Thorn.* Edited by José Limón. Houston: Arte Público Press, 1997.

Kanellos, Nicolás. "Folklore in Chicano Theater and Chicano Theater as Folklore." *Journal of the Folklore Institute* 15, no.1 (1978): 57–82.

Orchard, William, and Yolanda Padilla. *The Plays of Josefina Niggli: Recovered Landmarks of Latino Literature.* Madison: University of Wisconsin Press, 2007.

Perez, Domino Renee. *There Was a Woman: La Llorona from Folklore to Popular Culture.* Austin: University of Texas Press, 2008.

Rebolledo, Tey Diana. *Women Singing in the Snow: A Cultural Analysis of Chicana Literature.* Tucson: University of Arizona Press, 1995.

Saldívar, Ramón. *Chicano Narrative: The Dialectics of Difference.* Madison: University of Wisconsin Press, 1990.

CHICANO SPANISH

A dialect of Mexican Spanish found in the American Southwest, Chicano Spanish varies greatly depending on region. Its presence reflects primarily and most importantly the phenomenon of languages in contact in addition to slow linguistic acculturation because of immigration, the border and social experience. Spanish spoken by Chicanos is not considered standard Spanish due to nonstandard lexical items such as those reflecting English influence. These are either referred to as Anglicisms or, among Chicanos, *pochismos*. Most studies of Chicano Spanish fall into the realm of sociolinguistics, an interdisciplinary concerned with a range of topics: language, dialect-variety, attitude and behavior toward language, and speech communities. Folkloric studies, on the other hand, are concerned with how the language is used to convey stories, legends, song, etc.

Why does Chicano Spanish exist? One view states that Chicano speech is the result of political and economic dominance due to military conquest. This resulted in the imposition of English. Other perspectives view these changes as an invasion on the Spanish language. While Spanish has been spoken continuously since 1598, forms of Spanish have changed from generation to generation. What results is a linguistic diversity that cannot easily be pegged to all individuals: complete linguistic assimilation (to English), or different forms of bilingualism (fluent to unstable).

The sources of Chicano Spanish are also of interest. Texas Spanish draws from northeastern Mexico, while New Mexico/Colorado's use of archaisms draws from sixteenth-century Castilian Spanish. Arizona Spanish is influenced by migrations from the northern Mexican state of Sonora while California Spanish draws from Arizona Spanish. In California, however, Spanish is also changing as immigrants from all parts of Mexico and Central America affect Spanish there.

The historic interaction of cultures has led to a word play of languages. Loanwords are contained in the history of Spanish in the Americas: from the numerous Indigenous terms adapted into Mexican Spanish to English loanwords which shape Chicano Spanish. Urbanization, mechanization of agriculture, industrialization and growth of agribusiness contributed loanwords. As early as 1905 Aurelio Espinoza found 135 loanwords in New Mexico. Some indicate measurement; e.g., money in the following examples: *cuara, nicle, dola*. Some, occupations: *jobe, weldedor, emplastador, factoria, troquero*. Others, consumer goods: *overoles, suera, balun*. Then also, foods: *aiscrin, jeli, lonche*.

Other characteristics of Chicano Spanish are seen with the use of *caló* and code-switching (switching languages in a phrase, a word, or mid-sentence), a switch from one language to another as a form of substitution (*¿Cómo te fue en el dance?*). *Caló* synthesizes different varieties of Chicano language and reflects a generation in the midst of acculturation: Finally, *caló* made its way into the Southwest via immigration. Its peak development was in the 1940s and 1950s when it was associated with Pachucos. Two unique examples of *caló* can be found in José Montoya's poem "El Louie," or in Luis Valdez's film/play *Zoot Suit*.

Although Chicano Spanish is often viewed negatively by speakers of standard Spanish, it actually displays enormous creativity in its adaption to an English-speaking environment. It follows strict standard Spanish rules of grammar for the conjugation of verbs when adapting English ones. For example, the English verb "push" when adapted to the Spanish language is conjugated as if it were a standard "-ar" -ending Spanish verb such as "hablar."

Table 1.

Puchar (Puch + -ar)	
Yo pucho	nosotros puchamos
Tu puchas	ustedes puchan
El pucha	ellos puchan
For the English verb "watch" it becomes	
Guachar (Watch + -ar with the Spanish pronunciation of the "w")	
Yo guacho	nosotros guachamos
Tu guachas	ustedes guachan
El guacha	ellos guachan

Most English verbs can be incorporated into the Spanish language by adding to the English infinitive the "-ar" ending of Spanish verb infinitives and conjugating as if it were a Spanish verb such as detailed above.

Folklore, i.e., folksongs, proverbs, riddles, games, and folk plays as well as other aspects of cultural production were essential for maintaining Spanish. But traditional folk expressions are largely found to be in traditional Mexican Spanish. How does Chicano Spanish fit into this? Through pronunciation and grammar, one can clearly distinguish between Chicano Spanish and Mexican Spanish. One hears, "It's just Spanglish!" Spanglish being the word often used to designate Chicano Spanish which is perceived to be a mixture of Spanish and English.

Chicano Spanish and folklore should be understood as a form of linguistic performance, a method of using language to present aspects of culture. Forms of expression include historical discourse—not the academic kind but an informal, unofficial variety where discussions reflect the use of memory and insight. This could be a talk on an old church or family events. Also, proverbs or *dichos*, which are sayings that provide moral learning, provide insight into forms of knowledge traditionally handed down via the oral tradition from one generation to the next. However, the growing use of English among the third and fourth generations accounts for a diminished use of this form of expression.

Nevertheless, during the Chicano Movement of the 1960s and 1970s, it was a tremendous source of creativity for Chicano and Chicana authors. Its use was generously sprinkled throughout the works of authors and was a key element incorporated in the artistic expressions of most Chicano/a authors.

Lately, folklorists have begun to examine humor as a form of expression. For example, the prominent jest in Texas has to do with misunderstandings in language. Cross-cultural in nature, these forms of jokes examine misunderstanding whether it is an Anglo who is the cause or the Chicano. The point of these forms of humor inadvertently addresses questions of language and its importance in the area of communication. And it is here where one learns the full flavor of Chicano Spanish. With humor, the participants tell their jokes and stories utilizing their linguistic experience in Chicano Spanish

Of late, Chicano Spanish has come of age in literary folklore, in part because it reflects generational changes in that process, say, from oral traditions to writing novels. In addition to short stories, poetry, theater, and film, Chicano Spanish expresses the thoughts and experiences of Chicanos not always evident in traditional folklore. There is also the sense that the use of Chicano Spanish creates a form of resistance in the manner in which the expression takes place. Chicano poetry of the Chicano Movement is a prime example. Musicians utilize traditional music, but with lyrics in Chicano Spanish; songs like "El Quinto Sol" use codeswitching to convey political-historical messages about social conditions in the Americas.

CARLOS F. ORTEGA

See also: Caló (Folk Speech); Folk Speech and Folklore; Valdez, Luis

Further Reading

Fuentes, Dagoberto, and José López. *Barrio Language: First Dictionary of Caló.* Los Angeles: Southland Press, 1974.

Reyna, José R. *Raza Humor: Chicano Joke Tradition in Texas.* San Antonio: Penca Books, 1980.

Saldívar, Ramón. *Chicano Narrative: The Dialectics of Difference.* Madison: University of Wisconsin Press, 1990.

Stavans, Ilan. *Spanglish: The Making of a New American Language.* New York: Harper Collins Publishers, 2003.

West, John O. *Mexican-American Folklore: Legends, Songs, Festivals, Proverbs, Crafts, Tales of Saints, of Revolutionaries, and More.* Little Rock, AR: August House Publishers, 1988.

CHICHARRONES

Essentially, *chicharrón* is a food made from pig skin. Throughout the world, there are numerous variations of this delicacy. However, the word "*chicharrón*" is merely a name for what, in many parts of Latin America, is almost a major food group. Even so, there are regional differences in how people eat *chicharrones* and what they call them. Despite these regional differences, it is important to recognize the initial influence that the Spanish explorers and conquistadores had on introducing the pig to the New World, for the customs that emigrated came from the same regions as their human counterparts, especially Castile, Extremadura, and Galicia.

According to Rabbi Joseph Telushkin's (1991) *Jewish Literacy: The Most Important Things to Know about the Jewish Religion, Its People and Its History*, Christopher Columbus's diary begins in the following way: "In the same month in which their Majesties [Ferdinand and Isabella] issued the edict that all Jews should be driven out of the kingdom and its territories, in the same month they gave me the order to undertake with sufficient men my expedition of discovery to the Indies." On July 30th, 1492, the Jews were expelled from Spain. Furthermore, in *Spain: A Country Study,* Solsten and Meditz (1988) stated that 1492 also marked the overthrow of Granada and the hundreds of thousands of Moslems living there. In Spain, there was a great sense of urgency in enforcing religious conformity as it was assumed that religious unity was necessary for political unity.

Benjamin Joseph Zadik (2000), in his in-depth study *The Iberian Pig in Spain and the Americas at the Time of Columbus,* explained that throughout the everyday contact between old Christians and new *conversos* (new Jewish converts) and *moriscos,* there were periodic irritation and conflict over dress, speech, customs and, above all, food. It could not have been easy for either of these abstemious cultures to quickly take up pork into their food habits. Although there were exceptions, for the most part, these religions had considered the animal impure, sinful, and unclean. The religious doctrines forbade them even to touch the pig, so the thought of eating one must have been a humiliating sacrifice. In Spain, during these times, it was actually a display of loyalty to publically slaughter a pig. Ultimately, the Spanish had formed a connection with the pig over a millennium, and it was this culture and diet they would bring to the Americas.

In 1493, on the second voyage leaving Spain, Columbus brought eight pigs that were not slaughtered and that proved to be pivotal in transforming the New World. The arrival of pigs predated the arrival of cows in the New World, and the pigs played a vital role in the conquest and colonization of the Americas. Although the horses, dogs, and asses that the Spanish brought with them were crucial as instruments of war, pigs proved to be the primary source of sustenance for their soldiers during the first part of the Spanish invasion.

In addition to the basic survival of the Spanish soldiers, pigs were essential to progress and stability of the colonies. They provided a potential source of income and were used five to twenty times more than other livestock. Pigs were cheaper and smaller than cows for the voyages. Columbus perceived that the future of what he thought were the Indies, under Spanish control, necessitated the agro–pastoral economy and way of life the Spanish were accustomed to. Later, during the year 1519, Hernán Cortés landed at Veracruz on the coast of what is now called Mexico. In the 300 years that followed, the region included all of what is now called Central America and the Southwestern United States and California. Cortés also relied heavily on the various supplies provided by pigs. The Spanish explorers and conquistadores were predisposed primarily to pork as its meat provided sustenance for them. *Salazones, jamones,* and *embutidos* were some forms of salted and prepared pork that were able to be stored for later use. Pork fat provided a substitute for olive oil, which was not readily available in Mexico and other parts of the New World, and it was also used for soap and candles.

In addition to its various uses, the various cuts of pork were used to distinguish classes of people. Pork was thought to be a preferred animal that fed all classes; that is, the nobles got the best cuts while the subjected peasants got the feet, organs, and lesser cuts. The social role of the pig was also important when the Spanish clergy set up the missions. The religious orders attempted to convert the natives and teach them to raise pigs in the process. Communicating a preference for pork was one way the Spanish definitely established a sense of elitism through the use of food. For example, Father Bernardino de Sahagún, the Spanish Franciscan missionary and compiler of *el Códice Florentino* has been noted as emphasizing the importance of teaching the natives to "eat that which the Castilian people eat because it is good food, that with which they are raised; they are strong, and pure, and wise . . . you [the natives] will become the same way if you eat their food" (Zadik 2000, 57).

Despite this sense of paternalism, some Indigenous groups valued the added source of sustenance that pigs provided, and they simply fit in with native hunting practices better than cattle. Also, pigs were low-maintenance animals because they ate scraps, needed less care, and reproduced quickly. Despite these attributes, it is very important to note that other Indigenous groups found the pig dirty and disgusting. The responses of the Indigenous people to European imports and customs were not uniform. Because of their own dietary preferences, which included maize, beans and other vegetables, and fruits as well as seeds, *hierbas* (collard greens), and regional fowl or fish, many Indigenous people were opposed to eating pork due to the pigs' dirty habits and their association with the invading Spanish.

It is a well-known fact that the pigs and other new goods introduced by the Spanish irrevocably changed the diet of the Indigenous nations. Diseases ultimately caused a rapid decline in the overall native population. Zadik (2000) has explained that crowd diseases such as smallpox and influenza were primary causes and that pork itself was noted for transmitting several diseases, including brucellosis, leptospirosis, trichinosis, tuberculosis, and anthrax (60). Pigs had the potential to not only directly affect the native populations, but they also had the ability to indirectly affect them by contaminating the other regional animals that came in contact with the native peoples, even those that abstained from eating pork at the time. The cornerstones of the Spanish diet consisted of olive oil, meat, wheat, and wine. Warnings by reporters, such as one from Citlaltepec against adapting such habits, had been issued. It was noted that *comiendo carne de vaca y puerco*—not to mention *manteca*—*y bebiendo vino* would lead to unhealthy habits and result in detrimental effects among the native populations (Zadik 2000, 64).

Eventually, many Indigenous-Hispano cultures throughout Latin America would incorporate the pig as a staple in their national cuisines. This is still true even five hundred years after the arrival of the Spanish in the New World as they knew it. *Chicharrones* (most commonly referred to as fried pig skins) have come to be a familiar food in places such as Argentina, Bolivia, Brazil, Colombia, Cuba, Dominican Republic, Guatemala, Honduras, El Salvador, Mexico, Nicaragua, Panama, Peru, Venezuela, and even Puerto Rico and the Philippines, among others. Some of these countries use other variations of meats, such as chicken, mutton, or even beef. Also, some of these countries do not use the pig skin exclusively, but rather prefer to use pork meat for their dishes. This is so, for example, in parts of Latin America that use pork meat as the primary ingredient in a stuffing for *arepas* or *pupusas*, or as the meat portion of various stews and soups.

However, those that specifically use the skin, use it after it has been seasoned and deep fried. In many parts of Latin America, fried pig skins may be eaten as a snack or appetizer. In Mexico, the fried pig skins are also typically eaten in a *taco* or *gordita* with green or red sauce. Obviously, *chicharrones* can be prepared, served, and enjoyed in numerous ways depending on specific localities. Although there are several types of regional varieties, *chicharrones* frequently take on two forms—one is served as a main dish and the other is eaten as a snack or appetizer—*botana* or *antojito*. Bob Mrotek (2009) has provided a very useful and extensive description of *chicharrones*, specifically as to how they are prepared in Mexico. There are several types of pig skin that come out of the *carnitas* cooking process that fall under the category "*chicharrón*" depending on what part of the animal they come from. In some places, the fat located under the skin is very thin and thus the *cueritos* are mostly thin pieces of skin. In other places, however, the layer of fat under the skin is very thick such as on the back and the belly. This fat clings very stubbornly to the skin and the two are very hard to separate. This is also where much of the lard comes from that is rendered out during the making of *carnitas*.

This type of *chicharrón* is often used to make *chicharrones en salsa verde* (fried pork skins in tomatillo sauce) or *chicharrones con chile* (fried pork skins cooked with some variation of a sauce whose base consists of *chiles serranos* and *jitomates*). It is soft, gelatinous, and spicy and is often served with *arroz mexicana* (rice with tomato, garlic, carrot, and onion). Commonly, among many rural populations, it is recognized as a delicious and popular dish. There is another form called *lonja de cerdo* (or fatback) which consists of small squares of skin with fat. The small squares are about one half inch thick and come from the back of the pig. These are fried in a pan until the lard is rendered out and they turn brown and crispy.

There are other forms of *chicharrón* where the lard has been mostly rendered out and they are in a firm or "dry" state. The snack and appetizer versions of *chicharrones* come from this drier form. Mroteck (2009) has noted that the first of these is called *cuero duro* meaning "hard skin" and often just called *duro*. This is made from pieces of skin from which most of the subcutaneous fat and hair has been removed by scraping. The pieces of skin are then boiled in water and hung up to dry for about twenty-four hours. Then they are placed in vats of very hot vegetable oil until the skin "puffs up" and becomes thick and light like a piece of foam. The skin is drained and left to cool and harden into sheets. *Duro* can be used in several different ways. It is often used as an *antojito* or *botana* (appetizer or snack) served in hand-sized pieces with a *salsa picante* like *salsa Valentina*. The rich complexity of the pig, specifically, in its form as the Latin American delicacy *chicharrón*, is layered by a unique history that has been both maintained and altered by the diverse peoples of the Americas.

Silvia Toscano Villanueva

See also: Maíz; Frijoles (Beans); Salsa (Sauce)

Further Reading

Mroteck, B. "Chicharrones." 2009. [Website] Retrieved December 12th, 2010 from Mexico Bob's blogspot.

Solsten, E., and S. W. Meditz. *Spain: A Country Study*. Washington, D.C.: GPO for the Library of Congress, 1988.

Telushkin, J. *Jewish Literacy: The Most Important Things to Know About the Jewish Religion, Its People and Its History*. New York: William Morrow, 1991.

Zadik, B.J. "The Iberian Pig in Spain and the Americas at the Time of Columbus." Master's Thesis, University of California, Berkeley, 2000.

CHILDREN'S SONGS AND GAMES

The songs and games of children around the world are emblematic of the folk process and under examination simultaneously demonstrate the variety and the basic similarities among world cultures. Literally passed from generation to generation, from mother to child, from sibling to sibling, lullabies, knee-dandling rhymes, and finger and toe naming and counting rhymes exist in every culture, as do the circle games and nonsense songs of older children. The songs and games of Latino children are no exception to the rule.

Circle Games ("Arroz con leche")

The Spanish-speaking world has given us many circle game songs, among them "A la rueda" ("Round and Round"), "San Serení" (also known as "San Cerolín," "San Severino," and "Los talleres de la vida" ("The Careers of Life"), "Tengo una muñeca" ("I Have a Doll"), "Juan Pirolero," and "Naranja dulce" ("Sweet Orange"). However, the most famous of all of these is "Arroz con leche," or "Rice Pudding," a circle game known in various versions in Spain, in every Spanish-speaking country, and among Latinos/as in the United States. The in-depth exposition of its numerous variants and the different games that can be played with it which follows illustrates the general process by which all of the other material mentioned in this article has evolved.

While nearly everyone in the Spanish-speaking world knows the song and the game, there is great variation in the words sung and the way the game is played. It is probably this very flexibility that has insured its longevity. Below is a version from modern-day Spain (a variant of the lyric in parentheses) which tells the story of a man or woman who wishes to marry a widow or widower. Children hold hands in a circle with one in the middle and walk around singing as follows:

> Arroz con leche / Me quiero casar / Con una viudita (una señorita) / de la capital (que sepa bailar) / Que sepa coser / Que sepa bordar (planchar) / Que ponga la mesa (Que sepa abrir la puerta) / En su santo lugar (Para ir a jugar).
>
> Rice pudding / I want to marry / A widow (a girl) / From the capital city (Who knows how to dance) / Who knows how to sew / Who knows how to embroider (iron) / Who sets the table (Who knows how to open the door) / In her holy place (To go out and play).

Here the circle stops moving and the child in the middle sings as follows:

> Yo soy la viudita (el viudito) / La hija (el hijo) del Rey / Me quiero casar / Y no hallo con quién.
>
> I am the widow(er) / The king's daughter (son) / I want to marry / But to whom, I don't know.

Then he or she turns around pointing to one child and saying "*Con éste/a sí*," (With this one, yes), then pointing to another, saying, "*Con éste/a no*" (With this one, no). Then the child turns back to the first one singled out and says, "*Con este / a señorito / a / Me caso yo*" (With this one / Am I going to marry). The song then begins again with the couple dancing briefly in the middle until the original widow or widower goes off to join the circle, leaving the new one to choose a new partner.

In its life in the Americas, the song and the game were both simplified in some places and enlarged upon in others. A rather elaborate version comes from Puerto Rico which is played among boys and girls much as described above, but with more words and acting. The circle moves around a "*viudita*" or "*viudito*" singing the words as above with some minor variations. When the widow announces her indecision about her choice, the circle starts to move again, singing: *Y siendo tan bella / ¿Ni encuentras con quién? / Elige a tu gusto / Que aquí tienes cien.* (And as beautiful as you are / Can't you find one? / Pick the one that you like / Of the hundred you have here).

Then the widow touches one and says "*Contigo sí*" (With you, yes), touches another and says, "*Contigo no*" (With you, no), then returns to the first one and gives a hug, singing, "*Contigo, mi vida, / Me casaré yo*" (With you, love of my life, I will wed). The new "widow" is then left in the center, the former takes her place in the circle, and the game continues.

The following versions show how the lyric to the song has become democratized on its journey to the United States:

> Yo soy la viudita / De Santa Isabel / Me quiero casar / Y no encuentro con quien / El mozo del cura / Me mandó un papel / Y yo le mando otro / Con Santa Isabel / Mi madre lo supo / ¡Qué palos me dio! / ¡Malhaya sea el hombre / Que me enamoró! / Con éste si / etc.

> I am the little widow / From Santa Isabel / I want to marry / And don't know to whom / The priest's servant / Sent me a note / And I sent him another / With Santa Isabel / My mother found out / What a beating I got / I feel sorry for the man / Who falls in love with me! / With this one, yes, etc.

Here the "little widow" not only still has to answer to her mother, but in her exchanging notes with the priest's man she is setting her sights rather low. Furthermore, the song is sung completely from the female point of view as is the version below:

> Arroz con leche / Me quiero casar / Con un mexicano / Que sepa cantar / El hijo del rey / Me manda un papel / Me manda decir / Que me case con él / Con éste si / Con éste no / Con éste mero / Me caso yo.

> Rice pudding / I want to marry / A Mexican / Who knows how to sing / The king's son / Sent me a note / Asking me if / I would marry him / With this one, yes. / With this one, no. / Only this one / Shall I marry.

There is no mention of a widow, and it is obvious that the girl is only interested in being wooed by someone who "knows how to sing"; the king's son does not impress her at all. The old-world story of the little widow with all the attainments of a lady—and presumably a tidy fortune—being able to choose her next husband, has come down to every little girl being able to exercise the same freedom and making a "love match"—even if her mother disapproves.

In many instances, the game has been simplified so that the child in the middle simply closes his or her eyes and spins around and whomever he or she points to becomes the next to dance in the center. In other cases, it is a game played by girls only. When a "husband" is chosen, the two girls hug and retreat to the outside of the circle to clap and sing along until one "widow" is left unwed. She loses and the game starts again. However, the game is also played by mixed groups of prepubescent boys and girls where a boy goes in the middle, spins with his eyes closed, and then must kiss or hug the girl to whom he has pointed. If he chooses not to do so, he must pay a forfeit of some kind agreed upon at the start of the game. (It can be surmised that most ten-year-old boys choose the forfeit.)

Up to now, no mention has been made of the music for this game song which has surely played a part its longevity. The old-world melody is sung in a fast 3/4 or 6/8 rhythm and has remained relatively intact with minor variations; nearly everyone will change a note here or there, especially children. However, the real transformation of the piece from Europe to the Americas is in the rhythm. While some people of Mexican or Central American heritage guard the 3/4 or 6/8 feel so common in Mexican folk music, on its journey to the United States the song has in most cases taken on a 4/4 feel. Furthermore, in listening to the versions sung by most people of Caribbean heritage, one can hear the unmistakable three against four feel so typical of Afro-Cuban music, and often the melody has been somewhat leveled, giving it less melodic movement but more rhythmic propulsion.

The melody also serves as the basis for another circle game from Mexico which is played in much the same way as the simplified versions of the game described above. However, the lyric has the seemingly completely unrelated text given here:

> A guanchilopostle, / A huanchiloé / A ver señorita / qué tal baila usted. /
> Oh, chepi, chepi, chepi, / oh, lero, lero, lé.
> To Guanchilopostle / To huanchiloé / Let's see, miss / How well you can dance. /
> Oh, chepi, chepi, chepi, / oh, lero, lero, lé.

No translation is given for most of the lyric here because while the words of the first couplet appear to be of Native American origin (perhaps Nahuatl), they are generally sung as nonsense syllables. The same case holds for the second couplet, in which "chepi, chepi" is the signal for the child in the middle to start spinning with eyes closed, and "lero, lero" is roughly equivalent to "la la la" in English songs. The wish expressed in the earlier-cited version of *"Arroz con leche"* for a *"señorita que sepa bailar"* is here turned into a direct request for the *"señorita"* to show what she can do.

The real interest of this song to this discussion, however, is that in some collected variants "chepi, chepi, chepi" has been changed to "chequi, chequi, chequi," which recalls the Puerto Rican children's circle game *"Cheki, morena."* The lyric is quoted here for comparison:

> Cheki, morena, cheki. / Cheki, morena, ¡Jue! / ¿Qué a dónde está / Ese ritmo caramba /
>   Del merecumbé?/
> Un pasito a'lante / Y otra para atrás / Y dando la vuelto, dando la vuelta, / ¿Quién se
>   quedará? / ¡Jue!
> Shake it, brown girl, shake it. / Shake it, brown girl, hey! / Where is that wild rhythm /
>   Of the merecumbé? /

A little step forward / And another to the back / And spinning round and round / Who will be the next? / Hey!

In this case, "cheki" has been assumed to be a transliteration of the English "shake it," a staple phrase in Afro-American children's songs, from "Little Sally Walker" ("Shake it to the east, / Shake it to the west, / Shake it to the one / That you love the best") in the United States, to what is probably more influential in this case, the West Indian circle game song, "There's a Brown Girl in the Ring"—the *morena* of "*Cheki, morena.*"

The obvious musical and thematic connections between these different songs for a similar game—"*Arroz con leche,*" "*A Guanchilopostle,*" and "*Cheki, Morena*"— not only bear testimony to the undeniable confluence of Spanish, Native, and African influences on Latino culture, but also to the universality of the circle game and its role as a common denominator among these once disparate cultures. It is not at all difficult to see that much of the blending of cultural attitudes and practices that is Latino culture developed almost imperceptibly on the playgrounds of the New World.

Perhaps the most interesting feature of this seminal text is its adaptability. Something about the song and its connection with a dessert that has probably graced the Hispanic table since the Arabs brought rice and cane sugar to Spain in the second half of the first Christian millennium resonates with children and adults alike. As with many of the songs and rhymes that follow, it has often served quadruple duty as a lullaby, a nursery school game, a girls' jump-rope song, a sort of counting-out game, and later as a rite of passage as a kind of "spin the bottle" courtship game, thus transcending not only time and place but the vagaries of developmental changes.

There is one other immensely popular and well-known circle game song that deserves mention in this connection, "*La víbora de la mar.*" The game is played something like "London Bridge" with two children holding hands raised high for the others to pass under as they sing the following:

> A la víbora, víbora de la mar, de la mar, / Por aquí pueden pasar. /
> Los de adelante corren mucho, / Los de atrás se quedarán, / Trás, trás, trás. /
> Una mexicana, que frutas vendía, / Ciruelas, chabacanos, melón y sandía. /
> Campanita de oro, / Déjame pasar, con todos mis hijos, /
> Menos éste de atrás. / Tras, tras, tras. /
> Será melón, será sandía, / Será la vieja del otro día!
> To the serpent, sea serpent, the sea, / You can all pass by here. /
> Those ahead run fast, / Those at the back will stay / Back, back, back. /
> A Mexican woman, who was selling fruit, / Plums, apricots, melon and watermelon, /
> Little gold bell, / Let me pass, with all my children, /
> Except the one at the back, back, back! /
> It'll be melon, it'll be watermelon, / It'll be the old woman from the other day.

The last time "*trás, trás, trás*" is sung, the two children lower their arms to trap whoever is passing under at the time. That child must then pick "*melón*" or "*sandía*" and in this way teams are determined for a game of tug of war. This elaborate counting-out game can be used to pick sides for any game of course, and sometimes is only sung up to the first "*tras, tras, tras*" when the trapped child is led out of the game. In another instance of a children's game doing double duty, this song is often sung at weddings in the Southwestern United States with the bride and groom raised on chairs to make the arch and others being hoisted in the air to extend the bridge as the game continues.

Lullabies

In discussing children's folklore, one should never underestimate the role mothers and young girls play in communicating the tradition from one generation to the next. The earliest connection children have to song is often the lullabies, or "*canciones de cuna*" (cradle songs), sung to them and the hand and feet play games that caregivers use to amuse them. Traditionally young girls have been given this responsibility, leaving their mothers free to do other work. In this case, any song can become a lullaby if sung in a quiet, soothing manner, and indeed folklore collectors in the Southwestern United States have found instances of everything from the previously cited play songs to "*La Cucaracha*" and "*La Llorona*" being sung as lullabies.

That said, the most widely sung lullaby in the Spanish-speaking world is "Duérmete, mi niño." The most common version in print goes as follows:

> Duérmete, mi niño. / Duérmete solito, / Que cuando despiertes / Te daré atolito. / Duérmete, mi niño. / Duérmete, mi sol, / Duérmete pedazo / De mi corazón.
> Go to sleep, my child. / Go to sleep, all by yourself, / And when you awake / I'll give you atole to drink. /
> Go to sleep my child. / Go to sleep, my sun. / Go to sleep, you little piece / Of my heart.

The reference to *atole*, a sweet Mexican drink of various flavors thickened with corn meal, identifies this as a Mexican version.

However, this identification matters little, and it is hardly worth quoting other variants because there are nearly as many as there are mothers. The melody of the song is traditionally contained within the sixth degree of the scale and suggests no harmonization beyond the tonic and the dominant, which leaves it wide open for embellishment or improvisation. The repetitive lyric framework invites the singer to add whatever pet names she likes to lengthen the song. While they are not usually printed in collections, mothers often sing versions that warn the child to go to sleep before "*el cuco*" or "*el cucuy*" (the "boogie man") comes to eat him up or take him "down below." This sort of improvisation is found to some degree among all cultures, but it is especially common in Native American tradition, in which the improvisation of lullabies is often one of the first skills expected to be learned by young girls, as well as in various African song traditions. This African and Native influence clearly plays a role in this aspect of the Latino tradition.

Finger and Toe Enumerations

After lullabies, the most important songs sung to babies are hand and feet games and finger and toe numerations to keep the child amused. A mother or other caregiver will take the baby's hand and moving it in rhythm chant: "*Que linda manito / Que tiene el bebé / Que linda, que mona / Que bonita es*" (What a pretty little hand / The baby has / How pretty, how cute / How beautiful it is). Or patting the baby on the head with its own hand she will sing: "*Azótate la mocita / Con la mano en la cabecita*" (Pat the little child / With a hand on its little head). When the child is older and gaining greater awareness and motor control, the caretaker takes the child's finger, gently pokes the opposite palm with it and sings, "*Pon, pon, pon / El dedito en el pilón. / Pon, pon, pon, / El dinerito en el bolsón*" (Put, put, put, / The little finger in the palm. / Put, put, put, / Your change in your purse). Another of these goes, "*Cinco lobitos / tiene la loba, / cinco lobitos / tras de la escoba*" (Five little wolves / Has the mother wolf / Behind the broom): the "mother wolf" grabs each little finger as she says "cinco lobitos," then sweeps them all up in the broom.

One toe enumeration goes: *Cuando voy / A la casa de Peña, / Con la patita / le hago la seña. / Ven acá / Burrito viejo, / Daca la pata / De conejo.* (When I go / To my friends' house / With my little paw / I wave "hello." / Come here / You old donkey / Give me the paw / Of the little rabbit). (The whole foot is grabbed up and waved at "*le hago la seña*" and "*la pata de conejo.*") There are many such finger enumerations in which various names and characters are created for each finger. There is a simple one that names each finger from little finger to thumb this way: *Chiquito y bonito; Señor de los anillos; Tonto y loco; Lamecazuelas; y Mata piojos* (Teeny and handsome; Mr. Ring-finger; Foolish and crazy; Pot-wiper; Louse-killer). ("*Matapiojos*" [louse-killer] is just a step away from the etymological root of the actual word for the thumb in Spanish, "*pulgar*" which is derived from "*pulga*," flea.)

Following the lead of this is a game in which the adult takes each finger in turn from little finger to the thumb, saying, "*Éste, chiquito y bonito. Éste, señor de anillitos. Éste, tonto loco. Éste se va a la escuela / lame cazuelas. Y éste se lo come todo*" (This one, teeny and handsome. This one, Mr. Ringman; This one, crazy fool. This one goes to school / licks the pot. And this one eats everything up!). With "*y éste se lo come todo*" the adult may grab all the fingers under the thumb or pretend to eat them all up. A variation on this theme goes like this: "*Éste compró un huevito. Éste encendió el fuego. Éste trajo la sal. Éste lo guisó. Y éste pícaro gordo ¡se lo comió!*" (This one bought a little egg. This one lit the fire. This one brought the salt. This one cooked it. And this chubby little rascal ate it all up!).

Once out of the crib, there is no need to stop with fingers and toes. The following familiar game has been collected in many places and in many variants, but it is really just a dressed-up excuse for tickling. The adult acts the part of a butcher chopping first at the knee, then the thigh, then the arm, then the shoulder, and saying while doing so, "*Cuando vayas al mercado, no compres carne de aquí, ni de aquí, ni de aquí, ni de aquí*" (When you go to the market, never buy meat from here, or here, or here, or here). Then, while the adult picks a favorite spot to tickle, come the words, "*sólo de aquí!*" (only from here!).

These finger plays in turn become integrated into social play as the child gets older. A counting-out rhyme game played by children of Puerto Rican heritage called "*La vieja y las papayas*" begins with children putting their hands on a flat surface with all their fingers spread out. The leader goes around the circle pinching each finger in turn while repeating the following rhyme:

> Una vieja fue a la playa / A buscar una papaya. /
> La papaya no servía / Vete vieja con tu porquería.
> An old woman went to the beach / To find a papaya. /
> The papaya was no good. / Old lady, go on with your foolishness.

Whoever's finger is pinched on the last word puts this finger out of play and the game continues until one child has hidden all of his or her fingers. He or she becomes the leader of the next game.

Knee-Dandling Games

Other games toddlers enjoy are what folklorists refer to as "knee-dandling" games. Given that it was the Spanish who first brought horses to the New World it is little wonder that in the Southwestern United States we find numerous horse-themed knee-dandling games in Spanish. One such is sung by an adult like this, with the child bumping up and down on the knee as if riding:

> Caballito, caballito / No me tumbes, no me tumbes: / A galope y a galope
> Recio, recio, recio. / ¡Qué viva Antonio!
> Horsey, horsey / Don't you throw me, don't you throw me! / Gallop and gallop /
> Hold strong, hold strong, hold strong. / Long live Antonio!

Another goes like this:

> De esos caballos que vienen y van / Ninguno me gusta / Como el alazán
> Hágase pa' acá / Hágase pa' allá
> Que mi caballito / Lo atropellará.
> Horses come and horses go / But I don't care for any / As I do for the sorrel /
> Go this way / Go that way / So that my little horse / might knock him off.

Yet another variant of this has been collected and goes as follows:

> De los caballitos / Que vienen y van / ninguno me gusta / como el alazán. /
> De cuatro caballos / que me han regalado / a mi el que me gusta / es el colorado. /
> De esos caballos / que vende usted / ninguno me gusta / como el que se fue.
> Of all of the horses / That come and go / I don't care for any / As I do for the sorrel. /
> Out of the four horses / That were given to me / The one that I like / Is the roan. /
> And of those horses / that you are selling / I don't care for any as much /
> As the one that's gone away.

This wry comment on the capricious nature of our affections is, of course, lost in laughter as the child's bottom falls through the grown-up's knees.

One last horse chant, perhaps the simplest, recalls the water game "Motor Boat" that parents play with children in English. Here the knee-bounces begin slowly and increase in tempo as the adult names the following gaits:

> Al paso, al paso, al paso / Al trote, al trote, al trote, / Al galope, al galope, al galope!
> To the walk, walk, walk / To the trot, trot, trot, / To the gallop, gallop, gallop!

If this abundance of horse-themed games seems unusually large to the average Anglophone American, it is then perhaps more surprising to discover the preponderance of the donkey in Latino folklore.

Teaching Songs

A popular burro song for young children is "*Mi burrito está enfermo*" (My Donkey Is Sick). A line is added to the chorus as each verse is sung, challenging the memories of the singers. Here is one version:

> A mi burro, a mi burro, / Le duele la cabeza, / Y el médico le manda /
> Una gorrita negra, / Una gorrita negra / Y mueve las patitas.
> My poor burro, my poor burro / His head hurts. / And the doctor ordered /
> A black cap / A black cap / And move your little hooves.

Then the donkey's throat hurts, his ribs hurt, his heart hurts, and finally he gets well, but the doctor always orders something more so that the final verse is a long list of prescribed remedies:

> Trocitos de manzana, / Gotitas de limón, / Chaqueta amarilla, / Una bufanda blanca, /
> Una gorrita negra, / Y mueve las patitas.
> Apple slices, / Lemon drops, / A yellow jacket, / A White scarf, /
> A black cap, / And move your little hooves.

This type of song is only as short as the imagination of the singers, and the longer it gets, the more fun children have with it. The hidden agenda in this type of songs is to teach the children vocabulary such as the parts of the body, colors, and different nouns.

Equally as entertaining though more a test of stamina than memory is a "teaching" song of obscure origin which is found nearly everywhere and appears to be of Spanish origin called "*Los Elefantes*" (The Elephants). The charm of this song is that it can repeat for as long as the singers wish to continue it and to as high as they can count, the image that it conjures up becoming sillier and sillier as it goes:

> Un elefante / Se balanceabea / Sobre la tela de una araña / Y como ésta no se rompía
> (Como veía que resistía) / Fue a llamar / A otro elefante (A un camarada) /
> Dos elefantes / Se balanceaban etc.

> An elephant / Was swinging / On a spider web / And when it didn't break (As he saw
> that it held up) / He went and called / Another elephant (friend) / Two elephants /
> Were swinging etc.

These elephants do not appear to have any particular cultural significance but teach children to count and make children laugh.

Another fun song which is enjoyed by all ages is called "*La Tía Mónica*" (Aunt Monica). It can be sung and played in a circle with one person leading the group, or children may take turns demonstrating Tía Mónica's moves as they go around the circle. The chorus goes as follows:

> Yo tengo una tía / Llamada Mónica / Que cuando va a bailar, / Le dicen "u la la."
> I have an aunt / named Monica / And when she starts to dance / Everyone says
> "Ooh la la!"

The leader then demonstrates how Tía Mónica moves her eyes while dancing, and everyone imitates the example and sings along as follows:

> Así mueve los ojos, / Así, así, así / Así se da una vuelta, / Así, así, así.
> She moves her eyes like this, / Like this, like this, like this. / She spins around like
> this, / Like this, like this, like this.

The song continues naming body parts down to the feet and finishes with "*todo el cuerpo*" (the whole body), at which point everyone falls apart giggling as they try to put together all the crazy moves they invented during the song. The song is obviously designed to teach body parts.

The Future of the Tradition

So far, despite the desire of many Latino children and parents to assimilate into the broader Anglo culture, there has been a generally conservative trend in the preservation of children's folk culture. That is to say, parents tend to sing the lullabies that were sung to them as children, and bilingual children tend to play the games and sing the songs that their parents did. Furthermore, the constant influx of new immigrants from Latin America to the United States provides a source of contact with and renewal of Latinos/as' folk traditions. However, it cannot be denied that as Latinos/as become more upwardly mobile and as immigrant parents break their traditional patterns of work and play in the United States, much of the traditional means for the passing on of this material will be lost. So the continuance of this conservative trend is in some doubt.

Indeed, the very existence of the great number of collections of Latino folksongs, rhymes, and games for children bears witness to the sense of loss some Latino parents already feel. The work of such collectors, adaptors, and popularizers as Alma Flor Ada and José-Luis Orozco fills a void for many parents and educators who desire to pass on some of their heritage to their children. To do so, they need to learn or relearn material that belonged to their parents' world but which they missed out on or have forgotten. In preserving this legacy and presenting it bilingually and in formats that are readily accessible to any parent who can read, as well as to the average teacher of language or of music, these authors do us all a great service. Educational trends toward bilingual and multicultural education and more world language instruction in pre-school and elementary school are bound to make extensive use of these authentic songs and games for the teaching of language and socialization, and this can only be good for the preservation of the tradition.

Yet there is a great deal that could be lost if these works alone were to become the canon, and educators the sole transmitters of the tradition. The current of improvisation inherent in the Native American and African roots of the tradition, as well as the rhythmic subtleties and linguistic nuances in the music and the texts are best communicated in the traditional way—mother and father to child, sibling to sibling, neighbor to neighbor. The dominant language of a culture generally takes precedence when absorbing "foreign" material into its tradition. This can be seen in the case of the other songs cited here in which material of African or Native American origin has been absorbed into or replaced by material in Spanish. The influence of the subordinate linguistic cultures is now apparent only, though strikingly, in performance practice. It is too soon to predict what the result of the mingling of Spanish- and English-speaking traditions which is Latino culture will have on its children's folk music.

Yet children are harsh critics and are certain to give long life to those songs and games which suit their desire for fun and silliness and have music that is easy to sing, move to, and remember, regardless of the language in which it is preserved.

JOSEPH FLOOD

See also: African Influence on Latino Folklore; Afro-Colombian Music; Chicano/a Literature and Folklore; Folk Narratives: Folk Tales, Legends, and Jokes; Folk Tales

Further Reading

Ada, Alma Flor, and F. Isabel Campoy. *Mamá Goose: A Latino Nursery Treasury*. New York: Hyperion, 2004.

Bernier-Grand, Carmen T. *Shake it, Morena! and Other Folklore from Puerto Rico*. Brookfield, CT: Millbrook Press, 2002.

Cantú, Norma E., and Olga Nájera-Ramírez, eds. *Chicana Traditions: Continuity and Change*. Urbana: University of Illinois Press, 2002.

Nava, Yolanda, ed. *It's All in the Frijoles*. New York: Fireside, 2000.

Orozco, José-Luis. *De Colores and Other Latin-American Folk Songs for Children*. New York: Dutton Children's Books, 1994.

Orozco, José-Luis. *Diez Deditos*. New York: Puffin, 2002.

Treviño, Rose Zertuche. *Read Me a Rhyme in Spanish*. Chicago: American Library Association, 2009.

CHILE AND ITS FOLKLORE

Due to its unique geography, the "crazy" geography of Chile, as Benjamin Suberca-seaux, a well-known Chilean writer, characterized it, the long and narrow country on the west side of the Andes Mountains in the Southern Hemisphere differs in some respects from other Latin American countries vis-à-vis its history, customs, and folklore influences. The territory that encompasses contemporary Chile was a distant and sparsely populated southern region of the Four Sectors of the Inka Tawantinsuyo, that is, the Inca Empire. It did not have, as other territories conquered by Spain did, an advanced Indigenous civilization whose rulers needed to be toppled such as was the case for the Aztecs and the Incas. Instead, the Spaniards who ventured south from Peru encountered first the inhospitable Atacama desert, known as the driest place in the world, and then, upon their arrival at the Central Valley's fertile lands, they faced the fierce opposition of the Mapuche tribes, the "people of the land," as they called themselves. The Mapuche Indians were so fierce that not even the Incas had been able to fully dominate them.

Constrained by geography, weather and Indigenous resistance, the Spaniards settled in the Near North (Norte Chico) and the Central Valley, a 700-mile-long region to the south of Santiago. The Central Valley was ideal for settlement since it has an excellent Mediterranean climate highly suitable for farming and for raising cattle. The area is protected from weather extremes by the Andes Mountains to the east and the coastal range to the west. As the Spaniards moved south, founding cities and fighting the Araucanians, or "bellicose people," as they called the rebellious Mapuches, they began establishing agricultural concerns and began laying down the foundations for what today constitutes the proud tradition of wine making and fruit and vegetable production that is exported and sold all over the world.

In Chile the Spaniards developed an agrarian way of life different from that of the large plantations, haciendas and *latifundios* common in other Latin American countries. Given the smaller nature of the agricultural settlements, there was no need to import black slaves for labor. The predominance of Spanish and mestizo ethnic groups over Indigenous and African peoples characterizes Chilean *criollo* culture and forms the basis for a contemporary Chilean identity. As the years went by, and especially after the country's independence from Spain (1818), the new republic promoted the development of the southern region, opening it up to European immigrants. Furthermore, the war effort with Peru brought Chile a large territory of desert land, rich in minerals and saltpeter deposits. This newfound wealth attracted immigrants from Europe and the Middle East. Today Chilean life is a rich component of these various ethnic groups. Its folklore, though, seems to be dominated by the *criollo* tradition of Central Chile which was established in the colonial period as well as by Indigenous elements in the other areas of the country.

Chile was first explored in 1536 by Diego de Almagro, one of the Spaniards who had conquered the Inca Empire. Almagro, however, encountered insurmountable difficulties and was forced to return to Peru. It was not until 1541 that Pedro de Valdivia, another officer in Francisco Pizarro's army, founded the city of Santiago and that the region began to be colonized. The area north of Santiago, or Norte Chico as this area is called, was developed as a mining and agricultural sector with two main urban settlements, La Serena and its port, Coquimbo. North of this region is the seemingly infinite desert that stretches all the way to southern Peru. After the Colonial period, it became the richest region of the new independent nation due to its mining interests and its large deposits of saltpeter.

The Central Valley area stretches from Santiago to the southern part of Chile where the rainy, cold forest predominates. This southern part of Chile is the main territory where the Indigenous tribes reside; a frontier which was not colonized until the nineteenth century, when the Chilean government opened it up for settlement to European immigrants, mainly from Germany and Switzerland. The southernmost section of the country, the one that stretches from the Isle of Chiloe to the tip of the continent in Cape Horn encompasses a region consisting of numerous fjords. It was mostly uninhabited until the twentieth century. Even today the only populated area extant there is the city of Punta Arenas which is located on the Strait of Magellan. This land is known as Patagonia and was developed specifically for raising sheep.

Thus, this long, thin stretch of territory encompassing the Chilean nation runs about 3,998 miles from its northern border to its southern tip and is divided into three geographic regions: North, Central, and South. And each section exhibits its own distinct cultural characteristics. In addition to the mainland, there is also Easter Island (Isla de Pascua), an exotic component located 2,000 miles off the coast of Chile in the middle of the Pacific Ocean and a reminder of Chile's maritime character. Easter Island was acquired in 1888, a time when Chile had maritime aspiration in the Pacific, an ocean that, as the National Anthem sings hopefully, "is a promise of a future splendor" for the nation.

Of the three regions cited above, the central one, where most of the Chilean population of about 15 million resides, constitutes the main component of Chilean tradition: its *criollo* culture. In a similar manner to other Latin American countries, it has a strong Hispanic element. However, it differs from most of the other countries in that it exhibits a weaker influence from the Indigenous cultures and very little from the African diaspora. The Indigenous population in the territory at the beginning of Spanish colonization was small and sparse, and even today it represents a very low percentage of the general population. There is a small concentration of Aymara people in the northern region and the Mapuche people in the south. Other Indigenous groups from the southern part of the country have been extinct for several years and are only a cultural memory. Because the agricultural production in the Central Valley did not require a large number of workers, as in the case of plantation agriculture, few black slaves were brought to the country during the colonial period, and those few were sold when slavery was abolished in 1823.

Most folkloric manifestations today come from the Central Valley and are related to the agricultural life extant there. Of particular interest for folklore studies are the *huaso*, or cowboy, the *china*, or maiden, and the *roto*, or poor laborer who can be a farm worker, a miner, or a man of all trades in the city and seaports. All of them, *huaso, china* and *roto,* are either white or mestizo. In addition to the Spanish and Indigenous components that predominate in the region there are also other European groups that arrived in small numbers after Chile obtained its independence from Spain in 1818. They tended to settle in urban centers, mostly Valparaiso and Santiago. In the beginning of nineteenth century the most numerous group of immigrants were from England, but eventually other countries were represented also. Europeans emigrated from Northern Italy, Germany, France, and later in the nineteenth century, from Croatia and from Christian groups in Lebanon, Syria and Palestine. The contribution of these peoples to the Chilean folklore is rather small as they did not form communities large enough to disseminate and perpetuate their folkloric traditions, except among their own families. One area where there is notable influence is in the area of eating customs. Particularly interesting in this respect is the case of the general custom of tea time (*la hora del té*), or *las onces* (eleven o'clock), a mixture of the traditional Spanish *merienda*, the English tea time and morning "eleveners," and the German *Abend*.

Among the festivities related to agricultural work, the most important ones are the *vendimia*, or the autumn collection of grapes and their stomping for the production of wine, and the rodeo—the main folkloric spectacle of the central region. The rodeo is the festivity that combines in one activity the most salient elements of Chilean folklore. The rodeo itself consists of a series of maneuvers undertaken by the *huasos* or cowboys to prove their ability in the control of cattle. These are done at a *medialuna*, the rodeo arena, originally built as a round arena flanked by a strong wall of slightly tilted wood beams covered in sections with thorny branches from the Chilean trees or other similar native brushes.

The central figure of the rodeo is the *huaso* and his mount, a short, agile horse especially bred for cattle management. In earlier times large herds of cattle were brought from Argentina through the high passageways across the Andes, a feat that required extreme endurance and ability from the cowboys. Due to the difficulty of cattle roundups which require both expertise and daring, the *huaso* and his horse of necessity stimulated the production of a complex and highly decorative equipment, from the leather reins and saddle to the silver harness and spurs. This equipment requires a well-developed production of traditionally made products which keep the old designs and technical ways of making the equipment. The Chilean saddle is by itself an impressive piece of art and evidences skillful craftsmanship in leather. From the tanning process to the engraving workmanship, leather has a prominent role in Chilean folkloric art production. Another area of artistic leather work involves boot making. Chilean cowboy boots tend to be long, reaching above the knee to protect the legs and thighs, and have decorative tassels; they are also an important assessory to the *huaso* who wears them with pride. The fancy leather boots are worn together with silver spurs, which can reach a radius of several inches; they have bells which ring loudly since they jingle when the *huaso* walks and dances the national folk dance—the *cueca*. The *huaso* typically wears a large woolen poncho that reaches almost to the floor during winter months. However, when he is up in higher elevations he changes his clothing for a more festive outfit, especially during rodeos or for other types of celebrations. The most common festive dress the *huaso* wears is the *manta*, a colorful, short, square poncho profusely embroidered with motifs that frequently include the *copihue,* Chile's national flower. Under the *manta* the *huaso* wears a short jacket not unlike the one used by Andalusian horsemen; likewise, the hat worn by these men has its origins in Andalusia.

La china, or the maiden, who is the feminine counterpart to the *huaso*, wears a colorful dress in the style of Andalusian dresses, although it is shorter and with

A rider, flanked by a companion, maneuvers a bull into position during a rodeo in Chile. (Getty Images)

less frills. On the other hand, women who ride horses in the rodeo use a sober, long riding skirt, vest, and boots, similar also to those used by Andalusian women.

It is customary for the *huaso* and the *china* to dance a *cueca* at the end of each rodeo. The *cueca* is a dance that evolved from Spanish and, most likely, African dances as well. Traditionally, the music for this dance is played by musicians playing instruments that include guitars, harp, silver spurs or other percussion instruments. A singer, most frequently a woman, accompanies the musicians. Sometime in the nineteenth century, the accordion was introduced to take the place of the harp.

Similar to the rodeo, the *fiestas patrias*, or the celebration commemorating Chilean independence from Spain, takes place on September 18th and 19th of each year. This national holiday features in addition to the obligatory military parades the *cueca,* which is danced throughout the day. Other colonial dances such as the *pequen* and *refalosa* are less common and have more of an old-times folkloric character.

As stated earlier the northern part of Chile is a desert. It runs from the Peruvian border in the north and stretches to Bolivia in the northwest down to the Valley of Aconcagua located north of Santiago. Few cities and seaports were founded there and these were constructed mainly because the mines needed them. The area was inhabited by Aymaras when the Spaniards made their incursions there in the sixteenth century, and even today it retains some of the traditions and folk ways of this Indigenous people. This is particularly true with respect to the religious festivities that take place there in honor of the Virgin Mary; the two most important ones are La Tirana and Andacollo. The latter is the name of a mining town that traces its history back to the period of the Inca Empire. A truly colorful celebration, this festivity in honor of the Virgin Mary combines pre-Columbian dances, music and other festive paraphernalia with later additions brought by the Catholic Church and the influence of Spanish missionaries.

The southern region, which includes territories that were colonized much later than the other regions of the country, mostly in the second half of the nineteenth century and in the twentieth century, evidences a strong influence from European settlers, Germans in the continental territories and Croats in the extreme south. The islands located in the fjords region had no inhabitants, except for the largest one, the Isle of Chiloé, which had a small population of Indians, whites of Spanish descent, and mestizos from the times of the colonial period. Folklore in these southern lands is richly characterized by the traditions of the Mapuche tribes who have inhabited these lands for centuries, before the arrival of European colonizers. The forested lands that covered the regions with a rich variety of trees play an important role in their traditions. Most salient among those is the *copihue*, the national flower symbol, and the *canelo*, a sacred tree under which was signed the treaty that in 1803 put an end to the centuries-long conflict between the Mapuche people and the Spanish colonial and later the Chilean government.

The *alerce*-growing region with centuries-old towering trees is central to the lives of those living in the area since these trees do not rot under the humid, rainy weather and serve as an excellent material for building houses and other buildings. Particularly beautiful are the houses and churches built entirely of wood and covered by *alerce* shingles, an architectural design that contrasts with the whitewashed adobe walls of the old colonial Spanish model that predominates in the central region and in most Latin American countries.

The cold rain forest offers also abundant resources for the traditional medicine practiced by the *meicas,* and for myths and legends inhabited by fantastic and frightening monsters like *imbunches*, *traucos*, witches, and Pillán himself, the demonic character of innumerable traditional stories. *La calchona*, a half-woman half-animal fantastic folk entity, is featured in many of the folk tales of the region.

The Isle of Chiloé, whose people feel comfortable on both land and sea, is reputed to be the center of a rich lore of terrifying myths and legends. The Caleuche, or the phantom vessel, is one of these legends and perfectly expresses the fears mariners and fishermen have to face while working at sea. Similar to the Flying Dutchman of European sea lore, this vessel appears as a ghostly presence in the fog or the storm and serves as an omen of danger and misfortune for those navigating the treacherous icy waters of the fjords and the open sea.

Folk musical instruments are an important part of Chile's folklore. Different types of musical instruments are popular in the three major regions of Chile: in the central part of Chile popular folk instruments include the guitar, harp, *guitarrón*, *charrango*, *pandero*, *tormento*, and *cacharaina*. For the southern part of Chile, the instruments that are more common are the guitar, violin, *rabel, bombo Chilote, matraca*, and accordion. The instruments used in the northern part include, besides the ever present guitar, the *quena* (*kena*), *pincullo* (*pinquillo*), *pusa* (*sicura*), *tarka*, *erke*, *charango*, *ocarina*, *caja*, *bombo nortino*, *triángulo*, and *matraca*. Musical instruments of exclusively Mapuche origin, such as the *kultrun* and the *trutruca*, are used only in ceremonies and festivities purely Indigenous.

Folkloric celebrations include several dances, with a regional version of the *cueca*. For example for the northern part of Chile there are the *Cueca Nortina*, *Cueca Criolla*, *Cueca Campesina*, *Cueca Valseada*, *Cueca Larga*, *Cueca Cómica*, *Cueca Robada*, *Cueca Porteña*, *Cueca Chilota*. The folk dances from Chile are equally as varied as the instruments cited above, especially those from the central region: *cueca, vals, corrido, la porteña, el gato, la jota, el pequén, la refalosa, la sajuriana, el repicao, la polka, la masurca, el cuando*, and *el aire*.

With respect to folk food some special dishes are popular during the various holidays celebrated throughout the year. *Pan de pascua* (Easter bread), for example, is eaten during the Easter season; *cola de mono* is a festive drink made with Kalua and cream, *pastel de choclo* is a corn-based cake. Some foods have rather quaint names such as *calzones rotos* (literally "pants with holes"); this is a type of dish that consists of fried bread and is flakier than doughnuts. There are also *locas con mayonesa, torta de mil hojas* (similar to Greek dessert), *Brazo de Reina, Leche Nevada*. A mainstay dessert dish is called a *manjar* (literally a delicacy).

Sea food, as might be expected given Chile's geography and long coast bordering the sea, has a strong presence in Chilean cuisine. *Centollas*, sea urchins, giant mussels and giant *percebes*, oysters, clams and crabs are eaten in different preparations, raw or cooked. Peculiar to the cooking of the region is the *curanto*, an elaborate clam bake done on a hole lined with hot rocks and covered with the huge leaves of a forest tree. The hole is filled with sea food, fish, pork and pork sausages, chicken and two types of potato, *chicha* and *cacho*.

María Herrera-Sobek

See also: Argentina and Its Folklore; Bolivia and Its Folklore

Further Reading

Castillo-Feliú, Guillermo I. *Culture and Customs of Chile*. Westport, CT: Greenwood Press, 2000.

Pino-Saavedra, Yolando, ed. *Folktales of Chile*. Translated from the Spanish by Rockwell Gray. Chicago: University of Chicago Press, 1967.

Plath, Oreste. *Folklore Chileno*. Santiago: Editorial Nascimento, 1979.

Plath, Oreste. *Geografía del mito y la leyenda chilenos*. Santiago: Editorial Nascimento, 1973.

CHILES (PEPPERS)

Together with corn, squash, and beans, chiles or chili peppers constitute one of the great culinary contributions of the Americas to the world. Since his first voyage to the continent, Christopher Columbus noticed the use of the fruit of these plants as condiment and noticed that they were somehow stronger than the peppers already known in Europe, a plant to which they are not related at all. The common chili

A man hanging chili peppers for drying in Isleta, New Mexico in 1940. (Library of Congress)

pepper or *capsicum* is native to the Americas where it has been known since the first civilizations appeared on the continent, and it is believed to have been part of the native American diet since over seven thousand years ago, or earlier, since prehistoric peppers have been found in ancient burials in Peru. In fact, there has been evidence of its cultivation and consumption all over the Americas; and as soon as it was taken to Europe, it became also very popular in the Old World as well. Several travelers and explorers have left testimony of how important it was for the Indians in that they claimed that if they did not have any chili peppers with their meals it was as if they had not eaten.

The early European chronicles of the Americas mentioned that in Mexico and Central America, all kinds of vegetables, soups, meats, tamales, tortillas and even drinks were seasoned and cured with chili peppers, sometimes in amounts that would be intolerable for the European palate. In general they agree that the heat and taste of the chili peppers is at first unpleasant to the uninitiated, but remark how pleasant it seems to be to those who are used to its pungent flavor and heat. In fact, the plant was brought to Europe by the first Europeans who had actually discovered the New World in their search for new routes to the spice trade of Asia. All through the Middle Ages the spice trade was a source of wealth, particularly for countries with easy access to the Mediterranean, but also for those, like Portugal, that looked for new routes to the East and to the commerce of spices; towards the end of the Middle Ages, there is a period known as the era of explorations that resulted in travels around Africa and Asia and the discovery of America.

With the discovery of America, chili peppers (*capsicum annuum*) were added to the list of important spices and became a worthy rival of those from Asia. Soon after their discovery in the Americas, chili peppers spread all over the world and became favorites in Asia, Africa and even Europe. Spices had been an important commodity since the Ancient World, but became even more important in the late Middle Ages and for sure contributed to the transition from feudalism to capitalism in Europe. From that moment on, spices were consumed regularly by the upper classes, but even the poor had a moderate access to them. For hundreds or even thousands of years, spices were known, yet uncommon and therefore expensive. Among ancient cultures, like the Romans, Greeks, Arabs, and the people of India, spices were already an important commodity. Particularly prized were black pepper and ginger, but sweeter spices like nutmeg, cardamom, clove, and cinnamon were also appreciated. In Europe, they became important with the rise of the bourgeoisie commercial class.

Most Europeans used the different spices from all over the world in cooking, as condiments and preservatives, but they were also valued, perhaps even more, for their medicinal properties. The pungent flavor and burning sensation of some spices were not unknown to the Europeans who had black pepper, mustard, and ginger. But it was the discovery of the American chili pepper that revitalized the spice trade. Columbus himself wrote that they were more abundant and of better quality as condiments than the known black or melegueta pepper. Therefore soon after their discovery chili peppers were taken to Europe, first by the Spaniards and Portuguese, who took them to Africa and Asia where they started to cultivate them, and then by other Europeans. There are records of chili peppers being cultivated in Spain, Portugal, Italy, and even Moravia as early as the 1500s. Many contemporary cultures use chili peppers in their cuisine, but most of them are outside of Europe. The fact that it was very easy to transport and cultivate chili peppers in other tropical, semitropical, and Mediterranean climates means that there was never a huge commerce, since they could be grown and consumed locally, and in part that explains the low demand.

Nonetheless, this adaptability and the fervor with which it was embraced speak of the importance of chili peppers as a culinary contribution to the world. An American plant used as a condiment that became very important for cuisines as distant as Indian, Thai, Chinese, and North African is a testimony to its importance. Chili peppers most likely originated in Peru and from there migrated to Mexico, or they originated simultaneously in both places. However, ever since pre-Columbian times, the diversity of chili peppers and their importance for Mexican culture have been greater than for any other American culture. There are numerous accounts of the importance of chili peppers for the Aztecs as well as the diversity of species found. Bernardino de Sahagún and other early historians mention the different kinds of chili peppers grown, based on quality, availability, way of cultivating or picking them, and season, as well as how their commerce was regulated in the famous market of Tlatelolco in the ancient capital of the Aztec empire. Chili peppers have remained important in Mexican cuisine, and today most likely Americans associate them with Mexican or Mexican-influenced cuisine such as that found in California, New Mexico, Texas, and Arizona.

Some of the most popular Mexican chili peppers are the following:

Very Hot

- Cayenne very hot pepper: a long, hot pepper either green or red depending on the season. The green variety appears in the summer, and the red, considerably hotter, in the fall.
- *Habanero* pepper: a small, round, hot pepper with some hint of fruit and a yellowish color. Perfect for salsas, it can be sliced and seasoned with salt and lime juice.
- *Manzanilla* pepper: a similar pepper to the *habanero*, except for its reddish or green color.
- *Serrano* pepper: a small, long, green chili pepper that is usually boiled or charred and mashed in a *molcajete* or mixed in a blender with tomatillos, onions, cilantro, and salt to make *salsa verde*.

Hot

- *Jalapeño* pepper: a pepper similar to the *serrano* chili pepper, except not as hot; it is used in the same way as well as in *guacamole* and *pico de gallo*.
- *Manzana* pepper: similar to manzanilla, but smaller and round, related to *habanero*, but not as hot.
- Cherry pepper: a red, small, round chili pepper that is perfect in salsas or pickled.
- *Chile güero*: a similar pepper to the jalapeño, except that it is of a pale yellow color.

Mild

- *Poblano* pepper: one of the largest chili peppers, green and mild, perfect for stuffing. These are the peppers used in the classic *chile rellenos*.
- *Chilaca* pepper: similar to the *poblano* pepper, the *chilaca* is longer and thinner. It is usually added to soups or stews and is perfect for a Mexican favorite, *rajas con crema*: a dish of peeled, seeded *chilacas* simmered in a sauce of sour cream and sprinkled with grated *cotija* cheese.

Many of these chili peppers can also be consumed dry. The most popular are: (1) *Chile ancho*, which is a dry *poblano* pepper. When dried, it turns dark brown or even black and it has a smoky, mild taste. (2) *Chile pasilla*: a dry *chilaca*, long, wrinkled, and dark and of a mild flavor. (3) *Chile guajillo*: similar to the pasilla, but darker and of a very smooth skin. It is a little stronger in flavor than the *chile pasilla*. (4) *Chile mulato*: a dry green chili pepper. When dry, the *mulato* becomes very dark and its flavor stronger. (5) *Chile chipotle*: a dry, smoked jalapeño with a very strong and rich flavor. It is perfect for salsas, adobos, and stews; it can be canned and used in many dishes or just as a condiment. (6) *Chile de árbol*: a bright, red, dry chili pepper that is hotter than most of the other dry chili peppers and is the favorite for red salsas blended with tomatoes, onion, garlic and salt. (7) Dry *habaneros*: a dry variety of the fresh *habanero*. Usually they become darker and their flavor more concentrated. Most of these dry chili peppers will have to be soaked, rehydrated and seeded before using them.

RAFAEL HERNÁNDEZ

See also: Tamales; Tortilla

Further Reading

Heiser, Charles B., and Paul G. Smith. "The Cultivated Capsicum Peppers." *Economic Botany* 7.3 (July–September 1953): 214–227.

Long-Solís, Janet. "El abastecimiento de chiles en el Mercado de la ciudad México–Tenoch-titlan en el siglo XVI." *Historia Mexicana* 34.4 (April–June 1985): 701–714.

Soustelle, Jacques. *Daily Life of the Aztecs on the Eve of the Spanish Conquest.* Stanford, CA: Stanford University Press, 1970.

Wright, Clifford A. "The Medieval Spice Trade and the Diffusion of the Chile." *Gastronomica: The Journal of Food and Culture* vol. 7.2 (Spring 2007): 35–43.

CHILI QUEENS

Chili is believed to have been perfected in San Antonio, Texas, by the "chili queens" of the Military Plaza who set up make-shift stands to sell their spicy concoctions all through the night to customers who rode in from all over the Texas prairies for a taste of the aromatic chili. The term "chili queen" (or "chile queen") was most famous in the 1880 and 1890s. The chili queens operated near or in the Alamo (Military Plaza). They were moved to Market Square in 1887 and had stands in Haymarket Plaza as well before being forced to shut down their business in 1937. Chili queens refined the art of making chili in the Plazas. They added to the recipe, innovating new variations, and competed with one another to try to sell the most with the tastiest medley of ingredients. According to San Antonio natives, the chili queens reigned supreme for over 200 years, although historians do not document them making and selling chili before 1880. However, they had sold other types of Mexican food. The queens were mainly women of Mexican descent, though some Anglo American women also participated. These *Tejanas* and other Texas women all engaged in the friendly competition of the cook-off, each attempting to bring in the highest number of customers and have their chili deemed the favorite. However, there is an even more complex and interesting history behind the origin of the chili queens of Military Plaza.

The chili queens of San Antonio are a celebrated historical group of women. These resourceful and creative culinary mistresses fed locals and tourists alike an intoxicating menu of foods laced with the flavor of spiced red chilies. Red chilies themselves originated in the Americas and are a staple of many different Latino recipes. Chili queens expanded on the Southwest tradition of cooking spiced meat and ground chili powder together into a sensational stew that singed the tongue and cleared the sinuses. Red chilies are known for their tongue-burning heat. The chili itself was commonly concocted as a stew made with dried red chilies and spiced beef. The chili queens made their spicy food outdoors over mesquite fires. They also served a variety of dishes along with the chili including tamales, tortillas, chili con carne and enchiladas. The chili queens set up their makeshift kitchens in Military Plaza until it became the site of City Hall in 1889. Subsequently, they sold their dishes in Market Square until the erection of the Municipal Market House in 1900. They then moved their cooking operation to Haymarket Plaza and Milam Park. In 1893, there was a "San Antonio Chili Stand" at the Chicago World's Fair. These chefs of Southwest cuisine worked in the plazas of downtown San Antonio for two centuries and are still commemorated each year at a Chili Festival in the culturally rich and economically thriving Central Texas city.

The chili queens would normally cook their chili at home and then load it onto festively decorated chili wagons, along with pots, crockery, and all the other gear necessary to feed the crowds in the Military Plaza. The site was named thusly because a group of Spanish soldiers frequently camped out at that spot and enjoyed the chili queens' cuisine. Mesquite fires kept the chili warm while the queens squatted beside their wagons waiting to make a sale. They often hung colored lanterns and offered wooden stools to their customers. Hungry customers would sit on wooden stools to enjoy the stew. The site was popular for the spicy taste of the chili queens' wares, affordable price, bustling atmosphere and air filled with music. These open-air kitchens attracted a wide variety of customers. The crowds were made up of both *Tejanos* and Anglos, soldiers, cowboys, locals and tourists, families, businessmen, singers and other musicians who entertained as all manner of people enjoyed the chili. San Antonio was also a meeting place for theatrical groups from the East and West who often gave performances and tried their first bowl of the spicy stew. An entire meal cost under a dime. Many people were attracted by the low cost of the food, as well as the company, entertainment and other novelties in the square. This scene endured throughout the night until dawn when the vegetable vendors took the place of the chili queens. The Military Plaza was affectionately known as "La Plaza del Chili con Carne." The chili queens originally had stands in Military Plaza, Haymarket, and Alamo Plaza but eventually the city confined them to Haymarket Plaza only.

The Texas newspapers' historical accounts of the chili queens were romanticized ideals of the kinds of women who sold their wares in the town plazas. They were often described as dark and mysterious ladies, compelling and sensual. According to accounts of the *Dallas Morning News, Forest and Stream,* and the *Daily Light*, chili queens were often young and attractive women, who led men into the plaza with the delicious aroma of their spicy foods. Two especially famous women named Sadie and Martha were repeatedly mentioned in the articles. Tall tales of duels and scorned lovers were told throughout the region, and the chili queens were immortalized forever in Texas folklore as prolific, passionate ladies of the night, who tempted soldiers, poets and powerful politicians and businessmen alike to venture into the plaza late at night to enjoy the sumptuous hodge-podge concoction. The chili queens originally set up their carts to make money from a relatively simple and inexpensive type of nourishment embodied in the chili dishes. Cultural outsiders that sought to capture the quaint ritual, however, eventually exploited the picturesque attraction of the rudimentary restaurants. While the flirting and witty banter was documented extensively by Anglo males, the regional custom of family gathering and cultural idiosyncrasy is unique to the history of San Antonio, which was a community made up of a cornucopia of flavors and traditions from Mexico and America, the land originally belonging to Mexico for many years before the Treaty of Guadalupe-Hidalgo allowed the United States to annex a third of Mexican territory to the United States after the United States–Mexican War in 1848.

Ultimately, the impact of Mexican and American Southwest cooking on the cuisine and culture of the United States is undeniable, though Mexico does not directly claim the recipe for chili used in most American incarnations of the spice and meat blend. The Chicago World's Fair in 1893 featured a "San Antonio Chili Stand." The queens have been immortalized in song by the troubadours that serenaded people in the plaza and in writing by Stephen Crane and O. Henry. The chili queens' saga goes back nearly 200 years. Images of the plazas of San Antonio and the women called "chili queens" can be viewed at the University of Texas Institute for Texan Cultures in San Antonio.

Unfortunately, the rule of the chili queens came to an end in the late 1930s when the Health Department permanently shut down their business and ended a time-honored tradition in San Antonio. The women were unable to conform to the strict rules and regulations enforced on restaurants and had to close due to complaints about flies and improperly washed dishes. Some chili queens opened indoor restaurants and continued to sell their delicious concoctions such as Mrs. Eufemia López and her daughters, Juanita and Esperanza García. For a short time in 1939, chili queens were again allowed in plazas in San Antonio, but the return was short-lived and the stands were forced to close again after the beginning of World War II.

The legacy of the chili queens continues throughout Latino communities, especially in the Southwest and most devotedly in Texas. San Antonio pays homage to the chili queens by staging re-enactments in historic Market Square. It is called the "Return of the Chili Queens Festival" and is sponsored by the El Mercado Merchants. This tribute to chili, the state dish, began in the 1980s and is held annually during the Memorial Day Celebrations. Those attending the festival can find arts and crafts, music, dancing, and of course, chili.

ADRIANNA M. SANTOS

See also: Chiles (Peppers); Enchiladas; Tamales; Tortilla

Further Reading

Jennings, Frank W. "Popular Chili Queens Graced San Antonio Plazas." [October, 2007]. The University of the Incarnate Word. *The Journal of the Life and Culture of San Antonio.* http://www.uiw.edu/sanantonio/jenningschiliqueens.html.

NPR. "Hidden Kitchens: Talking Recipes." #1 Original San Antonio Chili. [October, 2007]. NPR. http://www.npr.org/templates/story/story.php?storyId=4108397.

NPR. "Hidden Kitchens: The Kitchen Sisters. The Chili Queens of San Antonio." October 2007]. NPR. http://www.npr.org/templates/story/story.php?storyId=4107830.

CHIMAYÓ

Chimayó, often referred to as the "Lourdes of America," attracts over three hundred thousand people a year who come to visit the Catholic adobe sanctuary, El Santuario de Chimayó (originally called Nuestro Señor de Esquipulas). Located 40 miles south of Taos and 24 miles northeast of Santa Fe, Chimayó is about ten miles east of Española in the Sangre de Cristo Mountains. It is on Highway 76, often called the "High Road to Taos," and cuts through beautiful old Spanish villages and scenery that Georgia O'Keeffe captured in her landscapes. The name Chimayó is derived from a Tewa Indian word for a local landmark, the hill of Tsi Mayoh. The town is unincorporated and includes many neighborhoods, called *plazas* or *placitas*, each with its own name, including El Potrero de Chimayó (Chimayó commons) and the Plaza del Cerro (plaza by the hill).

The historic Spanish mission of El Santuario de Chimayó in New Mexico, where pilgrims come to pray for healing. (Dreamstime.com)

While there is no written testimony for the story of the sanctuary, tradition maintains that in 1810 on Good Friday of Holy Week, Don Bernardo Abeyta, a member of the fraternity of Jesus Nazareno or Penitentes, was out performing penances and saw a bright shining light emanating from the ground near the Santa Cruz River. Digging up the lit ground with his bare hands, Abeyta discovered a crucifix with a dark Christ figure on it. A local priest, Father Sebastián de Alvarez, brought the crucifix to Santa Cruz, but three times it disappeared and was later found back in its hole. By the third time, everyone understood that the crucifix wanted to remain in Chimayó, and so a small chapel was built on the site.

The cross, which the people named El Señor de Esquipulas, was believed to be miraculous and pilgrims from all over made journeys to visit it. It was soon discovered that the earth from the hole it was in was sacred and had curative powers, increasing the pilgrimages to the shrine. These grew so numerous that the chapel had to be replaced by the larger, current adobe mission in 1816. The crucifix which began the original shrine still resides on the chapel altar, but its healing powers have been overshadowed by *el posito*, the "sacred sand pit" from which it sprang. Each year during Holy Week thousands of people make a pilgrimage to Chimayó to visit the Santuario and take away a bit of the sacred dirt. While nearly twenty tons of dirt a year are said to be taken by devotees, *el posito* always remains filled. Pilgrims who walk a few yards or a hundred miles claim to have been cured there of diseases, infirmities, and unhappiness. The walls of the sacristy are hung with discarded crutches, hospital ID bracelets, eye patches, before-and-after photographs, and other paraphernalia that are left as evidence of healing. *Milagros*, small metal stampings in the shapes of arms, legs, hands, and ears also decorate the chapel to signify miraculous recovery.

The church is decorated in the traditional Mexican folk style that features a large gold screen behind the altar, or *reredos*, decorated with various religious symbols and with devotional art introduced in the eighteenth century by Spanish missionaries and local artisans that include *retablos*, small oil paintings on tin, zinc, wood or copper; *santos*, carved and painted figures of saints; and *bultos*, brightly colored sculptures of *santos* (saints) or other religious figures carved from the wood of trees that grow in New Mexico: cottonwood, cottonwood roots, aspen, and pine. A favorite saint of those who visit the sanctuary is Santo Niño Atocha, who is believed to leave the chapel at night and wander the countryside, helping those in trouble. The statue is said to reappear in its niche with wet feet and its shoes worn out from its charitable errands, which has prompted many pilgrims to bring offerings of baby shoes to the chapel and place them at the Santo Niño Atocha's feet.

The history of Chimayó reflects the unique cultural heritage of New Mexico's mixture of Indian, Spanish, Mexican, and Anglo influences. Long before Abeyta's discovery of El Señor de Esquipulas, the Tewa Indians of San Juan Pueblo considered the area sacred and would make midsummer pilgrimages to their sacred hills and mountains to clean shrines, sweep the trails, and pray for rain. Shortly after the Pueblo Revolt, 1680–1692, several groups of Spanish colonists settled in the northwestern section of the fertile Chimayó Valley. The colonists were hard working, independent farmers, and artisans whose occupations included weaving, day labor, and stock raising. They came to the area in hopes of receiving the title *hidalgo* (nobleman) if they stayed. Frequently they were granted land, building lots, subsidies, and farming implements for their new life of hardship on the frontier.

According to archives from Durango, Mexico, a priest from Guatemala who came to Chimayó with the original settlers carried a large crucifix with him when he would minister to the surrounding Indians and pueblos. It is most likely that the cross carried by the priest was a copy of the original miraculous black Christ carved in 1595 at the request of Indigenous people in Esquipulas, Guatemala. In 1810, the Santa Cruz River flooded and the priest's remains and crucifix were unearthed. Older people remembered him as the Father from Esquipulas and associated the name with the cross. When Abeyta discovered the cross, he along with nineteen other families from El Potrero sought and received official permission to build the church. The sanctuary was privately owned until 1929 when it was purchased from the Chavez family and donated to the Archdiocese of Santa Fe.

Another important cultural feature of Chimayó includes its weaving tradition. Known today for high-quality woven goods, Chimayó is famous for the weavings of the Ortega and Trujillo families. Many shops contain their work as well as fine arts and crafts from the region. One of New Mexico's oldest restaurants is located in Chimayó—Rancho de Chimayó—which is well known for traditional New Mexican cuisine. Two other historic places to visit in Chimayó are Casa Escondida (the "Hidden House"), an intimate and serene inn built in the Spanish Colonial adobe style, and Rancho Manzana, now a luxurious B&B and cooking school located on the Plaza del Cerro and originally built as a residence and mercantile store in the mid-1700s.

Danizete Martínez

See also: Pilgrimages (Peregrinaciones)

Further Reading

Calamari, Barbara, and Sandra DiPasqua. *Holy Places.* New York: Viking Studio, 2002.
Chimayo. http://chimayo.org.
Kay, Elizabeth. *Chimayo Valley Traditions.* Santa Fe: Ancient City Press, 1987.

CHIRRIONERA

Folklorists who study the *chirrionera* among Mexican American or Hispanic women discuss the lore that surrounds the "vaginal serpent" theme as it relates to anxieties surrounding pregnancy, women's vulnerability to sexual assault, and female reflections of culturally assigned roles. As is the case with much of the folklore that details the private spaces of women, there is a dearth of information on the cycle of legends and beliefs surrounding women and serpents, or other small reptiles such as lizards or water dogs that either pursue or enter the female reproductive system as a form of sexual assault. The accounts are useful for considering the relationships between sex roles and folklore as well as social strictures, anxieties, and psychologically repressive attitudes surrounding assigned cultural roles. The variants of the *chirrionera* must not be taken at face value but, rather, in their cultural context.

The binomial name for *chirrionera* in *Diccionario de mejicanismos* (1989) is listed as *Masticophis flagellum*, a species of nonvenomous snake commonly referred to as coachwhips or whip snakes that range throughout the southern United States and the northern part of Mexico, typically in grassland areas. Stories of the mythical *chirrionera*, or *chirrionero* as it is also called, are found in Mexico and throughout the state of Texas. Scholars generally agree that there are two cycles of legends that pattern the folklore of the *chirrionera*. The first body of lore centers on vaginal serpents or serpent-like creatures that crawl into women's vaginas. "Milk stealing" serpent lore surrounds snakes that enter the home of a woman who has a nursing baby in the home. The snake may hypnotize women and is sometimes known to crawl into the bed of a lactating woman to steal or suck her breast milk.

Writings on the relationships between the *chirrionera* and *axolotls* date to the late nineteenth century in west Texas. The axolotl is another name for the water dog, and both names refer to the larvae stage of the salamander. In many of these early accounts, women and especially young girls are warned about the dangers of bathing in waters inhabited by axolotls, especially during their menstrual cycle, as the creatures smell the blood. Women may become mortally impregnated with axolotls or an axolotl entering a woman may remain in the body of a woman just as long as a human fetus.

Women are taught to stay in groups so as to remain protected from the mythological *chirrionera*, which is known to whistle at solitary women. Often, young women or girls who are suspected of being pregnant because they have been left alone to walk in the woods are not pregnant at all but instead have had one of these creatures slip in unnoticed. The *chirrionera* may be exorcised by a *curandera*. If not exorcised, the creature may gestate and the girl may in turn give birth to many such creatures that may strangle or devour her. Some women have related stories of a *serpiente diablo* (devil serpent) or a *cincuate* that invades a pregnant woman's womb to suffocate her unborn baby.

The tales inculcate a fear of sexual assault by often invisible lizard-like or snake-like entities. Small reptiles that penetrate and often destroy female bodies reflect the fears and anxieties concerning women's vulnerability to sexual assault as well as pregnancy anxieties. Scholars and folklorists reveal how the narratives point to the Hispanic woman's anxiety over bearing and raising children as a primary function of domestic life. The tales may also indicate one means whereby Mexican American women are conditioned from an early age to fear, distrust, and ultimately attach negative emotions to sexual acts. The narratives are connected to female views of culturally assigned roles that emphasize a necessary sexual purity during adolescence, at which time Hispanic girls are watched much more closely than boys of the same age.

Folklore about snake-like creatures entering and existing within the human body present a complex area for analysis, and they share motifs with the "bosom serpent" tradition collected in other parts of the United States. Although the stories involve the same animals (primarily snakes, lizards, and water dogs), *chirrionera* stories collected in Texas and Mexico reflect a specifically female viewpoint that underscores feminine fears of annihilation and penetration.

It is significant to note that in the tales, women are frequently shamed and humiliated. Often, the only way out of such shame and humiliation is death. In Hispanic culture, the world is a precarious place for females, especially females who venture out alone. This is a message that begins in childhood. Indirectly and symbolically, the encoded message of the many *chirrionera* variants reveals the inculcation of psychologically repressive attitudes towards sex. The stories condition women to fear sexual violation from an early age and shift the burden of abuse and misuse of women by others onto the female herself. Some scholars, however, indicate how the narratives overturn the ostensible wife/mother role of self-sacrifice and nurturance. The stories reveal how women are taught to distrust their own sexuality and how they—through lack of heeding the many warnings via storytelling and personal narrative—are the instruments of their own suffering.

Although the tales ostensibly emphasize a woman's vulnerability and helplessness, there are also male-oriented narratives that may be expressed as variants of the "*vagina dentata*" (vagina with teeth) story. In such variants, men are cautioned to abstain from penetrating the woman for fear of death.

CORDELIA E. BARRERA

See also: El Diablo; Espíritus Malignos (Evil Spirits); Folk Medicine; Spirit Possession and Exorcism

Further Reading

Cardozo-Freeman, Inez. "Serpent Fears and Religious Motifs among Mexican Women." *Frontiers: A Journal of Women's Studies* 3, no. 3 (1978): 10–13.

Griffith, James. S. "Quetzalcóatl on the Border? Mestizo Water Serpent Beliefs of the Pimería Alta." *Western Folklore* 49 (1990): 391–400.

Jordan, Rosan A. "The Vaginal Serpent and Other Themes from Mexican-American Women's Lore." In Rosan A. Jordan and Susan J. Kalčik, eds. *Women's Folklore, Women's Culture,* 26–24. Philadelphia: University of Pennsylvania Press, 1985.

CHISTES
See Jokes

CHOLOS/CHOLAS

Cholos is a disparaging term often used to denote the Chicano gang subculture and is characterized by a distinctive dress pattern, the use of *caló* speech, an assortment of hand gestures, and often interpreted as the cultural successor of the pachuco. In a broader sense, *cholo* is sometimes used to refer to members of the lowrider car culture or simply to Chicanos who have been influenced by the attitudes and dress patterns made popular by the Chicano gang lifestyle.

Ideas as to the roots of the word *cholo* are numerous. The most popular theory is that *cholo* comes from the Nahuatl *xolotl* (pronounced cholotl), meaning a mixed breed dog, and was used in a derogatory way to address people of combined Spanish and Amerindian ancestry. In written form, the earliest appearance of the word *cholo* is found in a Peruvian book by Inca Garcilaso de la Vega called *Comentarios Reales de los Incas.* The book is composed of two volumes, first published in 1609 and 1617 respectively, and uses *cholo* to describe a child born to parents who are of Black and Amerindian ancestry, and it is a term still used today with a similar connotation in different parts of Latin America. *Cholo* again appears in print in Hubert Bancroft's series *History of California,* when in volumes 4 and 5 (1841–1845 and 1846–1848) Bancroft refers to the Mexican soldiers who were of lower caste as "*cholos*" and "thieves and pickpockets." The single salient characteristic in these depictions is that the *cholo* is a person of mixed Amerindian ancestry.

The *cholo* as a Chicano gang member, also known as *vato loco,* is characterized by an attire consisting of plaid or flannel shirts with only the top buttoned or buttoned up to the neck that go over large white T–shirts. These are accompanied by loose-fitting khaki pants, or shorts that extend beyond the knee to the upper or middle of the calf, are at least a size larger than needed, and creased in the front. Colors of the pants consist of black, navy blue, gray, or brown. The pants are held up with black cloth belts clasped together by a chrome metal buckle, which often displays the first or last initial of the wearer, usually in calligraphy. In addition, white tube socks that rest high on the calf are also popular. The colors of particular gang affiliations are displayed where possible, such as getting a red or blue cloth belt and using socks that have two horizontal colored stripes at the top. Certain brands of clothing are given preference: pants are often Ben Davis or Dickies and shoes are often Converse or Nike Cortez shoes. Jewelry in the form of a crucifix pendant, watches, and stud earrings are popular. Common hairstyles consist of having a shaved head, a fade, or slicked back hair, all of which can be accessorized with a bandana.

The female counterpart of the *cholo* is the *chola,* and the two dress patterns have many similarities. *Cholas* are also known to wear oversized pants of comparable style, held up by identical belts, and they tend to wear the same types of shoes. Key differences are that *cholas* are slightly more revealing in their clothing, dressing in halter tops or in tight T–shirts that rest above the midsection, in addition to wearing the flannel or plaid shirts. Heavy makeup consisting of dark eyeliner, penciled-in eyebrows, and lip liner are noticeable features. Their hair is generally worn long and teased or put into a high ponytail, and hairspray is often used. Accessories of gold bracelets, rings, and dangling earrings, such as large hoop earrings, have also come to distinguish *cholas*. Bandanas are also worn by *cholas,* and both groups are known to prominently display tattoos, usually done with calligraphy.

The fluidity of fashion trends at different time periods, however, means that there is an extensive amount of commonly practiced variations of *cholo* and *chola* dress and hairstyles, varying significantly between different communities; this can include the wearing of items such as denim jeans and sports jerseys. The unifying aspect in the disparate forms of *cholo* and *chola* dress is meticulousness in appearance, manifesting itself as perfectly creased and ironed clothing for both genders, well-groomed facial hair for men, and considerable care in the application of makeup for women. This attentiveness to appearance as well as the use of oversized clothing is attributed to the pachuco culture of the 1930s and 1940s, known for its use of the zoot suit.

Another cultural trait believed to be inherited from pachucos is the use of *caló* speech, which went into forming the pachuco dialect. Like pachucos, *cholos* may use culture-specific colloquial terms, such as *orale*, *vato*, *ese*, etc. These slang words are joined by English idioms, such as *funds*, *fool*, *wassup*, etc., and help to create a uniquely *cholo* dialect.

The conflation of the *cholo* lifestyle with gangs gives the *cholo* a uniquely defiant street style symbolized by the use of an assortment of hand gestures to indicate particular gang affiliations. These gang signs are numerous, can be done with either hand, and differ significantly between neighborhoods. Commonly, when displaying a gang sign, the hand is held in front of the chest, center-oriented, with the arm nearly parallel to the ground, usually at a slight incline upward. Hand signs are also done with the hand positioned near the face and with the elbow stretched outward in line with the torso.

There is considerable conflation of *cholos* with the lowrider car culture, causing many people who drive lowriders to be referred to as *cholos*. In some ways, this is understandable due to the fact that this specific car culture was for a long time predominantly composed of Chicanos. Also, there are unifying aspects between the two groups, such as music interests, particularly oldies from the 1940–60s. The ten-volume collection of CDs known as *Lowrider Oldies*, for example, contains numerous songs that have also come to identify the *cholo,* such as the song "I'm Your Puppet" by James and Bobby Purify. In addition, many *cholos* are known to drive lowriders, but many others own a wide assortment of vehicles. The lowrider subculture, however, necessitates that to belong one needs to own a lowrider, and there are numerous owners of lowriders who are not *cholos* or even Chicanos. Essentially, while there may be overlapping between the two subcultures in terms of members and outlying interests, the two are still distinct.

In the United States, the term *cholo,* while applied to varying subsets of people, still carries a negative connotation and consequently is not often used as a means of self-identification, but rather tends to be imposed upon a group of people by outsiders, which may add to the ambiguity of the particulars of its definition. In recent years though, the *cholo* subculture has gained considerable traction in the media with the song "Lean Like a Cholo," released in 2007 by Down AKA Kilo. Other singers such as Gwen Stefani and Fergie have also attempted to emulate the *chola* style in some of their music videos. This type of media attention has helped to disseminate the cultural traits of the *cholo* into a wider population, many of which are not gang-affiliated.

ERIC CÉSAR MORALES

See also: Caló (Folk Speech); Lowriders

Further Reading

Castro, Rafaela G. *Chicano Folklore: A Guide to the Folktales, Traditions, Rituals and Religious Practices of Mexican Americans.* New York: Oxford University Press, 2001.

Hallcom, Francine. "Gang Girls." *An Urban Ethnography of Latino Street Gangs in Los Angeles and Ventura Counties*, n.d. http://www.csun.edu/~hcchs006/18.html.

CHRISTMAS (NAVIDAD)

Latinos/as celebrate the Christmas season, *La Navidad*, from the first week of Advent, through February 2nd, the *Candelaria*. Many rich and faithfully observed traditions, both solemn and festive, make this season among the most significant holidays in Latino cultures. In Mexico and parts of the United States, the Christmas season is distinguished with dramatizations that reenact, through community-based Christmas pageants, various aspects of the biblical Christmas story. Some Christmas traditions began as sacred practices in the church, but have since expanded into private or community events, either exclusively (such as the *piñata*) or in addition to religious observations (such as the Feast of the Immaculate Conception). Other practices that are central to Christmas in Latino cultures, such as the *misa de gallo*, maintain liturgical significance but are supplemented with traditions at home and in the community, which help people prepare for the event. Poinsettias, *luminarias*, and *piñatas* characterize the look of Christmas, while *tamales, buñuelos*, and bread pudding help define the taste of Christmas.

Feast-Day Celebrations of the Christmas Season

The Feast of the Immaculate Conception

December 7th marks the first pre-Christmas celebration for Latinos/as, especially those of Colombian heritage. People decorate the fronts of their houses and their porches with hundreds of colored lanterns and candles. The lanterns are crafted with wood in the form of a pyramid. Each side is lined with colorful cellophane. Families stay up all night celebrating. At dawn on December 8th, the revelers commemorate the feast day of the Virgin of the Immaculate Conception. This day celebrates the belief that the Virgin Mary was free from sin at the moment of her conception of Christ. Over the next three weeks, children burn sparklers (called Bengal Lights) and set off small fireworks.

The Feast of the Virgin of Guadalupe

In North and South America, the Feast of the Virgin of Guadalupe is part of the liturgical calendar and celebrated on December 12th. Tradition maintains that on December 9th, 1531, Juan Diego saw a vision of a young woman, surrounded by light, who instructed him, in his native Nahuatl language, to build a church in her honor on the land where they stood on Tepeyac Hill near Mexico City. When he returned home and told Fray Juan de Zumárraga what he saw and heard and of the lady's request, the bishop asked for proof, a sign that the vision was, indeed, real. Juan Diego returned to the place where he had seen the apparition. When she appeared to him for the second time, he told her of the bishop's response. The lady directed Juan Diego to take the flowers growing behind him on the Hill of Tepeyac to the bishop. Because it was winter and no flowers should be growing, this would serve as sufficient proof. He cut the flowers and carried them in his poncho to the bishop. When he arrived, Juan Diego opened his cloak to show the bishop the blossoms. The flowers fell to the floor and the two men found, imprinted on the fabric, the image of the young lady who had appeared to him.

This story was recorded in the late 1640s in both the Spanish and Nahuatl languages. This image of the Virgin of Guadalupe is one of the most recognized religious and cultural images in Mexico. The narrative of the apparition, along with prayers and the feast day, help people prepare for Christmas. Specifically, Our Lady of Guadalupe, who appeared to Juan Diego and spoke his language rather than the Spanish of the conquerors, suggests to believers that God's promise through his Son is meant for all of humanity. Many people make pilgrimages to the *Basílica de Guadalupe* and attend celebrations in her honor. Our Lady of Guadalupe is seen today as a national and cultural as well as religious icon.

Las Posadas

Las Posadas, meaning "the inns" or "the lodgings," begins nine days before Christmas. Traditionally, part of the posada procession is performed during each of the nine days, a *novenario*, as part of a religious observance: each day represents one month of the Virgin Mary's pregnancy. Through the course of the *novenario*, children and adults reenact Mary and Joseph's trek from Nazareth to Bethlehem, where they looked for, and were denied, shelter repeatedly. Coordination of the event is often a group effort in which neighborhoods, families and friends, churches, or community organizations assemble actors, musicians, guests, locations, costumes, and parties.

The Procession

On the evening of December 16th, participants gather, often offering prayers. Two children play the role of Mary and Joseph. In some places, the children carry images, *misterios*, of Mary and Joseph. In others, the children wear robes meant to resemble biblical-era garments. In rural areas, Mary may ride through the procession on a donkey. Often, a child dresses as an angel and leads the holy couple, followed by the group, through the procession. Other children may dress as angels, shepherds, kings, or livestock. Musicians and guests follow the three leading children, holding candles and singing songs. In some cases, the path of the procession is lined with *luminarias*. Based on the Gospel of Luke, the group travels from one house to another asking for shelter through the song of the *peregrinos*, or pilgrims. In keeping with the gospel, the homeowner, playing the part of innkeeper, denies the request, also through song:

> *Peregrinos* (Pilgrims):
> *En nombre del cielo*
> *os pido posada,*
> *pues no puede andar*
> *ya mi esposa amada.*
>
> In the name of heaven
> I ask for lodging
> because my beloved wife
> can no longer walk.
>
> *Posaderos* (Innkeepers):
> *Aquí no es mesón,*
> *sigan adelante.*
> *Yo no puedo abrir,*
> *no sea algún tunante.*
>
> This is not an inn;
> continue ahead.
> I cannot open the door;
> You might be a rogue.
>
> *Peregrinos* (Pilgrims):
> *Venimos rendidos*
> *desde Nazaret.*
> *Yo soy carpintero*
> *de nombre José.*
>
> We come exhausted
> from Nazareth.

I am a carpenter,
by the name of Joseph.

Posaderos (Innkeepers):
No me importa el nombre,
déjennos dormir,
pues que yo les digo
que no hemos de abrir.

The name is not important to me.
Let us sleep;
I tell you,
we won't open the door.

Peregrinos (Pilgrims):
Mi esposa es María;
es reina del cielo,
y madre va a ser
del Divino Verbo.

My wife is Mary;
she is the queen of heaven,
and mother to be
of the Divine Word.

Posaderos (Innkeepers):
¿Eres tú José?
¿Tu esposa es María?
Entren peregrinos,
no los conocía.

Are you Joseph?
Your wife is Mary?
Come in, pilgrims;
I didn't recognize you.

Todos (Everyone—to a different tune):
Entren santos peregrinos,
peregrinos, reciban este rincón.
Aunque es pobre la morada,
os la doy de corazón.

Enter holy pilgrims,
accept this humble home.
Even though it's a lowly dwelling,
I give it wholeheartedly.

This denial process may happen one time or several times during the procession, based on the arrangements made by organizers. Ultimately, at a pre-arranged home, the group is welcomed into the house, and the entire group sings the final verse of the posada song. A nativity scene is prepared with space for the children to bring their own statues and images in the places reserved for them. In some cases, the costumed children take their places around the manger as living members of the nativity scene. The people gather around the nativity scene for prayers before the celebration begins. Small bags or baskets of candy, fruits, and nuts, *colaciones*, are distributed along with other food and drinks. Songs are sung, and the home-owner usually provides a piñata filled with candy and nuts to add to the festivities. This process is repeated each of the first eight nights of the *novenario*. On the ninth night, the traditional *Las Posadas* procession ends at a church where Christmas Eve *misa de gallo*, the midnight mass, is celebrated.

Although the traditional *posadas* are held over a nine-day period, many Latino communities today make adjustments to the event based on local traditions, or limitations of time, money, weather, or people. Such alterations might include shortening the duration of *Las Posadas* from nine nights to one night or hold-ing the processional entirely indoors in an apartment building, church, or other location. Puerto Rican communities incorporate a vaguely similar door-to-door singing practice into their Christmas traditions. With each song, the carolers ask for admittance into the house to eat the well-loved Christmas fare, including sweets, roast pork, and rice with pigeon peas. Such foods are mentioned in the Christmas songs.

History of Las Posadas

The concept of *Las Posadas* may have been borrowed from the European medieval mystery plays, performed by members of the clergy, which dramatized Bible stories for largely illiterate audiences. Because such plays were performed increasingly for entertainment by members of the public, the Church banned them by the fifteenth century. In the sixteenth century, St. Ignatius Loyola instituted a *novena* of prayers to be offered on the nine days before Christmas. St. John of the Cross, later in the century, added a religious dramatization to the nine days of prayer, a custom which Spanish missionaries took with them to the Americas. They used it to teach the Christmas story to Native Americans. As part of a religious observance, these dramatizations were solemn events. Eventually, however, lay people took over the organization of them, and they became more festive through time.

Today, *Las Posadas* is performed in many Latin American countries, including El Salvador, Guatemala, Honduras, Nicaragua, Ecuador, Venezuela, and Colombia. It is also prevalent in the United States, especially in the southwestern states. The cities of Albuquerque, New Mexico and San Antonio, Texas both host large-scale public *Las Posadas* events.

Piñatas

Piñatas can be found at a variety of celebrations including birthday parties, but they are perhaps most frequently enjoyed during the Christmas season. Piñatas are traditionally made with a clay pot filled with candy, small toys, nuts, and fruit. The pot is decorated with papier-mâché, paint, tissue paper, crepe paper, and sequins.

Today, the pot is usually left out; instead, the body of the piñata is made entirely out of papier-mâché.

At the party following *Las Posadas*, and at other holiday gatherings, the piñata hangs from a rope suspended from a beam or pulley in the ceiling, usually outdoors in a garage or patio, or from a tree branch. An adult or older child takes hold of the rope, which controls the movement of the piñata. One child is blindfolded and a stick is placed in his or her hands while the other children stand back. An adult turns the blindfolded child in several circles, after which the child swings in the supposed direction of the piñata. The adult in charge of the rope tries to keep the piñata just out of reach of the stick. Each child takes a turn swinging at the piñata while wearing a blindfold. It usually takes many strong hits to break the piñata, and often the piñata does not break until several children have hit it. When it breaks, all the children run toward it, gathering the goodies that have fallen out of it into bags.

In the Americas, the piñata was originally intended to be part of Christian instruction incorporated by early Spanish missionaries into the existing Mayan and Aztec practices that involved breaking clay pots. The decorated pot represented Satan, who deceives people with a pleasing appearance. The pot was traditionally decorate with seven cones, each with streamers attached to their tips. The cones represented each of the seven deadly sins: greed, gluttony, sloth, pride, envy, wrath, and lust. The sweets and trinkets inside the piñata represented earthly temptations. The blindfold represented faith, which is maintained despite the lack of visual evidence, and thereby defies evil. The disorientation created by turning the blindfolded participant represents the trials of the faithful. The piñata is kept above the heads of participants and observers. This reenacts the practice of looking for heavenly, rather than earthly, rewards. The stick represents virtue, as it ultimately overcomes evil (symbolized by the piñata). The piñata filling, when it falls out after the piñata is finally broken, represents the gifts of heaven.

Today, the religious symbols of the piñata have largely given way to its entertainment value. They have become a common part of celebrations in Mexico, the southwestern United States, and Central America.

Misa de Gallo (Midnight Mass)

Translated literally, *misa de gallo* means rooster's mass. The first Christmas masses were held on Christmas morning. However, from the fifth century to the thirteenth, Roman officials held mass during the night as well, at about three in the morning: the hour in which the rooster typically begins to crow. In time, the mass was moved to midnight. A third mass, held at daybreak, was also incorporated into Roman Catholic tradition during the fifth century. Each of the three masses focuses on a particular theme. The "Angels' Mass" (*misa de gallo*, midnight) celebrates the relationship between the Father and the Son, the "Shepherds' Mass" (at dawn) focuses on the human birth of Christ, and the "Mass of the Divine Word" (Christmas morning) celebrates the birth of Christ in the human heart. Each year at midnight on December 25th, the pope presides over *misa de gallo* in Rome, and the mass is usually televised.

La Pastorela

Las Posadas are not the only dramatizations that take place during the Christmas season. *La Pastorela*, meaning "pastoral" (Shepherds' Play), is a play often performed outdoors in the afternoon or evening during the last weeks of December. Sometimes *La Pastorela* is performed in a church just before the *misa de gallo* (Christmas Eve midnight mass), in a public space open to the community, or in a private home. Performances can vary in length anywhere from half an hour to three hours or more. The story is told through song, dialogue, dance, verse, costumes, and sets. Most *pastorelas* have been passed down through oral tradition for generations. Because of this, the plotline of the play has been subject to variation. Although there are many different versions of *La Pastorela*, they all tell the same basic story, portraying the conflict between good and evil through a mix of Christian teaching, folklore, and lewd comedy.

Procession and Plot

As the title suggests, the storyline of the play follows the journey of shepherds to Bethlehem to meet the newborn Jesus. However, along the way, they are met with a variety of obstacles. The most important shepherds, Bato and Tubal, walk onto the stage just behind Saint Michael. Following Bato and Tubal are Gil and Lipio, then Bacirio and Cojo. Next is Gila, the pure shepherdess who is dressed in white. Finally, and intentionally distant from Saint Michael, Hermitaño and Bartolo enter. Hermitaño represents the person who is led astray by worldly desires, while Bartolo embodies laziness and the expectation of undeserved payment.

As the shepherds enter, they sing, thereby revealing their identities to audience members. The singing continues as Gila makes dinner for the shepherds. While everyone is asleep, Lipio and Tubal stay awake to watch the sheep during the night. During their watch, Luzbel (Satan) appears. He tells them that he will try to bewilder them so that they will not know of Jesus' birth. Throughout the play, Luzbel attempts to trick the shepherds and audience alike through lengthy and poetic speeches. Luzbel and Saint Michael engage in battle throughout the play, each trying to win the souls of the shepherds. Luzbel tempts Hermitaño to kidnap Gila and to question his faith. While Hermitaño is watching the flock at night, thereby trying to make amends for his weaknesses, Lipio and Tubal, jubilant, find him and tell him the news of Jesus' birth, which was announced to them by the angel Gabriel. Saint Michael finally defeats Luzbel and comforts the shepherds. The shepherds gather gifts for the Christ Child. They are all eager to begin their journey, except for Bartolo who must be coaxed out of bed to join the party of travelers. Saint Michael binds Luzbel for a thousand years and the play ends happily, with the shepherds' arrival in Bethlehem.

History

La Pastorela is part of a medieval tradition of cyclical dramas in the Catholic Church. Because *La Pastorela* depicts the life of Jesus, the life of a Saint, and the battle between good and evil, it falls into all three categories of cyclical dramas: mystery plays, miracle plays, and morality plays. The purpose of these plays, including

La Pastorela, was to give the largely illiterate public access to a more complete understanding of Christianity and faith through visual imagery and language they could understand. The plays helped the public understand how the principles of Christianity related to their own lives, particularly because the actors were usually ordinary people, rather than trained actors, who worked hard to memorize lines and put together their own costumes.

Eventually, the plays moved away from the church and onto public stages. They became highly entertaining folk dramas with plots adjusted for the masses and ribald humor. In the fifteenth century, the Church banned what it viewed as inappropriate adaptations of the gospel and Christian teaching. Although the plays were banned in Europe, Spanish missionaries used them to teach the gospel to Native Americans who did not understand the religion or language of the Spanish. Missionaries likely introduced *La Pastorela* to Native Americans in the sixteenth century.

In our time, local townspeople, professional and semi-professional acting groups, schools, cities, and churches perform or sponsor performances of *La Pastorela.* In the United States, it is especially prevalent in the states that border Mexico. In 1991, Luis Valdez wrote and directed a popular film version of the play set in rural Texas, featuring Linda Ronstadt, Paul Rodriguez, Robert Beltran, Cheech Marin, Miguel Sandoval, Flaco Jiménez, and Freddy Fender.

Poinsettia

Among the more popular Christmas decorations is the poinsettia plant, also known as *Flor de Noche Buena* (Christmas Eve Flower). It grows indigenously in Mexico and Central America. Many people mistake its colorful leaves (which are most often seen in crimson for the holidays, but also grow orange, pale green, pink, or white) for flowers. Aztecs named it Cuetlaxóchitl and used it as a red dye and a fever-reducer.

The plant's popularity likely stems from a Mexican legend in which a young girl could not afford to purchase flowers to honor the birth of Christ. When she prayed for help, an angel came to her and directed her to gather weeds as an offering instead. As she neared the church, the weeds turned into poinsettias. An alternate version of this tale tells of a poverty-stricken boy who was unable to afford any gift for the Christ child. Along the way to church, he noticed a bush growing beside the road. He decided to cut a few branches as his offering. As soon as he cut them, the branches turned into beautiful poinsettia plants. When he placed them at the foot of the manger at the church, the stars on the Virgin Mary's robe began to shine and a bright star appeared in the eastern sky outside. A very different story suggests that a girl died of a broken heart on Christmas Eve while pining over her lost love. Drops of blood fell from her to the earth, and from them grew the blood red leaves of the poinsettia plant.

Another possibility for the poinsettia's proliferation at Christmas time is that Franciscan monks distinguished it as a Christmas plant in the seventeenth century. The leaf pattern in the shape of a star symbolizes the Star of Bethlehem, which shone at the infant Christ's birth. The deep red color of the plant's leaves represents the love that faithful people have for Christ. The color also signifies the blood of the firstborn sons killed by Herod in his search for Jesus and the blood shed at Jesus' crucifixion.

Food of the Christmas Season

Certain foods characterize the Christmas season for Latinos/as. Turkey, native to the Americas, is often served at Christmas Eve dinner. A salad of fruits, beets, and nuts, called *Ensalada de la Nochebuena*, or Christmas Eve Salad, might also be served along with tortillas, meat, and hot chocolate spiced with cinnamon. *Buñuelos*, fried flour dough sprinkled with cinnamon and sugar, are served at Christmastime and at the New Year. *Tamales* are popular in much of Latin America, the Caribbean, and in some areas of the United States. They are made of steamed corn-based spread and are often filled with meat, beans, cheese, or vegetables, but can also contain a sweet fruit-based filling. Making *tamales* can be a lengthy process. During the Christmas season, families often get together and make large batches of them for distribution among themselves. In the Spanish-speaking Caribbean, roasted pork, rather than turkey, is the favored meat. To complement the main dish, Puerto Rican cooks offer *arroz con gandules*, or pigeon peas and rice, and bread pudding.

Holidays of the Christmas Season

For many Latinos/as, Christmas is not the only holiday of the Christmas season. *Día de los Inocentes* is the first post-Christmas holiday that some Latinos/as celebrate. The day remembers King Herod's search for Jesus through the murder of innocent young children. The holiday is celebrated by playing practical jokes on people. In some cases, the practical joke specifically involves borrowing a treasured item with or without the owner's permission. Later, a little toy or worthless bauble is given along with the returned item. The person duped in the joke or whose belonging was taken is called an *inocente*, "innocent."

Celebrated on January 6th, *Día de los Reyes Magos* is known in English as Three Kings' Day, the Feast of the Magi, and Epiphany. On this day, the Christian church commemorates the three kings' arrival in Bethlehem with gifts for the infant Jesus. The holiday remains a significant part of the Christmas season in Latino cultures. It is on this day, rather than Christmas day, that many Latino children receive their gifts of the Christmas season.

In the evening, the *Merienda de Reyes* takes place. The *Rosca de Reyes* is featured at this event. The *rosca* is a sweetbread baked in the shape of an oval ring and decorated with colored sugar and candied fruit. *Roscas* come in a variety of sizes, depending on the number of people present to enjoy them. Along with the *rosca*, tamales and hot chocolate might be served. Concealed inside the *rosca* is a plastic figure of the baby Jesus. The baby is hidden as a representation of the need to keep Jesus safe from Herod's search for him. Each person cuts a slice of the *rosca* with a knife, symbolizing the Christ Child's peril while Herod's decree was in effect. The person whose slice contains the plastic baby is expected to host *Candelaria* celebration on February 2nd.

Michael McGuigan, left, as one of the kings, plays with the children during El Museo del Barrio's 34th annual Three Kings' Day parade on January 6, 2011, in New York. The Three Kings' Day Parade is an annual celebration in New York City that commemorates the most festive day of the winter season in Latin American culture. The celebration is designed to pay tribute to the day that the three kings came to visit baby Jesus. (AP/Wide World Photos)

The *Candelaria*, or Candle Mass, honors the presentation of Jesus at the temple six weeks after his birth, where, following Jewish custom, he was presented to God. Also at this time, Mary fulfilled the purification rites after having given birth. While at the temple, Simeon and Anna recognized the baby as the Messiah who would be a light to the world. In keeping with this theme, candles are traditionally brought to the church to be blessed. Additionally, on this day the figure of the infant Jesus in the nativity scene is presented with a new gown by the designated *padrino*, or godparent, often the same person who found the plastic figurine in his or her slice of *rosca* on January 6th. After the *Candelaria*, the nativity scene and all of the Christmas decorations are put away until the following year, and the Christmas season officially comes to a close.

CHRISTINE NORQUEST

See also: Buñuelos; Las Posadas; Los Reyes Magos (The Three Kings); Pastorelas (Shepherds' Plays); Rosca de Reyes; Tamales; Virgin of Guadalupe: History and Fiestas Guadalupanas

Further Reading

Arias, Miguel, Mark R. Francis, and Arturo J. Pérez-Rodríguez. *La Navidad Hispana: At Home and at Church*. Chicago: Liturgy Training Publications, 2000.

Del Torre, Miguel A. *Hispanic American Religious Cultures*. Vol. 1 of *American Religious Cultures*. Santa Barbara, CA: ABC–CLIO, 2009.

Gulevich, Tanya. *Encyclopedia of Christmas*. Detroit: Omnigraphics, 2000.

Hispanic Christmas–Navidad Hispana: Decorations, Foods, Music and Traditions [Online 2007]. Hispanic Culture Online. http://www.hispanic-culture-online.com/hispanic-christmas.html.

Kanellos, Nicolás. *Noche Buena: Hispanic American Christmas Stories*. New York: Oxford University Press, 2000.

Menard, Valerie, and Cheech Marín. *The Latino Holiday Book: From Cinco de Mayo to Día de los Muertos—The Celebrations and Traditions of Hispanic-Americans*. New York: Avalon, 2004.

Santiago, Esmeralda, and Joie Davidow, eds. *Las Christmas: Favorite Latino Authors Share Their Holiday Memories*. New York: Vintage, 1999.

CHUPACABRA

The *Chupacabra* or goat sucker took its place among a long list of mythological creatures recognized in Latino folklore in the mid-1990s. Unlike the long list of regional gnomes, *duendes,* forest spirits and humanoids such as *La Llorona* or Wailing Woman, the *Chupacabra* entered our imagination almost overnight and is ever present.

The *Chupacabra* first appeared in 1995 around rural farms and villages on the island of Puerto Rico. First goats (hence the name) and then other barnyard animals such as chickens and pigs were mysteriously killed at night. When a woman from the small town of Canóvanas claimed the first sighting and description of the creature, the event was quickly reported on the island newscasts. Her description was later debunked but it was too late to expunge it from entering the realm of folklore.

Once the voracious world of Spanish-speaking comedians appropriated the event and spun it with the already rich folklore of the rural people of Puerto Rico, it was inevitable that an entity that had not existed in the lexicon of the people became an overnight popular icon: this entity is the legendary *Chupacabra* goat sucker.

The *Chupacabra* reportedly attacked barnyard animals, sucking them dry of blood without spilling a drop on the ground, which in and of itself was miraculous. All of the other known carnivores and predators of barnyard animals such as vampire bats, coyotes, wolves, raccoons, badgers and possums, all relatively small mammals, were known to make a mess of their prey. In almost all previously known cases, such as a fox in the hen house, the local dogs vigorously announced the intruder and were fearless of it. However, with a *Chupacabra* attack there were often no alerts of any kind sounded to warn people. The *Chupacabra* entered the barnyard and exited without being noticed. The *Chupacabra* caught the imagination of many cryptologists in that it was similar to the "cattle mutilations" of the 1970s and 1980s. The rash of bloodless cattle has never been solved while theories abound, UFO experiments and Satanic cults being the most popular culprits to blame in these cases.

The blood-sucking method of killing was most unsettling for the rural folk since this was an action of an animal they did not know and could not identify. When several "eyewitness" reports were compiled in an artist's sketch, the story of this new addition to crypto-zoology sent the conspiracy theorists into a frenzy. Most remarkable was that the unknown blood-sucking entity could not be identified by experts from the various descriptions given, thus making it entirely new and mysterious. The *Chupacabra* stood on hind legs and seemed to be a biped about four feet tall with claw-like features on both its toes and fingers. It is said to have a single row of spines from the top of its head and down along its back. Most troubling is the description of its head as consisting of a flat nose and small mouth. These are identifiable and can be compared to other animals but its eyes were described as consisting of very large, dark ovals and having a similar shape as those of space aliens but red in color.

During 1995, and for several years thereafter, numerous sightings of the *Chupacabra* continued in Puerto Rico. Reported richly, sightings began to be made in almost all Spanish-speaking countries of the Americas including on the United States border with Mexico. Predictably *Chupacabra* sightings would occur after every new report. The new urban legend was fueled by a sort of *Chupacabra* hysteria.

The numerous Spanish-language UFO and paranormal magazines in Mexico and beyond began to publish articles on the *Chupacabra,* and the leading Spanish television syndicates produced programs for the Spanish-speaking world on this new phenomenon. Eventually, very popular TV programs in the United States began to produce stories on the *Chupacabra*. Many associated the *Chupacabra* with the numerous UFO or unidentified flying object sightings in Latin America. The island of Puerto Rico has long been a hotbed of UFO sightings, especially underwater sightings. That is, UFOs are regularly seen coming to and from inland lakes and landing or taking off from offshore underwater bases.

Speculation had it that the *Chupacabra* was the result of an alien experiment gone wrong. Maybe it was even a human-alien hybrid. Either way, its ability to perform feats never seen before such as jumping long or high distances and being able to suck blood from animals with single puncture wounds seemed strange enough to fit the developing theories.

Within a short period of time *Chupacabra* sightings began to be reported on rural ranches and farms in northern Mexico and in south Texas along the border. The mysterious death of a barnyard animal combined with the failure of the family dogs to alert the owners was cause to call the sheriff and the news reporters. Local experts on the paranormal were sought for comment and for awhile the *Chupacabra* frenzy circulated everywhere. *Chupacabra* masks were fashioned for children at Halloween, an unpopular former Mexican President was dubbed *El Chupacabra* and a mask was made of his likeness in the form of a *Chupacabra*, and *Chupacabra* piñatas were all the rage. The small Texas town of Zapata located on Falcon Lake on the Texas-Mexico border began a *Chupacabra* festival every summer with the best *Chupacabra* costume contest and a *Chupacabra* parade.

In the ten-year period between 2000 and 2010, many alleged Chupacabra sightings and shootings have been made throughout Texas. Ranchers claiming to have shot the *Chupacabra* have not had DNA examination identify the carcass as anything other than a mangy hairless coyote or coyote-dog hybrid.

Sightings in other states of the Union and in non–Latin American countries are infrequent but continue to be reported. To date, no one has been able to produce a *Chupacabra* dead or alive. The Spanish-speaking media continue to keep the *Chupacabra* urban legend alive by publishing articles and so-called eyewitness accounts. Meanwhile the *Chupacabra* has taken its place in Latino folklore as an unknown and scary animal that one should be wary of in the night. However, simply stated, the *Chupacabra* does not exist.

Antonio Noé Zavaleta

See also: Coyote; Duendes; Greater Mexico and Its Folklore; La Llorona (The Wailing Woman); Puerto Rico and Its Folklore

Further Reading

Corrales, Scott. *Chupacabras and Other Mysteries.* Murfreesboro, TN: Greenleaf Publications, 1997.

Newton, Michael. *Hidden Animals: A Field Guide to Batsquatch, Chupacabra, and Other Elusive Creatures.* Santa Barbara, CA: ABC–CLIO, 2009.

Radford, Benjamin. *Tracking the Chupacabra: The Vampire Beast in Fact, Fiction, and Folklore.* Albuquerque: University of New Mexico Press, 2011.

CIHUACÓATL

Cihuacóatl (Snake woman) was the principal Aztec goddess associated with midwives, fertility, and motherhood. She was the patron goddess of *Xochimilco* and her temple there was the most magnificent. Fray Diego Dúran reported that for *Cihuacóatl's* feast day, a female slave was purified, and dressed as the goddess. For the 20 days prior to the feast day, the impersonator was feted in banquet after banquet—and all the time kept inebriated. On the day of the goddess, the woman was sacrificed and her blood sprinkled on the stone image of *Cihuacóatl*.

Like many of the Mexican female deities, *Cihuacóatl* had multiple aspects. She was sometimes benevolent and other times caused poverty, adversity, and depression. As a harbinger of bad news she twice warned the Aztecs of impending doom, crying that she and the other gods would soon abandon them. Apparently, the goddess foresaw the destruction that was to be wrought by the Spanish invasion. In the guise of a wailing woman with uncombed dirty hair bringing bad tidings, this aspect of Cihuacóatl may have been a precedent for *La Llorona*.

Representations of the goddess depicted her as a fearsome grimacing skull-faced old woman dressed as a warrior with an eagle feather shield and brandishing a weaving batten. Midwives called upon *Cihuacóatl*, particularly for difficult births. In childbirth, a woman was engaged in her own battle and she was encouraged to show the courage of *Cihuacóatl*. Metaphors drawn from warfare are strongly associated with childbirth. New mothers were praised and likened to eagles and jaguars, which were also the highest-ranking warrior societies of the Aztec military. *Cihuacóatl* was a powerful deity so great that her slightest presence could cause grave injury. Those that visited a new mother and child had to rub their joints with ashes to protect themselves from the residual power of the goddess.

Women that died in childbirth were mourned like deceased warriors and admired for having achieved a good death. Their spirits would transform into an Eagle Woman—deities that resided in the sky and captured the setting sun every day. However, the corpses of women that died in childbirth harbored the negative energy of Cihuacóatl which posed a potent danger to all nearby. Burial of such women was done quickly and secretly in the darkness of night with the body removed from the home by breaking through a wall. After interment at a crossroad (the dead were usually cremated), the husband kept vigil for four nights. It was vital that the burial spot be secret and guarded since warriors and thieves desired amulets from the corpse. The former wanted talismans for warfare and the latter means to cast spells on their victims to render them paralyzed.

Cihuacóatl's most important role was in the creation of humans for this the fifth world. She took the bones that *Quetzalcóatl* (Plumed Serpent) had retrieved from the realm of the Lord of the Dead. *Cihuacóatl* ground the bones into a fine meal in her jade bowl which was then moistened with sacrificial blood provided by *Quetzalcóatl*. From this *masa* (dough) *Cihuacóatl* fashioned human beings. Creation, then, sprang from the complementary efforts and powers of both male and female. This reflects the ancestral Mesoamerican principle of duality which was a fundamental aspect of their world view. As a mother/father pair, *Cihuacóatl* and *Quetzalcóatl* demonstrate the significance of dualism as the word *coatl* can mean "serpent" and/or "twin."

This organizing principle of dualism in Mexican society is also seen in Aztec political organization. European terminology has been inappropriately applied to the functioning of non-western societies. In the case of the Aztec, the supreme leader has uncritically been called "emperor." However, the Aztec term for the highest political office was the *Tlatoani*—which means "he who speaks for" the people. The *Tlatoani* did not, however, rule with impunity. The second highest head of state was the *Cihuacóatl*. Although the term referenced the goddess, the position was held by a high-ranking male. These two leading political offices divided the work of governing into external and internal spheres. The *Cihuacóatl* oversaw the administration of the capital Tenochtitlan while also being in charge of the army, sacrifices, and acting as senior advisor to the *Tlatoani*. During important state rituals, the *Cihuacóatl* dressed in the attire of the goddess. For the Aztecs, the state was a larger version of the household with an external/male and internal/female realm. The *Tlatoani* and *Cihuacóatl* functioned in parallel as father and mother to the Aztec people. Although the *Cihuacóatl* was selected from the high nobility, he could not succeed the *Tlatoani* at his death. Ultimately, after the death of *Moctezuma*, Cortés called together the Aztec nobility to demand gold. As a final barb, the *Cihuacóatl* speaking to/through *La Malinche* made a circumspect, if not lewd, statement about the sexual relationship between the Spaniard and his translator. While this *Cihuacóatl* did not hold the office of *Tlatoani*, he did, in the end, demonstrate the highly prized Aztec ability of sophisticated speech.

CARLEEN D. SÁNCHEZ

See also: Aztec Empire; La Llorona (The Wailing Woman); Malinche; Quetzalcóatl

Further Reading

Clendinnen, Inga. *Aztecs: An Interpretation*. Cambridge: Cambridge University Press, 1991.

Dúran, Fray Diego. *Book of the Gods and Rites and the Ancient Calendar*. Translated and edited by F. Horcasitas and D. Heyden. Norman: University of Oklahoma Press, 1971.

León-Portilla, Miguel, and Earl Shorris. *In the Language of Kings: An Anthology of Mesoamerican Literature—Pre-Columbian to the Present*. New York: W. W. Norton & Co., 2001.

Miller, Mary, and Karl Taube. *The Gods and Symbols of Ancient Mexico and the Maya: An Illustrated Dictionary of Mesoamerican Religion*. London: Thames and Hudson, 1993.

CINCO DE MAYO (MAY 5TH)

The following points must be highlighted at the outset regarding the Mexican American holiday celebration called "Cinco de Mayo," which falls on May 5th:

1. The event commemorates the Battle of Puebla, fought on May 5th, 1862.
2. It is not Mexico's Independence Day, which was September 16th, 1810, some 50 years earlier.
3. The holiday celebrates a victory achieved by the Mexican people, who fought and won a battle against seemingly insurmountable odds.

In 1862, the United States was in the middle of a civil war. Had the South acquired a strong foreign ally, the Confederacy may have won the war and the United States would have split in two. In 1862, a possible ally was just across the Mexican border—an invading French Army under General Laurencez. At the time, the French Army was considered the greatest military force on the globe. For nearly 50 years—since the defeat of Napoleon I at Waterloo, Belgium, in 1815—the French had won an unbroken string of victories in Europe and Asia. In 1862, the French landed at Veracruz, along with forces sent by Queen Isabella II of Spain and Queen Victoria of Great Britain. These European troops had come to collect the debt owed to their countries by Mexico—a debt that Mexican President Benito Juárez had officially suspended because the country was essentially bankrupt. Juárez, who served five terms as President of Mexico (1858–1872), was the first Mexican leader who lacked a military background, and also the first full-blooded Indigenous national ever to serve as President of Mexico and to lead a country of the Western Hemisphere.

Refusing Juárez's proposed compromise to repay the debt two years later, the European forces seized the custom house at Veracruz. They intended to intercept the customs payments in exchange for their debt. After some time, Spain and Great Britain reached an agreement with Juárez and the armies of those two countries left Mexico. The French, on the other hand, stayed and marched to Mexico City.

Many in the U.S. had opposed the Mexican-American War of 1846–1848 and the American expansionism of the 1840s known as "manifest destiny," which called for American acquisition of Mexican territory. Among these critics of manifest destiny was John Quincy Adams, the sixth president of the United States (1825–1829). Adams had declared in 1838 that in a war with Mexico "the banners of freedom will be the banners of Mexico; and your banners [the United States],

I blush to speak the word, will be the banners of slavery" (*Speeches of John Quincy Adams* 1838, 119).

Since this sentiment was still strong in the 1840s, President James K. Polk ordered General Zachary Taylor to march into territory in dispute with Mexico in 1846 in hopes of provoking the Mexicans into firing the first shot. A young lieutenant by the name of Ulysses S. Grant, who was part of the expedition, put its purpose succinctly: "We were sent to provoke a fight, but it was essential that Mexico commence it" (*Memoirs,* quoted in W. S. McFeely, *Grant: A Biography,* 1981, 30). That same lieutenant, years later, would suggest the possibility that the horrors of the Civil War were God's punishment for the war with Mexico; he was convinced that the entire Mexican enterprise was part of a conspiracy to increase the number of slaveholding states in the Union (González 1988, 20).

If the Mexicans held their fire, Taylor was ordered to continue advancing until he drew fire. When this happened, Polk protested vehemently, and Congress declared war on Mexico. The war was brief, ending on February 2nd, 1848, with the signing of the Treaty of Guadalupe-Hidalgo. Under the treaty, the United States acquired the present-day states of New Mexico, Arizona, California, Utah, Nevada, and part of Colorado, and made good the 1845 annexation of Texas. Mexico received a payment of $15,000,000.

France had significant interest in halting the rapid growth of the United States, which was beginning to threaten the economic position of the European powers. If Napoleon III, the nephew of Napoleon I and ruler of France, was successful in conquering Mexico, the possibility of marching north to aid the Confederates in dividing the United States was very real.

The American victory over Mexico in the 1840s emptied the Mexican treasury and led to financial disaster, thus causing Juárez to suspended payments to France, which, in turn, incited Napoleon III to act against Mexico. President Abraham Lincoln and the United States needed Mexico to hold back the French troops until the Confederacy could be defeated and Lincoln could deploy American troops on the border to aid Juárez.

Early on May 5th, 1862, General Laurencez led 6,000 French troops toward Puebla, just 100 miles from Mexico City. Expecting the attack was General Ignacio Zaragoza, a Texas-born Mexican, who was ordered to defend Puebla with a force of 4,000 troops, many of them agricultural workers armed with antiquated rifles and machetes. The battle would take place in a muddy, uneven field.

To show his contempt for the Mexicans, General Laurencez ordered his troops to attack through the middle of their defenses, the strongest part of the Mexican position. The French cavalry went through ditches, over adobe ruins, and toward the slope of Guadalupe Hill. The Mexican army stood its ground. General Zaragoza had no experience in military tactics but was a veteran in guerrilla warfare. He released a herd of stampeding cattle ahead of his infantry as a buffer for his troops as well as to confuse the French. He then ordered his troops to attack. Although carrying few firearms, the Mexicans had many farm implements, such as shovels, pitchforks, scythes, and machetes; they also had a large quantity of rocks, leading to the battle cry *"Hasta con piedras"* ("even with rocks"). The ferocity of the Mexican attack drove the French to Orizaba, where the pursuing Zaragoza attacked the French again, forcing them to flee to the coast.

Since that day, May 5th, 1862, no foreign army has ever again invaded the Americas. If it were not for the victory at Puebla by Mexican peasants, the history of the United States could have been very different. El Cinco de Mayo is a recasting of the old and perennial story of David and Goliath: with the weak fighting against the strong; justice pitted against oppression; and the apparently powerless against the seemingly invincible. It symbolizes the Mexican people standing up for their right to freedom, self-rule, self-expression, and self-determination. But more than that, "El Cinco de Mayo" symbolizes, for people in both Mexico and the United States, the spirit of courage in the face of insurmountable odds, ethnic pride in one's cultural heritage, and the realization that struggle and sacrifice are required to maintain that heritage. Understanding the true significance of "Cinco de Mayo" celebration is important because, as an old African proverb says, "Until the lion has its own historian, tales of the hunt will always glorify the hunter."

CALEB ROSADO

See also: September 16 (Mexican Independence Day)

Further Reading

Adams, John Quincy. *Speeches of John Quincy Adams.* Washington, D.C.: Gales and Seaton, 1838.

González, Justo. *The Theological Education of Hispanics,* New York: The Fund for Theological Education, 1988.

McFeely, W. S. *Grant: A Biography.* New York: Norton, 1981.

Miles, Donald W. *Cinco de Mayo: What Is Everybody Celebrating?* Lincoln, NE: iUniverse, 2006.

PBS. http://www.pbs.org/kpbs/theborder/history/timeline/10.html.

COATLICUE

Within the pantheon of Aztec or Mexica deities, Coatlicue, the decapitated earth goddess, is considered one of the most ancient and strangest figures. Though her name means "she with the skirt of serpents" in Nahuatl, Coatlicue is also referred to as the eater of filth, the earth mother and the beheaded goddess. Culturally, this goddess also shares attributes with the mother goddess Tonantzin, and for this reason is sometimes likened to the Virgin of Guadalupe. Because of her similar characteristics with the Aztec deity of filth, Tlazolteotl, such as the power to transform into a seductress capable of cleansing the sins of humans, Coatlicue also serves as a goddess of love in addition to her role as both creator and destroyer of life. Because of such dichotomous complexity, Coatlicue also symbolizes the ambivalence in nature. Despite the diverse attributes including agriculture, fertility, war, death and power, many contemporary Chicana artists reinterpreted the goddess as a symbol of feminine strength and creativity.

The religious practices surrounding Coatlicue are similar to other Mexica (Aztec) practices that involve ritual bloodletting and human sacrifices. The beheaded goddess was celebrated twice a year in the House of Darkness, her temple in Tenochtitlán. The first was the spring ceremony of Tonzozontli, in which the flayed skins of sacrificial victims were placed in a sacred cave along with the bones of war captives. This ritual, celebrating the oncoming rain season and harvest, was also believed to cure illness in the Mexica population. The second was the Quecholli, the autumnal ceremony of the hunt. In the Quecholli, a woman who represented Coatlicue was decapitated and her skin, as in Tonzozontli, was flayed and given as an offering to the earth goddess.

Statue of Coatlicue (Mother of Gods) displayed in the National Museum of Anthropology and History in Mexico City. (Dreamstime.com)

In the religious mythology of the Mexica, Coatlicue is the mother of the sun and warrior god Huitzilopochtli. In one tradition she was worshiping on the Mountain of the Serpent when a ball of feathers descended from the sky to impregnate her. Coatlicue's miraculous pregnancy enraged her daughter Coyolxauhqui, the Goddess of the Moon, who believed it to be the results of her mother's immorality. Coyolxauhqui gathered her 400 brothers (the stars) to storm the mountain and slay Coatlicue. From the womb Huitzilopochtli warned his mother of the attack and told her that he would protect her (other traditions, however, say one of her loyal children warned her). When the 400 brothers reached the mountain summit, Huitzilopochtli had been born fully grown and in full battle regalia. He vanquished the invaders and beheaded Coyolxauhqui, throwing her body down the mountainside where it was torn to pieces.

In another myth Coatlicue warned the Mexica people of their demise. While Coatlicue awaited the return of her son Huitzilopochtli to Aztlán, the emperor Motecuhzoma I sent his magicians to console her. When they arrived at the goddess's home, she asked about the original ancestors who left Aztlán and was surprised to hear that they had died, for death was unknown to the ancients of Aztlán. She then told the magicians that Huitzilopochtli and the Mexica would lose every city in their possession. Only after her son's defeat and the ruination of the Mexica Empire would he return to her.

A third legend of Coatlicue involves the creation of the world and her transformation into the earth through self-sacrifice. When mutilated, her hair became the grass, flower, trees and other vegetation. Her skin became the fertile soil that spread over the earth; her eyes filled with water, becoming the wells and springs from which the Mexica drank. From her nose she formed hills and valleys, and her mouth became a protective cave for her people to reside in.

Apart from the transformative blazon of Coatlicue's features, the physical imagery of this powerful and frightening goddess is exemplified by the archaeological artifacts that survived the Spanish Conquest. The statue of Coatlicue (now at the National Museum in Mexico City) features the goddess in a cruciform shape standing eight feet tall. The statue, dating between 1487 and 1520, was discovered in 1790 when the Spanish viceroy ordered an excavation to resurface the Zócalo, the central plaza of Mexico City. The Coatlicue statue is a bicephalous figure with two viper heads rising from her shoulders and facing each other. As snakes writhing from dismembered body parts often represent blood flowing from the body in many Meso-American cultures, the double serpent gives credence to the epithet of beheaded. At her waist Coatlicue wore a skirt made of woven snakes and upon her neck a necklace made of human hands and hearts with a pendant of a skull. Her feet are the claws of jaguars.

Some twentieth-century Mexican and Chicana artists repeated these physical features in their portraits of Coatlicue. The early-twentieth-century Mexican painter Saturnino Herrán, for example, used the image of the Aztec goddess in his painting *Coatlicue Transformed* (1918). Over the re-creation of the fifteenth-century statue of the goddess, Herrán painted a faint outline of a crucified Christ demonstrating a convergence of European and Indigenous religions and cultures in Mexico. Diego Rivera's mural *Detroit Industry, South Wall* (1932–1933) also contains a section reminiscent of Coatlicue. Abounding in geometric elements, Rivera's goddess is veiled in the image of a factory machine creating a technological and modern vision of an Amerindian past. While her contemporaries used the images of this Aztec goddess, Frida Kahlo's self-portrait *Roots* (1943) contains elements of the story of Coatlicue's death and sacrifice. In the self-portrait, the artist is lying on the ground with several open wounds or holes in her body. From those openings burgeon the roots and branches of plants, an image that brings to mind the Mexica vision of the creation of the world and Khalo's self-portrayal as the goddess.

Contemporary artists also use Coatlicue as a backdrop to their paintings. For example, the Chicana artist Alma Gómez uses the Coatlicue image in her *Corazón Sagrado / Sacred Heart* where at the center, she paints a human heart surrounded by the necklace of four hands and two sacrificial hearts that Coatlicue wears. The pendant, in place of a skull, is a portrait of an elderly woman. Another contemporary rendition of the goddess is the mural of Coatlicue designed by Susan Yamagata and featured in San Diego's Chicano Park. Similar to Herrán's portrait, Yamagata inscribes Christian imagery into the Aztec myth: Coatlicue is standing with arms open in a cross; in one hand she holds a sun and in the other a globe displaying the Americas (reminiscent of the myth of St. Christopher, in which the Christ child is holding the world in his hands). Yamagata also distinguishes her image of the Coatlicue by making the two snakes face away from each other, as opposed to being eye to eye.

While visual representations of Coatlicue have been important in the cultural development of the Mexica goddess, her role within literature has also provided fruitful transformations, especially among Chicana authors. Poets like Pat Mora, Ana Castillo and Sandra Cisneros use the image of Coatlicue as a conceit representing feminist creative force in their poetry often layering humor over their words. Helena María Viramontes also uses various characteristics similar to this Aztec goddess in her novel *Under the Feet of Jesus* to describe many of the female protagonists.

Many Chicana intellectuals also appropriate the goddess as a symbol representative of female strength derived from an Amerindian cultural past that subverts preconceived, western binary systems. Ana Castillo's *Massacre of the Dreamers*—her collected essays on Xicanisma based on Paulo Freire's concept of *conscientização* (Critical Consciousness)—uses Coatlicue as an example of a non-Western vision that goes beyond binary opposition. For Castillo, Coatlicue offers an alternative possibility where the features of life and of death may coalesce without any inherent contradiction. Likewise, Gloria Anzaldúa is best known for her vision of Chicana Mestizaje centered around the appropriation of such Aztec monster goddesses. She combines various female goddesses of the Meso-American mythological and religious traditions to contrast them with phallocentric imagery of power. However, she is also conscious of the many shared characteristics between Coatlicue and the feathered serpent god, Quetzalcóatl. Though Anzaldúa, like many Chicana feminist and Xicana theorists, interprets Coatlicue as a monster figure, she too sees the Mexica goddess as a cultural motif that signifies strength, vitality and creativity in the female form.

CHRISTOPHER ALEX CHABLÉ

See also: Aztec Empire; Aztlán; Chicano/a Art and Folklore; Cihuacóatl; Greater Mexico and Its Folklore; Huitzilopochtli; Quetzalcóatl; Tonantzin; Tonantzin in Chicana Literature and Art; Virgin of Guadalupe: History and Fiestas Guadalupanas

Further Reading

Anton, Ferdinand. *Women In Pre-Columbian America*. Translated by Marianne Herzfeld. New York: Abner Schram, 1973.

Anzaldúa, Gloria. *Borderlands/La Frontera: The New Mestiza*. San Francisco: Spinsters/Aunt Lute, 1987.

Anzaldúa, Gloria. *Entre Mundos/Among Worlds: New Perspectives on Gloria E. Anzaldúa*. Edited by Ana Louise Keating. New York: Palgrave Macmillan, 2005.

Contreras, Sheila Marie. "From La Malinche to Coatlicue: Chicana Indigenist Feminism and Mythic Native Women." In *Blood Lines: Myth, Indigenism, and Chicana/o Literature*, 105–132. Austin: University of Texas Press, 2008.

Parkinson Zamora, Lois. *The Inordinate Eye: New World Baroque and Latin American Fiction.* Chicago: University of Chicago Press, 2006.

Rebolledo, Tey Diana. "From Coatlicue to La Llorona: Literary Myths and Archetypes." In *Women Singing in the Snow: A Cultural Analysis of Chicana Literature*, 49–81. Tucson: University of Arizona Press, 1995.

Ruether, Rosemary Radford. "Tonantzin-Guadalupe: The Meeting of Aztec and Christian Female Symbols in Mexico." In *Goddesses and the Divine Feminine: A Western Religious History*, 190–219. Berkeley: University of California Press, 2005.

COCKFIGHTING

See Pelea de Gallos (Cockfighting)

COLCHAS (QUILTS, QUILTING)

In Chicana communities, the term "*colcha*" refers either to the quilting tradition found in northern Mexico and in the Southwest or to the embroidery art found most commonly in New Mexico and Colorado. The quilting appears to have come from the French presence in the area during the nineteenth century. Various quilters have been recognized as masters and have traveled to Washington, D.C., to present at the American Folklife Festival. One such quilter, traditional quilter María Soliz from San Ygnacio, Texas, would follow the traditional way of preparing the wool batting; a contemporary quilter of *colcha*s from San Antonio is Manuela Olivarez who has instituted some innovations and uses regular commercial cotton or polyester batting.

Materials—Batting

The traditional *colcha* quilting tradition uses wool batting, 100% cotton fabric and thread. The wool batting was most common in rural Chicana communities where the product was plentiful. The traditional way of washing the wool using ash to remove the lanolin and then preparing it by carding is almost an unknown art today. But some quilters who used this method remain and have changed and transformed the process to use commercial products such as Stanley Home products degreaser to wash the wool.

The Quilting Frame

The frame is often homemade with two-by-fours and requires a heavy fabric edge where the quilt fabric is attached. The frame, constructed so as to accommodate for a child's quilt to a king-size quilt, will serve the purposes of the quilter; the frame is held together with steel rods inserted into drilled holes to mark the size of the quilt.

The Fabric

Five yards of solid fabric matched to an equal length of a print (nowadays it is usually a cotton blend to avoid shrinkage) is attached to the frame. Traditionally the fabric matched the kind of quilt desired; for example for wedding quilts it was customary to use a satin pastel-colored fabric. For everyday quilts, it was a floral print; sometimes it came from large twenty-five pound sacks of flour or sugar. Nowadays the fabric is bought in fabric shops and often the quilter will select thematic—seasonal—or Disney character prints for children's quilts. The tradition has changed and often a grandmother will quilt an appropriately colored quilt for a child going off to college. After the wool is prepared, two layers of carded wool are placed on the print fabric, the solid one on top to sandwich the batting. The solid fabric has been previously marked for stitching using traditional patterns that have been passed down from generation to generation.

Patterns

The most common patterns are floral or geometric designs that are traced via tracing paper; occasionally the pattern has been cut out with cardboard and it is laid on the solid fabric for marking either with a quilting pen or with a thin bar of soap.

Needles and Thimble

The correct and well-fitted thimble is as important as the needle; size should be appropriate for the fabric and batting. Often grandmothers would pass on their thimble to their granddaughters to use.

After the quilting materials—fabric and batting—have been mounted, the hand stitching begins; quilters use quilting thread and a quilting needle. The quality of the quilting and the reputation of the quilter depend on the number of stitches per inch; usually ten stitches per inch is the mark of a master quilter.

Colcha Embroidery, most commonly found in New Mexico and Colorado, uses a special embroidery stitching technique that originated with the early European settlers to the area from Spain; indeed many of the bright colors and designs hearken back to Spanish traditional embroidery floral patterns. Initially the traditional embroidery graced coverlets and other bed clothes such as pillow cases, in addition to the traditional altar cloths and as decoration on clothing; however, in the twentieth century along with other traditional arts that came to be known as Santa Fe Style, the embroidered cloths moved to the decorative arts category and began to appear as wall hangings.

As evidence of how this traditional art is considered folk art, we point out that pieces of *colcha* embroidery art are housed in the International Folk Art Museum and the Museum of Spanish Colonial Art in Santa Fe, New Mexico as well as in the Albuquerque Museum. In addition, the National Endowment for the Arts awarded a 1994 Heritage Fellowship to Frances Varos Graves, a *colcha* embroiderer from Ranchos de Taos, New Mexico.

NORMA E. CANTÚ

See also: Paper Arts (Papel Picado, Papier Mâché, and Kites)

Further Reading

Benson, Nancy C. *New Mexico Colcha Club: Spanish Colonial Embroidery & the Women Who Saved It.* Albuquerque: Museum of New Mexico Press, 2008.

Cantú, Norma E., and Ofelia Zapata. "Mexican American Quilting Traditions of Laredo, San Ygnacio and Zapata, Texas." In *Hecho en Tejas: Texas-Mexican Folk Arts and Crafts*. Texas Folklore Society, no. 50. Denton: North Texas University Press, 1991, pp. 77–92.

MacAulay, Suzanne P. *Stitching Rites: Colcha Embroidery along the Northern Rio Grande*. Tucson: University of Arizona Press, 2000.

Wroth, William. *Weaving and Colcha from the Hispanic Southwest*. Santa Fe: Ancient City Press, 1985.

COLONIAL ART

To more fully comprehend the origins and affinities of Spanish colonial art in the Americas, it is imperative that one first acknowledge that the use of the term "colonial" has of late come into question in some quarters. Among Mexican scholars, the three centuries that encompass what has traditionally been referred to as the Colonial era (AD 1521–1821) are more appropriately referred to as the *virreinato*, viceroyalty, or Vicegeral era as per its emergence within the *virreinato de Nueva España* or viceroyalty of New Spain (Mullen 1997). The viceroyalty of Peru was in turn established in 1542 and subsequently partitioned into the viceroyalties of *Nueva Granada* (1718) and *La Plata* (1776). The period of the *virreinato indiano* or Indian viceroyalty is largely synonymous with that period identified with the *Imperio Español* or Spanish Empire created by Royal Decree on 12 October of 1535, and coming to an ignominious end with the *Tratados de Cordoba* on 24 August of 1821. This period corresponds with the installation of Viceroy Antonio de Mendoza in Mexico City in 1535 and culminates with the signing of the treaties that ended the Wars of Independence from Spain in 1821.

During this period, architectural historian Robert Mullen (1997, vii) estimates that some 100,000 churches and civic buildings were built in New Spain or Mexico in the period spanning 1530 through 1800. Accordingly, in the period prior to the end of the eighteenth century, some 70,000 churches and 500 monasteries were erected by Hispanic and Amerindian builders. According to art historian Gauvin Alexander Bailey (2005, 51), the New World variant of the Catholic Church can be credited with "the largest and swiftest building campaign in the history of the world." He further identifies the distinctive architectural developments in question with three major time frames that include a formative era spanning the 1540s through the 1600s, the transitional phase extending from 1650 to 1750, and the age of fulfillment interpreted to extend from 1750 to 1800. While the architectural history in question has been proposed for what today constitutes Mexico and Central America, these developments are readily identified throughout those areas of the Americas where the Iberian tradition left its mark.

While Iberian or Hispanicized architecture, architectural sculpture, and ecclesiastical works are among the most enduring vestiges of the colonial or viceregal artistic traditions of Latin America, the arts of that era spanning the three centuries extending from 1521 through 1821 encompass a particularly large universe of materials, methods, and applications. The principal artistic media of the era included stone and wood sculpture and statuary such as *santos* and *bultos*, polychrome (fresco) murals and portable arts, including paintings produced in oils, tempera, and a variety of mineral pigments, feather paintings, glazed tile mosaics, tin- and lead-glazed earthenware pottery, lacquer ware, jewelry in precious metals, bronze casting, Spanish metal work, glass wares, textiles, tapestries, banners, illuminated manuscripts, calligraphy, engravings, drawings, cartography, music, literature, poetry, and a world of devotional art. For our purposes, we will characterize the arts of the colonial or viceregal period in terms of architecture, sculpture, painting, and folk art more generally construed.

Viceregal and Colonial Architecture

During that period encompassing the three centuries identified with the expansion of the Spanish Empire in the Americas (AD 1521–1821), several major European artistic and stylistic traditions form the basis for the emergence of Colonial or Viceregal arts in the Americas, specifically, North, Middle, Central, and Andean South America. Among those traditions that served as the core for the emergence of a Hispanicized New World artistic framework, the Spanish architectural tradition owes its origins to the Gothic tradition formulated in Spain, including such styles as those embodied in the Early Gothic (twelfth century), High Gothic (thirteenth century), *Mudéjar* Gothic (thirteenth to fifteenth centuries), *Levantino* Gothic (fourteenth century), and *Isabelline* Gothic (fifteenth century). The Spanish Gothic, as such, formed the basis for the earliest European-inspired architectural and sculptural traditions in New Spain, and thereby, the New World. The Gothic style was in turn born of Renaissance and Romanesque artistic and architectural styles and traditions. The Renaissance style of architecture sought to evoke the conscious revival of ancient Greek and Roman traditions in art and architecture through the integration of semi-spherical domes, semi-circular arches, and the symmetrical arrangement of columns, lintels, pilasters, and statuary. This style originated in Italy in the early fifteenth century and reached its apogee by the beginnings of the seventeenth century, and much of that art and architecture influenced as such conjures a return to antique and ancient styles derived from both Greek and Roman archetypes in architecture, painting, and sculpture. Such embellishments and the influence of antiquity defined the Renaissance, and ultimately, the earliest reformulations of this tradition in sixteenth-century Mexico and Peru. By contrast, while examples of both the High Gothic and *Mudéjar* Gothic styles may be found throughout the Americas, the stone vault within the nave of the convent church of *Santo Domingo, Yanhuitlán* (Oaxaca), and the wooden vault within the *Mudéjar*-style nave of the convent church of *Asunción de Nuestra Señora* (Tlaxcala), provide dramatically distinctive examples of the Gothic tradition and its manifestation in Mexico.

The Gothic Style

The international medieval style identified with the Gothic cathedrals of Europe was introduced into the Americas early in the sixteenth century, and saw some of its most elaborate and celebrated manifestations in Mexico City, Mexico, and Lima, Peru. This style, which originated in France, is largely characterized by the integration of pointed rib vaults, steep spires, and delicate tracery windows into architectural contexts. The addition of bright polychrome paintings and sculpture produced a level of realism touted as "startling" in its effect on the viewer. The thirteenth- through sixteenth-century *Catedral de Santa María de Burgos* in Castilian Spain, the twelfth- through sixteenth-century *Cathédrale Notre-Dame de Chartres* in France, and the twelfth-century all-Gothic Cathedral of Welles in England, all exemplify early examples of the Gothic style in Europe. Ultimately, the Gothic architectonic tradition melded with both Renaissance and Plateresque styles in Mexico and Peru to achieve a New World synthesis in the earliest European-styled structures of the Americas. In viceregal Mexico, architect Claudio de Arciniega (c. 1520–1593) of Burgos, Spain, drew inspiration from the Gothic cathedrals of his homeland to design the sixteenth- through early-nineteenth-century *Catedral Metropolitana de la Asunción de María* in Mexico City. The *Catedral Metropolitana* was ultimately completed under the direction of architect Manuel Tolsa in the early 1800s, and as such, the copula and tall lantern, and statuary integrated into the façade, reflect the neoclassical style. By contrast, architectural historian Robert James Mullen has noted that the lower rectangular portions of the Cathedral exemplify the "severe Renaissance style" (Mullen 1997, 90). Flanders constituted the "cultural capital of the late Gothic," and this source ultimately imposed a powerful influence on the spread of the Gothic tradition into Spain and Portugal, and thereby, the New World. Finally, it should be noted that while the *Mudéjar* Gothic styles of Spain clearly derive from Islamic influence over the Iberian Peninsula for the period extending from the eighth through fifteenth centuries, this architectural tradition nevertheless proved to be among the most persistent stylistic sources to

The Metropolitan Cathedral (*Cathedral Metropolitana*) in Mexico City. (iStockPhoto.com)

manifest itself in the structure, embellishment, and key architectural elements of viceregal monuments throughout the Americas from the fifteenth through nineteenth centuries. Employing complex geometric patterns in inlaid wood furnishings, ceilings, and cut stone veneers, Islamic artisans and their Iberian protégés produced architectural and artistic creations that span exemplary productions from Alhambra, Spain, to Quito, Ecuador, and the *Mudéjar* embellishments of the early California mission of *San Carlos Borromeo del Río Carmelo* among others. Its resurgence in the late eighteenth and early nineteenth centuries in the Mission churches of *Alta California* is a testament to its cultural impact and longevity in the Americas.

Mexican Baroque

The Baroque artistic and historical era originated in Rome with the resurgence of Catholic culture in the wake of the Protestant Reformation, and Counter-Reformation, and this tradition first transformed Mexican colonial and viceregal architectural and sculptural styles in the early decades of the seventeenth century (Bailey 2005, 412). Spanning the period of circa 1590 to 1750, Baroque was first adopted internationally in Spain, France, and Holland, and swept into Latin America more generally by the mid-seventeenth century. In Europe, this artistic movement was dominated by the works of famed painters, sculptors, and architects, including Caravaggio (1571–1610), Annibale Carracci (1560–1609), Pietro da Cortona (1569–1669), and Gianlorenzo Bernini (1598–1680).

Art historian Gauvin Alexander Bailey makes the distinction between Baroque and Renaissance styles in so far as Mexican Baroque heralds an "increased interaction of structural forms and . . . a greater love for ornament and fanciful shapes" (Bailey 2005, 412). Where architectural embellishment is concerned, Gauvin Alexander Bailey sees Mexican Baroque as constituting a more three-dimensional and dramatically distinct artistic formula. Mixtilinear patterns, consisting of mixed aggregations of straight lines and curves, predominate in this artistic format. According to Yale Institute of Sacred Music theologian Jaime Lara, "any student of art history knows that Spanish baroque images are never static or stoic; they are in intense movement, windblown by the presence of the spirit, electrically charged by contact with the divine" (Lara 2009). In New Spain, Mexican Baroque, with its hybrid melding of European and Mesoamerican Indigenous forms, ultimately redefined the artistic tradition in a frenzy of architectural, sculptural, and polychromatic embellishment unlike that known anywhere else in Europe or the Americas.

By the late eighteenth century, this stylistic tradition was transformed into one dominated by particularly decorative and fanciful forms of ornamentation identified with *Rococo*; that is to say, Ultrabaroque or *Estípite-Baroque* in Spanish and Latin American contexts. In New World venues, the term Ultrabaroque or *Estípite-Baroque* is generally used to identify this particularly ornate form of artistic embellishment. The styles of this era were identified with Louis XV of France (1715–1774) and popularized in Germanic contexts as well. According to Bailey (2005, 417), where architecture is concerned, "structure gave way to embellishment, and in painting, forms lost their solidity through ever-looser brushwork and lighter, pastel colours."

The Ultrabaroque variant of this tradition was popularly identified in Spain as *Churrigueresque*, and a key characteristic was the reliance on the dissolution of structure and forms of embellishment reliant on a profuse body of ornamentation. In such contexts, structural elements appear more decorative than functional.

Neoclassical Style

A severe and regulated version of classicism, Neoclassicism dominated Europe and Anglo America from the mid-eighteenth century to about 1830, and was prevalent in Latin America from the 1780s until well into the Independence era. Linked to both the idealism of the Enlightenment, and that veil of sobriety, morality, and logic sought by the Bourbon monarchy in the wake of its diminished control over its colonies, the resurgence of Greco-Roman architectural styles signals this era (Bailey 2005, 415). It thereby became the architectural language of the art academies of the time, such as Mexico City's *Real Academia de San Carlos*. Many sixteenth- through eighteenth-century cathedrals and churches in Mexico were subjected to cycles of modification and retrofit that transformed preexisting Gothic, or Renaissance and Baroque, styles of iconographic and/or architectural embellishment into hybrid variations on the Neoclassical styles of the late eighteenth and early nineteenth centuries. In one such instance, the late-nineteenth-century interior of the sanctuary and nave of the *Catedral de Puebla*, with its beautifully crafted Baroque façades, was ultimately modified into one largely centered on the Neoclassical styles in vogue at that time. To that end the colonial *retablo mayor* or altar screen was replaced by the monumental Neoclassical altar that now stands in its place within the *Catedral de Puebla*. One of the few remaining colonial or viceregal artistic features remaining within the reconstituted Neoclassical interior of the *Catedral de Puebla* is the mural painted within the cupola or domed vault of the apse by Cristóbal de Villalpando (Mullen 1997, 99).

Extending the discussion of colonial art beyond institutional or civic-ceremonial architectural and artistic styles and traditions necessarily requires consideration of those furnishings and forms of portable and plastic arts intended to enhance the spiritual, political, economic and social landscapes of the built environment. Where colonial or viceregal arts are concerned, it is first important to acknowledge the wealth of media, diversity of forms, and those culturally and regionally distinctive manifestations that are beyond the scope of this essay. Hybrid and multi-ethnic sources of inspiration continue to inform the proliferation of folk art forms in the American hemisphere, and thereby present challenges well beyond the scope of this treatment. The following discussion treats only a select sampling of those colonial or viceregal art forms deemed most influential on the emergence of the broader Latin American artistic and folk traditions of today.

Paintings and the Liturgical Arts

Throughout the Americas, colonial art and its production were inextricably linked to the society, politics, and religion of the viceroyalty, and those Amerindian nations subject to the mandates of both Church and Crown for the period under consideration. Diverse cultural traditions, and the colonial artistic sensitivities of the viceroyalty, necessarily informed the hybrid artistic productions by men and women of Indian, *mestizo*, *afromestizo* or black, Asian, *criollo*, and European origin. As such, these diverse ethnic sources and influences worked their way into the arts of the colonial or viceregal eras. A particularly significant source of influence on the arts of the viceroyalty was that emanating from the many craft guilds and academies that emerged throughout the Americas as a direct response to the growing demand for liturgical and elite works of art.

Where the paintings of the viceroyalty of New Spain are concerned, those that have drawn the lion's share of attention are those identified with the liturgical arts. Interpretations and depictions of *Nuestra Señora de Guadalupe* and *San Juan Diego* by Zapotec Indian painter Miguel Mateo Maldonado y Cabrera (1695–1768) are among the most celebrated such works in New Spain and Latin America more generally. Miguel Cabrera, who is best known for the so-called *casta* paintings, has been deemed one of the greatest artists of the period (Castro Mantecón and Zárate Aquino 1958). The *casta* paintings in particular exemplify the visual practices of late-eighteenth-century New Spain by way of depicting what art historian Magali Carrera (2003) deems to reflect the broader regulatory narratives of that time. As a favored artist of both the Archbishop of Mexico and the Jesuit Order, Cabrera was often commissioned to execute liturgical works ranging from the first ever portrait of San Juan Diego to various studies of the agave or palm fiber *tilma* or mantle of Juan Diego that bears the apparition of Our Lady of Guadalupe. His works as such drew on both liturgical and state-sanctioned icons and imagery appropriate to the viceroyalty and its visual narratives, and this was in turn informed by those artistic and architectural traditions prevalent in New Spain or Mexico. Ultimately, Cabrera's art, like that of so many of his contemporaries, and those many others who would follow in his footsteps, conveyed their craftsmanship through the guilds of their time, and their prevalence in the missions, churches, and cathedrals of that time.

Derivative Arts and Folk Traditions

The liturgical arts spread rapidly through the Americas with the adoption of the Hispanic Catholic faith. With each new founding or dedication of a church or monastery, paintings and statuary commissioned in Mexico City or Lima, Peru, were conveyed to these new theaters of conversion. As with the missions of *Alta California*, each painting was accompanied by a copy in paper or other media, and it was this copy, or an original, that was forwarded to the site of the next mission founding on the frontier. By so doing, such copies were reproduced by Spanish, *mestizo*, *afromestizo*, or other native artisans and neophytes formally or informally schooled in the arts of the frontier. Such works of art then became the subject, and craft specialty, of folk art traditions within given communities.

The dynamism inherent in the folk art traditions of Latin America, and the rapid proliferation of types and media, thereby served as yet one additional conduit for the dissemination of the arts of the viceroyalty in the Americas. Created by local artists employing local materials, the shared and collective or popular dimensions of folk art productions served to hasten the dissemination of established institutional forms in both urban and rural community contexts. While such derivative traditions in folk art manufacture typically centered on the fabrication of functional or utilitarian items such as copper- and tin-backed *retablos* for home altars or elaborately embellished *majolica* vessels for kitchen use, such art forms typically integrated religious, celebratory, and sacred or symbolic elements into their iconographic vocabulary. Moreover, given their utilitarian or other functional nature, much of that art that once comprised the colonial Latin American folk art tradition has not survived, particularly as it was often "used, worn out, and discarded" (Oettinger, Jr., 1992, 3). As such, much of that which survived the passage of time and the elements is specific to the arts of religious devotion and related obligations, and includes paintings, frescoes, murals, *retablos*, feather work, *encochados*, *casta* paintings, hymnals, prayer boards, religious statuary such as *bultos* or *santos*, cast metal bells and reliquary, carved wooden crosses, ceramics, and a wide variety of textiles. The syncretic or hybrid blending of Indigenous, or pagan, and Christian art forms thereby served to satisfy both local tradition and the demands of the new Catholic hierarchy.

Colonial Art in Perspective

The identification and discussion of colonial or viceregal art within the context of a tome devoted to Latino folklore serve to acknowledge the pivotal role of those European traditions introduced into the Americas, and transformed by way of Indigenous adoption and the hybrid melding of New World ethnic, religious, and cultural forms. Clearly, colonial art constitutes the aesthetic and iconographic substrate for much of what is today deemed to comprise Latin American and Latino folk art. The inherent hybridity and dynamism of that cultural melding born of the admixture of the art of the *virreinato* with that of Indigenous traditional forms and concepts continue to fuel the proliferation of Latin American folk arts in ever new and innovative ways. Whether conveyed through the medium of traditional folk arts, or expressed via post-modern and popular forms of urban art, the impact of the colonial era remains a significant source of artistic influence in the propagation of traditional Latin American art forms. The resurgent interest in such hybrid centuries-old traditions is necessarily embedded in a host of modern forms, not the least of which include the otherworldly paintings of Frida Kahlo, with their *retablo*-like folk Catholic qualities; or in the portrayal of Mexican folk heroes rendered in the air-brushed murals of lowrider automobiles from communities throughout the U.S. Southwest. Ultimately, both colonial art and its folk art derivatives continue to make their presence felt throughout those areas once dominated by both the Spanish empire and the Hispanic Catholic Church of the Americas.

RUBÉN G. MENDOZA AND SHARI RENÉ HARDER

Artist Marie Luna works on a *retablo* in her Los Lunas, New Mexico studio. (AP/Wide World Photos)

See also: Chicano/a Art and Folklore; Mission Art and Architecture

Further Reading

Bailey, Gauvin A. *Art of Colonial Latin America*. London: Phaidon Press Ltd., 2005.

Carrera, Magali M. *Imagining Identity in New Spain*. Austin: University of Texas Press, 2003.

Castro Mantecón, Javier, and Manuel Zárate Aquino. *Miguel Cabrera, pintor oaxaqueño del siglo XVIII*. México: Instituto Nacional de Antropología e Historia, Dirección de Monumentos Coloniales, 1958.

Early, James. *The Colonial Architecture of Mexico*. Dallas: Southern Methodist University Press, 1994.

Early, James. *Presidio, Mission, and Pueblo: Spanish Architecture and Urbanism in the United States*. Dallas: Southern Methodist University Press, 2004.

Edgerton, Samuel Y. *Theaters of Conversion: Religious Architecture and Indian Artisans*. Albuquerque: University of New Mexico Press, 2001.

Lange, Yvonne. *Mission San Xavier del Bac: A Guide to Its Iconography*. With Richard E. Ahlborn. Photographs by Helga Teiwes. Tucson: The University of Arizona Press, 2004.

Lara, Jaime. "The Hispanic Aesthetic in Religious Art and Architecture." *Faith and Form Magazine*; *Journal of the Interfaith Forum on Religion, Art and Architecture* 41.3 (2009).

Mendoza, Rubén G. "Cruising Art and Culture in Aztlán: Lowriding in the Mexican American Southwest." In Francisco A. Lomelí and Karin Ikas, eds. *U.S. Latino Literatures and Cultures: Transnational Perspectives*, 3–35. Heidelberg, Germany: Carl Winter-Verlag, 2000.

Mullen, Robert J. *Architecture and Its Sculpture in Viceregal Mexico*. Austin: University of Texas Press, 1997.

Quirarte, Jacinto. *The Art and Architecture of the Texas Missions*. Austin: University of Texas Press, 2002.

Rosenak, Chuck, and Jan Rosenak. *The Saint Makers: Contemporary Santeras y Santeros*. Flagstaff, AZ: Northland Publishing, 1998.

Schuetz-Miller, Mardith K. *Building and Builders in Hispanic California 1769–1850*. Santa Barbara, CA: A Santa Barbara Trust for Historic Preservation, Presidio Research Publication, 1994.

Weigle, Marta, Claudia Larcombe, and Samuel Larcombe, eds. *Hispanic Arts and Ethnohistory in the Southwest: New Papers Inspired by the Work of E. Boyd*. Santa Fe, NM: Ancient City Press, 1983.

COMADRE/COMPADRE

Literally translated, comadre and compadre mean co-parent, co-mother, or co-father. Comadres and compadres can refer to the relationship between parents and godparents of a child, to a close friend or confidant, or to a genre of folk tales that relate stories of gossips and braggarts. The godparent relationship is also known as *compadrazgo* and appears in works such as *Don Quixote*. The relationship may be formalized through the Catholic sacraments or may be a less formal bond between close friends.

Comadre/compadre relationships originated in medieval European Catholicism as a way of strengthening relationships between people in a community. When a child was born, his or her godfather (*padrino*) and godmother (*madrina*) became compadres with the child's biological parents via baptismal rites. A marriage would mean that the parents of the bride and of the groom would become compadres. These formal relationships were not legally binding but were socially binding, and those who did not act as expected would face dishonor in the community. Compadres' responsibilities include treating a child as if he or she were their own, assuming care of a child should the biological parents die, and extending money or resources to their compadres if needed. Compadres may sponsor a child's subsequent Catholic sacraments (i.e., baptism, confirmation), a *quinceañera*, or other significant events in a child's, adolescent's or adult's life.

Even though the *compadrazgo* tradition originated in Spain, comadre/compadre stories and relationships exist throughout the Caribbean, Mexico, and Central America, throughout the United States where Hispanics reside, and South America. The bonds of compadre relationships strongly unite unrelated members of the working classes, while for the upper classes, compadre relationships solidify familial bonds. Occasionally, the compadre relationship strains economic ties between families and leads to a folk tradition that begins to use compadre as a signal for an imminent betrayal. A famous example is when a poor man threatens to ask the devil to be his compadre and gets his wish.

Along with the religious implications, comadre/compadre relationships carry less formal meaning and have spawned a folklore all their own. Compadre, in folk speech, can also refer to a braggart or loud-mouth, while comadre can mean someone to gossip with. A folklore tradition premised on two compadres, one rich and one poor, exists within the Mexican American community. The stories often focus on the poor compadre's (the *pobre*) need for food. As he goes to the rich compadre's (the *rico*) house, he expects the *rico's* wife to give him food. When the comadre denies him food, the *pobre* tries to wheedle it out of her. If this fails, he begins to plot against the *rico* and his wife. Fundamentally these stories reveal the basic expectation surrounding compadre relationships—that whatever one needs, the other will give if he has it. The folk tales focus on the stinginess of the comadres and the cleverness of the poor compadre. Other variations on these tales contain a smart compadre and a slow compadre with the two of them taking on outside society. Like other folk tales that celebrate the poor and working classes, these compadre tales reveal the folly of the rich and allow the poor to triumph over the rich through wiliness, intelligence, and daring. Riley Aiken has collected several of these tales.

Ana Castillo has described modern comadre relationships by seeing in these relationships a potential for women to identify more with other women. The comadre relationship calls for a reversal of the male-oriented nurturing women do regularly toward a woman-centered ideal of care in which a comadre might engage beyond baby-sitting or loaning money. She might cook dinner one night or read poetry to her comadre as they build a relationship that is not dependent on the male-defined stereotype of women's friendships. This subverts the idea that a comadre is a stingy gossip as shown in the folk tales; rather, she is an extension of the ways that women mother and care for their communities and each other. One particularly good example of how Castillo envisions this comadre relationship appears in her 1993 novel *So Far from God*. Through a comadre relationship resistance to patriarchy, capitalism, and oppression is possible. This theme actually mirrors that of the folk tales with the triumph of the poor over their wealthy counterparts.

Leigh Johnson

See also: Baptism; Bautizo (Baptism): Rites, Padrinos, and Celebrations; Matrimonio and Pedida de Mano (Marriage and Engagement); Quinceañera

Further Reading

Aiken, Riley. *Mexican Folktales from the Borderland*. Dallas: Southern Methodist University Press, 1980.

Delgadillo, Theresa. "Forms of Chicana Feminist Resistance: Hybrid Spiritualities in Ana Castillo's *So Far from God*." *Modern Fiction Studies* 44.4 (1998): 888–916. Available from Project Muse.

"A Spoon for Every Bite." Cinco Puntos Press. Joe Hayes tells a compadre tale in Spanish and English. http://cincopuntospress.blogspot.com/2008/08/storyteller-joe-hayes-tells-spoon-for.html.

CONJUNTO

Conjunto music, also called Texas-Mexican *conjunto*, is the traditional social and dance music of Mexican Americans in South Texas. Among the most distinctive Latino folk musical styles developed in the United States, *conjunto* music stands as an enduring symbol of musical artistry, working-class culture, and community life, and *Tejano* identity. *Conjunto* music and the dance culture that evolved alongside it had a unique, syncretic development in the early 1930s in the hardworking Mexican American communities of San Antonio and the Rio Grande Valley. It has continued to evolve as a distinct style; now there are considered discernable important sub-regional variants in San Antonio, Corpus Christi, and the Rio Grande Valley. The heart of *conjunto* music remains in Texas, where it continues to be played at clubs, festivals, dances, parties, and community events and where it stands as the epitome of working-class Mexican American culture and regional identity.

The word "*conjunto*" means group in Spanish, but in Texas the name refers to a specific musical genre style with a defined structure, repertoire, style, and social context. *Conjunto* music is closely related to the *Norteño* music of Northern Mexico in origins and instrumentation but there are important differences between the two. *Conjunto* is principally a driving dance music with less of an emphasis on singing *corridos*. *Conjunto* singing style is also different, tending to be higher pitched than *Norteño* singing and with different, often smoother harmonies and a greater reliance on the polka beat (2/4 time) in songs. Both kinds of music feature the diatonic button accordion, but in *conjunto* the accordion playing is generally faster, more constant, and more ornate than it is in *Norteño* music. *Conjuntos* often sing *ranchera* songs, but the music emphasizes dance music like polkas, waltzes, two steps, *redovas*, *schottisches*, *huapangos*, and, more recently, the popular *cumbias*. *Conjunto* music is also related to, but distinct from *Tejano* music, a contemporary genre of popular music with different instrumentation and a broad commercial appeal.

Conjunto music is a virtuosic music based upon two essential core instruments—the diatonic (usually three row) button accordion and the bajo sexto, a twelve-string Mexican bass that is used to punctuate the off-beat and make ornamented runs between chord changes. The accordion, which appeared in a variety of forms in the region in the early 1870s and became popular among Mexican Americans in Texas since at least the 1890s, is the lead instrument in *conjunto* music. The distinctive sub-regional styles of *conjunto* in the Rio Grande Valley are generally defined by differences in how the accordion is played. As *conjunto* music has evolved, the accordion has become almost exclusively used for the melody line of the music, and many modern players do not play the bass buttons at all. Other instruments have been added progressively to *conjunto* music since it was first developed, particularly the bass (first upright bass, called *tololoche*, and now the standard electric bass) and the drums. Occasionally *conjuntos* include saxophone or guitar but the combination of accordion and bajo sexton is essential.

The origins of *conjunto* music in Texas date to the end of the nineteenth century, when European instruments began to be imported into south Texas, and traditional Mexican *Orquestas Típicas* adopted accordions, violins, and musical structures like the polka. This area of the state also had significant communities of German, Polish, and Czech immigrants who brought their music with them. Mexican Americans absorbed this kind of music, with the polka foremost, though the different ethnicities were separate politically and socially from the *Tejanos*. *Conjunto* was created from a hybrid of these different styles by innovators remaking this music with a distinctly regional flavor for their own working-class Mexican American audiences.

The principal scholar on *conjunto* music, Manuel Peña, dates the beginnings of the *conjunto* music to 1936 when Narciso Martínez recorded the polka "La chicharronera." Martínez, referred to as "El Huracán del Valle" ("the hurricane of the Valley"), is considered the father of *conjunto* music not only for his early recordings, but because he set and popularized *conjunto* polka style with his fast, staccato technique. Martínez also played with the great bajo sexto player Santiago Almeida, who set the standard for the core of the classic *conjunto*

Joel José Guzmán, a noted accordionist, at his home in Buda, Texas, in 2001. (AP/Wide World Photos)

sound. Though he helped create the music as a distinct style, Martínez was never a full-time musician. Other formative *conjunto* musicians in the 1930s were Pedro Ayala and Santiago Jiménez, who played accordion in a more traditional style but wrote many of his own songs that became *conjunto* standards and also brought the tololoche (contrabass) into the music for the first time. The 1930s were a vital time in the development of the music, but it was not until after World War II that the style was fully defined.

Following World War II, a number of very important *conjunto* musicians helped to perfect the evolving and newly popular style by the mid-1950s. Principal innovators included Valerio Longoria, who pioneered new accordion tunings, sang *rancheras* as well as playing polkas, and introduced *boleros* to the style. Another significant figure was Tony de la Rosa of Corpus Christi, who became one of the most popular accordionists with a country-influence style that first brought drums into *conjunto*. In the 1950s, El Conjunto Bernal helped to transform *conjunto* music with a level of musical skill and three-part harmony singing that created a new standard on both accordion and bajo sexto.

By the 1950s, *conjuntos* brought the music throughout Texas and the United States where *Tejanos* had migrated, and new record labels like Ideal, Falcon, Joey, and Freddie distributed the music. *Conjunto* music has been dominated by men since it began, but there are important female artists, such as accordionist Eva Ybarra. Though rooted in tradition, the music remains open to stylistic developments. Major modern players of *conjunto* music like Flaco Jiménez, Esteban Jordan, and Joel Guzmán have absorbed elements of rock, country, R&B, and even Latin jazz, without diminishing the music's core *Tejano* identity.

Dancing is closely associated with *conjunto* music, starting in the formative years with *baile de negocio* in which female dance partners were paid per dance. In recent years *conjunto* music had flourished in ballrooms, clubs, and the civic and family functions of Texas-Mexican life. In San Antonio, *conjunto* dancing can be considered as much a regional specialty as the music which spawned it, particularly the unique, highly stylized and emotive *tacuachito* (opossum) style of dancing. *Conjunto* music and dance continue to be sustained by a rich respect for tradition while flourishing in the twenty-first century.

DANIEL S. MARGOLIES

See also: Afro-Colombian Music; Folk Instruments

Further Reading

Peña, Manuel. *The Texas-Mexican Conjunto: History of a Working-Class Music*. Austin: University of Texas Press, 1985.

Tejeda, Juan, and Avelardo Valdez, eds. *¡Puro Conjunto! An Album in Words and Pictures*. Austin: University of Texas Press, 2001.

CONJURO/HECHIZO (MAGIC SPELL)

A *conjuro* (also called a *hechizo*) is a magic spell, literally meaning to "conjure" up a spirit or demon." That is, through the use of witchcraft to call forth a spirit. The commission or casting of spells is also known as a *trabajo* or "a work of witchcraft." The *conjuro* is an ancient practice common throughout the world. The spell may be ordered for personal protection, for money acquisition, for a personal relationship, or for any other desired objective. The *conjuro* may be purchased from a professional who performs *conjuros*, or simple magic spells may be conducted even by the person who wants one. The *conjuro* or conjure requires that one believe in the efficacy of magic and that a person is knowledgeable about performing the spell or knows someone who can administer it professionally.

Historically, minor conjures or *conjuros* existed as part of the lore that is passed down from generation to generation, so even children know something about secret words and spells such as reciting "abracadabra" over a simple act of magic.

Passed on orally, this knowledge of the occult becomes part of family lore, and within any single culture one family may believe and practice it more than others. For most, the child's knowledge of magic fades from memory at or before adolescence. From adolescence onward, conjuring generally becomes the business of witches and its use is passed on by word of mouth from one satisfied customer to the next, who recommends the services of a particular witch.

With the widespread availability of books some of the very first to be printed along with the Bible were those related to esoteric knowledge containing spells, amulets and talismans such as the *Book of Solomon* and many others condemned by the Church. More recently with the advent of the Internet, the world of the magic spell has become available to all at one's fingertips. Specialists are still considered necessary for advanced and particularly nefarious witchcraft involving the command of evil spirits and demons. The simplest way to understand a *conjuro* is to think of it as some magical act that summons supernatural powers to perform acts on earth. In the Latino and Latin American world, the belief in and the use of magic is so common it is thought to be normal. Many conjures are perceived to be harmless or benign. In fact, this is never true. With *conjuros*, there is always a winner and a loser and in the world of magic it is believed that there is always a price to pay to the supernatural no matter how simple the act requested is. For example, if a *conjuro* is used to "make someone love me," then there is a gain and a possible loss of that person loving someone else. That simple change in the process of the balance of the natural order using supernatural intervention creates an imbalance that must be repaid. When *conjuros* are much more insidious and attempt to cause someone great harm, including death, a very serious spiritual debt is believed to be created. People who conjure professionally are called witches or *brujas*; they are not themselves protected from the negative effects and are generally thought of as having "sold their soul to the devil." The message is that any use of a *conjuro* no matter how simple has a consequence and should not be a parlor game.

During the 1960s, through the turn of the century, the international and multilingual New Age movement popularized the supernatural practice of magic. Witchcraft in general has experienced a boom in popularity in the last forty years that has redoubled in recent years through access online.

Latinos/as have developed, over the course of 500 years in the New World, a belief system for witchcraft, which combines medieval Catholicism and folk Catholicism mixed with Indigenous belief systems and extraneous beliefs from around the world. This ever-changing Latino New Age movement has made magic conjuring more popular today than ever before.

There are literally hundreds of Website businesses on the Internet dedicated to all forms of *conjuros*. Each of the major Latin American regions including the United States and Mexico has professional witches who operate thriving long-distance businesses. That is to say, someone in Chicago or Los Angeles may log-on and order a *conjuro*, which is intended to affect someone at home in a city in Guatemala or the other way around.

Before the age of pre-made and pre-packaged items sold in *botánicas* and *hierberías,* when a *conjuro* was ordered, the *bruja* would ask the petitioner to obtain certain objects including samples of hair, human excrement, soiled undergarments, cemetery dirt, holy water, and many other objects as needed for the spell. Alternatively, the witches would obtain the necessary objects themselves. Today, many objects which are used in conjures are readily obtainable in Mexican product stores or specialty stores called *hierberías*.

The most common *conjuros* deal with the circumstances of everyday life, for example, love and romance. Innocently, young Latinos/as are easily influenced by their cohorts who use a combination of card divination and spells to attract boys or girls to them. A more advanced step would be to cause the breakup of a couple and cause the romantic attraction to the person ordering or casting the spell. While these actions may seem innocent enough, in reality they are not and, once begun, may perpetuate a lifetime of belief and psychological dependency on magic. In some cases *conjuros* may escalate to cause the breakup of a marriage and the death of one of the partners. While many or most persons do not believe that this is possible to do through the use of magic, there have been many notable legal cases where witches were either directly or indirectly involved in the death of a person for whom a *conjuro* was intended.

Other popular uses of magic include *conjuros* for getting money and luck; for finding and keeping a job, or protecting a new business; for personal protection and for one's health and the ever popular "*tapa boca*" or don't tell (literally cover the mouth), "law stay away" or "just judge." Often the *conjuro* requires a photograph of the person or persons to be affected by the spell. Sometimes, the photograph is sealed in a jar and buried with the intention that the persons to be affected are sealed away and/or are dead to the world.

Professional *conjuros* are performed by the *bruja* and either maintained by them or are disposed of magically by them. However, it is common for the *conjuro* to require some actual intervention at the home, business, or workplace of the person at whom the *conjuro* is directed. Very often when a *conjuro* is detected by an opposing *curandera*, they will order that the home, yard and business be cleansed of the effects of a *conjuro*. When a *conjuro* has been ongoing for some time it has probably escalated in intensity, meaning that all sorts of witchcraft objects are probably located in one's yard or buried under trees or placed on porches on window sills and even inside homes. Since it is common for *conjuros* to be ordered against one's own relatives and in-laws, witchcraft objects may easily be placed inside the home. Very common in the creation of *conjuros* is the use of powders, pastes, oils and candles in addition to written and folded papers.

Hechizos or *conjuros*, that is to say "works" of witchcraft, are often very subtle, and knowing this the Latino or Latin American family is always suspicious of strangers coming into the house or objects thrown into one's yard or property. Finally, some Latina mothers will advise the family never to accept food from someone they do not personally know because it is believed that one of the most common ways to cast a *conjuro* on someone is to get them to eat it through food products that go directly to the soul.

ANTONIO NOÉ ZAVALETA

See also: Brujería (Witchcraft); El Diablo; Espíritus Malignos (Evil Spirits); Folk Medicine; Spirirt Possession and Exorcism

Further Reading

Scheffler, Lilian. *Magia y brujería en México.* Mexico City: Panorama Editorial, 1993.

Tamara. *Brujería: hechizos, conjuros y encantamientos.* Mexico City: Grupo Editorial Tomo, 2002.

Zavaleta, Antonio, and Alberto Salinas, Jr. *Curandero Conversations: El Niño Fidencio, Shamanism and Healing Traditions of the Borderlands.* Bloomington, IN: AuthorHouse, 2009.

CON SAFOS (C/S)

Con Safos, more commonly depicted as C/S in shorthand, is a traditional way for Chicano artists to signal the completion of a piece of work, most often seen on graffiti. There are many variations of the *con safos* symbol, ranging from the simple C/S to having the *C* and the *S* enclose the author's name. In whichever appearance, the basic structure is constant: the letters "C" and "S" are always clearly legible and are always offset from each other, either by dots, a dash, a hyphen, an "X," or some other variation.

The exact meaning of these words is vague but a colloquial understanding of the phrase depicts it as meaning "with respect" or "with safety," and the phrase stands as a symbol to other graffiti artists to keep the work safe and to show respect by not altering it. In addition, for the author, the symbol may act as a final seal, attesting that one's work is finished, providing a sense of completion. The late Chicano poet and writer José Antonio Burciaga interpreted the *con safos* symbol as acting as a "barrio copyright," granted safety by an honorable code of conduct among Chicanos. Other popular definitions include "this cannot be defaced," "whatever touches this returns to you," "the same to you," and "don't mess with this."

The phrase itself is a part of *Caló*, Chicano folk speech. Etymologically, the phrase is a combination of two distinct words: *con*, which is Spanish for "with," and the Chicano word *safos*, which is a derivation of the Spanish verb *zafar*. According to the Royal Spanish Academy (*La Real Academia Española*), the definition of *zafar* includes the following meanings that are all pertinent to our understanding of *con safos*. They are: (i) to let go of or release something, (ii) to free oneself from a nuisance, (iii) to excuse oneself from a specific activity, and (iv) to wash one's hands of an affair, commitment, or obligation. The first and second definitions are most in line with the contemporary use of *con safos*, since the phrase is meant to signal a finished piece and protect it from attack, freeing it from insults.

Aside from graffiti, there are numerous other instances where *con safos* was used. In the 1940s and 1950s, a variant of *safo*, the word *safis*, was used by Chicanos playing marbles. Children would yell out "*safis!*" if the marble slipped out of their fingers before being shot out. By exclaiming the word before another child grabbed the marbles, the shooter would get another turn. Currently, some Chicano children still say the word *safo* or *safos* in children's play activity, understood to mean "safe" or "not it." It is used when a child is expected to do something that no one wants to do; he or she will scream "*safo!*" or "not it!" It is in these instances that the third and fourth definitions of the word *zafar* may be most appropriate.

During the Chicano movement in the 1960s and 1970s, many Chicano writers and artists used C/S in signing their work, such as articles, flyers, posters, and murals. This was especially important with works that were political or cultural in nature, as *con safos* is a phrase unique to Chicanos, not found in other Latino groups, and cultural identification was a strong component of the Chicano movement. Currently, the symbol for *con safos* can be found at the end of electronic messages, as well as letters, short essays, and even in books or sections of books, such as in *Drink Cultura: Chicanismo* by José Antonio Burciaga.

Con safos has also made numerous appearances in Chicano naming practices. For instance, it was used as the name of a Chicano magazine, *Con Safos: Reflections of Life in the Barrio*, which was first published from 1968 to 1970 and republished from 1994 to 1996; in the 1980s, an East Los Angeles rock-soul band called themselves *Con Safos*; and more recently in 2007, a Mexican restaurant/bar in Madison, Wisconsin, bore the name *Con Safos*. More importantly, the phrase has even been given as a first name to some Chicano children.

Alternatively, *con safos* has also appeared as a hand sign, characterized by an outstretched hand, palm outward towards an opponent, with the fingers bent down, covering the palm, acting as a shield. In this way, the hand signal reiterates the intent of the written symbol, as a protective device that deflects criticisms.

Eric César Morales and Julián Antonio Carrillo

See also: Caló (Folk Speech); Chincano/a Art and Folklore

Further Reading

Castro, Rafaela G. *Chicano Folklore: A Guide to the Folktales, Traditions, Rituals and Religious Practices of Mexican Americans.* New York: Oxford University Press, 2001.

"Con Safo: Contemporary Chicano Art from Joe A. Díaz Collection." Exhibition guide. National Museum of Mexican Art. Chicago. http://www.nationalmuseumofmexicanart .org/downloads/ConSafos-exhibit-guide.pdf.

Grider, Sylvia Ann. "Con Safos: Mexican-Americans, Names and Graffiti." *The Journal of American Folklore* 88, no. 348 (April–June 1975): 132–142.

CORRIDO (BALLAD)

The *corrido* is a type of Mexican folk ballad that recounts the story of a common person (often it is a man) whose actions against greater odds or an oppressive authority elevate the figure to the status of hero. Hearkening back to the earliest ballads and romances of Europe, the *corrido* is at once a variation on a form as well as unique among oral folk ballads. Though the Mexican *corrido* flourished in several distinct locations in Mexico for so long that a specific date for its origination is unverifiable, it is the *corrido* of the border between the United States and Mexico (hereafter the Border) that has come to be the version most associated with the *corrido*.

The theme of the outlaw or the rebel marks the majority of Mexican *corridos* and, as such, makes it similar to other folk ballads such as the English "Lord

Randal," the Australian "Ned Kelly," and the African American "John Henry." In these ballads, the individual confronts an untenable decision: either he must face a challenge in which a Pyrrhic victory will be the consequence of the hero's struggle against his oppressor, or the hero can relent in his pursuit to overcome his oppressor. In each of these example ballads, the hero respects personal honor above all else. Thus, the choice to allow the perceived outrage or challenge to go unchecked is never an option. Likewise, the heroes of *corridos* struggle against these greater forces, and in doing so, are elevated to the level of epic heroes. The *corrido* functions as a popular song form, as entertainment, and as a creative outlet for challenging perceived social injustices. Thus, the Mexican *corrido* apotheosizes oppressed individuals into champions of the particular issues for which they struggle. Ironically, this antiquated song form has

This drawing by José Guadalupe Posada shows a simply dressed woman singing the story of *La Cucaracha*. "Cucaracha" literally means cockroach, but during the Mexican Revolution this term was synonymous with "camp follower" and referred to women who would follow and live with their male partners in the war camps. (Library of Congress)

been used in recent years to sing about such illicit activity as drug smuggling and trafficking, resulting in a song form dubbed the "*narcocorrido*." This, in many ways, is akin to the glorification of violence and drug trafficking in so-called "gangsta rap," yet a truly analogous relationship would be if gangsta rap used an older ballad form, say, in the manner of "John Henry." For example, hip-hop music appropriates and "samples" existing music to create a newly "remixed" song form. The *corrido*, even today, still uses the same basic formal qualities that were used in "The Ballad of Gregorio Cortez" and even earlier *corridos*. Despite this controversial use of this endearing song form, the *corrido* remains as relevant to today's Mexican Americans as it was during the Mexican revolution that provided fodder and the impetus for the explosion of *corridos* in the early nineteenth century. It shows no signs of waning in popularity.

Structure

Corridos tell straightforward narratives without the use of metaphoric or extravagant poetic language. This characteristic directly reflects the song's form name, which derives from the Spanish word *correr*—"to run." The *corrido* does not utilize a chorus per se, nor is there a bridge, which would necessitate a coda. The result of this is that the *corrido*, which relates a narrative (i.e., a story with a discernable plot), never seems to pause or stop until the song's close. Thus, the song is always running. Most *corridos* use quatrain (four-line) stanzas without a refrain or chorus. Without this periodic restating of a refrain to emphasize a certain point, the *corrido* seems to always be pushing forward, moving the narrative on to its inexorable conclusion.

Corridos come in varying lengths, from as few as four stanzas to as many as forty-eight. Most tend to follow a specific structure and common formula, though *corridos* do deviate from one to the next. The variability of poetic meter and rhyme scheme is not particularly useful in attempting to characterize the *corrido*. However, a majority of Mexican *corridos* are octosyllabic with a rhyming pattern of abcb per stanza. This is to say that, in any given quatrain, the second and fourth lines rhyme. Many *corridos* utilize a third-person narrator who is simply relating the *corrido's* events and is thus aligned with a balladeer who is most noticeable at the song's opening and closing. In these instances, the song's narrator and the song's performer become one, so that the performer seems to relate the song's events as if he was a witness to the events without explicitly stating so, or perhaps he has received the news of the *corrido's* events from some other source and is now relating this to his audience. Through this blending of narrator and performer, the songs take on the quality of both a news event and a history lesson. Indeed, the events are recounted in such a direct and unembellished way that the song poses as an instance of realism, yet it is carefully crafted to give the events an epic feel. In addition, some *corridos* are narrated by the protagonist himself, though this is not as prevalent. Of course, this would change the dynamic between the balladeer and the narrator, as the balladeer (narrating the events as if he were the protagonist), narrator, and protagonist are, in effect, aligned. The result is that such *corridos* have less of a news event or history lesson feel and more of a performance feel, in the sense of an actor inhabiting a particular role.

A catalogue of the *corrido's* structure was put forth by Armando Duvalier in 1937, when he identified particular devices within this ballad form that differentiate it from other ballad forms. In particular, Duvalier delineated six crucial components, which he called primary "formulas" in the Mexican *corrido*. These six primary formulas are: the singer's initial address to the audience; place, time, and name of the main character; antecedents to the arguments of the main character; message; main character's farewell; and composer's farewell. These characteristics of the *corrido* are applicable to the majority of *corridos*, and further, all need not appear in a single instance. For example, a *corrido* may not have the "composer's farewell" but may have the rest of Duvalier's primary formulas. In this sense, Duvalier's work is very much in the manner of Vladimir Propp, the

Russian formalist who performed a similar type of cataloguing of the Russian folk tale in which he identified specific plot points which appeared in these tales (he identified thirty-one functions, as he called them). Of course, it is important to note that the *corrido* form was long established before any scholars attempted to quantify and characterize them. In addition, the *corrido* has evolved over centuries, resulting in a variability of form. Thus, while there is not a definitive structure for the *corrido*, it does have key characteristics—many of which Duvalier identified in his 1937 study. These characteristics were further refined by Vicente T. Mendoza, John Holmes McDowell, and Américo Paredes, among other *corrido* scholars.

History

Many cultures have some version of the ballad form that originated early in their history. As they are essentially short stories in verse form, they are intended to be consumed by an audience just as any narrative art is created to be enjoyed. Setting these verses to music quickly allowed ballads to become both memorable and popular among audiences. Moreover, since ballads focus on events that directly reflect the common folk, they tend to become symbolic of the struggle of these people. Truly, it is an art form that invites participation. Early ballads were not written down only to be enjoyed by the literate, but rather, the ballad's fluid nature allowed for improvisation, emendation, and regionalization of their performances. Since ballads often were not originally transcribed, many of them are lost to history. However, those that have been recorded and preserved allow for an understanding of this very important form of artistic expression.

Another factor working against the ballad form is the fact that it is undoubtedly an art form for the masses. This fact, until relatively recently, proved a hindrance for most of recorded history. In Britain, the ballad was seen as unworthy of critical study despite the interests and work of such people as Bishop Percy, Sir Walter Scott, and Robert Burns. Scott in particular performed an enormous service on behalf of the ballad when he published his *Minstrelsy of the Scottish Border.* Without Scott's work, it is conceivable that many of these Scottish ballads would have been lost, or at the very least, unavailable for critical study.

Scott's work is particularly illustrative and useful for conceiving of the Mexican *corrido*. Paredes himself notes the similar historical contexts for Scottish-English border ballads and the Mexican *corrido*. Scott was able to preserve a great many of the extant Scottish ballads, despite criticism for his heavy-handed editing of the ballads he transcribed. Without such a devoted admirer of ballads as Scott, a great many of the Mexican border songs did not outlive the lives of those who performed and listened to them. Despite this, thousands of variants of Mexican *corridos* have survived in various forms, including broadsides, early recordings, etc., as María Herrera-Sobek notes in her book. These extant *corridos* have become the foundation for critical study of this literary form.

Specifically, the Mexican *corrido* is a descendant of the Spanish *romance* and especially the Iberian *chansons de geste*. This relation accounts for the epic nature of the *corrido* and the ease with which the narrative elements of the ballad are able to move from quotidian events to a near-mythologized version of the subject matter. In addition, as the *corrido* arose in the borderlands on either side of the Mexico/Texas border in the early decades of the nineteenth century, an area rife with conflict, war, etc., a natural proclivity of subject and purpose became an inextricable quality of these so-called border ballads. The *corridos* became a vehicle for expressing perceived injustices and extolling the virtues and bravery of Mexican men. As a result of this emotionally charged context, *corridos* became sources of inspiration as well as an integral part of Mexican identity and, in particular, the successive Mexican American generations that continue to flourish in the American Southwest.

Subjects and Themes

Flowing from the military exploits of revolutionaries such as Pancho Villa and Emiliano Zapata, *corridos* related the events surrounding these skirmishes and battles not unlike news reports. But the *corrido* subject matter is not limited to matters of great significance, relatively speaking. For example, the *corrido* of Celaya references the defeat of Pancho Villa by Álvaro Obregón. Quite often, however, the *corrido* used such misfortunes as might be expected of the common folk. And especially, these subjects often stem from localized disputes between men (though there is typically an indication that one of these men in the *corrido* is somewhat oppressed by the other). This characteristic of the *corrido* contributes greatly to its popularity among the masses. These ballads narrate real events to which the audience (often men of the same class and station in life as the *corrido*'s characters) would most certainly relate. In such *corridos*, the protagonist is often caught up in a situation that forces him to make a decision that will change his life from that moment, often for the immediate ill. This decision or complication sets two options before the protagonist. The first option, the one never selected by the protagonist, is to allow a perceived injustice or dishonorable act to go unchecked and unchallenged. Though an implicit option in the *corrido*, this option to "turn the other cheek" is never conceived of by either the protagonist or the troubadour as a viable option worth mentioning. In what José Limón called the "heroic world of the *corrido*," personal honor is the most exalted attribute in the protagonist's (and by extension the *corrido*'s audience's) value system. The implication here is that the honorable man will do whatever is necessary to maintain personal honor—whether this means to break the law, kill many men, face overwhelming odds, and so forth.

It is easy to see how this freedom from the constraints of law and, arguably, reason, raises the protagonist's actions to the level of the epic. However, it must not be assumed that this disregard for personal safety or logic is attributable to a psychological disorder or mental defect or overwhelming passion. On the contrary, the *corrido* positions the protagonist's actions as the only logical course of action he is able to take. In fact, it is for this very reason that the protagonist of the *corrido* is imbued with a certain disregard for established social authorities when called upon to do so—he becomes the kind of hero who operates under an ethical or moral code, which privileges a personal sense of right that again hearkens to the medieval romance and the chivalric code. Yet unlike the medieval romance, the Mexican *corrido* often ends with the hero defeated or voluntarily surrendering. Like the classical Greek tragic hero, the hero of these ballads fights on in spite of the knowledge of his outcome. And like the tragic heroes of antiquity, audiences elevate this struggle to the realm of the epic. Men such as Juan Nepomuceno Cortina and Gregorio Cortez, pushed to action by Anglo law enforcement, soon entered into the pantheon of Mexican heroes thanks to the *corridos*.

The Ballad of Kansas (*El Corrido de Kiansis*)

Although there is evidence of Mexican *corridos* as far back as the 1830s, the first preserved *corrido* is "*El Corrido de Kiansis*." As with most songs originating in the oral tradition, the exact composition date is uncertain, though it is clear that it was being sung between 1860 and 1870. The subject matter of this *corrido* concerns a cattle drive from Kansas to Mexico, and the difficulties of the drive provide fodder for an epic rendition in this ballad. While this ballad and others similar in theme extol bravery while performing dangerous and exhausting work, the *corridos* would take to a more personal theme—the theme of one man standing up for his rights in the face of an oppressive agency. This seemed almost bound to happen, as Anglo and Mexican methods for their respective cattle enterprises served as a site for tension and contestation. In "*El Corrido de Kiansis*," the lowly (in socioeconomic terms) vaquero (or Mexican cowboy) rises above the Anglo cattle rancher in power because the vaquero is the substance that drives the cattle industry. The vaquero's prowess as a horseman and his bravery in the labor and danger-riddled cattle industry are exalted in the ballad. As the cattle industry provided a convenient means for the Anglo to dispossess the Mexican of his land, this historical moment of confluence between the United States and Mexico would lay the foundation for the problematic neighbors these nations would become, but it also enabled a proliferation of *corridos* that would cast the dispossessed-but-brave Mexican against the powerful-but-cowardly Anglo American.

There are at least two versions of "*El Corrido de Kiansis*" that have been translated by Paredes. In both, a Mexican protagonist tells of a dangerous cattle drive to Kansas. The Mexican vaqueros are in some manner compared to Anglos, and each time the vaquero surprises the Anglo with his amazing ability to swim and handle huge herds of cattle—in one version where thirty Anglos fail to handle five hundred head of cattle, it takes only five Mexican vaqueros to wrangle and pen the steer in only *fifteen minutes*! Each of these versions also highlights not only the physical prowess of the vaqueros but also the differences between the Anglo and the Mexican. Thus, the Mexican had established a hero figure in the vaquero who, as in American "tall tales," could perform at a superhuman level with an inexhaustible supply of courage and bravery at his disposal. This figure would easily transition to the Mexican revolutionary, as well as the post-revolutionary Mexican American living under the Anglo American legal system.

The Ballad of Gregorio Cortez (*El Corrido de Gregorio Cortez*)

Perhaps the most famous Mexican *corrido* is the "Ballad of Gregorio Cortez," an assertion made clear by the amount of critical scholarship and more recent music "covers" by Mexican artists such as Ramon Ayala and Los Tigres del Norte, as well as a Hollywood adaptation starring Edward James Olmos. The breadth of academic and popular attention to this particular *corrido* has, for good or ill, made "The Ballad of Gregorio Cortez" a default prototype for this song form. While it does serve as an outstanding exemplar of the Mexican *corrido*, it should be emphasized that the *corrido* is an extremely variable and nuanced literary form in spite of its formula-driven structure. In addition, a preponderance of the foundational critical work on "The Ballad of Gregorio Cortez" rests on Américo Paredes's book *With His Pistol in His Hand: A Border Ballad and Its Hero*. For an in-depth examination of this particular ballad, its subject, its historical contexts, Paredes's text is the nonpareil.

The ballad is based on a real man named Gregorio Cortez Lira, who in 1901 shot Sheriff W. T. Morris in response to Morris's shooting of Gregorio's older brother named Romaldo. The investigation of a horse theft proved to be the impetus for this disastrous event, strengthened by a communication error between the brothers and the sheriff. This would not only prove to be highly significant in the subsequent events, but it would also be highly symbolic of the cultural and language divide between Mexican Americans and Anglo Americans at the time. Paredes's account is that Sheriff Morris asked for Gregorio, ostensibly to question him regarding a recent horse theft. Morris's translator, with his limited use of Spanish, used the work *caballo* as the word for the animal without realizing it is a specific type of horse, in this case meaning "stallion." Gregorio had indeed purchased a *yegua*, which translates specifically as "mare," and so, when asked if he had purchased a stallion, he said, no. Morris took this as a barefaced lie, and soon the situation turned ugly. The misunderstandings escalated until Morris turned his gun on the Cortez brothers, shooting Romaldo first. Gregorio, in defense of his brother and himself, shot Morris.

From this extremely brief sketch of these events, one can already see that all of the ingredients for a *corrido* are in play here. Two brothers, farmers by trade, are engaged in life and death matters with an authority figure. Additionally, we have a dichotomy set up between Mexican Americans and Anglo Americans that also has a power dynamic in its subtext. There is also a moment of decision for Gregorio, who, as the title indicates, is the protagonist of the *corrido*. On the one hand, Gregorio can stand aside as the due process of law takes its course. On the other hand, Gregorio can disregard what he should do in the eyes of the law and follow a personal code of honor, which is to say, he can defend Romaldo. Gregorio, naturally, seeks the course of action that corresponds to his personal sense of honor while disregarding the artificially made Anglo American law.

The facts from which the *corrido* generally arises are, mostly, of little concern and are only incidental to its power. In other words, the actual facts of the event are typically reshaped as they are adapted for the ballad in any case. Paredes's account of his own research on "El Corrido de Gregorio Cortez" is that one never hears the entire narrative in one sitting, owing to the highly variable nature of the oral transactions of these folksongs from person to person. Many of the events surrounding the narrative of the *corrido* that go unstated are filled in by the many regional variations of the song, as well as the discussions which are motivated by the *corrido's* performance. As with most legends, the line between fact and imagination quickly becomes blurred in the life of a *corrido*. Ultimately, "*El Corrido de Gregorio Cortez*" became popular especially during the time of the Mexican revolution, and served as a template of sorts for the exploits of Pancho Villa, Emiliano Zapata, and Joaquin Murrieta.

Corridos and Women

The Mexican *corrido* is inherently a male-dominated enterprise. With little exception, the balladeers and composers of *corridos*, the subject matter, and even the audiences have been male. Social factors are undoubtedly an influence in this phenomenon, but this is not to say that there is a complete absence of the female in the Mexican *corrido*. María Herrera-Sobek has effectively changed conceptions of the supposed absence of the female in the *corrido*. In her *The Mexican Corrido: A Feminist Analysis*, Herrera-Sobek defines four female archetypes within the *corrido*, employing a feminist archetypal criticism in her examination. These four female archetypes are the Good and the Terrible Mother, the Mother Goddess, the Lover, and the Soldier. Although not a part of her central project, Herrera-Sobek also acknowledges the presence of other female archetypes in Mexican *corridos*, such as the Daughter, the Wife, the Virginal Sweetheart, the Sister, the Mother-in-Law, the Acculturated Woman, and the Independent Woman. While of particular interest to scholars of feminism and archetypes, Herrera-Sobek's book opens an avenue for the exploration of the role and presence of the female within the Mexican *corrido*. *The Mexican Corrido: A Feminist Analysis* provides an excellent corollary to the androcentric studies of Vicente T. Mendoza, John Holmes McDowell, and Américo Paredes. In considering a more generalized approach to the Mexican *corrido*, Herrera-Sobek's book reminds us that while the *corrido* is often about the defiant man with his pistol in his hand, the woman is just as important in this tradition—even if the woman's role is at times only implied within any given *corrido*. As if to underscore this point, women such as Lola Beltrán and Linda Ronstadt have recorded stirring renditions of the Mexican *corrido*, reminding us that women are very much an integral part of this particular folk art. One example of the *corrido* that relies heavily on a female character is "*Contrabando y Traición*" (often translated as "Smuggling and Betrayal"), written in the early 1970s by Angel González and made famous by the band Los Tigres del Norte. This particular example of the *corrido* is not only a relatively recent instance (in comparison to those written in the early decades of the twentieth century), but it has a female protagonist as well.

Indeed, the saying goes that hell hath no fury like a woman scorned. So too with *Camelia la Tejana*, the female co-protagonist in "Contrabando y Traición." Along with Emilio Varela, Camelia leaves San Isidro by way of Tijiuana, bound for Los Angeles with car tires filled with marijuana. Of course, there is one major obstacle in their way: the Border and the immigration officers who patrol it. It soon becomes apparent that the complication in the song is not the Border, but rather the love Camelia feels for Emilio. When the two safely arrive in Los Angeles and exchange the drugs for money, Emilio reveals that he intends to part ways with Camelia for the love of his life who is waiting for him in San Francisco. Stunned by this apparent betrayal of the heart, Camelia blasts Emilio no less than seven times, taking the money and leaving the gun—never to be heard from again.

"Contrabando y Traición" highlights the idea that the *corrido* uses relevant and current subject matter. In addition, Camelia's role as a partner (both in the business and romantic sense) gives her prominence in the *corrido*, confirmed with matter-of-fact finality with her complete disappearance after the murder of Emilio. The ubiquitous Anglo American oppressor only serves as a diversion to the *corrido's* outcome, though it should be noted that Camelia is of Texas origin, San Antonio to be specific. Perhaps more striking, "Contrabando y Traición" seems to be the seminal *corrido* that treats with the subject of drug smuggling, giving rise to the "narcocorrido." "Contrabando y Traición" achieved such a popular reception that it inspired a Mexican feature film in 1977, and in March 2010, an opera titled *Only the Truth,* which opened in Mexico City.

The *Narcocorrido*

The drug trade and trafficking industry has become, of the late 2000s, the dominant Border-issue other than immigration, though some argue the two are strongly related. The *narcocorrido*, a subgenre of the *corrido*, is in many respects a more controversial ballad form. Structurally it differs little from the *corrido*; its key difference rests in the emphasis on personal gain through violent means and the resulting actions (and consequences) of drug trafficking. As a result of the *narcocorrido's* glorification of drug smuggling and violence, many Americans and Mexicans have called for an end to this genre of music. But because it utilizes the extremely popular *corrido* form and continues to exalt outlaw figures, the *narcocorrido* does not seem to show any signs of waning, despite the violence surrounding and central to the music artists producing these songs.

Smuggling has been a part of the *corrido* for most of its history. Even before Los Tigres del Norte released "Contrabando y Traicíon," there were *corridos* that recounted the tequila-smuggling exploits of the Prohibition Era. However, in the 2000s the violent themes and subjects of the *narcocorridos* have moved into the personal lives of the songwriters and performers of these ballads. Many *narcocorrido* singers have been murdered, often in a gruesome manner, and some have argued that this was retribution by a drug cartel that was unfavorably portrayed in certain songs. Along with Los Tigres del Norte, a *corridista* named Chalino Sánchez began writing *corridos* with specific drug traffickers in mind, and often at the behest of these individuals. Sánchez survived several attempts on his life (once, while at a concert, someone in the crowd shot Sánchez, and Sánchez pulled his own handgun and returned fire from the stage). Sánchez was finally murdered in 1992 after a concert. Since then the world of the music artists and the world that they sing about merged.

Essentially, because the *narcocorrido* artists use actual events and people as the material for their songs, they might offend certain drug lords who might be a part of the song's audience. In this case, the *corrido* is not simply extolling brave acts, entertaining eager (but mostly passive) audiences, or reporting on newsworthy events. The *narcocorrido* engages with its subject matter in a dangerous and potentially deadly way, to the point that the drug trade takes it upon itself to silence the songs of which they disapprove (i.e., music artists are murdered, it is believed, because of certain *corridos* they have written and performed). Yet, a confluence of technology (the Internet and YouTube) and devoted audiences keeps these songs from being silenced.

Elijah Wald's *Narcocorrido: A Journey into the Music of Drugs, Guns, and Guerrillas* does an excellent job of tracing the history of this particular type of *corrido*. The intriguing parallel he identifies is between the *narcocorrido* and "gangsta rap." While this comparison is not truly analogous, it is true that each song form exalts illicit behavior and is extremely popular with its respective audience. But unlike the relatively recent advent of gangsta rap, the *narcocorrido* continues a lengthy engagement with the song form—so much so that current *narcocorridos* are nearly indistinguishable in form from the early Border ballads. Thus, as has been the case since their inception, *corridos* continue to capture and mobilize current trends to create new outlaw figures for the times.

CHRISTOPHER GONZÁLEZ

See also: "Ballad of Gregorio Cortez"; Limón, José Eduardo; McDowell, John Holmes; Narcocorridos; Paredes, Américo

Further Reading

Herrera-Sobek, María. *Mexican Corrido: A Feminist Analysis.* Bloomington: Indiana University Press, 1990.

Herrera-Sobek, María. *Northward Bound: Mexican Immigration in Ballad and Song.* Bloomington: Indiana University Press, 1993.

Limón, José. *Mexican Ballads, Chicano Poems: History and Influence in Mexican American Social Poetry.* Berkeley: University of California Press, 1992.

McDowell, John Holmes. "The Corrido of Greater Mexico as Discourse, Music, Event." In Richard D. Bauman and Roger D. Abrahams, eds. *"And Other Neighborly Names": Social Process and Cultural Image in Texas Folklore.* Austin: University of Texas Press, 1981.

Paredes, Américo. *With His Pistol in His Hand: A Border Ballad and Its Hero.* Austin: University of Texas Press, 1958.

Wald, Elijah. *Narcocorrido: A Journey into the Music of Drugs, Guns, and Guerrillas.* New York: HarperCollins, 2001.

COSTA RICA AND ITS FOLKLORE

Costa Rica's folkloric expressions are in many ways similar to those of neighboring Central American countries. However, this tiny nation the size of West Virginia has experienced a distinctive historical development resulting in unique idiosyncratic manifestations and cultural traditions—from peculiar linguistic nuances and inventive speech forms, to world-renowned folk art best embodied in its painted

Traditional Costa Rican home with ox and cart.
(Allihays/Dreamstime.com)

oxcarts, to a rich spiritual life centered around the adoration of the Virgin of Los Angeles.

Costa Rican culture owes its formation to the historical convergence in its land of diverse civilizations and the varied geographical and climatic factors that shaped their development. Part of a geological bridge between North America and South America that facilitated the migration of flora, fauna, and people from both land masses, Costa Rica's pre-Columbian landscape was characterized by the intermingling of cultural groups from the northern Mesoamerican tradition and the southern Chibchan influence, as early as 11,000 B.C. The diverse and highly localized nature of Costa Rica's Indigenous cultures—which in turn contributed to the shaping of colonization and settlement patterns by Europeans later on—is reflected in the regional folkloric differences still discernible today. For example, the Chorotega culture of northwestern Costa Rica (which constituted the southernmost edge of Aztec influence in the Central American isthmus) transcended the particularly devastating impact of Spanish conquest and colonization on its people, bequeathing the modern-day province of Guanacaste a rich cultural heritage distinguished by corn-based culinary traditions, distinctive pottery and crafts, and a strong regional identity. Likewise, the network of Huetar cultural areas that spanned from the central Pacific coast past the central mountains and plateaus and into the Caribbean watershed, helped solidify Costa Rica's noticeable population distribution landscape in modern times—which unlike other Latin American nations heavily favors settlements in the intermountain valleys and nearby lowlands rather than on the coast. The same can be said for the southern region of the country and the remote Talamanca Mountains, which were dominated by the Brunka culture. Able to resist most colonization attempts by Europeans, the Brunkas have managed to keep many of their customs (weaving, animistic spiritual practices, and a diet based on root crops) alive, with their former domains remaining as Costa Rica's last frontier and the local folklore being heavily impregnated by their traditions.

In addition to this complex Indigenous heritage, Costa Rica's folkloric expressions have been shaped by transatlantic influences—especially Spanish and African, but also from other European nations and even from Asia. The first European sighting of the country is attributed to Christopher Columbus on September 25th, 1502, near what is now the port city of Limón on the Caribbean coast. Early Spanish explorers gave this land the name of Costa Rica ("Rich Coast"), captivated by its lush natural beauty and the sight of gold jewelry worn by native inhabitants. Costa Rica's native population was relatively small and spread out compared to the large population centers elsewhere in the Americas. But that didn't prevent the Spaniards from capturing and sending thousands of local Indians as slave labor to Peru and other regions in the Spanish colonies. Decimated by the slave trade and disease, most of the country's Indigenous groups eventually succumbed to Spanish power or were integrated into the incipient colonial economy—which relied on export crops such as cacao and indigo dye and small cattle ranches.

Small, rugged, deprived of precious metals and too distant from the main administrative centers of Mexico and Guatemala, Costa Rica was one of Spain's poorest and most isolated provinces in the New World. Partly because of its isolation, a distinct society of small, European-descended landowners concentrated in the country's Central Valley slowly evolved and became the nucleus of the Costa Rican nation—later forming the basis of a national rhetoric of "whiteness," "equality," and "exceptionalism" that helped shaped the young nation following independence from Spain in 1821, but which has also deepened the marginalization of minority groups such as Indians and blacks. Fiercely autonomous from the beginning, Costa Rica resisted attempts during the nineteenth century to establish a Central American Federal Republic, choosing instead to remain an independent state. Cultivation of coffee as an export product during this period (which brought along many British and German entrepreneurs to the country) had a profound impact on Costa Rica's economy and society—further consolidating the agrarian, *campesino* culture of its colonial past and creating an elite of coffee-growing barons, whose wealth gave rise to an oligarchy that has permanently influenced the political and social institutions of the country.

Construction of a railroad between the capital of San José and the Caribbean coast in the late nineteenth century by U.S. investors and the subsequent banana boom (which saw the immigration of numerous West Indian, Italian and Chinese workers) turned Costa Rica into a plantation-nation—a system fomented by earlier liberal reforms that sought economic and social progress but which was heavily influenced by foreign corporations and interests. In the first part of the twentieth century, protests by organized labor against the banana companies and demands from civil society for better protections for citizens led, among other things, to the labor rights and social security reforms of the 1940s—unprecedented accomplishments in the region. A new society of professionals and business owners was also emerging, challenging the country's oligarchy. Both groups clashed in the Civil War of 1948 over alleged fraudulent elections. This proved to be another turning point in Costa Rica's history, leading to the dissolution of the army, nationalization of banks and industries, promotion of health and education, and consolidation of a democratic system unmatched in Latin America. Costa Rica has since managed to develop a fairly stable and diversified economy and middle class, avoiding the bloody armed conflicts that engulfed most of Central America in the late twentieth century. A "culture of peace" has emerged as a result, which is an intrinsic component of Costa Rica's psyche, identity and folklore today.

Music and Dance

When the term "folklore" is used in Costa Rica, it typically refers to either music or dance. While folkloric expressions are certainly not limited to these two types of cultural products, they provide—perhaps more vividly and palpably than others—a striking revelation of the three forces that have energized and enriched the country's culture: Indigenous, European and African.

Indigenous Heritage

Native Costa Ricans created numerous musical instruments, some of which have become part of the modern musical repertoire. They include several types of *maracas* (made with dried *jícara* gourd and playing a key role in shamanic rituals), the *siaköl* (a wooden drum), and the *ocarina* (a small, clay wind instrument that has become a popular souvenir at local crafts markets). Other instruments that evolved post–European contact are the *quijongo* (a single-stringed instrument) and the *chirimía* (a kind of clarinet made of wood or clay). A few Indian songs have survived over time, including "*La Canción del Cazador*" (Song of the Hunter) and the funerary hymn "*El Baile de los Huesos*" (Dance of the Bones). The syncretism between Indigenous and Spanish religious beliefs is well illustrated in "*El Baile de la Yegüita*" (Dance of the Little Mare) and "*La Danza de los Promesanos de Esquipulas*" (Dance of the Promise Keepers to the Christ of Esquipulas)—both originated in Indian communities in the province of Guanacaste in honor of the Virgin of Guadalupe and the black Christ of Esquipulas. Perhaps the most unique of Indian dances is "*El Baile de Los Diablitos*" (Dance of the Little Devils or Spirits), which is still performed every year by the Boruca Indians of southern Costa Rica. The four-day, year-end festival commemorates the struggle between the Boruca and the Spanish conquistadors (and in a way, their modern struggle to preserve local identity in the face of increased Westernization). Local men wear elaborate, brightly painted masks made of balsa wood and play the part of the *diablitos* (representing their ancestors). They ceremonially fight against a bull (which represents the invading Spaniards). While at times it seems that the bull has killed the *diablitos*, the Boruca spirits prevail in the end. The influence of this dance on Costa Rican mainstream folklore is evident in the popular celebrations known as *mascaradas*—in which individuals dressed up in handcrafted masks and colorful costumes (there are always a devil and a bull among them) chase festival-goers around the town plaza and dance to live music. Despite increased urbanization, the masquerade has remained an indispensable component of Costa Rica's holiday celebrations both in small towns and cities.

Música Folclórica

What is known in Costa Rica as "*música folclórica*" refers mostly to songs and rhythms that came during colonial times, little by little mixing with aboriginal traditions and other cultural infusions. One element that seems to characterize most traditional Costa Rican music is the universal use of the *marimba*, which has even been officially declared the "national instrument of Costa Rica." Notwithstanding the many influences that are evident in Costa Rican music, there is a definite Spanish flavor in the tunes and dances that have become popular "classics" in this country, enjoying both wide dissemination and long duration and often performed at school gatherings, official government ceremonies, and patriotic holiday celebrations. Interestingly enough, most folkloric music and dances originated in or were heavily influenced by the province of Guanacaste—which chose to annex to Costa Rica instead of to Nicaragua in 1824 and whose idiosyncrasy has been clearly marked by the culture of the cattle hacienda. The *tambito*—whose name is a diminutive of the word *tambo*, a hut where *sabaneros* or cowboys slept—is regarded as the most Costa Rican of all rhythms. Among the best-known *tambitos* are "*Caballito Nicoyano*" (Little Nicoyan Horse) and "*Así Es mi Tierra*" (My Land Is Like This). Other popular musical expressions include "*El Punto Guanacasteco*" (Costa Rica's official "national traditional dance"), which is a type of *zapateado*, or dance characterized by a lively rhythm punctuated by the striking of the dancer's shoes. *El punto* is often accompanied by *bombas*—improvised poems recited by a dancer in the middle of the song. It's important to mention other musical expressions that, although introduced more recently and "foreign" in origin, have taken roots in Costa Rica and enjoy widespread acceptance. Examples of them are the *danza*, brought from Mexico; the *pasillo*, introduced by Colombian immigrants and adapted to Costa Rican taste, frequently performed as a patriotic dance called the "Pasillo Guanacasteco"; and the *bolero*, the most beautiful of which is "*Noche Inolvidable*" (Unforgettable Night).

Afro-Caribbean Music

African influence deserves special mention when accounting for Costa Rica's musical universe. The province of Limón, defined by the cultural heritage of Afro-Caribbean immigrants, became a unique enclave of bilingual blacks whose music has preserved traditional English songs from the islands combined with Spanish music from the mainland to yield a rich repertoire of songs in English, Spanish, and Spanglish. Denied Costa Rican citizenship and even banned from crossing into Central Valley for the longest time, black music nonetheless permeated Costa Rica's musical fabric and became a staple at traditional *bailes* and in popular *turnos* (fairs) all over the country. Popular Afro–Costa Rican rhythms include calypso, *mento*, *quadrills*, *sinkit*, square dance, and reggae. Among the traditional instruments associated with Limón music are the *marimbola*, the banjo, the *tumbadora*, the ukulele and the *quijongo*.

Arts, Crafts, and Traditional Food

Costa Rican folklore also finds a source of inspiration and a showcase of originality in its artistic expressions, the skill of its artisans, and the delightful spreads of its dinner table. As is the case with music and dance, all of these manifestations of the country's folklore are the result of centuries of fusing cultures, influences, and traditions. The ingredients may be Indian, European, African or Asian, but the result is unmistakably Costa Rican.

Identity in Objects: From Indian Art to Costumbrismo

The production of popular arts and crafts in Costa Rica gravitates toward two main motifs: Indigenous-inspired objects and the depiction of bygone bucolic customs, landscapes and architecture (known as *costumbrismo*).

Artisans in the country are still heavily influenced by the themes and techniques inherited from their native ancestors. Costa Rican Indians were particularly skilled in the production of polychromatic ceramic vessels, gold and jade jewelry, and elaborate corn-grinding *metates*, among many other relics housed in the country's many museums today. Craftsmen and craftswomen in the town of San Vicente de Nicoya, for example, still produce exquisitely painted pottery following the techniques used by the Chorotegas some 4,000 years ago. Balsa wood masks (previously mentioned in this article) and hand-woven articles of clothing made by Boruca Indians have become popular in artisan markets. Furthermore, the emergence of tourism as one of Costa Rica's most profitable industries in the past couple of decades has opened up spaces for artisans to revive and commercialize their work. Replicas of Indigenous artifacts—from gold and jade pendants to ceramic ceremonial effigies to *metates* to anthropomorphic statuettes—are common at galleries and markets in tourist towns.

More traditional Costa Rican folk art seems to be obsessed with *costumbrista* themes. Just as occurred in the literature of the early twentieth century, *costumbrismo* in arts and crafts emerged as an effort to capture those elements that defined "authentic" Costa Rican culture—which accounts for the fact that most of these depictions revolve around landscapes and activities of the Central Valley, where most Costa Ricans live. A recurring theme is the *casa típica*, a traditional adobe rural homestead brightly painted in white and blue with red clay roof tiles (the three colors of the national flag) and often shown surrounded by bougainvilleas and with mountains as the background. Along with portrayals of *campesinos*, coffee farms and oxcarts, the *casa típica* and its accompanying elements have become a visual cultural motif. While literature and other art forms moved past *costumbrismo*, folk art has held on to these nostalgia-evoking motifs as they have made their way into the country's permanent consciousness as well as into the main shelves at crafts and souvenir markets.

The Costa Rican Oxcart: Unique in the World

One element of Costa Rican folk art that can claim to be completely unique—not only in Central America and the rest of Latin America, but throughout the globe— is the painted oxcart. While oxcarts have been used in many parts of the world to transport goods and people, nowhere have they been so intricately and brightly decorated as in Costa Rica. From full-size, functional oxcarts to tiny ones meant as house decorations or souvenirs, artists in the western Central Valley town of Sarchí still create these wooden masterpieces. There are a few *boyeros* (men who guide oxen with long spears known as *chuzos*) left in the country's rural areas who use oxcarts as their main form of transportation or to carry crops to market, but for the most part oxcarts today are a cultural motif and source of Costa Rican identity. Costa Rican farmers began using oxcarts some 200 years ago, quickly adapting Spanish types that had spokes in their wheels to local needs by developing compact wheels so that mud would not get stuck in between the spokes. When painted, the spokeless wheels resemble Aztec discs such as the Stone of the Sun. Many things were carried in these rustic vehicles, but coffee was and continues to be their most prized load. Around 1900, owners began painting those wheels and others parts of the oxcart, first to protect them from the harsh tropical weather and later as a way of differentiating their vehicles from others. Geometrical patterns were first used, particularly in the area of Cartago, while the folks of Sarchí showed their preference for floral motifs and those in Puriscal depicted animals. Whichever the case, it is said that no oxcart decoration pattern is ever repeated, as painters combine basic design elements in different ways in each new project. In 1988, the Costa Rican oxcart was named a "national symbol of work," for beautifully representing the country's early years of progress and economical growth. In 2005, UNESCO declared it a "masterpiece of mankind's intangible cultural heritage."

Gallo Pinto and Tamales: Costa Rica's Culinary Folklore

On a daily basis, Costa Ricans preserve and carry their cultural heritage through food. The country's food is not spicy, but is flavored with plenty of natural spices and herbs such as garlic and cilantro. The most common ingredients in Costa Rican cuisine reveal the country's main cultural influences: corn and beans (Mesoamerica), root crops such as *yuca* and *ñampí* (southern Chibchan cultures), rice (Spain), and plantains (Afro-Caribbean). The national breakfast is known as *gallo pinto*, a combination of leftover rice and black beans from the previous day's meals, tossed with lightly sautéed onion, cilantro, and red bell pepper and usually accompanied by fried eggs, *chorizo*, or tortillas and *natilla* (sour cream). This hearty breakfast is flavored with *Salsa Lizano*, a brown spicy sauce used widely by local cooks in a variety of meals and much sought after by Costa Ricans living abroad. The traditional lunch is called *casado*, or married man, a humorous allusion to the kind of repetitive meals a man purportedly expects once he marries. It includes rice, beans, fried ripe plantains, salad and either beef, chicken or fish—but it can also include ingredients as varied as eggs and spaghetti. Other *platos típicos* include *olla de carne*, a meat stew with boiled chayote, field corn, tubers, potatoes and green plantains; party favorite *arroz con pollo*, steamed rice colored with *achiote* (annatto) and mixed with carrots, peas, cilantro, and juicy shredded chicken; and *picadillos*, which are dishes made with ground beef and finely cubed vegetables such as potatoes, chayote, carrots and green beans.

In Costa Rica, Christmas wouldn't be the same without a batch of freshly made *tamales*. The foundation of the Costa Rican *tamal* is in the *masa*—a mixture of ground corn, vegetables, spices and pork broth for which there are numerous recipes passed down from generation to generation. A small portion of the *masa* is spooned onto banana leaves, then topped with pork, steamed rice and vegetables of the cook's choice: usually carrots, green beans, peas and red bell pepper. Each *tamal* is carefully wrapped in the leaves and tied with twine, then boiled in large pots. For many families, especially in rural areas, *tamal*-making is an involved affair, which includes cutting banana leaves, cleaning them and lightly roasting them over the fire (to make them flexible); grinding corn and preparing the *masa*; and assembling the *tamales* on a large table, each member of the family being responsible for adding his or her designated ingredient. *Tamales* are eaten with a cup of coffee, another staple of Costa Rican cuisine, or *aguadulce* (a hot drink made from solidified blocks of sugar cane juice).

Costa Rican cuisine is also rich in regional dishes. The Western town of San Ramón is famous for its *cajetas* (sugary confections made from creamy milk); *chorreadas* and other corn dishes are popular in Guanacaste; seafood and *ceviche* (lime juice–marinated fish) are abundant in the Pacific town of Puntarenas; while cuisine on the Caribbean coast is rich in coconut milk– and oil–flavored dishes and has popularized *patí*, a spicy meat empanada, throughout the country.

Linguistic, Poetic, and Narrative Folklore

Two of the most compelling and telling aspects of Costa Rica's peculiar idiosyncrasy are linguistic—and only a few words at that. Costa Ricans call themselves "Ticos" or "Ticas," a nickname resulting from their peculiar tendency of using the Spanish diminutive "-tico" in almost every sentence, thus minimizing the proportions of anything too good or too bad. Ticos, meanwhile, describe their way of life as "*pura vida*" (pure life), a testament to their laidback existence and disdain for complications and conflict. Both their nickname, and their exuberant two-word response to questions about life and the state of things, have transcended the linguistic realm to capture the essence of who Costa Ricans are and how they perceive their place in the world and the homeland they hold so dearly.

Other peculiarities of Costa Rica's speech include the unique way, among Spanish speakers, that Ticos pronounce the trilled "r"—which is softened and slurred so that the "r" in "Costa Rica" sounds like the "s" in the English word "decision." Costa Ricans, particularly men, constantly refer to each other using the derogatory word "*mae*"—an ironic variation of the Spanish term *majo*(a), someone who is beautiful or richly dressed—and whose equivalent in modern English would be the expression "dude." And then there is the word "*upe*," which Costa Ricans use when knocking on someone's door or attempting to find out if someone is home. This is short for "*Virgen de Guadalupe*," which used to be part of an old way of announcing the arrival of a person in someone else's house. The language spoken by Afro–Costa Ricans—a combination of standard English, Jamaican Creole and Spanish known locally as *Mekatelyu*—also has some unique linguistic quirks of its own; one that has become popular throughout the country is the phrase "*Wa'apin, man?*" (What's up, man?).

There are few other aspects of Costa Rica's linguistic and poetic folklore that are distinctive in their own right. The Spanish *copla* (improved poem) appears in Costa Rica in two main forms: the *bomba* and the *retahila*. *Bombas*, popular with the cattle ranchers of the Guanacaste plains, are four-verse poems typically recited by men at town festivals to incite or in response to a contest of wits; while *retahilas* are longer, quickly spoken improvised poems that sometimes tell a story. Related to these expressions, although shorter and spoken without their cadence and musicality, is the *piropo*—a type of flirtatious remark that is extremely common in this country. The *piropo* can be only one or two words, and it may not even have a verb in it, but the message is clear: a boy has seen an attractive girl on the street and wants to exteriorize his feelings about her, whether nicely or crudely. It is such a popular and accepted institution (although some complain about it, considering it vulgar, disrespectful and utterly chauvinistic) that any time a voluptuous lady or one wearing skimpy clothing is seen in a public space, everybody expects the *piropos* to begin flowing with lots of gusto: "*muñeca*" (doll), "*qué cosa más linda*" (what a beautiful thing)—the nicer ones; or "*ricura*" (literally "delicious," but really meaning "hot"), among the lustful ones. It is important to note, however, that women sometimes use *piropos*, too.

Other linguistic creations characteristic of Costa Ricans include *decires*, whether these are witty comparisons: "*más tallado que calzón de puta*" (tighter than a whore's panties); or words of wisdom: "*aunque la mona se vista de seda, mona se queda*" (the female monkey may dress in silk, but it's still a monkey). *Choteo* (crafty humor) is an essential part of Costa Rican folk talk, and there are several levels of jokes Ticos tell: *chistes* are ways to turn into humor things that cannot be said publicly, criticism in disguise; *chiles*, as the name implies, are hotter and should be said in private not to hurt sensitivities; and finally there are *chismes*, forms of gossip that have become institutionalized in all spheres of public life.

Folk Tales

Costa Rica's popular narrative tradition is rich in folk tales from a plethora of sources and with various intents. One legend of the Chorotega tradition tells the tragic story of the lovers Tenori and Eskameca. Eskameca was bathing in a pristine lake of the region when a monster emerged, scaring her almost to death and making the waters dark and disgusting. Upon hearing this, her fiancé Tenori decided to go kill the beast and, having exhausted all his arrows during the fight, jumped into the lake to make sure the monster was dead. However, neither he nor the creature ever emerged. The nearby Tenorio Volcano became a symbol of the young man's courage, and the poor Eskameca eventually turned in a pink Jabiru stork—which the locals claim sometimes is seen with a male stork, known as *galán sin ventura* (charmer without fortune), emerging out of the lake and flying together at sunset. Other Costa Rican folk tales are aimed at teaching people about the consequences of their actions. One particularly well-known is the tale of the *Cegua* (from the Nahualt *cihuatl*, or woman). The *Cegua* is a beautiful lady all dressed in black who appears on the dark roads to men who are drunk or even gentlemen who are returning home late. If the man offers her a ride on her horse with lascivious intentions, the woman's face turns into that of a horrifying horse, driving the man mad. This story has been turned into a play and also into a film, set in Costa Rica's colonial times. Another popular story, told by older people to kids especially on scary nights, is that of the *Cadejos*—a man who was turned into a black dog with fiery eyes for being a drunkard, and whose eternal punishment is to roam the roads at night carrying a rattling chain, seeing other drunks safely home.

Spirituality, Celebrations, and Public Spaces

Whether through religious traditions or civil celebrations, Costa Ricans love to express themselves and find enjoyment in public activities, aided by the country's spectacular weather year-round. As a society founded on agriculture and influenced by native beliefs, Costa Ricans see life and time as cyclical processes—thus being drawn to the perpetuation of rituals and investing heavily in the celebration of holidays that mark the cycles of their inner and outer realities.

Religious Traditions and Popular Beliefs

Despite its Indigenous past and the co-existence of a wide range of spiritual practices and orientations in the country, Costa Rica's social life and cultural traditions show the indelible imprint of Catholicism over the past 500 years. From the time of the first Spanish settlements and even into the twenty-first century, the town's church—prominently built on its central plaza in front of the local park—has been a key space for congregation and identity-building and a powerful institution that extends its reach into all spheres of public and private life.

The best example of this extraordinary influence is the adoration of the Virgin of Los Angeles, Costa Rica's patron saint and unequivocal cultural reference. Similar to Our Lady of Guadalupe in Mexico, the legend of the Virgin of Los Angeles has its origins in colonial times in the former capital of Cartago, where a small stone statue of the Madonna appeared in front of an Indian girl at a spring. Speaking through the girl, the Virgin asked for a place of worship to be built at the site of her miraculous apparition. Because the

Priests carry the patron saint of Costa Rica, La Virgen of Los Angeles, through a crowd of hundreds of Catholic faithful making the traditional pilgrimage to the Basílica of Los Angeles in Cartago, Costa Rica, about 20 miles southeast of the capital of San José. The holiday is celebrated every year on August 2. (AP/Wide World Photos)

statue was made of dark volcanic rock, the Virgin came to be known as *La Negrita*—a symbol of the syncretistic blending of Christian and native beliefs and the *mestizaje* of Costa Rica's population. An impressive basilica has since been built for the Virgin, and every August 2nd, upwards of two million people from all over Costa Rica and even neighboring countries flock to Cartago in a pilgrimage (known *La Romería*) to honor *La Negrita* or to ask for miracles—many walking hundreds of kilometers as penitence. Throughout the year, many worshippers go to the basilica to drink water from the original spring, which is believed to be holy, and to ask for cures for all sorts of ailments. Costa Ricans also worship saints, including traditional ones such as San Isidro (saint of farmers) and San Antonio (who is believed to help you find a mate); but also local saints such as Dr. Ricardo Moreno Cañas, a famous surgeon who believers claim has performed miraculous cures throughout the decades. Other popular manifestations of religious life are the *rosarios*—public prayers organized at individual homes, led by a professional *rezador*, and often accompanied by musicians and lots of food; *rosarios* are typically dedicated to the Child Jesus after the New Year but are also an integral part of the after-burial vigils known as *novenas*.

Still, Costa Rica's spiritual landscape is not limited to Catholic rituals. Evangelical churches and followers are increasing in number and influence. Blacks in the Caribbean continue to attend the Protestant churches of their ancestors and perform ancient African rituals, such as *Obeah*. A strong Jewish community is also present in the country, most of which emigrated from Poland in the middle of the twentieth century. Indigenous populations carry on their animistic practices, highlighted by the elaborate cult of Sibö among the Bri-Bris. One element of Indian belief has spilled over into mainstream Costa Rica: that of the *curandero*, or healer, with many Ticos resorting to these figures for their purported magical cures.

Popular Celebrations and Holidays

In addition to the previously mentioned *Romería,* many of the landmark celebrations of Costa Rican culture are based on or at least inspired by Christianity. *Navidad* (Christmas) is the most popular of them all, characterized by the consumption of lots of food and drink (especially *tamales* and *rompope*, or rum eggnog) and the globalization–smitten but still surviving belief that the Child Jesus—not Santa Claus—is the one who brings presents. Other religious holidays are *El Día de Todos los Santos* (All Saints' Day, November 2nd) and *El Día de San José* (March 19th). Other holidays in the country are patriotic, most notably April 11th—which commemorates the 1856 Battle of Rivas in which the Costa Rican army defeated filibusters from the southern United States who were attempting to turn the young Central American nations into slave colonies. Other celebrations in Costa Rica can be both religious or civil. During the dry season months (December–March), Costa Rican towns organize many festivals, some of which are dedicated to the local patron saint (*fiestas patronales*) while others have nothing to do with religion (*fiestas cívicas*). Traditionally, these fiestas feature exhibits, food stands, masquerades, *pasacalles* (parades), *cimarronas* (bands made up of local musicians), *topes* (horsemanship parades), Costa Rican–style bullfighting (the bull, which is not hurt, runs after improvised *toreros* in the arena), and in some rural towns traditional games such as *palo encebado* (waxed pole) and *carreras de cintas* (horse races in which riders try to place a ring onto a pole at a gallop). The *carnaval*, a cultural staple in the Caribbean city of Limón but celebrated in other parts of the country as well, is a unique folk tradition, highlighted by magnificent *comparsas*—skilled groups of colorfully clad dancers and musicians who parade down the streets for hours. *Fútbol* (soccer) is central to Costa Rican life not only as a favorite leisure activity, but also as a deep-rooted cultural institution that sometimes is referred to as a "second religion." So are *bailes* (dances), perhaps the activity through which Ticos of all ages express their *joie de vivre* to the fullest. Also important in the culture are *quinceañera* parties, at which fifteen-year-old girls symbolically cross the threshold into adulthood and society.

The Pulpería: The Most Public of Costa Rican Spaces

No description of Costa Rican folklore would be complete without referring to the *pulpería*—the neighborhood store that in bygone times was the epicenter of socialization and distribution of news and which even today is the cornerstone of community interactions. In rural towns, *pulperías* are more like a general store, offering everything from groceries to hardware. Because many small towns have only one *pulpería*, or because oftentimes it also includes a bar and a billiard room or has the only public phone in town, this type of store has been central to identity-building in Costa Rica. Even in large urban centers today, which abound with modern supermarkets and imported big-box stores, tiny corner *pulperías* have remained a recalcitrant part of the landscape—perhaps because their relaxed atmosphere and the personalized service offered by the *pulpero* remind Costa Ricans of a simpler way of life in which warm human interaction and a little bit of neighborhood gossip were the spice of existence.

Costa Rican Folklore in the United States

Unlike other Latino groups that have had an important historical presence in what is today the United States or Latin American countries that have contributed large numbers of immigrants to this nation, Costa Rica has had little impact on U.S. culture and folkloric traditions. With a small population of just over four million, Costa Ricans have migrated to the United States and other countries in relatively few numbers. Most Ticos living in the United States come from poor rural areas where economic opportunities are scarce, have established themselves in this country only in the past two decades, and are heavily concentrated in the Los Angeles and New Jersey/New York areas. Hence, the reproduction of Costa Rican customs and folklore in the United States is still in its early stages. A few traditions, however, have traveled along with these expatriates and are beginning to take hold in their adopted communities. Worship of the Virgin of Los Angeles is one of the most prominent aspects of Costa Rican folklore in the United States, with many Ticos carrying small images of the *La Negrita* around their necks for protection and creating small altars accompanied by candles to pray to their patron saint at home. As the number of immigrants has increased to tens of thousands, a sense of community has developed, with Costa Rican–style bars, restaurants and *pulpería* stores sprouting in areas of New Jersey. Online communities are also becoming a tool for Ticos living abroad to keep alive their strong sense of national origin.

MAURICIO ESPINOZA-QUESADA

See also: Christmas (Navidad); El Salvador and Its Folklore; Tamales

Further Reading

Biesanz, Mavis Hiltunen, et al. *The Ticos: Culture and Social Change in Costa Rica*. Boulder: Lynne Rienner Publishers, 1999.

Chacón, Albino, and Alvaro Dobles. *La travesía azarosa de los textos: Folklore literario y literatura folklórica en Costa Rica*. Heredia: EUNA, 1992.

Harpelle, Ronald. *The West Indians of Costa Rica: Race, Class, and the Integration of an Ethnic Minority*. Montreal: McGill-Queen's University Press, 2001.

Helmuth, Chalene. *Culture and Customs of Costa Rica*. Westport, CT: Greenwood Press, 2000.

Láscaris, Constantino. *El costarricense*. San José: EDUCA, 1985.

Lizano, Víctor. *Leyendas de Costa Rica*. San José: Editorial Soley y Valverde, 1941.

Palmer, Steven, and Iván Molina, eds. *The Costa Rica Reader*. Durham, NC: Duke University Press, 2004.

Ramírez Sáizar, J. *Folclor costarricense*. San José: Editorial Imprenta Nacional, 1983.

Salazar Salvatierra, Rodrigo. *Instrumentos musicales del folclor costarricense*. Cartago: Editorial Tecnológica de Costa Rica, 1992.

COYOLXAUHQUI

Coyolxauhqui (Face Painted with Bells) was an Aztec goddess associated with either the moon or the Milky Way. She was the daughter of Coatlicue and Mixcóatl, and sister to 400 siblings (the stars) called the Centzon Huitznauhtin.

According to some accounts, Coatlicue (she with the skirt of serpents) was sweeping one day when she found a tuft of feathers. These she tucked into her skirt and later found herself inexplicably pregnant. Coyolxauhqui and the Centzon Huitznauhtin were outraged at their mother's indiscretion and illegitimate pregnancy. They conspired to kill their mother for the shame she brought upon the family. However, one Centzon Huitznauhtin had a change of heart and warned the fetus of the impending attack. Just as Coyolxauhqui and the Centzon Huitznauhtin were moving to attack their mother, she gave birth to the fully formed, and forewarned, Huitzilopochtli (the Sun God and War God). In a flash of anger over the intended matricide, Huitzilopochtli killed Coyolxauhqui by cutting off her head and limbs which were thrown down the side of Coatepec Mountain. Later, however, Huitzilopochtli tossed Coyolxauhqui's head up into the sky to become the moon so that Coatlicue could see her every night.

Coyolxauhqui Disk

In February 1978, electrical workers were working at the corner of Argentina and Guatemala streets near the *Zócalo* in Mexico City. Seven feet below the surface, they hit a large stone. Subsequent archaeological work revealed a massive engraved stone that shows Coyolxauhqui just after her death at the hands of Huitzilopochtli. The disk had been laid at the base of the *Templo Mayor*, the massive twin pyramid dedicated to Huitzilopochtli and Tlaloc (the Rain God).

The iconography on the disk identifies the image as Coyolxauhqui. The primary identifiers are the bells carved on the cheeks. There is a skull tied around her waist which references Coyolxauhqui's relation to her mother Coatlicue. Like her mother, Coyolxauhqui had pendulous breasts which identify her as a mother goddess. It has been suggested that the vanquishing of Coyolxauhqui by her brother denotes the conquest of the male over female, the assertion of the masculine over the feminine.

The position of the disk at the base of this stone mountain is significant in that after war captives were killed, their bodies were cast down the side of the pyramid to land at the foot of the symbolic mountain. Just as Huitzilopochtli had killed his enemies, the Mexica (Aztecs) killed theirs.

Symbolism

It has been argued that this Aztec myth represents the victory of the Mexica over other societies. Huitzilopochtli, the patron deity of the Mexica, led them from their homeland of Aztlán to the Basin of Mexico. From a symbolic perspective, the story of Huitzilopochtli's fantastic birth and ability to vanquish numerous and powerful enemies foreshadows the Aztec success in warfare and conquest. Ritual death and dismemberment of enemies reenacted the story of their patron deity's origin.

Additionally, Huitzilopochtli was a solar deity while Coyolxauhqui was a lunar goddess. A common theme in pan-Mesoamerican religion is the constant struggle between light and dark, day and night, chaos and order. This struggle was signified for the Aztecs in the conflict between the two powerful magician gods. The Mesoamerican worldview was dualistic and it was important to maintain the tension between opposing forces. There could be no light without dark and no birth without death. Imagery of Coyolxauhqui reminds us that this duality could be personified within a single individual. As such, this goddess was maternal (life giving) and destructive (life taking).

The motif of sibling rivalry underscores the relationship between Coyolxauhqui and Huitzilopochtli. In this, Huitzilopochtli stands for the Mexica people. When the Mexica arrived at the Basin of Mexico after their migration from Aztlán, they found the region heavily populated. The Mexica would spend some time in an unfavorable position vis-à-vis already established and powerful city states such as Texcoco and Tlacopan. Ultimately, the Aztecs would gain the upper hand over their neighbors through deft political alliances and military might. The Tlatoani Itzcoatl, who became emperor in 1427, rewrote Mexica history, providing them with noble origins. The story of Huitzilopochtli's victory over his half-brothers and sisters provided legitimacy for the rise of the Aztecs over their former rulers. This victory was literally set in stone and placed at the foot of the iconic house of the Aztec patron deity for all to see and remember.

In a similar manner to other mythic gods and goddesses in the Aztec pantheon such as Tonantzin, Coatlicue, Quetzalcóatl, and Huitzilopochtli, Coyolxauhqui has become an important iconic figure in Chicana political thought and philosophy as well as in art and literature. She appears in the paintings of such renowned visual artists as Santa Barraza and Irene Pérez as well as in the writings of Cherríe Moraga and other poets and novelists.

CARLEEN D. SÁNCHEZ

See also: Aztec Empire; Aztlán; Coatlicue; Huitzilopochtli; Quetzalcóatl; Tonantzin; Tonantzin in Chicana Literature and Art

Further Reading

Clendinnen, Inga. *Aztecs: An Interpretation.* Cambridge: Cambridge University Press, 1991.

Dúran, Fray Diego. *Book of the Gods and Rites and the Ancient Calendar.* Translated and edited by F. Horcasitas and D. Heyden. Norman: University of Oklahoma Press, 1971.

León-Portilla, Miguel, and Earl Shorris. *In the Language of Kings: An Anthology of Mesoamerican Literature—Pre-Columbian to the Present.* New York: W. W. Norton & Co., 2001.

Miller, Mary, and Karl Taube. *The Gods and Symbols of Ancient Mexico and the Maya: An Illustrated Dictionary of Mesoamerican Religion.* London: Thames and Hudson, 1993.

COYOTE

The word "coyote" is derived from the Nahuatl word "*coyotl*," which refers to several types of canines of the Americas such as wolves and foxes in addition to coyotes (also commonly called prairie dogs). The term may, however, conjure meanings other than the animal, most notably the trickster among Amerindian cultures, as well as a human trafficker along the U.S.-Mexican border.

To begin, the coyote is a mammal indigenous to Continental North America whose Latin name is *Canis Latrans,* meaning "barking dog." However, the origin of this species is difficult to pinpoint because of its hybrid nature; it is believed to have stemmed from the interbreeding of various different canines: wolves, foxes, and dogs (both feral and domestic). Additionally, discrepancies exist among scientists who have identified between 16 and 19 sub-species of coyotes.

Though the coyote is the number one predator of livestock in the United States, this animal is an omnivore and sustains itself primarily on plants and small rodents in addition to scavenging. Found across the entire North American continent, the coyote's habitat ranges widely, from the deserts and mountains of the American Southwest and northern Mexico to the forested areas farther north and even in some areas of Central America. The coyote has even become environmentally adaptive to human settlement and can be found in some populous suburban areas due to the annihilation of larger predators. The city of Los Angeles, for example, is said to be the residing ground of over 3,000 coyotes.

Physically, the color of a coyote's coat ranges from gray to reddish brown. They are typically smaller than a wolf, with a narrow and pointed snout, smaller paws and shorter legs. However, coyotes are significantly larger than foxes.

Socially, coyotes communicate through a series of yipping, barking and howling though their behavior varies. Sometimes this canine can be found in packs whereas others hunt and live either alone or as a pair with a mate. As for the pups, they are born in underground dens dug by the female.

The multifaceted characteristics of the animal have also influenced the mythology of the American Southwest where the coyote has come to represent the figure of the "trickster," as well as a creator, a cultural hero believed to have secured fire and daylight for humans and to have originated the creative arts.

In other traditions the coyote is represented as a sacred clown, a fool in humorous tales, as opposed to an ingenious one, often bested by other figures of Native American religion and folklore. Like its biological counterpart, this trickster is represented as a hybrid figure who possesses the power of transformation in many traditions. Though the coyote plays the role of trickster in the American Southwestern folk traditions, other Native American cultures ascribe this role to animals such as the Raven in the Pacific Northwest or the Great Hare among Eastern nations. However, playing either the role of trickster or sacred clown, its purpose is to maintain and reinforce the health of the moral and social order.

Though the coyote has acted as a standard character of traditional oral tales this figure has emerged as a central figure in poetry. The coyote has been a central motif in works like Joy Harjo's "Grace." In addition to Harjo, Native American authors such as Simon Ortiz and Thomas King have also been lauded for their use of coyote imagery as trickster and clown. For example, King's 1992 book *A Coyote Columbus Story* tells of how this trickster accidentally conjures the explorer Christopher Columbus into existence.

Though the coyote has a positive cultural connotation in the American Southwest, during the eighteenth and nineteenth centuries the term "coyote" became increasingly used among the Spanish-speaking population in the areas that are now New Mexico and Arizona as a pejorative term against biracial people, specifically the child of a Spaniard and a Native slave. In this sense the term is derived from the hybrid characteristic of the animal.

However, throughout the twentieth and twenty-first century "coyote" has become slang used to refer to a person who traffics immigrants across the Mexican border. Opening the polemical issues of border relationships between Mexico and the United States, coyotes have been studied in mainstream political and social magazines and newspapers. Varying from *Forbes* to the *New York Times*, countless articles have been written about human traffickers. Reports from the United States 2000 census, for example, estimate the presence of 9 to 11 million undocumented immigrants. Many of theses news reports have surmised that the majority of undocumented immigrants in the United States work menial jobs and are oftentimes paid in cash by middlemen arrange jobs for them. Additionally, the issues of undocumented immigration have been extensively studied in the social sciences. Ted Conover's *Coyote*, for example, presents his firsthand experience with Mexican citizens attempting to cross north to the United States and employing the highly mobile coyotes. Much like the animal counterpart, the coyote is presented as elusive and adaptive to the harsh environments of crossing.

Furthermore, for the past three decades immigration has been at the forefront of politics relating to the issues of not only border security but the North American Free Trade Agreement. For governments to insure a feeling of security through the border of the United States and Mexico, the two nations have established checkpoints throughout Mexico to monitor the movements of Mexican citizens as well as foreigners in Mexico, primarily Guatemalans and other Central Americans. Additionally, these points have been set up to monitor bus lines entering the United States. In some cases the border patrol has attempted to arrest even the drivers for human trafficking.

Regarding border security, many sociologists have begun to analyze the border patrol as an increasingly militarized institution. For example, Tim Dunn's book *The Militarization of the U.S.-Mexico Border* has viewed the border space in terms of a war zone where a police force (the Border Patrol) is attempting to control the civilian populations of the regions. This situation is exacerbated by the intertwining relationship between the police and the military (i.e., the military loaning equipment to the Border Patrol, empowering military personnel to make arrests, the use of the National Guard in some states to aid the Border Patrol).

In addition to the militarization of the border, theorists have been attempting to break away from the idea of a fixed border between the United States and Mexico. The mutability of a national border stems from a Chicano phrase "We didn't cross the border, the border crossed us" that refers to the annexation of Mexican territories after the Treaty of Guadalupe at the end of the Mexican-American War. Additionally, Chicana theorist Gloria Anzaldúa in her *Borderlands* briefly mentions that U.S. expansion has not stopped at the border but continued into Mexico where U.S. companies have partnered with powerful landowners. This union of Mexican and American capital and business conglomerates, according to Anzaldúa, has set up the system of *maquiladoras* along the northern border of Mexico.

This symbiotic relationship, which Anzaldúa refers to as a continuation of the conquest seeking to exploit the Native population, has been the background of an immigrants' right movement under the motto "no one is illegal." The theoretical basis of the argument is that since business capital has been open between the two countries (through NAFTA, for example) labor must also be able to freely move between them. The argument presented by authors like Mike Davis and Justin Akers Chacón in their *No One Is Illegal*, demonstrates not only the inaccessibility of immigrants to freely enter the United States but also the struggle of the Latino working class to curtail the power of globalized capital, the Delano Farmworkers' strike being a leading example.

In addition to the socio-political importance of coyote and immigration, literary production has presented numerous examples. The Chicano novel, *The Road to Tamazunchale*, published 1975 by Ron Arias features a protagonist immigrant from Peru. An additional example is that the coyote acts as the central image and metaphor in Ruth Behar's book *Translated Woman*, where she claims to be a "literary coyote" bringing the testimony of Esperanza across the border.

CHRISTOPHER ALEX CHABLÉ

Further Reading

Anzaldúa, Gloria. *Borderlands / La Frontera: The New Mestiza*. San Francisco: Aunt Lute Books, 1999.

Bauer, Erwin, and Peggy Bauer. *Wild Dogs: The Wolves, Coyotes, and Foxes of North America*. San Francisco: Chronicle Books, 1994.

Behar, Ruth. *Translated Woman: Crossing the Border with Esperanza's Story*. Boston: Beacon Press, 1993.

Conover, Ted. *Coyotes: A Journey Through the Secret World of America's Illegal Aliens*. New York: Vintage Books, 1987.

Davis, Mike, and Justin Akers Chacón. *No One is Illegal: Fighting Racisim and State Violence on the U.S.-Mexico Border*. Chicago: Haymarket Books, 2006.

Dunn, Tim. *The Militarization of the U.S.-Mexico Border: Low-Intensity Conflict Doctrine Comes Home*. Austin: University of Texas Press, 1996.

Lopez, Barry H. *Giving Birth to Thunder, Sleeping with His Daughter: Coyote Builds North America*. Kansas City: Universal Press Syndicate, 1977.

CUARESMA (LENT)

Cuaresma (Lent) is a period of approximately forty days in the Christian tradition that prepares the believer for the arrival of Holy Week (*Semana Santa*) and Easter (*Pascua*). The forty days also commemorate the time Jesus Christ spent fasting in the desert after being baptized and prior to commencing his public ministry. It is widely followed amongst Christians: Roman Catholics, Lutherans, Methodists, Presbyterians and Anglicans / Episcopalians are all supposed to observe it. These denominations encompass over 70 percent of all Latinos/as, according to the 2003 Hispanic Churches in American Public Life survey.

Cuaresma commences on Ash Wednesday (*Miércoles de Ceniza*) and finishes on Maundy Thursday (*Jueves Santo*), but the dates of these vary depending on the year. Cuaresma can therefore start anywhere from February 4th to March 10th, and finish from March 19th to April 22nd. Due to its length, cuaresma includes many liturgical celebrations, including half of Holy Week.

Cuaresma is generally understood as a time of penitence and reflection for the believer. It corresponds to two different periods in Jesus's life, both marked by personal sacrifice: his forty days fasting in the desert after being baptized, time during which he was tempted by Satan (the start of his public ministry), and his Passion (the end of his ministry). While there are many different ways to follow this time of reflection on Jesus's sacrifice, the most common is fasting or abstinence from certain products. The Catholic Church prescribes that believers abstain from eating animal meat on Ash Wednesday and every Friday of Lent. Many believers from all denominations also choose to abstain from a certain product or habit during Cuaresma, though this is highly individual and born out of custom and not doctrinal requirement. Prayer is also meant to be taken up with renewed vigor, as are charitable acts towards others. Other widespread practices amongst Christian denominations are the changing of the color of the priest's robes to violet, and the veiling of church statues after the fifth Sunday and until the Easter Vigil (the U.S. Conference of Catholic Bishops leaves this up to the discretion of the individual priest). Finally, in Roman Catholic, Lutheran and Anglican / Episcopalian liturgy, the hymn lyrics *Gloria in Excelsis Deo* and *Alleluia* are omitted from the mass throughout Cuaresma.

Because of its length, Cuaresma includes many important liturgical dates, each with its own prescribed ritual. Ash Wednesday and Palm Sunday (*Domingo de Ramos*) are the most universal in their observance and ritual. On Ash Wednesday the officiating priest or bishop draws a cross on the forehead of believers after services; the believer is supposed to keep the cross on his or her forehead until it fades away. Catholics consider this one of the most important days of penitence, and many of them fast during the day. The ashes employed to draw the crosses are usually those of the palms used during the previous year's Palm Sunday services. On Palm Sunday, the officiating clergy's vestments are supposed to be deep red. Other important liturgical dates which take place during cuaresma are Laetare Sunday (*Cuarto Domingo de Cuaresma* or *Laetare*), and the first days of Holy Week (Holy Monday, Holy Tuesday and Holy Wednesday; *Lunes Santo, Martes Santo, Miércoles Santo*). Maundy Thursday marks the end of Cuaresma, which therefore does not include the most important dates of Holy Week, known as the Easter Triduum (*Triduo Pascual*): Good Friday, Holy Saturday and Easter Sunday (*Viernes Santo* or *de la Pasión*, *Sábado Santo* or *de Sepultura*, and *Domingo de Pascua* or *de Resurrección*).

Beyond these general characteristics, observance of Cuaresma showcases a rich tapestry of traditions and customs, which both set Latinos/as apart from mainstream celebrations and individuate Latino communities from one another. Traditions can

César Tacalco prays during Palm Sunday mass at St. Bernard's Church, in Riverdale, Maryland, March 16, 2008. (AP/Wide World Photos)

be national, regional or familial. Food is one of the primary examples of this. The obligation to abstain from meat on Fridays calls for creativity in creating special Cuaresma dishes, and communities and families often have special fish or vegetable recipes for this season. A favorite amongst the Mexican American community is the *capirotada*, a bread pudding soaked in mulled syrup (made of water, brown sugar, cinnamon and nutmeg) with sugar, cheese, raisins and walnuts. The dish is highly symbolic of the season, with the bread representing the body of Christ, the syrup being his blood, the raisins standing for the nails on the cross, the cinnamon sticks being its wood, and the cheese representing the Holy Shroud.

Another feature of Cuaresma, and particularly of its last two weeks, is religious processions, which are greatly popular amongst Latinos/as. Processions are highly idiosyncratic, and often involve music and carrying a figure of Jesus, Mary or a particular saint to or from a Church; active participation in them is usually restricted to members of the organizing group (*cofradías*). Processions are more typical of Catholic rather than Protestant worship, and Latino ones have their roots in the Spanish celebrations of *Semana Santa*, still highly prevalent in contemporary Spain. Their observance is therefore one important differentiating factor between the Latino and mainstream American religious experiences, the latter being more focused on the pre-Christian symbols such as Easter eggs, the Easter bunny, and so forth. Processions like those of Palm Sunday, the Stations of the Cross (*Vía crucis*) and those organized by the Penitente brotherhood in New Mexico and Colorado take place during Cuaresma. Their observance does not only extend to Latino Catholics, as Latino Protestants are also known to participate in *Vía crucis* processions. However, it must be noted once again that the most important and spectacular processions (particularly those of Good Friday, which often re-enact Jesus's crucifixion, or the *Tinieblas* ones that commemorate the cosmological disruptions caused by his death) fall beyond the purview of cuaresma as they occur during the Easter Triduum. Similarly, though the *Vía crucis* can be performed any Friday of cuaresma, it is often reserved for Good Friday. Cuaresma is possibly best identified with a spirit of individual penance and reflection rather than with the communal outpourings of religiosity of the processions.

Other features of Cuaresma are the inclusion of *alabados* at mass at the start of Holy Week, and the practice of Penitente initiation rituals. Cuaresma also holds a special significance amongst Latinos/as as it is the period immediately following (and the justification for) traditional pre-Lenten carnivals. These carnivals are widespread practices throughout Latin America.

DAVID JIMÉNEZ TORRES

See also: Alabados; Brazil and Its Folklore; Los Penitentes

Further Reading

Avalos, Hector, ed. *Introduction to the U.S. Latina and Latino Religious Experience.* Boston: Brill Academic Publishers, 2004.

Barbezat, Suzanne. "Lent in Mexico." Web site: About.com Guide. Accessed December 14th, 2010.

CUBAN AMERICANS AND THEIR FOLKLORE

Cuban American popular culture and folklore is the product of a complex and ever-evolving set of interactions between pre-revolutionary Cuban cultural forms and the ongoing reinterpretation of the island's African, Hispanic and Indigenous Caribbean heritage in light of this community's displacement from their homeland. In the five decades following the 1959 Revolution, the beliefs, customs and cultural traditions of the Cuban diasporic community have been re-imagined by several generations of Cuban Americans, whether born in the United States or more recently arrived from the socialist nation. Constantly evolving in response to the historic experience of Cuban Americans as political exiles and, as is increasingly common since the end of Soviet subsidies to the island after the 1991 collapse of the USSR, as economic migrants, Cuban American folklore reflects and helps constitute the diverse range of racial, class, gender, sexual, religious and political identities within this community. At the same time, its ongoing development has been in dialogue with the cultural production and folklore of other Spanish-speaking and Anglo American peoples in the United States. It has thus served to differentiate Cuban Americans from other Latina/o communities at the same time that it has contributed to the development of a pan-ethnic "Latino" culture and identity in the U.S.

Discussion of Cuban American folklore naturally begins in Miami, the historic destination of the majority of Cuban immigrants who came to the U.S. after the Revolution. Though a large Cuban community resides in Union City, New Jersey and smaller numbers live in New York City and Los Angeles, more than eighty percent of Cuban Americans call Miami-Dade County home. Since the 1980s, a growing number rent or have purchased homes in the suburbs; nonetheless, the historic and cultural center of this upwardly mobile ethnic community continues to be Little Havana, a neighborhood due west of downtown Miami, where a majority of first generation émigrés settled. Little Havana continues to host a thriving ethnic economic enclave where Cuban Americans and other Latina/os can shop, dine, conduct business, receive medical care and legal advice, attend church and theatre performances, go to school, and even be buried exclusively in Spanish. This vital neighborhood thus serves as a home base for Cuban American political, economic and social institutions, and acts as a repository of Cuban American popular culture and folklore, keeping alive the customs, traditions and idiosyncrasies of this highly visible and influential Miami Latina/o community.

Since the early 1960s, émigrés have channeled their nostalgia for the lost homeland into remaking Little Havana's public spaces in the image of the Cuban city from which it takes its name. At the heart of this neighborhood is SW 8th Street, known to locals simply as "*Calle Ocho*," which is lined with Cuban-owned grocery stores, *botánicas* offering herbal remedies and religious items, furniture stores displaying the wooden rocking chairs popular with elderly Cubans, and innumerable restaurants, *cafeterías*, open-air lunch counters, small cigar factories, art galleries and *talleres*, music and souvenir shops. Little Havana's public spaces visibly manifest the community's shared love of their nation, their anti-communist worldview and unflagging commitment to securing the eventual liberation of their island

Cuban Americans play dominos at Máximo Gómez Park in the Little Havana section of Miami, Florida. (AP/Wide World Photos)

homeland from its authoritarian government. At the corner of SW 8th and 15th Street, Máximo Gómez Park is filled with elderly Cuban men who gather to play nine-dot dominoes, smoke cigars, and discuss sports, politics, and their memories of pre-revolutionary life on the island. Two blocks down *Calle Ocho* at 13th Street, a small park and monument honor the memory of Brigade 2506 members who died in the failed 1961 Bay of Pigs invasion. This park is a frequent meeting point for anti-Castro demonstrations and political rallies. Patriotic murals, small Cuban flags, maps of the island, and images of Independence-era heroes like José Martí are prominently displayed in shop windows throughout the neighborhood.

Conspicuously absent from Little Havana are the iconic images of Fidel and Ernesto "Ché" Guevara that have sometimes been adopted by other Latina/o groups, including Chicana/o and Puerto Rican activists who have been inspired by the Cuban Revolution's anti-imperialist and internationalist politics. Unlike other Latina/o barrios across the United States, Little Havana is also largely free of graffiti, which, when it appears, is usually limited to an occasional anti-Castro slogan or invocation of "Cuba Libre!"

Language, World View, and Identity

The Spanish language, which Cuban Americans share with most other Latin American origin peoples, is more than just a functional means of communication. Rather, it is the vehicle through which the unique Cuban American identity and worldview, with all their distinct beliefs, values, and idiosyncrasies, are transmitted.

By 2004, more than one third of Cuban Americans were U.S.-born and English-dominant; however, a majority of the second and third generation remain fluent in Spanish, though they may increasingly resort to "Spanglish," a localized synthesis between the languages they speak at home and school or work, in expressing their bicultural identities. Spanish remains overwhelmingly the dominant language spoken in Cuban American homes, and many elderly and first generation émigrés conduct their daily lives almost exclusively in their mother tongue. This shared mother tongue continues to play an important role in the lives of Cuban Americans of all generations, reinforcing extended family ties and reaffirming their cultural identity and sense of attachment to their island homeland.

Since the early 1960s, elders have worked to pass on their mother tongue to younger generations, at first in the hopes of a quick return to Cuba, and then as a means of protecting their familial and cultural identity against the threat of acculturation. Grandparents and parents often use Spanish as the vehicle for transmitting Cuban nursery rhymes, lullabies and songs, and nostalgic recollections of pre-revolutionary life on the island to U.S.-born or raised children with limited experience of the homeland. It is also a medium for communicating Cuban history, patriotic values, and anti-Castro/anti-Communist beliefs to children, and for inculcating them with parents' and grandparents' democratic, capitalist and pro-U.S. worldview. The Spanish-speaking Cuban American home thus functions as a repository of both *Cubanía* and exile political ideologies, as communicated through the child-rearing practices, folklore, and domestic rituals of family life. The deliberate continued use of Spanish fosters younger Cuban Americans' pride in their families and cultural heritage, reproduces elders' commitment to the ongoing struggle (albeit mostly rhetorical) for the political liberation of their homeland, and nurtures the second and third generations' feelings of attachment to an island they may have never visited.

The nostalgia and anti-Castro convictions which make up such an important part of Cuban American daily life have been reinforced in exile literature. This first appeared in the patriotic poetry and lyrics, inspired by Cuba's beloved national poet and hero of the Independence War, José Martí, that were published in exile periodicals beginning as early as 1960. The nostalgia and political mythology of the exile community were further developed in early Spanish-language testimonials and novels like Andrés Collado's *Enterrado Vivo* (1960) and, as time passed, continued to inspire works such as Ramiro Gómez Kemp's *Los Desposeídos* and José Sánchez-Boudy's *Lilayando*, which also explored the problems of political disaffection, loss and cultural displacement among an exile community now in its second decade away from the *patria*. Though much of this writing was dismissed by literary critics as thinly disguised political propaganda, it nonetheless offers an important record of the collective anger, confusion and homesickness that united the exile community.

By the 1980s, the arrival of a significant number of Cuban artists and intellectuals who had become disenchanted with the Revolution, including writers Reinaldo Arenas and Heberto Padilla, sparked a new level of literary sophistication among exile writers. However, the highly politicized emotions of nostalgia and loss have continued to fuel the literary productions of second and third generation Cuban Americans, many of whom write in English. Among the most commercially and critically acclaimed Cuban American authors is Oscar Hijuelos, whose 1989 novel

The Mambo Kings Play Songs of Love was awarded the Pulitzer Prize for fiction. A long tradition of personal and political memoirs also continues to flourish among Cuban Americans, many of whom now also choose to write in English, including Carlos Eire's 2003 *Waiting for Snow in Havana: Confessions of a Cuban Boy*, which he followed with 2010's *Learning to Die in Miami: Confessions of a Refugee Boy*. Nostalgia, loss and identity have similarly inspired Cuban visual arts since the 1960s, in the paintings, sculptures and mixed-media creations of artists including Juan González, María Brito-Avellana, César Trasobares, and Ana Mendieta.

Cuban Americans also use their language to conduct their daily lives and to express their ethnic identity and sense of belonging to a unique cultural community. Spanish provides friendly and gregarious Cubans with a shared idiom for interaction and conversation, elaborate storytelling and the exchange of *chistes* or jokes, and heated debates about baseball and politics, all of which make up an important part of the Cuban vernacular tradition. Older Cuban immigrants especially enjoy sharing anecdotes about past and present conditions on the island, and are quick to offer mocking stories or jokes about Fidel Castro or impersonations of the revolutionary leader. Political humor also forms the basis for many amateur theatre productions and stand-up comedy routines which can be seen at small theatres in Miami's Little Havana and other Cuban neighborhoods. These forms of expression allow individuals to deal with a painful collective history in ways that evoke laughter, rather than tears or anger. This vernacular tradition can also be observed on the island, albeit less overtly, where Cubans frequently share jokes about harsh living conditions, scarcity and political issues and events.

Higher rates of Spanish fluency and use among Cuban Americans compared with other Latina/o communities may be explained by several factors. These include the relatively higher educational levels of first and subsequent generations of Cuban immigrants; and, in Miami, an ethnic enclave where business, healthcare, legal and commercial activities can all be conducted exclusively in Spanish. Miami's large Cuban community has also benefited from a broader range of bilingual educational programs, schools, and Spanish language media. Cuban Americans enjoy access to major Spanish–language television stations like *Univisión* and *Telemundo*, both of which broadcast across the U.S. and into Latin America from Miami, as well as local TV channels like Miami's *Mega TV*. They are thus able to regularly view talk shows, news programming, musical and variety shows, and *telenovelas*, or serial soap operas, in their home language and tailored to their tastes and interests.

Cuban Americans are also avid radio listeners. Miami has more Spanish-language radio stations than any other U.S. city, including WQBA *La Cubanísima*, which broadcast traditional Cuban music, news and political commentary, and sports coverage. Radio shows also foster Cuban Americans' ongoing ties to the island and to one another, transmitting messages to family members in Cuba, broadcasting telephone interviews with political dissidents on the island, and sharing information on exile organizations, events and services. Radio thus continues to play a crucial role in maintaining Cuban culture and folklore in the United States. Cubans also enjoy broad access to Spanish-language print media. They get news from *El Herald*, the Spanish-language edition of the *Miami Herald* that began publication in 1976. They are also avid consumers of a wide range of Spanish-language editions of popular U.S. magazines, including *People* and *Cosmopolitan*, and are loyal readers of the locally produced *periodiquitos* that are distributed free of charge in drugstores, *bodegas*, barber shops and *cafeterías*.

Through the continued use of Spanish at home, in their neighborhoods, and sometimes at work, Cuban Americans share their history, culture and political ideology with one another and with the next generations. Their vernacular and literary traditions, as well as the vibrant Spanish-language media that serves this community, serve as repositories of *Cubanía*, allowing Cuban Americans to proclaim their pride in their shared identity, foster familial and community ties, and express their ongoing hopes for the liberation of their island *patria*.

Religion

Religion is an important element in the cultural heritage Cuban émigrés brought to the United States. Religious identities and practices reinforce Cuban Americans' sense of community and belonging, helping to preserve their ethnic identity and serving as a vehicle for the transmission of distinctive beliefs, values and traditions. Whether they are Jewish, Protestant, Catholic, or adherents of African-origin religions like *la Regla Lukumí*, Cubans are often deeply religious or spiritually aware. Their varied and oftentimes syncretic religious practices and beliefs underlie Cubans' shared worldviews and find expression through their daily lives, culture and folklore.

The overwhelming majority of Cubans are Roman Catholic. Though attendance at Catholic services is lower among Cuban American youth than previous generations, it is nonetheless significantly higher than among the U.S. population in general. Like many other Latina/os, however, Cuban Americans' religious identity is often more personal than institutional. Though Cubans make up more than half of Miami's 800,000 Catholics, and many parishes in Miami–Dade County and other Cuban neighborhoods offer services in Spanish, Cuban Catholics are as likely to engage in prayers and other religious activities at home as they are at church. Their Catholicism is characterized by devotion to the Virgin Mary and the saints, as much as or more than worship or prayers to Jesus Christ or God the Father. The personal nature of Cuban American Catholic faith is creatively expressed through the household and garden shrines which many erect in honor of *La Virgen de la Caridad* or the Virgin of Charity, patroness of their island homeland. Saint Barbara and Saint Lazarus, or Santa Bárbara and San Lázaro, also enjoy the special devotion of the Cuban American community. Even nominally Catholic Cubans often enjoy an intimate spiritual relationship with one or more of these Catholic saints, on whom they rely for comfort, guidance or divine intervention in the problems and challenges of their lives.

This personalized faith nonetheless has historically played an important role in constituting the exile community's identity, especially since more than 80 percent of the first wave of émigrés were Catholic and counted Fidel Castro's persecution of the church as among their reasons for fleeing the island. The intertwining of religious and political identities that characterized the early Cuban American community was dramatically manifested in efforts by early exiles to have a shrine built in honor of their island's patroness. Constructed in 1966 in Miami's Coconut Grove, *La Ermita de la Caridad* offers displaced Cuban Americans a spiritual retreat in the heart of the urban landscape and stands as a visible reminder of the intertwining of religion and politics in the history of the exile community.

Catholic holidays and feast days play an important role in the cultural life of the broader Cuban community, even among those who do not profess a Catholic identity. The ritual year begins with the January 6th celebration of *El Día de los Reyes*, or Three Kings' Day, on which many Cuban parents give gifts to their children, either instead of or in addition to those received on Christmas. Since the 1970s, Miami's Cuban families have also flocked to *Calle Ocho* on Three Kings' Day to view a lively annual parade, featuring high school marching bands and community-sponsored floats, held in honor of *los Reyes*. In late February, Cubans celebrate *carnaval*, a tradition that dates back to the Spanish colonial era. Now largely a secular event characterized by parades, folkloric music and street fairs, *carnaval* originated in the Catholic pre-Lenten celebrations that marked the beginning of the period of fasting and penance leading up to *Semana Santa* (Holy Week) and *La Pascua* (Easter).

On September 8th, Cubans celebrate the feast day of *La Virgen de la Caridad del Cobre*, the patron saint of their island homeland. On this day, the Cuban faithful gather to revere a statue of *la Virgen* as it is carried by procession to a place of honor at a special mass held in her name. After the conclusion of *la misa*, worshippers shower *la Virgen* with flowers and offer prayers of praise and supplication to their patroness. This annual commemoration was celebrated for many years at Miami's Orange Bowl; in recent years, however, celebrations in honor of *la Caridad* have been held at the University of Miami campus in Coral Gables. On December 4th, Cuban Americans celebrate the feast day of Santa Barbara, and on December 17th, they mark the feast of San Lázaro with processions and masses. In Cuban neighborhoods in Miami, New Jersey and New York, Cubans also organize to hold yearly processions in honor of the patron saints of their *municipios* or island hometowns. Finally, on December 24th and 25th, Cuban American mark what is perhaps the most important event of the holiday cycle. Christmas is joyfully celebrated by many Cuban Americans, regardless of their religious beliefs, according to homeland tradition, which includes family gatherings, feasting and, for many Catholics, *la misa de gallo* midnight mass on *la Nochebuena* or Christmas Eve.

Just as Cuban Catholics' personal beliefs and practices often reveal the historic influence of African religious beliefs and rituals, many Cuban Americans, including some baptized and practicing Catholics, also adhere with varying levels of commitment to a religion popularly known as *Santería*. The religion correctly known as *la Regla Lukumí* is a syncretic faith that evolved during the colonial era as a consequence of the massive importation of African slaves to the island. It is based on a synthesis of Catholic mythology and European spiritist practices with the pantheistic Yoruban religious tradition originating in what is now Nigeria. Devotees of "the rule of *Lukumí*" worship a pantheon of deities called *orishas*, presided over by *Olofín*, the Creator and Father who is also venerated as Jesus Christ, the Sacred Heart, or the Holy Spirit; under his rule are a number of lesser gods including *Obatalá*, god of peace, purity, reason, and protector of doctors and lawyers, who is also represented as the *Virgen de las Mercedes*; *Elegguá*, the trickster and lord of the crossroads, also known as the Holy Child of Atocha; *Ogún*/St. Peter, the god of iron and warfare; *Yemayá/La Virgen de Regla*, goddess of motherhood and fresh water; *Ochún/La Virgen de la Caridad*, goddess of love, sexuality, marriage and pleasure; *Babalu-Ayé*/Saint Lazarus, healer of illness and protector of sick children; and *Changó*/Saint Barbara, god of thunder, lightning, drums and war.

Adherents of *la Regla Lukumí* follow the religious and moral teachings passed down to them by their spiritual elders and priests (*santera/os* or *babalawos*). Their journey of faith begins with a year-long period of religious apprenticeship during which they learn the prayers, oracular narratives, sacrificial rituals, and herbal remedies and potions that form the basis of religious practice. This apprenticeship culminates in a week-long initiation, during which they are inducted into the faith by spiritual godparents or *padrinos*, and establish a tutelary relationship with a select group of *orishas*. They then practice their faith in affiliation with *casas* or houses of worship in Miami and other Cuban and Latina/o neighborhoods across the United States. The best-known of these *casas* is the Church of the Lukumí Babalu-Ayé in Hialeah, famous for its successful 1993 Supreme Court battle to win legal recognition of the *Lukumí* religion and their constitutional right to perform traditional religious rituals that include animal sacrifices.

At home and in their houses of worship, initiates of *la Regla Lukumí* engage in individual and collective prayers, participate in cleansing and healing rituals, offer sacrificial gifts of fruit, sweets, tobacco, spirits, and animal blood on altars dedicated to their *santos*, and participate in other religious ceremonies honoring their *orishas*. These ceremonies include the singing of praise songs, call-and-response chants, and dances to evoke the presence of the gods. Dancing is often accompanied by sacred *Batá* drumming, with different percussive rhythms corresponding to each of the *orishas* being called upon. Collective singing, dancing and prayer may lead to the trance-like possession of the priest or priestess leading the ceremony, or of one or more members of the religious community in attendance.

Like Cuban Catholics, the *Lukumí* faithful commemorate a number of religious holidays and saints' days. During the first week of January, Cuban American *babalawos* make divinations and share their predictions about the blessings, catastrophes, and challenges of the coming year, and offer advice on how devotees may best achieve health and wealth for themselves and their loved ones. These divination practices, known as *la Letra*, are widely discussed in Cuban American newspapers and on Spanish-language radio. *Lukumí* adherents also celebrate their spiritual birthday or *cumpleaños* on the anniversary of their initiation into the faith, and offer special worship and sacrifices to their tutelary *orishas* on their feast days. On September 8th, the *Lukumí* faithful join many Catholics Cubans to pay respects to *la Virgen de la Caridad* as a representative of the goddess *Ochún*, while on December 4th they honor *Santa Barbara* and her *orisha* counterpart *Changó*. On December

17th they revere *San Lázaro/Babalu-Ayé* with processions and religious services, most famously in Hialeah at the popular San Lázaro Catholic Church.

Membership in the *Lukumí* ritual family, as in other Cuban American religious communities, provides practitioners with a spiritual identity and moral code. It also establishes ties between them and other members of their ritual house, living and dead. Participation in this religion also reinforces cultural and historical ties to Cuba through interactions with Cuban priests and priestesses in the United States and during trips to the island. Practitioners come from a variety of racial backgrounds and, increasingly, from other Latina/o and non-Latina/o communities. The growing popularity of this religion may reflect some Cubans' and Latina/os' disenchantment with Catholicism and other organized religions; however, it is also attractive for less spiritual reasons. Many uninitiated clients also turn to *santera/o* priests for counseling and support, for help to cure illness or win a lover, and to invoke or thwart perceived supernatural forces. The religion thus also functions as an informal system of medical and mental health care for individuals who, for a variety of reasons, may be unwilling or unable to access these services in U.S. hospitals or clinics. It also offers a link to the cultural traditions and history of Cuban Americans' island homeland, providing a sense of security to many who fear losing their cultural identity as a result of acculturation to U.S. ways of life. As such, *la Regla Lukumí* provides its faithful with a sense of continuity with the past and a way of dealing with the social, economic, political and cultural challenges of daily life in the United States.

Not all Cubans profess a Catholic or *Lukumí* religious identity. Approximately twenty percent of Cubans in the United States belong to Protestant Christian denominations, the most prominent being Baptist, Methodist and Assembly of God, while a growing number also attend services at Seventh Day Adventist congregations and at Jehovah's Witnesses temples. A small Jewish Cuban community also attends services at the *Círculo Cubano Hebreo* and Cuban Sephardi Hebrew temples in south Miami Beach. Like other Cuban Americans of faith, many Protestant Christians also maintain transnational ties to Cuba through religious organizations.

Music and Dance

Music and dance are an essential part of Cuban American life. Cubans take enormous pleasure and pride in their rich and varied musical heritage; however, music also plays an important role in maintaining familial and community ties for this community. It is also a primary signifier of Cuban American identity and a key means of maintaining cultural continuity with the past and with the lost homeland.

Traditional Cuban music is a happy byproduct of interactions between African, Spanish and European musical styles on the island. West African musical techniques, including polyrhythmic drumming patterns and call-and-response chanting and singing styles, were carried to Cuba by African slaves during the seventeenth through the nineteenth centuries. African musical traditions continued to find expression in, first, Afro-Cuban religious rituals and then, by the late nineteenth century, in new forms of fusion with Spanish music. This fusion led to the emergence of the secular, percussion-driven folkloric music today called *rumba*. Encompassing three basic styles—*Yambú, Columbia, and Guaguancó*—rumba music first appeared in poor and marginal neighborhoods in the cities of Havana and Matanzas. It was not widely accepted by the island's white Spanish population until at least the 1920s. Previously, both Spanish colonial and early republican laws prohibited Afro-Cuban religious practices in which music played an important role; they also restricted the performance of religious Batá drumming as well as other forms of Afro-Cuban music and social dancing. However, by the 1920s, a movement known as *afrocubanismo* began to assert the importance of African-origin cultural traditions to the Cuban national identity, leading to a new interest in and appreciation of this previously denigrated musical tradition. Though the *rumba*-styled music that emerged in this period had often been simplified and adapted to white tastes, it nonetheless represented a new openness to Afro-Cuban cultural expressions that had been repressed during the colonial and early republican eras.

By the turn of the nineteenth century, as a growing number of Afro-Cubans moved from the countryside to the city, other fusions between Afro-Cuban music, Spanish guitar and vocal music, and European brass band music began to appear. Afro-Cuban music took on an increasingly secular character and grew in popularity as it was performed more and more frequently in public, most dramatically in the pre-Lenten *carnaval* parades that pulsed with the infectious percussion and wailing *corneta china* of *congas* and *comparsas*. The ongoing process of musical cross-pollination taking place in Cuban cities also helped the Spanish *boleros* so popular with the island's white elite to evolve into a new musical genre known as *habanera*, ideal for both listening and dancing.

Within the first two decades of the 20th century, popular music had taken on many of the rhythmic and melodic structures that still characterize it today. It relies on the syncopated rhythm of *la clave*, resonant sticks that are struck against one another to produce the 1–2–3, 1–2 beat that underlies most traditional and contemporary Cuban music. Together with other percussion instruments including the small *bongo* drums and the larger congas or *tumbadoras*, *la música Cubana* is polyrhythmic, compelling, and always highly danceable. Its catchy beat is further enhanced by the use of *cencerros* (cowbells), *maracas, guiros* (notched gourds scraped with a stick), and more recently by the addition of *timbales* (metal drum, cowbell and cymbal kits), all of which create a lively and spontaneous sound that provides an excellent foundation for dancing.

Traditional Cuban music is played by three distinct types of groups. The earliest groupings, known as *Septetos*, were trumpet-led string ensembles that featured guitar, *tres* (a small nine-string guitar), bass, percussion and vocals. The *Septeto* is identified with the traditional Afro-Cuban and rural musical style known as *son*. Combining African rhythms with the structure, melody and romantic lyrics of southern Spanish country music, the *son* has long been associated with the Cuban *guajiro* or peasant farmer. Its lyrics, rich in romanticism and humorous double entendre, extol the serenity of the Cuban countryside, describe the hardships of agricultural labor, and celebrate the beauty and sensuality of "*la mulata*," the mixed-race Cuban woman who remains an important symbolic presence in

Cuban popular music as well as the focus of much fascination, anxiety and desire in the island's popular culture and folklore.

A second traditional grouping is the *conjunto*, which evolved in the 1930s in response to the influence of European brass band and U.S. Dixieland jazz ensembles. The stylistic predecessor of the musical genre today known as *salsa*, *conjuntos* emphasize a brassy, upbeat sound, and feature a lead singer or *sonero* and a chorus. Musical instruments include trumpets, trombones, percussion, especially *conga* drums, and occasionally piano and bass. More formal dance orchestras known as *Charangas* reveal an especially strong European influence; they are led by a flautist, who provides the intricate melodies accompanied by violins, percussion and timbales.

Among Latin musical genres, Cuban styles have had the most significant influence on U.S. popular music. As early as the 1920s, an Americanized version of Cuban music became popular in the United States, sparked by the popularity of the song *"El Manicero,"* first recorded in 1921 by Don Azpiazu and the Havana Casino Orchestra. The resulting "rumba" craze led to the emergence of big bands like the Xavier Cugat Orchestra, which played Anglicized Cuban dance music throughout the next two decades. By the 1940s, a big band "mambo" sound was sparked by the popularity of a new band, Machito and his Afro Cubans, who combined American jazz with traditional Afro-Cuban rhythms, vocals and instrumentation. Machito and other Cuban musicians working in New York City nightclubs quickly established the city as the center of Latin music in the U.S. At the same time, on the west coast Pérez Prado offered a simplified and brassy version of the "mambo" which grew increasingly popular with a non-Latin market. By the mid-1950s, he had also introduced U.S. audiences to the simpler and highly danceable *chachachá* music originally played by *Charanga* ensembles like *La Orquesta Aragón*.

By the 1960s, Afro-Cuban music had undergone an even deeper fusion with North American musical idioms, especially African American styles like rhythm and blues, in the working class barrios of New York City. The result was a new style known as Latin *Bugalú*, which combined Cuban piano *montunos* and Spanglish lyrics with R&B and jazz stylings, most famously in Joe Cuba's runaway hit "Bang, Bang." By the early 1970s, this ongoing fusion with African American and other Afro-Latino and Caribbean musical styles had produced the up-tempo, urban dance music now known as *salsa*, first performed in New York's Cheetah nightclub to an exhilarated pan-Latina/o audience.

During the same decade, a regional variation on these new pan-Latin rhythms known as the "Miami Sound" further blended Cuban and Caribbean musical elements with U.S. pop, rock and jazz. By the end of the 1970s, Emilio and Gloria Estefan's Miami Sound Machine had graduated from playing school dances and wedding receptions and began to be featured in local recordings and concerts. By the 1980s, the band's popularity had exploded across the nation, transforming them into the first Latin crossover band to enjoy long-lasting success on the U.S. pop charts. While Gloria continues to perform as a solo artist, she has returned to her Cuban musical roots with nostalgic albums like *Mi Tierra* (1993) and *Alma Caribeña* (2000). Meanwhile, her husband Emilio has dedicated himself to producing an ever-expanding number of Latin American and U.S. Latina/o artists.

Together, they have arguably been the single most important force in converting Miami into the capital of the Latin crossover market.

A number of famous Cuban and Cuban American artists have lived and performed in the United States. The most beloved of these include Chano Pozo, Mario Bauza and La Lupe, Mongo Santamaría and Cachao López, Paquito D'Rivera, Olga Guillot and the internationally beloved Celia Cruz, known as *la reina de la salsa* until her death in 2003. More contemporary artists include the exile idol *salsero* Willy Chirino and *la sonera* Albita Rodríguez, who recently left the island for the U.S. and now hosts the musical variety show *"La Descarga con Albita"* on Miami's *Mega TV*. Trumpeter Arturo Sandoval is a regular on the U.S. Latin jazz circuit and owns a jazz club in Miami Beach. Cuban American musicians have also ventured into the U.S. pop market, including two-time Grammy winner Jon Secada, and since the late 1980s, into the growing rap market. Mellow Man Ace, godfather of Latina/o hip hop, Cypress Hill members Sen Dog and B Real, and popular rapper Pitbull all boast Cuban origin.

Contemporary music is popular among the Cuban American community, especially among the second and third generations, but more traditional *son*, *guajira*, *danzón*, *rumba*, *mambo* and *chachachá* rhythms continue to be broadcast on Spanish radio stations and are enjoyed wherever Cuban Americans gather, at home celebrations, public ceremonies and festivals, and danced to at social events like weddings and anniversary parties. Second and third generation Cuban Americans also learn to play these musical styles, at home from parents and grandparents, and through piano, guitar, drum and singing lessons at small music schools in Little Havana and in Cuban neighborhoods in New Jersey, New York and Los Angeles. This steeping in their ancestors' musical traditions leads many younger artists to mine Cuban folkloric styles for inspiration, and traditional instrumentation, rhythms, and lyrical themes reappear in innovative ways in many contemporary songs and live performances.

Afro-Cuban religious practices and musical traditions remain an especially important source of inspiration for many Cuban and Cuban American musicians, and through contact with other Latina/o artists, have become part of a shared vernacular among Latina/o artists. The shared African religious idiom underlying much Caribbean Latin music is expressed in two tracks on Puerto Rican *salsera* La India's 1993 debut, *"Mi Primera Rumba"* and *"Yemayá y Ochún."* A more commercial collaboration, the 2000 duet *"Tres Gotas de Agua Bendita"* by Gloria Estefan and Celia Cruz, also speaks to the layering of traditional Cuban musical structures and elements in contemporary and "pop" music, as well as to the syncretic religious identity and worldview many Cuban Americans share with other Latina/os in the United States.

Cubans enjoy hearing their traditional and contemporary music performed live in nightclubs, cabarets, concerts, and in the open air on *Viernes Cultural*, a street fair held the last Friday of each month on Little Havana's *Calle Ocho*. The Little Havana Kiwanis Club also sponsors the United States' largest Cuban and Latin music festival. Since 1978, the *Festival en la Calle Ocho* has been held every March on SW 8th St., where for several days multiple stages showcase the best Latina/o artists from the United States and around the world. In recent years, the *Calle Ocho* music festival has drawn more than one million visitors; the event has had a profound impact on Miami's economic and cultural landscape and has increased its visibility as a world center of Latin music and culture.

Cuban Americans' relationship with contemporary music produced on the island continues to be complex. Many young Cuban Americans rediscovered a love for traditional Cuban music after the 1997 U.S. release of the *Buena Vista Social Club* album and Grammy-award-winning documentary film, inspired by U.S. artist Ry Cooder's journey to the island the previous year. However, since the 1960s, Miami Cubans have frequently boycotted concerts and shows offered by touring revolutionary artists; though this practice is less common today, more stalwart exiles continue to object to those who choose to patronize artists from the socialist nation. Non-political music from Cuba is nonetheless increasingly accepted by Cuban Americans, and albums by the island's pre-eminent artists and groups are now available in many U.S. music stores. Some of the island's most popular bands, including Los Van Van and La Charanga Habanera, have also performed to large appreciative audiences in Miami and frequently travel to other U.S. cities to entertain Latina/o and non-Latina/o audiences. Indeed, highlighting the continuing links between island and U.S. resident Cuban artists, La Charanga Habanera performed live on the Miami TV show *Pellízcame, Que Estoy Soñando* during their autumn 2010 international tour; this television show is hosted by Carlos Otero, one of Cuba's most popular artists before he left for Miami in 2007.

The popularity of Cuban music and its enormous historical contribution to contemporary Latin musical genres, especially salsa, make music one of the most important realms in which Cuban American folklore has influenced the development of a pan-ethnic Latina/o culture in the United States. Much of the music that the Anglo mainstream identifies as "Latin," is Afro-Cuban or Afro-Caribbean in origin or in influence. Similarly, Latina/os from different Latin American backgrounds have adopted this "*música tropical*" as a signifier of pan-ethnic *Latinidad*, learning to dance *salsa* for pleasure and profit, taking on new roles as cultural entrepreneurs as performers or instructors of this style of dance.

Food and Cooking

Food and cooking also play an important role in Cuban American daily life, as they do among many Latina/o communities in the United States. In addition to offering pleasure and sustenance, food and the rituals associated with its distribution, preparation, presentation and consumption provide threads of continuity with the homeland and help Cuban Americans to continue to express their cultural identities in the United States. They are also deeply intertwined with Cuban and Latina/o customs of at-home hospitality, extended family and community ties, and play a central role in celebrations, commemorations, and other familial and social events.

Cuban food is a hearty and flavorful fusion between European and African culinary traditions, blending Spanish/Iberian and African ingredients and cooking techniques with those indigenous to the Caribbean. It has also been influenced over time by other world cuisines and by the changing availability of foodstuffs and prepared goods imported to the island from the United States and elsewhere. During the colonial era, Spanish conquerors brought beef, pork, rice, *bolillos* (buns made from wheat flour), olives, olive oil and citrus fruits to the island. African-origin and local foods including tubers such as *malanga*, *boniato* and *yuca* (cassava), as well as local fish and shellfish, are equally important elements in Cuban cuisine. Tropical fruits, including plantains, bananas, papaya, guava, and avocado, also play a central role in Cuban cooking, as do the condiments of garlic, onion and lemon juice, which make up the "*sofrito*" of sautéed ingredients that form the base of many Cuban stews and casseroles, and are combined with lemon, lime or sour orange juice in marinades and dressings for meat, chicken and fish dishes.

Many of the island's most popular drinks, both alcoholic and non-alcoholic, are derived from the island's plentiful sugarcane crop. These include *guarapo* or sugarcane juice, which has long served as a source of energy for Cuban laborers and their families, *agua de coco*, or fresh coconut juice, and fruit milkshakes or *batidos* made with mango, papaya and mamey. Cuban rum, most famously made by the Bacardi family corporation which left the island for Puerto Rico after the 1959 revolution, and presently on the island by the Havana Club distillery, is consumed worldwide in *Cuba Libres*, *Mojitos*, and *Daiquiris*. Rum, like tobacco, is also used in *Lukumí* rituals and is offered as tribute to the saints and *orishas* on household altars.

Cuban coffee is also an important element of the Cuban American diet and lifestyle. Strong, dark and heavily sweetened with sugar, it is drunk from small demitasse cups at home after meals, over conversation, and at open-air cafés and bakeries in Cuban neighborhoods, where *un cafecito* or *un cortadito*, cut with a splash of milk, may accompany an aromatic *puro*, hand-rolled in one of Little Havana's more than twenty small cigar factories. Whenever and wherever coffee is drunk, it is always accompanied by the exchange of news and gossip, and serves to punctuate spirited discussions about baseball and politics.

Cuban Americans enjoy shopping for traditional foodstuffs in the *bodegas* that line the thoroughfares of Cuban neighborhoods in Miami's Little Havana and other Cuban neighborhoods in New Jersey, New York and Los Angeles. These small, family-run grocery stores sell a full line of Cuban and Latina/o foods, condiments and spices. Cubans also buy fruits, vegetables and tropical tubers from open-air markets and from itinerant peddlers who sell produce and cold drinks from their pickup trucks and cars at busy intersections. Cuban *carnicerías* (butcher shops) also offer a complete selection of specialized cuts of meat, and bakeries offer delicious Cuban pastries and desserts. In addition to offering products not easily available elsewhere, *bodegas* and other Cuban shops and marketplaces are important social institutions in their own right, providing the opportunity for conversation, gossip, and the exchange of news and information. *Bodegas*, butcher shops and bakeries also distribute Spanish-language newspapers and magazines and hang posters advertising concerts, theater and dance performances, and other community events in their windows. By serving as a central gathering site for Cuban Americans from different neighborhoods and socioeconomic groups, these public spaces and the food shopping rituals associated with them play an important role in enriching community life, fostering ethnic solidarity, and strengthening Cubans' cultural identity.

Cubans traditionally follow the Spanish custom of eating a light breakfast of bread and *café con leche*, a heavy, leisurely mid-day *almuerzo*, and a light late evening *comida*. However, as second and third generation Cuban Americans adapt to U.S. ways of eating and to the demands of dual career households, many have given up this custom or reserve it for weekend meals with the extended family. Though many Cuban American families continue to eat a diet heavy in traditional foods, the chance to eat more elaborate meals, too time-intensive to prepare regularly at home, draw Cuban Americans to the hundreds of restaurants that thrive in Miami's Little Havana and the neighborhoods of Westchester and Hialeah as well as in Cuban New Jersey, New York, and Los Angeles. Many of these restaurants are patterned and named after restaurants in pre-revolutionary Cuba, and continue to be operated by their previous owners or their children; their décor features photographs, paintings and murals that introduce second and third generation Cuban Americans to the bustling Havana streets and rural landscapes remembered with such nostalgia by their parents and grandparents. Among the most famous of these dining establishments are Lila's in Westchester and Victor's Cafe and Versailles Restaurant in Little Havana.

Favorite dishes eaten at home and in restaurants include *bistec de palomilla*, a thin sirloin steak smothered in sautéed onions, *ropa vieja* and *picadillo*, shredded beef or ground beef hash in tomato sauce, and pot roast or *boliche*. Cuban Americans share an undying passion for pork dishes, especially *masas de puerco*, fried chunks of marinated pork, and *puerco asado*, tender and garlicky roast pork served with rice, black beans, and accompanied by fried *platanos maduros* or boiled yuca drenched in garlic and olive oil *mojo*. Chicken is also eaten grilled, breaded, or stewed with vegetables and saffron rice in *arroz con pollo*, and fish and shrimp are served fried with garlic or *enchilado*, swimming in a Spanish tomato sauce. Cuban Americans also love desserts, including rich rum-soaked *dulce de leche* cakes, guava- and mango-filled pastries, custard flans, and coconut, sweet potato, rice and egg puddings (*arroz con leche* and *natilla*).

Cuban Americans also enjoy eating at the crowded and inexpensive *cafeterías* which offer *pan con lechón*, Cuban sandwiches made with ham, pork, and Swiss cheese on grilled French bread, as well as the ever-popular *medianoches*, a smaller *Cubano* served on a soft roll fried in egg batter. Or they may stop for a quick *frita*, or Cuban-style hamburger topped with fried shoestring potatoes, at a street corner stand. In New York City, Cubans and non-Cubans continue to flock to the few remaining *Chino-Cubano* restaurants run by descendants of Havana's once thriving Chinese immigrant enclave, where they enjoy Cubanized versions of Chinese dishes like chop suey and lo mein.

Food and drink, like music, are at the heart of Cuban holidays and commemorations, from christenings and anniversaries to elaborately catered *Quince* debutante parties. They are central to the celebration of feast days in honor of *santos* or *orishas* and the coffee-fueled all-night *velorios* or open-casket wakes held in honor of deceased family members. The most joyful of all Cuban American gatherings, however, is the annual celebration of *la Navidad*. Cubans traditionally celebrate Christmas on *la Nochebuena*, or Christmas Eve, when extended families and friends gather at home to talk, laugh, sing and dance, and open the gifts displayed around a Christmas tree or *nacimiento* (nativity scene). Drinking *sidra* (cider) and snacking on seasonal delicacies like roast chestnuts, *turrón* or nougat candies, praline-like *cocitas*, and *buñuelos*, fried pastries topped with powdered sugar or syrup, they impatiently await the late evening holiday meal of *lechoncito* or tender roast suckling pork accompanied with beans, rice, yuca, and radish salad. Though the *lechón* is customarily slow-roasted in a banana-leaf-topped charcoal pit in the backyard, many Cuban American families have adapted this custom to their busier lifestyles in the United States, and order their pre-cooked *lechoncitos* from supermarkets and restaurants. Before partaking of the holiday meal, many families may ask an elder relative to say grace or blessings over the meal, and a toast is often offered, usually concluding with the ritual expression of hope that the upcoming Christmas will be celebrated *"el año que viene en la Habana"*—next year in Havana. The evening's events often conclude with prayers for departed relatives and, if the family is Catholic, with attendance at a *misa de gallo,* or midnight mass, at a local church.

Food and drink, whether eaten at home, in restaurants, or on special occasions, or carried or shipped to friends and relatives living outside the Miami, New Jersey, and New York *barrios* where they are widely available, serve to express and reinforce Cubans' distinctive cultural identity. They also reveal Cubans' shared history with other Caribbean Latina/os, other African-origin communities, and indeed with many immigrant ethnic communities, where the values of extended family and community are expressed through rituals of hospitality and solidarity that center on eating and drinking.

Clothing and Adornment

Cuban Americans, like Cubans on the island, are often stylish and image-conscious people who are fastidious about personal grooming and enjoy shopping for clothing, accessories and toiletries. Though they most commonly dress in modern western clothing, they also continue to use special-occasion clothing and accessories that signify their Cuban heritage and identity. The most famous of these clothing items is the traditional *guayabera*, an embroidered linen or cotton button-down shirt that can be worn for formal as well as informal events. *Guayaberas*, with either short or long sleeves, are most commonly worn by men. Variations of this style are also commonly worn in the Yucatán Peninsula of Mexico and in the Philippines, countries that share Cuba's Spanish cultural heritage.

Folkloric costumes worn by dancers and other performers in Cuba reveal the blending of the island's Spanish and African heritages. They include elaborate *carnaval* costumes and headdresses, women's folkloric dresses with long, full skirts and ruffled embroidered blouses, sometimes worn with cloth turbans. Men's folkloric outfits consist of loose cotton and linen shirts and pants, topped with a neckerchief or tied with a sash, similar to those worn by Afro-Latina/os in Colombia, Venezuela, the Dominican Republic and Puerto Rico. Another important element of folkloric dress is the woven *Yarey* hat, the symbol of the Cuban *guajiro* that was immortalized by singer Celia González in the song "*Quien Ha Visto por Allí Mi*

Sombrero de Yarey?" Adherents of the Lukumí religious tradition may wear clothing and accessories that reveal their spiritual identity or signify their status as religious apprentice or initiate. Initiates may dress in all-white clothing, shave their hair, and cover their heads with hats or cloth turbans as symbols of purity and respect; they may also wear an assortment of *collares*, colorful beaded necklaces whose distinct patterns signify the individual's devotion to specific *orishas*.

Conclusion

Cuban American folklore is rich, varied, and ever-evolving. It finds expression through the U.S. Cuban community's shared language, worldview, literature and art, through its reinvention and use of public space, and in its religion, music and dance, food, styles of dress and adornment, and familial and social rituals. Following the 1959 revolution, the beliefs, customs and cultural traditions of the Cuban diasporic community have been re-imagined by several generations of Cuban Americans, whether born in the United States or more recently arrived from the socialist nation, and they continue to evolve in response to the historic experience of Cuban Americans as political exiles and economic migrants from the *patria*. The constant reinvention of Cuban American folklore serves both to preserve the cultural distinctiveness of this diverse and upwardly mobile community even as it facilitates, through contact and conversation with other Latina/o cultural traditions, the emergence of a shared pan-Latina/o identity in the adopted homeland.

ANITA CASAVANTES BRADFORD

See also: African Influence on Latino Folklore; Afro-Colombian Music; Arroz con Leche (Rice Pudding); Christmas (Navidad); Conjunto; Puerto Rico and Its Folklore; Rumba (Rhumba)

Further Reading

Atwood Mason, Michael. "'I Bow My Head to the Ground': The Creation of Bodily Experience in a Cuban American Santería Initiation." *The Journal of American Folklore* 107, no. 423 (Winter 1994): 23–39.

Boswell, Thomas D. *The Cuban American Experience: Culture, Images and Perspectives.* Lanham, MD: Rowman and Littlefield Publishers, 1984.

De la Fuente, Alejandro. *A Nation for All: Race, Inequality and Politics in 20th Century Cuba.* Chapel Hill: University of North Carolina Press, 2001.

Díaz, Guarione M. *The Cuban American Experience: Issues, Perceptions and Realities.* St. Louis: Reedy Press, 2007.

González-Pando, Miguel. *The Cuban-Americans.* Westport, CT: Greenwood Publishing Group, 1998.

Ortiz, Fernando. *Cuban Counterpoint: Tobacco and Sugar.* Durham, NC: Duke University Press, 2003.

"DANCING WITH THE DEVIL" LEGEND
See Bailando con el Diablo

DÉCIMA

The *décima* is an octosyllabic ten-line stanza, rhyming *A B B A A C C D D C*, and Spanish in origin. Although ten-line stanzas of a different design were used and performed with some frequency as early as the fifteenth century, the above variant is the most well-known and is accredited to Vicente Gómez Martínez Espinel (1550–1624), the acclaimed Spanish writer and musician of the *Siglo de Oro* (the Spanish Golden Age). The *Siglo de Oro* refers to a period of artistic and literary florescence in Spain, which began in 1492 with the completion of the *Reconquista* (the Christian recapturing of the Moorish-controlled Iberian Peninsula) and the voyages of Christopher Columbus to the New World, and ended roughly with the death of the last prominent writer of the period, Pedro Calderón de la Barca, in 1681. The *A B B A A C C D D C décima* form, often referred to as the *décima espinela* or simply *espinela*, appeared at the height of this period in 1591 with the publishing of Vicente Espinel's *Diversas rimas*.

(A) *Suele decirme la gente*
(B) *que en parte sabe mi mal,*
(B) *que la causa principal*
(A) *se me ve escrita en la frente;*
(A) *y aunque hago de valiente,*
(C) *luego mi lengua desliza*
(C) *por lo que dora y matiza;*
(D) *que lo que el pecho no gasta*
(D) *ningún disimulo basta*
(C) *a cubrirlo con ceniza.*

The *espinela's* poetic dominance ultimately trumped the use of pre-existing ten-line stanzas commonly referred to as *copla real*, a few of which existed in the general form of *A B A A B C D C C D*.

Crucial to its emergence as a popular poetic form in Spain was its use in *controversia*, a form of verbal dueling between rival poets. This tradition was long established by *juglares* (juggler and minstrel troubadour poets) in the Middle Ages. The *juglar* is first mentioned in Spanish historical accounts in the eleventh century, although its antecedents date back to the ninth century in royal courts. Still, it was in the greater region spanning southern France, northern Spain, and northern Italy where such artists made their living performing for audiences through music and poetry as charlatans, acrobats, mimes, and so on, and went on to establish the poetry, music, and art of the *juglaresca*. Their performative work was key to developing the *controversia* or *contrapunto*, which in the *Siglo de Oro* served to give a particular vitality to the *décima* as a form used in poetic controversy.

The popularity of the *décima espinela* in Spain undeniably contributed to its emergence in Latin America. Along with other Spanish poetic and musical forms and genres including the *alabado, romance, copla, pregones, música profana,* and *música divina*, the *décima* and *controversia* also came to exist in Latin America in the late sixteenth century. Sources suggest its diffusion in Latin America occurred by means of the Catholic Church's evangelical efforts and labors, as clergy attempted to Christianize Indigenous populations with the aid of song and poetry, and as a result of colonial aristocratic popularization, as the cosmopolitan sensibilities of Spanish soldiers, *conquistadores*, and colonial officials gained favor.

To date, the *décima* is performed throughout Latin America and among Latinos living in the United States, although its use has all but disappeared in Spain. It exists and is practiced in a variety of performative contexts, all with their own nuances, stylistic traits, and functional features. These New World *décima* traditions have been infused with African, Indigenous, and Mestizo influences to produce rich, poetic practices intimately tied to bodies of folk-song and music and dance traditions. The *décima* exists in Argentina, Brazil, Chile, Colombia, Cuba, Ecuador, Mexico, Panama, Peru, Puerto Rico, the Southwestern United States, Uruguay, and Venezuela. Further, verbal dueling, in line with the *controversia* tradition, is also common in these places. There exist the *paya* in Chile, *punto* in Cuba, *seis* in Puerto Rico, and *valona* in Mexico, among others. *Decimistas*, or *decimeros*, usually begin with a *planta*, a base-stanza to be glossed or expanded upon that often takes the form of a quatrain rhyming *A B A B* or *A B B A*, and proceeds to poetically render each line of the *planta* with a corresponding *décima*. Such an exercise serves to demonstrate the *decimista's* improvisational talent and poetic competence *vis-à-vis* another performer, as each is expected to respond in kind with *décimas* of their own. Further, *décimas* are often thematically grouped into two categories in accordance with their content. *Décimas* of a religious orientation are referred to as *décimas*, or *canto*, *a lo divino* (of the divine) and those concerned with more worldly themes are *décimas*, or *canto*, *a lo humano* (literally of the human, but of the secular more appropriately). Although *décimas* exist that do not readily fit into either of these categories, these groupings are commonly used; they serve principally as markers that frame performance, thus allowing for the use of particular types of *décimas* within the varied Latin American and Latino traditions.

ALEX E. CHÁVEZ

See also: Alabados; Romance

Further Reading

Behague, Gerard. "Latin American Folk Music." In Bruno Nettl, ed. *Folk and Traditional Music of the Western Continents*, 179–206. Englewood Cliffs, NJ: Prentice Hall, 1973.

Clarke, Dorothy Clotelle. "A Note on the Décima or Espinela." *Hispanic Review* 6 (1938): 155–158.

Espinel, Vicente. *Diversas rimas.* Salamanca, Spain: University of Salamanca, 1980.

Jiménez de Báez, Yvette. *La décima popular en Puerto Rico.* Xalapa, Mexico: University of Veracruz, 1964.

Linares, María Teresa. "The Décima and Punto in Cuban Folklore." In Peter Manuel, ed. *Essays on Cuban Music: North American and Cuban Perspectives*, 1–23. Lanham, MD: University Press of America, 1990.

Mendoza, Vicente T. *Glosas y décimas de México.* Mexico City: Fondo de Cultura Económica, 1957.

Menéndez Pidal, Ramón. *Poesía juglaresca y juglares: Aspectos de la historia literaria y cultural de España.* Madrid: Centro de Estudios Históricos, 1924.

Menéndez Pidal, Ramón. *Los romances de América y otros estudios.* Buenos Aires: Espasa-Calpe, 1943.

Navarro González, Alberto. *Vicente Espinel: Músico, poeta y novelista andaluz.* Salamanca, Spain: University of Salamanca, 1977.

Orta Ruiz, Jesús. *Décima y folclor: Estudio de la poesía y el cantar de los campos de Cuba.* Habana, Cuba: Ediciones UNION, 2004.

Paredes, Américo. "The *Décima Cantada* on the Texas-Mexican Border: Four Examples." In Fellows of the Folklore Institute, eds. *Journal of the Folklore Institute*, 91–115. Bloomington: Folklore Institute, Indiana University, 1966.

Velázquez, Guillermo, ed. *Poeta, dame tus razones: Tres trovadores campesinos queretanos.* Querétaro, México: National Council for Culture and Arts, 1993.

DESCANSOS

Descansos have a long tradition in the Hispanic Southwest. The term derives from the Spanish word *descanso*, which means a short rest or resting place, and the tradition dates to the early days of Spanish exploration and settlement in the Americas. In the Southwestern United States and among Hispanic cultures in particular, *descansos* are handmade memorials, or physical shrines, that are erected to memorialize the spot where a person was killed in an automobile accident. *Descansos* are memorials as well as folk art that mark the spot where the soul has left the body. An important aspect of these roadside markers is that they are highly public and generally face the roadside or highway.

The practice of memorializing the place where a loved one has met the shadow of death can be traced to ancient Spanish funeral rituals in the old villages of New Mexico. Traditionally, *descansos* marked the places where funeral processions, led by priests and followed by mourners (mostly women) dressed in black, paused to rest on the journey between the church and the *camposanto*, or cemetery. Often four to six men carried the coffin. If the *camposanto* was some distance away, the men would periodically pause to rest; they lowered the coffin and placed it on the ground. These resting spots were marked with a cross, a bundle of juniper or

This memorial has been placed along the side of the highway to remember a person who died there, as well as to remind other drivers that this can be a treacherous part of the road. (Greg Biggs/Dreamstime.com)

piñon sprigs, or a small pile of stones. The association was thus created between a road travelled, an interrupted journey, and death as a destination. In time, this processional practice of rest and contemplation found expression in marking the location of fatal accidents along roads and interstates. Today many people regard roadside crosses as sacred but not necessarily religious.

In the twenty-first century, *descansos* are almost always handmade and vary a great deal in form and style. *Descansos* are vernacular and incorporate any number of changing elements, including fresh or plastic flowers, ribbons, photographs, handwritten notes, religious objects such as rosaries and saint statuettes, seasonal decorations such as Christmas ornaments or Easter eggs, and even car parts collected from the wreckage of the accident. Handmade wooden crosses often, although not always, distinguish the centerpieces of these memorial assemblages.

The memorials reflect varying belief systems and aesthetics, and there is controversy surrounding their status as religious offerings. *Descansos* often reflect the needs of the maker, rather than the personality of the person in whose memory the marker is erected, and the imagery and iconography of most *descansos* are often highly personal. *Descansos* are found placed along the roadside on either rural or major urban thoroughfares from Texas to California. In the twenty-first century, these handmade memorials are increasingly found in states as far north as Delaware and Pennsylvania, and throughout the midwestern states of Kansas, Iowa, and Illinois.

Scholars note that some who experience the loss of a loved one may erect a cross or marker on the spot where the soul left the body in the hope of placating an otherwise aimlessly wandering spirit that may haunt those who fail to venerate the spot. Others erect *descansos* as spontaneous expressions of grief, which serve as public tributes to the loss of a loved one. Many who erect the shrines do so in the hope that the public memorials will serve as reminders to motorists to drive safely and never leave one's home in anger, or without kissing loved ones goodbye.

Descansos serve as reminders of human mortality. They are performative sites enmeshed in the everyday lives and ritual practices of individuals who seek to actively redefine a given space as they work to transform public sites into private realms of memory and reverence. Because *descansos* in various shapes and sizes are increasingly found nationally and even globally, institutional attempts have been made to halt or regulate their usage. Although the memorials are based in tradition and therefore are typically outside of the control or jurisdiction of state or local authorities, *descansos* generally fall under the auspices of local districts, and so policies and regulations vary from state to state.

In the United States, individual states, cities, and other municipalities have laws governing the height, width, and distance of *descansos* from the roadside. Some people are offended by them and regard them as unwanted intrusions into their personal space. Such controversy is frequently an innate component of the performance of traditional customs in public places. Some states, such as New Mexico, have made it a misdemeanor to remove or in any way damage or vandalize the shrines. Critics maintain that *descansos* promote Christianity and violate the lines between church and state.

Some scholars discuss the roadside memorials as part of a dynamic memory network that is influenced by such diverse factors as participants' relationship to the deceased, religious affiliation, city ordinances, and cultural influences. *Descansos* may serve as primary or secondary sites of memorialization; this often depends on accessibility and cemetery policies and regulations. Some memorials are supported by the efforts of the international organization Mothers Against Drunk Driving (MADD).

In 2007, Kansas-based independent filmmaker Melissa Villanueva produced and directed the documentary *Resting Places*, narrated by the Irish actor Liam Neeson. The film tells the story of three mothers who maintain roadside *descansos* and explores the controversy surrounding what many call an increasingly worldwide phenomenon.

CORDELIA E. BARRERA

See also: Yard Shrines

Further Reading

Anaya, Rudolfo, Juan Estevan Arellano, and Denise Chávez. *Descansos: An Interrupted Journey, Tres Voces.* Photographs by Juan Estevan Arellano. Albuquerque, NM: El Norte Publications, 1989.

Barrera, Alberto. "Mexican-American Roadside Crosses in Starr County." In Joe S. Graham, ed. *Hecho en Tejas: Texas-Mexican Folk Arts and Crafts*, 278–292. Denton: University of Texas Press, 1991.

Kennerly, Rebecca M. "Locating the Gap between Grace and Terror: Performative Research and Spectral Images of (and on) the Road." http://www.qualitative-research.net/index.php/fqs/article/view/396/860.

Santino, Jack. *Spontaneous Shrines and the Public Memorialization of Death.* New York: Palgrave, 2006.

DÍA DE LA RAZA

Día de la Raza is the Spanish name of a holiday, literally meaning "Day of the Race," though often interpreted as "Day of the People," and is celebrated annually on October 12th corresponding with Columbus Day. This distinction between "race" and "people" is notable because "*raza*" in Spanish, unlike its English counterpart, refers to a group of people in a similar cultural and class group. Furthermore, the word "*raza*" can additionally mean people of the working class.

Names for the holiday differ historically in Latin American nations: *Fiesta de la Raza, Día de Colón, Día de la Cultura,* or *Día de la Hispanidad.* The holiday, first celebrated as early as 1792 in the Spanish colonies and the United States, commemorated the arrival of Christopher columbus in the Americas. However, in the first decades of the nineteenth century, this celebration fell out of favor in Latin America upon the onset of the wars of independence and due to anti-Spanish sentiments throughout the continent.

Nearly a century after its creation the holiday would reemerge under a different social context. In 1885, the recently founded Spanish organization *Unión Ibero-Americana* helped promote the holiday as *Día de la Hispanidad* as an attempt to strengthen the economic and social relationships between Spain and her former colonies. However, they had little success as the largest contemporary celebration was held in the United States during the World's Columbian Expedition in Chicago in 1893.

The holiday evolved further as in 1913 the Mexican chapter of the *Unión Ibero-Americana* renamed it "*Fiesta de la Raza*" as an attempt to focus on the role of Spain as the foundation of Latin American cultural heritage rather than on the discovery of America. Continuing this new tradition, Argentine president Hipólito Yrigoyen decreed on October 4th, 1917, the creation of *Día de la Raza* as a national holiday to be celebrated later that month. However, the controversy arose because of mixed views toward Spain regarding the suppression of Native American cultures.

Throughout the rest of the twentieth century, controversy surrounding the holiday grew in countries with large Native American populations. By the end of the century, Native groups led various demonstrations against the holiday, claiming that it is designed to perpetuate European dominance in the Americas and to suppress Indigenous cultures. The largest of such demonstrations occurred in 1990, when Native American representatives gathered in Quito, Ecuador to organize against the celebrations of the 500-year anniversary of Columbus's voyage.

In contrast, *Día de la Raza* became a celebration of Latino heritage as opposed to the American version of the discovery celebrated through Columbus Day in the United States. Additionally, the Spanish-named holiday recognized the mixture of Indigenous and Spanish cultures. As a Latino community–oriented holiday, the date has been set by numerous Latino organizations as a focal point to mobilize against anti-Hispanic sentiments and the scapegoating of Latinos in the United States. In addition to the political nature of *Día de la Raza* in Latino communities in the United States, cultural presentations representing all of Latin America often accompany the celebrations.

CHRISTOPHER ALEX CHABLÉ

Further Reading

Deardshell, Peter. *Europe and Latin America: Returning the Gaze.* New York: Manchester University Press, 2000.

Pachum, Ilan. "Origins and Historical Significance of Día de la Raza." *Revista Europea de Estudios Latino Americanos y del Caribe* 76 (2004): 61–81.

DÍA DE LOS MUERTOS (DAY OF THE DEAD)

Día de los Muertos (Day of the Dead), or *Todos Santos* (All Saints) as it is sometimes called, is an annual celebration of life and death observed throughout Greater Mexico during which time celebrants welcome home the spirits of their deceased loved ones with *ofrendas* (offerings) of food, drink, and other cherished personal items and then commune with them at their grave sites. The Day of the Dead marks the one time during the year when the dead may return, if only for a few hours, to visit their loved ones and to enjoy the pleasures they had known in life. Traditionally, festivities are held between the evening of October 31st and November 2nd but some communities begin parts of the celebration as early as October 27th. Throughout Mexico, *el Día de los Muertos* is primarily a private, family-based ritual that culminates in a public, community celebration. The practice of observing *el Día de los Muertos* has also found a home in the United States where festivities are largely public and represent an opportunity for community building and cultural affirmation for urban Chicanos and Latinos.

History of the Ritual

Like most Mexican traditions and religious practices, *el Día de los Muertos* is a syncretic ritual with elements borrowed from both Spanish Catholicism and pre-Columbian religious beliefs. The Day of the Dead comes out of the Indigenous belief in three deaths: the first death is the physical death of the body; the second death, the death of the spirit, comes with the spirit's return to mother earth and ascent to the sun; and the third death is the death that Indigenous peoples truly feared—the death of the soul that occurs after there is no one left alive to remember or welcome the soul home. *El Día de los Muertos* represents a means through which to spare ancestors from this third death.

El Día de los Muertos has been observed throughout Mexico for almost 3,000 years. The Florentine Codex contains records of two Aztec feast days: *Miccail-huitontli* and *Miccailhuitl,* which can be translated as "Feast of the Little Dead Ones" and "Feast of the Adult Dead." Together, these feasts were known as *Tlaxochimaco* (The Offering of the Flowers) or *Xocotl uetzi* (Fruit Falls)—festivals which were held in the ninth and tenth months of the Aztec year. When the Spanish arrived in the New World, they moved these feast days to coincide with the Catholic observance of All Souls' Day and All Saints' Day in an attempt to convert the Indigenous population to Catholicism.

As a result, All Souls' Day and All Saints' Day merged with the harvest rites of *Mictlantecuhtli* into the syncretic rituals we are familiar with today. The Folk Catholic traditions of bringing food offerings to the dead meshed well with the Indigenous practice of offering grave-goods for the departed's use in the afterlife. The Catholic belief in heaven and hell added a new dimension to the Aztec belief in *Mictlán*, an afterlife that was determined by how an individual had died, not by how he or she had lived.

Welcoming Home the Dead

El Día de los Muertos is the most visibly celebrated festival of the year in Mexico. This is particularly true of Mexico's rural areas where preparations for the Day of the Dead may be carried out throughout the year but explode with activity in the days preceding the feast. Rural markets are at their most impressive in the days before *el Día de los Muertos,* and brightly colored flowers, candies, and paper goods are seemingly everywhere.

Rural areas are also more likely to begin practicing *Día de los Muertos* rituals earlier than revelers in urban settings who might only recognize November 1st and 2nd as days of celebration. In these communities, the Days of the Dead begin on October 27th, when the hungry and thirsty souls of those without families or friends are welcomed with water hung from vessels outside of people's homes and crusts of bread. These souls might alternately be welcomed into a village's church, where a single offering provided by the community awaits their return.

The next night, October 28th, marks the time when those souls who died violently are cautiously welcomed back. Many consider these souls malevolent spirits who are unable to find peace in their afterlife and fear these unfortunate spirits. These fears stem from Aztec beliefs that the quality of our afterlives is dictated by the manner in which we die, not the manner in which we lived. For this reason, those souls who died by accident, murder, or other violent means are offered sustenance at a safe distance. Food and water are placed outside of the home for returning spirits to find, but their souls are not welcomed back into the home out of a fear that they may not leave or cause problems for the living while they visit.

On October 30th, the souls of those children who died before being baptized and who therefore dwell in limbo are welcomed home for a few hours. The next night, the souls of baptized children are allowed to return and are welcomed back into their homes. As with the other souls who have returned, the time shared with them is fleeting, and they must return to their afterlife by the following afternoon.

The late afternoon of November 1st brings with it the beginning of an impressive celebration. Church bells ring all afternoon to welcome the souls of the adults. The Faithful Dead, as they are sometimes called, arrive throughout the evening and join their families at the home altar where they find *ofrendas*, or offerings, laid out in their honor. Families first acknowledge the most recently deceased loved one before welcoming home their other ancestors.

Public and Private Rituals

Traditionally, *el Día de los Muertos* is primarily celebrated privately in the home with family and close friends. The feast days mark a time of family reunion both for the living and the dead. This is particularly true in some areas in Mexico where it is customary for family members to travel to the homes of relatives who have lost loved ones within the last year to pay their respects in a ritual that resembles a Catholic wake. Family members gather around the *ofrenda* and drink *atole*, a hot drink made with cornmeal and cinnamon that is sometimes flavored with fruit or chocolate, and sit in quiet reflection. The ritual culminates at sundown, when family members travel to the cemetery with food and drink to commune with the dead at their gravesites. By now, the graves will have been cleaned and tended to by the women in the family and the men will have repainted the headstones or tombs in bright colors and made any necessary repairs.

When families move to the cemetery on the last night of the Days of the Dead, it will be for a community celebration. Celebrants bring food and potables in offering to the dead and to share with one another. The distribution of food amongst the living represents an important element of Day of the Dead rituals as it symbolically reaffirms community ties and social relationships.

At the cemetery, women will take their places graveside to pray for the departed while men socialize amongst one another. Candles will be lit to represent each departed soul. Mariachis, or other traveling musicians, might attend to play songs for the enjoyment of both the living and the dead.

On these nights it is also common to witness masked *comparsas* take place through village streets. Men in masks perform amusing skits in return for a few coins or a warm drink. These performers will, in the tradition of oral *Calaveras*, offer up some witty, but biting epitaph for the living members of a family in exchange for a small payment.

When night falls on the second day of November, the festivities will come to a close. The souls of the dead will return to their afterlife. The dead who linger will be hurried on their journey by masked "mummers," whose job it is to frighten away the souls who dawdle in the world of the living.

Ofrendas

Day of the Dead *ofrendas*, or offerings, have historically constituted the most private aspect of *Día de los Muertos* celebrations. Today, however, elaborately constructed *ofrendas* play a central role in public, community-oriented Day of the Dead celebrations. Depending on local traditions, the construction of the home *ofrenda* begins on either the 30th or 31st of October. The assembly of the *ofrenda* is a family activity in which every family member who is able participates.

The construction of the *ofrenda* is premised on the Indigenous Mexican belief that souls require nourishment—even after death. For this reason, families provide food and drink to the souls of their dearly departed on the one night of the year during which they are able to return to commune with the living. *Ofrendas* are usually constructed on a table or platform that has been covered with a decorative cloth—either a crisp white cotton or an embroidered table-cloth—although more recently, the introduction of festively colored plastic sheeting has become increasingly popular even in rural settings. Sometimes levels will be fashioned out of empty boxes to form a pyramid shape and then covered with the tablecloth. The *ofrenda* is usually positioned as close to the family altar as possible as, like the permanent altar, it constitutes an important element of the family's spiritual practices.

Upon the *ofrenda* table, families will artfully arrange food, water, sweets, candles, flowers, and statues of saints or prayer cards. The specific items featured on the *ofrenda* will vary according to the *gustos* (likes or tastes) of the person to whom the offering is being made. The use of sugar skulls—skulls molded from granulated sugar and meringue powder, left to harden and then decorated with brightly colored icings and bits of colored tin foil and sequins—upon which the name of the deceased is printed has become increasingly popular for use in *ofrendas*. Should they be available, photographs of the deceased will occupy a position of prominence on the altar as will any mementos that held special meaning to the dead. Copal, a resin derived from plant sap and used as incense to cleanse the space of evil spirits, will then be burned to lead the souls of the dead back home. There, a woven mat laid in front of the *ofrenda* table awaits the returning souls so that they may rest after their long journey. Personal cleansing items such as soap, combs, razors, and toothbrushes are often placed next to the *ofrenda* alongside a washbasin, mirror, and towel so that the souls of the dead may "freshen up" when they return.

In some regions of Mexico, families will construct an *arco* (arch), which represents the universe, out of cane and place it above the *ofrenda* table. The *arco* is then decorated with some combination of flowers, various food items, and palm leaves. In Tzintzuntzán, Mexico, the *arco* is an elaborate structure that might be constructed in the form of an angel or a bird before being decorated with flowers and candied fruits. These costly *ofrendas* are usually reserved to honor the dead who have passed into spirit within the last year. Day of the Dead offerings are as unique as the people they are dedicated to, but some elements remain consistent across regions: the inclusion of food, water, candles, and the tissue paper garlands known as *papel picado*.

The Four Elements

Traditionally, the *Día de los Muertos ofrenda* contains four components symbolic of the four basic elements: earth, air, fire, and water. Earth is represented in the *ofrenda* as a crop item—i.e., food. In many of Mexico's corn-based cultures (the Maya, the P'urhepecha, etc.), corn holds both spiritual and cultural significance. Corn harvested in October is used to make a variety of foods such as *tamales* and *gorditas* which are then offered up alongside *moles*, breads, and seasonal fruits and vegetables. In some regions, the tamales made for the *Día de los Muertos ofrenda* are wrapped to resemble a five-point star, a geometric shape symbolizing the *Atomo Divino*—the soul of the dead in its celestial afterlife.

The second element, air (or wind), is represented in *ofrendas* through the incorporation of *papel picado*—tissue paper squares cut to form pictures and elaborate designs. *Papel picado*, an Aztec art form that predates Spanish conquest, can be made at home by folding tissue paper and using small, sharp scissors to cut out the negative space in the design. However, more often than not, *papel picado* is created by skilled artisans who use a chisel (called *fierritos*) to cut through up to fifty sheets of tissue paper at once. *Papel picado* is used for a wide variety of holidays and celebrations throughout Mexico—the colors and designs changing according to the occasion. *Papel picado* made for the Day of the Dead typically features skulls and skeletons engaged in various activities, religious symbols, and images of offering tables. These brightly colored delicate tissue squares, which can resemble lace, are then strung together to form a banner and hung above and in front of the *ofrenda* platform so that they may flutter in the breeze.

One of the most well-known *papel picado* artists, Herminia Albarrán Romero, is the 2005 recipient of the National Heritage Fellowship in Folk and Traditional Arts from the National Endowment of the Arts (NEA). Albarrán Romero, who learned her craft at the knees of her mother and grandmother in Tlatlaya, Mexico, has exhibited her *papel picado* art in museums throughout the United States and is a frequent contributor as both an *altarista* (altar maker) and paper artisan to Day of the Dead workshops. Her recognition by the NEA and the various commissions she has received for her work are evidence of the impact that folk arts connected to *el Día de los Muertos* have had on U.S. culture.

The third and fourth elements, water and fire, are represented quite literally in *ofrendas*. Water is left on the offering table in decorative jugs so that the spirits may quench their thirst after their long journey home. Families that are more connected to the Catholic aspects of the Day of the Dead may choose to bring this element into their *ofrendas* by including a bowl of holy water—water blessed by a Catholic priest.

Fire is incorporated through the inclusion of lit candles. Tradition dictates that four candles should be lit to symbolize the four directions and that one candle be included on the *ofrenda* for each soul being remembered. An extra candle is typically included on the offering table in remembrance of forgotten souls. These candles represent hope and faith and are left to burn throughout the night so that no soul will be left in darkness. If possible, the candles burned for the purpose of inclusion in the *ofrenda* are purchased especially for the occasion and burned in new candleholders.

Food

Aside from its role in representing one of the four basic elements of the *ofrenda* (i.e., earth), food plays a significant role in Day of the Dead rituals. Food is the means through which the living are able to maintain a relationship with the dead. The food offered as part of an *ofrenda* is imbued with spiritual meaning, and for this reason it cannot be consumed by the living until the souls have departed back to their afterlife. Mexicans do not believe that the dead actually consume the food offered to them. Rather, they understand the food as a sort of evidence of connection between the living and the dead and believe that the returning souls appreciate the effort put forth on their behalf.

El Día de los Muertos is also the only time of the year during which certain foods become available. One of these food items is a baked good known as *Pan de Muertos* or Bread for the Dead. The baking of this yeast bread begins before October 30th and is a task carried out by the men in a family or by a local baker. Though considered a sweetbread, *Pan de Muertos* is virtually unsweetened. Sugar is used to dust the tops of the bread, but none is used in the dough. Instead, *Pan de Muertos* is flavored with orange water, anise seeds, and nutmeg.

The most common shape of the bread is a round, flat bun with two strips of dough shaped like bones forming a cross over the top. However, different towns often offer regional variations on the classic shape. For instance, the bread can be formed in the shape of a person, in the form of a heart, or in the shape of an animal. Among the P'urhepecha, the bread is often formed in the likeness of a rabbit called *aguani*, which also represents a man.

A dazzling array of skeleton-themed sweets is also available during Day of the Dead festivities. Skulls, skeletons, and coffins are crafted out of sugar and chocolate and offered at home altars and given to friends and loved ones. In many ways, the food prepared for *el Día de los Muertos* takes on the function of maintaining community among the living. This is evident not only in the purchase of confections as gifts, but also in the practice of sharing the *ofrenda* food after the spirits have departed.

According to custom, food is brought to the cemeteries to nourish the departing souls as they leave on their long journey back to the afterlife. When the souls have left, the special foods prepared especially for the occasion are shared with family, friends, and neighbors as a sort of offering to the community. This practice is an integral part of maintaining community connections, particularly in rural areas.

Flores para los Muertos *(Flowers for the Dead)*

Flowers, which symbolize the brevity of life, are an essential element of the Day of the Dead *ofrenda*. Though many different flowers are used in Day of the Dead celebrations, one flower has become a national symbol for the festival: the marigold. Also called *cempasúchil* (the flower of 400 lives), *k'etsikarhani*, or *cempoaxotchil*, the marigold holds a revered place in pre-Columbian religious history. According to legend, *cempasúchil*, which comes from the Nahuatl words *cemposalli*, meaning "twenty," and *xochitl*, or "flower," making marigolds the "flower of twenty petals," were miraculously gifted to the Nahua by Tonatiuh, their sun god, so that they might honor their dead. Today, the marigold continues to be featured prominently in all aspects of Day of the Dead rituals.

Marigolds are used in the construction of the floral arches, garlands, wreaths, crucifixes, and five-point stars that accompany *ofrendas* in many regions and in the decoration of gravesites and home altars. In addition to its decorative uses, the marigold serves a practical purpose in Day of the Dead rituals. Prized for their bright coloring and potent fragrance, marigolds are thought to attract the souls of the dead to the *ofrendas* prepared for them. Families will often scatter marigold petals forming a path from their front doors to the *ofrenda* waiting within the home. In smaller towns, families might even lay a floral path from the cemetery to their front doors to lead the dead home. In larger towns where this is not possible, a family might still scatter a path of marigold petals in the direction of the cemetery to ensure that the souls of the dead make their way safely to and from their final destinations. The petals of the marigold are also thought to possess cleansing properties, and families will often use them to form a cross on the floor in front of the *ofrenda* so that the souls may be cleansed of their sins and guilt when they tread upon it.

The use of other varieties of flowers in *Día de los Muertos* celebrations will vary regionally and according to which flowers are available locally. Some of the more commonly used flowers are Cockscomb, or *Mano de León* (lion's paw), a brilliantly hued magenta blossom, *Flor de ánima* (Flower of the Soul), a flower similar to the orchid, and various species of orchids. Notable among these orchids are a variety referred to as *Joskua tsitsiki*, or "starflower," a purple orchid with white hues which represents the spirit of the deceased. The bloom's star shape references the spirit's conversion into a star after it returns to the sun. The *Parakata tsitsiki* or "butterfly" is a yellow orchid with brown hues which represents the human psyche, and the yellow color of the *Tiringui tsitsiki*, an orchid with distinctive markings, represents the golden color of the soul. These join the more common gladiolas and carnations in typical Day of the Dead celebrations.

Ofrendas *for Children*

The souls of dead children, or *angelitos* (little angels), are typically welcomed home on the evening of October 31st, but in some regions of Mexico, celebrants of *el Día de los Muertos* differentiate between the souls of children who died before being baptized and other children. In these communities, infants in limbo, as the unbaptized are thought to be, are believed to return on the 30th of October. *Ofrendas* set out for the souls of children are smaller and less lavish in scale than those created for adult souls. Offering tables are often smaller in scale and are sometimes decorated with miniature table settings and small portions of food. The exception to this will come in the case of offerings made to children who have died within the previous year, which can be quite lavish. For instance, in some parts of Mexico it is customary for the godparents of a recently deceased child to offer an *arco*, an elaborate arch, which may be made to resemble many forms but which is always covered in flowers, breads, fruits, and candies, to the parents of the deceased on October 31st. Tradition dictates that the parents will offer a meal in thanks for the offering or the *arco* and then bring the arch to the child's gravesite where it will remain until the end of the Day of the Dead feast days.

Offerings to children often include favorite or new toys, candies or other sweets, and milk. Depending on availability, junk food such as soda or commercially packaged candies and chips may be set out. Some families choose to purchase new clothing for their returning children.

Ofrendas *for Adults*

When the spirits of the deceased adults return on November 1st, no expense is spared to prepare the *ofrendas* for their arrival. If the soul being welcomed home has died within the last year, the *ofrenda* will be particularly lavish as *el Día de los Muertos* will likely represent the family's first opportunity for closure. Because *ofrendas* are made to cater to the tastes of the returning souls, offerings made to adult souls will contain elements not present in those constructed for children. *Ofrendas* for adults might feature an alcoholic beverage favored by the dead in life—a special tequila or a favorite beer. If the departed was a smoker, cigarettes or a favorite pipe may be laid out on his or her behalf. As with children, snacks enjoyed by the returning souls in life will be brought to the offering table. These offerings are made to remind the dead of the things they had loved in life. The spiritual needs of the returning souls are also attended to as family members will include statues of saints with whom the dead felt connected or of the Virgin in the *ofrenda*.

Skeletons/Calacas

Skeletons have become synonymous with the Day of the Dead for those removed from Mexican rural settings. Rarely featured in the *Día de los Muertos* celebrations of small, rural towns, skeletons take center stage in urban Day of the Dead celebrations—particularly those in the United States. In urban Mexican communities, skeletons make their presence felt via festively decorated sugar skulls, paper cutouts in bakery shop windows, papier-mâché skulls and skeletons—both large and small, plastic and *barro* (red clay) toys and figurines, a dizzying assortment of candies and chocolate made in skeleton and skull molds, intricately crafted *papel picado*, and face-painted revelers.

These skeletons are not morbid in nature nor do they reflect a fascination with death as some might suggest. Rather, these whimsical skeletons are a means through which the living may poke fun at the foibles of human existence. These *calacas* remind us that death is not something to be feared or worshiped, but rather embraced as an inevitable part of life. The popularity of these skeleton figures is due in large part to the influence of José Guadalupe Posada's (1852–1913) now iconic images of skeletons in the afterlife.

Posada's artwork and mastery of the written *calavera* gained national prominence during Mexico's turbulent *Porfiriato*, the years during which Porfirio Díaz (1830–1915) ruled as President. *Calaveras*, the Spanish word for skulls, in this case refer to amusing, sometimes biting, epitaphs written for friends, loved ones, and public figures and circulated during Day of the Dead celebrations. *Calaveras* are sometimes written for the dead and read as part of the nocturnal festivities held in cemeteries but they are just as often composed for the living and either performed for the amusement of an audience or circulated via printed flyers or pamphlets. Posada endeared himself to the Mexican public by producing engraved images of decadent skeletons accompanied by witty *calaveras* that ridiculed the rich and those in political power. Posada's images worked to show that, in death, we are all equal regardless of the social class we occupied while living.

One of Posada's most famous images, "La Calavera Catrina," a portrait of a skeleton attired in the finery of an upper-class woman, is one of the most widely recognized examples of this political work and has become an iconic symbol of *Día de los Muertos* celebrations both in Mexico and the United States. Indeed, Posada's ubiquitous Catrina has become synonymous with death itself. La Catrina's image graces everything from mouse pads and rubber stamps to T-shirts. The famous *Dulcería La Catrina*, a candy shop in Guanajuato, Mexico, uses Posada's Catrina as a store logo. Posada's skeletons have given death a recognizable face.

Posada's influence is evident in the work of the renowned Linares family. In tribute to Posada's work, Pedro Linares re-created Posada's engravings using his own three-dimensional papier-mâché and cartonería *calavera* figures. The Linares family (Pedro Linares [1906–1992]; Enrique Linares [b. 1933]; Felipe Linares [b. 1936]; Miguel Linares [b. 1946]) has, for over 100 years, worked in the artisan craft of papier-mâché and cartonería. Working with paper, cardboard, and wheat-flour paste, the men of the Linares family have created skeletons both small and grand in scale that have been internationally celebrated for their artistry. The Linares' *calacas* reside in the permanent collections of the Museum of Modern Art in Mexico City, the Centre Pompidou in Paris, Disney World's Epcot Center, the Fowler Museum of Cultural History in Los Angeles, the British Museum in London, and in galleries all over the world.

Taking inspiration from Posada's practice of using *calacas* as a means to convey political messages or comment on current events, the Linares family has used their art to depict world events of both local and global significance such as the 1986 Mexico City earthquake and the 1945 bombing of Hiroshima and Nagasaki. Also like Posada, the Linares use *calacas* to mock both the living and the dead, creating skeletons in the images of corrupt politicians as a means of social critique. Though the Linares' work is now considered collectible art, the family began by creating ephemeral objects designed to be used during Day of the Dead celebrations and then discarded or burned afterward. That the Linares' work has reached the level of prominence that it has speaks to the influence and impact Mexico's Day of the Dead festivities have had on a global cultural stage.

Tourism

Tourism promoted through state intervention has had a significant impact on the ways in which the Day of the Dead is celebrated in some parts of Mexico. The Day of the Dead's carnivalesque atmosphere—replete with whimsical skulls and skeletons—has proven to be an irresistible draw for tourists who flock to Mexico to marvel at the colorful celebration. The voyeuristic nature of the tourists' enjoyment of the feast day has inspired Mexican writer and journalist Carlos Monsiváis to comment on "the cameras [which] have come to outnumber the candles in the cemeteries": "Kodak takes possession," and "Mexico has sold its cult of death and the tourist's smile is anthropologically satiated" (Carmichael and Sayer 1991, 9).

In a study of the effects of tourism on Day of the Dead celebrations in the state of Michoacán—where the festival is called *Noche de Muertos* (The Night of the

Dead), Stanley Brandes writes, "The impact has been to convert a relatively minor ritual event, in which a small proportion of the town participated and virtually no outsiders showed much interest, into one in which thousands of city people clog the streets with traffic, television cameras flood the cemetery with glaring lights, and the town becomes more or less a great stage prop for a ritual drama. In this drama native townspeople participate as actors but outsiders run the show" (2006, 71). Brandes reports that state intervention into tourism related to Day of the Dead activities in Michoacán began in 1971.

Prior to 1971, *Noche de Muertos* rituals consisted of a mass, the construction of home altars, a candlelight vigil in the cemetery (known as *la velación*), public offerings or *ofrendas* made to the dead and then shared with the community, and then culminated with a practice referred to as *el doble*—the slow ringing of church bells. This ringing of the bells—a service performed by local youth—is a practice that had been accompanied by community-sanctioned door-to-door begging (either for food or money) and a shared feast prepared and consumed by the youth (Brandes 2006). These simple, religiously grounded activities have changed significantly as a result of state intervention.

Today, *Noche de Muertos* has taken on the tone of a carnival and is referred to informally as *la Feria de los Muertos* (The Fair of the Dead). The Ministry of Tourism has introduced several cultural performances into the feast celebrations so that now the celebration of *Noche de Muertos* includes theatrical performances and exhibitions of regional dances which are put on primarily for the benefit of tourists from both within Mexico and abroad (Brandes 2006, 78–79). In addition to these new performed events, the introduction of craft competitions and open-air marketplaces with vendors selling everything from pottery to food has also come with the influx of middle-class tourists. For better or for worse, these changes have had the effect of commercializing what was once a deeply religious and spiritual celebration and have turned the Day of the Dead into a globally recognized symbol for Mexico and Mexican identity.

Celebrating the Day of the Dead Outside of Mexico

The Day of the Dead is celebrated throughout urban centers in the United States as part of a public display of cultural affirmation. Throughout the country, city streets come alive with processions featuring face-painted revelers dressed as skeletons and mariachis playing traditional Mexican music. Participants carry large-scale papier-mâché skulls and skeletons—some of which can reach fifteen feet in height—and marigold-encrusted altars. Spectators are encouraged to attend these processions dressed in Day of the Dead costumes. Celebrations typically include altar-building contests in which altars are placed on public display and Day of the Dead workshops for both adults and children.

Though these types of celebrations are held all across the United States, some of the oldest, and most well known, are held in the Southwest. San Francisco's Mission Cultural Center for Latino Arts and East Los Angeles's Self Help Graphics both organize festivals that are considered major annual events in their respective cities. These festivals, which began as a way for Mexican and Mexican American communities to maintain positive connections to their cultural heritage, have become an opportunity to practice community activism. Day of the Dead altars are frequently constructed along themes that have an impact on the community such as police brutality, violence against women, and immigrant rights.

The growing popularity of Day of the Dead events in the United States has opened the door to commoditization of what was once a deeply spiritual religious practice. Processions are now held with corporate sponsorship, and many have critiqued the events as an opportunity for consumerism to run rampant as vendors have come to play an increasingly important role in the celebrations. The Day of the Dead's evolution from religious ritual to cultural spectacle is made glaringly evident in the annual celebration held at Los Angeles's Hollywood Forever Cemetery—purportedly the only cemetery in the country to open its gates to the Día de los Muertos festival. Here, for only $10, Hollywood hipsters are invited to take part in an "authentic" Day of the Dead celebration complete with Aztec dancers and an altar-building competition.

Alexandra Mendoza Covarrubias

See also: Altars; Calaveras (Skulls); Día de los Muertos: Migration and Transformation to the United States; Paper Arts (Papel Picado, Papier Mâché, and Kites)

Further Reading

Andersson, Daniel. *The Virgin and the Dead: The Virgin of Guadalupe and the Day of the Dead in the Construction of Mexican Identity*. Göteborgs Universitet, 2001.

Andrade, Mary J. *Day of the Dead: A Passion for Life—Día de los Muertos, pasión por la vida*. San Jose, CA: La Oferta Publishing Co., 2006.

Brandes, Stanley. *Skulls to the Living, Bread to the Dead: The Day of the Dead in Mexico and Beyond*. Malden, MA: Blackwell Publishing, 2006.

Carmichael, Elizabeth, and Chloë Sayer. *The Skeleton at the Feast: The Day of the Dead in Mexico*. London: British Museum Press, 1991.

Congdon, Kristen G., Catalina Delgado-Trunk, and Marva López. "Teaching About the *Ofrenda* and Experiences on the Border." *Studies in Art Education: A Journal of Issues and Research* 404 (1999): 312–329.

Day of the Dead in Mexico, Day of the Dead Resources. www.dayofthedead.com.

Día de los Muertos/Day of the Dead, Day of the Dead Resources. www.azcentral.com/ent/dead/.

Greenleigh, John. *The Days of the Dead—Los Días de los Muertos*. San Francisco: Collins Publishers San Francisco, 1991.

Harlow, Gwen. Ofrenda, Day of the Dead Resources. www.ofrenda.org.

King, Judy. Los Días de los Muertos (the Days of the Dead), MexConnect. http://www.mexconnect.com/articles/1427-los-dias-de-los-muertos-the-days-of-the-dead.

Norget, Kristin. *Days of Death, Days of Life: Ritual in the Popular Culture of Oaxaca*. New York: Columbia University Press, 2006.

Nutini, Hugo G. *Todos Santos in Rural Tlaxcala: A Syncretic, Expressive, and Symbolic Analysis of the Cult of the Dead*. Princeton, NJ: Princeton University Press, 1988.

Sayer, Chloë, ed. *The Mexican Day of the Dead: An Anthology*. Boston: Shambhala, 1994.

DÍA DE LOS MUERTOS, MIGRATION AND TRANSFORMATION TO THE U.S.

El Día de los Muertos, or the Day of the Dead, is one of the biggest holidays in Mexico, an important observance throughout Latin America, and a major Latino celebration in the United States. A colloquial term referring to the period of All Saints' Day and All Souls' Day in the Roman Catholic liturgical calendar, the "Days of the Dead" are observed, respectively, on November 1st and 2nd. The two days are conceptualized as one holiday throughout Latin America, with both days implied in a variety of popular expressions such as *Todos Santos* (All Saints' [Day]), *El Día de los Difuntos* (The Day of the Deceased), *La Fiesta de Todos los Santos* (The Feast of All Saints' Day), *El Día de los Fieles Difuntos* (The Day of the Faithful Departed), *La Fiesta de los Finados* (The Feast of the Deceased), and *El Día de las Animas Benditas* (The Day of the Blessed Souls).

The celebration's key practices include sprucing up family graves by weeding, cleaning, and repainting them; refurbishing old headstones and crosses; placing flowers and candles on graves; constructing shrines or "altars" in homes or at gravesites; preparing special holiday foods or drinks; and attending Catholic Church services. These customs are carried out in diverse ways from country to country and vary from region to region within countries.

In some places, the holiday is celebrated via the standard Roman Catholic rituals of All Saints' Day and All Souls' Day, such as attending Mass, participating in novenas, and praying for the dead using rosary beads. In other areas, these official Catholic rituals are mixed with popular practices of folk Catholicism such as shrine-making, grave adornment, street processions and nocturnal vigils. And in regions with large Indigenous populations, such as the southern states of Mexico and rural areas of Guatemala, El Salvador, Bolivia, Peru, and Ecuador, the holiday period is celebrated through a fusion of official Catholic All Saints' Day rites, unofficial Catholic folk customs, and pre-Christian Indigenous rituals for honoring the ancestors.

In the worldview of the Aztecs, Maya, Olmecs, Mixtecs, Zapotecs, Aymara, Quechua and other aboriginal peoples of Latin America, maintaining harmony between the worlds of the living and the dead was a crucial spiritual belief before the arrival of Europeans. Festivals to honor the dead via the construction of harvest altars were held throughout the calendar year in conjunction with regional growing cycles. It was commonly believed that the spirits of the dead and the deities were always present among the living and had to be properly cared for on a daily basis, especially during the Days of the Dead, to ensure the well-being of oneself and one's family.

Centuries-old practices of honoring the ancestors via the creation of altars, ritual drinking of alcohol, ceremonial dancing, and other oblations for the dead were so deeply rooted in Latin America's Indigenous populations that Catholic missionaries found it impossible to eradicate these "pagan" activities. In dynamics of forced religious conversion and Indigenous cultural resistance that have occurred throughout the global Catholic diaspora, native rituals for remembering the dead were "tolerated" by missionaries, incorporated, and relocated to correspond with the Roman Catholic liturgical dates of November 1st and 2nd.

An example of the amalgamation of Indigenous and Catholic spiritual practices is the tradition of creating altars for the dead called *ofrendas* or "offerings." Elements commonly placed on Day of the Dead *ofrendas* in Mexico, Central America, and South America include pre-Columbian foods such as maize, squashes, grains, fruits, legumes, tortillas, and fermented alcoholic beverages customarily offered to the dead before the imposition of Christianity. In ancient Mesoamerica, marigolds and *copal* incense made of pine resin were integral elements of altars for the dead, along with valuable commodities such as salt, cacao, shells, and other forms of monetary currency (all of which are still placed on *ofrendas* today). Pre-Columbian elements are combined with Catholic iconography such as images of saints, Jesus, the Virgin Mary, crucifixes, rosary beads, statuettes of angels, and devotional saints' candles. Photos of the deceased may also be placed on altars.

In pre-Christian America, most communities were agricultural and the bounty of the land was crucial for the continuance of society. Ancestors were thought to be deeply involved in a family's ability to reproduce (both successful harvests and healthy offspring), so altars paying tribute to the dead were constructed at each harvest, when bountiful food offerings were possible. Ritual fertility dances were also performed during these festivities for the dead.

In the Indigenous worldview, death was not considered the end of life, but rather, a stage in the continuum of life, necessary for regeneration. The symbolic association of life (harvest, fertility, sexuality) and death is visible in the contemporary Day of the Dead celebrations of southern Mexico and the Andes, where breads shaped like babies (new life) are baked specifically for this holiday, and fertility and courtship rituals have traditionally been performed (Buechler and Buechler 1971, 84).

Latin American Indigenous beliefs regarding the afterworld differed starkly from Christian Europe's teachings about the relationship between the living and the dead, resulting in distinct cultural meanings associated with All Saints' Day and All Souls' Day. According to the official Catholic doctrine, dominant in Europe and among those Latin Americans who identify more with European than Indigenous cultures, the souls of children and other sexual innocents are believed to ascend directly to heaven, while those of adults suffer indefinitely in purgatory, a place of punishment for past sins. The role of the living, in this belief system, is to pray to the saints on November 1st, and pray for the souls in purgatory on November 2nd, hoping to hasten their journey to heaven. However, Indigenous peoples have given these dates other significance, based on pre-Columbian beliefs that the souls of children and adults visited the earth on separate dates. In regions of Mexico, Central America, and South America, the period of October 31st to November 1st is popularly designated as the time when the souls of children visit the earth, and the evening of November 1st through the dawn of November 2nd, the time when the souls of adults arrive.

Historically, Christian Europe has had frighteningly apocalyptic formulations of death, including medieval anguish about the end of the world, the eerie figure of the grim reaper clutching a sickle, and notions of hell as a place of excruciating pain. In contrast, pre-Columbian cultures viewed the afterworld as a desirable province offering peace from earthly suffering. In the Indigenous worldview, deceased loved ones are assumed to be in a positive place, free from the tribulations of life, and the Days of the Dead are a family reunion time when reciprocal relationships between the living and the dead are reaffirmed via lavish commemorations.

Contemporary Day of the Dead Customs in Latin America

Mexico

Many Mexicans visit cemeteries between October 30st and November 2nd, to clean, refurbish, and decorate gravesites. *Papel picado* (intricate, colorful, crepe paper cut-outs) made for festive occasions in Mexico and Central are ubiquitous during these days, adorning everything from tombs and altars to churches, homes, stores, schools, restaurants, and hotels. In some areas of the country, nocturnal cemetery vigils are held to await the visiting souls, and home altars are constructed to honor the dead. The southern regions of Oaxaca, Michoacán, Puebla, Chiapas, Vera Cruz, and Yucatán, home to Mexico's highest concentration of Indigenous peoples, are famous for their painstakingly elaborate *ofrendas* for the dead. These often include tables laden with *pan de muerto* ("bread of the dead"), salt, grains, coffee, soda pop, the fermented corn drink *chicha* or the agave alcohol beverage, *pulque*, tamales, *mole*, photos of the departed, candles, and Catholic iconography. Various-sized shelves or crates may be used to create multi-leveled altars, which may be crowned with large arches or square frameworks overlaid with marigolds and/or hanging fruits (said to be gateways to welcome the spirits home). These spectacular works of art, created by Indigenous peoples for generations, have gained worldwide attention, attracting millions of tourists to Mexico each year, including photographers, filmmakers, journalists, and university researchers.

Unlike the rest of Latin America, Mexico also has humorous "pop culture" manifestations of the holiday. In contrast to rural communities that hold Day of the Dead processions in which participants walk together from the church to the cemetery holding foods and decorations to place on gravesites, urban areas of Mexico hold boisterous street parades in which participants carry giant skeleton puppets, dress as skeletons, or wear other motley costumes. The most prominent symbol of Mexico's Day of the Dead is the *calavera* or "skull," often made of papier-mâché, clay, wood, plastic, metal, or cut-out tissue paper. In particular, edible white sugar skulls decorated with colored icing have become internationally recognized symbols of the Day of the Dead. Piled on trays by the dozens in shops and open-air markets, these treats decorate *ofrendas* and are often exchanged between family and friends as tokens of affection. Mexico's Day of the Dead skull art also takes the form of marionettes, gigantic puppets, chocolates, toys, masks, paintings, statues, posters, mobiles and more. With humorous expressions that mimic the living and mock everyday behaviors, these images are said to be reminders of the brevity of life and inevitability of death, urging people to appreciate life today, since death may be just around the corner.

In addition, Mexico has a style of humorous poetry also known as "calaveras." Emerging in urban Mexico in the mid-nineteenth century as a carry-over from nineteenth-century Spanish literary lampoons or *pasquines* (Carmichael and Sayer 1991, 58; Tinker 1961, 20), these satirical stanzas are written and published, often anonymously, during the Days of the Dead. The poems may touch on any theme and often take the form of joking "obituaries" for corrupt political leaders and other public figures. The custom of writing satirical verses during the Days of the Dead, also practiced in Guatemala and El Salvador (where poems are called "bombas" rather than "calaveras"), is part of annual school curricula in Mexico, where local and national competitions are held for the pithiest epigrams.

A latter-twentieth-century rendition of *calaveras* to emerge in Mexico is seen in the miniature figurines known as *calaveritas*. About two inches in height, these mini-skeletons humorously reenact scenes from daily life, including weddings, funerals, sporting events, workplace scenarios, and drunken brawls. Sometimes accompanied by written captions, a significant number of *calaveritas* express commentary on socio-political issues, spoofing the wealthy and condemning corruption, hypocrisy, and exploitation. They have become popular collectibles among students, urbanites, and international tourists.

In Mexico, Day of the Dead has become an exuberant popular and commercial fiesta, complete with televised parades, concerts, theater productions, dance performances, *ofrenda* competitions, "discos for the dead," and a variety of other secular activities. Businesses, schools, and universities are encouraged by the government to construct *ofrendas,* and Day of the Dead tours are marketed to tourists from around the world.

Central America

Guatemala provides a good example of how Day of the Dead observances can vary widely within a relatively small country. The towns of Santiago Sacatepéquez and Sumpango, for example, are known internationally for their Day of the Dead kite-flying celebrations in which Maya K'akchikel villagers fly ornate kites (many larger in size than a house) in the cemeteries to help traveling spirits find their way back to earth. Notes to the dead are often attached to the kite strings, ascending into heaven as a kind of telecommunication with the dead. To the delight of hundreds of participants and onlookers, a festival atmosphere prevails in and around the cemeteries, with vendors selling food, flowers, candles, and the hot corn porridge, *atol de maíz.* Whether elaborate tombs or simple mounds of dirt, graves are lovingly adorned with flowers, candles, and foods for the dead.

In the tropical Atlantic Coast region of Izabál, Guatemalans repaint cemetery tombs in vibrant colors, re-carve wooden crosses, lay wreaths of flowers on graves, and hold family picnics in the cemeteries. In the town of Salcajá, Day of the Dead is celebrated with nocturnal candlelight vigils in the cemetery, where mementos and flowers are brought to the graves and most of the town turns out to await the visiting souls. Adults carve small gourds (*chilacayote*) with intricate geometric designs, placing candles inside to create lanterns, while children go door-to-door, ritually begging for candles to illuminate the cemetery. During the night of November 1st, friends and neighbors keep watch by family graves and reminisce together about the departed. The atmosphere is happy, as children frolic, marimba music is played, and the sweet smells of candles, marigolds, lilies, and copal incense fill the air. A similar nocturnal celebration occurs in the town of Huehuetenango, where people walk from tomb to tomb serenading the dead with their erstwhile favorite tunes (a practice that also occurs in areas of Mexico, El Salvador, and South America). In the capital, Guatemala City, small altars are set up in homes, stores, restaurants, bus terminals, and market places. Trips to the cemetery tend to be more cursory than in rural areas, and great emphasis is placed on the preparation of Guatemala's most famous Day of the Dead food, *el Fiambre* (a cold dish made of varieties of finely chopped sausages, meats, fish, poultry and vegetables). Garifunas (Central Americans of Afro-Caribbean descent living along the Atlantic Coast of Guatemala, Belize, Honduras, and Nicaragua) observe the holiday by preparing special meals and creating ancestral altars comprised of foods, liquor, and articles of clothing formerly belonging to the deceased. During the Days of the Dead, some Garifunas pour liquor around graves and send small rafts carrying fire, water, and flowers to sea.

In El Salvador, colorful waxed paper flowers and paper chains adorn tombs, and wreaths of flowers or fresh pine boughs are placed on graves. *Ojuelas*—sweet, fried tortillas drizzled with honey—are made specifically for this holiday and sold at busy food stands around the cemeteries. Families leave small mementos by graves, sometimes tape letters to the tombs of loved ones, and may hire musicians to play songs at the tombs of the dead. In Nicaragua, families also adorn graves, light candles in the home for deceased family members, and prepare *buñuelos* (fried dough pastries) and tamales.

South America

There are many similarities between Andean and Mesoamerican Day of the Dead festivities. Bolivian rituals of the Aymara people include creating elaborate harvest altars for deceased relatives, often framed by arches made of sugar cane. These are laden with candles, fruits, vegetables, breads, grains (such as quinoa), and alcohol. In addition, altars include coca leaves and special breads called *guaguas* that are baked in the shape of babies. In the evening, family members, comadres, and compadres (symbolic relatives connected via godparent relationships), friends, and neighbors visit each other to pray in front of home altars and share the specially prepared foods. The praying and eating continue all night, while boys go from house to house singing and collecting bananas and oranges as offerings for the deceased in exchange for their songs. On November 2nd, communities gather in the graveyards and each family creates an altar by their family's gravesite, arranging foods, candles and flowers. Praying, singing, and ritual fertility dances occur in cemeteries and town squares (Milne 1965, 162; Buechler and Buechler 1971, 84).

In Peru, tombs are adorned with colored paper decorations, flower wreaths, and freshly painted crosses. Pots filled with roasted pig, tamales, breads, and other *alma micuy* (meaning "favorite foods" in the Quechua language) are carried to the cemetery and presented as offerings for the dead. After a Catholic priest blesses the offerings, the food is shared with family and friends (Milne 1965, 162–163).

Similar festivities have been documented in rural Argentina in the Cochinoca, Rinconada, Santa Catalina and Yavi regions where, from the evening of October 31st through November 2nd, kitchen tables are converted into *ofrendas* comprised of meals, special breads, fruits, jams, cocoa, and chicha. Vigils and prayers for the souls are held during the night and ceremonies are performed among compadres. In the regions of Tafi and Tafí Viejo, Tecumán, families make *ofrendas* filled with fruits and doll-shaped *guaguas* and prepare special meals for the dead. They carry pots of food to family tombs and arrange portions by the gravesites for the souls of the deceased. Similarly, in Andean areas of Colombia, cloth is draped over tombs during November 1st and 2nd, converting them into *ofrendas* of candles, flowers and the foods most enjoyed by deceased relatives.

In Ecuador, a blood-like, blackberry drink called *colada morada* is prepared during the Days of the Dead, along with the doll-shaped *guaguas* found throughout the Andes. Indigenous Quechuas visit cemeteries to clean and restore grave markers, placing offerings of flowers, *guaguas,* and fruits at family graves, praying, and picnicking in the cemeteries. In Quito, cemeteries are packed on November 1st and 2nd, as people clean, refurbish, and decorate family graves with flowers, candles, *guaguas* and other decorations.

Throughout Latin America, there are ethnic, race, and class differences that influence levels of participation in the celebration. Generally speaking, upper- and middle-class urbanites (usually more affiliated with European than Indigenous cultures) adhere to more muted official Catholic observances of the holiday, while Indigenous communities engage in more elaborate harvest-oriented festivities.

Day of the Dead in the United States

Since at least the 1890s, Mexican American families in South Texas and the Southwest have visited local cemeteries on November 1st and 2nd to clean and decorate gravesites. These customs resembled the grave-decorating customs of other Catholic ethnic groups and did not include Indigenous practices such as making harvest-laden altars or burning copal incense. Nor were *pan de muerto* or sugar skulls part of early Mexican American practices. Before the 1970s, most Mexican Americans did not identify with (or know much about) Mexico's Indigenous cultures, and followed folk Catholic, rather than Indigenous All Saints' Day and All Souls' Day customs. Texan and Southwestern customs for honoring the dead were carried out because of the religious beliefs of participants, and were not performed for a public audience.

The 1960s and 1970s marked a decisive period in U.S. history, when people of color were deeply engaged in struggles to gain civil rights and respect from the mainstream Anglo society. The Chicano Movement blossomed in California and the American Southwest as a political and cultural movement working on a broad cross-section of issues affecting the Mexican American community, such as farm workers' rights, improved educational opportunities, voting and political rights, and the celebration of collective histories and cultural traditions. Chicanos, a self-identifying term for Mexican Americans engaged in radical political and cultural work, also sought to counter historically negative stereotypes of Mexicans in the U.S. media via the creation of literary, theatrical and visual art that celebrated Mexican American ethnicity, history, and culture.

At this time, many racial minorities in the United States were attempting to learn about and reclaim their cultural roots—languages, clothing, art, music, rituals, and other ancestral traditions that were lost in the processes of slavery, colonization, reservation systems, and forced assimilation. Historically, public approbation of Latino cultures had been rare in the realm of U.S. arts, education, and the mass media. When Latino heritage was acknowledged at all, it was not Indigenous but Spanish art, music, and literature that were lauded. As a rejection of this Eurocentric mentality, Chicano artists and educators enthusiastically embraced Mexico's Indigenous cultures. Traveling to southern Mexico, the country's most "underdeveloped" region with the highest concentration of Indigenous peoples, Chicanos studied Indigenous languages, Mayan weaving, Aztec *danza* and other arts. There, they observed Indigenous *Día de los Muertos* celebrations and, deeply moved by their spirituality, visual aesthetics, and community-building power, decided to recreate these rituals in the United States.

Since most Chicanos (the majority of whom were born and raised in U.S. cities) did not grow up celebrating *el Día de los Muertos*, their interpretations of the commemoration were based on customs they had read about, observed in Mexico, or seen in Mexican films. Many Chicano artists were inspired by Mexican engraver José Guadalupe Posada's (1852–1913) politically satirical *calavera* imagery, published widely in nineteenth-century Mexican broadsheets. They began to create stylistically similar skeleton caricatures that critically commented on California's politicians, urban youth, and other political topics. Others modeled their work on the traditional *ofrendas* of southern Mexico, while still others made altars that showcased ironic expressions of Catholic iconography as political commentary linking the church with histories of sexism, racism, or colonization. These eclectic and experimental *ofrendas* emerged in secular spaces (art galleries, community centers, museums, schools, parks, and commercial venues) as a form of popular culture. The term "popular" here refers to cultural practices that are derived from folk culture, commodified for intended consumption by large audiences, and utilized to signify new meanings. This is not to say that U.S. Day of the Dead rituals are devoid of spiritual significance, but that they routinely occur in secular contexts as "art" or "ethnic culture" and are not primarily undertaken as acts of religious devotion. Their principal goal is not the fulfillment of moral obligations to the dead, but the public celebration of Chicano/Mexican/Latino identity.

Rather than focus exclusively on deceased individuals personally known to the altarmaker (as occurs in Latin America), Chicanos have used the altar format to publicly commemorate (and teach about) the "collective ancestors" of the Latino community—iconic writers, artists, and political figures ranging from Che Guevara and Pancho Villa to Frida Kahlo, Celia Cruz, Tito Puente, and Rubén Darío. "Altar installations" (the term used by Chicano artists to describe the *ofrendas* they make in public spaces) can be comprised of mixed media such as sculpture, oil

Day of the Dead parade in Hollywood, California. These celebrations have their roots in pre-Columbian Aztec and other native festivals memorializing departed loved ones, and occur annually on November 1 and November 2, coinciding with similar Roman Catholic celebrations of All Saints' Day, and All Souls' Day. (Zepherwind/Dreamstime.com)

paints, silkscreen, mobiles, collage, computers, televisions, sound systems, video footage, and interactive websites. Day of the Dead celebrations in the United States include events such as altar exhibitions, community altar-making ceremonies, street processions, cemetery rituals where participants may decorate graves, hold vigils, pray, sing, or dance in honor of the dead, screenings of documentary films about the Day of the Dead, educational lectures, performance art, and poetry slams (where participants publicly read poems or tell stories about the departed).

Chicano Exhibits and Events

The first recorded *Día de los Muertos* celebrations in the United States occurred in 1972, organized separately by the Latino art galleries, Self Help Graphics in Los Angeles, and La Galería de la Raza, in San Francisco. Self Help Graphics, a community-based visual arts center in East Los Angeles, hosted a Day of the Dead procession in which people dressed as skeletons and walked to a nearby cemetery. None of the Chicanos who helped organize this event were personally familiar with the Day of the Dead, so they took their cues from the three founders of Self Help Graphics (Mexican artists Antonio Ibáñez and Carlos Bueno, and Italian American nun Sr. Karen Boccalero), who knew about the celebration (Venegas 2000, 47). Within a couple of years, the celebration attracted the participation of the larger Chicano artist community, and a plethora of silkscreen prints, posters, paintings, performances and other Day of the Dead–inspired art soon emanated throughout greater Los Angeles. Over time, Self Help's annual Day of the Dead procession grew to include music, Aztec danza, giant *calavera* puppets, "low rider" cars, and decorated floats. Workshops were held at the gallery to teach the public how to make *papel picado,* sugar skulls, plaster skeleton masks, and *ofrendas.* Inspired by Self Help, community centers, schools, libraries, art galleries, museums, folk art stores, city parks and commercial venues throughout Los Angeles later developed annual Day of the Dead programming.

In the same year of 1972, the Chicano art gallery La Galería de la Raza, located in San Francisco's predominantly Latino Mission District, held the city's first Day of the Dead *ofrenda* exhibit. Organized by artists René Yáñez and Ralph Maradiaga, together with other artists, including Carmen Lomas Garza and Yolanda Garfias Woo, the exhibit and related educational workshops evolved into annual traditions. In 1981, La Galería organized a Day of the Dead street procession with a small group of people who walked around the block holding candles and photos of deceased loved ones. Within a few years, it burgeoned into an exuberant annual manifestation of thousands. Today, San Francisco's Day of the Dead procession includes Aztec blessing rituals and danza groups, outdoor altars, sidewalk chalk cemeteries, giant *calavera* puppets, skeletal stilt walkers, Cuban Santería practitioners, bagpipe players and a Jamaican steel drum band on wheels. Sacramento, Chicago, New York and many other U.S. cities now hold Day of the Dead processions and events in honor of the dead (Marchi 2009).

La Galería's annual Day of the Dead exhibits ranged from traditional *ofrendas* to high-tech video displays and websites, to cross-cultural installations done by students and artists from diverse ethnic and racial backgrounds. This small gallery had a profound influence on the future shape of Day of the Dead celebrations in the United States, both in encouraging hybrid experimentation and "mainstreaming" the altar format. Chicana curator Tere Romo notes that the Galería's "most significant contribution to día de los Muertos and Chicano art history" was the new direction in which it took *ofrendas.* Artist Rene Yáñez, in particular, transformed the altar format into an "environmental space" and pushed altar making into the realm of contemporary art while remaining respectful of the traditional *ofrenda* as a source of inspiration (Romo 2000, 38). La Galería's exhibitions and activities generated city-wide recognition and inspired parallel celebrations at galleries, schools, and museums across the city, state and country.

Political Meanings of the Celebration

Initiated as one of the most prominent manifestations of the Chicano Movement, U.S. Day of the Dead exhibitions and events communicated politically on a number of levels. In the spirit of social critique found in Mexican *calavera* poetry, *calaverita* figurines, and the satirical caricatures of José Guadalupe Posada, Chicano artists utilized the holiday's focus on remembrance to criticize U.S. government and corporate policies that cause death on a local, national, or global level. From their onset, a significant number of U.S. Day of the Dead activities encouraged moral reflection about "life and death" issues, via the mediums of altar exhibits, street processions, vigils, art work, and poetry. For example, since the 1970s, Day of the Dead altars, displayed in museums, art galleries, community centers and other public spaces, have commemorated California farm workers victimized by pesticide poisoning and exploitative labor practices. Such altars typically contain farming implements, California-grown produce such as lettuce, strawberries and grapes, pesticide cans, photos of deceased farm workers, and news clips about ongoing labor struggles. They often include photos of Mexican American labor leader César Chávez (1927–1993), founder of the United Farm Workers' Union (UFW). Such labor-related altars continue to appear at Day of the Dead exhibits today, critiquing the North American Free Trade Agreement (NAFTA) by drawing attention to "the death of organized labor" in the US and parallel worker exploitation and environmental contamination taking place in transnational factories located in Mexico. Each year, in cities across the United States, Day of the Dead altars focus on labor and immigration issues by commemorating the thousands of Latino migrants who die in attempts to cross the US-Mexico border in search of jobs. Other political themes honored during U.S. Day of the Dead events have included altars in memory of AIDS victims (drawing attention to the disproportionate level of AIDS in Latino and African American communities); youth killed by drug-related violence in US cities; victims of domestic violence and gay bashing, and victims of US-funded wars in Vietnam, El Salvador, Guatemala, Colombia, Afghanistan and Iraq (Marchi 2009).

Transnational Day of the Dead

While U.S. Day of the Dead celebrations began in California and were quickly embraced by Mexican American communities in Chicago, Texas and the Southwest, they gradually expanded throughout the rest of the country during the latter twentieth century, as Latinos/as migrated to areas of the country with little or no previous Latino presence. Today, Day of the Dead celebrations are held throughout the Midwest, the East Coast and even Alaska and Hawaii. Latinos with ancestry from Mexico, Guatemala, El Salvador, Honduras, Ecuador, Bolivia, Peru, Colombia, Argentina and elsewhere participate in U.S. Day of the Dead celebrations, along with non-Latinos of various races and ethnicities who are captivated by the tradition. As Latinos have come into contact with new areas of the globe, Chicano-style Day of the Dead celebrations have been held in Canada, New Zealand, England, Ireland, Scotland, Spain, Japan, Australia, Prague and elsewhere, making it an increasingly transnational celebration (Marchi 2009).

REGINA MARCHI

See also: Altars; Calaveras (Skulls); Chicano/a Art and Folklore; Día de los Muertos; Paper Arts (Papel Picado, Papier Mâché, and Kites)

Further Reading

Buechler, Hans, and Judith Buechler. *The Bolivian Aymara.* New York: Holt, Rinehart and Winston, Inc., 1971.

Cadaval, Olivia. "The Taking of the Renwick: The Celebration of the Day of the Dead and the Latino Community in Washington, DC." *Journal of Folklore Research* 22 (1985):179–193.

Carmichael, Elizabeth, and Chloe Sayer. *The Skeleton at the Feast: The Day of the Dead in Mexico*. Austin: University of Texas Press, 1991.

Guatemalan Day of the Dead kite making. http://grupoquepasa.com/other/the-kites-of-santiago-sacatepequez/.

Marchi, Regina. *Day of the Dead in the USA: The Migration and Transformation of a Cultural Phenomenon*. New Brunswick, NJ: Rutgers University Press, 2009.

Masuoka, Susan. "Calavera Miniatures: Political Commentary in Three Dimensions." *Studies in Latin American Popular Culture* 9 (1990): 263–278.

Milne, Jean. "November: All Saints and All Souls." In *Fiesta Time in Latin* America, 162–172. Los Angeles: Ward Ritchie, 1965.

Oakland Museum of California. *El Corazón de la Muerte: Altars and Offerings for Day of the Dead*. Oakland: Oakland Museum of California, 2005.

Photos of Day of the Dead celebrations in San Francisco: http://www.sfmission.com/dod/ and in Los Angeles: http://www.ladayofthedead.com/gallery.html.

Romo, Tere. *Chicanos en Mictlán*. San Francisco: Mexican Museum of San Francisco, 2000.

Tinker, E. *Corridos & Calaveras*. Austin: University of Texas Press, 1961.

Turner, Kay, and Pat Jasper. "Day of the Dead: The Tex-Mex Tradition." In Jack Santino, ed. *Halloween and Other Festivals of Death and Life,* 133–151. Knoxville: University of Tennessee Press.

Venegas, Sybil. "The Day of the Dead in Aztlán: Chicano Variations on the Theme of Life, Death and Self-Preservation." In T. Romo, ed. *Chicanos in* Mictlán, 42–43. San Francisco: Mexican Museum of San Francisco, 2000.

DICHOS (PROVERBS)

The English term which best describes *dichos* is "sayings." They are composed of concise, stand-alone statements typically laced with wit and humor, independent of further explanation. *Dichos* are commonly accepted as an expression of the common man's, the folk's, wisdom and their observations of ordinary life. They may convey opinions, teach lessons, offer counsel, or bring emphasis to a specific talking point. On occasion the English "proverb" is used in reference to *dichos*, but generally considered too scholarly to transmit their populist characteristic; this is particularly true of its Spanish equivalent, *proverbio*. *Refrán* and "refrain" are deemed inadequate because these imply a back-story or additional context. When *dichos* are placed at the center of various interdisciplinary studies, literary critics, social scientists, folklorists, and linguists attest to their cultural, social and educational significance and their merit in the development of social attitudes, morals, and social behaviors.

Interest in the study and compilation of *dichos* dates back to the seventeenth century; evidence of their usage may also be traced to Spanish medieval times. The tradition of sayings in the vernacular of Spanish speakers throughout Latin America, the United States, and the Iberian Peninsula signals their dissemination across the New World to be a consequence of the Spanish conquest. Although lexical variances may occur from country to country, or region to region, their message remains intact. In *Cada oveja con su pareja / Cada abeja con su pareja*, similar to the English "birds of a feather flock together," where the words *oveja* (sheep) and *abeja* (bee) are interchanged, but the message is the same (each sheep or bee with its own kind). Not all *dichos* are necessarily of Spanish origin; some form part of the European saying tradition as evidenced by their exact English equivalents: *No dejes para mañana lo que puedes hacer hoy* (Don't put off till tomorrow what you can do today); *No todo lo que relumbra es oro* (All that glitters is not gold). Yet, others are considered to have developed regionally; *El que nació para tamal, del cielo le caen las hojas* (For him who was born to be a tamale, heaven will provide the husks) is considered to be an authentic Mexican proverb; this most likely is due to the use of the regional word *tamal*. In a literal translation the intent of a specific saying is often lost, so it is important to bear in mind that it is the central message of *dichos* that is foremost.

Scholar Américo Paredes expounded on *dichos'* pluralistic aspect and recognized that they represent the knowledge of many, but express the wit of one. Here, Paredes is commenting on the creativity of the poet responsible for stringing together the perfect series of words which transmit the folk's invaluable tidbits of wisdom. Identified by folklorists as true proverbs or proverbs proper, these free-standing statements have distinctive linguistic structures. One such pattern offers the sense of balance, which separates two equally weighted sides: *Barriga llena, corazón contento* (Full belly, content heart). Other characteristics that may contribute to the pleasing poetic effect include the introduction of rhyme, *Obra empezada, medio acabada* (A task begun, is half done), where the ending vowel sound is repeated. Contrasting words also complement the balance of structure. In the following the use of *mucho* (much) and *poco* (little) demonstrates that big talkers take little or no action; *Mucho ruido, poco trabajo* (Much noise, little work).

When *dichos* are looked at in isolation, their central messaging may appear contradictory, as illustrated by the English "If at first you don't succeed try and try again" and "A leopard can't change its spots." For this reason it is important to be aware of the purpose and the context in which sayings are uttered. They have various purposes. To advise someone against business ventures with friends and family one may say, *Entre dos amigos, un notario y dos testigos* (Between two friends, a notary and two witnesses). To persuade the listener to come around to your way of thinking, *Más vale doblarse, que quebrarse* (It is better to bend than to break). Sayings can simply offer the speaker the opportunity to express an opinion or to say something about a situation, like noticing that those who complain the loudest get what they want or need: *El que tiene boca, a Roma va* (He who speaks up, goes to Rome). The didactic purposes of *dichos* are especially useful to families and community in the rearing of children and guiding adolescents' social behavior: as a warning against lying, *La mentira es como el maíz, sola sale* (A lie like corn, comes out on its own), or to discourage unsavory friendships, *El que con lobos anda, a allular se enseña* (He who keeps company with wolves learns to howl).

YOLANDA GODSEY

See also: Adivinanzas (Riddles)

Further Reading

Arora, Shirley L. "Proverbs in Mexican American Tradition." *Aztlán* 13 (1982): 43–69.

Burciaga, José Antonio. *In Few Words/En pocas palabras: A Compendium of Latino Folk Wit and Wisdom.* San Francisco: Mercury House, 1997.

Cobos, Rubén. *Refranes: Southwestern Spanish Proverbs.* Santa Fe: Museum of New Mexico Press, 1985.

Paredes, Américo. "Folklore, Lo Mexicano, and Proverbs." *Aztlán* 13 (1982): 1–11.

DICKEY, DAN WILLIAM (1953–)

Dan William Dickey is an educator, scholar, and musician who is perhaps best known for his work with Mexican corridos. As a musician, he has toured domestically and internationally with two groups—Los Romanceros and Chaski—and has been featured in several films.

In *The Kennedy Corridos,* published in 1978, Dickey collected twenty-one corridos—predominately from Texas but several from California as well—circulating in Mexican American communities in the years after the assassination of President John F. Kennedy. Under the guidance of his thesis advisor, seminal folklorist Américo Paredes, Dickey argued that Mexican Americans shared a special relationship with the nation's first Catholic president whose Irish heritage made him an outsider in the political arena. Furthermore, Dickey showed that the corrido—a tradition thought by some to be dead in the years leading to Kennedy's assassination—had lain dormant, waiting to be summoned by a particularly emotional and shocking event. The Kennedy assassination proved such an event.

In 1979, Dickey teamed with fellow researchers to compile a collection of migrant border ballads, which document the music and experiences of ethnic Mexican migratory workers in the Texas borderlands. This collection, funded by the National Endowment for the Humanities, includes sixty songs from migrant workers in south Texas, as well as photographs of musicians and environments, and oral interviews. The records of this project are housed in the University of Texas at Austin Benson Latin American Collection.

In addition to documenting and analyzing Latino music, Dickey also performs it on the *guitarrón*—a Mexican six-string acoustic bass—with his music trio *Los Romanceros*, which Dickey co-founded in 1982. The group can be seen in the recent video *Songs of the Vaqueros*, released by the Wittliff Gallery of Southwestern and Mexican Photography, in which Dickey acts as both scholar and musician. Dickey also plays guitar, *cuatro*, and *charango* with the Latin American folk music and education group Chaski, which has toured across the country and internationally; Dickey joined the group in 1991. Their most recent recording, *Viracocha*, was released in 2005. Dickey has also taught Mariachi, Andean music, and Marimba ensembles at the University of Texas at Austin.

Dickey is currently dean and teaches Spanish at The Lower School at St. Andrew's Episcopal School in Austin, Texas, where he has taught since 1981. At present, he is working on a traveling exhibit of Mexican Corridos de Pizcas (cotton picking songs) in the 1920s.

NICK BRAVO

See also: Corrido (Ballad); Mariachi

Further Reading

Chaski homepage. http://www.chaskimusic.com/.

Dickey, Dan William. "Corridos y Canciones de las Pizcas: Ballads and Songs of the 1920s Cotton Harvests." *Western Folklore* 65 (Winter, 2006): 1–28.

Dickey, Dan William. *The Kennedy Corridos: A Study of the Ballads of a Mexican American Hero*. Austin: The University of Texas Press, 1978.

DUENDES

Duendes are creatures referred to as "*gente menuda*" (little people) that appear in the folklore of Spanish-speaking communities throughout the world. The word "*duende*" is often translated into English as "dwarf" or "elf," and the creature itself is thought to originate in Scandinavian mythology. Depending on the storyteller, *duendes* are portrayed as mysterious creatures that rarely interact with humans, spirit-like beings that make random appearances, or demonic beings that prey on the lazy, the wicked, and the filthy.

In Spain, several types of *duendes* are spoken and written about. The *follet* is the most popular *duende* in Cataluña and is thought to have a kind disposition, even though it has the tendency to appear during the night and scare people in ways that ghosts would. Other *duendes* like the *boiet insular* are tiny enough to fit inside of a cane. They have long nervous tails that move incessantly. If human beings are able to catch sight of one of these creatures, the *boiet* quickly disappears behind clouds of black smoke. The island of Ibiza is home to the *barruguet ibicenco*, a seemingly crazy *duende* that uses his small size to sneak up on people in their homes, especially if they are women. The *barruguet ibicenco*, with his strong arms and goat-like beard, has a deep, manly voice that does not seem to correspond with the size of his body. It has been hypothesized that belief in this particular *duende* has origins in Egypt (Aracil, 2000).

One famous story, "*Barruguet de San Lorenzo*" published in Miquel Ferrer's *Diccionario de secretos de Ibiza*, tells of a countrywoman who was traveling by donkey to sell goods in the city. Upon hearing a baby's cry from the path, she dismounted and picked up the infant. When he continued to cry, she offered him her breast so that he could eat, and after he sucked she realized that he had left bite marks. She examined his mouth and noticed that he had an entire set of teeth. Upon hearing her exclaim, "You have teeth!," the *duende* made a statement that could be interpreted as the word for male genitalia—perhaps a lewd reference to his own (Aracil 2000).

Duendes have appeared in so many works of classic Spanish literature that a set of criteria for the creatures was developed by Julio Caro Baroja in his book *Algunos Mitos Españoles* (1974). The *duende* that he recognizes adheres to one or more of the following descriptors: demon-like, domestic, terrorizes by screaming or laughing in the house, a keeper of hidden treasures, able to convert into carbon or smoke upon being spotted by humans (as in the case of the above-mentioned *boiet insular*), and similar to spirits of the dead. Although the origin of most all *duendes* is uncertain, the creatures definitely became a fundamental component of Spanish culture, even beyond classic literature. In the sixteenth century, a law existed that said anyone who moved into a home and realized later that it was infested with *duendes* was free to abandon it (Caro Baroja 1974).

In Mexico, *duendes* appear in stories either to punish someone who has misbehaved or, simply, to cause a little mischief. In her article "The Elves of Old Mexico," Mary Blake recounts several *duende* stories told to her by a 73-year-old man from León. In one example, she tells how pesky *duendes* can be driven away; the dishes must be left out, and corn-meal dough must be left on the *metate*. In addition, if anything bad happens, the cause must always be attributed to the *duendes*. A person must say, for example, "This cut (or this fall or this pain) is for the *duendes*." However, one must be prepared for the consequences that come with this. The *duendes* might, indeed, disappear, but then your hens might lay fewer eggs, your fields might bear fewer crops, and your pigs might grow thin.

In New Mexico, the most popular idea about *duendes* is that they appear to frighten the lazy, the wicked, and the filthy. One woman revealed the common belief that *duendes* live together in an isolated place—perhaps underground—from which they emerge at night to steal provisions and clothing. They may also be found in remote sections of the forest, where they exist peacefully amongst themselves and where human beings are not permitted. In one New Mexican story, when a family moves from one house to another, a "lazy" and careless daughter leaves a broom at the old house. At the discovery of this oversight, a *duende* suddenly appears and descends slowly from the roof with the broom in his hand, saying, "Here it is!" This is one example of the way in which *duendes* appear in stories to scare someone who has not done something one should have.

While the little creatures known as *duendes*—or their English counterparts of "dwarfs" or "elves"—exist in the folklore of many other communities around the world, the word "*duende*" is, perhaps, most often associated with the Andalusian poet Federico García Lorca. In an effort to popularize flamenco music and dancing—an art form previously relegated to the outcasts of Spanish society—García Lorca began to speak of it as having *duende*. The word *duende,* in this sense, is loosely translated as "energetic instinct." It is characteristic of the spirit—very much inspired by the *duende* creature—that takes possession of an artist. And although it does not frighten the audience, this type of *duende* is considered to be equally mystifying.

KATIE SCIURBA

Further Reading

Aracil, Miguel G. *Guía de seres fantásticos de los países catalanes: Cataluña, Valencia, y Baleares: Duendes, hadas, vampiros, ogros, y demás criaturas fantásticas* Barcelona: Indigo, 2000.

Blake, Mary. "The Elves of Old Mexico." *The Journal of American Folklore* 2, no. 104 (1914): 237–239.

Caro Baroja, Julio. *Algunos mitos españoles.* Madrid: Ediciones del Centro, 1974.

Espinosa, Aurelio M. "New-Mexican Spanish Folk-lore." *The Journal of American Folklore* 23, no. 90 (1910): 395–418.